THE RUSSIAN FOLKTALE
BY VLADIMIR YAKOVLEVICH PROPP

THE RUSSIAN FOLKTALE
BY VLADIMIR YAKOVLEVICH PROPP

EDITED AND TRANSLATED BY

SIBELAN FORRESTER

FOREWORD BY JACK ZIPES

WAYNE STATE UNIVERSITY PRESS

DETROIT

© 2012 by Wayne State University Press, Detroit, Michigan 48201. English translation
published by arrangement with the publishing house Labyrinth-MP.
16 15 14 13 12   5 4 3 2 1

Library of Congress Cataloging-in-Publication Data

880-01 Propp, V. IA. (Vladimir IAkovlevich), 1895–1970, author.
  [880-02 Russkaia skazka. English. 2012]
  The Russian folktale by Vladimir Yakovlevich Propp / edited and translated by Sibelan
Forrester ; foreword by Jack Zipes.
    pages ; cm. — (Series in fairy-tale studies)
  Includes bibliographical references and index.
  ISBN 978-0-8143-3466-9 (paperback : alkaline paper) — ISBN 978-0-8143-3721-9 (ebook)
  1. Tales—Russia (Federation)—History and criticism.   2. Fairy tales—Classification.
3. Folklore—Russia (Federation)   I. Forrester, Sibelan E. S. (Sibelan Elizabeth S.), translator,
editor.   II. Zipes, Jack, 1937–, writer of added commentary.   III. Title.   IV. Series: Series in
fairy-tale studies.
  GR203.17.P77713 2012
  398.20947—dc23

                                                                      2012004220

Published with the assistance of a fund established by Thelma Gray James of
Wayne State University for the publication of folklore and English studies.

Designed by Chang Jae Lee
Typeset by Newgen North America
Composed in Alexei Solid and Arno Pro

To N. B., the emperor—you know who you are.

CONTENTS

FOREWORD

TOWARD UNDERSTANDING

THE COMPLETE VLADIMIR PROPP

JACK ZIPES

FOR MANY YEARS NOW Vladimir Propp has been famous in the West mainly for his innovative study, *Morphology of the Folktale* (1928), first published in English in 1958. His other major work, *The Historical Roots of the Wonder Tale* (1946), was partially translated into English in 1984 in *Theory and History of Folklore*, a crude pastiche with sundry articles and a misleading introduction by Anatoly Liberman. It was suggested—and Liberman is not the only scholar to have done this—that Propp had yielded to communist pressure and abandoned his "genuine" commitment to true scholarship to become a Marxist ideologue when he published *Historical Roots*. Moreover, other Western scholars spread the same false rumors, arguing that Propp's so-called formalist approach to folklore had been considered heretical in the Soviet Union, that Soviet folklorists were all obliged to follow a party line of orthodox historical materialism, and that Propp was largely ignored as a folklorist in the Soviet Union. Nothing could be further from the truth, and thanks to Sibelan Forrester's scrupulous and meticulous translation of *The*

Russian Folktale, first published posthumously in 1984, it is now possible to gain a fuller understanding of Propp's development as a folklorist and the monumental contributions he made not only to Russian folklore but also to international folklore.

The Russian Folktale is based on lectures that Propp delivered at Leningrad State University in the 1960s and represents the culmination of his thinking about the genesis, relevance, and structure of the Russian folktale. Unfortunately, Propp died in 1970 as he was preparing the lectures for book publication and could not put the finishing touches on them. However, thanks to notes by his former students, his lectures were eventually published as a book and complement *Morphology of the Folktale* and *The Historical Roots of the Wonder Tale,* so that we are now in a position to grasp Propp's comprehensive approach to folktales and folklore in general.

In his insightful essay, "V. Ya. Propp: Legend and Fact" (1986), Kirill Chistov, a former student of Propp's, clarifies certain "myths" that had been spread about Russian folklore and Propp's status as a folklorist. First, Chistov explains that Propp was never regarded as a formalist in the Soviet Union but rather was considered a structuralist and an innovative folklorist. Without any training in folklore, Propp used a structuralist approach to analyze the Russian wonder tale long before structuralism became fashionable in the West during the 1960s. Second, Chistov demonstrates that Propp's *Morphology of the Folktale* was well received in the Soviet Union when it appeared in 1928 and was discussed and cited by many scholars until and after his death in 1970. In fact, Propp was never censored by the Soviet academy or government. Chistov demonstrates that Propp never abandoned his morphological approach to the folktale, nor was he forced to recant this approach. In contrast, it took the West thirty years to finally recognize the value of Propp's approach by bringing out the first translation of *Morphology of the Folktale* in 1958, when structuralism became popular in Western intellectual circles. Because many Soviet works in folklore had been published between 1930 and 1970, there had never been a linguistic barrier to publishing *Morphology of the Folktale,* only a lack of favorable conditions in the West. In short, Propp was ignored more in the West than he was in the Soviet Union. Once translated, however, Propp's work had a great impact, even though it was pegged as some kind of formalist study. Consequently, Propp's early works have never been fully understood in the West even when he endeavored to explain his attachment to history, ethnography, and anthropology in articles and essays.

The Russian Folktale, I hope, will rectify some of the misleading impressions of Propp's work that various critics have disseminated. As Forrester points out in her preface, Propp intended from the very beginning of his career to work within a historical-anthropological framework; he wanted to include a chapter on the historical origins of the wonder tale in *Morphology of the Folktale* and would have preferred to use the term *wonder tale* in the title rather than just *folktale*. In fact, he could have been even more exact by using the term *Russian wonder tale*, because his focus in *Morphology of the Folktale* was primarily on a hundred tales from the huge groundbreaking collection published by the great Russian folklorist Aleksandr Afanas'ev. The tales selected by Propp from this nineteenth-century collection all belong to the category of wonder tales (Aarne-Thompson-Uther tale types 300–749) registered in *The Types of International Folktales: A Classification and Bibliography*.[1] In other words, there is a an "organic" development in Propp's work on folktales from the 1920s to 1970 that is made eminently clear in *The Russian Folktale*.

As Propp explains in *The Russian Folktale*, he believes that in order to establish what constitutes a genre, one has to demonstrate that there is a constant repetition of functions in a large body of tales. The purpose of his *Morphology of the Folktale* was to establish the thirty-one functions of the wonder tale and then later in *The Historical Roots of the Wonder Tale* to trace the origins of the functions and genre to rituals and customs of primitive peoples. Propp, never a Marxist or a communist, was evidently strongly influenced by the British anthropological school of Edward Tylor, Andrew Lang, and Sir James George Frazer, which he describes in the early chapters of *The Russian Folktale*. Indeed, *The Russian Folktale* is a book that brings together his structuralist leanings with his profound interest in the evolutionary process that brought about the genre of the wonder tale. But it is also more than just a summary of his own work and interests, for it was intended to provide a general history about the rise of folklore studies in Russia and Europe.

Although Propp was not a trained folklorist, he had a masterful command of the history of folklore by the time he began delivering the lectures that formed *The Russian Folktale*, and he provides important information about European folklore studies, debates, and collectors in the nineteenth and twentieth centuries, always with a focus on Russia. He then substantially reviews and supplements the theses that he had introduced in *Morphology of the Folktale*, distinguishing carefully between plots, motifs, and functions. His discussions of various tale types are illuminating. In writing about the genesis of the wonder tales and their connections to rituals, customs, and myths, he is always cautious in making claims, but it is important to note that he neither idealizes the common people nor interprets the history of folktales from a Marxist or historical materialist viewpoint. Propp was interested in belief systems and initiation rites that contributed to the formation of narrative structures, and he tried to trace these through history. Some of the parallels he draws cannot be substantiated, and many might not apply in particular cultures. But, as I have tried to stress, Propp was first and foremost interested in Russian cultural developments, and many of his discussions of initiations and characters, such as Baba Yaga, are highly stimulating; his propositions are convincing and can best be understood within the framework of Russian history.

Interestingly, Propp does not limit himself to wonder tales in this book. There are illuminating chapters on novellistic, cumulative, and animal tales. His analysis of totemism and animal tales is particularly insightful, and his final chapter on storytellers, performance, and biography reveals that Propp was at the cutting edge of new developments in international folklore studies that have become major areas of research.

Of course, certain notions in Propp's book are outdated or not fully elaborated. Some of the discussions are narrowly limited to folklore studies in the Soviet Union. Nevertheless, Propp was not narrow himself. He was familiar with international debates, mainly in Europe, and he was a modest and tolerant thinker who did not have an ax to grind. Propp dedicated himself to a tiny aspect of folklore studies, and his small first book, *Morphology of the Folktale*, which incorporated the seeds of his curiosity about the origins of a particular genre, namely, the Russian wonder tale, blossomed belatedly through many translations in the latter half of the twentieth century to make its mark throughout the world. *The Russian Folktale*, published for the first time in English, adds a much-deserved exclamation mark to his notable scholarly work that spanned fifty years of original research.

PREFACE

VLADIMIR PROPP AND

THE RUSSIAN FOLKTALE

SIBELAN FORRESTER

VLADIMIR PROPP is the most widely known Russian folklore specialist outside Russia today, thanks to the impact of his 1928 book *Morphology of the Folktale.*[1] *Morphology* has done more than influence our understanding of folklore. It decisively shaped contemporary narrative and textual studies and semiotic theory of all kinds, and some have argued that it gave birth to structuralism.[2] But *Morphology* is only the first of Propp's contributions to scholarship. This volume is his late book, *The Russian Folktale*, translated for the first time into English.

The Russian Folktale is as important for what it tells us about Propp as for its topic. It illuminates and contextualizes Propp's insights on wonder tales within the broader context of the Russian folktale as a whole. Two sections have particular value for today's reader: Chapter 2 treats the history of study and theories of the folktale and addresses in detail the Finnish school, with its system of tale types. After many discussions of how the achievements of Propp's *Morphology* might be integrated with the Aarne-Thompson index, it is fascinating to see Propp's own take on the issue toward the end of his life. Chapter 3, devoted to the wonder tale, summarizes the main points of *Morphology* and incorporates the conclusions of Propp's 1946 book, *Historical Roots of the Wonder Tale*, which was originally intended as a section of *Morphology* and clarifies the intentions of that project. The five chapters devoted to different varieties of folktales dwell on numerous individual tales and tale types, comparing the Russian tales to Classical myths and tales from other traditions. Besides a thorough introduction to the Russian folktale, therefore, *The Russian Folktale* gives a summary overview of Propp's scholarly position and thought. Anchored by his insights into the structure of the wonder tale, it reveals his approach to folklore more globally. This book is a crucial source for appraising Propp's thinking and his continuing relevance to folklore scholarship and narrative studies in general.

The book has indicative idiosyncrasies as well. A contemporary reader will notice the copious Soviet-style references to the standard luminaries—not only Friedrich Engels but also Vladimir Lenin and Maxim Gorky, hardly known as experts in the field. Propp was not merely protecting himself with mechanical citations—that kind of caution was no longer a matter of life or death by the 1960s, when he wrote *The Russian Folktale*. Propp's original insight was meant to conclude with the project that became his dissertation and then the *Historical Roots of the Wonder Tale*; isolating the moves and functions of the wonder tales' master narrative would let the scholar tie each one to the tales' origins in rituals of initiation or death, based in the primitive religion and material culture of the deep East Slavic past. Like a late nineteenth-century anthropologist, Propp assumes that folkloric material from more "primitive" cultures can be used to penetrate that Russian past, because every society (as historical materialism teaches) moves through the same obligatory stages of development. Propp's theoretical assumptions, which now appear antiquated, must have allowed him to continue his research more or less in harmony with the inflexible historical and philosophical underpinnings of Soviet Marxism. After he introduces the genre of the folktale, the first two chapters of *The Russian Folktale* present the history of collecting and theories of the folktale in ways that are quite distant from today's reader. Propp assumes that there used to be a single underlying narrative of initiation, based in the life of a forest culture at the stage of hunting and gathering and early (garden) agriculture, and that the outlines of the initiation ritual had blurred in the wonder tales that evolved from primitive myths. This is oddly similar to the sun-seeking mythological school, whose limitations Propp criticizes. His discussion of animal tales refers frequently to totemism; he even suggests that agglutinative languages (a group that includes several languages spoken on Russian territory) are more primitive in mentality than languages that have grammatical inflection. Propp's scholarly references are not only dated but also disappointingly Eurocentric.

Several factors condition this orientation toward the past: Propp's own philological education, limited access to publications from other parts of the world, and the ideological pressures exerted on Soviet scholars. Propp's approach was essentially the safe one, although he too faced attacks in the years after World War II. Citing classic Marxists helped him to carry on working in peace in an era when even astronomy textbooks had to conclude with a chapter on "Marxism-Leninism in the Cosmos."[3] Moreover, the Marxist vision of societal development from primitive matriarchy through various stages leading up to feudalism and capitalism did not contradict Propp's vision of human history. Last but not least, in the Soviet period the past could be a kind of safe zone for inquiry, whereas letting the critical energy of folklore move too close to the present would have involved risks for a scholar.[4]

Propp resembles many Soviet and post-Soviet semioticians in striving to recover and reassemble elements of the distant past through deep reading of the structures of folklore and other surviving materials (chronicles, sermons, etc.). This reconstructive impulse can be seen as a response to the loss of Russian traditional culture and Soviet historical trauma. Most cultures begin to study and collect folklore when educated, literate individuals (be they local elites or representatives of a colonizing nation) perceive the danger that oral lore might pass away in the face of modernization (literacy, industrialization, and eventually competition from media and popular culture); thus folklorists' attitude toward their material often includes an element of mourning. In the case of Russian folk culture, this pathos is compounded by the vast and often violent destruction of peasant life in the Soviet period. Peasant life was considered dangerously backward and was more often suppressed than valued. Collectivization, industrialization, and forced population transfers had a huge impact on the Russian village, where folklore once flourished. The idea that the past could be reconstructed, at least as an idea or an ideal, held understandable appeal for Soviet scholars who valued the past and regretted its losses. This approach to folklore and traditional culture has emerged even more strongly in the post-Soviet period. Indeed, recent editions of Propp's collected works, with their cover titles printed in an archaic, Old Russian–looking font, suggest that his books may appeal not only to students and scholars of folklore but also to Russian neo-pagans.

Finally, in some cases Propp's Marxist interpretations are usefully thought provoking, as when he argues in Chapter 4 that the Aarne-Thompson tale-type index dilutes and obscures the social point of satirical tales about masters or priests and hired men because it fragments one type into a number of more limited and specific types, several of which may occur within a single satirical tale collected in Russia.

Propp commented that he possessed the "curse" of perceiving patterns, and his sharp eye and thoughtful analysis of the economy of form in various genres and media are in harmony with Soviet structuralism or Tartu-style semiotics. His role in folkloristics shares important elements with that of Aleksandr Afanas'ev, whose famous collection of tales Propp used as the basis of his *Morphology* and later edited for republication. Afanas'ev did little fieldwork; instead, he edited, published, and systematized tales he received from others. Propp too relied on other collectors, and his work credits them generously for what they achieved in the field and for the theoretical implications of their practice. M. V. Ivanov rightly compares Propp's scholarly opus to James George Frazer's *Golden Bough*.[5] Assimilating an amazing amount of material, Propp homes in on the aesthetic and ritual structures that give traditional societies dignity and psychological depth. His readings on many adjacent topics enrich the pages of *The Russian Folktale*.

AFTER ATTEMPTING IN THIS introduction to place *The Russian Folktale* in the context of Soviet and Western folklore scholarship, I outline its contents and give a brief survey of Propp's life and work. I end with a translation note. At the end of this volume, I have added a basic bibliography of works on Russian folklore and other works by Propp available in English.

PROPP AND SOVIET FOLKLORE STUDIES

As Jack Zipes points out in his foreword to this volume, Propp's reception in the West was distorted in ways that were typical of the cold war. It was also difficult for many Western readers to understand the position of a Soviet folklorist. Folklore study in the Soviet Union, including Propp's own scholarly work, was shaped by the vexed position of the "folk." The Soviet Union from the start was supposed to be a country of peasants and workers.[6] Even in the later twentieth century, most Russians had close ties to the countryside and its folklife whether or not they themselves had grown up in cities. On the other hand, the application of "scientific" Marxism, as it solidified in the 1920s and 1930s, suggested that traditional culture, including traditional folklore, would and should soon wither away. Anatoly Liberman, in his edition of Propp's *Theory and History of Folklore*, points out the essential contradictions in the position of folklore as Soviet ideology defined it.[7] Even before the 1917 revolution, Bolsheviks were suspicious and often hostile toward the village, at least in part because villagers were especially devoted to religion, that "opiate of the people" and competing ideology. The uncensored energy of folklore made it suspect in a highly controlled public discourse; many a Soviet citizen wound up in jail or a labor camp after indulging in another popular genre, the political joke.[8] In any case, the genres of traditional folklore that were still lively in the late 1920s were often channeled by folklorists into centralized, homogenized folk performance ensembles or into "fakelore," which celebrated heroes such as Lenin or Stalin and the new Soviet reality.[9] Meanwhile, villages were collectivized, and large parts of their population were liquidated, sent to Siberia for resisting collectivization, or moved en masse to work in urban factories. From another direction, the electrification of rural Russia helped radio, popular movies and music, and eventually television to displace traditional pastimes such as telling folktales.[10] Russia's rural culture today has lost much of what it had in the 1920s, when Roman Jakobson asserted a living culture of folktales in villages around Moscow.[11] Propp's diary records the sorry state of the villages where his visitors were doing provincial fieldwork in the 1960s.[12]

Propp's intellectual relationship to Marxism, again, remains an open question. The classic texts of Marxism (Engels especially) had a great deal to say about traditional societies, even if one of the orthodoxies was that traditional society and national folklores would be left behind in the evolution through capitalism to socialism and eventually communism. At least Marxism, unlike some spheres of Bolshevik rhetoric, recognized the value of the past and suggested ways to connect that past with folklore collected more recently. Thus a well-chosen quotation could either buttress an argument or pay dues to Soviet scholarly style without distorting one's own content too much—and perhaps both. Liberman writes, "Marxist ideas pervade everything Propp wrote between 1928 and the mid Sixties. . . . Propp used a pool of quotations that allowed him to feel safe under the most diverse circumstances."[13] Liberman's irritation with Propp's Soviet scholarly practice, and especially his Marxist quotes, mars and overlengthens his introduction to the scholar's work in *Theory and History of Folklore* in a way that was understandable in 1984. Clearly, folklore (and the ways it was presented and understood) remained a lively zone of contention in the late cold war era. For today's reader, the signs of Soviet practice in Propp's work can serve as reminders of the role of ideology in scholarship wherever it is practiced; perhaps we can become equally sensitive to the ideological markers in scholarship that is closer to us.

How much Propp personally believed in it all is hard to say; it was certainly true that in the 1930s and 1940s scholars less careful or less lucky than Propp could pay with their lives. Quotations from Engels, Lenin, and Gorky are all over *The Russian Folktale*. Yet the author wrote in his diary about a colleague, "He's a significant scholar, but ruined by fear. He quotes Marx endlessly under every assertion."[14] The reader may judge how much Propp's references to Marxist classics add to the work or distort it and how much they reflect or inform the scholar's beliefs, suggesting productive approaches to folk creativity and fieldwork or simply standing as a sign of his times.

OVERVIEW OF *THE RUSSIAN FOLKTALE*

The Russian Folktale sprang from a *spets-kurs*, or advanced course, that Propp taught toward the end of his life; he was still at work on parts of it when he died, and some sections have been supplemented with notes taken by Propp's students. It was first published in 1984, fourteen years after Propp's death. The book may have been left unfinished, but the course was clearly well organized. One can see elements of the oral style, as the lecturing professor repeats an idea for emphasis or pauses a moment to let students prepare to focus on the important information he is about to convey. Drawing on both Russian and Western folklore studies, Propp offers a thoroughly grounded introduction to the Russian folktale, the development of folkloristics in Russia, and the study of folktales in general, as understood in his time and place. He himself emerges as a broadly interested intellectual. He approaches the folktale as a truly interdisciplinary topic, rooted in the concrete everyday life of the Russian people. Where *Morphology* examines the building blocks of the folktale (Propp compared its approach to the study of skeletons in establishing biological morphology), *The Russian Folktale* looks at folktales from every angle: their origin, setting, and performance and the character of the people who performed and collected them. Propp's own appreciation of beauty informs his discussion of the tales and their relationship to literature and other arts.

In the Introduction Propp stresses the attractiveness and ubiquity of folktales and their role in the origins of European literature. He briefly discusses the use of folktale plots in contemporary culture, especially ballet and opera. He traces the outline of the Russian word *skazka* (folktale) and compares it to the terms used in other European languages. He examines several definitions of the folktale, declaring them all inadequate, and suggests possible elements of a more adequate definition. A long section discussing adjacent folk verbal genres ends with a helpful list of examples for these genres (myth, memorate, *legenda*, *predanie*, folk book, and *skaz*)[15] as well as the anecdote. He mentions the Finnish school, which he addresses in greater detail in Chapter 2.

In Chapter 1 Propp presents a history of folktale collection, beginning with the surviving traces of folktales in old Rus' and Muscovy. He lists various publishers and collectors of Russian tales and the role of folklore in the rise of Russian secular literature, with numerous examples. Propp clearly prefers the collectors who were leftists and thus fitted the Soviet image of a politically progressive nineteenth-century intelligentsia, but the brief biographies also show that tsarist repression could have unintended and fruitful side effects, as educated men (and occasionally women) exiled to unfamiliar regions became interested in the local lore and began to collect, translate, and publish it.

In Chapter 2 Propp gives a history of folktale study and theories, concentrating on Russia from the eighteenth century onward but discussing developments in Western Europe as well, especially English, French, and German studies. Propp traces the gradually evolving understanding of the genre of the folktale and enumerates the achievements as well as the shortcomings of each school. In typical Soviet style the Russian scholars tend to be smarter and more subtle than the Western scholars they followed, foreshadowed, or challenged. In this chapter Propp discusses (among others) Afanas'ev (as a theoretician rather than a publisher of folktales), Fedor Buslaev, the formalists, Ol'ga Freidenberg, Nikolai Marr, Aleksandr Nikiforov, Aleksandr Pypin, Aleksandr Veselovskii, and the Russian Orientalists; among Western European scholars and movements, he discusses Joseph Bédier, Theodor Benfey, James Frazer, Jacob and Wilhelm Grimm, Andrew Lang, Max Müller, Edward Tylor, the Finnish school, the migrationist school, and the mythological school, all in roughly chronological order but referring back (or forward) to theorists or theories relevant in other periods. After criticizing the Finnish school in *Morphology*, Propp recognizes the value of the tale types and then enumerates their flaws. He declares that the Soviet practice of his own period, the theory of stadial development, is the last word in theory and methodology: It was just a matter of applying Marx and Engels to the best of what came before! One should note, though, that Propp treats each topic with balance, crediting it for its improvements before turning to a critique.[16] Clearly he views scholarly theory as another process of evolution, tending ever closer to perfection.

Chapter 3 is devoted to the wonder tale, which Propp defines by its formal characteristics and the generic traits advanced in his introduction. This substantial chapter usefully combines the matter of Propp's *Morphology of the Folktale* with the most interesting conclusions of *Historical Roots of the Wonder Tale*. (One might argue that it is better written than *Morphology* and more inspiring than *Historical Roots*; the best parts of both books go into *The Russian Folktale*.) In this chapter Propp outlines the major moves in order, providing copious examples. Then he mentions a number of the best known Russian tales: "Sivko-Burko," variants of "Amor and Psyche" (segueing into Aksakov's "Little Scarlet Flower" and the related "Feather of Finist the Bright Falcon"), "The Firebird," "Truth and Falsehood," and tales of persecuted stepdaughters. The last section advances his ideas on the most ancient foundations of the wonder tale, as elaborated earlier in *Historical Roots of the Wonder Tale*. He connects, for example, Pushkin's verse tale "Tsar Saltan" with Classical mythologies.

Chapter 4 covers "novellistic," that is, everyday or realistic, folktales, which can share traits with wonder tales but often differ from them entirely: They are much more various in composition. They are not formulaic but closer to life, even if they do involve elements of magic, and are most often entertaining or humorous. Propp considers the novellistic tale a later development and points out that these tales criticize the upper classes and the clergy (surprise!) even more than typical peasant character flaws. He gives a summary of the most common plot types—tales of wise maidens, robbers, fools, bad wives, and so on—and ends by considering adjacent genres, seventeenth-century urban tales ("Shemiaka's Judgment") and moralistic tales (such as tales of great sinners).

The brief fifth chapter considers cumulative tales, distinguished by their agglomerative structure. Examples include "The Turnip," "The Fly's Chamber," and "Kolobok" (The Gingerbread Man). The Russian repertoire includes only about twenty types of cumulative tales.

Chapter 6 treats animal tales. Propp finds it unsatisfactory to distinguish these as having animals as main characters, but agrees that they nevertheless do form a distinct class of Russian tales. He compares them to fables (which he considers a later form), to the Western European animal epos (*fabliaux* and the tales of Reineke the Fox), and to animal tales from Native Americans and other "primitive" peoples, speculating that they originate in a totemistic system (because telling the tale of a crafty animal magically confers that luck and craft on the hunter). Here too some of Propp's insights reveal an outmoded theoretical framework.

In the seventh and final chapter Propp turns to the life of the folktale as a performative genre, stressing collecting methods that not only seek to give the fullest possible information and the most accurate possible recording but also elicit the most natural performance (spontaneous, not rushed). Propp speculates on the types of tale-tellers and critiques other folklorists' attempts to categorize them, citing examples from Russian and Soviet collections. He also conveys his appreciation of the individual personalities of the tellers and his pleasure at the distinct qualities of their versions of tales.

The bibliography at the end of the book includes all the sources Propp cites in *The Russian Folktale*, both Russian and European, as well as other references cited by the editors of the Russian edition or by me.

A BRIEF BIOGRAPHY OF VLADIMIR PROPP

Because of our distance from *Morphology of the Folktale* (first published in 1928 but translated into English only in 1958) and because of Propp's private nature as a person, it may not occur to readers of *Morphology* that they know nothing at all about Propp's life. In a substantial 2005 article dedicated to the 110th anniversary of Propp's birth,[17] M. V. Ivanov stresses the scholar's reserve and tendency to maintain a certain distance from others. Ivanov traces this characteristic to Propp's German upbringing, although it was surely heightened by life in the Soviet Union during years of fear and trauma, and it surely helped him to survive.

Vladimir Yakovlevich Propp was a folklorist, ethnographer, philologist, (unpublished) poet, language pedagogue, and mentor to many outstanding younger scholars. He was born in 1895 in St. Petersburg, Russia, to parents of Volga German background. His father came from a family of German colonists in the Saratov region; he worked for Schmidt Brothers trading house, supplying flour to the many German bakeries in St Petersburg. Propp's mother kept house and cared for the couple's seven children. Before the revolution the family was prosperous enough to buy a summer estate in the Saratov region. Johann Jakob Propp died in 1919; Anna Propp (née Beisel) died during the blockade of Leningrad in 1942.

Propp was christened Hermann Woldemar in the Evangelical Lutheran Church, and his childhood unfolded largely in St. Petersburg's long-established German colony. He spoke German with his mother (Russian with his father and siblings) and attended German primary and secondary schools. His early life seems to have been emotionally impoverished. Propp entered St. Petersburg University in 1913 and began studying German philology, also composing philosophical poetry in German. After the beginning of World War I, he switched to Russian philology, a choice that perplexed and displeased his family. He changed subjects not only out of patriotism or a wish to be *Russian* but also because his experience with fellow students suggested that Russian intelligentsia life was more congenial than what he had known at home. In his autobiographical work, "The Tree of Life," the narrator asks, "Can there be a fate more tedious than to be born a German, a Jew, or a Pole in the great Russian Empire?"[18] Nevertheless, Propp never lost his connection to German language and culture. He taught German at the university until the 1950s, and many pages of his late diary were written in German.[19] He was educated as a philologist, not a folklorist, and everything he knew about folklore was self-taught, although of course folklore played a crucial role in nineteenth-century German (and Russian) literature and culture.

Propp graduated from St. Petersburg University in 1918 and began teaching German in Petrograd schools. He married Kseniia Novikova (with whom he had worked as a nurse for World War I wounded), and they soon had two daughters. In 1918 he began his first book, *Morphology of the Magical Folktale* (a contemporary Western scholar would translate the term "magical folktale" as "wonder tale"). Propp worked slowly on this innovative study, seeking no outside direction. When he felt ready, he showed the manuscript to older scholars he respected: Boris Eikhenbaum, Dmitrii Zelenin, and Viktor Zhirmunskii. All three were impressed by the work, and Zhirmunskii agreed to publish it.[20] *Morphology* came out in 1928 from Academia publishers, with two important changes. First, the publisher removed the word *magical* from the title in hope of better sales, although Propp's analysis in fact applies only to wonder tales, not to other categories of folktales. Second, Zhirmunskii persuaded Propp to remove a chapter on the origins of the tales in order to develop it further in a separate study; this eventually became Propp's 1939 doctoral dissertation and then his second book, *Historical Roots of the Wonder Tale* (1946). Removing this chapter, as it turned out, made *Morphology* more vulnerable in the years ahead to accusations of formalism—defined in the Stalinist period as an "idealist" emphasis on form to the detriment of properly socialist content. *Morphology* was close to the formalists not only in its achievements but also in the involvement of people associated with that school in its publication.[21]

In 1932, Propp was arrested by the Soviet secret police (the GPU) and apparently spent some months in solitary confinement. We do not know why he was arrested, although 1932 was still a "relatively vegetarian" year compared to the later 1930s. His family speculated that it was because he continued to correspond with a former student who had emigrated, but neither family recollections nor GPU archives record the reason for Propp's eventual release. This is a puzzling part of his biography; his late diary refers to it only obliquely. Given his continued employment as an educator, he cannot have spent as long in jail as some sources suggest. At about the same time, perhaps in part because of the arrest, his first marriage was ending.

In 1937, Propp was invited to teach German philology at Leningrad State University (LGU)—his own alma mater under the city's new name. He gradually began teaching folklore as well and then Russian philology, once that department merged with the folklore department. He joined the Institute of Russian Literature in the famous Pushkin House, although he was later expelled from the institute in one of the era's many scholarly purges. In 1937 he married Elizaveta Yakovlevna Antipova, who taught English at LGU, and their son was born in the late 1930s. The family lived in a tiny semi-basement apartment full of books. In 1941 both Propp and Antipova were in Leningrad as the siege began. As university personnel, they were evacuated over the ice of Lake Ladoga along with their son in 1942; thus they survived the war when many others did not (including Propp's mother and a valued colleague, folklorist Aleksandr Nikiforov). LGU was moved to Saratov, and Propp lived and taught there until the university returned to Leningrad in 1944. At that point, most likely because of his German name, his passport was taken away and the dean of the university had to make strenuous arguments to get him back to Leningrad.

Propp's second book, *Historical Roots of the Wonder Tale*, was based on his 1939 doctoral dissertation, which argued that the structure of the wonder tale reflects its origins in initiation and funeral rites. Delayed by the war, the book was published in 1946. This was just in time to attract the kind of vicious attacks many other scholars and writers faced in the late 1940s, as Stalin's cultural henchman Andrei Zhdanov tightened control over Soviet discourse, which had been strategically relaxed during the war. The tension damaged Propp's health. He had a heart attack in 1950, and heart trouble cast a shadow of fear and physical discomfort over the rest of his life.

As mentioned, it is impossible to say how much of the Marxism in Propp's books and articles reflects true faith and how much was a protective camouflage. *Morphology* makes no mention of Marxism, and Propp never joined the Communist Party. Late in life he wrote many critical comments about Soviet scholarship and everyday life in his journal.[22] He even stood up to party hacks at the university while he was chair of the department of Russian literature at LGU, to the delight of many of his younger colleagues.

After Stalin's death in 1953 and the ensuing Thaw in the Soviet Union, Propp could allow himself to write more candidly in his letters and diary, although even there he may sound oddly isolated (e.g., he always refers to his wife formally as Elizaveta Yakovlevna). Propp's third book, *The Russian Heroic Epos*, was published in 1955, and *Russian Agrarian Festivals* appeared in 1963. He edited and wrote a new introduction to the 1957 three-volume edition of Afanas'ev's classic *Russian Folk Tales*, the most important Russian work of its kind for general readers and scholars (reading it had inspired his *Morphology*).[23] The most influential work of those years, however, was *Morphology of the Folk Tale*, translated into English in 1958 at the suggestion of the great linguist Roman Jakobson. This edition brought Propp international attention and renown at home. The 1969 Italian translation of *Morphology* included an afterword, in which Propp responded (finally) to Claude Lévi-Strauss's 1960 critique and declared himself not a formalist but a structuralist.

Propp retired from teaching in the mid-1960s but continued writing. He composed and refined parts of the course on the Russian folktale that form this volume, and he worked on the book *Problems of Laughter and the Comic*, published posthumously in 1976. Freed from the heavy teaching load he had always carried, Propp enjoyed playing piano, reading classical novels and poetry, taking photographs, and welcoming former students and colleagues when they visited. His diary details serious reading on Russian icons and church architecture, seeking the same kinds of patterns he had found in folktales. Propp died in Leningrad at the age of 75 in August 1970, after yet another heart attack.

Translator's Note

I have adapted and compressed somewhat the style of Propp's work in order to minimize repetition and rhetorical gestures that are less effective in writing than in a lecture hall. (Propp worked very hard on the lectures, practicing his delivery, although former students recalled him as much less flamboyant in style than many of his colleagues.) Except for authors who are widely known under other spellings (Tolstoy, Gorky), I have used the Library of Congress system of transliteration to make for a quick transition to library catalogs in further research. Russian scholarly style typically gives an author's initials (for the first name and patronymic) plus last name, for example, V. Ya. Propp. Whenever possible, I have changed these initials to the first name to fit Western practice, except when Propp spells out a full tripartite Russian name, indicating someone especially important.

The sometimes cryptic sections of text set in smaller type between a pair of lines were incomplete in Propp's manuscript or were missing and reconstituted from notes of his students. I have retained them here only when they help trace the course of his presentation. References to entities that no longer exist have been left in the text, because they mark Propp's own time (e.g., the German Democratic Republic or Soviet cities now renamed). Where Propp mentions famous Russian artists or cultural figures, I have added their first names to make them easier to find for the curious.

Propp uses a few Russian words whose translations would be ambiguous or clumsy, such as *rusalka* (the mermaid-like Russian female nature spirit), *bogatyr'* (the superheroic main characters of folk epic songs), and *legenda* and *predanie* (genres of folk narrative prose mentioned in Propp's introduction). These are defined on their first appearance and are then left in Russian throughout the text; their plurals are in Russian as well (e.g., *rusalki*), because the alternative is an awkward hybrid with an English ending. The crucial word *skazka* has been rendered as "folktale" or sometimes (to avoid monotony) "tale" throughout most of the book, but it is left as *skazka* in the parts of the text that describe its evolution or etymology; *narodnaia skazka*, literally "folk folktale," is rendered as "folkloric tale," although the word *folkloric* suggests a stylization, and the point here is precisely that the "folk folktale" is not a stylization. This distinguishes the folktale proper from *skazka* tout court, which can also refer to literary fairytales, such as Aksakov's, or tales in verse, such as those by Aleksandr Pushkin or Marina Tsvetaeva. This ambiguity reflects the benefits and hazards of using a term that the people themselves use rather than a scholarly neologism whose meaning can be kept under control.

Notes in the text belong variously to Propp himself, to the editors of the 1984 edition (Kirill Chistov and Valentina Eremina),[24] or to me; notes and other additions by the Russian editors are given in square brackets with the initials CE, whereas my notes also appear in brackets and are labeled with my initials (SF). Titles of books or articles in the body of the text have been translated into English; those in the notes have not been, although the titles have been shortened for space and the publication information has been omitted (the complete reference information can be found in the bibliography). All sources cited are listed in the bibliography at the end of this book, and I offer a separate section in the bibliography for recent works in English on Russian folklore, folktales, and ethnography and of works by Propp in English translation.

ACKNOWLEDGMENTS

I would like to thank Jack Zipes for his inspiration and encouragement of the translation. Marina Rojavin gave me precious stylistic advice, and David Birnbaum offered invaluable support with rendering of archaic Russian and with bibliographic searches. Lou Wagner, Professor Emeritus at Allegheny College, generously let me take advantage of his unparalleled familiarity with *Morphology of the Folktale* and his sharp eye for all kinds of detail. The two anonymous readers for Wayne State University Press provided provocative and extremely helpful comments, especially concerning this introduction. Donald Haase has had excellent suggestions all along, and working with Annie Martin, also of Wayne State University Press, has been a great pleasure. Finally, I wish to express my gratitude for a James A. Michener Faculty Fellowship from Swarthmore College, which funded a second sabbatical semester as I worked on this translation.

THE RUSSIAN FOLKTALE
BY VLADIMIR YAKOVLEVICH PROPP

INTRODUCTION
IN PRAISE OF THE FOLKTALE

IT WOULD SEEM THAT we all have a clear empirical idea of what a folktale is. Perhaps we preserve poetic recollections, remembering a tale from childhood. We intuitively feel its charm, we enjoy its beauty; we dimly understand that we are face to face with something quite significant. In other words, it is a poetic sense that guides our understanding and evaluation of the folktale.

A poetic sense is absolutely essential for understanding the folktale—and not only the folktale but any work of verbal art. This sense is a natural gift. Not everyone has it, and some very good people lack it. No one knows why some of us are born with inclinations, abilities, and an interest in mathematics while others are gifted in chemistry, physics, or music. The humanities occupy a somewhat particular place among the sciences. A botanist does not necessarily have to understand the beauty of the flower whose structure and growth he studies. However, an aesthetic reception is quite possible here too. Academician Aleksandr Fersman understood the beauty of rocks from the time of his childhood. Such receptivity and sensitivity are all the more necessary for people who work with any of the arts, including the folk arts. A person who lacks such a sensitivity, vocation, or interest should take up something else. At the same time, a poetic reception, although essential for understanding the folktale, is not yet sufficient. It is fruitful only when combined with strict methods of scholarly study and research.

A scientific or scholarly approach has greatly advanced the study of the folktale. There is such an immense body of literature that a mere bibliographic list of titles of works on the folktale and collections that have been published all over the world would make up a thick volume. Before World War II, scholars in Germany began publishing an encyclopedia of the folktale (*Handwörterbuch des Märchens*); several volumes came out before the war interrupted. In the German Democratic Republic a new edition of this encyclopedia is being prepared, in conformity with contemporary scholarly demands.[1] An Institute of German Folk Studies has been created under the auspices of the Berlin Academy of Sciences. Since 1955 this institute has published an annual review of everything that is taking place in Europe concerning the study of the folktale (*Deutsches Jahrbuch für Volkskunde* [The German Folklore Annual]).[2] The International Society for the Study of Narrative Folklore periodically convenes international congresses and publishes a special journal, *Fabula*.[3] The Institute of Russian Literature (the Pushkin House) is a part of the Academy of Sciences of the USSR, and it includes a special sector for folklore that publishes an annual journal, *Russian Folklore*.[4] A bibliography of Russian folklore is in preparation.[5] Even so, scholars have not completed all that is to be done, and their work will continue.

My task is not to produce a broad, comprehensive, monographic study of the folktale or to reveal all the problems associated with it. I will open the door to this treasure house only slightly, so as to peek in through the crack.

The folktale's range is enormous, and studying it has required the work of several generations of scholars. The study of the folktale is not so much a discrete discipline as an independent science of encyclopedic character. It cannot be imagined in isolation from world history, ethnography, the history of religion, the history of forms of thought and poetry, linguistics, and historical poetics. The folktale is usually studied within national and linguistic boundaries. We too will proceed this way: We will study the Russian folktale. Strictly speaking, however, this kind of study will not reveal all the issues connected with the life of the folktale. The folktale must be studied with a comparative method, using material from all over the world. Folktales are spread throughout the whole world. No people lack them. All the cultured peoples of antiquity knew the folktale: ancient China, India, Egypt, Greece, and Rome. It is enough to recall the tales of the *Thousand and One Nights*—a collection known to the Arabs from the ninth century—to feel the greatest respect for Arabic folktale art. The peoples inhabiting the Asian part of the Soviet Union possess an unusually rich trove of folktales: the Buriats, Tadzhiks, Uzbeks, Evenks, Yakuts, and many others, as well as the peoples of the Volga and the European North. Armenian and Georgian folktales, like the tales of other peoples of the Caucasus, are famous throughout the world. All this has been painstakingly collected, recorded, and studied. Only a trifling part of it has been published.

I would also digress if I started to list all the peoples of the world and their folktales. Every people has its national tales, its own plots. But there are also plots of another kind—international plots known all over the world, or at least to a whole group of peoples. It is remarkable not only that folktales are so widespread but also that the tales of the world's peoples are interconnected. The folktale symbolizes the unity of peoples, who understand one another in their tales. Folktales pass widely from one people to another, disregarding linguistic or territorial or state boundaries. It is as though the nations conspire and work together to create and develop their poetic wealth. The idea that the folktale should be studied on an international scale has dominated scholarship for a long time, especially in the era of the Grimm brothers, who cited a huge number of variants of tales from all the peoples of Europe in the third volume of their *Children's and Household Tales*. I digress slightly here, but I want to mention that on the hundredth anniversary of the 1812 appearance of the first volume of the Grimm brothers' collection, in honor of that date, German scholar Johannes Bolte and Czech scholar Jiří Polívka began publishing an enormous work titled *Notes to the Tales of the Brothers Grimm*. They continued the work the Grimms had begun, adding variants of folktales not only from Europe but from the whole world to the 225 tales in the Grimms' collection. The list of variants takes up three thick volumes. They also published two volumes of material for study of the history of folktales among various peoples. Publishing these *Notes* took about twenty years (1913–32).

To give some sense of the dissemination of folkloric tales and individual plots, let me cite one example: the tale of the fool who tricks everyone. The fool travels to the city to sell the hide of a bull he has killed. Along the way he happens to find a treasure, and he says that he got the money by selling the bull's hide. His fellow villagers slaughter their bulls too, but they are unable to sell them. The fool carries out capers: He receives a large sum when he sells a pot that supposedly cooks by itself, sells a whip or a flute that supposedly reanimates the dead, drives away someone else's cattle and says he found them at the bottom of the lake. His envious enemies jump into the water to find herds themselves, and they drown. The tricks may vary, but there are few variations, and the tale type is stable. This tale is known among the Russians, Ukrainians, Belarusans, Bulgarians, Czechs, Slovaks, Serbs, Croats, Sorbs,[6] Germans, and Polish Kashubians. The tale is known in Holland, Sweden, Norway, Denmark, Iceland, the Faeroe Islands, Scotland (but not England), France, Italy, Spain (among the Basques), Albania, and Romania. It is known among the Baltic peoples (the Lithuanians, Latvians, Estonians), the Finno-Ugric peoples (Finns, Hungarians), the Nenets, the Volga peoples (Udmurts, Mari, Tatars), and the peoples of the Caucasus and Asia Minor. It is also found in Afghanistan, in India (in several languages), and among the Ainu. It exists in Africa: on Mauritius, in Madagascar, the Congo, Tunisia, among the Swahili peoples, the Berbers, and in Sudan. In the Americas it is attested to in the Bahamas, in Jamaica, in Louisiana (United States), in Peru and Brazil, and in Greenland.[7]

The list of peoples who know this tale was long when it was published in 1915, but it is clearly incomplete. Some peoples' tales have been collected very little or not at all.

But if a tale that is spread throughout the world is an international plot in the fullest sense of the word, is there any sense then in studying one people's tales in isolation from those of other peoples—and is it even possible? In fact, it is not just possible; it is essential. First, each people, and sometimes each group of peoples, has national plots of its own. Second, even given a common subject, each people will create distinctive forms. The tale of the fool I mentioned is far from being merely a cheerful farce. Every people invests it with its own specific life and social philosophy, shaped by that people's material conditions and history. Russian tales of the fool are just as nationally specific as German, French, or Turkish ones. Third and finally, establishing comparative folklore studies on a worldwide scale is a matter for the fairly distant future. It demands a variety of prerequisites. One of these is full mastery, first and foremost, of all national material. Russians should first and foremost study the Russian folktale—it is our duty.

I will not ask how we can explain the folktale's universality. This topic still lies before us. The folktale's universality, its ubiquity, is just as striking as its immortality. All forms of literature die out at some point. The Greeks, for example, created great dramatic art, but the Greek theater of antiquity as a vital phenomenon is dead. Reading Aeschylus, Sophocles, Euripides, or Aristophanes today requires a certain preliminary study. The same can be said of the literature of any era. Who can read Dante now? Only educated people. However, absolutely everyone understands the folktale. It passes unhindered across all linguistic boundaries, from one people to another, and it has been preserved in that form for millennia. It is understood just as well by representatives of peoples who have not yet joined modern civilization, who are oppressed by colonialism, and by minds standing at the apex of civilization, such as Shakespeare, Goethe, or Pushkin.

This is the case because the folktale contains eternal, unfading values. These values will gradually reveal themselves to us. For now, I will limit myself to pointing out the poetry, the sincerity, the beauty, and the deep truthfulness of the folktale, its cheerfulness and liveliness, its sparkling wit, its combination of childlike naïveté with deep wisdom and a sober worldview. Of course, each text taken in isolation may contain defects or imperfections. These imperfections should not at all be glossed over, evened out, or concealed, as unfortunately often happens. The folktale reveals its treasures only in broad comparative study of each tale type. This requires labor and patience, but the labor will be richly rewarded.

THE FOLKTALE'S ROLE IN THE ORIGINS OF EUROPEAN LITERATURE

We are moved to study the folktale not only because of its folk poetic character and ethical virtues. Knowing about folktales is essential for all scholars of literature and especially literary history. The folktale played a large role in the rise and development of European literature. The folktale's influence on the process of literary development is bound to certain periods of this development.

We find no influence of the folktale and almost no trace of it in medieval Russian literature. Only in isolated cases do folktale motifs penetrate into hagiographic literature, as in the fifteenth-century tale (*povest'*) of Prince Peter and the maiden Fevronia, one of the loveliest tales not only in Russian literature but in the world. This old-fashioned, morally elevating tale is entirely shot through with folktale motifs.[8]

The situation in Western Europe was somewhat different, but medieval culture on the whole bore a clerical character both in Russia and in the West. This culture created grand monuments of architecture, visual art, and literature. We need only recall the cathedrals of Cologne, of Reims, the church of St. Basil the Blessed or the Uspenskii Cathedral in Moscow, the Kievan church complex. We need only walk through the rooms of medieval art in the Tretyakov Gallery in Moscow or the Russian Museum in Leningrad to get an impression of this art's grandeur. Medieval literature was equally subordinated to the religious worldview.

This art developed for centuries, but it could not last forever. The watershed came in the fourteenth century, in the epoch known as the Renaissance, or Rebirth, the epoch of humanism. The new art, centered in Italy, could no longer depend on or continue the Christian medieval tradition. Its forms were based on the pagan art of antiquity.

I will not speak here about issues of architectural and representative arts in the Renaissance. That would take me too far afield. The process of liberating the human being from captivity to the church's worldview and ascetic ideals also took place in the development of verbal art: Writers began to study Greek and Latin literature. But narrative art could not orient itself toward antique culture as much as the visual arts and architecture could. The new secular literature arose on the basis of national folklore, primarily narrative folklore and, first and foremost, the folktale. This explains the rise of one well-known figure of Renaissance literature, Giovanni Boccaccio (1313–75). His famous *Decameron* (1350–53), which marks the beginning of secular literature in Europe, is half composed of folk plots. Even those plots that are not attested in folklore are clearly not Boccaccio's own inventions but rather retellings of stories and anecdotes that were current in urban circles.

This orientation toward folklore is not an individual trait of Boccaccio; it is a sign of the times, a historical law and necessity. Boccaccio is only the most outstanding and famous of a whole group of novelists. His English counterpart is Geoffrey Chaucer (1340?–1400), with his *Canterbury Tales* (1387–1400). Twenty-nine pilgrims, simple people with various occupations, meet in a tavern on the road to Canterbury to visit the grave of St. Thomas Becket. At night and while traveling they exchange amusing stories, which a folklorist will easily recognize as folktales. Chaucer has only twenty-one stories, told in simple conversational language (though in verse), some with dialect elements. Here too, as in Italy, a new secular narrative literature of realistic character grew up from the soil of folktales.

The folktale's influence did not weaken after the Renaissance; on the contrary, it grew stronger. An imitation of Boccaccio, usually called *The Pentameron*, that is, "five-day collection" (*decameron* means "ten-day collection"), came out in Naples in 1634–36. The author, Giambattista Basile, was a simple soldier who had heard all kinds of unusual stories during his campaigns. The framing story is basically that a certain prince, to amuse the princess, hires ten women to tell one folktale each for five days. Together the result is fifty tales, all genuine Italian folktales in their plots, although narrated in literary language and style.

These works are all united by one common trait. They represent a kind of reaction against church and ascetic literature. Many are therefore aimed at the Catholic clergy, which is depicted satirically with all its failings. The human personality comes into its own, tossing off the chains of asceticism and religious exaltation or contemplation. It claims the right to ordinary human love. It is through folklore that the theme of love enters world literature. Let us note that the theme of love comes to lyric poetry from the folk song as well.

However, we should not conceive of the matter too simplistically, as though writers simply borrowed folklore plots and retold them. Things are significantly more complicated. The folktale is a source of varied plots, but the plots themselves undergo an essential reworking as they enter the orbit of literature. The aesthetics of folklore and the aesthetics of professional composition reveal deep differences, which gradually become obvious. A great deal has been written and said about the interrelations of folklore and literature. There are many works on Pushkin and folklore, Gogol and folklore, Lermontov and folklore, Blok and folklore, and so on. They describe folklore's beneficent influence on literature, and that is undoubtedly true. Folk creativity has been a source of inspiration for many writers, as Maxim Gorky noted. But at the same time people forget one thing: A writer who mines the treasures of folklore must not only accept the folk tradition but also overcome it. Scholars usually fail to demonstrate this. One may establish which plots Boccaccio borrowed from the treasury of the novellistic folktale, and many works have already done so, but Boccaccio is still not the same thing as folklore. We must determine the deep and principled differences, and this is possible only once we have fully studied the poetics of folklore and of the folktale in particular. The folktale is in essence a made-up story. Once folktales pass into literature, they take on the character of the novella, that is, of narratives that have a certain plausibility. They acquire exact chronological and topographic locations, their characters receive personal names, types change into characters, individual experiences begin to play a larger role, the setting is described in detail, and events are narrated as a chain of causes and effects.

What occurred in Western Europe in the fourteenth century took place significantly later in Russia, essentially in the seventeenth and eighteenth centuries. Secular literature arose then in Russia, on the basis of the folk narrative tradition. It arose in cities, and its creators and bearers were working people, the third estate. The *bylina* (epic song), which peasants had sung, moved onto the pages of manuscript books, where it was called a tale, a story, or a word, and it became the subject of reading for amusement.

Secular literature developed somewhat differently in Russia than in Western Europe. Russia had no writers like Boccaccio and his followers. But the rise of secular literature was essentially the same. The Russian secular tale arose anonymously. One may cite the seventeenth-century tale of Karp Sutulov, based on the tale of a priest, a deacon, and a sacristan who try to gain the favors of a beautiful woman. She invites them in one after another on the same evening and hides them all in a trunk full of soot. Her husband drives the trunk to market and releases them there, saying that they are devils. Gogol used this plot in his story "The Night Before Christmas" (A-T 1730).[9]

Still, folklore influenced secular literature less in its plots than in its realistic narrative style. Tales were created about the fox who goes to confession, Ruff, Son of Ruff (*Ersh Ershovich*), Shemiaka's Judgment, Savva Grudtsyn, Frol Skobeyev, and others.[10]

Some of these, like the tales of the fox confessor or Ruff, Son of Ruff, undergo a circular movement. Their plot is folkloric. They are creations of individual authors who remain unknown to us, but their images, motifs, and style come from folklore. The tales of Ruff, Son of Ruff and the fox confessor imitate the animal folktale—and they imitate it so well that these works have passed back into the sphere of folktales. They have become folklorized. This phenomenon has been the object of more than one study. They are literary tales with a folkloric basis, which thereafter returned to folklore.

I will not speak about the later development of Russian prose and its folkloric roots. I will touch on the *lubok* (woodblock) print folktales of the eighteenth century, such as *Bova, Eruslan Lazarevich*, and others. Russian tales of the seventeenth and eighteenth centuries, particularly the tales of the Petrine era, are unimaginable without the foundation of folk prose. They are studied by historians of literature. The most complete study, richly supported by materials, is by Vasilii Sipovskii.[11] A briefer outline can be found in any textbook or course on eighteenth-century Russian literature;[12] I refer anyone who is curious to these works.

I can add nothing new here. It is a task for scholars of literature, not for folklorists. We are studying the folktale, not the development of literature based on folklore. The examples I have cited only show the significance in principle of the folktale in the development of European literature. This process takes on a different character in the nineteenth century.[13]

Realist writers of the twentieth century no longer draw plots from folktales, but Maxim Gorky indicated how much a contemporary writer might learn from the folktale in his speech at the First Congress of Soviet Writers in 1934.

The Folktale and Contemporary Culture

There is, however, another sphere where the folktale has had a fruitful impact up to the present day. This is in the fine arts: musical and dramatic arts, ballet, and opera, as well as symphonic music. They have been influenced by verbal folklore and by musical folklore as well.

Mikhail Glinka's opera *Ruslan and Liudmila* is replete with folktale and musical folklore. Everyone, of course, will remember Rimsky-Korsakov's *Tale of Tsar Saltan* and *Kashchei the Deathless* and Sergei Prokofiev's *Love for Three Oranges*. Less well known are Iuliia Veisberg's operas *Jack Frost* (1930) and *The Magic Swan-Geese* (1930) and Marian Koval's *The Wolf and the Seven Kids* (1941). The Grimms' tales have been used in more than thirty German operas.

The ballets are more numerous: two ballets (by Ludwig Minkus and Rodion Shchedrin) based on the plot of the Little Hump-Backed Horse; *Sleeping Beauty* by Petr Ilyich Tchaikovsky; *Cinderella* by Sergei Prokofiev; *The Firebird, The Tale of the Runaway Soldier and the Devil,* and *The Fable of the Fox, the Rooster, the Tomcat, and the Ram* by Igor Stravinsky; *Ivushka* by Orest Evlakhov; and *Aladdin and the Magic Lamp* by Boris Savel'ev. In addition, the symphonic compositions include Nikolai Rimsky-Korsakov's *Scheherazade* and *Folktale for a Large Orchestra*; *Baba-Yaga* and *Kikimora* by Anatolii Liadov; and Sergei Prokofiev's *The Fool Who Out-Fooled Seven Fools* and *The Old Granny's Tale*. Folktales and musical folklore are the basis for the young opera and ballet arts in our [Soviet] national republics (e.g., Farid Iarullin's *Shurale*).[14]

It is curious, all the same, that there are no well-known or popular drama-tizations of the folktale. A folktale on stage without music would be simply tedious. The folktale's magical element turns to reality, without ceasing to be magical, only with music. The folktale is possible in the puppet theater, where there are many performances. It is just as impossible in cinema as on the stage, and for the same reasons (e.g., the tale of Never-Laugh).

Animated cartoons can be based on folktales, on the same basis as the pup-pet theater.

But the folktale is out of place in one sphere of the arts. This is visual art. True, there is no shortage of artistic illustrations of folktales. But, in my opin-ion, even the best of them (Ivan Bilibin, Elena Polenova) do not convey the folktale world; instead, they present a stylization. They correspond neither to folk ideas nor to the folktale spirit. I think the folktale cannot be illustrated in principle because its events take place outside time and space, whereas rep-resentative art transfers them into real, visible space. A folktale ceases at once to be a folktale. This is true even of the best paintings, such as Viktor Vas-netsov's *Alyonushka*. The picture is full of a genuine, lively lyricism. A girl sits on the pebbles by the water, sorrowfully hugging her knees, resting her head on them. Completely absorbed in her grief, she gazes straight ahead without seeing anything. It is a splendid painting, but there is nothing of the folktale in it except the title. Another painting by Vasnetsov, *The Flying Carpet*, is in-comparably weaker—simply a poor piece of work. The flying carpet hangs in mid-air, the princess sits on it calmly, and we don't believe any of it.

Brilliant and significant artists who have depicted folktales express them-selves more than they express the folktales. This is the case, for example, with Mikhail Vrubel''s *Swan Princess* or *Thirty-Three Bogatyrs*. It is typical Vrubel', but it is no folktale.[15] Yet I digress. One could write a whole book on the folk-tale's role in the development of European culture.

THE TERM *FOLKTALE* IN VARIOUS LANGUAGES

I began with the question of what the folktale is, but I did not answer the question. Instead, I indicated some of the folktale's qualities and its role in the origin and early development of European literature. We must return to the question, What is the folktale? What do we mean by the term? It is es-sential to have a scholarly definition of the concept "folktale." The other ques-tions that arise in the study of the folktale will depend on that definition.

What is a folktale? At first the question might seem entirely rhetorical, as though everyone knows the answer. Even scholars have advanced such opinions. Finnish scholar János Honti writes, "A one-sided definition of a concept that everyone knows is in fact superfluous: everyone knows what a folktale is and can use that sense to distinguish it from so-called related genres—the folk *predanie*, the *legenda*, and anecdotes."[16] Authors of some fundamental folklore surveys have made do without a definition of the concept and essence of the folktale.[17]

I note that Aleksandr Veselovskii, whose works on the folktale make up a whole volume, never gave his own definition of the folktale. This does not mean that these scholars had no personal understanding of the folktale. They had, but they never recorded it in exact definitions. Nevertheless, we cannot rely on a *sense*, as Honti suggests. We must lay out our point of view as precisely as possible. We cannot accept as folktales everything that is included in collections. In his review of Aleksandr Afanas'ev's collection, nineteenth-century scholar Aleksandr Pypin pointed out the motley nature of folktale material and the fact that "the concept of the folktale has now become very inclusive."[18]

We should first obtain as clear as possible a concept of the term *folktale* itself. I will begin by defining the Russian term *skazka* (folktale) and by studying the word *skazka* and how it is expressed in various other languages. Could such a survey reveal what the folk itself understands by the word *skazka*, what is invested in that notion?

Here we encounter some uncertainty. The peoples of the world, or rather the European peoples, do not as a rule distinguish this variety of folk poetry, using the most varied words to define it.[19] Only two European languages have created special words to express the concept: Russian and German.

The Russian word *skazka* is significantly more recent. It first appeared with its present meaning no earlier than the seventeenth century. Old and medieval Rus' did not know it. This does not mean that there were no folktales; rather, it means that the tales were originally described by some other word. We presume that one such word was *basnia*, corresponding to the verb *baiat'* (to speak), which is now obsolete, and the noun *bakhar'*. The twelfth-century sermonizer Kirill of Turov, listing the torments awaiting sinners in the other world, mentions under the fifteenth torment sinners who "believe in [predicting the future through] meetings, in sneezing, in tracks and in birds' singing, in enchantment, and who tell tales [*basni baiut*] and play the *gusli* [a folk instrument like a psaltery]." Another twelfth-century sermon (in the *Sermons of [Pseudo-] John Chrysostom)* depicts a rich man going to bed: "As he lay down and could not fall asleep his friends would stroke his feet. . . . Others would play music, still others were telling tales [*baiut'*] and performing sorcery."[20] Turns of phrase such as *polno basni-to skazyvat'* (stop telling stories) or *bab'i basni i durak liubit* (even a fool loves old wives' tales), cited in Vladimir Dal''s *Explanatory Dictionary,*[21] point to the fact that the term *basnia* in the living contemporary Russian language may include the meaning of *skazka*. Ancient Rus' did not know the word *skazka; basnia* served as its equivalent.

In the beginning the word *skazka* had a completely different sense from what it has now. It signified a spoken or written word, a document in force. We read in the notes of eighteenth-century memoirist Andrei Bolotov, "Then they (the peasants), being satisfied, created together with me a document [*skazka*] of affection."[22] In oral use *otobrat' skazku* (to take away a *skazka*) once meant "to take down testimony." In Nikolai Gogol's novel *Dead Souls, revizskie skazki* was the term for establishing, by means of revision, documented lists of the peasants who belonged to a landowner. But *skazka* could signify other things too. Ivan Turgenev's story "The Bailiff" gives, "We've drawn the boundaries, your honor, all through your mercy. We signed the *skazka* three days ago."[23]

The root of the term *skazka*, -*kaz*-, acquires a variety of meanings with different Russian prefixes, but the basic meaning of the root itself is some form of communication: *skazat'* (to say), *ukazat'* (to indicate), *nakazat'* (to punish, to make an example of), and so on. Serbian *kazati* means "to speak," and Czech *kazati* means "to prove, to demonstrate."

Therefore, until the seventeenth century the Russian word *skazka* signified something trustworthy, written or oral testimony, or a witness with legal strength. From the seventeenth century on we can trace another sense of the word *skazka*—one that contradicts the meaning just cited. A 1649 *ukaz* of Tsar Aleksei Mikhailovich reads: "Many men through unreason believe in dreams, and in meetings, and in tracks, and in birds' songs, and guess the answers to riddles, and tell impossible *skazki*."[24] Note that the word *skazka* appears here in the same context we saw in Kirill of Turov with *basni* (bird song, tracks, and the like), showing clearly that the word *basn'* was replaced by *skazka*. Here the word *skazka* already conveys the same meaning that we give it.

What conclusions can we draw from this outline? We can extract two markers of the folktale encoded in the word: (1) *Skazka* is recognized as a narrative genre (*baiat'* means "to narrate, to tell" [*skazyvat', rasskazyvat'*]);

(2) a *skazka* is considered an invention. (In Tsar Aleksei Mikhailovich's *ukaz* we have *skazki nebylye* [tales that never happened].) The Ukrainian language contains the word *kazka*, along with the word *baika*. Both signify not only a narrative but an invention unworthy of trust.

It is difficult to say how a word could receive a meaning opposite to its own meaning. Apparently those *skazki*, the testimonies taken during trials or investigations and so on, tended to be so undependable, so filled with lies, that the word *skazka*, which once meant a dependable document, came to signify a lie, an invention, something completely untrustworthy.

The ancient Greeks used the word *myth* to mean a folktale. They had no special word for the folktale.

In Latin, the word *skazka* is conveyed by *fabula*, but this word is not specific to the folktale either. It has many different meanings: a conversation, gossip, a topic of conversation, and so on (compare *fabula* in Russian, which means "a plot, the subject of narration"), but also a story, including a folkloric tale and a fable. It passed into German in the sense of *basnia* or fable. In German *Fabel* means a fable (*basnia*), and the verb *fabulieren* means "to tell an exaggerated story."[25]

I will not dwell on how the concept of the folktale is expressed in various world languages. Bolte has done this with great mastery.[26] I will discuss only three languages: Italian, French, and English. Italian identifies the folktale with the words *fiaba* and *favola*, which clearly descend from the Latin *fabula*, or the words *conto*, *racconto*, and others. The root *cont* generally signifies a count (compare the Russian root *chit*, as in *schitat'*, "to count"). French most often uses *conte*, which means "story," as in *raconter* (to narrate, to tell). For exactness they use *conte populaire* (folk story), *conte de fées* (fairy story, which actually only fits the wonder tale), *récit*, or *légende*.

The same is true in English. *Skazka* is conveyed by the word *tale*, which signifies a story in general or any kind of story. Dickens gave one of his novels the title *A Tale of Two Cities*. *Fairytale* is used on the French model. Tales meant especially for children are described with the term *nursery tale*. The words *story* and *legend* are also used.

Here again I might digress and take up the question of how to convey the concept of the folktale in various languages. Such a study might reveal why most peoples lack specialized terms and why they these terms do exist in German and Russian. I could state as many hypotheses as you like, but a scholarly solution would demand broad investigation.

Defining the Concept of the Skazka

I mentioned earlier that many scholars have made do without defining the concept of the folktale. Others, though, have offered definitions. Scholarly understanding of the term *skazka* has its own interesting history, which I will address in what follows. For now, I will cite two or three definitions and attempt to make sense of them. To make a complete study of the folktale, we must have at least a preliminary idea about this.

Bolte and Polívka gave a definition that has been accepted in Europe. It can be summarized as follows: Since Herder and the Grimm brothers, the folkloric tale has been understood as a story based on poetic fantasy, particularly one from the world of magic, an account not connected with the conditions of real life, which people at all levels of society listen to with pleasure, even if they find it unlikely or implausible.[27]

Can we agree with this definition? Although it has been widely accepted, it reveals a number of weaknesses.

First, defining the folkloric tale as "a story based on poetic fantasy" is too broad. In general, any work of literature is based on poetic fantasy. Even if we understand "poetic fantasy" as pure fantasy, things that are impossible in real life, then, for example, Gogol's story "The Portrait" or the second half of his story "The Overcoat" would have to be recognized as folktales.

Second, what does "particularly one from the world of magic" mean? The majority of folkloric tales (animal tales, novellistic tales) involve no enchantment at all. It is present only in the so-called wonder tale. This definition would exclude all folktales that are not wonder tales.

Third, a Soviet scholar would never accept the idea that a folkloric tale was "not connected with the conditions of real life." The question of the folktale's relationship to real life is complex. But it is wrong to consider it axiomatic that a folkloric tale is not connected with the conditions of real life, and to put that into a definition. We shall see that even the most fantastic folkloric tales grow out of the reality of various eras.

Finally, making it a formula that the folkloric tale provides aesthetic pleasure even if listeners find it "unlikely or implausible" suggests that a folkloric tale *might* be considered verisimilar or plausible, that it all depends on the will of the listeners. We have seen that the people have always considered the folkloric tale an invention. We must find a different definition.

An old rule of logic states, *Definitio fit per genus proximum et differentiam specificam*; that is, a definition is drawn through the nearest kind and the specific difference. In this case we should understand the nearest kind to mean the story in general, narrative. The folkloric tale is a story; it belongs to the sphere of the *epos*. But not every story can be called a folkloric tale. What kind of story may be called a folkloric tale? What is its specific distinction?

The first thing that may come to mind is that a folkloric tale is defined by its plots. Really, when we think of the folkloric tale, we recall the tale of the fox, the kidnapped princess, the Firebird, the priest and his hired laborer, and so on; that is, we imagine a whole sequence of plots. Yes, these plots really are specific to the folkloric tale, but nonetheless the folkloric tale is not defined by its plots alone.

In fact, the plot of a woman rescued from a dragon is possible in myth, in the *legenda*, in the *bylina*, in spiritual verses. It is not the plot that is specific to the folktale, but the *folkloric* form of the plot. Boccaccio rewrote plots he took from folktales in the form of novellas, and they ceased to be folktales. The plot of "Terentii the Guest" exists as a folktale, a *bylina*, and a folk comedy. The plot of the nightingale robber is possible for the *bylina*, but it is told in the form of a folkloric tale, especially in areas where the epic *bylina* no longer exists.

Plot is of crucial significance for understanding and studying the folktale, but the folktale nonetheless cannot be defined by its plots. What defines it, then?

If we compare genres, we see that their distinctness lies less in the range of plots than in the fact that their artistic form conveys different points of view. Each genre possesses a particular artistry that is specific to it, and in some cases to it alone. This specific trait must be isolated and defined.

A body of artistic devices that has taken shape through history can be called a poetics, and I would now say that folklore genres are defined by a specific poetics. Thus we arrive at the original, most general definition: The folkloric tale is a story (*genus proximum*—the nearest kind) that is distinct from all other kinds of narrative in its specific poetics.

This definition, made according to all the rules of logic, nonetheless does not reveal the folktale's essence; it must be supplemented further. If we define the folktale through its poetics, then we are defining one unknown by another, because this poetics has not yet been studied sufficiently. The concept of poetics also permits variant interpretations, different understandings. Nevertheless, the principle itself is important. If the poetics has not yet been sufficiently studied, that is a matter of time, not a difficulty in principle.

Aleksandr Nikiforov, an important folktale collector and researcher, set out to define the concept of the folktale in this way. He collected a great deal and worked on the practical methodology of collection. He published several specialized works on the folktale as a form; as a result, he was ideally prepared for a multifaceted understanding of the folktale.

Nikiforov's definition states, "Folktales are oral stories, known among the people with the purpose of entertainment, containing events that are unusual in the everyday sense (fantastic, miraculous, or everyday), and distinguished by a particular compositional and stylistic structure."[28] To this day, this definition has not lost its scholarly significance. It should form the basis of our understanding of the folktale and help us set it apart from other related formations.

This definition results from a scholarly understanding of the folktale, expressed in the briefest possible formula. It provides all the fundamental traits that characterize the folktale. The folktale, the tale told by the folk, is a folk narrative genre characterized by the form of its function in society. It is a story passed on from generation to generation by oral transmission alone. This distinguishes the folktale's function from the function of the artificial, or literary, fairytale, which is transmitted by reading and writing and is unchangeable. The literary tale, like other literary works of art, may come into use by the people and begin to circulate, produce variants, pass orally from person to person; in that case it too enters the folklorist's field of study. This is the folktale's first trait—still not specific to it but one that should be stressed and underlined.

Furthermore, the folktale is characterized as a story; that is, it is a narrative genre. This trait is not decisive either, because there are other folk narrative genres that differ from folktales (the *bylina*, the ballad). As I said, the word *skazka* itself suggests something that is *told*. This means that the people perceive the folktale primarily as a narrative genre.

Another trait Nikiforov noted is that the folktale is told for entertainment. It belongs among the entertainment genres. The great Russian critic Vissarion Belinsky noted this trait, and no doubt correctly, although it is sometimes disputed. Thus, for example, Vladimir Anikin asserts that the folktale pursues educational goals.[29] We cannot dispute the idea that it has an educational significance, but to say that it was created with the goal of education is definitely wrong. The folktale's entertaining character does not by any means exclude deep ideational content. When Nikiforov speaks of the folktale's entertaining significance, this means that it serves primarily aesthetic functions, that it is a genre with artistic goals and is thus distinct from all the forms of ritual poetry, which have applied significance, the *legenda*, which has moralizing goals, or the tradition (*predanie*), whose purpose is to convey information.

The trait of entertainment is connected with another folktale trait advanced by Nikiforov, namely, the unusualness of the events (fantastic, miraculous, or everyday) that make up its contents. Soviet scholarship set apart this trait of the folktale long ago, but Nikiforov added the essential point that its unusualness is understood not only as a fantastic unusualness (as in the wonder tale) but also as an everyday unusualness, which allows us to include novellistic folktales under the definition. He is undoubtedly correct in noting this trait, although I must say that it is more probably typical of folklore and the epic in general rather than one specific to the folktale. Epic folklore does not speak of general, everyday, workaday things. That may sometimes serve as a background for subsequent events, which are always unusual. But unusualness in the *bylina* is different from that in the folktale. There is a specifically folktale unusualness, and this should become the topic of our study.

Finally, the last trait Nikiforov advances is the folktale's special compositional and stylistic structure. We can unite style and composition under the common term of poetics and say that the folktale is distinguished by its own specific poetics. Let us add on our own account that this very trait is decisive in defining the folktale. This is the trait Nikiforov first advanced, recognizing it as a scholarly achievement. True, here one unknown (the folktale) is reduced to another unknown (its poetics), because the study of folktale poetics is still far from adequate. Nonetheless, the given definition is not merely a verbal formula. It points the way toward a real, concrete discovery of the concept of the folktale. By defining the folktale's nature through its poetics, we know what direction to follow in our ongoing studies; we must make a detailed study of folktale poetics and the regularities of that poetics.

In this way, we have a definition that reflects contemporary views of the folktale and enables further study.

One trait, however, is insufficiently developed, although Nikiforov did note it. This is that listeners do not believe the veracity of what is told. The folk themselves view folktales as inventions; we see this not only in the word's etymology but also in the Russian saying "A tale's made up, a song's the truth" (*Skazka—skladka, pesnia—byl'*). They do not believe the actuality of the events laid out in the folktale, and this is the folktale's fundamental, decisive trait. Belinsky himself noted it when, in comparing the *bylina* with the folktale, he wrote: "At the basis of the second kind of verbal work (i.e., the folktale) we always notice a second thought, we notice that the narrator himself does not believe what he is saying and is laughing inside at his own story. This is particularly true of Russian folktales."[30]

This is an essential trait of the folktale, although at first glance it may seem to be a trait that belongs not to the folktale but to the listeners. They are free to believe or not. Children, for example, do believe. Nevertheless, the folktale is a deliberate poetic fiction.[31]

Jacob Grimm tells an interesting story. One tale from the Grimms' collection ends with the words *Wer's nicht glaubt, zahlt'n Thaler*. This German saying means, "If you don't believe, pay me a thaler." One day a girl rang at the door of his apartment. When Grimm opened the door, she said, "Here's a thaler. I don't believe your tales." At that time a thaler was a large gold coin.

Not everyone agrees that the people do not believe in folktales. In his book *The Russian Folkloric Tale*, Vladimir Anikin says, "There was a time when people believed in the veracity of folktale narrations just as unshakably as we believe in a historical documentary story or sketch today."[32] This is not at all correct. True, there are individual cases where an object, plot, or story from folktale narrations entered the contents of non-folktale formations and those stories were believed. For example, Herodotus tells about how a crafty thief robbed the Egyptian king Rampsinit and married his daughter. Thanks to comparative materials, we now know quite well that this is a folktale. But Herodotus did not know, and he believed that it had all really happened. In our chronicles the tradition of the miraculous jelly of Belgorod represents a folktale from a cycle about fooling someone from another tribe, but the chronicler believed the tale. Even the enlightened Englishman Samuel Collins, Ivan the Terrible's doctor, passes on in his book about Russia the tale about Ivan the Terrible and the thieves, not realizing that it is a folktale; he conveys it as historical fact. Individual cases of people who believe in the veracity of the narration have occurred, but they are not typical of the folktale and its listeners among the broad mass of the people. If people believe a narration, then they are not taking it as a folktale.

Anikin needs this kind of assertion to prove that the folktale is realistic. It depicts reality, and therefore people believe it. The folktale consciously depicts reality, according to Anikin: "A millennium of original history opens before us through the folktale."[33] However, it is enough to pick up any textbook of history to see that this is not so. If Anikin says, "The folktale reproduces reality by means of fantastic invention," then this is nothing more than a paradox.[34]

Everything I have stated here gives us a particular and, for now, approximate impression of the folktale's specificity. To understand it more exactly, we must distinguish the folktale from adjacent genres, which I will now proceed to do.

The Folktale and Adjacent Genres

The Folktale and Myth

To distinguish the folktale from related genres, we must find some trait that produces this distinction. I will choose the trait that has been perceived from the very beginning of scholarly examination of the folktale, namely its implausibility, hence also disbelief in the reality of the events it narrates. This is not an external or accidental trait but one that is deeply internal and organic.

Correspondingly, the whole sphere of folk prose can be separated into two great divisions: stories people do not believe (all kinds of folktales belong here) and stories people do believe or used to believe. The latter type includes all the other genres of folk prose. What are those genres?

The folktale has been studied in relation to genres that presumably preceded its appearance. Among these, we must turn first of all to myth. The folktale's relationship to myth presents a great problem, one that has occupied scholarship from the beginning to the present day. For the moment we will not ask whether the folktale and myth are genetically related to one another. The vagueness of ideas about myth led the so-called mythological school to a dead end, as they asserted the invariable descent of the folktale from myth. For Soviet folklore scholars the myth is a formation from a much earlier stage than the folktale. The most primitive, most archaic of all peoples known to us had myths at the moment they were discovered by Europeans, but they did not have folktales as we understand the word. This too gives us the right to say that myth represents an earlier stage of development than the folktale.

The folktale signifies entertainment, whereas myth has sacral meaning. Nonetheless, scholarship on the folktale's relationship to myth has shown extreme disagreement. The German scholar Erich Bethe writes, "Myth, tradition, folktale are scholarly concepts. In essence all three words signify one and the same thing—simply a story."[35] Here the boundary between myth and folktale is completely erased, and erased as a matter of principle. Wilhelm Wundt considers the myths of aboriginal peoples to be folktales and creates a special term for them, *Mythenmärchen*.[36] Stories in circulation among aboriginal peoples are called myths (e.g., by Brinton),[37] folktales (Cushing),[38] legends (Rand),[39] or traditions (Boas),[40] or they are described by other terms (traditions, stories). The vagueness of this situation cannot be tolerated.

We shall describe as myths those stories of aboriginal peoples that are not, perhaps, presented as reality (this cannot always be confirmed or denied, because we see here a different type of thinking; the boundaries between invention and reality may not be fully recognized) but that are admitted as reality of a higher order; they partake of a sacred character. Among aboriginal peoples such stories have religious and magical significance. They may be part of or accompany rituals. Like rituals, myths are also intended to act on nature. Stories about animals, for example, are meant to bring good luck in hunting. Other myths are meant to act on the weather or to heal illnesses. They represent an original form of science, an attempt to explain the world, the origin of the universe or of parts of it—rivers, mountains, animals. Myths of this kind can be called etiological.

A completely different formation is presented by the myths of peoples who already know gods (Greek, Scandinavian, Hindu, and others). Classical mythology can serve as an example. When gods appear in human culture and human consciousness, a myth becomes a story about deities or demigods. The mythology of antiquity is one of the great achievements of human culture in the richness of its plots, its beauty, depth, and harmony. Unfortunately, this mythology is still little known in Russia. There are popular retellings, but popular retellings cannot replace the originals.[41] To give some impression of that mythology and also to cast more light on the difference between the folktale and myth, I will linger on one model, the myth of Orpheus and Eurydice. The plot of this myth has passed into European culture; Glück's remarkable opera *Orfeo ed Euridice* is based on it.

The myth is Greek. We do not know the Greek texts or how this myth was told among the people. It is mentioned by Aeschylus and in Euripides's *Argonauts* and is reflected in representative art. We know it best from Roman literary treatments. There are treatments in Ovid's *Metamorphoses* and in Virgil's *Georgics* (a georgic is a didactic poem about the charms of agriculture). Let me remind you that Virgil is the one who Dante, in his *Divine Comedy*, takes as his wise guide through the underworld. Roman literary treatments of the Orpheus and Eurydice myth must be recognized as splendid and highly artistic. I will give a retelling summarized from all the sources accessible to me.

Orpheus was a singer. His mother was Calliope, the Muse of epic song. Sometimes Apollo was called his father. Apollo gave him a lyre. When he played and sang, the birds would fly up, fish would swim to him, and the beasts of the forest would run to him. Even the trees and cliffs would listen to him.

Compare with the hero of the *Kalevala*, Veinemeinen. Consider rune 41, p. 284. In the end: the tears are pearls.[42]

Orpheus's wife was the naiad Eurydice. The naiads are female inhabitants of flowing water: springs and wells, rivers, lakes. They correspond to the Russian *rusalki* but as a rule are not malevolent; on the contrary, they are benevolent creatures distinguished by beauty and appeal. Eurydice was strolling in a flowering meadow with her friends, nymphs and dryads. (The nymphs are daughters of Zeus; they live, according to Homer, in the mountains, in groves, and on the shores of lakes and rivers. The dryads live in trees.) Such meadows always seem particularly beautiful to the Greeks. The natural landscape of Greece is the sea, valleys, and mountains, rocky and severe; therefore green meadows are the Greeks' most beloved landscape. Their favorite flower is the narcissus. The shepherd-god Aristeos was struck by the beauty of Eurydice and chased her. She fled and did not notice that she had stepped on a snake. The snake bit her, and she fell down dead. I cite Ovid (*Metamorphoses*, X, 8–10):

The young woman,
In the company of naiads wandering the green meadow,
Fell down dead, wounded in the heel by the snake's tooth.

Her friends—nymphs, naiads, dryads—mourned for her loudly. This means that all nature wept. Orpheus cried as well, and he sang. The birds and the clever deer listened to him. Virgil says:

He sang of her when the sun was rising,
He sang of her when the sun was setting.

But this could not bring back his beloved wife. So he decided to go down to the underworld, to the kingdom of shadows, to the ruler of that kingdom, the gloomy god Hades and his spouse Persephone. He addressed him with a song:

I have tried to bear it, the immeasurable grief,
Long have I struggled like a man.
But love is breaking my heart.
I cannot live without Eurydice.
And now I beg you, terrible, holy deities . . .
Give her up to me, my beloved wife,
Release her and return to her the life
That lost its flower too soon.
But if this cannot be,
Take me too into the number of the dead,
I will never return without her.[43]

And a miracle occurred. Everyone wept. The bloodless shades of the dead wept. Even the cheeks of the horrible Eumenides, whose hair was twined with dark-blue snakes, flowed with tears. Hades and Persephone, who had never known pity, felt it now. Persephone summoned the shade of Eurydice. This was a victory of love over death, pity over dispassion. But there was one condition:

Take her, but know this: only if you do not glance back
At the one who will follow after you, only then will she
Be yours. If you look back too soon,
Then you will see her no more.

We already know that in folklore the prohibition is always violated. Ovid describes their return:

Here in mute silence both already moved up the slope,
Up a dark steep path, swathed in unbroken gloom,
And they were already not far from the earthly border—
But fearing she might fall behind, and greedy to see her,
He cast his eyes back, and at once his spouse disappeared.

Virgil has Eurydice say:

Both I, your unhappy wife, and you, Orpheus, are undone
By your lack of reason! Here I am called back by merciless
Fate, and my eyes, already clouding with sleep, flood with tears.

Farewell! The great night seizes me and bears me away,
I can only hold out my powerless hand to you, but I
May be yours no longer![44]

So this narration ends. There is another myth about Orpheus—but we will not dwell on it. Orpheus continued to mourn his beloved wife. He paid no attention to other women. For his scorn of women he was torn apart by the maenads. This piece is literary in its workmanship.

It is quite clear that we have before us in essence not a folktale but a myth, a sacred story, one that people believed to be real. The Greeks believed in the existence of the underworld, believed in the god Hades and the goddess Persephone, believed in the existence of naiads and nymphs and in the terrible Eumenides. The myth of Orpheus and Eurydice was sacred truth for them.

Myths are already alive in the earliest society. By the way, a myth resembling the antique myth of Orpheus and Eurydice is found among the North American Indians. The hero of this myth is not a singer but an ordinary man. When his wife dies, he carries out a purifying bath and penetrates alive into the kingdom of the dead. He succeeds, despite various obstacles, and brings back his wife.

As I have already said, when the gods appear in human consciousness and human culture, myth becomes a story about deities or semideities. This is the whole of Classical mythology. I need not recall the myths of Prometheus, Zeus's abduction of Europa, the Argonauts, and so on. In their plots, composition, and fundamental motifs, myths may coincide with the fairytale. Thus there are episodes in the myth of the Argonauts that correspond fairly closely to our folktales, but they represent myth, not folktales. Jason is sent to Colchis to get the Golden Fleece just as the hero in our folktales is sent over thrice-nice lands to seize golden marvels. King Aeëtes will let him have the fleece if Jason first withstands a test: he must plow a field with two bronze-legged fire-breathing bulls.

Here mention the episode with the golden fleece. Draw more folktale motifs from antiquity from Bolte-Polívka and Herodotus.

Jason is supposed to sow the teeth of a dragon, which will immediately grow into terrible warriors, and he must kill all of them. Aeëtes's daughter, Medea, falls in love with Jason and helps him. Jason manages to do everything and flees with her in his ship. The king tries in vain to catch up with them.

All of this is a classical fairytale. Plowing a whole field and so on are difficult tasks. Medea is the princess-helper, as in many folktales. Finally, winning the wonders, winning the princess, flight and pursuit—all these are typical compositional motifs of the wonder tale. But Jason and the Argonauts is not a folktale but rather a sacred myth, despite all the resemblances between the compositional schemes. The contemporary folklorist cannot take a solely formal point of view. These myths were told with a purpose that was far from entertainment, although their plots were interesting. Myths were connected with cults. Cults were intended to act upon deities so they would help people. The difference between myths and folktales is thus a difference of social function. "The myth, having lost its social significance, becomes a folktale."[45] Myth is a story of religious order; the folktale is aesthetic. Myth is an earlier formation; the folktale is a later one. In this way, myth and folktale are distinguished not so much in themselves but in how people approach them. This means that folkloristics is a science not just of plots, texts, but also of the role of plots in the social lives of peoples.

Byl', Bylichka, Byval'shchina

Stories with religious content were still being told not long ago among the Russian people, and in fairly large numbers and a variety of types at that. They are current in Western Europe to the present day. Can we consider such stories myths as well? Perhaps they should be considered folktales? They cannot be considered folktales according to the criterion we have given, because they are presented as reality and people are firmly convinced of their veracity. They also cannot be considered myths, because they do concern deities whose worship is elevated into a cult in the state religion. People distinguish them from folktales, and Russians call them *byl'*, *bylichka*, and *byval'shchina* (memorates), all based on the root *byt'* (to be), which suggests something that really *was*. These names tell us that people firmly believed in their reality. I will use the same terms. They are more successful than the vague term accepted in West European scholarship, *Mythische Sagen*. Memorates are stories that feature such figures as the forest spirit, the water spirit, the field spirit, the house spirit, the *rusalka*, the bathhouse spirit,[46] and so on—that is, demonic beings who exert their supernatural powers on human beings for good or evil. Stories about meetings with such beings also make up the contents of the *byl'* (the forest spirit leads an old woman astray, brings her to his dwelling, and keeps her there as a nanny for his offspring). The subject of these stories can also be a person: not a living, natural person but rather a dead one, a ghost, a vampire, a werewolf, and so on. The subject may be nature, but not the nature that a person deals with in everyday life and has power over; rather, it is nature ruled by unknown powers, nature before which people are powerless, which they attempt to master using special magical means. For example, there are stories of ferns that flower on St. John's Eve. Stories of this kind are communicated not with aesthetic goals but with a certain tremor of horror and mystery, and people would never call them *skazki*. It is true that such stories are sometimes included in folktale collections, and they are in themselves valuable ethnographic and folkloric material, but they are not folktales. Dmitrii Sadovnikov includes more of this material than others, as he calls his collection *Folktales and Traditions of the Samara Region* (1884).[47] Sadovnikov understands the term *predaniia* (traditions) to mean precisely stories of this type. We find them in the collections of Afanas'ev, Nikolai Onchukov, Zelenin, Irina Karnaukhova, and others. Classifying memorates as folktales is a widespread error. Pushkin wrote of the folktale in *Ruslan and Liudmila*:

There are wonders there, there the forest spirit wanders,
Rusalka sits on the tree branches[48]

This means that Pushkin too considered these stories folktales. The mistake is completely understandable, given that in Pushkin's time there was still no differentiated concept of the folktale. The mistake continues to this very day. It is repeated in Iurii Sokolov's course on Russian folklore, where he includes memorates among the folktales.[49]

Analyzing memorates is not part of our task. Their plots are completely distinct, as are their origins, manner of performance, and poetics, so much so that the memorate should be separated from the folktale and studied with different methods. It is placed with the folktale because of the lack of study of folktales and adjacent genres; this cannot be supported. The Grimm brothers did not consider memorates folktales. They did not include any in their folktale collection, but they did give them a place in their *German Legends*, under the not entirely suitable name *Orts-Sagen* (place legends), because stories of this type usually have exact locations. Antti Aarne did not include memorates in his index of folktales either. Nikolai Andreev added an outline for a future index of stories of the memorate type to Aarne's index.[50] Andreev himself, not entirely successfully (and evidently following Sadovnikov), calls them *preda-niia*. However, this schema does not display a sufficiently precise understanding of the genre, because, alongside stories about dead people, devils, witches, nature and house spirits, and so on, he also suggests including stories about robbers, which, from our point of view, do not belong here at all, and also historical traditions, which represent a different genre, as we shall see.

In 1961 a remarkable index came out, compiled by the Finnish scholar Lauri Simonsuuri, under the title *An Index of the Types and Motifs of Finnish Mythological Narratives*.[51] This is a precise, logical, and superbly organized index of what we call memorates or, in Simonsuuri's terminology, "mythological narratives." In Russia this genre has received little attention from either collectors or researchers.[52] In Western Europe, on the other hand, the genre is intensively studied and problems connected to its study are discussed at international congresses. Several thousand texts have been collected in Finland. In recent years Russian expeditions (including student expeditions) have brought back new and interesting materials from this naturally moribund genre. It is obvious that these memorates are not folktales. We must qualify this, however, by saying that some of them may be transitional, borderline, or unclear cases. I have distinguished memorates from folktales by the qualities of their characters (nature spirits and so on) and their relationship to reality, that is, by two features at once. But their features may not coincide. Belief in the beings depicted in these stories might be lost, whereas the story remains as a pure invention. It is true that such cases are rare, because loss of belief usually causes disappearance of the story. But such cases are possible, they exist, and then we are dealing with intermediate formations, whose generic belonging must be decided on the basis of each case separately. The *byl'* may turn into an anecdote, as well as into a folktale. In its social function the memorate is a story with religious content; moreover, here it is still living, an active, pagan religion. The folktale, on the other hand, is a purely artistic story with no religious function at the present.

This shows us that until recently there were no precise differentiated concepts of the genres of Russian folk prose, even in Russian scholarship. I propose separating memorates—on the basis of their images from a pre-Christian religion that was still alive at the moment of the story's performance and on the basis of belief in the reality of the events described—into a separate genre, distinct from folktales. Study of the poetics and manner of performance of this genre will show its deep distinction from the folktale, whereas a historical study will show its different origins.

The Legenda

We must also distinguish the folktale from the *legenda*. The people have no term to define this genre. *Legenda* (legend) is not a native Russian word; it comes from church Latin. Latin *legenda* is the plural of a neuter participle (meaning literally "what undergoes reading"), and it was later incorrectly understood as a word of feminine gender in the singular. Like the memorate, the *legenda* has contents that are believed, but whereas the *bylichka* is composed of living remnants of pre-Christian folk belief, the contents of the *legenda* are Christian. The characters in the *legenda* are figures from the Old and New Testaments: Adam and Eve, the prophet Elijah, Solomon, Christ and his apostles (among whom Peter and Judas are especially popular), and also numerous saints. But holy beings from Christian religion are not the only characters in the *legenda*. There may also be people who have committed some grievous sin against fundamental Christian morality (which usually leads to the punishment and then to the sinners' moral salvation and cleansing) or else people who are taken alive to the other world, to heaven, hell, and so on.

The *legenda* differs from the folktale not only in its characters but also in its relationship to what is narrated. Its goal is not entertainment, but moralizing. The *legenda* is close in many ways to spiritual verses. Its origins are distinct from those of the folktale as well. The *legenda*, which reflects Christianity, could only appear relatively late, along with Christianity. If we move to non-Russian material, then we can assert that the *legenda* in general arises within a system of monotheistic religions. Thus, alongside Christian *legendy*, we can speak of Muslim or Buddhist ones. The Russian *legenda* comes in part from Byzantium, the source of Russian Christianity. Many legends have a literary origin and recall the Apocrypha.

The particular poetics of the *legenda* depends on all these particularities. Here its laws differ from the laws of the folktale. It is true that the *legenda* sometimes reveals the same compositional system as the folktale and that moralizing, pious tendencies are occasionally found in the folktale. However, an intent and detailed study of the folktale and the *legenda* will show that we are dealing with two different formations here. Afanas'ev was completely correct to separate *legendy* into a separate collection, *Russian Folk Legendy*, rather than putting them in his collection of Russian folktales.[53] Nonetheless, not everyone recognizes the division of the *legenda* as a particular genre. Aarne places them in his catalog of tale types, calling them "legendary narratives," and sets aside a hundred numbers for them (750–849). A monographic study of individual plots will show which pertain to the folktale, which to the *leg-enda*, and which to other genres.

As one example, I will pause to discuss the *legenda* of the two great sinners. It has been thoroughly studied by Nikolai Andreev.[54] Andreev's book grew from a seminar paper at Kazan′ University, written under the direction of Professor P. P. Mindalev and subsequently expanded. The study uses the methods of the Finnish school. At that time the tale of the two great sinners was known in forty-three variants, thirty-seven of them from the Slavic peoples. A person commits some kind of grievous sin. In most cases the sinner is a robber, but there are other treatments. In a few cases this plot is related to the myth of Oedipus: The sinner kills his own father and marries his mother without knowing what he is doing. In another case (used by Dostoevsky and known in other tale types), the sinner, after taking communion, does not swallow the wafer but spits it out and shoots at it. The wafer begins to bleed. In most cases, however, the sinner is a terrible robber who has killed ninety-nine people, looted monasteries, stolen things, and so on. The robber's conscience suddenly awakens. In most cases this happens for no reason ("The robber stole for many years and then got the idea of repenting"),[55] but narrators motivate the impulse in various ways. He discovers, for example, what kind of punishment awaits him in the other world, or, as in Gogol's "Terrible Vengeance," he is unable to die: Death does not come, but his soul is in torment. Death will not take him, and the earth refuses to receive him. Sometimes he is pursued by terrible dreams, and so on. He goes in despair to some elder or hermit, to ask him how to pray his sin away. Usually the elder puts a penance on him (to water a burnt log until it begins to grow; the burnt wood is often rooted on a mountain, water must be brought from a river flowing at the base of the mountain, and the sinner must go there and back on his knees). There are other forms of penance (e.g., tending a flock of black sheep until they all turn white), but the one I mention is encountered most frequently. The sinner spends many years in penance, but the burnt log does not grow. But then an even greater sinner rides past him, and he kills him. At that moment the burnt log starts to bloom. Who is this second man, the greater sinner? A lawyer, an extortionist, a tobacco seller, a merchant, a rich peasant exploiter, a priest. In one Belarusan variant the story runs: "He goes along and sees many, many people in the field. They are plowing, harrowing." We should add here that the action is set on Easter, considered the holiest day in the year, and that people are not supposed to work that day. I cite further: "What could this mean?" he thinks. "The first day of Easter, such a holy day that even the birds are celebrating, not weaving their nests, and here christened people are laboring." Coming closer, the sinner sees the overseer walking among the laborers, shouting and driving them with his whip. The peasants weep and complain, but "the overseer bellows as if he's damned, strikes them with his whip." The angry sinner picks up a stone, hits the overseer's head and shatters his skull. For this murder all his previous ones are forgiven. He finds death at last, dies on the spot, and his soul is saved (or, at the moment of the murder the burnt log bursts into bloom).[56]

The Belarusan variant is probably one of the most powerful. The sinner is saved because he kills another, even greater sinner. This second sinner is always a landholding noble, a merchant, a greedy peasant exploiter, a blood-sucker, an overseer, and so on. In Ukrainian variants he is an estate manager who is hitting graves with a stick, to drive even dead serfs to work. There are other cases, but the given form is predominant.

Nikolai Andreev's study has a purely formal character. It does not touch on the ideological contents of this folktale-*legenda*. Its idea is fairly clear. Killing a serf keeper is not only not a sin, it is a good deed, for which any sins at all, even the most grievous, are forgiven. This idea breaks through the multitude of genuinely Christian traditional concepts of sin, repentance, and salvation of the soul in the other world. This plot does not have worldwide distribution. It was born of Russian life with its terrible forms of serfdom, the peasantry's religious concepts, and the growth of indignation and protest. These contradict religious concepts and essentially replace them, although of course the peasants were not yet conscious of it at that time.

This plot is used by Nekrasov (part II, ch. 2).[57] According to Aarne it is a folktale, type A-T 756 C.

This legend of the two sinners (combined with another, about God's god-child) was also used by Leo Tolstoy. Here God's godchild is guilty of a person's death and repents, watering a burnt log. An even greater sinner passes him three times: a terrible robber who sings merry songs, with the songs sounding merrier when he has killed more people. But God's godchild does not kill him, as in the folk *legenda* Nekrasov uses, but teaches him and sets him on the path of truth: He persuades him not to ruin himself but to change his life. This second sinner repents and becomes a righteous man. Thus Tolstoy uses the folk plot in his own way as a lesson in his doctrine of nonresistance to evil by force, which is not at all present in the folk treatment.

The Skazanie *or* Predanie

There is one more genre that cannot be counted as a folktale, a genre we would most correctly call the *predanie* (legend, tradition) or the *skazanie* (tale, story, legend). Here we would place stories that are presented as historical truth and that sometimes even reflect or contain historical truth. If the legend is akin to the spiritual verse, then the *predanie* is to some extent kin to historical songs.

Skazaniia are stories that concern historical places or else historical personalities and events. The first kind is connected with a city, town, landmark, lake, burial mound, or the like. One of the most striking, artistic, and typical *skazanie* is the narrative of the drowned city of Kitezh. The second kind is connected with historical names: Ivan the Terrible, Peter the Great, Stepan Razin, Emelian Pugachov, General Suvorov, and others. There is no firm boundary between the two kinds. Thus there are *predaniia* connected with places and persons at the same time, describing historical occurrences (wars with the Poles, Swedes, French, and so on). However, we must take care when ascribing folkloric material to the category of *skazaniia*. We have distinguished the given genre based on a certain category of character or of historical names or events. However, this trait is not always decisive. The decisive factor is the poetics of each genre, and the poetics of this genre has been studied even less than the poetics of others. Thus the presence of the name Ivan the Terrible in a story is not yet enough for us to take that story as a genuine historical *predanie*. We are better acquainted with the poetics of the folktale, and we will take some similar texts as examples of folktales, despite the presence of a historical name. Evidently, on closer study many *predaniia* or *skazaniia* of this kind can be described as anecdotes. Nonetheless we need the category of such a genre, with the caveat that its theoretical study still lies in the future. The Grimm brothers undertook one of the first attempts at a theoretical definition of this genre in the preface to their *Deutsche Sagen*. They called the corresponding category *Geschichtliche Sagen* (historical sagas).

It follows that there can be no "historical folktales" in the sense that we can talk about historical songs or historical *predaniia*. It is true that Erna Pomerantseva accepted this term in her textbook on Russian folklore, under Pëtr Bogatyrev's editorial guidance, but she subsequently rejected the term and the concept.

Here is a model of a *predanie*: "Arakcheev was a very strict master—the dog! He had a lover who practiced black magic, who had power over him. She read in her books and knew everything that went on. For a long time they wanted to kill her, but they couldn't because of the books. Once they stole her books and ran to get her; she reached for her books but they weren't there. That's how she died. Arakcheev gave it all up then, all his business, and ran away."[58]

This genre is diverse; it not only allows further internal subdivision, it requires it.

The Folk Book

The folk book is closely related to the folktale, but it is nonetheless a completely different genre. The term *folk book* demands clarification. In Western Europe this term describes printed tales of folk provenance, reworked in novellistic form. They began to appear in Germany in the sixteenth century. They include works such as *Faust, Fortunato, Robert the Devil,* and *La Belle Melusine.* The young Friedrich Engels wrote a specialized article on these books.[59]

The folk book was a product of medieval urban culture, when the printing press took over the circulation of epic folkloric genres and reshaped them to suit middle-class tastes.

The folk book existed in Russia too, although the term did not catch on as a description of Russian materials. From Pypin's times, the *povest'* (a long tale or novella) was the accepted term.[60] Growing up on a folkloric basis, the folk book evolves into the bourgeois *povest'* and gives stimulus to the novel. Its sources are exceedingly varied, as varied as the folk books themselves. They are often the products of international folk connections and influences. Thus typical folk books include *Eruslan Lazarevich, Bova Korolevich, Meliuzina,* and *Peter Gold Keys.* They are of folktale descent, Eastern and Western. But some folk books have other origins. Their composition is complex. They are adjacent to hagiography, the *legenda,* and the literary tale. The folk book, which arose on a folkloric basis, may return to folklore and be narrated as a folktale. A significant part of the woodcut *lubok* folktales, which were published in Russia in large quantities in the eighteenth and early nineteenth centuries, can obviously be considered folk books. Folk books elaborated a characteristic language with splendid literary qualities, a special style, and special literary devices. Their language and their style influenced the folktale; some folktales are narrated in literary language. Folk books were exceedingly popular in Russia. Identifying the folk book with the folkloric tale is a methodological error. Yet it would be just as erroneous to study the folk book without regard to the folktale. They are adjacent, related, and intersecting genres; each, however, has its own internal particularity, historical fate, and forms of circulation.

Skazy

After the revolution a new term appeared in our scholarship: the *skaz*. The essence and contents of this term have caused many debates. Contemporary life is so vivid, so rich in historical and other events, that every person who is drawn into life as it unfolds and does not lack the gifts of observation, curiosity, and even some small talent for narration will have something to tell about. Here we see stories about things people saw, heard, or lived through, about the heroics of our era, about life now and before, stories of heroes of the civil war and World War II, recollections of meetings with great civic figures of our era, and stories of dramatic occurrences of all kinds. Should all that be recorded? Or should we perhaps record only folktales, memorates about the forest spirit, or historical traditions of the distant past? It is obvious that such stories should be both recorded and studied, although only, of course, if they are interesting in content and artistic in their form. The famous mourner Irina Fedoseva told El'pidifior Barsov her whole life story, and Barsov did well to record it. Her story is no less valuable than her lamentations. It is a deeply artistic, truthfully realistic story. The art of narrating something seen and lived was always present among the people, but it underwent particular development after the 1917 revolution. One great storyteller of the Soviet era, Filipp Gospodarev, told Leningrad folklorist Nikolai Novikov many interesting episodes from his life: his childhood, landowners, prisons, repression under the tsars. The style of his reminiscences recalls Gorky's autobiographical works. If Gospodarev had received an education, he could have become an important realist writer.

I have cited examples of autobiographical *skazy*, but the field of the *skaz*, its form and its contents, is much broader. *Skazy* do not belong among the folkloric tales, and they are not always folklore. But folklorists who record and collect such stories are nonetheless doing the right thing. So, for example, Semën Mirer and V. N. Borovik collected reminiscences and stories from workers who were present on the square at Finland Station (Lenin Square) when Lenin arrived in Petrograd in 1917.[61] Saratov folklorist Tat'iana Akimova organized an expedition following the steps of civil war commander Vasilii Chapaev's division and collected a whole book of stories about him. These

sometimes intermix reality with artistic invention, but they are always interesting from many points of view.[62]

The word *skaz* may have several possible meanings in Russian. We must
distinguish other kinds of *skazy* from the *skazy* described here. For example,
there are the so-called "secret *skazy* of the Ural workers." These are semifan-
tastic or wholly fantastic miners' stories of meetings with mountain spirits;
some of the miners believed in the stories' reality. There are realistic layers in
some of the stories, describing miners' encounters with entrepreneurs. Pavel
Bazhov heard stories of this kind and reworked them artistically into his story
"The Malachite Casket."

In belles lettres the word *skaz* was used, for example, by Nikolai Leskov,
who gave his story "Lefty" the subtitle "The *Skaz* of Cross-Eyed Lefty from
Tula, and of the Steel Flea." By using the word *skaz*, Leskov meant to underline the folk-narrative nature of his plot.

THUS THE QUANTITY OF genres of folk prose is fairly large and various.
Summing up what I have said about the genres that are close to the folktale,
but still distinct from it, we can boil our observations down to the following
(citing a vivid indicative example for each genre):

The **myth** of Orpheus
A **memorate** about the forest spirit
The *legenda* of the two great sinners
A *predanie* about Emilian Pugachov
The **folk book** *Eruslan Lazarevich*
The *skaz* about Chapaev

These genres do not exhaust the field of folk prose, all of which is custom-
arily placed in folktale collections. Nonetheless, distinguishing them gives us
some points of orientation as we start to find our way in this complicated
field. The division of genres I offer has the drawback of essentially relying on
the characters of the heroes, not on the genres' internal structure and poetics. However, I presume that a study of the poetics of the genres indicated
justifies their division. Of course, future research will contribute many other
changes and clarifications. I must point out that the division here is carried
out on Russian material and uses Russian terminology. I cannot include international terminology because there is no such international terminology

currently in existence. Thus the German word *Sage* is applied to all the genres established here (with the exception of the folktale) and besides that to the heroic epos; the word *legenda* is also used to signify all the genres described here, and it also signifies Classical myths, especially those in English. Russian terminology allows more exact and fine-grained definitions. In everyday language we too say "The *Legenda* of Stenka Razin" and so forth, but scholarly language does not permit such mixing.

The Anecdote

At first glance, the folktale's relationship to the anecdote is not entirely clear. The anecdote essentially comes down to the unexpected, witty dénouement of a brief narrative. The structure of anecdotes does not violate the generic traits of the folktale. Aarne includes anecdotes in a special rubric in his index of folktales, and in this case he is right in principle. He sets apart rubrics such as anecdotes about country bumpkins, spouses, women and girls, crafty people, priests, and so on. However, Aarne sometimes mistakenly includes long and complicated plots, such as "Nikola Duplenskii" or "Terentii the Guest," for example, in his list of anecdotes. Some of the narratives he placed among the anecdotes are unquestionably folktales. Afanas'ev similarly includes anecdotes in his collection of folktales. He combines a number of witty brief stories under the title "Folk Anecdotes" (numbers 453–527). However, the stories' brevity is a relative term and not a dependable feature. In the broader sense, the anecdote can include longer stories, such as the ones Afanas'ev places in his *Obscene Folktales*. In the preface to this edition Afanas'ev notes their sparkling wit and simple spirit. We may ask whether anecdotes have to do not only with the plots Aarne assigns to anecdotes (such as tales about country bumpkins and deceived spouses) and not only with folktales of the "obscene" type but also with a whole series of other tales that may be considered close to anecdotes. Here we find tales about crafty thieves, swindlers of all kinds, evil or unfaithful wives, lazy people, and so on. There is no basis for separating the whole sphere of folk humor from the folktale. Such stories can be combined as a particular kind of folktale, with a specific structure. Here we might question the folk anecdote's relationship to the literary anecdote, but this is just part of the question of the relationship of literary and folk literature. At the same time, anecdotes that were passed on orally in an urban sphere among the upper classes undoubtedly deserve study as well (see Pushkin's collection of anecdotes, for example), although they do not represent folklore as we now understand it. However, not everyone shares this view. Aleksandr Nikiforov writes, in his introduction to Orest Kapitsa's anthology, "The anecdote as such is distinct from the folktale. It has always had a strictly humorous purpose."[63] Nikiforov later dwells on the anecdote's folkloric particularities, but in our view, as I noted, they do not exclude the generic traits of the folktale.

Thus, unlike other genres examined here, anecdotes can be considered part of the sphere of the folktale, but there are anecdotes that cannot be counted here. The criterion in this case may be social: Folk anecdotes (i.e., anecdotes that arise and circulate in a peasant milieu) represent one form of the everyday folktale, whereas historical and other anecdotes, collected and exchanged in urban circles, have no relationship to folktales.

CLASSIFICATION OF THE FOLKTALE

The survey we have carried out here lets us orient ourselves among the genres of Russian oral prose and distinguish the folktale from them.

But this is not enough for study of the folktale itself. We must establish what types of folktales exist in general.

Once we distinguish the folktale from adjacent and related genres, we must bring folktale material itself into a system. I have already indicated that the world of the folktale is exceedingly manifold, varied, and mobile. Classification is important so that we can bring not only order and system into the colorful world of the folktale but also a purely cognitive significance. Combining heteronomic phenomena in a single series will lead to further errors. Therefore we must strive to combine folktale formations of the same type correctly. Various types of folktale differ not just in their external traits, the character of their plots, heroes, poetics, ideology, and so on. They also turn out to have a completely different ancestry and history and to demand different approaches in their study. Therefore correct classification is of prime scholarly significance. At the same time, we must admit that to this day Russian scholarship possesses no generally accepted classification of folktales. In Afanas'ev's historiographic survey, listed in the following paragraphs, we shall see what attempts have been made. No one of them can satisfy us completely. In any case, these attempts are nothing compared to the elegant classifications in the biological sciences (zoology and botany) or even in linguistics. This is because scholars have not yet found the decisive trait that could serve as the basis of divisions. Given the current state of scholarship, we must say that this trait ought to be the poetics of different kinds of folktales. A classification of this type would be genuinely scientific, and it would have the cognitive significance mentioned earlier. But the poetics of individual kinds of folktales has been as little studied as the poetics of the folktale as a whole. Therefore distinguishing types and varieties of folktales from the general repertoire encounters the same difficulties as distinguishing folktales from other genres of folk prose. Nonetheless the question should be resolved at least preliminarily, as a work in progress. We must recognize Aleksandr Afanas'ev's attempt as the best so far.

Afanas'ev was the first Russian scholar who encountered the compelling need to put an enormous and motley body of folktales in order. The first edition of his folktales in 1855–64 (we will speak of it later in more detail) had a somewhat chaotic appearance. Material was published in installments as it came into the publisher's hands. Not only folktales of one type, but even variants of one and the same plot were scattered through various volumes of this edition. When the first edition was complete, however, Afanas'ev perceived the need for some kind of order, and the second edition arranged the tales systematically (1873), although he did not live to see it (he died in 1871). Afanas'ev did not divide his collection into parts and did not give titles to the sections. If we do this for him, we obtain the following picture:

- Tales about animals (nos. 1–86), followed by a few folktales about objects (nos. 87 and 88) (e.g., "The Bladder, the Straw, and the Bast Shoe"), plants (nos. 89 and 90) (e.g., "The Mushrooms Go to War" and "The Turnip"), and the elements (nos. 91–94) (e.g., "Frost, Sun, and Wind" and "The Sun, the Frost, and the Raven").
- Wonder tales, that is, mythological, fantastic folktales (nos. 95–307).
- Folktales drawn from *byliny* (nos. 308–316) (e.g., "Il'ia Muromets and Nightingale," "Vasilii Buslaevich," and "Alyosha Popovich").
- Historical *skazaniia* (nos. 317 and 318) (e.g., "About the Tatar Khan Mamai" and "Alexander of Macedonia").
- Novellistic or everyday tales (no. 319 and the like).
- Memorates (no. 351 and others), that is, tales about dead people, witches, the forest spirit, and so on.
- Folk anecdotes (nos. 453–527).
- *Dokuchnye* (tiresome tales) (nos. 528–532).
- *Pribautki* (humorous sayings) (nos. 533–547).

Looking attentively at these categories, we can easily discern a certain lack of order, but that is easily resolved. Then the virtues of the classification become apparent. From our point of view, historical *skazaniia* and retellings of *byliny* do not belong among the folktales. The tiresome tales and humorous sayings are not folktales either, although they are of course close to them and may be included in folktale collections. The memorates fall in part among the everyday folktales, but they are easily distinguished from them. Aside from these imperfections, we get an elegant classification, including these major categories:

Folktales about animals
Folktales about people
   (a) wonder tales
   (b) novellistic tales

This schema is not suitable for African folktales. Tales there do not distinguish between people and animals.[64]

We could add smaller categories, represented by one or two cases, to these larger ones. Afanas'ev did not separate a class that has been established only recently: the cumulative or chain-form tale, such as "The Gingerbread Man" or "The Rooster Choked." This way, we obtain only four large classes: animal tales, wonder tales, novellistic tales, and cumulative tales. We too will adhere to this division. Afanas'ev took an empirical approach and found the proper approach, dividing the fundamental classes. Gradually, however, the need for a finer classification became obvious: subdivision into families, types, variants, and so on.

The Finnish School: Tale Types

A finer classification of tale types was suggested by Finnish scholar Antti Aarne. As folktale material was collected in Europe, it became more and more clear that the quantity of plots was relatively small, that many plots were international, and that in most cases new material represented variants of plots that had already been recorded and described. The question arose: Which plots are known to the European fairytale as a whole? Aarne answered this question. He took several major European collections and established the plots they included. Aarne described recurring plots as tale types. He compiled a catalog of types and published it in German as *Verzeichnis der Märchentypen*. This index came out in 1910 in Helsinki, in the series Folklore Fellows' Communications (no. 3). Aarne performed an invaluable service for world scholarship. Every type of folktale received a name and a number. The type number represents a code, that is, a conditional symbol signifying the tale regardless of the language it is recorded in. These codes have the same significance as the international Latin names of plants and animals or as chemical symbols. Folktales cannot be signified through their titles alone, because different peoples and even the same people may tell one and the same tale with different titles. And the titles may say nothing about the tale's contents. Really, what stories lurk under the titles "Sit-at-Home Frolka," "Elena the Wise," and so on? We will see later that Dmitrii Zelenin or the brothers Boris and Iurii Sokolov, for example, were obliged to give brief retellings of texts in order to provide indexes to their collections. This approach is obviously impossible when one is dealing with thousands and thousands of texts. Now, to signify a tale, it is enough to indicate the tale type number. Thus tale 707 is "Tsar Saltan." Under this number we will find a brief description of the contents of the folktale. For example, when a collector returns from an expedition and wants to communicate what folktales he found, he simply describes them with Aarne's numbers. The same is done to describe collections.

Since Aarne's index first appeared, it has become common practice throughout the world to append a list of types to a collection. If a researcher is occupied with one plot, say, "The Little Hump-Backed Horse," he has no need to read whole collections. He looks to see whether a certain collection includes type 531, and he knows at once whether the folktale he wants is present or absent in any collection in any language. The numerical system has even greater significance in describing archival materials and in compiling catalogs of tales preserved in an archive. I remember how I once turned to the Pushkin House archive while I was studying the tale of Never-Laugh. They graciously allowed me to examine any of their manuscript materials, but they could not tell me whether a certain tale was in the archive. This has changed now in a fundamental way. It is enough to look into the catalog, compiled according to Aarne's system, to establish at once whether a given tale is present in an archive, and, if it is, then in precisely which folder, in what collection, and on what page.

Aarne's catalog has received worldwide distribution and has become a part of international scholarship. It has been translated into many European languages. Professor Nikolai Andreev translated it into Russian under the title *An Index of Folktale Plots According to the System of Aarne.* This translation was published in 1929 by the Folktale Commission of the State Russian Geographical Society.[65] Andreev equipped the index with bibliographic references to the newest Russian collections. Thus, if a researcher is studying "The Frog Princess," he will find a list of Russian variants of this tale in the collections Andreev examined under tale type 402.

The quantity of plots turns out to be strikingly small. Aarne provided about 2,400 numbers for his index. In fact, there are fewer plots than this. Aarne understood, of course, that he had not exhausted the material, that others might find new types he had not foreseen. Therefore he left empty places in his numeration, blanks that could be filled in afterward. Thus, for example, after type 130 comes type 150. Twenty numbers are left free to be filled in the future. In point of fact, Aarne established fewer than 1,000 types. This way of distributing material makes it possible to supplement the index without breaking up and violating the order that has come into worldwide use, and researchers and publishers have used it widely. For example, when Andreev translated the index into Russian, he made several additions based on Russian material. Scholars from other countries have done the same. The supplements brought a certain lack of coordination and demanded accounting and reordering. This was done by American scholar Stith Thompson, who translated the index into English and took into account all the additions that had been made up to that time.[66] His translation was reissued in 1964 with further additions. To the present day, this edition is the standard by which the whole world orients itself. Here there are published bibliographic indexes (among others, Andreev's index) for each number, and each type also includes the newest research on that type. In this way, any researcher can determine right away all the published variants for each tale and all the works published on it in all European languages.[67]

These are the virtues of Aarne's index. Along with those, the index has many significant imperfections. Folkloristics has advanced significantly over the years, and this index already fails to satisfy contemporary requirements. We are compelled to use it for lack of a better one. I will not delve here into a detailed critique of the index; I will indicate only the most important imperfections.

Aarne did not define anywhere what is understood by the term *type* (Russian scholarship does not use this term). On the one hand, Aarne understands a type to mean a series of tales united by a common character. Thus type 1525 is called "The Crafty Thief." This type includes the most various plots (but far from all plots) about crafty thieves. This type is divided into subtypes (A, B, C, and so on), which is not done in other cases. The concept of a type is understood more broadly than the concept of a plot. On the other hand, sometimes fine distinctions of motif are understood as a type. Thus numbers 1000–1199 are given to tales about a devil or giant who is fooled. Each trick of the hero against a stupid devil receives its own number: A threat to make waves on a lake comes under type 1045, a racing contest has number 1012, a contest with throwing an oak log represents type 1063, and so on. Thus a whole folktale (Aleksandr Pushkin's "Balda") is broken up into parts, whereas the tale as a whole is not given.

Another imperfection of this index is the inconsistency of classification and its poor fit with the material. Thus wonder tales are divided into classes: a marvelous opponent, a marvelous spouse, a marvelous task, a marvelous helper, a marvelous object, a marvelous power or knowledge (ability), and other magical tales. From the outside all this looks elegant and logical. But in fact this classification is arranged according to traits that do not exclude one another. For example, the marvelous task is usually carried out with the help of a marvelous helper. In the tale "Sivko-Burko" the marvelous task is to jump up to the window of the princess and kiss her, and it is achieved with the help of the marvelous horse, Sivko-Burko.

One may point to several other imperfections in the classification. These mistakes are unacceptable from the scholarly point of view. Moreover, they create significant difficulties in using the index, namely, the categories are arranged in an entirely subjective way. To move from the index to the tale is easy, but the path from the tale to the index is very difficult. Collectors who wish to define their material according to Aarne must leaf through many pages and try out dozens of types before finding the necessary one. Thus the tale of the stepmother and stepdaughter falls into the class of the "magical task," but the tale "Cinderella," which, one would think, also involves a stepmother and stepdaughter, is found in the division of "magical helper." Nikolai Andreev was a virtuoso who could define any folktale instantly, but he could do this only because he knew the index by heart. A person who does not know it by heart is often placed in an impossible position. An alphabetical subject and name index to the typological index might offer a way out of that position. Stith Thompson set out to accomplish this.[68] If collectors working on a tale wish to define which type "Sivko-Burko" or "Tsar Saltan" or "The Frog Princess" belongs to, they look into the alphabetical index and find what they need right away. Unfortunately, Andreev's Russian translation is not equipped with such an index.

To this day there is no scholarly classification of folktales. This is clear even if we examine only the attempts made in Russian folklore textbooks. Thus, for example, Iurii Sokolov's classification essentially comes down to dividing the following categories: wonder tales (nos. 320–330), tales about animals (nos. 330–335), cumulative tales (no. 335), realistic tales (nos. 335–342), folktale-*legendy* (no. 342), folktale-*byliny* (nos. 342 and 343), historical legends and *predaniia* (nos. 343 and 344), and religious *legendy* (nos. 344–347).[69] All these genres are included in the system of folktales. The mistakes in Sokolov's classification are fairly obvious. They represent a step backward compared to Afanas'ev's classification, which distinguished folktales from *legendy* and created two separate collections. The Grimm brothers did not consider historical legends or *predaniia*, and they too were right. The difference between Sokolov's "folktale-*legendy*" and "religious *legendy*" remains unclear. We will see later why *byliny* cannot be considered folktales.

How can we escape this position? Let us take the classes Afanas'ev established as the basis. We will make subdivisions not according to Aarne, but by uniting folktales into groups according to the relatedness of their plots as a whole.

As I have already stated, Afanas'ev recognized the existence of three large groups of folktales: (1) animal tales, (2) fantastic (mythological) or wonder tales, and (3) novellistic tales. Afanas'ev did not specify his classification anywhere. The enormous material itself fell naturally into these groups. We will adhere to the classes Afanas'ev observed, but we will do so for different reasons.

1
THE HISTORY OF COLLECTION

AT FIRST GLANCE it seems easy to write down a folktale, as if anyone could do it without special preparation. What could be special about the history of folktale collection?

To some extent this is true. A folktale really can be written down by anyone who hears it. However, certain conditions must be observed if such a recording is to have scholarly value: One must know what to record, how to record it, from whom, and for what purpose. Views of collecting and recording folktales have changed sharply in this regard. These views depended in part and still depend on the general level of scholarship that treats folk creativity, the social-political views of the collector, and the goals of the collector.

It never occurred to anyone in ancient Rus' to write down folktales. The tales attracted not only official scorn, as something completely unworthy of attention, but also persecution. Telling folktales was forbidden, first by the clergy and the church and later by the government. Kirill of Turov, a twelfth-century sermonizer, threatened people who did magic, played the *gusli*, or told folktales with posthumous torments.[1] The church's hostile attitude toward folk amusements, including telling folktales, can be traced through the whole medieval period in Russia. Subsequent government bans added to this. An ukase of Tsar Aleksei Mikhailovich strictly forbids celebration of pre-Christian solstice rituals, guessing riddles, and telling tales. Nonetheless, the folktale existed among the people. We know this from indirect testimony. It even penetrated literature of a semihagiographic character, regardless of the persecution. In this regard the tale of Prince Petr of Murom and the maiden Fevronia, one of the most splendid Old Russian tales, is indicative; here the folktale is used artistically for religious and didactic purposes.

The change in attitudes toward the folktale came only at the end of the seventeenth century, and it developed during the eighteenth.[2] Peter's reforms, which brought Russia closer to the great European states, the development of cultural links with Western Europe, the founding of large-scale industry— all this led to a decline in the old feudal and patriarchal way of life in Rus'. Church culture began to lose its influence and significance, and a new, secular culture and literature appeared. This new secular literature in Russia had no tradition yet; it was newly created. But it had a foundation, and this was the verbal art of the people, which in its primary manifestations always had a nonchurch character and sometimes an antichurch tendency as well. This explains the medieval ban on telling folktales.

The urban middle and lower classes began to grow rapidly at the end of the seventeenth century. They began to demand a written narrative literature that could be read as well as told. The pious tales of the Middle Ages ceased to satisfy this milieu's literary demands.

The first stirrings came from Western Europe and reached Russia through Poland. Strange as it may seem, the first compilers of narrative collections were churchmen. The Catholic Church made a practice of giving instructive sermons during mass. These sermons tended to be abstract and boring, and parishioners would often flee at the beginning of the sermon. In order to keep them, to force them to listen, the clergy enriched their sermons with entertaining stories that had some moralistic or religious-philosophical interpretation. Collections of stories were created for such use. For folklorists, these collections are precious treasure troves. Their stories are folkloric to a significant extent. They were widely disseminated and popular and were translated into European languages as they made their way to Russia.

I will name only a few of the most important collections. One of the most capacious was *The Great Mirror*. It appeared in the Netherlands in Latin with the title *Speculum exemplorum* (The Mirror of Examples). These "examples" were understood to mean stories that had been given a moralizing meaning.

The *Speculum exemplorum* was first published in the Netherlands in 1481. In 1605, the Jesuit Johann Major translated the collection into Italian, giving it the title *Speculum magnum exemplorum*. The book was translated into Polish in 1633 and into Russian in 1677.[3]

In the West and also in Ukraine, *The Great Mirror* is a collection of examples to help clarify various assertions from church sermons. The Polish text has 2,300 stories; the Russian has less than half that many. The translation is not mechanical; it is adapted, freed from Catholicism.

The contents of the collection are composed of religious-didactic tales and anecdotes. The religious-didactic tales are stories in which the Virgin Mary plays a great role, saving people from temptation and misfortunes. For example, a certain bishop, after coming to power, abandons himself to worldly sins and temptations. Mary assembles a court of buried men— righteous dead men. Their skeletons rise from the grave; they condemn the bishop to punishment by death, and an angel chops off his head. In another example, a certain young warrior, handsome and chaste, begins to burn with impure passion for his lady at the devil's urging. He confesses his feeling to her, and she rejects him. He is tormented by this passion for over a year and finally asks a desert elder for advice. The old man advises him to pray to the Virgin a hundred times. He does so, and then once, coming out of church, he sees a beautiful woman holding his horse. The woman asks whether she is beautiful and whether she pleases him. He answers, "I have never seen such a woman." Then she asks, "Do you wish to be my bridegroom?" They are betrothed on the spot. She promises to marry him, but soon he dies. The beautiful woman was the Virgin Mary, and the marriage signified death.[4] Note the use of marriage and death in rituals and the identification of the woman as simply another woman, not the Virgin. There is a variation of this story in Boccaccio, where a husband gives orders for a youth to be smothered.

The second group of stories in *The Great Mirror* is composed of tales of the anecdotal type. For example, a man has an evil-tongued and quarrelsome wife. To test her, the man forbids her to bathe in a dirty puddle in their yard. Because of her accursed nature, she does just that. As punishment, the husband takes away all her good clothes. This tale is also found in *The Deeds of Rome*. This medieval collection was created in the thirteenth century. It has more secular elements than *The Great Mirror*. Rome is understood not only as ancient Rome but also as the Holy Roman Empire, that is, Western Europe. The compiler is unknown. "It was founded on the migratory tales that arose in various eras, both West and East."[5] "Almost every text is accompanied by moralizing interpretations in the spirit of Christian doctrine."[6]

A translation of *The Deeds of Rome* was made from a published Polish text around 1680–90 and exists in many copies. The highest quantity of texts is 39 (the Polish one has the same number; the Latin has 180). A translation was made in Belarus. It contains, for example, "The Tale of Pope Gregory."[7] It also recounts "The Story of the Seven Wise Men."

The *Deeds of Rome* collection was popular and is extant in a multitude of copies. Its homeland is reputed to be India,[8] but this is dubious. The tales are not attested in India; there are Persian and Arabic redactions, considered to be translations. There are Syrian, ancient Hebrew, and Greek translations; a Latin translation was made from the Hebrew in the thirteenth century, and the Latin text was translated into Polish in the sixteenth century and then into Russian. The oldest manuscript is from 1634. Like the others, it is a reworking.

Fifteen novellas are united by a frame narrative in *The Deeds of Rome*. One novella concerns the death of a king's wife. He marries a second time. He sends his son from the first marriage to Rome to study with seven wise men. Seven years later the stepmother asks the son (Diocletian) to return, secretly intending to kill him. The wise men read in the stars that if Diocletian speaks, he will be killed immediately. But the son sees in a dream that this silence should continue for only seven days. The stepmother tries to seduce her stepson but without success. She tears her dress and calls for help. Diocletian remains silent to all the accusations. Now a sort of competition for the prince takes place between the queen and the wise men. The queen tells a story about a king who died as a result of excessive trust in his son, and one of the wise men tells a story about women's craftiness and women's wiles. This continues for seven days; every day two stories are told. Every day the king wants to execute his son after hearing his wife's story, but after hearing the wise man's story, he delays the execution. On the eighth day Diocletian receives the gift of speech, he tells what really happened, and the king orders his wife executed.

Here there is no religious-clerical reworking. These are funny stories about examples of great craftiness.[9]

Besides these collections there are tales of a semifolkloric character, of Western and Eastern origin. The Western collections include, for example, the tales of *Prince Bova*, "Peter Golden Keys," "Melusine," "Vasilii the Golden-Haired," "Apollo of Tyre," and "Ivan Ponomarevich."[10] The Eastern tales include *Eruslan Lazarevich*. I will not discuss these, because their relationship to folklore is tangential.

Folk books. Stages. Extremely significant contents (see Sipovskii).[11] Pypin points to more than a hundred works of various kinds (Savchenko, 66).[12] The trade of recopying. *Lubok* (woodcut) editions with colored pictures.

Speaking of the collection, recording, and publication of folklore, I must mention the collection *Facetiae or Polish Jests*, translated in Russia in 1680.[13] This is a collection of funny stories with a farcical character. Many such amusing collections were in circulation in the West. They did not represent recordings of folklore in our sense of the word, but they did make extensive use of folklore plots. They have been little studied by our folklorists.

However, the naïve *lubok* editions soon ceased to satisfy the tastes of the bourgeoisie. Educated people considered them ridiculous. In his satirical ode "The Bigwig" (*Vel'mozha*) Derzhavin wrote:

> I read the poems *Polkan* and *Bova*;
> While over the Bible, yawning, I sleep.

It was considered poor taste for a nobleman to read *Polkan* and *Bova*. This negative, mocking attitude was passed on to the layers of society that were the main consumers of these editions. Demand for a literary, authorial folktale grew.

This demand was addressed by Mikhail Chulkov in his collection *The Mocker, or Slavic Folktales.*[14]

Summarize Chulkov and Levshin according to my general course. Also, Blagoi and Savchenko, 76–77. Then Kurganov.[15]

Kurganov's *Pis'movnik*, first ed. 1769; there were twelve editions in all.

Levshin, *Russkie skazki*, 1780–83. (See Blagoi's general course, 472–73; and Savchenko, 77–83.)[16]

Lekarstvo ot zadumchivosti i bessonitsy, ili nastol'nye russkie skazki (A Medicine for Pensiveness and Insomnia, or a Table Book of Russian Tales), published in 1786, 1793, 1815, 1819, and 1830. This book contains six folktales: (1) the story of the famous and powerful knight Eruslan, his bravery, and the indescribable beauty, princess Anastasiia Vakhrameevna; (2) the tale of the Tsar-Maiden (compare Pushkin); (3) the tale of the Seven Simons (compare Afanas'ev); (4) the tale about Suvor the invisible peasant; (5) the tale about Ivanushka the Fool; and (6) the tale about Prince Sil.

Dedushkiny progulki, ili Prodolzhenie nastol'nykh russkikh skazok (Grandpa's Strolls, or a Continuation of the Table Book of Russian Tales), published in 1786, 1791, 1805, 1815, and 1819. There are ten tales here, including the tale of the Firebird (Savchenko, 91).[17]

Skazki russkie (Russian Tales), containing ten different tales, collected and published by Petr Timofeev (Moscow, 1787). This collection is just as varied as the others. It also contains some genuine folktales (Ivanushka the Fool). It was very popular. It was republished under other titles until as late as 1865 (Savchenko, 91–92).[18]

Staraia pogudka na novyi lad, ili Polnoe sobranie prostonarodnykh skazok (An Old Tune in New Style, or a Complete Collection of Tales of the Simple Folk), in three parts, 1794–95. There are ten tales here, including one about Ivan Bear-Ear.

Vasilii Berezaiskii's *Anekdoty drevnykh poshekhontsev* (Anecdotes of the Ancient Bumpkins), 1798.

I have mentioned only the most significant. Savchenko lists twenty-one publications of a similar kind. These collections have been insufficiently studied.[19] They represent a motley mixture of genuine folktales with a variety of inventions that have little interest or artistic quality. Many of them have become great bibliographic rarities.

PUSHKIN

Based on what I have outlined here, it becomes clear what a great role was played by the folktales that Aleksandr Pushkin recorded.

In the history of Russian artistic culture, Pushkin was the first person who began to record tales from a simple peasant woman with full understanding of the folkloric tale's whole beauty.

At first glance, these recordings do not seem to represent anything special. From the point of view of contemporary requirements, these are what we would now call summary recordings. They preserve the backbone of the plot and a few expressions. But Pushkin's recordings nonetheless signify a watershed in the attitude of educated people toward oral folk creativity. It is an accepted opinion, and people usually write, that Pushkin recorded folktales in order to use them later. I consider this doubtful.

Nikolai Novikov has done a great deal of work toward establishing the complete Pushkinian texts in his book *Handwritten and Published Russian Folktales of the First Half of the Nineteenth Century*.[20] First and foremost, we must establish exactly what Pushkin noted down and from whom. He took down several folktales from his nanny, Arina Rodionovna, such as the tale of Tsar Saltan. Pushkin wrote this folktale down for the first time in Kishinev (1822); the next recording was made from the words of Arina Rodionovna (1824); and, finally, there is one more recording whose source is not clear (1828). Thus Pushkin wrote down this tale three times. He undoubtedly recorded the tale of the priest and Balda from Arina Rodionovna. This record shows that Pushkin valued not only the wonder tale, with its magical beauty, but also the brightly satirical folktale that was directed against the priesthood. Pushkin did not hide or retouch anything. On the contrary, he gave even sharper coloration to the people's mocking, negative attitude toward priests and tsars.

There is a fragmentary record of a folktale about Snow White. It is doubtful, though possible, that it came from Arina Rodionovna. Pushkin made use of it, but the Pushkinian tale in verse is richer and better structured than the text in question.

Pushkin used these three records of folktales he heard from Arina Rodionovna in his own creative work. Besides them, we have recordings that he did not use. He recorded the tale of Mar'ia the tsar's daughter from Arina Rodionovna. Its plot tells of the hero's marriage to the daughter of the king of the sea. Pushkin did not use this tale, but it formed one source of the tale of Tsar Berendei by Vasilii Zhukovskii. Zhukovskii's unctuous manner differs sharply from the realistic, folk manner of Pushkin's tales. He also recorded tales from Arina Rodionovna about the death of Kashchei, about the son of the tsar and the son of the blacksmith, and about the maiden kidnapped by the devil. Thus he recorded seven folktales from Arina Rodionovna; of these, he used three.

At the same time, Pushkin has tales that did not come from Arina Rodionovna's repertoire. His horizon was extraordinarily broad, and he made use of the most varied sources. Thus no records of the tale of the fisherman and the fish were discovered in Pushkin's papers, nor was the tale of the golden cockerel. The tale of the fisherman and the fish comes from the Brothers Grimm, and the tale of the golden cockerel is from Washington Irving.[21]

The tale of the she-bear is also not from Arina Rodionovna. In creating this tale, Pushkin used "The Old Story of the Birds," which is widespread in the Russian north. It is included in Mikhail Chulkov's collection. Chulkov's text was well known to Pushkin and was reflected in the given tale. Besides that, Novikov mentions a tale Pushkin told Vladimir Dal' (about St. George and the wolf). This tale is included in Dal"s complete collected works, with a note that Pushkin had told it. One of Pushkin's friends wrote down his telling of the tale of Foma and Erema. Novikov gives its text.[22]

What results do we observe? Of seven *skazki* or tales in verse that Pushkin wrote, two come from Arina Rodionovna, two from the Grimm brothers' collection, one from Chulkov's collection, and one from Washington Irving; the source for one tale (the dead princess, or Snow White) remains unclear. Pushkin never made use of four of the recordings he made from Arina Rodionovna, and we have evidence of two cases when Pushkin told tales orally that he never wrote down.

These data do not at all support the opinion that Pushkin wrote down folktales in order to make use of them himself. A whole series of recorded tales

Tale	Plot number in Novikov's collection	Oral source	Written source
Tsar Saltan	9	Kishinev notebook, 1822; Arina Rodionovna, 1824, 1828?	
Snow White	15	Arina Rodionovna (?)	Brothers Grimm (?)
Golden Cockerel		–	Washington Irving
Fisherman and Fish		–	Brothers Grimm
Priest and Balda	11	Arina Rodionovna	–
The She-Bear		–	Chulkov
Bridegroom		–	Brothers Grimm
Mar'ia the Tsar's Daughter	10	Arina Rodionovna	
Kashchei's Death	12	Arina Rodionovna	
Tsar's Son	13	Arina Rodionovna	
The Careless Word	14	Arina Rodionovna	
St. George and the Wolf	15	Unknown	
Foma and Erema	16	Unknown	
The Eagle-Tsar and the Birds	18	Unknown	
Kusukurpech and His Bride Sulu-Baian	19	Unknown	

were not used and, on the other hand, several of Pushkin's verse tales do not spring from his own recordings.

Pushkin did not take a utilitarian approach to folktales. His recording is not defined by a search for plots; it has significantly deeper roots. Pushkin's interest in folktales is characterized by the development of social consciousness in the leading intelligentsia of that time and by the evolution of Pushkin's own creative work. The folktale occupies a special place in his opus. Before Pushkin, the folktale belonged to the most deprecated kinds of folk poetry. This scorn was still displayed even after the appearance of Pushkin's *skazki*. The folktale was hardly known. Chulkov's and Levshin's editions, several small collections containing literary, reworked retellings, did not give a true reflection of the folkloric tale. A mass of imitations of folkloric tales of all kinds had cheapened this kind of folk poetry. The genuine folkloric tale was brought into literary, societal, and scholarly currency by Pushkin, who immediately revealed all the Russian folktale's remarkable artistic qualities.

For Pushkin, national culture is an original culture, connected with the history, everyday life, and traditions of the people and reflecting a national character distinct from the character of other peoples. From this point of view, folktales marvelously depict the Russian cast of mind and feelings, ideals, and aspirations: "Here's the Russian spirit, here it smells of Rus'."[23] Pushkin wrote to his brother from the family estate in Mikhailovskoe: "In the evening I listen to folktales—and by so doing I make up for the gaps in my cursed upbringing. What a charm there is in these folktales! Each one's an epic poem."[24] It is obvious that when Pushkin mentioned his cursed upbringing, he meant an education in the spirit that worshipped French language and French literature. In Mikhailovskoe, Pushkin began to recognize the significance of his native culture and native language even more strongly than before.

Arina Rodionovna was not the cause of Pushkin's turn toward folktales; the cause lies much deeper. Pushkin began to write down folktales while he was still in the south of the Russian Empire. But Arina Rodionovna's tales corresponded to a whole range of Pushkin's interests in Mikhailovskoe, and he began to record them.

Although Pushkin's recordings bear a summary character, they convey the plot with complete precision and sometimes also both the speech and the stylistic locutions of the storyteller. If we compare them with texts in Levshin's and Chulkov's collections or other editions of that time, we see immediately what a huge step forward Pushkin made. We see that his view of the folktale differs in principle from the view of the publishers of his time.

FROM PUSHKIN TO AFANAS'EV

Pushkin was not the only one to decant the folktale into literary and poetic form. His most outstanding contemporaries in this regard are Vasilii Zhukovskii, with his verse tales, and Nikolai Gogol, with *Evenings on a Farm Near Dikanka*, and later Pëtr Ershov, creator of the immortal "Little Hump-Backed Horse." After them followed a whole constellation of less famous writers who wrote literary fairytales based on French plots. The literary use of the folktale has been splendidly researched in Irina Lupanova's book.[25] These works belong in the sphere of literary history, not in a history of the collection and publication of Russian folktales.

Collection and publication of folktale texts proper continued in the same vein as it had even before Pushkin. We have a series of small collections, each containing five to ten folktales. True, they are far closer to the genuine folk-tale than were editions of tales from the eighteenth century, like the *Medicine Against Pensiveness and Insomnia.* They do not subject the plot to major changes, but the style and language are edited. The language is tailored to a supposedly folk style. Such editions include Bogdan Bronnitsyn's *Russian Folk Tales.*[26] This collection includes four wonder tales and one everyday tale. In his preface, Bronnitsyn asserts that the tales were noted down "from the words of the storyteller, a peasant man from near Moscow, who heard them from an old man, his father." However, this assertion raises doubts. Bronnitsyn writes of the tales, "There is a remarkable cast to the story, presenting for the most part a collection of Russian verse of various meters." The view that folktales were a kind of poetry was generally widespread at that time; it exposes the lack of understanding of the folktale style.

The collection *Russian Folktales, Told by Ivan Vanenko* came out the same year, 1838, containing six folktales.[27] Vanenko also issued several other books of "literature for the people." Both collections, Bronnitsyn's and Vanenko's, were judged severely by Vissarion Belinsky, who wrote in his review that they were unsuccessful attempts to imitate a fantasy version of the people. "The foundation of the tales is taken for the most part from genuine Russian folk-tales, but is so mixed up with their own inventions and decorations that they turn into something alien."[28] This condemnation, though severe, is unarguably fair. It applied more to Vanenko than to Bronnitsyn. Vanenko tricked his tales out in an especially buffoonish style. Belinsky was well acquainted with oral performance of folktales, which he had listened to; therefore he was able to judge how much editions like these corresponded or failed to correspond to the originals. It is interesting to note that other reviewers, although not so severe as Belinsky, likewise felt that Bronnitsyn was either deceiving his readers or else had let his storytellers deceive him. On the other hand, some reviewers praised both Bronnitsyn and Vanenko for their supposed fidelity to the simple people's narrations. These reviews show that a demand for publication of genuine folktales was already ripening. The leading journals of that time judged the publications that were coming out from that very point of view.

However, the idea that there was a need to publish genuine folktales made slow progress. Belinsky stood alone, we could say, when he wrote in his review of Vanenko's collection that folktales, created by the people, should be recorded as closely as possible to the way they were narrated by the people, not faked or reworked.[29] Belinsky also asserted that the Russian folktale had its own significance, but only in the form in which the folk imagination created it. Reworked and decorated, it made no sense at all.[30] But words like these did not reach the publishers of folktales. After his 1838 collection, Vanenko published a whole series of other small-scale collections, more or less identical in quality and style, which continued to come out until 1863. His *Russian Folktales* was reprinted five times in ten years. This means that there was a market for literary work of that kind. At the same time, there was a demand for the genuine folktale, as we can see from reviews that reflected the developing opinion of society. This explains the bifurcated line of development in collecting and publishing folktales: on the one hand, a tendency to publish folktales that had undergone literary reworking, and on the other hand, an aspiration to publish texts that were genuinely of the people.

The most significant representative of the first direction was Vladimir Dal'. Dal' reworked his folkloric tales quite consciously before publishing them. He put out two books,[31] which are weak from the artistic point of view and hold hardly any interest for folklorists. At the same time, Dal' had an enormous collection of folktales in his hands. We know he passed on to Afanas'ev as many as a thousand folkloric tales, recorded by him and by others. Afanas'ev used only 148 of them for his collection, noting with regret that "very few . . . are conveyed with respect for local grammatical forms."[32] Where these records wound up is not known; they have been lost. Why did Dal', who put out a classic dictionary of Russian proverbs and who published the remarkable dictionary of the living Great-Russian language, not publish genuine folkloric tales, preferring instead his own imitations? We can only explain it by the level of development of scholarship at the time.

Another, still more lamentable fact testifies to this: the publication not only of literary reworkings but of outright fabrications. Dal' did not present his tales as truly coming from the people, but that is what I. P. Sakharov claimed for his collection *Russian Folk Tales*, which came out in 1841.[33] His preface says that he listened to a hundred storytellers and chose the five best. He also writes that he used a manuscript from the Tula merchant Bel'skii. However, as early as the 1860s it was proved that in fact no such manuscript from a merchant named Bel'skii existed. Sakharov's tales are reprintings and retellings from prior editions. He retold *byliny* collected by Kirsha Danilov in the form of folktales. One of his tales, about Vasilii Buslaevich, combines texts from Levshin and Kirsha Danilov. The very long (60 pages) "Tale of the Novgorod Man Akundin and Prince Gleb Ol'govich" presents a retelling of Fedor Glinka's long poem "To Karelia, or the Captivity of Marfa Ioannovna

Romanova" (1830). I will not spend time on a detailed analysis and description of Sakharov's tales. Such exposure is not very interesting, and there is
something else of interest to us here. If Sakharov presented his editions as
genuine folktales, he did so because the genuine Russian folkloric tale had
already gained both interest and respect. The only problem was that people
did not know it; there was no place to read genuine folkloric tales. Even Belinskii, who so subtly criticized Vanenko and Bronnitsyn, took Sakharov's tale
of Akundin as genuine and discussed it in detail in his fourth article on folk
poetry in 1841.[34] This interest in genuine folktales led to the appearance of editions that had begun to attempt to convey folktales as exactly as possible. We
can consider these editions the forerunners of Afanas'ev.

To this day the activity of Ekaterina Avdeeva, a remarkable collector and
publisher of ethnographic and folkloric materials, has not been sufficiently
clarified and valued. As a child, she moved with her parents to Irkutsk. The
new setting awoke her interest, and she became an ethnographer of Siberia.
Her fundamental works, *Notes and Remarks About Siberia*,[35] *Notes on Old and
New Everyday Life in Russia*,[36] and several others, contain a multitude of valuable and refined observations, including those on the forms of old-fashioned
celebrations (see also her "Sketches on the Carnival in European Russia and
Siberia, in Cities and Villages").[37] She also published a splendid collection of
songs, *A Russian Songbook, or a Collection of the Best and Most Curious Songs,
Art Songs, and Vaudeville Couplets*.[38] She was the sister of Nikolai Polevoi, who
helped her in publishing. She was an intelligent and observant woman, able
to describe what she saw truthfully and simply. In 1844 she issued a small collection titled *Russian Folktales for Children, Told by Nanny Avdot'ia Stepanovna
Cherep'eva*.[39] These are six folktales about animals and one from the cycle
about persecuted stepdaughters. The tales are all in a single style, and their
language is close to genuine peasant speech. Evidently, the nanny Avdot'ia
Stepanovna was not a made-up character. It is possible that Avdeeva made
some insignificant corrections in the language, but as a whole this little cor-
rection is the first genuine recording from the mouth of the people. The collection was quite popular and went through eight editions by 1881.

Mykhailo Maksymovych's collection, *Three Tales and One Invention*, was
similar in character to Avdeeva's collection.[40] What Maksymovych called an
invention (*pobasenka*) is also a folktale ("Godmother-Death," A-T 332). All
these are genuine folktales, laid out in folk language. They have a more noticeable literary correctness, perhaps, than in Avdeeva, but as a whole these are
texts that one can trust. Maksymovych was a Ukrainian who became famous

with his *Little Russian Songs*,[41] used by Gogol in writing his remarkable article on folk songs.[42] Maksymovych was a botanist by profession. He held a chair at Moscow University but was transferred to the newly opened university in Kiev, where he received the position of rector. There he turned to the study of Russian and Ukrainian literature. He was a Romantic and a Ukrainophile, although he was far from being a nationalist. Where he recorded the tales is unknown. Judging by the presence of some Ukrainianisms, they were probably written down in Russian regions neighboring Ukraine.

All this demonstrates how great a need there was for a collection that would present genuine Russian folktales.

This need was met by the famous collection of Aleksandr Nikolaevich Afanas'ev (1826–71).[43] Afanas'ev came to the folktale as a theoretician, under the influence of the Grimm brothers and their school. His work as a theoretician and representative of the mythological school and as the author of the major three-volume work *Poetic Views of the Slavs on Nature* is already well known, and I do not wish to repeat myself. The collection *Folk Russian Tales* brought him worldwide fame. Afanas'ev could not have created so grandiose a collection without the cooperation and assistance of the Russian Geographical Society, founded in 1845. The Society included a division of ethnography, which became active in collecting ethnographic and folkloric materials. This was advanced by well-composed proposals, distributed locally. People from the most varied professions responded to the invitations and sent materials they had collected, which accumulated in the Society's archives in fairly large quantities. Afanas'ev had already acquired a certain renown with his articles, later combined in *Poetic Views of the Slavs on Nature*, and also with his active interest in folk poetry, and he was elected to the Russian Geographical Society. The Society's council resolved to prepare the folktale materials for publication. This offer suited Afanas'ev's wishes, because he had intended for a long time to publish a collection of folktales. The Society's offer was his opportunity to realize this idea.

Seventy-five texts were taken from the archive of the Russian Geographical Society for publication. The remaining materials were collected from the most varied sources. Afanas'ev himself recorded no more than ten folktales, in the Voronezh region where his family was from. He also made use of some records from his Voronezh friends. Through Pëtr Kireevskii he obtained the notes of P. I. Iakushin. Subsequently Dal', who himself concentrated on publishing proverbs, gave Afanas'ev his own huge collection of folktales. Besides that, Afanas'ev drew the best texts from old printed and *lubok* editions. He chose more than 600 texts in all for publication. The collection came out in installments. The whole collection comprised eight volumes and was given the title *Folk Russian Tales*. It was the first scholarly edition of genuine Russian folkloric tales, surpassing analogous editions in Western Europe in its richness. The marvelous artistic qualities of the Russian folkloric tale became widely known for the first time. Afanas'ev's edition far surpasses the Grimm brothers' edition in its scholarly qualities. Afanas'ev did not permit himself any kind of falsification, polishing, or literary reworking like what the Grimm brothers carried out. He included variants in his edition, which the Grimms had not done. The Grimms' tales aimed at a reader from the middle and petty bourgeoisie. Afanas'ev's edition pursued purely scholarly goals and strove to convey the tales exactly as they had been narrated in performance. His tales became one of the best loved and most popular books for Russian readers. They were reprinted several times in the nineteenth century. The last complete edition [before 1974—SF] came out in 1957.[44]

In the first edition, the arrangement of texts depended mainly on the order in which material came into Afanas'ev's possession. He provided the edition with commentaries in the spirit of the mythological school and pointers to analogous tales of other peoples. In the second edition (1873), as mentioned, the folktales were arranged systematically. The system Afanas'ev adopted was the first attempt at a classification of folktales, and in this regard too the collection surpasses that of the Grimm brothers, who placed tales in no defined order. The collection also has certain imperfections. Afanas'ev depended on his correspondents; therefore the quality of the recordings is uneven and mixed in character. The whole collection bears the stamp of Afanas'ev's views of folklore and the people. These imperfections are noted in a review by Nikolai Dobroliubov. Although recognizing Afanas'ev's achievements, Dobroliubov pointed out the need for completely different methods of collection, publication, and study of folk poetry.

Afanas'ev's collection also included some materials that could not see the light of day because of the conditions of censorship at that time. These were satirical folktales, aimed at tsars and landowners and containing satirical depictions of the clergy. Afanas'ev understood the great significance of these realistic folktales, although they were not amenable to mythological interpretation. He published these tales anonymously and without indication of the year of publication in Geneva, under the title *Obscene Russian Folktales*. Soviet editions of Afanas'ev include some of the most sharply satirical stories from the *Obscene Tales*.[45]

Afanas′ev′s third collection was *Folk Russian Legends*.[46] The legends are stories with characters from the Old and New Testaments: Adam and Eve, Noah, the prophets, Christ and his apostles, and also the saints. These legends may seem at first glance to express the church-going, moralizing inclination of the Russian peasantry. In fact, that is far from always the case. The legends express a negative attitude toward the church, the clergy, and sometimes even religion as such. With regard to this edition, the Chief Procurator of the Holy Synod, Count A. P. Tolstoi, wrote to the minister of education, complaining that "this book often speaks about Christ and the saints, and therefore the secular censorship should have consulted with the church censorship, but it did not do this: in this book the names of Christ the Savior and the saints are added to tales which offend pious feelings, morality and decency, and it is necessary to find means to preserve religion and morality from printed blasphemy and mockery."[47] The book sold out in an unbelievably short time, but the censorship laws forbade republication.[48] This ban lasted until 1914, when it was lifted and the book came out in a second edition. After the *Legends* were banned in Russia, they were published illegally in London.

Afanas′ev′s collection, for all its imperfections, has first-class scholarly significance to this day. But scholarship cannot rest at the stage of Afanas′ev′s achievements. Afanas′ev was the first editor of folktales who pursued scholarly goals, but he was not a collector himself in the proper sense of the word, because for the most part he published manuscript materials.

From Khudiakov to the Present

The fame of the first collector belongs by rights to Ivan Aleksandrovich Khudiakov (1842–76). His character and convictions were completely different from Afanas′ev′s. He was an active professional revolutionary, exiled to the Verkhoiansk *okrug* of Yakut *guberniia* for his involvement in Karakozov's attempt on the life of Aleksandr II (1866). Khudiakov was interested in folklore not just as a folklorist. He aspired to put folklore in the service of revolutionary activity and to use it as propaganda material. With this goal, he studied folklore not from books but by immediate communication with people. He traveled all through Riazansk *guberniia* and recorded folktales there. He wrote down some tales in cities too, in Kazan′ and Moscow. As a result, he compiled a large collection, which was published under the title *Great Russian*

Folktales.[49] This collection came out at almost the same time as Afanas'ev's installments, but it was different in an essential way. Khudiakov's is the first large collection of folktales recorded entirely by the publisher himself—and recorded accurately at that. The reputation of the first major collection of folktales taken straight from the people's mouth should belong to Khudiakov, not Afanas'ev. Khudiakov's work is the first integral collection of a new type. He did not convey the phonetic and other peculiarities of local speech and did not consider that necessary. However, he was able only in part to achieve the goals he was pursuing by collecting folktales. He writes in his preface, "Unfortunately, we must note that certain circumstances do not permit us to print many interesting folktales from our collection." By "certain circumstances," he means the pressure of censorship. For the same reasons, Khudiakov could not print any commentary to his collection. The most sharply satirical of the folktales, which express the mood of the peasants on the eve of the great reforms, did not make it into the collection. They were not preserved, as they were destroyed when Khudiakov was arrested.

Great Russian Folktales was not Khudiakov's only publication. He issued a collection titled *Great Russian Riddles*[50] and also an anthology of Russian historical songs, selecting the most patriotic and at the same time the most revolutionary. His preface cites Belinsky.[51] Khudiakov compiled a series of scholarly popular sketches on Russian history ("Ancient Rus'" and others), in which, in opposition to Karamzin and the official point of view, he demonstrated the ruinous nature of autocracy for Russia in a veiled but sufficiently clear manner.

In exile, Khudiakov continued the work he had begun. He compiled a Yakut grammar and dictionary and switched to recording Yakut folklore. Khudiakov was the first to value and record works from the highly artistic epic songs of the Yakuts, and he published them in splendid translations that preserved, as much as possible, the deeply national poetics of Yakut heroic songs. The manuscript was published many years after Khudiakov's death by the Eastern Siberian division of the Russian Geographical Society under the title *The Verkhoiansk Collection*.[52] Russian folktales and songs he had collected in Verkhoiansk were included here too. Khudiakov bore his harsh deprivations and loneliness with difficulty, and he ended his life in a mental hospital.

Ivan Gavrilovich Pryzhov (1827–85) also belongs among the folklorist revolutionaries. Pryzhov was unable to realize almost any of his many projects and ideas because of their sharply denunciatory character. He planned a work titled "A History of the State of Serfdom Primarily from the Testimony of the People Itself." As the title shows, this work was meant to be composed of oral testimony and stories from the serfs themselves. The same is true of his works "The History of Free Settlement in Russia" and "The Priest and the Monk as the Primary Enemies of Culture." These have not come down to us. For "The Priest and the Monk," Pryzhov collected thousands of folktales about priests and monasteries, but he was obliged to burn this collection in expectation of arrest, just as he burned his "History of the Free Settlement." What has come down to us (in most cases in fragmentary or distorted form), besides small articles and other works, are his sketches about holy fools and shriekers (*klikushki*), aimed against religious fanaticism and bigotry, and sketches of the history of beggars and the history of taverns, which reveal the ulcers of the Russian state and societal system based on examples of people who sank "to the depths."[53]

Pryzhov was arrested in connection with the Nechaev affair and sentenced to twelve years of hard labor and eternal exile in Siberia.

Although Pryzhov's collection of folktales has not come down to us, his name holds an honorable place in the history of Russian folkloristics. The fate his collection met shows us that far from every tale the people told was published. Afanas'ev was compelled to publish part of his tales in Geneva, Khudiakov had to burn part of his collection, and Pryzhov burned his whole enormous collection because the presence of tales reflecting the lives of the peasants and their views of this life would have threatened him with a sentence even more severe than what he received. This makes clear that Afanas'ev's and Khudiakov's collections, although they contain genuine, unfalsified folktales, nonetheless do not give a complete impression of the Russian folktale and its character. The same is true of later collections.

If we do not count small publications, more than twenty years passed after Afanas'ev's and Khudiakov's editions before the next major scientific collection appeared. This was the collection of the poet-democrat and ethnographer Dmitrii Nikolaevich Sadovnikov, who had the convictions of a man of the folk: *Folktales and Traditional Narratives of the Samara Region*, published by the Russian Geographical Society in 1884. Sadovnikov had a lively interest in the folklore of the Volga region. He wrote works on the lore of Stenka Razin, sketches of the Zhiguli region, and a large quantity of other works. He issued a large collection of riddles.[54] Sadovnikov was the author of the song on Stenka Razin, "From Behind an Island to the Main Channel," which was accepted by the folk and has not lost its popularity to the present day.

Folktales and Traditional Narratives of the Samara Region was published after the researcher's death, without introduction or commentary. Sadovnikov made an important innovation: He noted the place where he had made each recording and also the person from whom he made it. These remarks make clear that 72 of the 183 tales in the collection were recorded from one person, Abram Novopol'tsev. Sadovnikov was the first to draw attention to the living tellers of folktales. Novopol'tsev is, we might say, a classic of oral narration. In 1952 Ema Pomerantseva published his folktales as a separate edition and collected all the information she could find about him.[55]

Sadovnikov had planned to write an introductory sketch about Novopol'tsev as an outstanding master of narration. The tale-teller's repertoire is striking not only in its breadth but also in its variety of styles. Novopol'tsev had mastered both the style of the wonder tale, with its "rituality," and the buffoon (*balagur*) style of the comical and satirical folktale. He undoubtedly had an exceptional literary talent. Sadovnikov was thus the first to pay attention to the enormous individual gifts in the realm of verbal artistic creativity that the simple peasant milieu concealed. Sadovnikov had planned to equip his edition with an introduction and a commentary, but he did not have time to complete them. His edition has splendid scholarly qualities. Sadovnikov made all the recordings himself, and they are all distinguished by exactness. Sadovnikov did not preserve the grammatical and phonetic peculiarities of local speech, as Khudiakov did, because to understand the ideological and artistic nature of the folktale . . . [phrase unfinished in the original—SF].

After Sadovnikov's edition comes another pause of almost thirty years. During that time (in 1873) Aleksandr Gil'ferding's large collection of *byliny* came out. Gil'ferding established completely new principles of collection and publication. He wrote down and published *byliny* not only as textual material of interest to the philologist but also in connection with the whole life of the people.

Gil'ferding's collection has its material organized by tellers. It includes a biography of each teller and has a general introductory chapter, "The Olonetsk *Guberniia* and Its Folk Rhapsodists."

This principle of collection and publication was transferred to the folktale. In 1908 the Russian Geographical Society issued Nikolai Onchukov's large collection under the title *Northern Tales*.[56] Onchukov traveled throughout the region of Pomor'e and Pechora and wrote down folktales in Olonets and Arkhangel'sk *gubernii*. The collection included 303 folktales. Scholarship could no longer limit itself to the study of texts alone. The collection came out after the revolution of 1905. Society was greatly interested in the folk and, among other things, in the peasantry. Now the folktale was approached in connection with the whole life of the peasantry. Onchukov equips his collection with a large introductory chapter, "Folktales and Tale-Tellers in the North." This introduction gives a detailed description of the region. After the discoveries of Pavel Rybnikov[57] and Aleksandr Gil'ferding, the Russian north seemed to be the region that was richest overall in folklore—hence Onchukov's aspiration to collect folktales in the same place. He gives a detailed description of conditions of life in the north, the northern trades and ways of obtaining the necessities of life, the occupations of the inhabitants, and the forms of labor. Thus the conditions in which the folktale lives and is performed become clear.

Onchukov understood the necessity of studying the milieu where folktales exist. But that milieu breaks down into living people. Therefore Onchukov arranges his material by performer. He supplies a biography for each tale-teller, with a description of the person. Onchukov was the first to raise the question of needing to know and study the performer in order to understand the text better. In fact, it is not unimportant whether a folktale is told by an old nanny, a young peasant man, or a widely traveled soldier or sailor.

Onchukov's collection also includes recordings made by the prominent Russian linguist, academician Aleksei Shakhmatov. Shakhmatov had been making recordings even before Onchukov. His recordings are distinguished by ideal clarity. Here we have a phonetic record, as much as possible given the means of the Russian alphabet. (The international system of precise phonetic transcription did not yet exist at that time.)

Onchukov's collection is important for another reason too. After the revolution of 1905, the demands of censorship became somewhat weaker. Onchukov had the chance to publish some tales of the kinds his predecessors could not publish, primarily tales about priests. In distinction from earlier collections, where the wonder tale occupied the greatest part, this collection shows that the favorite, most widespread form of the Russian folktale is the everyday tale, realistic in the form of its narration and full of sharply satirical content.

In the aggregation of all these data, Onchukov's collection represents a significant step forward in the work of publishing folktales. Previous collections had offered no scholarly apparatus (introductory chapter, descriptions of the performers, indexes), and Onchukov's collection was the first equipped with such an apparatus. It also gives an index of names and objects and a glossary of dialect words. Nevertheless, Onchukov is far from the ideals that directed the revolutionary democrats or collectors such as Khudiakov and Pryzhov. He has little interest in the economic position of the peasants, and the data on trades are brief and accidental; in addition, he passes over the question of the social struggle and class hatred of the peasantry reflected in the folktales. Onchukov was unable to see what Vladimir Lenin saw in these tales at first glance.[58]

Onchukov's collection was published by the Russian Geographical Society, and from then on the Society took the initiative in the work of collecting and publishing folktales. In 1914–15 two big collections came out, by Dmitrii Zelenin, who became a corresponding member of the Academy of Sciences of the USSR. These were *Great Russian Folktales of Perm' Guberniia* and *Great Russian Folktales of the Viatsk Guberniia*,[59] which contained 1,311 pieces. Zelenin was one of the most significant Russian ethnographers, and these two collections observe all the rules of scholarship at his time. The material here is arranged according to tale-teller, as it is in Onchukov. There is also a description of the region, in this case the Urals. Details of the lives of the peasants who tell the folktales are indicated, and there is a splendid index. The significance of indexes must not be underestimated. Unfortunately, our collections often provide bad indexes or no indexes of any kind. The best indexes are the ones made by Zelenin for these two collections. If researchers are working on some kind of folktale detail or even a tale type, they can always establish, using the index, exactly what is in the present collection relating to the question that interests them. Besides that, Zelenin gave short retellings of all the plots as appendixes to his collections. Aarne's index had not yet been translated; therefore there were no references to it. The brief, schematic retellings, done by Zelenin with unusual skill, are very useful and allow readers to find their bearings quickly in the material.

Zelenin's collections also have certain deficiencies. The tales they contain are not as sharply satirical folktales as those in Onchukov's collection. Obviously, the peasants did not tell Zelenin everything. Besides that, Zelenin considered his collections a selection of traditional folktales; he considered it "out of place" to include the "everyday story-anecdotes" in them. This point of view must be recognized as erroneous.

The brothers Boris and Iurii Sokolov began collecting folklore in a way that was new in principle. They correctly considered that collecting folk poetry by genre did not essentially give a full picture of folk poetry and its role in the life of the peasantry. The collector who came only to get folktales would not record any songs, no matter how rich in them the region was. Because of collecting by genre, some regions would wind up with well-recorded folk-tales, others with *byliny*, still others with folk songs, and so on. The Sokolov brothers began to collect not by genre but by territory. That is, they attempted to encompass a certain region completely, to make a record of everything to be found there. For this they chose the Belozersk region. The book *Folktales and Songs of the Belozersk Region*, published by the Academy of Sciences, was a result of that expedition.[60] The Sokolov brothers described the difficulties they happened to encounter in detail. People did not believe them when they said they had come to record folktales and songs. Their interest in songs provoked distrust and indignation: "We have nothing to eat, and here they come from Moscow to get hold of songs."[61] The peasants distrusted the aristocrats from the city, took them for secret police, and were sure they would be taken away to jail if they told folktales. Local police assumed the collectors were secret political agitators and created all kinds of obstacles. All this makes clear that the Sokolov brothers heard and recorded far from everything that was current among the peasants, although they succeeded in softening their distrust to a significant extent. It turned out that the most widespread and popular form of folk verbal art was the folktale, which takes up two thirds of the collection. In second place comes the lyrical song, and other kinds of songs follow. Things are different now. The Sokolov brothers thought that one of their greatest tasks was to study the tale-teller as such, his individual traits, his style, his manner of performance. Although the folk master truly should be studied, the Sokolovs' mistake was in tearing the creative work of individual masters away from the creativity of the folk as a whole. In their work the problem of individuality replaces and displaces the problem of the people, their spiritual needs, and their art as a folk art. By doing so the Sokolovs abandoned Belinsky's demands that folk poetry be studied in the first place as poetry of the people. This explains why the Sokolovs were unable to understand the essence of the poetry they recorded. Instead, they attempted an abstract classification of "types of tale-tellers."

To sum up, we may say that the prerevolutionary scholars collected an enormous amount of factual material. Given the conditions of censorship and later also some scholars' incorrect understanding of their tasks, this material suffers from a certain one-sidedness. It represents poorly those tales that express the peasantry's revolutionary mood. But nonetheless even what was recorded reflects, as Lenin wrote when he got to know Onchukov's collection, "the hopes and expectations of the people" and testifies to its high artistic and poetic gift.

But at this point World War I began, then the revolution, and on its heels the civil war, and for a while the collection of folktales moved into the background. Only after surviving the basic difficulties of the first revolutionary period did interest in folklore come back to life, and with a force, a sweep, that could never have occurred before the revolution. If earlier collections of folktales would come out once in ten, twenty, or twenty-five years, after the 1920s they began to come out at a rate of several collections per year.

THE PRESENT

It is quite impossible to list all the editions, or even just the most important ones, and there is no need to do so. Thus I will just describe the fundamental trends, illustrating them with representative examples.

The work of collecting before the revolution depended on the individual initiative and personal enthusiasm of important individual scholars who, not sparing their strength, overcame tremendous difficulties in order to gather the precious pearls of folk creativity.

After the revolution, the work of collecting passed into the hands of scholarly organizations, which compiled thoughtful plans and used state funds to send out well-organized expeditions. A few of these establishments are the Russian Geographical Society, the Institute of Ethnography in the Academy of Sciences of the USSR, other scholarly research institutions, the Union of Soviet Writers, universities, pedagogical institutions, and local history museums.

One of the most remarkable Russian collectors, Aleksandr Isaakovich Nikiforov (1893–1941), began his work soon after the end of the civil war. Without denying the enormous amount of good prerevolutionary collecting that had been done, Nikiforov nonetheless considered the principles and techniques of this work erroneous. How was folklore collected before the revolution? A collector would arrive in a village, find out whether there were any good tale-tellers, write down everything they could tell him, and then travel on to the next village. Nikiforov found this unsatisfactory. He carried on his collecting work differently from his prerevolutionary predecessors. Once he arrived in a village, he would settle in for an indefinite period. Then he would begin to record a folktale from everyone who knew it, both great masters and ordinary performers. He would record children with particular attention and love, because often it is precisely children who love folktales and tell them in special ways. He tried to dig up each one. The picture that resulted was really quite novel and interesting. Nikiforov's method may be called the stationary method of complete recording. Nikiforov completed three expeditions. In summer of 1926 he traveled north of Lake Onega, in 1927 to Pinega, and in 1928 to Mezen'. He brought back 636 texts (196 from Lake Onega, 161 from Pinega, and 279 from Mezen'). This, therefore, is the largest collection of Russian folktales recorded from the mouths of the people. Really, only this kind of approach makes it possible to establish the exact plot composition of folk narrative art, to define that art's character as a folk art, a collective art. For the scholar the folktale is important and interesting not just as a work of art. The poorest, most fragmentary, incoherent text, even if it contains archaic layers, provides a great deal for the study of folktales as a whole—of plots, motifs, images. It may serve as valuable historical material for studying the most ancient concepts and the worldview of the tale-teller's own time. Such texts may also turn out to have ethnographic value. In his aims and his working technique, Nikiforov was undoubtedly correct. His error lay elsewhere. He considered that everything, even fragmentary texts that were artistically inferior, should be published as a whole. He submitted his collection to various publishers, but publishers refused to put out such an enormous, weighty collection with so many inferior or fragmentary texts. Then he appealed to Maxim Gorky for help. Gorky answered with a letter objecting to the unselective publication of works of folk creativity.[62]

Now, after several decades have passed, it is clear to us that each side was correct according to its own point of view. Every single text is important for scholarship. But it is specialists in the folktale who need these texts. There are not many of those, and if the texts are well preserved in archives, they will be accessible to any scholar. The broad masses of readers need the best examples, which will let them evaluate the marvelous creativity of the people on its merits. Nikiforov perished in the blockade of Leningrad and did not live to see his own collection appear.

Tell about the volume I [Propp] edited—*Northern Russian Folktales as Recorded by A. I. Nikiforov.*[63]

Subsequent collectors did not follow the path Nikiforov recommended. We may regret this, because complete collection does not exclude recordings from the finest master tellers; on the contrary, it includes them as well.

Basically, we can note two types of collections. Some collectors follow pre-revolutionary collectors while introducing essential improvements. The Soviet collector is not a nobleman who arrives from the city, whom local people distrust and therefore will not tell everything. Contemporary collectors know how to approach the performer, how to earn his trust. Contemporary collecting work proceeds according to a plan and is gradually covering the whole enormous territory of the Soviet Union.

It is impossible to list them all. There are two types of collections. The old type presents folktales from one area, presenting the best texts from the best performers.

Siberia

M. K. Azadovskii. *Skazki Verkhnelenskogo kraia* (Tales of the Upper Elensk Region), v. 1. Irkutsk, 1925, 1958. 22 tales.

A. Gurevich. *Russkie skazki vostochnoi Sibiri* (Russian Folktales of Eastern Siberia). Irkutsk, 1939.

The North

I. V. Karnaukhova. *Skazki i predaniia severnogo kraia* (Folktales and Traditional Narratives of the Northern Region). Leningrad, 1934.

N. I. Rozhdestvenskii. *Skazy i skazki Belomor'ia i Pinezh'ia* (Skazy and Folktales of the White Sea and Pinega Regions). Arkhangel'sk, 1941.

M. K. Azadovskii. *Russkie skazki Karelii* (Russian Folktales of Karelia). Petrozavodsk, 1947.

N. I. Savushkina. *Skazki i pesni Vologodskoi oblasti* (Folktales and Songs of the Vologda Region). Vologda, 1955.

The Urals

V. P Biriukov. *Dorevoliutsionnyi fol'klor na Urale* (Prerevolutionary Folklore in the Urals). Sverdlovsk, 1936.

Central Russia

T. M. Akimova. *Skazki Saratovskoi oblasti* (Folktales of the Saratov Region). Moscow, 1937.

V. I. Sidel'nikov and V. Iu. Krupianskaia. *Volzhskii fol'klor* (Folklore of the Volga). Moscow, 1937.

This list is far from including everything, only examples. See Akimova's *Seminar*, 1958.[64]

Along with this, a completely new type of folktale collection arose, one that was impossible before the revolution. The trust with which people in the village generally meet scholars from the city led them to tell collectors decidedly everything they knew. And it turned out that there were performers who knew several dozen folktales and could tell them for days in a row. (Compare this to Sadovnikov's and Novopol'tsev's collections.) The first to encounter this was the Leningrad linguist N. P. Grinkova, later a professor at the Herzen Leningrad Pedagogical Institute. She came to the Voronezh region while studying dialects.

Further, Kuprianikha. Grinkova, Novikova, and Ossovetskii, *Kuprianikha's Tales* (Voronezh, 1937).[65] All of them represent a new type of collection.

In those years it seemed that the tale-teller Baryshnikova (Kuprianikha) presented an exceptional, outstanding phenomenon, but it became clear that this was not so. It turned out that there are talents, masters, and connoisseurs of this kind in the heart of the people whose repertoire significantly exceeds Baryshnikova's.

For example, see Korguev, *Korguev's Tales* (1939), 115 texts in two volumes of about 600 pages, and Gospodarev, *Gospodarev's Tales*, recorded by N. V. Novikov 1941.[66] Other collections of the same type are Azadovskii and Ellasov, *The Tales of Magai [Sorokovikov]* (1942); and Gofman and Mints, *I. F. Kovalev's Tales* (1941).[67]

This is the general picture of intensive work in collecting. How many folktales were collected? By 1929, in Nikolai Andreev's count, about 10,000 folktales (texts) had been collected, of which approximately one-third were published in large collections, one-third in various small editions, and one-third preserved in archives. At present these figures are significantly out of date. No one, it is true, has counted all the material collected. But we will not be much in error if we increase that figure at least by a factor of 2. Changes occurred, however, not only in the quantity of collected material but also in the relationship of archival and printed material. So many folktales are recorded that it is impossible to publish all of them. And although a great deal is published in Russia, the published material makes up the lesser part; the greater part is preserved in archives.

Some theorists suggest that under such conditions it is no longer necessary to record new materials only to put them in the archives. This opinion is deeply mistaken. The quantity of new plots, it is true, is insignificant, and in most cases they record variants of plots that are already known, but these new variants represent material that is most valuable for the thorough, in-depth, and full historical study of the folktale and all the problems connected with folktales. Research lags far behind the work of collecting, but this will not always be the case. The folktale in its whole scope cannot be exhaustively studied by one person. It requires the work of well-prepared scholarly collectives, and it requires a protracted length of time.[68]

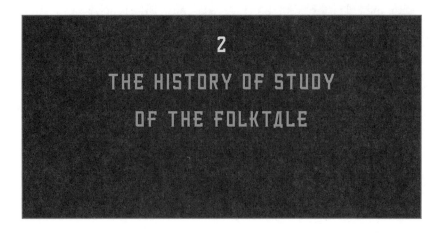

2
THE HISTORY OF STUDY
OF THE FOLKTALE

The Problem of Genre

Development of Concepts of the Folktale in the Eighteenth
and the Early Nineteenth Century

The history of the study of the folktale has been laid out in Russian schol-arship more than once.[1] Aleksandr Pypin, Mikhail Speranskii, S. Savchenko, Iurii Sokolov, and others outline the history of study of the folktale according to movements and their representatives. This gives us the chance, without repeating what has already been said, to focus the outline of our study around particular central issues. Each era, each tendency, and each individual scholar have put forward new issues, which were taken up in the further development of scholarship. The outline of the history of Russian scholarship on these is-sues corresponds in sum to the outline by movements.

The study of the folktale is part of the study of folk creativity as a whole. The history of this study is conditioned by complicated causes. It is conditioned by the country's social and political history, and it is one of the streams that create and reflect the people's self-consciousness.

This aspect of the topic cannot be unfolded here in detail; it is developed in Mark K. Azadovskii's book.[2] My task is to give an external history of the study of the folktale, to grasp primarily the scientific-technical, scholarly-side of this issue. As my introduction indicated, one of the central tasks in the study of the folktale is the definition of its generic markers. Whenever the folktale became an object of societal and scholarly attention, this task should justly have demanded some resolution, although the question was posed on a different plane than it is now.

Societal and literary interest in the folktale begins in Russia in the eighteenth century. However, this was interest not in the *folkloric* tale but rather in courtly romances of the French type, included in the French *Bibliothèques*.[3] Novels of this kind passed as "tales" (*skazki*). This is evident in the introduction to Levshin's *Russian Folktales*, which asserts that "the knightly tales included in the Paris Universal Library are nothing other than *bogatyr'* tales, and the French *Bibliothèque bleue* [Blue Library] contains the same kind of tales that are told among us by the simple people."[4]

Such a misunderstanding was possible only because the properly *folkloric* tale was not yet known. But this assertion is of interest to us, because it shows that people in the eighteenth century were already asking what the folktale was, even though they gave a completely incorrect answer, corresponding to the tastes of the era.

We see that in the beginning the folktale was understood and defined through some other related genre. In the French case the folktale was defined through what we would now call the courtly adventure novel. However, if we look carefully at Levshin's definition, we find in it the expression "*bogatyr'* tales." By *bogatyr'* tales Levshin means the *bylina*. The word *bylina* itself was not yet in currency (it was, as you know, put into use by Ivan Sakharov in his *Skazaniia of the Russian People*),[5] but *byliny* themselves were already known. In this way, we see that the courtly novel, the *bylina*, and the tale (*skazka*) are united in one common concept.

Despite all the naïveté and erroneousness of such a unification, we can still understand it to some extent, because in the final analysis novels of the type included in the *Bibliothèque bleue* spring from folk sources, and there is also a relationship between the *bylina* and the folktale. But the folktale was understood in another way as well; it was often identified with the literary tale.

The anonymous author of the article "A Glance at Tales or Folktales" (in the journal *Patriot*, 1804) declares that in writing his folktales, Nikolai Karamzin followed Marmontel. "'Poor Liza,' the first *skazka* written by him, captivated its audience and brought him fame." The reference to Marmontel is no accident. His *Contes moraux* (Moralizing Stories) was published in Russia too (the first translation was by Pavel fon Roum, 1764), and it passed to Russian readers the dual reading of the word *conte* as both "folktale" and "story" or "tale." The article "On Tales and Novels" (*Avrora*, 1806), where Marmontel establishes the influence of "Arabic and Persian tales" on the development of the novel, moves in just the same direction. Here the folktale and the novel are reduced to a single concept. The reference to Arabic and Persian tales is called up by the appearance in 1804 of Galland's translation of *The Thousand and One Nights*. Although this collection was read with great interest by all of Europe, it did not help in understanding the essence of the folktale. Here we may note that Pushkin too defined the folktale through another genre, namely, the long poem: "How charming these folktales are! Each one is a *poema*."[6] Defining the folktale through the long poem came naturally to Pushkin, who wrote a number of long narrative poems himself. Pushkin also retold folkloric tales in verse, and to him they sounded right only in that form. Pushkin's *skazki* are folktales in their plots, but in form they most resemble long poems. Although Pushkin's assertion is not really an attempt at a strictly scholarly definition, it nonetheless reflects an understanding of the folktale's nature that is typical of his time and of the poet himself.

Along with definition through a genre we see as different, we can observe the first attempts to define the characteristics of the folktale as such. Thus Aleksei Merzliakov, in his *Brief Rhetoric*, still shares Levshin's point of view entirely: "Knightly eras and fairytale kingdoms are the usual storehouses for this type of composition."[7] However, Merzliakov already attempts to establish the particularity of these "tales." He considers "implausible miracles" to be the fundamental feature of a folktale, and he calls them "invented narrations." This means that Merzliakov considers one feature of the folktale to be the implausibility of events and the fact that they are not presented as reality. In this way, Merzliakov was the first to define the essence of the folktale, and we cannot deny that his definition is to some extent correct, although he could not yet have been acquainted with the properly *folkloric* tale.

However, the *lubok* editions of folktales, as well as editions such as *Grandpa's Strolls* and *Medicine Against Pensiveness and Insomnia*,[8] were already providing some material that would allow folktales to be separated from other genres. Nikolai Tsertelev, in his article "A View of Old-Fashioned Russian Tales and Songs,"[9] attacks publications like Mikhail Chulkov's, which a whole generation read with pleasure; he calls them "tedious fantastic novels." This declaration shows us the beginning of a change in tastes. Such novels are already not identified as folktales. On the contrary, Tsertelev opposes them to folkloric tales, of which he distinguishes two kinds: "Some are *bogatyr'* stories, while others are folktales proper, so-called *skazki*." Under *bogatyr'* stories he understands the *bylina*, but Tsertelev is contradictory in his concept of "folktales proper, so-called *skazki*." On one hand, he tends to credit them with great antiquity: Folktales, songs, and proverbs represent "the infancy of the written verbal arts of all peoples." On the other hand, he talks about "composers" of folktales, revealing that he does not distinguish the folkloric tale from the literary tale and the literary fairytale. The literary tale of that time was moralistic. Charles Perrault had started to add morals to his fairytales, and in Russia Ippolit Bogdanovich composed moralizing fairytales, for example. This moralizing nature is ascribed to the folkloric tale as well. But if Perrault added morals, Tsertelev looks in the folktale itself for the moral hidden there. "Often the composer, not daring to speak the truth or wishing to be entertaining, hides it in inventions, leaving the reader to guess." He ascribes an allegorical meaning to the folktale. Thus, if in the tale of Malandrakh and Silikol (from *Grandpa's Strolls*) the tsar's son uses wings without his teacher's permission, putting himself in danger, this is supposedly "an allegory showing how dangerous it is for young people to give themselves over to their own wishes." Tsertelev interprets other tales and folktale motifs in the same manner. The folktale here is understood as a moralizing fable or parable, in which Marmontel's influence is undoubtedly felt.

In 1821 Nikolai Ostolopov published his *Dictionary of Ancient and New Poetry*, something like a literary encyclopedia—and here too there is a chapter about the folktale. For the first time, an attempt is made to distinguish the folktale from other genres: from the novel, the long poem, and parable, that is, from precisely those genres with which, as we saw, it tended to be united. Ostolopov's definition of the folktale foregrounds its implausibility: "A folktale is a narration of a made-up event. It may be in verse and in prose."[10] Like the epic, it demands invention, but, enjoying greater freedom, it crosses the boundaries of verisimilitude and even of possibility at will.

Thus the folktale is defined here from the perspective not of form but of content. The assertion that the folktale can be in verse on equal terms with prose shows us that the folktale is still not distinguished from the *bylina*. Aleksandr Shishkov, in his *Conversations About Verbal Art Between Two Persons, Alpha and Beta*,[11] has the *bylina* in mind when he speaks of *skazki*.

Thus we understand why Mikhail Makarov, in a series of articles in the journals *The Moscow Telegraph* and *The Telescope*, titled "Guesses About the History of Russian Folktales," considered it possible to speak of "*skazki* about Il'ia Muromets, Alyosha Popovich, and Dobrynia Nikitich,"[12] although he was speaking of *byliny*. Makarov was the first to attempt to understand the folktale through its past, through its history—although we will have something to say on that point later on. These attempts were distinguished by total fantasy. Therefore it is natural that the more serious scholarly attempts tried to make sense of the material that already existed. The young Izmail Sreznevskii, who turned to the study of Ukrainian literature and folklore in the small article "A Look at the Founding Works of Ukrainian Folk Verbal Arts,"[13] touched on not only Ukrainian but also Russian folktales. He made an attempt to classify the folktale, and, although that classification cannot be considered successful now, it was important in bringing scholarship to the correct path. Sreznevskii already clearly distinguished the folkloric tale from the *bylina*, the novel, the story. Under the concept *skazka* he included everyday folktales, anecdotes, and folktales about animals. As a representative of Ukrainian democratic romanticism who was well acquainted with the Ukrainian folk song, he was the first to recognize the *folk* character of the tale, when speaking of the folktale. Although he understood this term somewhat broadly, using it, for example, to cover "historical recollections" and "events from private life," merely recognizing that the folktale belongs to the *folk* is a great step forward.

Therefore we can say that by the 1840s a certain understanding of the character of the folktale had been achieved. The folktale was no longer identified with the novel, the tale, the parable, the *bylina*. The folk character of the folktale was understood, the diversity of structure of the folktale epos was recognized, and one of its fundamental features was marked, namely, the "unusualness" of the subject of narration, understanding the character of the folktale as an invention that is not presented as reality. Finally, the first, still entirely fantastic attempts were made to understand the past of the folktale. It is true that all these utterances were scattered and unsystematized, did not yet offer any direction, and sometimes still included erroneous or false concepts. But nonetheless a basis had been created for the foundation of a properly scholarly study of the folktale.

The 1840s–1860s

Until the 1840s, the fundamental question of folktale studies, the object of societal thought, was the question of the essence of the folktale as such. Beginning in the 1840s, study of the folktale (from various angles and with various methods) began to emphasize study of its past. The folktale was no longer related to any adjacent or similar genres; its specific traits and form ceased to be of interest. New problems of a historical nature were advanced. This was, without doubt, a great step forward. However, given the state of scholarship at the time, it was still too early to resolve the historical issues. This is a graphic example of how a historical study of folklore, undertaken without exact, clear concepts of the nature of its genres, cannot lead to success. The desire to get to know the past was in the spirit of that era. It was typical of both Slavophile tendencies and the related aspirations of the mythological school and of dilettantes from among the adepts of so-called Official Nationality.[14] This explains why the healthy beginnings established, for example, in Sreznevskii's writings did not receive further development and in part even regressed.

This has to do first and foremost with the representatives of so-called Official Nationality. Among them, Ivan Sakharov, Dmitrii Shepping, and Pëtr Bessonov wrote on the folktale.

As we already know, Sakharov's collection is made up not of genuine folktales but of retellings of various texts from the eighteenth century (see Chapter 1). In the foreword to this collection, Sakharov also states his own views, although it is difficult to catch their essence because they are not so much sober opinions as emotional exclamations. Their essence remains unclear, and they are mutually contradictory. First, he ascribes to the folktale great historical significance together with historical sources; then he denies that significance completely, polemicizing with Makarov. Sakharov evidently still does not distinguish folktales from stories and *byliny*. ("Russian folktales hold in themselves the foundation of the folk *byliny* and stories, beloved by our fathers and grandfathers"). Sakharov states one correct idea: that there are truly Russian folktales and borrowed tales, ancient tales, and new ones. Sakharov expresses himself only in order to nuance the meaning of "old" and "Russian" folktales, because "they have preserved our Russian family life; they have preserved our pure Russian language" (by this, Sakharov means his own sugary and overdecorated language, used to tell the tales). Sakharov's views come down to the idea that folktales awaken love for everything old-fashioned and truly Russian, as opposed to everything new and foreign, which Sakharov fights against and hates. His views have no scholarly significance.

The past has no concrete historical character for Sakharov; it is a kind of banner. From the scholarly point of view, Sakharov's work is important only in that it contains a series of valuable bibliographic references; his love for ancient things led him to search out some old editions of folktales.

Shepping's article "Ivan the Tsar's Son, a Folk Russian *Bogatyr'*"[15] takes the same tack. As the title shows, Shepping wants to see Ivan Tsarevich as an epic *bylina* hero. The folktale supposedly contains the most ancient core of the tradition, already spoiled in the *bylina*. Consequently, we see once again an emotionally colored extolling of ancient things in the folktale that even the *bylina* has not preserved. "Does not Il'ia in our folktales embody the very concept of our dear mother Russian land, with her hearty revelry, her powerfulness, her riches, and her warm Orthodox faith?"[16] Like the tradition of Il'ia, he writes, at some point there supposedly existed "traditions of Ivan," whose fragments have become folktales.

Shepping's praise of the old days and of Orthodoxy clearly gives away the value system he represented. The head of the Slavophiles, Konstantin Aksakov, spoke out against Shepping in his brief commentary "On the Difference Between Folktales and Russian Songs."[17] Aksakov uttered for the first time the simple and natural thought that folktales and *byliny* were different in form. Aksakov already knew that the *bylina* was sung, and he distinguished the *bylina* and the folktale not only by their form but also by the means of their performance, introducing a properly folkloristic principle: The *skazka* is narrated (*skazyvaetsia*), and the *bylina* is sung. For Aksakov, "the folktale and the song are different from the outset." The folktale is based on invention; the *bylina* speaks of something considered to have really happened. Thus, as we would put it now, Aksakov asserts the primarily aesthetic meaning of the folktale and the historical significance of the *bylina*. Correspondingly, it is not the folktale but only the *bylina* that expresses the people's spirit. "There is no sense comparing Ivan to Il'ia Muromets, a unique, entirely individual personage, a *bogatyr'* who is chiefly Russian, who expresses in himself the Russian land, the Russian people."[18] We should recognize that Aksakov's views are correct in their foundations and quite advanced for their time. But they were not accepted by his contemporaries: Aksakov remained entirely alone. In his response, Shepping attempted to argue against Aksakov, defending and even expanding on his previous views.[19]

Pëtr Bessonov's statements in the appendixes to the songs of Pëtr Kireevskii, which he published, are the same type of work.[20] Afanas'ev's collection had already appeared, and Bessonov himself had in his hands Kireevskii's splendid collection of *byliny*; that is, the conditions had been achieved for genuinely scholarly study of the folktale and of the *bylina*. However, we still find no such scholarly study in the works of Bessonov. For him the fairytale Ivan was a representative of pagan Rus', and he argued this in an entirely fantastic manner (with a pseudo-philological analysis of the name Ivan and a description of its dissemination). Furthermore, this Russian Ivan had entered a new period of life: that of the *byliny*. Bessonov identifies this collective Russian Ivan with Mikula Sedianinovich, with Il'ia Muromets (through the folktale of Sidnia), with Dobrynia (through the plot of the husband at his wife's wedding), and so on. In this way, the collective fairytale Ivan represents prehistoric Rus', whereas the heroes of the *byliny* are already historical. Bessonov makes the heroes of the *byliny* bear right-wing Slavophile ideals. The fairytale Ivan in some way becomes the representative of nomadic Rus', whereas the heroes of the *bylina* embody the people—the Slavic village council and the boyar domains. These were Bessonov's primitive concepts of Russian history, the historicity of the folktale, and the *bylina*.

Bessonov's manner of exposition is lengthy and ponderous. He makes a whole series of particular remarks, committing as he does so an enormous quantity of the most varied linguistic, historical, and folkloristic blunders, which we will not linger on here. Bessonov's views met harsh judgment even from some of his contemporaries.[21]

The interrelationship of the *bylina* and the folktale also interested the representatives of the mythological school. Generic questions were not urgently significant for the mythologists. Problems of the past predominate in their works, analyzed within the system of the Indo-European theory, which we will present in more detail later. But here too, a one-sided interest in the past leads to a misunderstanding of the present. The *bylina* and the folktale are united by a common origin. Fedor Buslaev, the theoretician of the epic, did not doubt that the folktale descended from the *bylina*.[22] Buslaev briefly formulated his view of the folktale in a course of lectures he read to the crown prince. Here he disputes the saying *Skazka—skladka, pesnia—byl'* ("a tale's made up, a song's the truth"), because both folktale and song (i.e., the *bylina*) contain mythological antiquity. The folktale, as a result of its prosaic form, has lost and distorted this antiquity. "What was once understood in songs as reality, as myth and belief, becoming distorted little by little afterwards, took on a fantastic character in the prosaic form of the folktale."[23] Aleksandr Kotliarevskii expressed a similar opinion.

Folktale theoretician Aleksandr Afanas'ev held a diametrically opposed point of view. For him it was not the *bylina* that came first but the folktale. As we have seen, he succeeded in providing a classification of the folktale; he also perceived the difference between the folktale and the legend. But he knew all of that empirically. In theory, the folktale was the most ancient myth for him, and both the *bylina* and the *legenda* came from the folktale. Thus he saw confirmation of the substantial unity of the folktale and the *bylina*; they represented different stages of historical development. Shepping expressed this idea even more straightforwardly in his article "The Cosmogonic Significance of Russian Folktales and *Byliny*."[24]

Orest Miller occupied a somewhat particular position with regard to the folktale's relationship to the *bylina*. In his "Analysis of Afanas'ev's Folktales,"[25] he argued against Aksakov, who considered the folktale and the *bylina* distinct from their origins, Buslaev, who traced the folktale's origins to the *bylina*, and Afanas'ev, who saw the *bylina* as deriving from the folktale. Miller asserted that both the folktale and the *bylina* had a single point of origin: the song, and the "mythical" song at that. Both folktale and *bylina* sprang from this mythical song.

Thus we see that attempts at a historical study of the folktale, as carried out by adherents of the theory of so-called Official Nationality as well as from other positions (representatives of the mythological school), did not clarify the question of the folktale's essence. Representatives of one and the same school resolved the fundamental question of the folktale's relationship to the *bylina* in diametrically opposite ways. All they achieved was an empirical understanding of both the folktale and the *bylina* as separate genres. But theoretically they were united once again, testifying to the misunderstanding of the specific nature of each of these genres.

After the mythologists there was no shift in understanding of the folktale for a long time. Study of the folktale died down to some extent, giving way to study of the *bylina*. Neither the democratic folkloristics of the 1860s, which valued above all folklore's ideological direction, nor the historical school, which treasured folklore's historical correspondences, brought anything new to the understanding of the folktale as a genre. They did not recognize the scholarly significance of the question and considered it possible to study the history and ideology of the folktale outside the question of its form and poetics.

Veselovskii

Aleksandr Veselovskii brought extraordinary new depth to the question of poetic forms, including the forms of the folktale. Veselovskii's thought was brilliantly simple: He never separated or opposed form and idea (or content). On the contrary, form was itself an expression of the idea. Historical poetics, Veselovskii wrote, "teaches us that there is a regularity in the forms of the poetry we inherited, worked out by a societal-psychological process, that verbal poetry cannot be defined by an abstract concept of beauty, and that it is created eternally in the people's combination of these forms with regularly changing societal ideals."[26] Veselovskii demonstrated in a series of concrete studies that form was an expression of worldview. His works include "From the History of the Epithet" (1895), "Epic Repetition as a Chronological Moment" (1897), and "Psychological Parallelism and Its Forms in the Reflection of Poetic Style" (1898).[27] However, he did not do this for the folktale. True, in "The Poetics of Plots"[28] he created the theory of the separability of motifs and plots and demonstrated this separation largely on the basis of the folktale. But this study, although illustrated with folktale examples, has broader significance and application for all genres of epic creation. The motif is the simplest unit of narration, not subject to further division. A plot is a combination of motifs.[29] This separation of motif and plot represents an enormous achievement, creating the preconditions for scholarly analysis of plots and analysis of their structure and allowing us to ask about their genesis and history. Both motif and plot, as well as their development, lack self-sufficient significance for Veselovskii; they are a reflection of everyday conditions and the development of a worldview.

For Veselovskii, the motif is primary to the plot from the genetic point of view. The folktale not only consists of motifs but is also created from them. His lectures on the history of the epos include a section on folktale schemata. "The more ancient a folktale, the simpler its schema, and the newer it is, the more complicated. Thus, our Russian folktale is already combinative, and those who speak of its ancientness rely on a false proposition that has not yet been sufficiently refined."[30] Thus, elaborating a poetics is a precondition for historical study of the folktale. Veselovskii himself, however, thought that he had insufficient support for his ideas, and he never published them. The

"Lectures" were reproduced only as a lithographed edition, first printed by Viktor Zhirmunskii in 1940. "The Poetics of Plots" also remained unfinished. In the "Lectures," Veselovskii shows the insufficiency of all existing theories. Hence his conclusion is that "the question comes down to the necessity of constructing a morphology of the folktale, which no one so far has done."[31] We can see that Veselovskii proposed a study of form as the basis for historical and any other study of the folktale. Of Veselovskii's numerous works, only one ("The Tale of Ivan the Terrible") concentrates on a particular folktale. But there are individual statements about the folktale's connection to other genres in many of his works. His reviews of published collections take up a whole volume,[32] but in them Veselovskii does not touch on the problem of genre; instead, he treats other questions, which we will mention later.

Formalist Works

Veselovskii's ideas could not be developed in either Russian or Western European scholarship, not only because the works containing these ideas were unpublished but also because they were essentially incomprehensible to the shallow, declining scholarship of the late nineteenth and early twentieth centuries. This was due to the wholeness of their conception and, at the same time, to the caution of scholars. The form and specific quality of the folktale was still misunderstood. Most scholars paid attention not to the whole, as Veselovskii did, but to details. The only European scholar who made a serious attempt to study the poetics of the folktale was Joseph Bédier,[33] who strove to capture and define how constant, stable elements in the folktale were related to the changing, variant ones (see S. F. Freidenberg's review in the *Journal of the Ministry of People's Enlightenment*, October 1906). Otherwise, the form of the folktale as such was not studied, although the individual formulas of the folktale were (e.g., in Basset's *Formulas in Folktales*).[34] Works were devoted to triunity in the folktale (e.g., Usener, "Rhein"; Lehmann, "Triunity and the Device of Gaining Strength Thrice in the German Folktale"; and Polívka, "The Numbers Nine and Thrice-Nine in Folktales of the Eastern Slavs"),[35] embellishments and ending formulas (Petsch, "Formulaic Endings in the Folk Tale"),[36] poetry (Kahlo, "Verses in Sagas and Folktales"),[37] and the riddle (Eleonskaia, "Some Observations on the Role of the Riddle in the Folktale"; and Kolesnitskaia, "The Riddle in the Folktale").[38] All these works broaden our knowledge of the folktale, cast light on details, but they do not resolve the basic questions of the folktale's essence or broaden Veselovskii's question about its historical forms as an expression of ideology. It is clear from Johannes Bolte's *Name and Traits of the Folktale* that the sum of details does not lead to a definition and understanding of the folktale's organic wholeness. Bolte's book lists a partial series of traits of the folktale (prosaicness, the presence of verses in the tale, introductory and final formulas, etc.); however, Bolte is compelled to admit that these traits are unstable.[39]

In Russian scholarship the question received some advancement in the works of the so-called formal school. The ideological leader of the school was Viktor Shklovskii.[40] I must add a cautionary note, however: There was no formal school in the proper sense of the word in Soviet folkloristics. There was such a movement in literary studies, and its influence was reflected in the study of folklore.

This movement had predecessors in the West. One of the most important and serious of its representatives was the Dane Axel Olrik.[41] He declared that the regularities observed in folk poetry were regularities of form as such and called them epic laws. Olrik examined repeating phenomena in folk creativity and made a series of truly interesting and valuable observations. Some of them are the laws of the gradual beginning (from calm to action), the ending that moves from movement to calm, repetition, opposites (the smart person and the fool, the good and evil persons, etc.), and the single line of action. These are understood as self-sufficient formal laws.

The Russian formalists confirmed the same thing. Thus Shklovskii objected to Veselovskii's elevating similarity of motifs to the level of a similarity of everyday and psychological conditions. "Coincidences are explained only by the existence of particular laws of plot formation."[42] Folklore is not "elevated" toward reality. The motif of incest is not evidence of hetaerism; animals helping the hero say nothing about totemism; a kidnapped woman in folklore does not testify to actual kidnapping, and so on. Shklovskii developed his thought in detail, critiquing Vsevolod Miller's work on the tale of Dido, who used craftiness to grab land (she demanded as much land as could be encompassed with a bull's hide, cut the hide into thin strips, and so encompassed an enormous space). Shklovskii argued that the plot could not spring from a custom of measuring land in that way because the plot is based on a deception.

Shklovskii's work made no attempts to explain the development of form. Such an attempt was made in my article "The Transformation of Magical Folktales," where processes of evolution come down to reductions, amplifications, exchanges, assimilations, and so on. I assert there that "the folktale must be examined in connection with its surroundings, with the environment in which it lived and still lives. Everyday life and religion will have the greatest significance for us here."[43] But this situation is not developed on the basis of factual material, and the form appears to alter according to its own laws.

Roman Volkov's work is formalist in the narrow sense of the word.[44] It is devoted to a cycle of plots about the "unjustly persecuted" (e.g., stepdaughters) and rests on comparison of variants among themselves, with motifs and their variants indicated by symbols. The whole of the work is in essence the signification of motifs by symbols (letters and figures).

The positions of representatives of this direction did not suit contemporary views of the essence of phenomena of spiritual culture, their origin, and development. But this does not mean that contemporary folkloristics rejects the descriptive principle in scholarship as one technical approach to the study and recording of phenomena. Otherwise they would have to reject, for example, descriptive grammar and the descriptive aspects of archaeology. Although the formalists overemphasized the significance of form, by ascribing to it an immanent regularity and self-sufficient development, the formal school nonetheless played a positive role in drawing attention to the least studied aspect of the folktale: its form.

Study of the Morphology of the Folktale

Russian scholarship has gradually reached the idea that a genre's specific traits lie in its form. Entirely independently, two scholars, Aleksandr Nikiforov and Vladimir Propp, realized that the study of the folktale should rely not on the study of characters as such but on the study of their actions, or functions, because these functions are stable elements of the folktale and because identical functions can be assigned to different characters. Nikiforov devoted a small comment to this topic, "On the Question of the Mythological Study of the Folk Tale."[45] My book *Morphology of the Folktale* [46] attempts not to fix individual scattered traits of folktale poetics, such as introductory and final formulas or tripling, but rather to investigate the wonder tale's structure, its composition. I had the unexpected insight that the composition of the wonder tale has a single type (for more detail, see Chapter 3, on the wonder tale). This allowed me to provide a scientific definition of this type of folktale. Thus Veselovskii's demand that we must "construct a morphology of the folktale" was partly fulfilled. If other kinds of folktales were also studied from this point of view, we would be able to give both a precise definition and a scientifically justified classification of the folktale. I do not declare the revealed regularity to be in any way self-sufficient or equivalent to a formal law. On the contrary, I reduced the folktale's regularity to regularities of a historical order, phenomena of everyday life, thought, or psychology and various forms of religion.

My subsequent works already approach the problem of regularity historically. The press and pedagogical literature recorded the view that these works supposedly testify to my shift onto new tracks. This is not correct, however. Descriptive and historical studies do not exclude each other; rather, they depend on one another. However, although the works cited created a certain basis for understanding the folktale's essence as a genre and for further historical study, the poetics of the folktale still do not exhaust the phenomenon of its composition.

Nikiforov's works attempt to broaden the framework of study of the folktale to include the question of style.[47] However, these are only small commentaries that contain interesting new ideas. They leave the elaboration and systematization of questions of folktale style for the future. Nikiforov's works consider form a phenomenon of an ideological order. There is still no historical perspective, but it becomes possible in principle; that is, the given works are not formalistic. Nikiforov's "Structure of the Chukchi Folktale as a Phenomenon of Primitive Thought" attempts to follow the historical-ethnographic path in the study of form.[48] One of Veselovskii's fundamental ideas, namely, the study of form as a historical category, would seem to be realized. However, the given work does not comprehend the genre of the folktale with adequate precision. Its concept of the folktale includes texts with incantatory and magical purposes, although from our point of view that kind of text is not folktale but myth. Similarly, Chukchi ideology is not sufficiently understood, and phenomena of form and thought remain unconnected. Nonetheless, it is important that the attempt to study form as a phenomenon of the order of thought is methodologically correct.

Nikiforov also made an attempt to broaden traditional concepts of the genres of the folktale. He distinguished the tiresome folktale[49] and the children's dramatic folktale[50] as special genres.

Nikiforov brought together many of his observations in his introductory chapter to Kapitsa's *Russian Folk Tale*.[51] Here, he gives the same definition of the folktale that we take as our starting point. It is characteristic of Nikiforov's works that, as a collector who observed the folktale's living existence, he subjected precisely that side of things to study, sometimes distinguished a genre by that feature, and thus even attempted to classify the folktale according to the forms of its existence (see more on this later).[52]

Nikiforov's definition works by way of poetics, and this kind of definition and understanding of the folktale's specific nature reflects the scholarly aspirations of the present day.

Nikiforov subsequently complicated his definition in work on the genres of the Russian folktale, bringing in the historical principle. With this Nikiforov wished to underline the significance of the historical principle in studying the folktale. However, the folktale's history is sufficiently complex and its study is such a difficult task that it cannot be subsumed within any overly brief formula. Although descriptive and historical studies are most intimately connected, their tasks are nonetheless distinct and cannot be united in a single definition.

The Problem of the Composition
of the Folktale Epic

If, as we have seen, the history of Russian scholarship has made certain advances in understanding the folktale's specific nature as a genre, even though the question cannot yet be considered finally resolved, then another field—the study of the folktale epic's composition and divisions of systematization—has achieved nothing essential since Afanas′ev's time. This is understandable too, given the general lack of work on folktale poetics. No fundamental trait has been found as the basis of a division that could serve as a foundation for further subdivisions. If we use purely abstract reasoning, there could be many such principles of division. For example, if we classify a folktale according to its characters, then we can separate out tales about people, demonic creatures, dead people, animals, elements, objects, and so on. Division by social traits would lead to establishing tales of peasants (with subdivisions), soldiers, barge haulers, townspeople, and so on. If we classified a folktale using the category of style, then we could discern fantastic tales, realistic tales, jesting tales, and so on. It is possible to assemble a great many such classifications. It is not a matter of creating more or less elegant divisions using all the rules of logic, however. The division must have real significance; that is, it must reflect the actual situation of things. A genuinely scientific division would follow one of the traits of folktale poetics per se, namely, the internal structure, or, more simply put, the composition. However, so long as the composition of the folktale has not been thoroughly studied, we cannot resolve the question of whether such a classification will be genuinely possible and useful. The question of classification is one of the most important in the system of each science, and it is to some extent decisive for understanding the material's composition and character. A classification should emerge from painstaking preliminary study; it should proceed from the material rather than being imposed from without. In our scholarship this preliminary study is still developing. Hence it is understandable that the attempts undertaken so far have not led to success. They are not connected with one another, do not proceed from one another, and do not produce a well-formed line of development.

Nonetheless, the question is of historiographic interest, reflecting the degree and character of understanding of the folktale in various eras. In Russia the first attempt at classification belongs to Izmail Sreznevskii. A romantic and an enthusiast of folk literature, he was the first person to understand the *folk* quality of the song and the folktale and attempted to introduce a system into the material that had already been accumulated. His article "A Look at the Founding Works of Ukrainian Folk Verbal Arts" distinguishes folktales by their degree of dissemination and stability. Some of them, "expressing the people's favorite ideas and recalling events and personages precious to its memory, have come to be general possessions of the people; others are attested in only a few places; the latter are extraordinarily important for history."[53] We may understand from these words that Sreznevskii divides folktales into folktales with international plots and historical *predaniia* or *skazaniia*, which generally have only limited range. But he also divides folktales by the character of their contents. Here he establishes three sorts: (1) mythical, among which he considers tales about evil powers, sorcerers (*znakhari*), dragons, and other "superstitions" (i.e., the variety we distinguish as memorates); (2) tales about personages or about historical events and private life (this category is not elaborated and remains unclear); and (3) tales that are "fantastic and humorous," among which Sreznevskii considers tales about animals (the *basnia* or fable of sister fox), the purely realistic (the tale of Foma and Erema), and the fantastic on an equal footing.

In its time Sreznevskii's classification was a step forward, as he already excluded *byliny* and adventure novels from the genre of folktales, but he did include the animal epos. By now his classification has only historical interest. The question of classification did not arise in Russia until the 1860s, when Afanas'ev's collection (1855–64) stimulated interest in the folktale and was reflected in its scholarly study. However, the representatives of the school of so-called Official Nationality did not yet understand the significance of Afanas'ev's collection as being genuinely of the people. For example, I. Snegirev, in his *Lubok Pictures of the Russian People in the World of Moscow*, still did not distinguish the folktale from the *bylina*, and he spoke of three types of folktales: (1) mythical, (2) *bogatyr'* (here Snegirev places the *bylina*), and (3) everyday tales.[54] As we see, he ignores the animal tale. Pëtr Bessonov's commentary to his edition of Kireevskii's songs reflects similar views. He does not include *byliny* among folktales, but nonetheless he calls folktales first and foremost "about the past, having to do with *bogatyr's*," understanding this to mean folktales based on *byliny*. After that come tales that are "about the past, but not about *bogatyr's*." Bessonov understands these as mythical folktales, although he avoids this term, as a scholarly enemy of representatives of the so-called mythological school. Further, Bessonov separates out the *lubok* folktales (as we can see, his principle of division is changeable) and, finally, everyday folktales, among which he puts animal tales, because, in his opinion, they are not "zoomorphic" but rather tales about people with later transference of human traits onto animals.[55]

The mythologists turned out to be much more sensitive, grasping the significance of Afanas'ev's collection in their own manner. As I said before, a pressing need for classification arose after the first edition of Afanas'ev's tales. Orest Miller proposed such a classification after publication of the tales was completed and the awkwardness of the unsystematic arrangement of Afanas'ev's first edition became evident.[56] First, Miller separates out mythical tales, counting 343 of them in Afanas'ev and subdividing them according to plot or, rather, into plot cycles (with ten of these in all). Next come moral-mythical tales, about fate, simpletons, prophetic dreams, truth and falsehood, unjust wealth, and so on. Miller's general view of the moral element in folk creativity motivates the separation of this category. The third category includes animal tales. The fourth includes tales based on *bylina* plots; the fifth includes tales that arose from literary influences (about Alexander the Great, Khan Mamai, Shemiaka's Judgment; Miller also includes here some tales about evil wives). Finally, Miller describes the last category as "tales that are purely descriptive of morals, in part of a protesting character, and protesting in part in the form of satire."[57] Among these Miller includes the tales of Ruff, Son of Ruff, Ivan the Terrible and Gorshen, and all anecdotes.

Miller's is the first scholarly classification. Afanas'ev undoubtedly made use of it, but he was far from accepting all of it (e.g., Miller does not distinguish moral-mythical tales, and the tale of Ruff is with the animal tales). This classification played a great role in the history of scholarship in Russia and, with Afanas'ev's corrections, even today it is correct in its fundamental traits, despite the inexactness and inconsistency of the principle of division. Miller himself considered his classification historical, that is, arranged "according to stages of historical development of this branch of the folk verbal arts."[58] We cannot say this of Miller's classification, however. In itself Miller's idea is a valuable aspiration, but we know now that arranging folktales by stages of historical development and classifying material in a static cross-section are two completely different questions. We need both static classification and a historical study of the folktale according to its forms of development. Miller's classification entered our scholarship precisely as a formal one, not a historical one. Subsequently, in his *Attempt at a Historical Survey of Russian Verbal Arts*,[59] Miller complicated his classification by strengthening precisely the historical element, but it gained nothing from this; rather, it lost. He arranged mythical folktales according to the forms of the struggle of light with darkness (light that is not personified; light that is personified in the form of marvels or animals of a golden hue, etc.).

Given Russian publishing practice, no one after Afanas'ev raised the question of classification because folktales were arranged according to their performers. But Ukrainian and Belarusan editions made attempts at classification that were critiqued by Russian scholars. So, Myhailo Drahomanov's *Little Russian Folk Predaniia and Stories*[60] established thirty rubrics for the variegated material he had collected. Veselovskii's review of the collection sharply attacked Drahomanov's division, reproaching him for not upholding the principle he himself had asserted: the old (autochthonic, ancient, pagan) and the new (Christian). He accepted Drahomanov's arrangement as only temporary and mnemonic and denied that it had the character of a scientific system. However, Veselovskii did not specify his own views on a possible classification and its principles. The third volume of Evdokim Romanov's *Belarusan Collection* contains animal, mythical, humorous, and everyday tales, and the fourth includes cosmogonic and "cultural" tales.[61] Legends, stories of dead people, devils, and so on are included here. The division of the third volume clearly comes from Afanas'ev, but it does not match the extremely arbitrary division of the fourth volume, which Nikolai Sumtsov indicated with particular sharpness: "*Legendy* show up in the section of mythical and everyday tales; here too are the facetious tales. Mr. Romanov puts folktales about rogues both in the mythical tales and in the 'cultural' tales."[62]

Besides classification by basic category, more refined divisions can be made according to plots and motifs. We find such a division in Pëtr Vladimirov's *Introduction to the Russian Verbal Arts*.[63] Vladimirov recognized three varieties of motifs: "First we will examine motifs of the animal epos, then motifs of mythological character . . . and, finally, motifs of ancient everyday, cultural character."[64] As we can see, this division follows the tradition springing from Afanas'ev. However, Vladimirov included motifs of grateful animals (e.g., Puss in Boots) and the language of birds or beasts among motifs of the animal epos. Here there is an obvious error: These motifs form part of the wonder tale. Thus Vladimirov's division is not a step forward. There is also no precision in the way he understands the motif; he considers both detailed parts of narrations and also whole plots as motifs. Vladimirov counts forty motifs, but this clearly does not exhaust the whole folktale repertory. Sumtsov's article on the folktale asserts the existence of 400 motifs, offering no foundation for his statement.[65] All the classifications in our courses and handbooks descend from Miller and Afanas'ev's division. This system was used by Aleksei Galakhov,[66] Vsevolod Miller in his lectures, Mikhail Speranskii in his course on the Russian oral verbal arts, and Iurii Sokolov in his course on folklore. In this way, Mikhail Khalanskii turned out to be wrong when he wrote in 1908, "At the present time such a division of folktales is being completely pushed aside."[67] Khalanskii divides the folktale epos into plots without uniting them into general rubrics, aside from animal tales, which he examines as a distinct group.

To what extent the question of the contents of the folktale epos, its genres, and their relationship to one another was still unclear even in the early twentieth century is shown by the volume of *Izvestiia otdela russkogo iazyka i slovesnosti* (News of the Department of Russian Language and Literacy) assembled by Aleksandr Smirnov, "A Systematic Index of Themes and Variations in Russian Folk Tales,"[68] published in three parts: animal tales, tales about animals and people, and tales of the struggle with evil powers. The phrase "about animals and people" naturally raises the question of the relationship of these tales to the animal tales. At the same time, those tales include "The Tale of the Goldfish," "The Rooster and the Millstone-Makers," "The Marvelous Ducks," "Emelia and the Pikefish," "Puss in Boots," "Sivko-Burko," and "Beasts' Milk," that is, any tales in which animals play some kind of role. The final part (the struggle against evil powers) encompasses mainly tales about fighting dragons. The index has no sequential numeration and cannot be used for practical purposes; as a system of classification it muddles what had already been at least somewhat clarified. The index was not completed.

The situation in Western European scholarship was no better than in Russia. As early as 1864 Johann Georg von Hahn counted forty folktale formulas in his introduction to *Greek and Albanian Folktales*.[69] In 1890 George L. Gomme counted seventy-six of them.[70] Arthur Christensen proposed a classification according to motifs and themes.[71] A magisterial index of motifs in folk verbal arts was undertaken by the American scholar Stith Thompson.[72] More interesting and complex was the classification of Wilhelm Wundt in his *Völkerpsychologie* (1903). Wundt arranges folktales according to their forms of development. The most ancient form is the mythological tale and fable. It develops, on the one hand, into the pure wonder tale and, on the other hand, into the biological tale and the fable in two forms: the purely animal fable and the etiological tale. Later formations are the jesting tale and the moral fable. Wundt's system is a result not so much of his own research as of his philosophical evolutionary and psychological conception.

Thus we see that Russian scholarship had worked out no generally accepted classification during a century of development. At the same time, such a great quantity of folktale material had accumulated in all countries that its description and inventory urgently required some kind of system, at least a preliminary one. This system was proposed by Antti Aarne in his 1910 index of folktale types, which we have already mentioned.[73] Aarne's system came into international use. The proposed classification is not scientific in the proper sense of the word. Aarne's index represents a reference book, a listing of plots. Listing demanded a certain order, and this order was created by Aarne.

Aarne divides folktales into three large varieties: (1) tales about animals, (2) folktales proper, and (3) anecdotes. This nomenclature is not entirely successful because it suggests that animal tales are not recognized as folktales proper. Animal tales are divided according to animal (the fox, other wild animals, wild and domesticated animals, people and wild animals, etc., through "other animals and objects"). This kind of classification reveals its irregularity only after detailed acquaintance. Thus the tale "The Sun, the Frost, and the Wind" falls into the rubric of "other animals and objects." The rubric "about people and wild animals" includes tales that not every folklorist would assign to the animal epos, for example, "Verlioka" (A-T 210*B) or the tale of the peasant man who shows a bear how to play the fiddle and traps its paws in a vise (A-T 151). The folktales proper are divided into magical tales, legendary tales, novellistic tales, and tales about the stupid devil. The narrowness of the category of tales about the stupid devil is obvious, compared to the broad categories of wonder, novellistic, and legendary tales. Each of these varieties is divided into subcategories. Wonder tales are divided according to their characters, but this principle is not maintained and there are divisions according to features that, as we noted, are not mutually exclusive. Legendary and novellistic tales are subdivided differently, according to motifs (for the legendary tales the divisions are reward and punishment, truth comes to the surface, and so on; for the novellistic tales the divisions are the hero marries a princess, fidelity and innocence, taming a shrew, and so on). We would consider the motif of the hero marrying a princess to be characteristic not so much of the novellistic tale as of the wonder tale, where it is often the dénouement. Finally, anecdotes are divided according to their characters (country bumpkins, husbands, women, etc.), but the principle is not maintained and subdivision by motifs (e.g., about happy chance) is added.

The imperfections of this classification are readily apparent. It cannot be corrected by removing individual defects. Its flaws are organic. It is not yet time for a correct classification, because the poetics of the folktale have not yet been completely studied. The given system of classification should be regarded only as an aid in creating an index, as a title for it, that is, as purely applied, not scholarly-cognitive. In Soviet scholarship Aleksandr Nikiforov spoke with particular clarity about the need to restructure the classification in his introductory article to Kapitsa's anthology and in his specialized work "Genres of the Russian Folktale," which I have cited.[74] In the first of these Nikiforov still followed the usual path. He counted five genres of folktale: introductions or flourishes, fantastic or miraculous tales, everyday tales, religious (legendary) tales, and, finally, children's tales. In some strange way he managed to pass over the animal tales. Nikiforov posed the question differently in "Genres of the Russian Folktale."[75] He underlined the importance and complexity of the question, its lack of a solution, and the need to find new principles of classification. He also suggested this principally new path. For Nikiforov the folktale is not a text or a plot but a complex entity in which forms of performance are also part of the contents. The idea is in itself undoubtedly correct. As an experienced and attentive collector, Nikiforov did not just read a folktale; it was as though he also saw and heard its performance. The living folktale is not a purely epic genre. He tried to organize the folktale precisely according to the forms of its performance. However, this attempt cannot be called a success by any means; one and the same folktale may indisputably be performed in different ways. Nevertheless, Nikiforov's attempt has great significance, not as a contribution to the classification of folktales but rather as a survey of forms of performance. We will speak of that later, in the chapter on the life and performance of the folktale (Chapter 7).

THE FOLKTALE AS MYTH

The Symbolic School

Scholarly interest in the folktale took shape in Russia in the 1840s and 1850s. This was the era of Fedor Buslaev's introduction, which we can count as the beginning of our discipline's history. But the field was not created all at once. It had a prescientific period, a period of scholarly guesses and fantasies. The folktale was interesting not only as such, not only as a contemporary phenomenon, which had to be accounted for, collected, described, but also from the point of view of its history, its past. The first hints came from Germany, defined by the retrospective interests of the Romantics. The folktale was perceived as a symbolic expression of the deepest wisdom. It seemed that at one time, in the distant past, this wisdom was public and open. The folktale was a myth. This poetic idea found its scholarship-forming expression in Friedrich Creuzer's once famous work *Symbols and Mythology of the Ancient Peoples, in Particular the Greeks.*[76] In the opinion of Creuzer and his adherents, myths are invented by individuals, in part by priests, who participate in philosophical study of higher symbols that are inaccessible to the crowd and present them for the use of the masses. Joseph von Görres understands this somewhat differently in his *History of the Myths of the Asiatic World.*[77] According to Görres's theory, the primeval person was a seer to whom the secrets of nature were open. The seer was the folk itself. All humanity spread over the world from one point—from some most ancient state somewhere in the heart of Asia, in the Himalayas. From there it carried ancient Eastern wisdom, preserved in the symbolic images of myth and folktale. As we can see, this idea contains the embryos of both the future Indo-European and the future Eastern theories. The theories of Creuzer and Görres have a reactionary character. Görres idealized the Middle Ages and later became a zealous champion of Catholicism. The teaching of the symbolic school is pseudo-historical and pseudo-mythological. In their argumentation, adherents of this school resorted to impossible linguistic rapprochements—for example, the supposed resemblance of the name Attila to the Atlas Mountains.

The influence of this tendency in Russia has still not been sufficiently studied. We can say with confidence, however, that it influenced Mikhail Makarov, whose series of articles on the Russian folktale for the first time touched on the question of its past and traced the folktale to a single ancient Asiatic source.[78] Folktales about Il'ia, Dobrinia, and Alyosha "are not yet the most antique ancientness. Prior to them . . . there is also something of the kind that still smells of the banks of the Gang or the Ganges."[79] True to the methods of the school, Makarov developed a theory that folktales came to Russia from the Asiatic East, with the Mongols as possible mediators. He called such tales Mongolo-Indian. Other tales took shape under the influence of Greek myths, but the Greeks themselves took their mythological "inventions" from Asia. In that way, Makarov had some concept of the migration of folktales in connection with historical events. Thus he writes that clashes with the Varangians and other neighbors led to the appearance of new folktales. Makarov described "Bova" entirely correctly as an "Italian-French tale," and he confirmed the Western origin of "Peter Golden Keys." In Makarov's opinion, "Eruslan" came to us "from the most recent Slavic peoples."[80]

Makarov's statements offer a motley mixture of correct and absurd assertions. The historical fate of folktales interested him more than their symbolic contents. Folktales conceal, in his words, "curious mysteries of an antiquity unfathomed until this time."[81] He did not attempt to decipher these secrets, by the way, but insisted on the folktale's ancient Asiatic origin, bringing the world of its magical objects together with fantastic Indian mythology and producing impossible rapprochements between the Russian language and Sanskrit (which he did not know). Many questions here—about the origin of the folktale, its original link with myth, the paths of dissemination and cultural influences, borrowings—were already harbingers of future scholarship. However, there was still neither method nor material with which to solve these questions.

Ivan Snegirev was another follower of this school. He considered proverbs a discovery of the ancient tsars, priests, and sibyls sent out among the people. He touched on the folktale only in passing, in his work *Lubok Pictures of the Russian People in the Muscovite World* (1861), where he proposed the classification we mentioned earlier. Acquainted with the Grimm brothers' theory, Snegirev also observed the international resemblance of folktales. He explained it not only by borrowing but also by a common prehistoric past. However, he imagined that past not in the spirit of Indo-Europeanism but as some kind of archaic time revealed by God. Such views did not prevent him from being a great connoisseur of folk illustration, and as a collection of materials his work has importance of the first magnitude.

Buslaev

The activity of Fedor I. Buslaev (1818–97) began in the 1840s. He encompassed all fields of folk creativity and united them in a single scholarly worldview. The folktale, strictly speaking, cannot be removed from his system and examined separately. We will limit ourselves to a brief description of Buslaev's activity as a whole.

From his first steps, Buslaev emerged as a professional scholar, not a dilettante, engaged in the advancement of European scholarship of his time. This scholarship was presented in the elegant system of Jacob and Wilhelm Grimm. Buslaev, as a leading scholar of his time, was expected to respond and in fact did respond to their teaching. There is a widespread opinion that Buslaev was an imitator of the Grimm brothers, bringing their theory to Russian soil and applying it to Russian material. That is not entirely true. The young Buslaev naturally accepted the most forward teaching of his time, to some extent making it his own. Thereafter he surpassed and overcame it, embarking on a new path of research.

The tales of the Grimm brothers (*Kinder und Hausmärchen*) came out in three volumes in 1812 (though marked as 1813), 1815, and 1822. Of those, the first and second volumes contain the preface and tales, and the third volume gives the scholarly apparatus. This was the first edition of genuine people's folktales, recorded for the most part directly from their performers. In some texts the dialect is preserved. It is true that Wilhelm Grimm subjected the texts to light editing, leveling them to a somewhat conditional folk style, but he did so with great tact and taste, not touching the plot. With this one reservation the texts can be recognized as genuine. This was an enormous achievement because it found a new and correct path to understanding the genuine folktale. The collection contains 200 tales and 10 children's legends. During the Grimm brother's lives, seven editions came out, each time with new prefaces and introductions. These prefaces were indeed a turning point in the history of our field. Besides that, Jacob Grimm stated his view of the folktale in a preface to Basile's *Pentameron*, which he and his brother translated, in his *German Mythology*, and in several articles.

The scholarly apparatus consisted of a bibliography of variants. Although some folktale material was known (from our point of view, not much), the amount was insufficient to see resemblances between the folktales of various European peoples. This is the significance of the third volume. For the first time the Grimm brothers posed the question that would occupy scholars for a whole century: the question of resemblance. Asking the question moved the study of the folktale onto a scholarly path.

The second problem the Grimm brothers posed for the first time was that of the folktale's origin. Once again, they posed it correctly. The problem still occupies scholars today.

The fundamental achievement of the Grimm brothers consists in a new, properly scientific phrasing of the questions of studying the folktale. Moreover, they not only posed the questions but also worked to resolve them. To understand how they approached these questions, we must keep in mind that the Grimms were not just folklorists, even not so much folklorists as they were philologists, linguists. Jacob Grimm's *German Grammar* laid the foundations of Germanic philology.[82] As a linguist Jacob Grimm took the only possible, the only scholarly position at that time: Indo-Europeanism. I do not need to lay out the fundamentals of that theory here. Suffice it to say that the principles of the Indo-European theory were transferred to the study of the folktale and that this initiated its scholarly study.

The problem of the resemblance of folktales was solved in the same way as the problem of the resemblance of languages: by asserting the existence of some ancient homeland of the European languages where a single people lived and spoke a single language. Gradual migration and settlement formed separate peoples, each already speaking a separate language, one that nonetheless preserved traits of earlier linguistic kinship. At the time of the Grimm brothers' activity, the Indo-European theory appeared so obvious that it demanded no particular proof. Thus the Grimms also never especially emphasized it, and they did not work to prove the theory's correctness for folktales. That seemed to them understood in itself, and it penetrates all their statements.

The second question, that of the folktale's origin, was more difficult to answer, and here it was impossible to rely on data from the adjacent science of linguistics. The Grimm brothers asserted the religious origins of the folktale.

What came down to us as a folktale was a myth during the period of Indo-European unity. Scholars did not yet have access to sufficient means to establish the character of that myth. They imagined that religion as the religion of a divinity and asserted that the folktale went back to *Göttermythen*—myths about gods.

In prefaces to the folktale editions these thoughts were uttered fairly clearly and precisely, but they nonetheless bore a declarative character, because the folktale was reduced to something unknown: to myth. Jacob Grimm undertook a grandiose attempt to establish the Old German pagan religion in his capital work, *German Mythology*.[83] Here he gathered, nugget by nugget, data relating to pagan cults of the ancient Germans. His fundamental source was the relics of those cults, and the folktale occupied an important place among them. Individual chapters speak of various aspects of the cult. Thus there are chapters devoted to the gods (Wotan, Donner), giants, trees, animals, the sky, the stars, day and night, and so on. The folktale's penetration by various elements of the original faith becomes apparent, although the study as a whole was not undertaken on behalf of the folktale.

These brief comments on the activities of the Grimm brothers allow us to understand the character of Buslaev's work better. Proceeding from the methods and assumptions of the Grimms, Buslaev followed his own path. He grew and developed, and his views cannot be understood as unitary and of a piece. His views of the folktale developed as well, in connection with general views of folk poetry. Buslaev made a definitive step forward in understanding folk poetry precisely as of the people. "We will define epic poetry as only the so-called indigenous, in opposition to the artificial."[84] Buslaev understands the properly folkloric character of folk creativity. The folk, for him, is not only an idea but a concrete historical given. In this regard Buslaev far surpasses the Grimms. He treasures folk creativity not because it reflects moral ideas in allegorical or symbolic form but because he sees in it "the foundation of the moral physiognomy" of the people. This foundation must be studied historically. Buslaev defines "scholarship about a people's traits" as follows: "It is as dispassionate as possible a study of everything Russian life has elaborated over the centuries and has taken organically for itself from what was imported from outside."[85]

Buslaev adopts the point of view of Indo-Europeanism. However, he is less interested in the formation of peoples and languages or the process of the migration of peoples. The past interests him because it is precisely in the deep past that the people's moral face took shape. Anyone who wants to understand his own people must understand that people's past. "All the moral ideas of a people in the primitive era make up its sacred heritage, its great individual antiquity, a holy bequest from ancestors to descendants."[86] These general views also define Buslaev's views of the folktale.[87]

Buslaev's individual statements on the folktale are scattered throughout many of his works. Buslaev dedicated his life primarily to the epos, the *bylina*. The epos for him is the most perfect and ancient expression of the people's moral idea. For him the folktale stands in the background, but Buslaev nonetheless devoted two specialized articles to the folktale, "Slavic Folktales" and "Migrating Tales and Stories."[88]

Buslaev's views were founded on the study of genuinely folkloric tales. By this time Afanas'ev had already begun publishing. Besides that, Buslaev brings Pantaleimon Kulish's *Notes on Southern Rus'* into his first article on Slavic folktales.[89] He knows Czech and Slovak folktales from Wenzig,[90] Wallachian tales from Schott,[91] Lithuanian tales from Schleicher,[92] and so on.

"Slavic Folktales" is a series of sketches or essays that are not connected with one another, with a short theoretical introduction. Buslaev values folktales for the same reason he treasures the epos: "It is the people's antiquity and traditions, from which the first foundations of its moral physiognomy took form."[93] Buslaev for the first time defines the folktale as genuinely folk poetry. "The poetic creativity of whole masses or generations and the creativity of an individual person flow together in this all-encompassing broad stream of folk poetry," he says, referring to the folktale.[94] From these statements it is evident that Buslaev treasures the folktale not for its artistic side but as a monument of antiquity, and for him this antiquity is a mythical antiquity.

The question of the folktale's mythical character in the past is connected with the question of the international resemblances of folktales. Buslaev is a convinced enough adherent of Indo-Europeanism that he does not consider it necessary to prove the theory's correctness. "There is not the slightest doubt that the most intimate relationship of these peoples in mythology, language, mores, and poetry is conditioned by the common historical descent of the Indo-European peoples from one source."[95]

For Buslaev the folktale was formerly a myth. He expresses this view with extreme precision and clarity.

> Like a fragment of prehistoric antiquity, the folktale contains in itself
> the most ancient myths, common to all the Indo-European languages,
> but these myths have already lost their meaning in more recent genera-

tions, updated by all kinds of historical influences; therefore, from the point of view of more recent ways of thought, the folktale has become an absurdity, an invention, and not reality. But with regard to the comparative study of the Indo-European peoples it offers material for the study of how each of the related peoples has adopted the common mythological heritage.[96]

These words contain a whole program for study of the folktale. In the past the folktale was a myth, and this myth can and should be reconstituted by way of comparative study.

From this we can see how enormous a step forward Buslaev made in understanding the folktale and concerning the methods of its study. He steps onto the historical and comparative path of study; that is, for the first time in Russian scholarship he stands on a genuinely scholarly foundation.

However, accurate application of the principles that Buslaev declared encountered one difficulty: From his point of view, no genuine myths had been preserved. Of course, Buslaev could not yet know that eventually the myths of aboriginal peoples would be collected and would show that the contemporary folktale is in direct genetic relation to them; that is, they would in essence confirm his theory. But so long as this genuine original antiquity was not in existence, Buslaev set out to reconstruct it from folktales. His essays on the folktale are occupied with this. From the genetic point of view, for Buslaev there is no specific difference between the folktale and the *bylina*. The *bylina* comes from ancient myth in just the same way, Buslaev thinks. The *bylina* is more ancient than the folktale, and Buslaev straightforwardly asserts, "The folktale comes from the *bylina*; that is, it is nothing other than a scattered and updated episode of the folk epos."[97] We know now that more recent scholarship has not confirmed this. Buslaev was misled by the presence of the same plots in the folktale and the *bylina*. In fact, in isolated cases a folktale did come from a *bylina*, for example, the tale of Il'ia and Nightingale the Robber (Afanas'ev 174),[98] the tale of Vasilii Buslaevich (Afanas'ev 176), and others. But Buslaev took this individual case of a folktale borrowing a plot from the repertoire of the heroic epos as a general law of the folktale's descent from the *bylina*. Buslaev also asserted (though without ever proving it using comparative examples) that the verse fragments often encountered in folktales are remnants of *bylina* form. "These verse remnants refer to the era when the folktale, still the same thing as a *bylina*, was an episode in the folk epos."[99]

The prosaic form of the folktale represents a later form of the epos. But, after starting on the path of prosaic development, the folktale loses its mythical traces; it acquires a "new appearance" and "it changes from a mythic episode into an entertaining novella."[100] In this way, Buslaev's view is far from one-sided. He observes the literary character of the folktale as well. He considers this kind of tale the most recent. Buslaev observed both borrowing and migration of plots even before Benfey drew attention to them. "Therefore, the more recent folktale may already take its contents from literary sources and even rework foreign stories translated from foreign languages."[101] We see the breadth of Buslaev's horizon, how he strives to include all the phenomena that concern the folktale in its historical development. We should recognize Buslaev's theoretical pronouncements as a great achievement not just for their own time: Many of Buslaev's views remain true to the present day.

From all the many perspectives that open in the study of the folktale, Buslaev values one side more than the others (and devotes to it not only general thoughts but also concrete research); that is the folktale's link to primitive religion. Although Buslaev moved extraordinarily far in his theoretical views and created a basis for further development in scholarship, the same cannot be said about his concrete assertions. Not many of them would pass into later scholarship.

There are nine essays on the folktale in Buslaev's article "Slavic Folktales." We will not stop to consider all nine but will give only select examples that characterize Buslaev's tendency and method. Such, for example, is his analysis of the tale of Ivas' and the Witch (A-T 327 C, "Ivashka, Zhikharko, and Others and the Witch"). The witch (a fox) lures a boy into her place by imitating his mother's voice; she wants to fry him, but her daughter winds up in the stove, and then she herself does. Buslaev did not yet know Afanas'ev's variants; for him the original text was the one Kulish had published. This is the only text of the tale he knows. What is his study's purpose? To uncover the "mythological meaning," that is, to define the original beliefs sedimented here. Buslaev declares that two independent *predaniia* are united here: one about Ivas', who lived in a boat and only came close to shore for a short time at his mother's call, and the other about the deceived witch, who eats her own child.

Buslaev's assertion is so inaccurate because he did not have sufficient comparative material. Ivas' does not live on the water. He is only fishing there; he lives with his parents. This mistake led to another—the idea that there are two traditions that could be combined. The folktale texts show that the motif of the deceived witch is an organic part of the plot and cannot be separated from it, whereas the boy who is fishing does not form part of the plot type and contains no plot development. However, Buslaev then discards the motif of the deceived witch, paying no attention to it at all.

In this way, we see here that the contents of the folktale, its divisibility or indivisibility, the relationship of parts to the whole, of motifs to the plot, are still far from clear. Buslaev separates out the plot of the boy who, in his opinion, lives on the water and returns home riding on geese. "The mysterious presence of Ivas' in the boat on the water and his miraculous rescue by a swan-goose probably exists in connection with some belief which lived among us as a whole and definite tradition [*predanie*], in a self-sufficient myth."[102]

For comparison, Buslaev brings in the "tradition" of the swan-knight (which, from our point of view, has nothing in common with the plot of Ivas'; Buslaev brings them together through the motif of riding home on a swan or goose). In the tradition of the swan-knight, six brothers are turned into swans by their stepmother's machinations, but their sister restores their human form and only one remains a swan. This swan takes his brother in a boat to rescue a woman who has been unjustly condemned. The brother saves her, marries her (or her daughter), but forbids her to ask who he is. She violates the ban, and the swan takes his brother away from her.

As I have already said, we consider these plots completely distinct and not comparable. Buslaev compares them and uses them to supplement one another. Thus the swan-children are born of a mother who was caught while bathing by a swan knight; he marries her. This is important for Buslaev, because it enables him to assert that the mother (and therefore Ivas''s mother) is "a personification of the element of water: the knight finds her bathing in the water; she is the maiden of the lake, Undine, *rusalka*. . . . Her children are the same kind of supernatural beings."[103] Further, he brings in other materials (the tale of Melusine). "Returning to the Little Russian tale, we now see its basic mythical motif clearly. Ivas' is a creature of the other world; he lives on the water, in a boat, and returns carried by a swan-goose. But his mythical relationship is already lost in the people's memory: He is no longer the son of a *rusalka* or of some kind of prophetic maiden, the white swan, but of a simple mortal; and the swan-goose, though it understands his speech, is no longer his brother."[104]

The Indo-European descent of the plot is buttressed by reference to a related plot in the tale of Bishma and the Mahabharata, where some of the characters are not people but gods. For Buslaev this is the plot's most ancient form, and it allows him to assert that the swan-children, just like the Ukrainian Ivas', are foreigners in the world—"beings who are not only supernatural in general, but creatures of divine descent, the personification of elemental deities."[105] With this the study concludes. The folktale's Ivas' turns out to be a distant descendant of the Indo-European water god.

The given essay is typical for Buslaev and his school. The imperfections of his method are completely obvious: comparison of whole plots and mutual supplementation according to one detail from plots that have nothing in common but this detail, that is, a weak technique of comparison; the arrangement of phenomena in supposedly historical order; and striving to see and reveal mythical antiquity everywhere. Thus Buslaev considers the tradition of the swan-knight an ancient folktale because it exists in verse form, making it a *bylina* for Buslaev. The tale of Bishma and the Mahabharata are still more ancient, because here it is already divinities who act; that is, it is as though the mythical form is preserved in its pure form.

Nonetheless, Buslaev's work on the folktale was a great step forward. His assertion of the folktale's religious origin does not provoke objections in principle. Buslaev steps onto the path not of abstract but of historical interpretation, applying a comparative method. Scholarship did not yet possess either a sufficient quantity of material or sufficiently refined tools for comparisons to allow realization of these tasks. In themselves, Buslaev's works represent genuine scholarship in its initial stage of development.

In other essays, Buslaev follows the same movement, revealing the mythical prototype of folktale characters, that is, primordial divinities. Here he commits the error of trusting the title of the folktale. If in a Slovak folktale a girl who was chased into the forest by her stepmother meets twelve old men, who personify the twelve months, then Buslaev sees in them a latter form of the most ancient divinities. He is more persuasive when he interprets the names of some days of the week, which were given the names of saints (Mother Friday, Mother Wednesday, and others), seeing here new designations of the old gods for whom the days were named, as the German Friday (Freitag) comes from the name of the goddess Freya. He hunts down traces of the old religion wherever possible. Following Wilhelm Grimm, he considers one-eyed giants personifications of the sun (the sun is the eye). In the fate of the folktale hero Florian, torn apart by water maidens and brought back to life, he sees (and not without good reason) traces or correspondences to the myth of Bacchus, torn up and brought back to life, and of the resurrected Osiris.

Buslaev devotes several essays to maidens—prophetesses and controllers of fate—and establishes their link with the maidens of fate, spinners, the Moirai. Once again, we should admit that this analogy is not wholly unfounded. He studies through folktales the mythic Slavic *rozhanitsy* and *vily* and the Russian *rusalki*. The range of his interests is exceptionally broad. So, when Buslaev leaves the territory of the folktale itself and studies concepts of were-wolves and shape changers, here too he succeeds in assembling interesting material and setting up some accurate analogies.

In this way, the direction of Buslaev's works was correct and should be considered scholarly. But we see now that there was not yet enough depend-able material to support his constructions, particularly concrete ethnographic material and material on the history of beliefs. His basic error was that he as-cribed belief in gods to people in primitive society, considering this the most ancient form of religious belief.

Buslaev later returned once again to the folktale in his brilliant article "Mi-grating Tales and Stories," but I will have something to say about that later.

Kuhn, Schwartz, Müller

A new direction of scholarship was founded by the Grimm brothers in Ger-many and by Buslaev in Russia. They declared the folktale a reflection of original myth. This thought was taken up, however, in a completely one-sided way, and interest in myth overshadowed interest in the folktale. Folkloristics, which by the 1850s and 1860s had already taken on a wide scale and demon-strated numerous, varied interests, turned into mythology and the science of myths. Younger followers of the new teaching narrowed and distorted it more than they developed it. Externally, it is true, there was a certain development in the taking up of new materials. Vedic poetry and the antique world were brought into the circle of comparative study. This was considered the sum total of antiquity.

Here we must cite Adalbert Kuhn and his once famous work *The Descent of Fire and of the Drink of the Gods* (1895).[106] The work is devoted not to the folktale but to the myth of Prometheus, yet it influenced subsequent study of the folktale. Kuhn for the first time brings in study of the Veda, the book of songs that were performed during sacrifices in ancient India. Finding a plot or even a hint of it in the Vedas meant proving a myth's Indo-European de-scent. Kuhn, a good Sanskritologist, finds the name of Prometheus in the Ve-das, where it supposedly signifies a driller. Interpreting Prometheus as a solar myth, Kuhn was the first to stimulate the movement that sought a reflection of the cult of the skies in every myth. Not only the sun but also the moon, stars, wind, storm clouds, and so on could be objects of veneration. This school can be called the mythological school. Its representatives declared themselves followers of the Grimm brothers, although we find no such interpretations either in their articles on the folktale or in Jacob Grimm's *Deutsche Mythologie*. It is true that Wilhelm Grimm devoted a work to Polyphemus, in which he interprets the eye of Polyphemus as the sun. But otherwise we see no attempts in the Grimms to interpret myths. The mythologists regard every myth, which means every folktale too, as a reflection of religious beliefs in the sun, moon, stars, and so on. Jacob Grimm indignantly rejects such an interpretive approach.

The new tendency is reflected most vividly in Wilhelm Schwartz's two-volume work *The Poetic Views of Nature of the Greeks, Romans, and Germans in Their Relationship to the Mythology of Primitive Times*.[107] The first volume, published in 1864, treats the sun, moon, and stars; the second volume, published in 1879, deals with clouds and wind, thunder, and lightning. This work is the first application of mythological exegeses, which boil any plot down to conceptions of heavenly phenomena. According to Schwartz's theory, mythology arises from observing the struggle of two forces, light and darkness. Their alternation and succession lead people to ponder the proximity and relationship between them. Day and night are imagined as a mother and son, brother and sister, and so on. The same is asserted for winter and summer. The victory always belongs to the principle of light. Thus Schwartz explains the motif of fighting a dragon as the sun's victory over the clouds that block it. We will not polemicize here with the goals of this school; today their lack of scholarliness and their complete arbitrariness are obvious. But in its time this school was so powerful that it overshadowed any genuinely scholarly study of the folktale.

The third major representative of this school in the West was Max Müller, a German by descent, who moved to England, took up a professorship at Oxford University, and wrote in English. Müller was a prominent Sanskritologist, editor and translator of the Rig Veda, and author of a history of Sanskrit literature, among other things. He brought nothing new to the interpretation of myths, considering them allegories linked to observations of heavenly life, primarily the sun. But Müller attempts to explain the origin of myths, to explain the very fact of allegory. He seeks an explanation in the area of linguistic phenomena. His theory in brief can be reduced to the idea that objects were originally signified by their characteristics. But because many objects have the same traits, objects could replace one another. Thus the eye gleams and the sun gleams; hence the sun is signified by the eye. A horse possesses speed, but the sun's ray also possesses speed; hence a horse can signify a ray of sun. A dragon and a storm cloud share the traits of mobility and darkness—and the storm cloud is termed a dragon. A multitude of objects and traits cover over one another; hence we get the signification of one object with different words, and the opposite—the signification of different objects with one word. A name can also be transferred from one object to another. Müller's whole theory can be called a theory of metaphors. Thus the dragon is a metaphor for a storm cloud and so on. Müller himself called the process of signification of some objects through others "the illness of the age."

The Russian Mythological School

The mythological theory shortly conquered the whole world. Works applying mythological exegesis began to appear in various countries. In Russia their main representative was Aleksandr Nikolaevich Afanas'ev. His first edition of folktales (1855–64) already supplied each tale with commentary in the spirit of the mythological school. Even before that, he had written a series of articles that later, in reworked and supplemented form, went into his fundamental three-volume work, *The Poetic Views of the Slavs on Nature*.[108] They united the lines of European and Russian scholarship. As the title shows, Afanas'ev follows Schwartz. Indeed, Afanas'ev proceeds in general precisely from Schwartz, not from the Grimms, as is often asserted. He follows the Grimms in part only in his plan, the arrangement of material. The origin of myth is interpreted in the spirit of Müller's theory of metaphors. The whole work is introduced by the chapter "The Origin of the Myth: The Method and Means of Its Study." This chapter's first words make clear its tendency: "The rich and, one might say, the sole source of various mythical conceptions is the living human word with its metaphorical and consonant expressions."[109] Afanas'ev lays out the phases of linguistic development according to Müller; moreover, he is convinced that language is liable to gradual spoilage and degeneration. The process of forgetting the primeval pictures leads to the formation of myths.

An object was depicted from various angles, and it received its full definition only in the multitude of synonymous expressions. But it must be noted that each of these synonyms, signifying a certain quality of one object, at the same time could also serve to signify a similar quality in many other objects and in that way link them among themselves. It is precisely here that we find the rich source of metaphorical expressions, which . . . is gradually running dry. Now let us imagine what a confusion of concepts, what a mix-up of notions must have occurred as the fundamental meaning of words was forgotten; and such forgetting, sooner or later, inevitably overtakes a people.[110]

Thus myth is created as a result of forgetting and confusion. The "fundamental meaning of words" is forgotten. Afanas'ev relies primarily on riddles as the most typical case of metaphor. Metaphors are the basis of omens, fortune-telling, charms (*zagovory*), ritual songs, spiritual verses, and, finally, folktales. Afanas'ev accepts without proof that the foundation is in the wondrous forces of nature, to which primeval man was supposedly close. "The subject of [the folktale's] narration was not man, not his societal worries and feats, but the diverse phenomena of all of deified nature." "Wonder tales are what is wondrous in the forces of nature."[111] From what follows, however, it is obvious that by nature Afanas'ev means exclusively the sky and phenomena of the heavens and the atmosphere.

The Poetic Views cannot be considered a piece of research dedicated strictly to the folktale. Its materials range far wider; it encompasses the whole field of folk creativity, folk beliefs, holidays, traditions, printed literature, and so on.

We must call Afanas'ev's research method exceedingly simple, even primitive. Afanas'ev gradually, with tremendous industry and fully armed with knowledge of the materials, draws a foundation under the whole motley world of the folktale's visual images and motifs; that is, he reduces them to some kind of atmospheric phenomena and thereby explains them, revealing what he supposes to be their true meaning. The chapter titles show him taking in the whole sphere of heavenly phenomena: "Light and Darkness" (Chapter II), "Sky and Earth" (Chapter III), "The Element of Light in Its Poetic Representation" (Chapter IV)—these are a few characteristic chapters of his work. But even in chapters devoted to the study of animals (Chapter XIV, "The Dog, Wolf, and Pig"), water (Chapter XVI), trees (Chapter XVII), giants and dwarves (Chapter XXI), and so on, the concepts he touches on inevitably come down to notions of thunder, the blizzard, the sun, storm clouds, the wind, and so on. Afanas'ev cannot be called a one-sided representative of the solar theory, the thunder theory, or any other. We find elements of all these theories in him in equal measure. Thus, examining the tale of the Firebird, Afanas'ev asserts: "The Russian folktale . . . mentions apples that ripen by night and are stolen by the Firebird: the poetic depiction of a thunderstorm, whose stormy breath tears the fruits from the tree—the storm cloud or the same thing—casts golden lightning and pours the living water of rain."[112] On the image of an old man with iron eyelashes (cf. Gogol's Vii), Afanas'ev, bringing in some comparative material, says:

> In Podolia . . . they imagine the Vii as a terrible destroyer, who kills people and turns villages to ashes with his glance; fortunately, his murderous glance is covered by thick brows and eyelids that cling close to his eyes, and they raise his eyelids with pitchforks only when it is necessary to destroy an enemy army or burn down an unfriendly city. The people's fantasy has drawn for itself the thunder god (Granddad Perun) in such a grandiose image; from beneath cloudy brows and lashes he casts his lightning glances and sends out death and conflagrations.[113]

The wondrous bird who lays a golden egg every morning is, for Afanas'ev, night, darkness, storm clouds from which the sun emerges,[114] and so on.

Afanas'ev's book made a strong impression on both scholars and the broader reading public and literary circles thanks to the abundance of material, the conscientiousness of its elaboration, and the simplicity of presentation. It was an event. All the most prominent scholars of that time reacted to it, and it was on the whole warmly received. Its methods and conclusions were already known in part from the first edition of the folktales, where the commentaries were more copious than in later editions. These commentaries went into *The Poetic Views*. In a review, Aleksandr Pypin noted Afanas'ev's "faithful approach in explaining folktale traditions," although "in explanations of the mythical significance of various folktales he goes too far, wishing to give even small details a place in the mythical concepts of the people."[115] In this way, even Pypin, who by that time had written his remarkable *Sketch of the Literary History of Old Russian Tales and Folktales,* objected not to mythological exegesis as such but only to its exaggeration and one-sidedness. The mythological interpretation also met no objection from the early Veselovskii, although he later spoke out with a harsh, shattering critique of the whole system. In the article "Comments and Doubts on the Comparative Study of the Medieval Epos" (1868), he writes, "We consider it necessary to warn that we are rebelling only against this narrow interpretation, not against mythological exegesis in general as applied to all the folk-poetic creativity of the Christian era."[116]

I do not know of a single review that rejected the work as a whole or pointed out the complete groundlessness of the method. On the contrary, a scholar as prominent as Aleksandr Kotliarevskii responded to *The Poetic Views* twice (as he had before to the folktales), after the second volume and after the third.[117] True, Kotliarevskii makes a series of critical observations, but these observations do not touch on the essence of the method. Kotliarevskii's criticism comes from the same position, from the same camp. But nonetheless Kotliarevskii is far from sharing Afanas'ev's passions. He is a strict and careful scholar, and some of his objections could essentially have undermined Afanas'ev's whole system. When Kotliarevskii reproaches Afanas'ev for not being sufficiently careful in his etymological rapprochements, for not being sufficiently critical in relation to written sources, and so on, these are still partial objections. Kotliarevskii lists intriguing examples. Thus, when Afanas'ev asserts apropos of "The Verse About the Dove Book" that the belief that the earth rests on three whales is mythical and that the whales embody storm clouds as gigantic water reservoirs, Kotliarevskii points to the literary, anecdotal source of this concept. "Whales—as bearers of the Universe—could not belong to Slavic mythology either, because the Slavs became acquainted with these animals at a very late date."[118] Afanas'ev makes a fair number of mistakes like this one, but the most serious objection is that Afanas'ev's point of view is not properly historical but rather psychological. Kotliarevskii demands inclusion of "historico-ethnographic forms from everyday life." From Kotliarevskii's point of view, this would broaden and deepen Afanas'ev's work; from our point of view, the introduction of properly ethnographic data would overthrow all Afanas'ev's assertions. Thus Kotliarevskii lingers on the concepts of the house spirit and the forest spirit. Afanas'ev asserts that they are thunder gods brought down to the earth. Kotliarevskii doubts this. "Was not the image of the forest spirit an immediate creation of the conditions of life and that epoch when, in the words of the chronicler, people 'dwelt in the forest, like any beast,' and does not the house spirit correspond to conditions of stable, settled life and its kinds of order!"[119]

We must recognize the outstanding Russian linguist Aleksandr Potebnia (1835–91) as the last major representative of the mythological school. His basic interests lie not in the field of folkloristics but rather in the field of linguistics, where he has extraordinary significance, though he was properly evaluated and recognized only in our day. In the early years of his work, Potebnia paid tribute to the general enthusiasm. The most important work for us is "On the Mythical Significance of Some Rituals and Beliefs." Potebnia does not distinguish the folktale as a particular genre; he seeks its mythic foundations (as in Yuletide, wedding, and other rituals). Moreover, he considers the folktale's mythic foundation to be the same as that of the rituals. I will not bring Potebnia's views into a system and linger on his views of the nature of myth. His method is the same as that of Afanas'ev and his Western predecessors, but all the same Potebnia is more careful, sometimes recognizing the powerlessness of mythological interpretations of every detail of a folktale. Thus, polemicizing with Afanas'ev, who asserts that heavenly fire in the folktale is the thunder god, Potebnia underlines its watery nature. Proceeding from the observation that sometimes in a folktale the dragon guards water, Potebnia writes that "a link with earthly water presupposes a link with heavenly water, that is, with the storm cloud."[120] The thunder god, more likely, is actually a demon, and the enmity between dragon and hero comes down to enmity with the thunder god. The copper and silver threshing floor where Pokatigoroshek battles is nothing other than the sky. The Kalina bridge, under which the hero fights, is the vault of heaven, and so on. The sun melts the storm cloud. But the storm cloud, for Potebnia, is Baba Yaga (her flight in the mortar is interpreted as the flight of a storm cloud), and Potebnia actually equates the witch with the dragon.

I have cited only a small number of Potebnia's interpretations, which show that his method, despite some individual particularities, is on the whole no different from the methods of his contemporaries. However, this refers only to his early work, "On the Mythical Significance of Some Rituals and Beliefs." On the whole, Potebnia cannot be counted as a member of the mythological school. In other folkloristic works, for example, devoted to the proverb and the saying ("From Lectures on the Theory of Literacy," the charm [*zagovor*], the song, the myth ["On Some Symbols in Slavic Folk Poetry"], "Little Russian Folk Songs"), Potebnia studied poetry and poetic creativity as a function of thought and cognition. His sphere was the problematics of poetics and the psychology of creative work, and here he accomplished an extraordinary amount. Potebnia touches on folktales in part in his work "On Dola and Beings Related to Her."[121]

THE PROBLEM OF HISTORICAL CORRESPONDENCES

The Crisis of the Mythological School and the Introduction of New Methods

By the 1870s the mythological school had worn itself out from within. The patent absurdities it had reached discredited not only the method itself but also the question of the folktale's origin. The problem ceased to be of current interest. New problems and methods came to the fore. The problem of resemblance received a new solution. Resemblance was explained as a result not of Indo-European unity but of borrowing, of cultural communication among peoples. When materials from non-Indo-European, including Semitic, peoples were brought into the circle of observations, it turned out that these people had the same tales as the Indo-European peoples, and the lack of grounding of the Indo-European conception became obvious.

Pypin and His Forerunners in the West

Aleksandr N. Pypin was the first to approach the study of individual plots from precisely this angle, in his remarkable book *A Sketch of the Literary History of Old Russian Tales and Folktales* (1858).[122]

Pypin had precursors in the West on whose works he relied, for example, Silvestre de Sacy with his work *Calila et Dimna ou fables de Bidpay en arabe* (Calila and Dimna, or Fables of Bidpay in Arabic) (1816) and John Dunlop with his classic *History of Fiction* (1814), later translated into German by Felix Liebrecht with a large number of additions. This work has retained its significance until the present day. It for the first time placed classic literary works on a broad, international scale in mutual relationship and dependence. We might mention Johann Georg Theodor Graesse, with his study *The Great Legend Cycles of the Middle Ages* (1842),[123] among other authors. Pypin researched the anonymous medieval tales, and he proved that many of them had an Eastern origin. The tales he investigated included tales about Akira the All-Wise, Solomon and Kitovras, Stefanita and Ikhnilat, tales from the *Gesta Romanorum*, translations of knightly romances ("Melusine," "Peter Gold Keys," "Prince Bova," and others). All these were translated tales whose sources were unclear, and Pypin established them. He clarified the path of penetration of these works into Russia from Byzantium, from the South Slavs, from Poland, and from the Romano-Germanic world. Pypin did not limit himself to establishing sources only from the point of view of Russian literature; he strove to discover the original source. Thus plots from Byzantium or from Poland (e.g., the *Gesta Romanorum*) may themselves have other origins. Pypin introduced the concept of the literary history of plots, which coincides with the concept of the migration of plots. "Byzantium, on the one hand, communicated to the Arabs the works of the brilliant period of Greek literature . . . on the other, itself became acquainted with the poetic traditions of the East, even the Indian epic, which reached it by way of Syrian, Arabic, and Persian translations; by way of the link with the Germanic and Romance peoples it also had access to the folktale wealth of Western Europe."[124] "This migration of poetic works was so ordinary and almost inevitable a phenomenon that every remarkable tradition or tale was dispersed everywhere and changed its physiognomy among different peoples, gained a lengthy literary history not devoid of characteristic particularities."[125]

In these works we already detect the range of interests and methods of a different tendency. The question of genesis is suspended; more accurately, Pypin accepts the mythological descent of folktale plots, but the question does not interest him. His focus of interest shifts to the tales' migration. On the other hand, this method is applied not so much to works in oral circulation as to classical written works, which were translated from one language to another. However, medieval literature is folkloric in its essence, and Pypin thoroughly examined the question of the interrelations of oral and written traditions. They interact and may have a common fate, although Pypin takes fully into account that oral transmission may not be accompanied by writing: "Many of our folktales have existed until now only in oral transmission, and therefore it is very hard to designate accurately both the range of their contents, and the ramifications of these works of the people's fantasy."[126]

Benfey

The most significant representative of the new method in the West was Theodor Benfey. In 1859 he published a collection of Indian folktales (and also fables, parables, and sayings) from the fourth century A.D., the Panchatantra (Five Books) in two volumes in German translation. The first volume contains an introduction, and the second a translation of the text and commentary. This edition became a turning point in the history of European folkloristics.

The first new and unusual thing was Benfey's phenomenal erudition; even the apparatus of such editions as the Grimm brothers', say, pales in comparison. A brilliant Orientalist and linguist, Benfey had mastered Indian, Mongolian, ancient Iranian, Syrian, Arabic, ancient Hebrew, and archaic, Byzantine, and Romano-Greek languages and materials. The text of the Panchatantra is contrasted (using Indian sources in various versions) with later translations into the languages listed. The old method of reconstructions, guesses, and etymological and other interpretations gives way to the method of critical analysis and comparison of texts.

This enormous mass of material is united by a general concept. It made up an entire epoch in the history of folklore scholarship. In his preface Benfey says, "Stories and especially folktales turn out to be primordially Indian. . . . My research in the field of fables, folktales, and stories of the East and West has led me to the conviction that only a few fables, but a great number of folktales and stories from India, have been disseminated almost over the whole world."[127] Thus Benfey declares the Indian descent of the whole plot treasury of prosaic folklore, with the exception of fables about animals, which he traces to classical antiquity on the basis of Aesop's fables.

Comparison of texts allowed Benfey to designate in general outline the epochs and paths of dissemination of Indian plots into Europe.

Benfey never laid out his views on the paths of plot dissemination from India in a connected and consistent form. Corresponding statements are scattered throughout his book and in his short articles. In the scholarly literature these views are usually laid out in simplified form, not entirely correctly. The best summary belongs to L. Kolmachevskii, who collected all of Benfey's statements on the question.[128] Indian works penetrated into the regions of Western Asia and farther—to Africa, and moreover not only into North Africa but also to the inhabitants of Senegal, to the Tuareg, Bantu, and other tribes, and to the far south, to the Bechuans and Hottentots.

The transfer points in the migration of Eastern traditions into Europe were Byzantium, Italy, and, by way of Africa, Spain. Earlier and more broadly, Indian works spread to the north and east of India and passed into Siam (today, Thailand). Beginning in the first century C.E., they constantly penetrated into China and Tibet along with Buddhist literature. Beyond the borders of Tibet the plots made their way to the Mongols. The Mongols passed on folktale material to the Russians, who in turn passed it to the Lithuanians, Serbs, and Czechs.

When he reveals the Indian roots of European folktales, Benfey simultaneously asserts their Buddhist origin. The stories of the Panchatantra have a moralizing character. Folktales were originally composed to spread Buddhist teachings among the people. Later, when Buddhism was driven out by hostile Brahmanism, the tales remained, but they took on a different character and different morals. It is in precisely this altered form that they came to us. Benfey attempts to search out the traces of Buddhist ideology in various translations and redactions of the *Panchatantra*.

Followers of Benfey in Western Europe and Russia

The new method quickly began to spread. Benfey founded the journal *Orient und Occident*, specially devoted to the study of Eastern influences, where he published a series of brief essays. The new direction seized every country. Here I list only the most significant names. In Germany we have Felix Liebrecht, who made a specialized study of the parable of Varlaam and Josaphat and proved its Indian descent. Liebrecht's articles are collected in the book *Scholarship on Peoples* (1879),[129] and he translated Dunlop's book into German. One outstanding connoisseur of the folktale was Reinhold Köhler, a tireless collector of variants, who studied the small and smallest motifs of folktales (*Articles on Folktales* [1894] and *Folk Songs* [1898–1900]).[130] A follower of Benfey in France was the famous Romanist Gaston Paris (*Oriental Tales in Medieval French Literature*, 1875).[131] At about the same time (1876–81), E. Cosquin began to publish his *Folktales of Lorraine* in the journal *Romania*; he later issued them as a separate book.[132] The edition was introduced by a theoretical chapter, which once again asserted the Indian origin of folktales. Aleksandr Veselovskii responded to this edition with an extended review.[133] Cosquin remained true to his views to the end of his life. His works are collected in two large volumes: *Folkloric Studies* (1920) and *Indian Folktales and the Occident* (1920).[134]

This theory had fewer followers in England. There the anthropological school was enthroned. But there as well we could point to a small work by Thomas Keightley, *Tales and Popular Fictions: Their Resemblance and Transmission from Country to Country* (1834), as well as the large two-volume study by W. Clouston, *Popular Tales and Fictions: Their Migrations and Transformations* (1834). Clouston's colossal work collected extremely valuable material on individual motifs and plots (the invisibility hat, animals who produce gold, grateful animals, and so on). The book does not represent a systematic study of the folktale repertoire. It includes only things that to some extent promise to reveal an Eastern and especially an Indian origin.

In Russian scholarship, as we have seen, Pypin was the initiator of a new movement. However, comparison of Pypin and Benfey reveals an essential difference. Pypin never asserted the Indian origin of the entire folktale repertoire. He posed the question of the source of borrowings carefully, and the source could be located either in the East (not only in India) or in the West— hence the different fates of different plots. We can see how much more objective and cautious Russian scholarship was in the person of Pypin. Pypin likewise understood that establishing the source and clarifying the "literary history" of a plot still had nothing to say about its genesis, that these are two distinct problems.

Adherents and followers of this theory introduced a series of corrections and supplements into Benfey's conception. The paths and time of penetration of plots into Europe were made more precise. The most vulnerable spot in Benfey's theory was the assertion of the folktale's Buddhist origin. Cosquin, for example, already knew that the Buddhists did not invent the folktale, but he allowed that Buddhists could have reworked them. The basic thesis of the Indian descent of the folktale remains unshaken. We have seen that Pypin allowed the possibility of the folktale's descent from myth. Benfeyists had to assert the still less plausible Buddhist origin; if they rejected that assertion, they had to reject the problem itself. Finally, Pypin raised the question of the possible lack of correspondence of oral and written transmission.

Vladimir V. Stasov was a striking representative of the new movement in Russia. Stasov cannot simply be reduced to Benfey either because, by his own admission, he became acquainted with Benfey's work only after he had begun his "Origin of the Russian *Byliny*."[135] It is not our task to evaluate this work as a whole (see the articles by Mark Azadovskii and A. M. Astakhova).[136] Stasov's study concentrates on two folktales, "Eruslan Lazarevich" and "The Firebird." From our point of view, "Eruslan" is not a folktale (in its origins), but generic distinctions were not as essential for Stasov as they are for us. It is precisely "Eruslan" that inspired him to write the whole work. Stasov was struck by the resemblance between "Eruslan" and an episode of Firdousi's *Rustemiad*. At first he imagined an unmediated borrowing, but after more detailed comparison he had to abandon that idea; the differences, which Stasov lists in detail, turned out to be too great. Stasov seeks other sources. He finds traits of resemblance in the Indian epic the Mahabharata, in the songs of the Tatars of Minusin, and so on. Thus there is no single prototype. As Stasov expressed it, "Eruslan is a mosaic of heterogeneous materials laid down over a length of time."[137] He studied "The Firebird" with the same method. Stasov did not find a direct prototype for this tale, but its individual elements coincide with similar motifs in various Eastern folktales.

We must describe Stasov's method as dilettantish. If Benfey's fundamental approach consists in seeing translation and transmission (in the folklore tradition) as identical, and even if we should on the whole regard this tactic critically, the very translation represents a definite scholarly achievement. Stasov's approach comes down to recognizing "resemblance-transmission," moreover one that invariably moves from East to West. If one motif of a Russian folk-tale coincides with the Mahabharata, another with "Shakhname," and so on, then Stasov will assert their borrowing regardless of their relationship to one another, to the whole, and to their history. Stasov is not so much a scholar as he is a talented and many-sided journalist. He needed to present a challenge to the Slavophile nationalist tendency, to deliver a blow to their false national-ist self-regard, and in this he was entirely successful. Stasov's work provoked a storm of indignation.[138] But it also follows from this that Stasov cannot be reduced to Benfey. His tactics are completely different.

Veselovskii

It was Aleksandr Veselovskii who truly posed the problem of international correspondences in Russia. What is more, he did so with a depth and critical acumen that left behind all that had been done in this direction in the West. His article "Notes and Doubts on Comparative Study of the Medieval Epos" breaks Stasov's method apart step by step: the comparison of tiny details, re-duction to a "lost" prototype, the ease with which Stasov explains differences by later changes, and so on.

However, Veselovskii's personal assertions are still fairly timid in this early article. He admits the mythological origin of the folktale, but, having shat-tered Stasov's method, he does not yet oppose to it his own understanding of the question of borrowing. As we might now say, he establishes the criteria of borrowing. Stasov's criteria are insufficient. "All of that is too little for the hypothesis of historical borrowing; we urgently await from him not only as full as possible a preservation of the idea of the whole in each individual case, but also preservation of the historical setting and details of the way of life in which the transfer took place."[139] The point of view of wholeness opposes Stasov's method of mosaicity. From that angle, Veselovskii allows the borrow-ing of such plots as Varlaam and Josaphat, Shemiaka's Judgment, and the like. This is an internal criterion, so to speak. The preservation of a name (Eruslan) may serve as an external criterion. In cases when one redaction is more com-plete and makes more sense and the other is briefer and more distorted, then we can posit either borrowing or else a common original source.

Veselovskii's views received full development in his doctoral dissertation, "The Slavic Traditions of Solomon and Kitovras and the Western Legends of Morolf and Merlin: From the History of the Literary Communication of East and West."[140] Although this work is not devoted to folktales in the narrow sense of the word, its method had great significance for the study of folk-tales. Here Veselovskii not only did not follow Benfey but took a completely independent path. It is true that the overall composition of the work has an external resemblance to Benfey's construction. The plot of Solomon arose in India, where it is linked to the name of the king Vikramadita ("Thirty-Two Tales of the Throne of Vikramadita"). From India the tradition moves into Iran. From Iran it is disseminated along two routes: on the one hand to the Jews and on the other hand to Byzantium. Veselovskii establishes the successive links and dates of transmission. The two paths take the given plots across the whole East and West.

However, this is only the outer schema. Veselovskii does not restrict himself to establishing the fact of borrowing, but he poses the question Benfey did not ask, namely, the reasons for borrowing. Historical communication does not always lead to the borrowing of folklore. For this there must be internal reasons, which lie in the sphere of a people's ideology, depending on its historical destiny and phenomena of a social order. Thus Veselovskii's attention centers not only on plot schemata and their coincidences and distinctions, not only on the geographic map, the expeditions, and trade routes, but also first and foremost on the living people as a concrete historical reality, as the creators and bearers of a tradition. Here he differs from both Benfey and Stasov, whose theory of borrowing led to the concept of the people's creative powerlessness.

This also explains Veselovskii's heightened interest in the very genres that are saturated with folk ideology—*legendy*, apocrypha, spiritual verses—and relatively lesser interest in the folktale. Hence we also see Veselovskii's heightened interest in heresies as expressions of the folk worldview. In part, Veselovskii linked dissemination of the plot of Solomon and Kitovras with the dualistic Bogomil heresy. He asked which social groups held this heresy. It had adherents among the bourgeoisie and even among educated people, but the most promising soil for its dissemination was among the people. "The reasons are comprehensible: simple people suffered more than anyone from the disorders and arbitrariness of feudal rulers, from the mass of evil that would descend out of nowhere in the form of famine, poor harvests, and enemy attacks. The people grew accustomed to this accident and fatalism and hence in conclusion to a particular principle of evil, independent and ruling the world."[141] The Bogomil heresy also created fertile soil for spreading the plot of the building of Solomon's temple with the help of Kitovras-Asmodei the devil and so on.

Such a view does not pretend to resolve the questions of genesis. Veselovskii carefully distinguished the problem of genesis from the problem of dissemination, and in his preface to *Slavic Traditions of Solomon and Kitovras* he wrote, characterizing Jacob Grimm's *Deutsche Mythologie* and Benfey's *Pantschatantra*: "These books do not exclude each other, just as both movements do not exclude one another."[142] This is not a "conciliatory attitude," as Savchenko would have it,[143] but a deep understanding of the essence of the question. In his 1887 review of Cosquin's *Contes de Lorraine*, Veselovskii already rejects the mythological theory as such. Nevertheless he objects here not to the question of how a folktale arose but to Cosquin's understanding of *origine* as the place of descent. Cosquin's point of view, which proceeded from Benfey with a few corrections (e.g., on the question of the folktale's Buddhist origin), could offer nothing new to Veselovskii because Veselovskii himself, as we have seen, had already moved significantly further. Therefore his reaction is fairly restrained and limited: "This theory [of borrowing] has much to recommend it: the word-for-word resemblance in the most insignificant details, presented in the folktales of various peoples, cannot be explained by anything other than migration."[144] But here Veselovskii allows that the schema of folktales may arise independently in various places. We have the right to speak of borrowing only when chance details testify to this. They explain neither questions of descent nor the rules of resemblance. Here, too, Veselovskii's favorite idea recurs in an extraordinarily precise and clear from: "The adoption of newly arrived folktale material is unthinkable without a certain predisposition of the receiving environment. Like is drawn to like, even if the resemblance is not absolute. . . . From this point of view, each folktale should contain both something familiar and something alien; the theory of borrowing takes hands with the theory of spontaneous generation."[145] The question is resolved in each case only by analysis.

The Mythologists' Attitude Toward Migrationism

As we see, Veselovskii considered it possible to combine the trends of mythologism and migrationism. Moreover, the mythologists themselves did not consider themselves vanquished either in Western Europe or in Russia. Jacob Grimm recognized Benfey's achievement and nominated him for election to the Academy of Sciences, giving a detailed, glowing description and evaluation. But this does not mean that he accepted his method; he stood by his previous convictions once and for all. Evidence of the power and dissemination of the mythological tendency also appears in the fact that the fundamental works of Wilhelm Schwartz, who considered himself a follower of the Grimms, appeared after Benfey's *Pantschatantra*. In 1870 Max Müller read a lecture on the plot of the day-dreaming milkmaid Pierette in which he demonstrated its Indian origin, tracing its migration through the East and Europe, and he did this with no less erudition and no less élan than Benfey. But Müller too stood by his views on the origin of plots in language and myth. In this way, the my-thologists not only did not dispute the Indian origin and migration of some plots in individual cases but also confirmed it. However, for them Benfey's theory was not an all-encompassing theory. On the question of the origin of plots, that is, on the genetic process, they essentially stood by their convic-tions, for Benfey had not discovered a genetic process. The appearance of the new school in Russia supposedly brought a crisis into the work of the mythol-ogists. Buslaev's preface to his collection of articles, *Folk Poetry*, is often cited.

> The so-called Grimm school, with its theory of the originality of the popular foundations of mythology, habits, and traditions, which I carried out in my research, had to give way to the theory of mutual com-munication between peoples in oral and written traditions. Much of what was accepted then as the heritage of one or another people turns out now to be chance borrowing from outside, taken as a result of vari-ous circumstances, more or less explicable by the historical routes along which these cultural influences traveled.[146]

However, these words do not at all mean that Buslaev had abandoned his position and accepted this new theory. Buslaev opposed the new theory, not because he remained true to mythologism but rather because for him mu-tual influence had always been one of the fundamental questions of his re-search and because he understood this communication far more profoundly than Benfey and his immediate followers. We have already seen that in the very concept of nationality, Buslaev, in counterbalance to the Slavophiles, in-cluded the creative reworking of other people's material. This was not a ques-tion of method, theory, or school for Buslaev but an element of his whole philosophy of life.

A negative attitude toward the new movement is already visible in Buslaev's review of Stasov's work (see the *Report on the Twelfth Award of the Count Uvarov Prizes*). He refuses to recognize Stasov's method as comparative. For Buslaev, borrowing is an "accidental" fact. (He also repeats these words in the preface to *Folk Poetry* and in his review of Orest Miller's *Il'ia Muromets.*) This means that for Stasov's work Buslaev does not question borrowing itself.

Buslaev had a completely different reaction to Veselovskii's "Slavic Traditions of Solomon and Kitavras" (see the *Report of the Sixteenth Award of the Count Uvarov Prizes*). We already know that this work does not follow Benfey's path and that it poses the question of borrowing in a principally different manner from Benfey. This is in part exactly what provoked Buslaev's enthusiastic response to Veselovskii's work, which, Buslaev says, "electrifies the reader, so to speak, inspires him, and provokes new considerations and observations on the broad field that the work itself so fruitfully cultivates."[147]

Buslaev showed what these "new considerations" were in one of his most brilliant works, the article "Migrating Tales and Stories."[148] The external occasion for this work may have been Max Müller's article "The Migration of Fables," in which, following Benfey's example, he traced the dissemination of the tale of the day-dreaming milkmaid who in the end breaks her pitcher. As we said before, Müller did not at all lower his banners when faced with the new teaching. He asserts that the fact of migration of such plots from one nation to another in historical time has no impact on his theory of prehistoric Aryan myths. Buslaev traced the dissemination of several plots, such as the milkmaid, the Matron of Ephesus (a wife, having lost her husband, is in such despair that she follows him into the sepulchre, but right in the sepulchre betrays him with a warrior she happens to meet there and gives her husband's body away to him), Shemiaka's Judgment, the Seven Wise Men, Virgil, and others. He did this not just to demonstrate the fact of migration; this was not Buslaev's focus. Just like Veselovskii, he mainly emphasized study of the people and the historical conditions in which the people lived. If Veselovskii's research still had not linked the folktale plot with ideology in such manifestations as heresies (to which Buslaev objected), Buslaev himself still took the people in the aggregate historical conditions of its existence. Following the migration of the plot, Buslaev also followed its alterations and established the internal reason for these changes. On the one hand, we have the gloomy, ascetic Middle Ages with their misogyny and, on the other hand, we have the cult of woman as sacred; we have the social and material conditions of life of the people and their traditional worldviews—the multitude of plots rests on this, their general resemblance. For one thing, Buslaev examined the plot of Virgil not from the point of view of borrowing the figure of Virgil from antiquity but from the point of view of the medieval refraction of elements of antique culture and the antique worldview.

What conclusion did Buslaev draw from his extraordinarily colorful, rich, and vivid international comparative materials? His conclusion was not just ahead of the scholarship of his time; it sounded strangely modern. By accepting the migration of wandering plots, however, Buslaev discerned a certain regularity of resemblance not based on borrowing but consisting "in the identical principles of everyday life and culture, identical ways of living and feeling, dreaming and exploring and expressing their life interests in word and deed."[149]

These words hold a declaration that, had his contemporaries accepted it, would have signified a move to a new path for all of folktale scholarship. Buslaev pointed out a new regularity, so far unnoticed by anyone: the dependence of ideological and artistic creativity on "identical principals of everyday life and culture," on "identical ways of living and feeling." He had not yet elaborated this new principle of explaining resemblances in material, had not formed the basis of his research. It was a new idea that Buslaev reached in his late years, but his contemporaries did not accept it. This misunderstanding of Buslaev has lasted, however, up to the present. The meaning of his article is generally and incorrectly explained as a concession to the new trend.[150]

Late Benfeyism in Russia

So, if representatives of the old classical scholarship had a restrained and critical attitude toward the new trend, while recognizing its good points, the newer generation came under Benfey's immediate influence and sometimes followed and imitated him blindly. It is true that Benfeyism as such was not widespread in Russia, but the influence of Benfey was nevertheless felt here too.

Myhailo Drahomanov (1841–95), a historian and classicist by education, did more in Ukrainian than Russian scholarship. Despite his Ukrainophilic inclinations, Drahomanov had a good understanding of the impossibility of an exclusively national study of folklore; this also reflected his societal-political views. Drahomanov's works, written in various languages and often under pseudonyms, were translated into Ukrainian and published in four volumes with the title *On Ukrainian Folk Verbal Arts and Writing*.[151] His early articles sometimes followed Benfey down to the details, asserting the Indian origin of plots he examined. See, for example, his articles on Cordelia-Zamarashka and on "The Best Sleep." Later, one notes the influence of Vsevolod Miller, who introduced Iranian materials and asserted the role of the Caucasus as a transit point. Such was the article "Shaggy Buniaka in Ukrainian Folk *Skazaniia*." In the article "Turkish Anecdotes in the Ukrainian Verbal Arts," Drahomanov revealed the Turkish influence on Ukrainian anecdotes, connecting it to the historical relations of the two peoples.[152]

Drahomanov's later and more significant works moved in the same direction. The article "Slavic Tales of Sacrificing One's Child"[153] lingered in detail on the motif of a god who wanders the earth and asserted the motif's Buddhist origin. Drahomanov claimed the same thing for the motif of sacrificing one's child for the life of another, although this motif was not attested in India. Similarly, in a monograph on Slavic tales about the birth of Constantine the Great, he asserted the Buddhist origin of the plot of Mark the Rich.[154]

Drahomanov displayed a broader horizon in his largest and most significant work, "Slavic Variants of the Oedipus Story."[155] By this time the anthropological school was already recognized, and that forced Drahomanov to reexamine his previous views not only of migration but also of plot origins. Following Lang, he allowed polygenesis, but he considered it possible to explain the process of origin mythologically. "All three scholarly trends have reasonable foundations," he wrote.[156] Correspondingly, he saw the Oedipus plot as a reflection of the myth of the powers of nature, reaching that conclusion by analyzing antique versions of the motif of incest. Subsequently the plot passed to the Slavs and into Europe by way of Byzantium, although Drahomanov did not yet know the Byzantine materials. Pětrin's discovery of Byzantine materials allowed Drahomanov's point of view to be overthrown. Nonetheless, he collected and compared a significant body of materials, and he describes some cases of dependence of certain texts on others quite persuasively.

Leonard Zenonovich Kolmachevskii applied Indianism to the study of the animal folktale in his fundamental work *The Animal Epos in the West and Among the Slavs* (1882), giving a rich critical survey of literature on the animal epos. Kolmachevskii decisively refuted the Grimms' view that the animal epos was nationally German, and he rejected the anthropological theory just as sharply. As one conclusion of this survey, he formulated the following thesis: "The animal epos in general owes its origin to the East, namely to India."[157] Western scholars, however, did not know Slavic and, in particular, Russian materials, although these tales have a striking resemblance to Western ones. Kolmachevskii examined the Slavic and Russian repertoire by plot and moreover brought in an enormous number of variants. The resemblance of variants forced him to conclude: "One may present a series of considerations and arguments, in view of which it is more than probable that the remarkable agreement of all variants can be explained only by borrowing."¹⁵⁸ Following Benfey, Kolmachevskii saw the origin of the animal epos in the antique fable. The animal epos passed into India from the antique world, and from India it went to Europe. Russian folktales about animals go back either to Eastern, Byzantine sources or else to Western ones. This was the general conclusion, proceeding from extraordinarily detailed comparison of the plots of the animal epos in all the variants then known.¹⁵⁹ Kolmachevskii recognized a properly Russian, folk origin for a small quantity of plots. Besides that, his book examines texts of the "romance of the fox" and their genealogical connection. Veselovskii responded to this work with a brief, welcoming review.¹⁶⁰

Vsevolod Miller occupied a somewhat particular place among Russian followers of the new theory. Miller dedicated himself for the most part to study of the heroic epic. His *Excursions in the Field of the Russian Folk Epic* (1892),¹⁶¹ and even earlier his *Ossetian Essays* (1881–87),¹⁶² were tributes to the new trend. Miller was one of our most prominent scholars of the Caucasus, hence the particular tendency of his works. Knowing Caucasian materials extremely well, he drew them into the orbit of scholarly observation and underlined their significance in the international folkloric exchange. But Miller also wrote a series of extraordinarily important works on the folktale.¹⁶³ His early works were still completely under Benfey's influence. His article "The Eastern and Western Parallels of One Russian Folktale" asserted the Indian origin of the tale of the lucky guesser.¹⁶⁴ This folktale, according to Miller, could have arisen only in India, because calling oneself "a belly" and so on is unnatural, whereas the Indian word *dzhihva* both signifies a belly and is at the same time a proper name. Miller accompanied the study of this tale with a series of theoretical arguments in a spirit of pure Benfeyism. His work on the collection of Hindu folktales, the *Virkramarkcaritram*, moves in the same direction. Miller later began to emphasize his Caucasian interests. In this field too he produced a series of extremely valuable works: "Caucasian Traditions of Giants Chained to the Mountains" and "Caucasian Traditions of the Cyclops."¹⁶⁵ Here he was far from the one-sidedness of the German migrationist school, and he weighed with extreme care the significance of the Caucasian materials that he himself had collected.

As we know, Miller later rejected the methods of the migrationist school completely and became one of the founders and a prominent representative of the so-called historical school. His studies of the folktale show less of the understanding of historicism characteristic of the Russian historical school than his work on the epic. Nonetheless, Miller attempted to subject the folk-tale as well to historical study of that kind, as in his articles, "On Tales of Ivan the Terrible,"[166] "On Songs, Folktales, and Traditions of Peter the Great,"[167] and "The Worldwide Folktale in a Cultural and Historical Light."[168] In the last of these works Miller attempted to find traces of a juridical tradition that once existed in the plot of dishonest seizure of land by measuring it with a skin cut into strips. As in the field of *bylina* studies, here too the aims of the historical school received a justified, though also one-sided, critique by the formalists.[169]

Bédier

Migrationism quickly became the leading movement in Western Europe. With the increased number of works, its weaknesses were more and more exposed, and this provoked Joseph Bédier's shattering critique.[170]

At present we cannot accept this critique in all its aspects. It is true that in our day the theory of the Indian origin of narrative folklore is even less ac-cepted than it was in Bédier's time. But it had tremendous significance in its day, and it allowed advancements in our scholarship. With the discovery that non-Indo-European peoples (the ancient Hebrews, the Arabs) had the same plots as the Indo-Europeans, the theory that Indo-European prehistoric unity was the reason for the resemblances of language and folklore was bound to collapse. Although its representatives did not surrender, mythological exege-sis was nonetheless doomed to defeat. However, the school's achievements were not limited to the negative, polemical side. They drew attention to one of the most important and complex phenomena in folklore: migration. Plot was no longer interesting as an abstract mythological schema but was examined in connection with its carrier, the people. This helped in understanding a whole series of phenomena correctly. The Indian origin of Varlaam and Josaphat, for example, is in no doubt. Although it recognizes the fact of migration and the need for its study, contemporary scholarship does not elevate this par-tial phenomenon into a general principle or law; borrowing does not, from our point of view, explain the phenomena of resemblance of folklore forma-tions as such. One weak side of the new theory, similarly, was the fact that the routes of borrowing (migration) were defined primarily by studying written, not purely folkloric works. Translation was considered to be transmission. By now we know that the paths of oral transmission need not coincide with written routes. Oral and written transmission can take place independently of one another.

These and a whole series of other shortcomings gradually had to be recognized, bringing sobriety and a critical attitude to the new theory. We owe the most brilliant critique to Joseph Bédier and his remarkable study of the *Fabliaux*, in which he attempted a historical study and unfolded an extraordinarily witty, merciless critique of migrationism. However, Bédier found no explanation of his own for the resemblance of plots, and he admitted that he was an agnostic in principle.

Russian Orientalism

Bédier's critique evoked a many-sided and various response. But there was one camp, or encampment (among the migrationists), where this critique did not penetrate much: the Orientalists. Psychologically, this is entirely comprehensible. A scholar who has devoted his whole life to studying Eastern materials is always likely to give these materials priority over Western materials, which he will consider derivative.

We can trace two fundamental lines or currents in the development of migrationism. One of them is Orientalism proper, with its assignment of plots depending on the author's specialty: Indian, Iranian, Mongol, or, as with dilettantes such as Stasov, Eastern in general. They begin to assert not only the Eastern but also the Western or other newly minted origin of the folktale. Thus we might speak of an Eastern school and a "school of borrowings," without meaning the same thing by these. The name *comparativist* has become accepted for representatives of the latter tendency in Russia.

R. P. Potapin was a continuer of the old Eastern school. Potapin was an outstanding Mongolist who knew northwest Mongolia excellently and made several expeditions there. The fourth volume of his *Sketches of Northwest Mongolia* contains folktales.[171] His major work, *Eastern Motifs in the Medieval European Epic*,[172] compared various Mongolian materials (among them a particularly large number of tales about Genghis Khan) with European and Russian epics and folktales. Potapin's comparisons were not always correct and persuasive, but he did succeed in revealing a whole series of genuine and interesting coincidences. Potapin's conclusions about the origins of the enormous body of material that he analyzed was likewise far from always convincing or free from strain. Nevertheless, his work was extremely significant in the enormous and varied amount of material it used for comparison. Among the folktales Potapin examined in more detail were the tales of "Handless"

(Chapter I), tales of thieves, Solomon (Chapter XIII), Mark the Rich (Chapter XX), and Eruslan Lazarevich (Chapter XVI).

Among the Russian Orientalists, a special place in the history of study of the folktale belongs to academician Sergei Ol'denburg. Ol'denburg always understood the enormous scholarly significance of the folktale. He was the organizer and permanent president of the Folktale Commission in the Ethnographic Sector of the Russian Geographical Society, whose *Survey of Works* opened with his article "The Exceptional Importance of the Study of the Folk Tale." Ol'denburg was an Indologist by specialty, but not so much a linguist as a historian of culture and of folk culture at that. His first major work, *Buddhist Legends and Buddhism*,[173] defined the range of his dominant interests. He had to assume a certain position with regard to the Indianist theory. The fullest expression of his attitude toward this theory and Bédier's book appeared in a series of articles under the general title *The Fableau of Eastern Origin*.[174] Ol'denburg gave a well-supported analysis of Bédier's book and revealed all its weak aspects. For example, Bédier, although rejecting the Eastern origin of the *fabliau* "Constant du Harel," knows only one of its Eastern versions. Ol'denburg cites fifteen of them. In those years Ol'denburg was an Indianist, asserting the Indian origin of the plots he was studying. Later, in the article "The Migration of the Folktale," he introduced a quantitative limit to Benfey's theory: "If we pose the question in such a way that the source of a great *many folktales* (the italics are ours) should be sought in India, then there could hardly be any objections to such a formulation."[175] For Ol'denburg the question of the migration of the folktale shifted from methodology to a great range of culture and history. The transference of folktales is "one of those links that binds peoples together, forces them to understand one another better."[176] Ol'denburg later shifted the emphasis of his "folktale interests" to the problem of the folktale's real existence and the methodological significance of this problem for its all-round study (cf. his so-called Sorbonne lecture, "The Folkloric Tale: Problems and Methods").[177]

The Russian Comparativists

As I mentioned, we can trace two lines in the development of migrationism: one Orientalist and one that we can conditionally call comparativist. A broad comparative study of variants and the routes of their dissemination, if one takes a more objective view of things, does not always lead to India or even to the East. For Russian materials, a Western origin can often be shown quite persuasively.

The representatives of migrationism are quite varied in their individual tendencies, the range of their interests, and their technical approaches and application of the comparativist and migrationist method. By this time other principles of the study of folklore were already being advanced along with the migrationist principle, and this affected the comparativist works of that time. We can observe an original and fertile combination of migrationism with historical study in the works of Ivan N. Zhdanov. His master's thesis, "Toward a Literary History of Russian *Bylina* Poetry,"[178] examined a series of folktale motifs connected with the *bylina*. His doctoral dissertation, "The Russian *Bylina* Epos,"[179] is a series of separate sketches, including essays directly related to the folktale. "The Tale of Babylon and the *Skazanie* of the Princes of Vladimir,"[180] published earlier, was completely devoted to the folktale and examined the Byzantine prototype and primeval folktale elements borrowed from the West in the tale of Barm-Iaryzhok, who set off for the Babylonian kingdom.[181] Among other folktale themes, Zhdanov lingers on the motif of the untold dream. He examines the folktale foundations of the *bylina* of Potyka, Vasilii Buslaevich (in which he sees an echo of the medieval legend of Robert le diable). The object of Zhdanov's study was the epic, not the folktale, yet in the epic it is often precisely the folktale elements that interested him. He called them "wandering legends and folktales," spoke of the epic's borrowings from the folktale, and followed the fate or "literary history" of the plots he studied. In some cases he established borrowing of plots that arose in the East by way of Western Europe. His manner of posing the question is expressed with particular clarity in an unfinished work devoted to the tale of Balthasar, about how a *bogatyr'*'s wife betrays Balthasar with a wandering minstrel.

At present we cannot agree with everything Zhdanov asserted. He derived common material between *bylina* and folktale, which the mythologists traced to Indo-European foundations, from borrowings, but it cannot all be explained by borrowings. It has deeper historical roots, which can be revealed and explained only by a detailed genetic study of the folktale and the *bylina*. For example, the link between Vasilii Buslaevich and Robert le diable that Zhdanov asserts is not presented convincingly. Nonetheless, Zhdanov brilliantly proves a series of literary influences, particularly in his work on the Babylonian kingdom.

The appearance and development of the anthropological school (see later discussion) also found an echo in the study of worldwide correspondences.

The one-sidedness and insufficiency of the study of migrations and borrow-ings gradually became clear. Ivan Sozonovich made a new attempt to unite these two directions, and in part that led to quite novel and important re-sults. His work, *Songs About the Maiden-Warrior and Byliny About Stavro Go-dinovich*,[182] were still fairly superficial combinations of analysis of "everyday foundations" and possibilities of the independent origin of plots among dif-ferent peoples, with an assertion of borrowing in some cases. Sozonovich had an insufficient understanding of the ethnographic, pre-historic basis of gen-esis, asserted in the Tylor-Lang theory. The question was posed much more deeply in one of his most significant works, dedicated to the plot of Lenore.[183] Sozonovich showed on the basis of archaeological and ethnographic data how belief in the possibility of bringing back the dead gives rise to the plot. In part, Sozonovich ascribed great significance to the prohibition on crying for the dead, in connection with this belief: The tears of those who are left behind disturb the deceased and provoke him to leave his grave. Sozonovich estab-lished versions and studied the influence of some on the others. He estab-lished borrowing on the basis of a criterion advanced by Veselovskii himself: a coincidence in details that could not be accidental. Sometimes, however, Sozonovich went too far, asserting, for example, that the Scandinavian saga of Helgi and Sigrup is a reworking of the ancient plot of Protesilaus's return from the afterworld to his wife Laodamia.

Another work by Sozonovich, "The Poetic Motif of the Unexpected Re-turn of the Husband During His Own Wife's Wedding, as She Is Preparing to Marry Another Man,"[184] is less successful. It brought together rich material on West European medieval and Slavic literary texts; in this regard the work has major significance. In the given work one can already see phenomena that are also characteristic of other authors and works of the time; gathering mate-rial becomes an end in itself. The phenomenon is entirely predictable for this stage of scholarly development, when materials were still scattered, uncol-lected, not grouped together, and not compared. All kinds of summaries of materials by plot or by some other trait therefore have great value, although the conclusions may be completely lacking or may no longer be persuasive at present.

Nikolai Sumtsov, an outstanding connoisseur of folklore and literature, was a characteristic figure for this stage in the history of Russian folklore scholar-ship. He wrote an enormous quantity of works, nearly 800. Judged by the general theoretical premises of his research, he may be called an eclectic. As a migrationist, he asserted not only the Eastern influence on the West but also a Western influence on the East, in part on the Mongols ("Echoes of Christian Legends in Mongol Folktales").[185] Sumtsov reveals the most various, intersecting, and intertwining routes of plot migration, sometimes combining his conclusions with arguments that clearly come from the mythologists or comparing his material with living folk beliefs. His work "The Husband at His Wife's Wedding" is telling in this regard.[186] First of all, he gave a rich survey of material. The survey is not very systematic, but it nonetheless made up the main value and the significance of Sumtsov's work. He then gave conclusions or observations with the basic goal of establishing which form was encountered most frequently. The work is studded with formulations such as "in almost all variants," "most often," and so on. We might call Sumtsov a forerunner of the statistical method, later elaborated by the Finnish school. Sumtsov's general conclusions are often unexpected and do not proceed from the material. So, for one plot he asserts that a ring that a husband threw into his wife's goblet "in distant antiquity was a symbol of eternity."[187] Then he gives the equally unexpected assertion that Alyosha and Dobrynia are historical personages (echoes of the historical school), and then he asserts that they too are borrowed. "Comparing *bylina* motifs about Dobrynia's quarrel with Alyosha over his wife with Western European tales and ballads negates the very possibility of original Russian creation in the *byliny* of Dobrynia's wife. The plot is obviously borrowed in all its component parts, and it follows a foreign model down to the arrangement of details."[188] These assertions are typical enough of Sumtsov's aims and method. But his numerous works bring together valuable, rich material, and no researcher can ignore them.

The migrationist tendency was dominant at the end of the nineteenth and the beginning of the twentieth century. It had numerous representatives both in Russia (Aleksandr Kirpichnikov, Iavorskii, Durnovo, Rezanov) and in the West. Gradually going into decline, it changed to the so-called historical-geographical school, attempting to refine its methods of studying the folktale but exposing the insubstantiality of its method, already obvious to us.

The Historical-Geographical, or Finnish, School

In Sumtsov's works we observed signs of a clear methodological decline. In this regard he is symptomatic. True, we see a rich selection of material, but we also see helplessness in the face of the material, unfounded conclusions, reduction of resemblances to borrowing, and rejection of independent folk creativity. This situation in Russian scholarship corresponded to the general situation in European scholarship of the time. Little by little, an enormous quantity of folkloric materials was piling up in every country. These materials demanded inventory and systematization, but the unsatisfactory state of folklore studies sparked the ambition to make methods of study more precise as well.

In 1901, the International Federation of Folklore Fellows was founded in Helsinki by Finnish scholar Kaarle Krohn, Swedish scholar Carl Wilhelm von Sydow, and Danish scholar Axel Olrik. The Federation's works came out in the form of a nonperiodic series titled Folklore Fellows' Communications (FFC). The Federation's goal was not just scholarly gatherings and contacts. It also stood for certain methodological positions. These positions were laid out by Finish scholar Antti Aarne in his *Guide to the Comparative Study of the Folktale*,[189] with regard to the folktale, and more generally by Krohn in his *Working Methods in Folklore*.[190]

The methods of study of the folktale that this school elaborated come down to the following approaches.

Study is generally devoted to one plot of some kind. First, a full and precise numbered list of all known variants of a given plot is established. Material is arranged according to an ethnic system, that is, by groups of peoples (Slavic, Romance, Germanic, Finno-Ugric, etc.) and within groups by individual peoples. Each people is designated by a symbol (e.g., RF would mean Romance, French; SR would be Slavic, Russian; SBe would be Slavic, Belarusan). We consider this the most important part of all the work of this school. Thus, for example, in one work Nikolai Andreev managed to establish 245 variants of the plot of the robber Madei, published as well as preserved in archives or in the hands of private individuals. Striving for exhaustive completeness is characteristic of the Finnish school. It was a great step forward compared with the work of previous decades, when far less effort was made to achieve exhaustive completeness of material. However, the aspiration also has an obverse side. Completeness can never be more than relative. Over the years material continues to increase, and new materials do not always confirm the correctness of earlier conclusions. Besides that, the quantity of recordings used for research is inconsequential compared to the thousands of cases of actual performance that take place among the people. From our point of view, the correctness of conclusions is defined not just by the completeness of materials (for which we may always strive) but first and foremost by the correctness of methods.

The second stage of a study is analysis of the material. The component parts of the plot, its motifs, are subjected to painstaking comparison and contrast. Every variant of each such part is established, in order to work out which forms are encountered most often. The most commonly occurring forms are declared the fundamental ones, that is, the primordial and most ancient ones. The aggregate of primeval forms of motifs gives the primeval form of a plot, its ur-form, or archetype, that is, the form from which variants developed. Studying the material according to peoples makes it possible to establish national and local versions (ecotypes).

We cannot recognize such an approach as correct. These researchers proceed from the presumption that each plot is created only once, in a certain place and at a certain time. However, plots can undoubtedly arise independently from one another, under common conditions that favor their origin. The Finnish school makes a narrowed, isolated study of phenomena, whereas our methodology demands the study of broad connections. We also consider the statistical method unacceptable. After a genuinely historical, not formal-statistical study, it may turn out that the archaic forms are not the ones encountered most often but rather the ones met more rarely and that more recent forms have crowded them out.

The third stage is establishment of the homeland of the plot and its history. Having set this goal for itself, the Finnish school calls itself historical-geographical. The establishment of a plot's geographic region of origin is produced in the same statistical manner as establishment of the ur-form. All data are painstakingly entered on a map. The homeland of a plot is defined by the maximal concentration of recordings among this or that people.

This approach is already incorrect, in that the frequency of recordings does not correspond to the actual state of things. In places where collecting has been intensive (e.g., in Russia, Ukraine, Germany, and Finland), there is a greater quantity of recordings than in places where collecting work was done less vigorously (e.g., in France). Enormous areas have been barely or not at all included or collected.

Finally, the history of plots and their movement from one people to another are established according to a whole series of oblique indicators.

Here we can describe only the fundamental methodological approaches of the Finnish school in their naked form. Of course, individual writers will not always adhere exactly to the schema given here; a whole series of other questions may arise in the course of a study. Clever guesses are advanced; a series of subtle and sometimes correct observations are made. But all that does not rescue the school from the fatal erroneousness of its methodological foundations and presumptions. The very fact that separate plots are studied in isolation is a methodological error for the folktale. The school does not take into account the law of portability of motifs from one set of tales into another. Each motif, as a rule, is examined only within the system of a given plot, whereas studying motifs across plots may indicate a completely different picture (let us recall Veselovskii's theory of motifs and plots). The school ignores the historical conditions of the plot's existence, studying only texts, sometimes even only schemata of plots. The study of folklore takes on a formalistic, unideological character. Nevertheless, we must admit that the major monographs that came out in the FFC series on the folktale and other forms of folklore (and on the history of religion, of agricultural rituals, etc.) have great significance and greatly broadened the horizon of our knowledge.

We must also recognize as a great achievement the fact that one of the school's active members—Aarne—created the index of folktale types. The school's methods demanded study of the folktale by plot, demanded the establishment of all plots in existence. The accumulation of materials revealed a limited quantity of plots along with their vast repetition in variants. How many folktale plots could be established, and precisely which ones? Aarne's index, which we spoke of earlier, offers an answer to this question.[191] It is true that the answer is still far from exhaustive. The index is composed on the basis of comparison of a set of large national collections. Aarne left unused numbers for plots that might be discovered in the future, and experience has proved him right. Over many years the ever broadening material has demanded revision and expansion of the index. A new edition, with many new types introduced, was created by the American scholar Stith Thompson.[192] This index is internationally accepted to this day.

True, the system of arrangement, the classification, is not satisfactory, but in the given case that is not so essential, because in practice the index serves the purpose of a reference work. Aarne's index is important in another way. It can also be used as the basis for composing indexes of national repertoires. Indexes have been composed according to Aarne's system, for example, for tales of the Scandinavian peoples. Nikolai Andreev applied it to Russian material.[193] For each plot he also gives a basic bibliography. Comparing a national repertoire with the international store of plots allows scholars to make valuable conclusions about the contents of the Russian folktale epos. If such indexes were composed for all peoples, it would be enormously significant for scholarship on the folktale.

The shakiness of the Finnish school's fundamental presumptions and the flaws of its methods caused a critical reaction in Western Europe. The most merciless critique belongs to A. Vesel'ski.[194] Finally, even Olrik, one of the movement's founders, was obliged to admit that folktale scholarship had reached a dead end; he spoke about this at the Seventh Northern Congress of Philologists in 1932.[195] However, the personal opinions he advanced about the possible ways out of the cul-de-sac turned out to be no better than the position of the Finnish school.

No school or movement in Russian scholarship corresponds to the Finnish school. Russia did not join the Federation of Folklore Fellows. Only Valter N. Anderson, a former professor at Kazan'University, can be considered close to this school's positions.[196] Nikolai Andreev published two large monographs in the FFC series.[197] He subsequently abandoned his earlier views, as we see in his other numerous folkloric works; he mentioned this himself, for example, at the anti-Fascist conference of the Folklore Section of the Soviet Academy of Sciences in 1936. Aleksandr Nikiforov gave an extraordinarily well-founded and withering critique in his reviews of Anderson's monographs *The Emperor and the Abbot* and *The Folk Anecdote About Old Hildebrandt*.[198]

Epigones and Eclectics

No new movements were founded in Russian scholarship at the beginning of the twentieth century. In Western Europe this was a time characterized by epigonism and eclecticism. The bankruptcy of methods was sometimes recognized, but shaky conclusions were blamed on the insufficiency of material. We can observe a striving toward large compilations, bibliographic or systematized works. These summaries, indexes, and encyclopedias have great significance as auxiliary aids for scholarly research, but they are not in their essence research. We have already spoken about Johannes Bolte and Jiri Polívka's five-volume *Comments* to the Grimm brothers' collection of folktales. The Grimms' modest, slender book (the third volume of their collection) has grown into five large volumes. Of them, the first three contain an index of variants to all the folktales in the Grimms' collection, including unpublished ones. This index encompasses all the peoples of the world and represents the life work of two of the greatest experts on the folktale. The fourth volume essentially contains surveys of folktale materials of the ancient world (Egypt, Babylon, Judea, Greece, Rome), the European Middle Ages of the sixteenth to eighteenth centuries, India, the Arabs and Jews, and a description of the work of the Grimm brothers. The fifth volume lays out the history of collection by peoples and gives a brief history of the theoretical study of the folktale. Besides the main authors, specialists in individual fields took part in the work. Both Bolte and Polívka wrote numerous works on the folktale. Polívka was a migrationist and Bolte a tireless collector of variants, which he published in the form of separate notes and supplements and in commentaries to the folktales he published.

The instability of Western European scholarship is particularly obvious in the example of Friedrich von der Leyen. He began as a migrationist, asserting the Indian origin of the folktale, paid tribute to Freudianism by asserting the origins of the folktale in dreams, and finally proposed returning to the Indo-European conception, with certain corrections and reservations.[199]

These data give an adequate description of the state of European scholarship on the eve of World War I. The creation of grandiose bibliographic works or of a handbook such as the *Handwörterbuch des deutschen Märchens*,[200] for example, which began to come out in 1931 and was the fruit of collective labor of the best specialists and scholars, reveals the internal contradiction between first-class mastery of the material and methodical helplessness and lack of principles.

THE PROBLEM OF WORLDWIDE UNITY

The Anthropological School

By tracing the development of folktale scholarship, we see that resemblance was one of the fundamental problems that occupied it for decades. This problem's solution in the last analysis comes down to two things: Resemblance is declared a result of an archaic unity of peoples, or it is explained by borrowing. The first school simultaneously produced a theory of genesis; the second did not in essence attempt to solve the problem. The mythological school operated with material from the Indo-European peoples; the school of borrowings, in its Orientalist variant, used material from Asia, the Mediterranean, and cultures that were oriented toward them in its general-comparativist variant—with materials from all Asian and European cultures. The roots of the mythological school are connected to some extent with linguistics, whereas the school of borrowings is tied to literary scholarship.

In the 1870s a new solution to the question was ripening in England, a solution that sprang not from linguistics and not from literary studies but from ethnography. After England's overseas colonization of peoples who stood at earlier stages of development, these peoples became the object not only of economic exploitation but also of scholarly study. Numerous expeditions and notes by scholars, travelers, missionaries, and merchants accumulated in an enormous mass of factual material, sufficient for broad generalizations. The cultures of peoples of the whole world could now be studied. The resemblances of cultural phenomena, including those among peoples who had never had any contact with one another and who were observed for the first time at a given stage of the development of scholarship, could no longer be explained by borrowing. Just as at one time the introduction of information about non-Indo-European peoples necessarily led to the downfall of the mythological theory, so the broadening of observations on a worldwide scale undermined the theory of borrowing. The resemblance of folkloric phenomena was now examined as an individual case of similarity of an ethnographic order. The resemblance of folkloric formations does not differ in principle from the resemblance of instruments of production, structures, utensils, or clothing. Neither primordial unity nor migration can explain it. Its roots, from the point of view of the new movement, are in the laws of the human psyche, and these laws are the same for all peoples. From this last trait, and also because the term *ethnography* in England corresponded to the term *anthropology*, the whole school was named anthropological.

It is already clear from what we have laid out that folklore as such does not stand at the center of this school. But its representatives also touch on folklore in the course of their ethnographic research, and these statements are extraordinarily important for us.

Tylor

The most complete expression of these tendencies was by Edward Tylor (1832–1917). His most important forerunners in Germany were T. Waitz and A. Bastian. Waitz was the first to produce a summary ethnographic work encompassing all the peoples of the world, and he came up with the concept of psychological unity.[201] Waitz was a philosopher-psychologist, Bastian a doctor who devoted himself entirely to ethnography and traveled over the whole globe. Bastian's works are extraordinarily numerous and various. One of his fundamental works is *Man in History: Toward the Founding of a Psychological Worldview*.[202] Bastian's theory cannot be surveyed here because it concerns the history of ethnography. We need only point out that Bastian was also occupied with primeval folklore. He has a large work on the mythology of the Polynesians.[203]

Speaking of Tylor's predecessors, we do not mean to assert that he depended on the scholars listed. Ideas are born because they meet the demands of the era. Tylor's significance for scholarship on the history of human culture is comparable to Darwin's significance in the biological sciences. His theory is a step toward a materialist understanding of the historical process. Here we may touch only on the small part of his work that relates to folklore. Tylor's fundamental works are *Researches into the Early History of Mankind*; *Primitive Culture*; and *Anthropology: An Introduction to the Study of Man and Civilisation*. Besides these, Tylor wrote an enormous quantity of smaller works. *Primitive Culture* exerted the strongest influence on the development of worldwide scholarship, including scholarship in Russia.

According to Tylor, all peoples follow an identical path of development. The peoples of contemporary Europe were once in the same primitive state where "savages" are now. This point of view greatly broadens the field of comparison. The sphere of comparison comes to include the culture and folklore of primitive peoples, whom European folklorists and Russian ones as well had completely disregarded. This folklore represents the earliest stage of development. In this way it not only broadens the circle of comparisons but also brings properly historical perspectives into their analysis for the first time.

Contemporary culture, according to Tylor, contains unrecognized or, as we would now say, reinterpreted remnants of this primitive culture. Tylor introduced the extraordinarily fruitful and important concept of survivals. The mythological school also asserted that a folktale was a remnant of a primeval myth, but what this primeval myth represented was completely unknown. The mythologists constructed it by way of abstractions and, moreover, constructed it incorrectly or took as primitive myth such late-stage phenomena as the Rig Veda, which already represent the product of a class and priestly culture. Now primitive man stepped forth in all his concreteness. He is described in the works of numerous ethnographic expeditions. Primitive mythology is the topic of several chapters in Tylor's work. This part of Tylor's theory is the most important and seminal for us. He speaks for the first time (in ethnographic science) of the unity of the historical process. Tylor sees this process as evolutionary, just as Darwin was an evolutionist. Development moves from the less perfect to the more perfect. Tylor demonstrates this based on the development of housing from caves to contemporary structures and the development of the tools of production from axes to contemporary factories. Spiritual culture, language, religion, and folklore are subordinate to the same process, although Tylor says little about folklore proper.

Tylor places phenomena of spiritual and material culture not in a conditional relationship but in parallel. They are united by mankind's spiritual activity. For Tylor, the psyche of the person is the same over the whole extent of his or her development, and it is the very thing that defines the unity of cultural phenomena. Tylor imagines the progress of this psyche as a development from the simple to the complex. The psyche of primitive man corresponds to the psyche of a child. It is distinguished from the psyche of contemporary man only by its primitiveness.

We cannot now agree with Tylor in this. The resemblance of cultural phenomena, of folkloric phenomena among others, does not define a psychic unity. For us, spiritual culture is a superstructural phenomenon, above the phenomena of material culture. Nonetheless, it is important for us that Tylor took the first steps in studying the thinking of primitive man.

The study of the psyche of primitive man led Tylor to the study of animism (from the Latin *anima*, "soul, spirit"). Animism is the worldview of primitive man. Primitive thought ascribes a soul or some kind of spiritual principle to all of nature, the whole surrounding world. Stones can speak, trees can bleed when they are cut, the sun may get married, and so on. Tylor establishes for the first time the essence of religion, no longer as belief only in the animacy of the sun, stars, and clouds but as recognition of the presence of some kind of spiritual principle in the world. This observation is indubitably correct, but the phenomenon of animism itself is more complex than it seems to Tylor. His basic works, for example, do not yet reflect the phenomenon of totemism, which was discovered later and which represents a great problem, reflected in only a few of his articles.

Lang

Andrew Lang (1844–1912) continued Tylor's work directly. Lang was more interested in folklore than Tylor was, and his work has primary significance for us. His fundamental works are *Custom and Myth*; *Myth, Ritual, and Religion*; *Modern Mythology*; *The Making of Religion*; *Magic and Religion*; *Social Origins*; and *The Secret of the Totem*. Lang translated the Odyssey into English, published Charles Perrault's tales and the Grimms' tales in English, and provided them with prefaces. He wrote the article "Mythology" for the *Encyclo-*

pedia Britannica (the only one of his works that has been translated into Russian). It is obvious from this list that Lang was more interested in phenomena of spiritual culture than in material culture.

Lang made an important step toward a materialist understanding of folklore. He introduced the phenomena of social life to the study of folklore, and particularly the folktale, for the first time. (Tylor's great works hardly touched on social life at all.) Social life takes its shape from social institutions. Lang reduced the resemblance of folkloric phenomena to the resemblance of social institutions. Thus for Lang the motif of the three brothers, where the youngest inherits the throne, comes down to the institution of minorate (i.e., the right of inheritance by the youngest). He explains the plot of Amor and Psyche through former marriage taboos and so on. Not all of Lang's explanations can now be accepted as correct. The important thing, however, is the principally new path that makes it possible to illuminate the origin of a great many folktale motifs and plots.

However, Lang was still not a materialist. Explaining the resemblance of folktale phenomena by the resemblance of social institutions is correct in principle for many motifs, but the resemblance of social institutions demands an explanation in its turn, and Lang explained that resemblance in a way that exposes the idealistic essence of his views. He explained the resemblance through the unity of the human psyche. An identical psychology defines identical social attitudes and institutions, and they in turn define the identity of folktale plots. A one-sided study of the folktale's primitive foundations leads to misunderstanding of the contemporary state of folk creativity. If the mythologists idealized the people, then Lang treated the people with scorn and rejected their creative role.

Frazer

The third significant representative of the anthropological school was James George Frazer (1854–1941). By the time he began to write, an enormous, almost unimaginable quantity of ethnographic material had accumulated. Frazer strove for full mastery of this material, including material from the ancient East and cultures of antiquity. His works are major volumes that represent an invaluable treasure-house for any ethnographer, historian of culture, and folklorist. He continues the line of his predecessors, studying folklore in its connection with religious concepts and social institutions. His capital work is *The Golden Bough*. It is devoted in essence to researching a form of the inheritance of power in which the heir kills his forerunner. In the past, the king governed not only the people but also nature. His subjects were convinced that the weather, the harvest, and the reproduction of livestock depended on him. The king was at the same time a priest. He controlled the weather not by rational means but by magic. This gives Frazer cause to study the essence and forms of magic in general. The pages devoted to magic belong among the classical achievements of European ethnography and folkloristics. According to Frazer's theory, the priest was killed when his magical power began to decline with age. It is clear from what we lay out here that Frazer accepts the religious origin of power. We cannot share this point of view, or Frazer's view of magic as a prereligious stage in the development of human consciousness. According to Frazer, magic, religion, and science represent three stages in the development of human culture.

The Golden Bough is Frazer's fundamental work, and it immediately won him worldwide fame. But Frazer's other works also had primary significance for folkloristics and, in particular, for the folklore scholar. *Totemism and Exogamy* contains valuable material for the study of the history of wedding customs, which play a large part in the folktale. *The Belief in Immortality and the Worship of the Dead* and *The Fear of the Dead in Primitive Religion* are important for study of tales about the other world, the folktale "Thrice-Ninth Kingdom." *Folklore in the Old Testament* addresses folklore in the proper sense of the word. This book reveals the folkloric origin of many biblical tales, considered sacred in Christianity. Frazer cites a huge amount of comparative material, and he explains its descent from earlier forms of human culture.

English scholarship has developed on the path Tylor established to the present day.[204] This direction was also characteristic of the main journals published by the English folklore society: *Folklore World*, *Folklore Journal*, and *Folklore*.[205] One major figure in this society was E. Hartland, who put out a magisterial study of Perseus, examining from an ethnographic point of view the plot of a girl who is put out for a dragon to eat and is rescued by a hero.[206]

France

In France the organ of the anthropological school was the journal *Melusine*,[207] founded by historian of religion Henri Gaidoz. Lucien Lévy-Bruhl was an important ethnographer-folklorist who followed not so much Tylor as the sociological teaching of Emile Durkheim. In distinction from Tylor, who proceeded from the psychology of the individual, Lévy-Bruhl studied the collective thinking of primitive peoples. This thinking differs qualitatively from the thinking of a contemporary person. Lévy-Bruhl called it prelogical. It does not follow cause and effect but relies on the law of complicity (participation); that is, it is a worldview in which a person does not separate his "I" from the world around him. This peculiarity of primitive thinking is studied in languages, systems of counting, rituals, and especially myths, to which the books *Mental Functions in Inferior Societies* and *The Primitive Mentality* are devoted (excerpts of both came out in a combined Russian translation, *The Supernatural in Primitive Thinking*).[208] Lévy-Bruhl's works have primary significance for the study of the folktale and its genetic links with primitive myth. We cannot, however, identify the social-psychological group, from which Lévy-Bruhl proceeds, as identical with the social collective, on which our work is founded.

The decadence of the ethnographic method can be observed in P. Saintyves's large theoretical work on plots in Perrault, *The Tales of Perrault and Parallel Stories*.[209] If the so-called mythologists interpreted the folktale by tracing it arbitrarily from mythic conceptions, here the folktale is just as arbitrarily reduced to various habits, rituals, beliefs, and so on. Thus the twelve fairies in the tale of Sleeping Beauty are interpreted as the twelve months of the year and the thirteenth fairy is the New Year; Little Red Riding Hood "signifies" the May queen, and so on. At the same time, however, some correspondences are guessed correctly. Thus Saintyves confirms the link of the tale of Tom Thumb with a ritual of initiation, without elaborating it on the basis of concrete material (see our later discussion on the works of Lur'e and Propp).

Responses in Russian Scholarship

The new tendency did not resonate widely in prerevolutionary Russian scholarship, which tended to move on a comparativist track. The only scholar who understood the new movement's significance in principle was Aleksandr Veselovskii. This does not mean that Veselovskii was subject to the immediate influence of the school. He came to the necessity of studying primitive culture and the development of social institutions independently, as he began to work on "historical poetics." The development of his own views should have brought him to the teachings of Tylor and his successors, but the idealistic elements characteristic of Tylor's theory are alien to Veselovskii. True, the first page of *The Poetics of Plots*, which speaks of the psyche and everyday conditions "in the first days of human habitation together," declares, "The one-dimensionality of this psyche and of these conditions explains the one-dimensionality of poetic expression among ethnicities who have never come in contact with one another."[210] However, it is evident from what follows that Veselovskii's focus is not so much on the psyche as on the everyday conditions. He derives a whole series of motifs from them. Veselovskii did not yet consider such a descent possible for a whole plot or for the combination of motifs. The unfinished *Poetics of Plots* gives a picture of stubborn work on the study of these everyday conditions. Veselovskii reviews for himself the whole literature on animism and totemism, exogamy, matriarchy, and patriarchy. Along the way he makes observations on the possible origins of individual motifs. He writes, "The story of Psyche would indicate to us an everyday environment where the break from exogamy to endogamy had occurred."[211] He traces back to totemism motifs of people descended from animals, people marrying animals, grateful animals, an infant nursed by an animal, and some others. In the motif of parthenogenesis (miraculous conception) he sees a reflection of matriarchal and patriarchal relations. All these are only hints, thoughts laid out in an abbreviated and fragmentary way, but even the fragments show how much deeper Veselovskii's views were than the constructions of the English anthropologists. He says nothing about "identity of the psyche." If the English anthropologists only lay out a path to a materialist understanding of folklore in their works, remaining idealistic in essence, then Veselovskii already takes the first step along this path. He does not follow the anthropological school so much as he overcomes it.

Otherwise, there were only occasional, sporadic reflections of this current in Russian scholarship, which as a whole adhered to other movements. L. F. Voevodskii developed the mythologists' idea on the basis of antique material; his book, *Cannibalism in Greek Myths*,[212] seeks traces of primitive everyday reality in Greek myths. One of the studies in M. N. Komarov's book *Excursions into Folktale Myth* is devoted not to solar myths (as with the mythological school) but to primitive conceptions of blood and their reflection in folklore ("One Epic Conception of the Meaning of Blood").[213] A. I. Kirpichnikov is more consistent. On the basis of material he has studied, he sees the independent generation of identical plots among different peoples, and at the same time he underlines not their psychological identity but the identical conditions of their lives.[214] Nikolai Sumtsov collected his short notes on ethnography and folklore in the book *Cultural Survivals*.[215] Ema Eleonskaia's specialized article, "Some Observations on the Survivals of Primitive Culture in Folktales,"[216] is devoted to traces of primitive culture in folktales.

In prerevolutionary Russian scholarship, questions about primitive culture could not be of immediate concern in the study of folklore. Only after the revolution, when our scholarship began to pursue a materialist understanding of the historical process, did the works of anthropologists and ethnographers turn out to be extremely necessary and useful for the construction of Soviet folkloristics and for culturally enlightening work. Some of Frazer's and Lévy-Bruhl's works were translated. It is not the method and not the worldview in these works that are important for us but rather the abundance of concrete materials and correctly established connections. The model for Soviet scholarship is not Frazer or Lévy-Bruhl but Friedrich Engels's work "The Descent of the Family, of Private Property, and the State,"[217] which examines phenomena of primitive and later cultures as phenomena of the historical process, defining them not by psychological identity but by the laws of development of the means of production and social relationships. In connection with his study's fundamental subject, Engels explained a series of phenomena in language and folklore by the way. Thus he defines the historical basis of the myth of Orestes. This plot is the basis of Aeschylus's *Oresteia*, but the plot is folkloric in origin. Engels sees the plot of Orestes, who kills his mother, who did in her husband for the sake of her lover, and of Orestes's revenge for his father (in which Orestes is subjected to the persecution of the Eumenides but is justified by a trial of the gods) as a reflection of the shift from maternal rights to paternal. Engels's works should be placed at the foundation of the stadial study of the folktale, which is one of the fundamental issues in Soviet folkloristics.

THE PROBLEM OF STADIAL DEVELOPMENT

Posing the Problem

After the October Revolution, a radical restructuring of methods of study began in the humanitarian sciences. There is no need to outline the foundation of dialectic and historical materialism here. Our task is to speak of their application to the study of the folktale.

Academician Nikolai Marr advanced the principle of stadial or stage-by-stage study of the development of languages. Correctly understood and utilized, this principle applies the method of dialectical materialism to phenomena of spiritual culture, including folklore.

By the principle of stadial study we mean study of the development of society in stages, defined by the aggregate of material, social, and spiritual culture, where phenomena of spiritual culture turn out to be arbitrary, a superstructure above a social-economic base. Development occurs in a regular way, conforming with historical necessity. However, the same societal law plays out in different ways with different peoples, and their development (conditioned by that law) does not occur with identical speed. We define that development not from the point of view of chronology but from the point of view of its level and of the forms at each stage.

We find such an understanding in embryonic form in individual cases and also in the person of its most advanced representatives. So, in a series of lectures delivered in 1884, Veselovskii says, "We may say with certainty that the Homeric poems stand at a later stage of development than the folk poetry of our day."[218] This means that monuments of folklore that were written down late, sometimes in the nineteenth or twentieth century, preserve traces of earlier stages of their existence. But folklore does not remain unchanged over the course of its sometimes millennial existence. Traces of later stages are also etched on it, right up to the present. We could call this phenomenon polystadiality. The task of scholarship lies in separating the layers of texts according to the materials sedimented in them, from the most ancient to the contemporary. Their interrelationship with the social-economic base allows us to define their genesis and the cause of their alterations, their fading, and new formations.

It is clear from all that I have said that the phenomenon of resemblance does not constitute a problem. Indeed, the *absence* of such a resemblance would be more difficult to explain.

The Works of Soviet Scholars and Their Forerunners

Studies of the folktale at various stages of societal development present particular value for the study of folklore according to the principles I have outlined.

The study of the creativity of primitive peoples in foreign nations was not considered a persuasively necessary task in Russian scholarship. But, as we saw, an extraordinary amount was accomplished in European scholarship.

In Russian scholarship, it was most often the representatives of the revolutionary-democratic intelligentsia who paid attention to the ethnic groups who populate our country. It is not my task to give a description of the study of small ethnic groups by Soviet scholars. (I may only indicate here the possibility of such study in principle.) As the most important I will list the collections of V. G. Bogoraz (Tana) on Chukchi folklore, L. Ia. Shternberg on the Giliak, V. I. Iokhel'son on the Iukagir, and Ivan Khudiakov and S. V. Iastremskii on the Yakut. These materials (except for Khudiakov's) are accompanied by introductory articles and commentary. It is telling that all the collectors and researchers listed were political exiles. Their work had significance as translated and splendidly edited material for future historical generalizations. After the revolution this work continued and was carried on in a fairly interesting way.[219] Research proper into aboriginal materials was poorly represented in Russian scholarship before the revolution, and the influence of the anthropological school was visible in some of the individual works mentioned.

The importance of such study in principle was recognized only after the revolution. Solomon Lur'e indicated the link of the folktale with primitive rituals for the first time in the Russian literature in his work "The House in the Woods." It is devoted to the motif of a girl who visits brothers or robbers who live in the forest and also to the cannibal's house in tales of the Tom Thumb type and a series of similar motifs.[220]

The work of Vladimir Propp carries out a systematic investigation of the magical folktale from the point of view of its genetic connection with the world of primitive rituals, conceptions, and beliefs. He considers the motifs or plots of the magic tree on a grave,[221] the reflection in folktales of the institution of "men's houses,"[222] the tale of Never-Laugh and the whole complex of phenomena connected with ritual laughter,[223] the motif of miraculous birth,[224] and motifs of incestuous marriage and parricide.[225] These works trace the most ancient stage of the folktale and examine its prefolktale foundations and the genesis of its individual parts.

The question of the origin of the magical folktale as a whole is raised in Propp's monograph *The Historical Roots of the Wonder Folktale.*[226]

The distinction between these works and those of the English school is that they explain the resemblance of folktales not by the identity of the human psyche but by their regular connection with the forms of material production, which lead to identical or similar forms of social life and ideology.

One difficulty of stadial study is that we do not have a precise and generally recognized periodization of the stages of development of human society. Lewis H. Morgan laid the foundation for such a periodization.[227] Friedrich Engels devoted the fifth chapter ("Prehistoric Stages of Culture") of his work

The Origin of the Family, Private Property, and the State to this question and elevated it to the height of a principle.

Since then, material has accumulated in enormous quantities, and it demands more differentiated and exact definitions than could be given seventy or eighty years ago. We are often obliged to make do with the overly general categories of clan structure, slaveholding agrarian state, and so on.[228]

Besides what might be defined in general outlines as the primitive stage, Russian scholarship has studied the stage whose typical expression is classical antiquity. The cultural and general human significance of antiquity is so great that interest in it was bound to be reflected in the study of the folktale, both in Europe and in Russian scholarship before and after the revolution.[229] Russian scholarship after the revolution particularly developed the question of the folktale's significance for the study of antiquity, but it was touched on in earlier work as well, for example, by Kiev scholar V. P. Klinger and St. Petersburg professor Faddei Zelinskii. Klinger's *Folktale Motifs in Herodotus's "History"* could stand up with the best European works on the same theme.[230] Two of his other works connect materials from antiquity with the contemporary stage of folklore (*Animals in Antique and Contemporary Superstition* and "Two Antique Folktales About the Eagle and Their Later Echoes").[231] Here antiquity is examined as a source, a nursery for later cultural phenomena. Zelinskii takes the same position in his work "The Ancient Lenore."[232] The significance of antiquity for later cultures and for the contemporary world is one of Zelinskii's fundamental ideas. This idea, however, represents something distinct from the principle of stadial development in the study of folklore, although the two are not mutually exclusive. Zelinskii examined the popular folkloric foundations of antique comedy in his work on folklore comedy in Athens (*Märchenkomödie in Athen*). One of his most significant achievements, still insufficiently valued by folklorists, was the discovery of a special internal law of folkloric epic works, which Zelinskii called the law of chronological exclusion. This law, in brief, specifies that in folk epic poetry it is impossible to have parallel simultaneous events in two theaters of action.[233] Zelinskii traces this law in the *Iliad*, where it is, in essence, already violated. It can be traced in the folktale in its pure, original form. This law is indispensable in the study of folktale poetics; it is one of the fundamental regularities of folktale composition.

Academician Mikhail Pokrovskii later worked on the relationship of Roman comedy to folklore.[234]

In the indicated works from before the revolution, the principle of stadial study of the folktale is not yet conscious. It receives full development only in

Soviet scholarship. Russian classical philology of our day does not represent "philology" in the narrow sense of that word. Folk creativity is studied as one of the foundations of ancient literature. Today, folklore acquires enormous significance in scholarship on antique culture. Contemporary folklore can open our eyes in many ways to the nature and sources of the great works of this culture. Ivan Tolstoi's works, exemplary in their abundance of material and strictness of method, move in this direction. We can offer only a brief survey of them here.

The first of this series of works—"Circe's Enchanted Beasts in the Poem of Apollo of Rhodes" (1929)[235]—cites folkloric material only incidentally. "Unsuccessful Doctoring: An Antique Parallel to the Russian Folktale" (1932) is already devoted entirely to one folktale plot.[236] Eleven Russian and two antique versions are analyzed, taking Western European material into account. The exceptional state of preservation of precisely the Russian material allows a series of conclusions concerning the form of the antique versions. Russian materials allow Tolstoi to overturn the theory of the priestly origin of this plot, to judge the relative age of the two antique versions, and so on. We find an entirely new approach, compared with the works of Sozonovich and Sumtsov on the same theme, in one of the most significant works of Soviet folkloristics: Tolstoi's article "The Return of the Husband in the *Odyssey* and in the Russian Folktale" (1934).[237] Russian material makes it possible to decipher a whole series of details, and it confirms the theory of the folktale basis of the *Odyssey*. The article "The Ritual and Legend of Athenian Buffoonery" (1937)[238] is important in giving rare ritual material for cumulative folktales. The article "Euripides's Tragedy *Helen* and the Origin of the Greek Novel" (1939)[239] studies the interrelationship of three genres (tragedy, novel, and folktale) on the basis of one plot. Here the folktale turns out to be the primary genre, which allows judgment about the sources of Euripides's tragedies and a whole series of extremely to-the-point and important observations. The article "The Strongman Bound and the Freed Strongman" (1938) belongs to the same type of work.[240] This work confirms the peasant origin of the plot about the capture of a strong man, a forest creature, who possesses magical powers and grants the wishes of his conqueror, after which he is released. Detailed analysis of the plot allowed Tolstoi, aside from other observations and conclusions, to decipher the depiction on an Eleutherian vase from the sixth century B.C.—leading a bound strongman to the king. We may ask about the connection of this plot with the cycle of traditions about Solomon and Kitovras.

In the small work "'Callimachus's 'Hecale' and the Russian Folktale of Baba Yaga" (1941),[241] Tolstoi uses the Russian folktale to give a more complete interpretation than what antique materials allow of the old woman Hecale, at whose home Theseus spends the night on the eve of one of his feats, the capture of the bull of Marathon. Here Tolstoi collects and compares rich material concerning the motif of a hero who spends the night before undertaking a feat with an image in the antique world analogous to Baba Yaga. The work "Folktale Language in Greek Literature" (1929)[242] also has great significance. Although its topic is the antique folktale, Tolstoi's observations cast light on the language (syntax) of the Russian folktale.

Iosif M. Tronskii also devotes a great deal of attention to the folktale. His work "The Myth of Daphnis"[243] mentions folktale material in passing and does not yet have decisive significance. However, his later work "The Antique World and the Contemporary Folktale" offers a substantive and theoretically well-founded comparison of antique plots in myth with the same ones in folktales.[244] The position that "the folktale reproduces the old contours of the plot with more precision than the Greek epic" cannot be accepted without qualifications, but it is complicated by examination of the historical destinies and social nature of the folktale and myth. The work applies this approach to the plot of Polyphemus. The contemporary folktale allows us to understand and explain "the confused progress of the story in Homer." The same views are applied to the myth of Peleus and Thetis (the forced marriage of a man with a woman of divine descent, afterwards violated). "A Cretan folktale, written down in the nineteenth century, allows us to gather together the scattered details of the old tradition of Peleus and Thetis."[245] The same method is used to analyze other motifs. Studying the social nature of the folktale and myth allowed Tronskii to offer a new understanding of the relationship of the myth to the folktale. "A myth that has lost its social significance becomes a folktale."[246]

The listed works advance the development of social-historical study of the folktale; they have primary significance for the folklorist, although the folktale is not the primary topic of investigation here. They do not ask or resolve what a folktale itself represents at the antique stage of societal development, although they offer rich material for its solution. Including folktale material helps clarify the origin and character of the antique material, but this does not solve the question of the descent of a plot or the method as such. The folktale plot itself springs from a stage more ancient than antiquity. Representatives of classical philology do not as a rule address this more ancient stage.

In this regard, a somewhat particular place among scholars who work on antiquity belongs to Ol'ga Freidenberg, who also invested a great deal of effort in the study of folklore. Freidenberg's works are characterized by the application of paleontological analysis. Nikolai Marr introduced the method of paleontological study for the study of languages. Its essence comes down to uncovering elements and foundations of a more ancient stage in the later condition of a language. This method is not in essence comparative, although it does not exclude broad application of comparative materials for confirmation of the positions it advances. We could refer to it as introspective. The method is also applicable to the study of plots. If the stadial historical method proceeds from top to bottom, from the ancient to the new, then the paleontological method, on the contrary, proceeds from the new to the ancient. Establishment of the most ancient, prehistoric stage cannot always be confirmed by materials, and then it is constructed by practitioners of the given movement. Both approaches—from ancient to new and the reverse—ought to work in harmony, although reconstructing the prehistoric stage without introducing factual materials follows an exceedingly dangerous and slippery path.

One of Marr's contributions is that he does not limit himself to the formal side of language in the study of languages; he brings study of the meanings of a word and their transformations to the foreground. The rightness of this approach for studying languages is completely obvious. But transferring this principle to folklore would demand a fundamental justification. Every word "means" something. But whether a myth or a folktale "means" anything is not a question that can be simply confirmed or negated; it demands a critical examination. At the same time Marr, not a folklorist, ascribed a semantics to the myth without reference to comparative materials on primitive peoples. Marr refers to the prehistoric era as cosmic and correspondingly speaks of the cosmic consciousness. No folklorist or ethnographer who is well acquainted with the narrowness of the primitive person and his conceptions of space could accept this. Cosmogonic myths are a phenomenon of a later stage. Marr speaks of the plot of *Tristan and Isolde*: "G. Paris's proposition that in Tristan we have the sun, transformed into a hero of love, has been brilliantly justified,"[247] but it is clear to the folklorist that Paris, a typical migrationist, helpless in questions of genesis, is paying tribute to the old mythological theory, tracing every plot and motif back to solar myths, without asking when the cult of the sun actually appears in the historical development of peoples. This is the danger of the given method: Uncritically applied, it returns us to the era of arbitrary interpretation of myths and folktales. Not every tactic of studying language can be transferred to folklore and its study.

The application of similar methods necessarily leads to confirmation of the metaphoricity of myth and attempts to semanticize these metaphors, which were already being undertaken by Max Müller.

The most consistent principles of paleontological analysis are applied in the collection of articles that Marr edited on the plot of *Tristan and Isolde*. The collection's goal was formulated in several articles ("to reveal paleontological semantics").[248] However, this semantics turns out to be either various for one and the same image or else unchanging for what we would consider the most various motifs. Thus battling a dragon represents either "the motif of the solar hero's struggle with the darkness of death" or else "vanquishing a dragon means 'taking possession of a woman,' 'coupling,' 'marrying.'"[249] At the same time, the sun is not only the hero himself, but, for example, the ring lovers exchange.[250]

On the whole, this authorial collective defined the problem correctly: "to trace various plot formations in connection with alterations in socioeconomic structures."[251] But as a consequence of the great quantity of completely arbitrary interpretations, the problem cannot be considered resolved. One article deals with the Russian folktale ("Motifs of Tristan and Isolde According to Materials of the Russian Folktale").[252] Other articles are each dedicated to some people—from the Celtic and Germanic to the peoples of the ancient East and antiquity (including the Russian folktale and Mordvinian folklore). The problem also remains unresolved because individual articles provide no picture of the stages of development in comparison with previous stages.

Freidenberg introduces folktale material in her articles "The Blind Man over the Abyss," "The Myth of Joseph the Beautiful," and "Folklore in Aristophanes."[253] The basic plot in the last article is about a man in disguise who spies on women's festivities (in part a Russian Mikula the Joker).

Freidenberg's major work, which is typical of a certain group of students and followers of Marr, is her book *The Poetics of Plot and Genre*.[254] Among minor works that follow the same path, we could mention R. L. Erlikh's article on crafty thieves[255] and S. S. Sovetov's "One of the Images of 'Fire' and 'Water' in Serbian and Slavic Folktales."[256]

Russian scholarship has been less interested in the stage represented by ancient Egypt than in the antique stage. Relatively abundant folktale materials have come down to us from Egypt, and they have been the subject of extremely painstaking study in Western European scholarship.[257] In Russia we may point to the splendid critical edition *The Ancient Egyptian Tale of the Two Brothers*, with copious comments and folkloristic parallels, prepared by Vladimir Vikent'ev.[258] Iurii P. Frantsov was occupied with research on the Egyptian folktale.[259] Both these works, though properly in Egyptology, have great significance for comparative-historical study of the folktale.

The tale of the two brothers has been subjected to comparative study in Russia. Israil' Frank-Kamenetskii compared it in detail with the Georgian folktale.[260] This allowed Frank-Kamenetskii to elaborate on the question of this famous folktale's structure. The resemblance of these Georgian and Russian folktales is explained by a single "mythological substrate," which Frank-Kamenetskii declares is the solar myth.[261]

The stage represented by the Russian Middle Ages is not witnessed by any immediate materials.[262] A. Vesel'skii published medieval folktale texts in German translation with detailed commentary and a most valuable bibliography (*Folktales of the Middle Ages* and *Monastic Latin*).[263] Not a single folktale text has been discovered on Russian soil. We can ascertain the existence of folktales through their indirect reflections. These are found in denunciatory literature, in the sermons of Kirill of Turov and of Serapion of Vladimir, in the Missive of Fotii to the Novgorod archbishop Iona (1416), and in the ukase of Tsar Aleksei Mikhailovich to his generals (1649). The existing testimony is collected in S. V. Savchenko's book *The Russian Folkloric Tale*, which also provides a summary of all the traces and residues of the folktale in Old Russian literature, beginning with the chronicles and finishing with the notes of Collins. This collection does not pretend or aspire to completeness. The task of compiling a complete index of traces of folktales in surviving monuments of Old Russian literature is still not complete today. Nikiforov made a valuable survey of folklore of the Kievan period in the first volume of his *History of Russian Literature*, published by the Academy of Sciences of the USSR.[264]

Nikolai Andreev on the History of Folklore

Today we may consider that the need for a stadial historical study of folklore is generally accepted in the Soviet Union. It is recognized both by adherents and students of Marr and by scholars who remained outside the range of influence of his teaching. Nikolai Andreev belongs among the latter. He made the first attempt to establish the principle of such a historical construction (in the article "The Problem of the History of Folklore"). However, this first attempt cannot be called successful. At the time Andreev did not yet fully understand the folktale's specific nature as a creation of the people. He tended to presume that the creative role belonged to the ruling classes and that the people only accepted what had been created on high: The creative process took place in boyar circles and came to an end once the boyars became courtiers.[265]

Later, Andreev, in his article "Folklore and Its History,"[266] came to reiterate his first article's position in an altered form. He recognized folklore as "genuine creativity of the people." He presents here an essentially stadial principle of study, although he does not use the term *stadial* (*stadial'nyi*). According to Andreev, early stages of the development of folklore can be studied on the basis of peoples who are now at earlier stages of development. The folktale originates in pre–class society. Thus folktales about animals are created in the stage of totemism. In a class-stratified society the people's creativity penetrates to the upper reaches. Folklore, including the folktale, loses the mythological and magical character that characterizes it in early stages. It is precisely then (in the fifteenth and sixteenth centuries) that novellistic folktales also arise in Russia. Andreev describes the period from the seventeenth century to the first half of the nineteenth century as the era of serfdom. At this time the folktale takes on a more pronounced peasant character and greater social sharpness. At the same time, both wonder tales and humorous tales express the people's optimism. By that time, folklore was dying out in noble milieus. The next period is defined as capitalist. Class stratification of the peasantry leads to the same kind of stratification of folklore. Finally, erasure of the boundaries between folklore and literature is characteristic of the period of proletarian revolution and socialist construction. Folklore becomes the general creativity of the people. Genres that are not in harmony with the era die out, others change their forms, and still others are only now being created. This is Soviet folklore in its process of becoming.

Such is the first and, for now, the only attempt in our scholarship to encompass the fundamental landmarks of the development of folklore, including the folktale. Complete elaboration of this question is a matter for the future. Creation of a history of the folktale, not along general lines but in all its concreteness, demands thorough elaboration of every stage in isolation with reference to all existing material.[267]

3

WONDER TALES

General Description of the Wonder Tale

Let us proceed to an examination of the wonder tale. This is probably the most splendid variety of artistic folk prose. It is full of high ideals and elevated aspirations. However, before we can speak of the wonder tale's artistic qualities, we must discuss what the term *wonder tale* means.

Stable and Variable Elements of the Magical Tale

The wonder tale (*volshebnaia skazka*) has so vivid a character, is so distinct from all other forms of the folktale, that Afanas'ev was right to separate it from the other kinds. What first presents itself when we speak of the magic tale is the sort of plots that are typical of it. In truth, folktales such as the tale of the Three Kingdoms, Copper, Silver, and Gold; Finist the Bright Falcon; the Frog Princess; the Seven Simeons, each with some kind of magical power, who win the princess; the Firebird, dragon slayers, and many others undoubtedly represent wonder tales.

We can speak of the motifs of the wonder tale in the same sense. It is obvious that motifs such as building a magic palace in a single night, a hero's invisible helper, or a hero who flies to a different kingdom on an eagle or a flying carpet are motifs typical of the wonder tale. Therefore in most cases the concept of the wonder tale is defined through its plots and motifs.

Here is what Aarne does in his index, for example. He sets aside 450 numbers for the category of the wonder tale (300–750), which are still far from all being filled. As new tales are found, they might be brought into the index in their own places. There are lists of motifs of exactly the same kind. We know of Stith Thompson's ambitious attempt to create a complete list of the motifs of all folk literature, which encompasses six volumes. Of these, the last volume is an index to the index.[1]

What features define the concept of the wonder tale? Which tales form part of this category, and which do not? Afanas'ev, for example, considered the tale of the fisherman and the fish not a wonder tale but an animal tale. Was he right or not? His original thought was that wonder tales are fantastic (or have some quality of the fantastic) and involve enchantment. We cannot acknowledge this trait as scholarly or even as exact. Take, for example, the tale of the evil and unfaithful wife. When her husband discovers her infidelity, she turns him into a dog. He finds a way to recover his human form and, in turn, transforms his wife into a mare and uses her to haul water. Aarne considers this a wonder tale, because enchantment plays a role in it. I cannot agree with that at all. This is a novellistic folktale of the purest kind. Not every folktale that includes enchantment belongs among the wonder tales.

Without going into detail, we will say that the wonder tale must be defined not by some vague concept of enchantment but rather by the regularities that typify it. Scholarship in general is concerned with regularities. They can be established in the field of folklore too.

Regularity begins when there is repetition. A scientific law is always founded on repetition. The concept of a law includes repeatability. The wonder tale truly possesses a kind of characteristic repetitiveness. Everyone who has read a large quantity of folktales knows that, along with all their variety and all their color, folktales have a uniformity, so that by the middle of the tale an attentive or experienced listener or reader can already predict what will happen next.

The character of this repetitiveness must also be established and studied. What is it that repeats in the folktale?

Let us compare some plots from the cycle of folktales about stepmothers and stepdaughters (A-T 480 = AA 480*B, *C):

1. Because his second wife hates the daughter from his first marriage, a man takes his daughter out into the forest to be a servant to Baba Yaga. Baba Yaga gives the girl all kinds of household tasks to do: "She gave the girl a basket of material to spin into yarn, told her to heat the stove, to store up all kinds of provisions," and so on. The stepdaughter does such a good job with the work that Baba Yaga rewards her richly. Then the stepmother sends her own daughter into the forest, but this one does not want to do anything. Baba Yaga "breaks her up," and the man brings her bones back home (Afanas'ev 102).[2]

2. A stepmother hates her stepdaughter. To get rid of her, she puts out all the fires in the house and sends her to Baba Yaga to get fire. Yaga meets the girl with the words, "If you live and work with me awhile, I'll give you fire." She assigns her a whole series of tasks; the girl manages to do everything. Baba Yaga gives her a flame, which burns up the stepmother and the stepmother's daughter.

3. An old man's wife, his second wife, orders him to take his daughter from his first marriage into the forest. Jack Frost (Morozko) tries to freeze her, but she answers his questions so meekly that he takes pity on her and gives her rich rewards. The old woman sends her own daughters into the forest. They behave arrogantly, and Morozko freezes them to death.

4. A stepmother hates her stepdaughter. Her father takes her out into the forest and leaves her in a dugout house. A bear lives in this dugout. The bear plays hide and seek with her, but he can't catch her. The bear rewards her richly. The stepmother sends her own daughter into the forest. This one is afraid, and the bear bites her (Afanas'ev 98).

For now I am giving only a schematic plot in the briefest summary. The number of examples could be greatly increased.

Let us look more closely at what happens to the girl in the forest. At first glance, her adventures are all completely different: Baba Yaga forces her to do all the housekeeping; Jack Frost tries to freeze her; a bear plays hide-and-seek with her, and so on. Afanas'ev considered all these different tales, and the Aarne-Andreev index also shows them as distinct. At the same time, if we try to define what the girl undergoes in a logical way, then we can conclude that these actions are the same in all cases: She undergoes a test, after which she is rewarded if she passes the test or punished if she fails. A test, a reward, and a punishment—those are the repeating, constant elements of these tales. All the rest may change. The characters differ; in our examples they are Baba Yaga, Jack Frost, and a bear. Their actions are different as well: Baba Yaga gives the girl housekeeping tasks, Jack Frost tries to freeze her, the bear plays hide-and-seek with her. But they are all doing one and the same thing: They are testing and rewarding the stepdaughter and punishing her stepsisters.

The difficulty is how to give a correct definition of equivalent actions. We can refer to actions that have significance for the development of the plot as *functions*. From the examples cited we see that it is precisely these functions that make up the stable, repeating elements of wonder tales, whereas all the rest are variable elements.

We will study the wonder tale first and foremost not through its plot and not through its motifs but by the characters' functions. We will see what results from that and how the results we obtain might apply to the study of plots.

But before we do so, we must ask whether the repetition of functions in fact extends over the whole sphere of wonder tales. Perhaps our observations are correct only for tales about stepmothers and stepdaughters and will turn out to be wrong for other plots.

To answer this question, let us compare the following cases too:

1. A king gives an eagle to a daring man. The eagle flies the daring man to another kingdom.
2. A hero receives a horse from his grandfather. On the horse he flies away to another kingdom.
3. A sorcerer orders a hero to draw a boat on the sand and get in it.
4. A princess gives Ivan a ring. Strong young men come out of the ring and take Ivan away to another kingdom.[3]

This time the examples are taken from various plots. Nevertheless, we once again have the same kind of repetition as in the tales of stepmothers and step-daughters. The conclusions are self-evident. This obligates us to study the functions of the folktale. We will try to define how many functions are known in the wonder tale in general.

Getting ahead of ourselves for a moment, we can say that the number of functions is quite limited; there are hardly more than thirty in all. Further, we will have to ask one more question about the nature of their sequentiality. We will see that, although certain variations and rearrangements are possible, on the whole the sequentiality is always the same. Not all tales include all the functions, but this does not influence the regularity of their sequence, one after another. This will lead us to conclude that wonder tales are all of one type in their construction. The sequentiality of functions can also be called the composition of the folktale. This means that wonder tales are characterized by the uniformity of their composition. This is precisely what serves as their distinguishing trait. Correspondingly, the genre of wonder tales can be defined not by the presence of elements of enchantment and not by a list of plots but by their construction or composition; moreover, this can be done with complete precision. The most difficult thing is to give a logically correct definition of the function. Function and action are not entirely the same thing. I repeat that the function of a fairytale character is an action that is defined from the point of view of its significance for the development of the plot. The function in the listed cases may be transportation to the place of a quest, and flight may be a form of realizing this function. One and the same action may fulfill different functions. Thus a devil may sail in a ship. But that is not yet a character's function. What functions consist of is evident only from the significance that a given act has for the general course of the action. Thus travel on a ship may serve the function of transporting the hero to the place of his feats. But it also might represent his fleeing or, on the contrary, giving chase, and so on. We will discuss the details later.

We will examine the magic tale from the point of view laid out here. The whole variegated, brilliant world of folktale images will open up before us along the way.

The Opening

"In a certain kingdom, in a certain state"—thus the Russian wonder tale begins, with a slow and epic pace. However, this slowness is deceptive. The folktale is full of the greatest tension. It is by no means static. It never describes or characterizes; instead it strives for action.

The formula "in a certain kingdom" points to the spatial indeterminacy of the setting. The introductory formula is typical of Russian folktales. It corresponds to temporal indeterminacy in the tales of other peoples: *es war einmal* (German, "there was once"); "once upon a time"; *il y avait une fois* (French, "one time there was"). We sometimes find this kind of formula in Russian tales: "In the old years there stood a little village" (Afanas'ev 149), but this formula has a bookish whiff and is more typical of the *legenda* than of the folktale, whereas the opening "in a certain kingdom" is typical precisely of the wonder tale, as though to underline that the action takes place outside time and space.

Then comes a list of the characters. There lived "an old man and an old woman" or "a peasant man"; "he (she) had three sons"; "a king had three daughters of indescribable beauty"; and so on. This is far from a realistic depiction of a family. The opening situation usually includes people from two generations, older and younger. They are the future characters of the narration, and the folktale never introduces a single superfluous character. Each character will play his or her role in the narration. Characters of the older generation usually take care of sending the hero away from home; the younger generation leaves home, in various forms and with different kinds of motivation. The hero's social position does not play an essential role here. The hero may be a king's son or a peasant's. But there will be, of course, a certain difference in setting the stage of their surroundings.

The initial or introductory situation sometimes stresses the characters' well-being. Everything is arranged marvelously. The son and daughter are "so well-born, so good." "There lived a super-rich merchant; he had a daughter who was amazingly beautiful." Daughters are always unusually beautiful, "so that it can't be told in a tale, nor written with a pen." The tsar has a splendid garden—in the tale of the Firebird, it is a garden with golden apples. If the tale begins with sowing, for example, then the seeds always sprout wonderfully, and so on. It is easy to note that such well-being serves as a contrasting background for future misfortune; this happiness itself prepares us for unhappiness.

The initial situation is sometimes epically extended. The old people are childless; they pray for the birth of a son. The hero is born in some miraculous way. We meet the motif of miraculous birth in a variety of plots and in different forms. If there are three brothers, the youngest is usually considered a fool. He lies on the stove and does nothing: "He sat around in the soot and snot." But this is only outer appearance, which contrasts with his inner qualities. This fool who is despised by everyone is the one who later achieves fabulous feats. He turns out to be an unselfish hero, he rescues the princess, he attains the greatest happiness. But all this is only in the future. If the hero is born in a miraculous way, he grows quickly, "not by the day, but by the hour." Three brothers sometimes argue about their superiority, test their strength. The youngest always turns out to be superior.

All these forms of epic description do not in themselves represent functions. I mention them in passing, although the motifs themselves deserve attentive study. The action begins when some kind of misfortune occurs.

Misfortune steals up quite unnoticeably. Everything begins when one of the characters listed in the opening situation leaves home for a time. Thus a prince goes on a long journey and leaves his pregnant wife alone. A merchant departs "for foreign lands" to trade, a prince goes to war, a peasant goes away to work in the forest, and so on. We call this function temporary absence. It means that the old and the young, the strong and the defenseless, are separated. Defenseless children, women, girls remain alone. This prepares the ground for misfortune. A heightened form of absence is the death of the parents. It is especially often the father who dies, leaving the whole kingdom to his young, inexperienced son, and the son himself is entrusted to some kind of male caretaker. We get the same effect of dangerous separation with the absence not of the older but of the younger characters. Ivashechka goes off to fish, and his granny lets him go with great reluctance, but as a sign of affection she dresses him in a clean shirt and a little red belt (A-T 327 C, F; Afanas'ev 106–108 [U], 110–112). The king's daughters go off to stroll in their garden: "Then the beautiful princesses went out into the garden to stroll, to see the red sun, and the trees, and the flowers," and so on (A-T 301; Afanas'ev 140). Children go into the forest to pick berries or simply to take a walk.

The absence is often accompanied by prohibitions. An especially vivid form of prohibition is the forbidden storeroom. The father, as he is dying, forbids his son to go into one room of the palace: "Do not dare to look into that storeroom." Most frequent of all, though, are prohibitions on going out of the house: "Many times the prince tried to persuade her, commanded her not to leave her high chambers." We have a heightened form of this prohibition in cases where children are not only told to stay inside but are also put in a deep underground place, where they sit without light, or when a daughter is confined in a high tower, where she likewise cannot see the light of day, is not supposed to touch the ground, and receives food through a window. The prohibitions in folktales are extraordinarily various. So, a horse warns the hero who has found a golden feather, "Do not pick up the gold feather; if you take it, you'll know grief" (A-T 531 = 531 K; Afanas'ev 169). The prohibition in folklore is always violated. Otherwise there would be no plot. Prohibition and violation form a paired function. There are many such paired functions in the folktale. I am giving a formal description of the folktale, looking for now at its composition. But formal study does not mean a formalist study. It is the first step of a historical-genetic study. I will give a historical study of the folktale as a whole separately, but certain elements can be examined in isolation. This will do some harm to the shapeliness of the outline, but it will add to our understanding.

Prohibitions are an important and interesting cultural-historical element. We can define an era and its character by what it would prohibit. We could study all the prohibitions in the folktale systematically. I will not give the whole system, but I will pick out a few especially indicative cases.

[According to his students, here Propp summarized the arguments of his book *The Historical Roots of the Wonder Tale.*—CE][4]

One type of prohibition—not to leave the house, to sit locked up—is among the most ancient and fundamental. We will not here touch on other types of prohibitions with less complicated prehistories. We will encounter one of them—with the motif of the forbidden lumber room—later.

Violating the prohibition leads, sometimes at lightning speed, to some misfortune, some kind of unhappiness. A dragon carries away the princesses who leave their chambers behind and come out to stroll in the garden. Ivashechka is carried off by a witch; in the lumber room the prince sees the portrait of a rare beauty, falls down in a faint, and has no peace until he decides to leave home; and so on. Violation of the prohibition provokes the original misfortune. The misfortune will later provoke counteraction, putting in motion the folktale's whole course of action. Thus the original misfortune represents the founding element of the opening. There are special characters for realization of this function (prohibition and violation): dragons, Baba Yaga, unfaithful servants, animals, thieves, etc. These characters can be called antagonists, opponents, enemies of the hero. When the prohibition is violated, these antagonists may appear instantly, no one knows from where ("wherever you came from"). For example, the princesses just go out to stroll in the garden despite the prohibition, and the dragon flies down and carries them away. But the appearance of the antagonist can happen in another way.

Another example is the offering of the apple in "The Magic Mirror" (Snow White). See Propp, *Morphology of the Folktale*, pp. 38–39, functions IV and V[5] and VI and VII.[6] The first seven functions represent a kind of preparatory section.

After appearing and tricking his prey, the antagonist causes some kind of harm. The forms of this misfortune or harm are extraordinarily varied; most often we encounter the form of abduction. A dragon abducts a princess or a peasant's daughter; a witch abducts Ivashechka. When the course of action is complicated, when it essentially starts again from the beginning, the brothers take away the bride or the hero's treasure or magical tools. The Firebird steals golden apples, a general hides the king's sword, and so on. It is interesting that some cases do not logically represent abduction but still provoke the same course of action as an abduction. The servant blinds her mistress and puts the eyes in her pocket. Subsequently the eyes are recovered and returned to their proper place.

When a person abducts someone else, it comes down in essence to separation, disappearance, and this disappearance may take place in various ways, not just by abduction. Thus, for example, in the tale of the Frog Princess the prince violates the prohibition by burning his wife's frog skin, and she disappears forever, flies away. The effect here is just the same as if someone had abducted her. She flies away from him with the words, "Farewell, seek me beyond thrice-nine lands in the thrice-tenth kingdom."

The forms of the original, plot-engaging misfortune are quite various, and it is impossible to count them all here. Being driven away from home, substitution, murder or the threat of it, sorcery, vampirism—these are a few forms of that original misfortune.

Lack

However, not all wonder tales begin with a misfortune. Sometimes the misfortune's equivalent is a situation in which something is in short supply or missing. The effect turns out to be the same as an abduction. The hero, for example, sets out to find himself a bride. On this path he may encounter the same kind of adventures as though he had set out to rescue an abducted princess. Stolen objects correspond to some kind of marvelous or magical objects that are lacking in the beginning of the tale. Thus, for example, an old king is ill ("his eyes have grown poor"). He sends his son to get the apples of youth and the water of life. In other words, a lack or shortage presents the morphological equivalent of abduction.

But whether a folktale begins with a misfortune or with a lack, this misfortune or lack must come to the hero's attention. In these cases the king raises a cry. "The tsar raised a cry. Would no one come forward to find the tsaritsa?" Corresponding to this lack is the moment when the lack is realized. A family is living peacefully, but then it suddenly turns out that something is missing. Sometimes this lack is not motivated by anything external. For example, there are three sons. "Then their mother and father got the idea of finding wives for them." Sometimes a motivation for its realization is introduced. This goal is served, for example, by the forbidden woodshed, where the hero sees the beauty's portrait; then he sets off to find her.

Thus we see that in a typical wonder tale the whole plot motivation comes down to sending the hero away from home. In sum, we can say that the plot engagement is composed of elements that prepare a misfortune (a temporary absence; a prohibition and its violation), the misfortune itself or a corresponding lack, pleas for help or sending the hero away, or the hero's own wish to exert a counteraction. He asks permission to go, asks for a blessing, and so on. And, finally, the hero leaves home.

Types of Heroes

We have examined several typical cases of misfortune as such, but we have paid no attention to who experiences the misfortune. The initial situation includes characters from the older and younger generations, and a misfortune may happen with either. This does not, as we shall see, influence the course of action, but it does influence the character, the type of hero. In one case the hero sets out to remedy someone else's misfortune. He searches for abducted princesses or queen, he goes to battle a dragon, he gets the apples of youth for his father, and so on. This hero is a seeker. We might also include the hero who sets out to find himself a bride in this type. In the other case he is driven from his home, as is a stepdaughter or a child stolen by a witch or the Handless Girl (Afanas'ev 280). Sometimes after an abduction the tale follows the suffering Tereshichka, and there is no seeker in the tale. This kind can be called a hero-victim. A tale may begin not only with misfortune or lack but also in other ways (e.g., the tale of Sivko-Burko), but we will analyze those cases later.

Gift Givers

The moment after leaving home is the tensest, the most intense for the hero in the course of the action. He leaves by guesswork, knowing neither the road nor the goal. He walks along, "following his nose." It is precisely here that the formula most often applies: "He rode near or far, high or low, the deed is not so quickly done as the tale is spun."[7] The hero is cast upon the caprice of fate and sometimes even falls into despair and weeps. The formula "a tale is quickly spun" is interesting in one regard: It seems to underline the nonreality of time in which the action is completed. It cannot be calculated, and never is calculated, in real periods of days, weeks, or years.

The composition, in consequence, does not develop logically. At this point it is as though the chain has broken, and what follows is not prepared by what comes before. It is an arena where things may appear by chance. To a significant extent this element of chance defines the fantastic character of the wonder tale. Theoretically, the number of possible forms of further development is infinite. What happens next? A writer could set his imagination free; if we took a hundred or a thousand writers who did not know the folkloric tale and told them "Write a continuation," then the hundred or thousand writers would all write different things.

But in the folkloric tale this is not the case. The folkloric tale has regularities, and the people will not move beyond their borders. If there are cases that go outside these regularities (e.g., with literate or well-read tale-tellers), then that kind of departure is not an aesthetic achievement but rather a violation of folktale aesthetics.

Of a thousand possible accidentalities there is always only one, but its forms are extraordinarily various. We will examine a few of these forms.[8]

The wonder tale's composition is defined by the presence of two kingdoms. In one kingdom the tale begins: "In a certain kingdom, in a certain state." Some tale-tellers add, "and that is just the one we live in." This kingdom is opposed to another, located "beyond thrice-nine lands," which is called "the thrice-tenth kingdom." Baba Yaga ("old woman," "hag") is the guard at the border; she guards the entrance into that distant world. The entrance passes through her hut. Beyond its borders is the dark forest (the hut stands on the edge of the forest) and the thrice-tenth kingdom. In long tales, where the hero will encounter a multitude of adventures, the style of the tale changes at the moment when he reaches the little hut. The tale's beginning tends to be realistic (with the exception of the figure of the old king): peasant men and women, a hut, family life and family troubles, mowing and other kinds of agricultural work. From this moment folktale fantasy comes in strongly, and the real peasant world is forgotten. What happens in the little hut?

Baba Yaga lives in a little hut. She is a complex, far from monosemantic personage. When the hero-seeker comes upon Baba Yaga, she gives him an unfriendly welcome. She recognizes him as an enemy by his smell: "Foo-foo-foo! Before now you couldn't smell the Russian odor, couldn't see it. Now the Russian odor lies down in the spoon, rolls itself into your mouth" (Afanas'ev 137).[9] These words already characterize her as belonging not to the human world (Rus') but to some other world. Comparative study of this image shows that Baba Yaga guards the boundary of the other world and the entrance to it. She lets only the worthy pass through. The hero is never disturbed by her welcome. "Hey, old woman, don't scold. Come down off the stove and sit on the bench. Ask me, where are we riding to? I'll tell you a good story."[10] Baba Yaga calms right down at this kind of answer. "Baba Yaga got down off the stove, came right over to Ivan the Bull's Son, bowed low to him."[11]

This is the benevolent type of Baba Yaga, the gift giver and adviser. She shows the hero the path. From now on he knows where to go. Sometimes she gives the hero a magical horse or eagle, which the hero rides to the thrice-tenth kingdom.

This is the basic function of Baba Yaga from the point of view of development of the action. She gives the hero magical objects or a magical helper, and the action moves to a new stage.

Baba Yaga belongs in the broad category of the folktale donor. Meeting with a donor is a canonical form of development of the action. He or she is always met by chance, and the hero earns or somehow otherwise obtains a magical object. Possession of the magical object defines success and the story's outcome. Baba Yaga also behaves as a donor when a stepdaughter finds her way to her. In those cases, however, there is always an extraordinarily stressed moment—the moment of testing. It can also be traced in "male" tales (i.e., the hero is a boy or a man), but in forms that are less clear. Baba Yaga tests the hero or heroine. If the tale is "female," the test has the character of domestic work: making up a bed, beating the featherbed, hauling water, stoking the stove, and so on. In this case the gifts do not bear a magical character but represent material wealth. The tale ends with a reward. The stepdaughter returns home.

We have a somewhat different type of Baba Yaga when she herself drags children to her hut or when lost children come to her hut as they wander. She wants to cook and eat them. The children are always saved; they sometimes manage to stuff her into the oven and, as they run away, they take a magical object that saves them from pursuit and sometimes also some kind of fabulous riches.

Baba Yaga is far from being the only donor. There are figures related to her in character, perhaps representing a weakened form of her. These are all kinds of old women or old men, met by chance, who also point out the road and, even if they do not immediately give a magical object or helper, suggest how to find it (e.g., how to get or raise a magical horse).

But there are also donors of a completely different type. We can count grateful animals among them. The hero is hungry; he is already taking aim at a bird, but she begs him to spare her: "Don't eat me! Some day I'll come in handy." Sometimes the hero does a favor on his own initiative for an animal who is in trouble. He covers fledglings who are getting wet in the rain, pushes a beached whale back into the water, and so on. In all cases there is no direct testing, but nonetheless the hero displays responsiveness, benevolence, which is rewarded. The animals either give him one of their own young or put themselves at his disposal, telling him the words to summon them. In these cases a magical helper once again comes to the hero in the form of an animal.

We have a similar case in the tale "The Magic Ring." The hero buys a cat and dog from boys who are torturing them. The cat and dog turn out to be magical and subsequently help the hero win a princess. In other cases the hero sees a man who cannot pay back a debt and frees him from execution or torture. The redeemed debtor turns out to be an all-powerful helper. More rarely, the hero buries a dead man whom people refuse to bury, and he acquires his helper in the person of the grateful dead man. In the tale of Eruslan this corresponds to the head under which the hero finds the sword.

In all these cases, the magical helper or magical object is given as a reward. But they can also be obtained by craft (see later).

There is no need to list all the relevant characters here. The important point for us is to establish that they all belong to one category from the point of view of the action: With their help, the hero receives a magical object, and he is also sometimes preliminarily subjected to a test (the functions of the test and receiving the magical object).[12]

Let us look at a few examples of the hero's test and reward. There are a great many of them. (Several are cited in *Morphology of the Folktale*.)[13] It is not a matter of listing as many cases as possible but of understanding the given motif's part in the composition. This moment is not merely formal. The folktale is a creation of the most ancient times, but it contains a certain unconscious life philosophy of the people represented by the tale-teller. In the folktale, strictly speaking, everything is predetermined. The hero gets his hands on a magical object or magical helper and with its help achieves all his goals. This may sound like fatalism. But no, it is not fate at all. When the hero leaves home, he cries, he does not know where to go or what to do; he meets someone or something on his way. These meetings are quite various, and the hero may react to the future donor's actions in different ways.

Here we should point out that there is one more category of character: the false hero. This may be, for example, the blood daughters of the stepmother, the hero's older brothers, smart people, or any kind of people in general. They react to the donor's actions not as the hero does, but negatively. Thus, for example, when they find their way to Baba Yaga or Jack Frost, the blood daughters cannot and do not do anything; they answer arrogantly. In the tale of Sivko-Burko the older brothers refuse to sit on the father's grave. The hero does not know he is being tested. We may generalize: Each encounter in life, even the most fleeting, can be considered a test. We are surrounded everywhere with testers and people being tested; all our life at any moment is a test.

The folk consciousness divides all heroes only into positive real ones and negative false ones. There is nothing in the middle. The negative hero is punished; the positive one rewarded.

Moreover, sometimes the hero reacts first negatively but then positively; that is, the hero does not at first show his positive qualities. Such cases would seem to violate the laws of folktale poetics, but this is not so. They lend a lifelike truthfulness to the images of the heroes. Let us cite an example. A peasant's son has set out to fulfill the errand of a childless king: "Who could serve as doctor so the queen will become pregnant?" but he himself does not know how to do this. "He runs into an old woman, who says, 'Tell me, peasant's son, why are you so thoughtful?' He answers her, 'Be quiet, you old bat, don't bother me!' Then she runs ahead and says, 'Tell me your heavy thought; I am old, I know everything.' He thinks, 'Why did I scold her? Perhaps she does know something.'" He tells her about his misfortune, and she gives him advice: He must catch a golden-winged fish and give it to the queen to eat (A-T 519; Afanas'ev 136). The fact that the peasant's son answers rudely in his haste does not yet make him a negative hero. He regrets his rudeness, and from that moment his fate changes.

However, cases in which the hero acts first negatively and then positively are still quite rare; we must search for them. Psychologization and repentance are not in the style of the folktale. These external violations, however, represent an undoubted artistic achievement. They break up the schematicism; they lend the hero's character a lifelike verisimilitude.

The hero's character is fully clarified only at the end of the folktale, but we should linger now on several typical traits of this image.

In the wonder tale the hero is either a tsar's son or a peasant. This has no influence on the development of the action. The hero's external appearance is never described, but the listener imagines him as handsome. He is an idealized hero. His fundamental characteristic is generosity. He acts not for himself, not for his own benefit, and not in his own name. He always sets someone free, rescues someone. Even when he is looking for a bride, he finds a girl in trouble, enchanted, captive, in the power of a dragon. He frees her, saves her—he earns his princess. These qualities are not asserted directly in words anywhere. They flow from the action. In Pushkin's "Tale of Tsar Saltan" we find "You, prince, are my savior, / My powerful rescuer." The swan princess says this to the prince once he kills the kite, actually a sorcerer and enchanter who had her in his power.

The situation and motif—rescuing a girl from a monster's power—are entirely folkloric, but these words could never be said in folklore. The folkloric tale is modest, restrained, chary of words and praise, and the hero achieves his feats simply, without words, as something that is understood, and he never demands or receives any kind of praise.

When we have three brothers, the hero is always the youngest. He is a fool, despised by everyone; he sits on the stove, in the cinders, in the dirt. He is called Ivan Behind-the-Stove, Ivan Cinders. The heroine is sometimes (primarily in tales from Western Europe) named Cinderella, from "cinders," or Dirty-Face (Zamarashka). But unprepossessing external form is an envelope that contrasts with unusual internal beauty—spiritual strength, nobility. This is revealed when the hero is tested; it also appears in his further actions. The older brothers, the clever ones, never withstand the tests. They always suffer defeat, which springs from their internal lack of moral foundation; they think only of themselves, of the reward. The same applies to the old woman's blood daughters, who are opposed to the stepdaughter. They set off into the forest as she did, hoping to receive the same reward, but they do not withstand the test, and instead of a reward, they earn a harsh and well-deserved punishment. How is the hero tested? It is easiest of all to establish this in the "female" folktales. In the tale "Baba Yaga" (A-T 480 = AA 480*B, *C; Afanas'ev 102), a witch orders a girl to spin "a big basket of material, to stoke the stove, to provision everything." This is a test of housekeeping abilities, so important in peasants' everyday life. But that is not the main thing after all. The work is too much for her. She cries, but then little mice appear; she feeds them, and the mice help her. A variant of this tale says that the girl, before going to Baba Yaga, stops by to see her aunt, and the aunt gives her advice: "My niece, a birch tree will whip into your eyes there—you tie it back with a ribbon. The gate will squeak at you there and slam—you pour a little oil on its hinges. There the dogs will try to bite you—you throw them a bit of bread. The cat will scratch at your eyes there—you give it a bit of ham" (A-T 480*E; Afanas′ev 103). The girl does all this and acquires helpers, who help her withstand the test. Here there is an adviser. But there are no advisers, for example, in the tale "Jack Frost." Jack Frost wants to freeze the girl, but she answers him meekly and patiently ("It's warm, dear Jack Frost! It's warm, father!"), and he lets her go and rewards her. Her stepsisters react in an entirely different way; they scold each other with bad words ("sleepy mug," "dirty snout"), and they answer Jack Frost's questions with "You go to the devil! Are you blind? Look, our hands and feet are frostbitten" and "Get lost, go to all the devils in the ravine, disappear, you cursed one!" (A-T 480 = AA 480*B; Afanas′ev 95). In the tale "Baba Yaga" (A-T 480*B; Afanas′ev 102), the blood daughter hits the mice with a rolling pin. She behaves similarly in other variants of this tale. What qualities does the heroine reveal? Thrift, industry, restraint, endurance, patience, modesty, meekness, readiness to do a favor and to help. The stepmother's blood daughters have the opposite traits: reluctance to work, laziness, rudeness and lack of self-control, impatience, arrogance, self-love, egotism. All these are probably later introductions. Folktale heroes are not psychologically elaborated characters; they are types who pass through all the plots. In all the tales of the cycle about the stepmother and stepdaughter the positive type is one and the same. It reflects the ancient ideals of the Russian peasant. To the present day, these ideals are distinguished by beauty, wholeness, and persuasiveness.

This female ideal matches the ideal of the male hero. We have already seen that in the tale of Sivko-Burko the hero displays honor and love for his father, whose last request he sacredly fulfills. The father rewards him with a magical horse. In the tales of the grateful dead man, the hero rides on the dead head, the skull. He piously buries this skull, and then the grateful dead man becomes his invisible helper. It is curious that we have the same motif in the *bylina* of Vasilii Buslaevich. But Vasilii Buslaevich is a rebel. He smirks and kicks the dead head with his foot, then trips over the grave and perishes. His death is tragic. In the magical fairytale there is no rebellion, and there is nothing tragic in the moment of the test.

The motif of grateful animals is widely distributed. The hero is hungry; he takes aim at a bird, meaning to kill it, but it begs for mercy, and he spares it. In another tale he sees fledglings getting wet in the rain, and he covers them with his cloak. The bird gives the hero a fledgling, who later turns out to be magical, an all-powerful helper of the hero. He sees a whale stranded on the seashore. He pushes it into the water, and the whale later helps him travel to the thrice-tenth kingdom. In the tale of Emelia the Fool, Emelia catches a pike. It begs him to let it go, the fool does so, and it later becomes his helper. By the pike's order Emelia gains everything he wants and ends up marrying the tsar's daughter. In the tale "The Magic Ring" the hero asks his mother for permission to go out of the house. She gives him a hundred rubles. He sees people beating a dog and pays all he has to buy it, the whole hundred rubles. Another time he meets boys who are taking a cat to drown it. He buys the cat for a second hundred rubles; that is, he does an unreasonable, "foolish" thing. His mother drives him away from home, and the cat and dog become his prescient helpers; they help him find the princess's ring and the princess herself (A-T 675; Afanas'ev 165–167 [283]).

I have taken a few choice examples, but they already clearly show the kinds of qualities the hero reveals upon being tested. First and foremost, this is the quality opposite to egoism. It is the ability to understand another creature's condition and suffering, compassion for the oppressed, the weak, those who need help. It is a kind of humaneness. The hero fully reveals his traits later, in the course of the action. We already know that he always acts as a rescuer, a savior, and here he knows no fear or doubt. One may presume that the hero's lofty human qualities represent later accretions. Along with these high moral qualities, the hero sometimes reveals unusual physical qualities, which are essential for completion of the feat. He alone, for example, can move the rock covering the entrance to the underground world where the princess he seeks is to be found. His brothers cannot do it. He lifts, throws aside, and catches in flight a heavy beam, which his brothers cannot lift. But there are also quite different cases. He masters his magical object not only by withstanding a test but also by way of deception and craftiness (A-T 530, Afanas'ev 184; A-T 518, Afanas'ev 562; A-T 566, Afanas'ev 192).

The problem of craftiness is one of the most complex problems of folktale poetics. Craft is the weapon of the weak versus the strong. Therefore craftiness in the folktale is not only not condemned but becomes heroic. The motif of the arguers belongs here, for example. In a forest the hero meets two giants or two forest spirits who cannot figure out how to divide marvelous things they have found in the forest between them: a tablecloth that lays itself with food, a flying carpet, seven-league boots, an invisibility hat. The hero sets about making peace between them and says, "Run down this road as fast as you can, and whoever overtakes the other after three miles will get the whole trove." While they are running, he takes the wonderful objects himself, sits on the flying carpet, and flies away (A-T 518; Afanas'ev 562). From our point of view, the hero's morality in this case is not entirely above reproach, but the motif reflects the morality of a different era, when a weak person could prevail in the difficult struggle with nature and power only by trickery. In these cases the tricked ones are always stronger than the hero. They are not ordinary people but forest spirits or giants. But the weak person turns out to be stronger than giants and forest spirits. Later, when we study animal tales and novellistic tales (Chapters 4 and 6), we will see that deception and fooling someone compose their primary plot axis. There we will attempt to find an explanation for this. Now we can simply say that the hero or heroine with a morally elevated image is a later layer in comparison with the hero who achieves success by any means. The hero of the wonder tale achieves success without particular effort, thanks to the fact that he has a magical object or a magical helper at hand. This object, as we know, is given to him, passed along. He meets the donor by chance, but the magical equipment of the hero is no accident. He has earned it. In this way, the high moral qualities of the hero are not an addition; they enter organically into the logic and structure of the narration.

Magical Helpers and Magical Objects

The hero meets the donor, as we can see, by chance. This is the canonical form of the donor's appearance. The transfer of a magical object or magical helper introduces a new character. If it is a living creature—a person, a spirit, an animal—it can be called a magical helper. If it is an object, then it is a magical object. They function in the same way. Thus both a horse and a flying carpet take the hero to another kingdom. The most ancient form of magical helper is, without a doubt, a bird, in the folktale usually an eagle or some fantastic bird. The bird is an ancient cult animal. People assumed that after death a person's soul turned into a bird or flew away on a bird. The hero sometimes has to feed the bird. This helper's only function is to carry the hero to the thrice-tenth kingdom. The bird is a zoomorphic form of helper; there are many of these in folktales.

We encounter the eagle relatively rarely, but we come upon the magical horse far more often. It is not possible to give a full analysis of this image here.[14]

The folktale horse is a hybrid creature, combining a horse and a bird. He is winged. The cult role of the bird passed on to the horse when the horse was domesticated. Now it is no longer a bird that carries the souls of the dead but a horse. But it must have wings in order to fly in the air. Along with that, its nature is fiery. Smoke pours from its ears, sparks scatter from its nostrils, and so on. It also reveals traits of a chthonic nature. Before it begins to serve, it is under the ground. It has a link with the world after death. There are tales in which the hero receives the horse from his dead father.

The horse's functions are fairly various. The first is carrying the hero through the air, over thrice-nine lands, to another kingdom. Later he helps the hero vanquish a dragon. He is wise, prescient; he is the hero's true friend and adviser.

Grateful animals also belong among the zoomorphic helpers. We have already spoken of the way they are acquired. Baba Yaga may also give or loan the hero the most various helpers, such as a wolf, a vixen, or a frog. It is as though zoomorphic helpers represent a particular category.

Another group is made up of anthropomorphic helpers of a fantastic character. These are all kinds of experts with an unusual ability or art, such as Gorynia, Dubynia, and Usynia, who move mountains and forests and stop rivers. Furthermore, Studenets can cause an unusual frost, Ob″edalo and Opivalo can eat whole bulls and drink forty barrels of wine at a time, Begoun runs so fast that he has to have one leg tied, and others.

Finally, a third group of helpers includes invisible spirits, sometimes with peculiar names (Shmat-Razum [Rag-Sense], Nevidim [Invisible], etc.). They appear when called; and to call them, you must know the formula of incantation, turn a magic ring, and the like. A horse is summoned either with the formula "Stand before me like a leaf before grass" or with the help of tinder. The devil may also be an invisible helper who suddenly appears.

This, of course, does not exhaust the list of helpers. We indicate here only their broadest groups.

The helpers, for all their variety, are united by functional identity; that is, they complete one and the same action in various forms. We shall see later what it is that their help to the hero represents.

Magical objects can be united with magical helpers in a single category. In the folktale objects act just like living beings, and from that point of view they can conditionally be called characters. Thus the self-cutting sword slashes the dragon itself or the ball of twine unrolls and shows the way.

If the world is rich in magical helpers, then the quantity of magical objects is almost infinite. There is no object that cannot play the role of a magical object in some circumstance. Here we find tools (sticks, axes, canes), various weapons (swords, guns, arrows), means of transportation (boats, carriages), musical instruments (pipes, fiddles), clothes (shirts, hats, boots, belts), jewelry (rings), and household objects (tinder, a whisk broom, rugs, tablecloths), and so on.

This peculiarity of the folktale, namely, that an object may function like a living being (along with its other peculiarities), defines the character of its fantasticality.

If the images of magical helpers and magical objects are extremely various, their actions, on the contrary, are extremely limited. The monotony of these actions is concealed or colored by the variety of actors and forms of action.

Speaking a priori, the hero should be able to demand countless and quite various services of his magical helper. However, this does not happen. The hero makes use of his helper with strictly limited goals.

Observing the fate of the fairytale hero, we are obliged to assert his complete passivity. Everything is done for him by his helper, who turns out to be all powerful, all knowing, or prescient. The hero sometimes even spoils things rather than helping. He often does not obey his helpers' advice or violates their prohibitions and thereby brings new complications into the course of the action, as in the tale of the Firebird. Nonetheless the hero, once he has received the magical object, is no longer following his nose. He feels confident, he knows what he wants, and that means he will reach his goal.

But here we should utter one caveat. The hero does not walk so much and so often as he flies through the air. This is the first function of the helper or the magical object. They bring the hero through the air over enormous distances. Consequently, we can identify the function of transportation. The object of his quest is located "over thrice-nine lands," in the "thrice-tenth kingdom." The fairytale composition is founded to a significant extent on the existence of two worlds: one the real one, here, and the other the magical, the fairytale, that is, the unreal world, where all earthly laws are suspended and different ones obtain.

Although this other world is quite distant, it is possible to reach it in a moment if one possesses the proper means. The horse or eagle carries the hero over forests and seas, or he flies away on a flying carpet or in a flying ship or on a boat that sails through the air. The speed of flight is especially stressed when the hero is carried on the shoulders of the devil, the forest spirit, or some invisible spirit. Then his hat flies off in the wind.

However, flying through the air is not the only form of transport. The hero may simply ride on a horse or sail on a ship or even go on foot. In all cases the other kingdom is thought of as far away, which is sometimes underlined by details (iron footwear and the like). The other kingdom may be located not only far away, across the sea over thrice-nine lands, but also deep under the ground or under the water or, on the contrary, high in the mountains. In such cases the hero is lowered on straps or cables or else climbs up a ladder.

We will briefly identify the function of taking the hero into another kingdom as transport. Transporting the hero is one of the basic functions of the helper.

The Outcome

The thrice-tenth kingdom is never concretely described. It differs in no external way from our own. There "the light is the same as with us; and there are fields, and meadows, and green groves, and the sun is warm" (Afanas'ev 222). Sometimes this kingdom is represented by a city. "There the dark-blue sea spread out before her, broad and spacious, and there in the distance the golden cupolas on the high chambers of white stone burned like the glow of a fire" (Afanas'ev 235). Nevertheless, it is still "other." A terrible tsar or a tsar-maiden rules it. It is not always populated by human beings: Sometimes it is a serpent kingdom. The abductors of a girl—an eagle, a falcon, a raven—carry her away to their avian kingdom, the bear to the bear kingdom, and so on. Here the hero must meet with the abductors or possessors of the object or person he is searching for. His antagonist is located here, and here too is the object of his quest. In this kingdom he will be impressed by unusual palaces (Afanas'ev 128–130). The palace is sometimes guarded by dragons or lions; the palace and garden may be surrounded by a high wall, with strings stretched over it.

Here the hero is destined to do battle with his opponent. The clearest form is fighting a dragon. The motif of fighting a dragon is international, but the Russian folktale preserves it in a vivid and relatively developed form. Victory over the dragon would also be impossible without a helper or a magical weapon. The horse often tramples the dragon with its hooves.

Following the development of the action, we can identify the function of the battle or struggle and victory. Victory over the dragon marks the liberation of the girl it abducted or captured. The given function is paired with the function of abduction; that is, it can be viewed as a resolution.

And in fact, if the goal of the quest is some kind of object—a thing or a wonder (a firebird, the apples of youth, the water of life, and the like)—then getting what is sought, as a rule, is followed by the return. Battle or struggle is not an obligatory element in these cases. Naturally, obtaining the person, the princess, the mother, the girl proceeds from the course of action as a result of victory. But when there is no struggle (for the most part this is linked with a situation where lack is the motivator or complication), the sought-after object must be obtained somehow and carried away. If we look closely at the form of winning it, we will see that it represents a theft. The whole task consists in fooling the guards, putting to sleep or taming the lions and dragons, or not waking them, not touching the strings that are tied along the bottom of the wall. The hero always seizes his booty himself, whereas the helper usually tells him how to do it. Not only objects may be stolen; people can be stolen too. Thus, to steal the princess, a horse turns into an old beggar and begs for alms. "While the lovely maiden was taking out her purse of money, Ivan the peasant's son jumped out, grabbed her in his arms, covered her mouth so tightly that she could not make even the slightest sound" (A-T 531; Afanas'ev 185).

Abduction is not the only basic form of the outcome, although it is the leading one. With a magical helper or object, the hero undoes the original misfortune in forms that correspond to the plot opening. The abducted or sought-after one is stolen, the enchanted one is freed from enchantment, the murdered one comes back to life, the captive is liberated, and so on. Here the hero reveals his heroism, his craftiness, wisdom, and aptitude. The fact that this is always done by magical means does not cheapen his heroism at all. It is a special, specifically folktale heroism, distinct from the heroism of epic poetry, which bears a completely different character.

We have been able to establish that winning the girl has a dual character. She is either freed (and then happy to be rescued when the hero appears) or, on the contrary, she is taken by force. This has no significance for the composition of the tale. In both cases a marriage follows, but this marriage is sometimes prepared by special actions, which represent the onset of complications.

Complications

In cases where the hero finds a princess who has been captured by a dragon and talks with her while waiting for the dragon to fly back, he sometimes falls into a *bogatyr'*'s sleep, from which it is impossible to wake him. "Princess Martha had a little pen knife, she took it and cut Prince Ivan on the cheek. He awoke, leapt up, did battle with the dragon," and so on. The significance of this is specified only afterward: She recognizes the hero by the little scar. We can establish the function of marking the hero. Sometimes the princess binds up his wound with her handkerchief and afterward recognizes him by that handkerchief. In essence, we have here a concealed or preliminary form of betrothal. We see the same effect when the hero is given a ring by which he is later recognized. The same function is carried out later in completely different conditions, namely, when he carries out a difficult task. He flies up to her window on a horse. "He flew about the tsar's courtyard, so that he broke all twelve windows and kissed the princess Peerless Beauty, and she put a brand right on his forehead" (A-T 530 A; Afanas'ev 183). In these cases she either kisses him on the forehead or strikes him with a sealing ring; hence a golden star begins to burn on his forehead.

This function is already the harbinger of some kind of complication, separation, although this complication, even in the presence of the function of marking, is far from an obligatory element.

Having gained the object of his quest, the hero returns. We establish the function of return. The return may lead to arrival back home, and with that the tale ends. But this is often not the case. Return sometimes takes the character of flight, which is directly linked with abduction as the form of the feat. On the return path the hero may be subject to a chase, from which he is always successfully saved. The forms of persecution or pursuit may be quite various. The chase may occur earlier as well, when the hero reaches the hut of Baba Yaga and after that (usually when children are the heroes) goes home. Baba Yaga flies after the hero, but he has stolen her comb, a pebble, and a towel, which he throws behind him so that they turn into a forest, mountains, and water. Sometimes flight and pursuit accompany a series of consequent transformations into various animals. This form is most often encountered in tales of the crafty knowledge type. A sorcerer chases the hero in the form of a wolf, a pike, a man, a rooster. A dragoness flies after the hero, opening her maw from earth to sky, and tries to swallow him. We must also consider as a special form of pursuit the case where dragons' wives stand on the heroes' path, turning into various tempting objects: an apple tree, a well with a silver drinking horn (A-T 325; Afanas'ev [235] 249–253). The hero slashes at these wells, gardens, and other tempting objects with his sword, and they bleed.

But even after successful rescue from a chase, the hero's fate is still not decisively settled. True, he arrives home, or more accurately, comes to the gates of the city or some field not far from his home, and so on. To his misfortune, his unsuccessful and worthless brothers are there. For some reason (the folktale is not concerned with rational motivation) the hero lies down to rest right here and falls asleep. The brothers quickly steal all his booty (the bride, marvelous object, etc.), and they either kill him or throw him into a deep abyss.

Here the folktale, in essence, begins over again. The misfortune that occurred to the hero is now just the same kind of plot opening as in the beginning. Development proceeds in the same manner. The hero once again acquires and applies a magical object, and so on. This means that a folktale can consist of two or more parts, which may be called moves. It is as though a second round, or pass, or circle of actions begins. It leads once again to the hero's return. This time the hero actually arrives at home but does not announce himself. He stops at the home of some shoemaker or goldsmith or the like or enters the king's service as a stable boy, a cook, a gardener, and so on. We establish this function as unrecognized arrival.

Meanwhile his brothers or the other false heroes, having claimed his booty and his bride, also claim his rights: They pretend to the hand of the princess. This is the function of the pretensions of the false hero. In another form, we have just the same thing in cases when a hero fights and kills a dragon, and the episode is witnessed by some general or water carrier hiding in the bushes. The hero falls asleep, and the false hero abducts the rescued princess and passes himself off as the victor.

The Difficult Task

The princess does not marry the thief in either case. To get rid of the false hero, she demands fulfillment of several conditions, knowing that for the false hero they are unrealizable. They can be carried out only by the real hero, who has magical means in his possession. The purpose of the difficult task is not only to frighten away the false hero but also to discover, attract, or find the real hero.

The motif of the difficult task is one of the most popular and varied motifs in the magical tale. The given motivation (to find the real hero) is only one of many possible motivations. In the tale "Sivko-Burko" the task is brought forward in the form of a summons to all the people. It may proceed without any antagonistic attitude toward the false groom and without antagonism toward any future groom. This is underlined by the complete inaccessibility and unreachability of the bride. In such a case the task may be assigned not by the princess but by her father.

The tasks are extraordinarily various. Functionally they are united by one trait: They can be performed only by a hero who possesses the very same magical object or helper that corresponds to the task. Thus the presence of a flying horse is linked with the task of kissing the princess on her balcony from horseback. The presence of helpers such as Frost-Cracker, All-Eater, All-Drinker, Hawkeye, Adept, and the like is linked to the task of sitting in a hot bathhouse while Frost-Cracker freezes it; eating an enormous quantity of bulls, which All-eater consumes with ease; building a castle with the fine young men from the magic ring, and so on. I cannot list all the tasks known to the folktale here. I will note only a few. One such task is to get hold of the wedding dress, ring, and slippers that the princess had in another kingdom. The hero is tested with riddles, he must demonstrate his ability to hide, he must enter a contest with a *bogatyr'*-maiden, milk a herd of wild mares, obtain seventy-seven mares, build a palace in a single night and the bridges to it, and so on. In all cases it is the magical armament of the hero that is being tested. Because the hero possesses this magic preparedness, he always manages to carry out the task.

It is essential to note that the motif of a difficult task is not compatible with the motif of fighting a dragon or the forms of battle that correspond to it. According to this trait, we can establish two types of tales: those that develop through the motif of the battle and those that develop through the motif of the difficult task. If they are combined in one text, then the tale always forms two moves; the first develops through a battle and the second through a difficult task. We can establish a third type as well, which includes neither of these motifs—for example, the cycle of tales about stepmothers and stepdaughters. This observation could serve as the foundation for a scholarly classification and systematization of the magical tale.[15]

Marriage and Crowning of the Hero

The tale can now proceed to the marriage and crowning of the hero. But there are still some undeveloped motifs that demand to be carried to the end.

The fulfillment of a difficult task, naturally, leads to recognition of the hidden hero. He may be recognized by the brand on his forehead, by a star, a scar, a handkerchief, and so on. The false hero, on the contrary, is exposed and punished. The punishment is always mentioned briefly, whereas the exposure, on the contrary, is sometimes elaborated in complex forms, to the point where everything is told from the beginning in the presence of the false hero, who is exposed by that very story.

Now there are no more impediments to the final outcome. The hero actually gets married and becomes the tsar. Before this he has sometimes changed his appearance, his external looks, in a magical way (transfiguration). For example, he crawls through the ears of a horse or bathes in boiling milk and emerges young and handsome. The marriage usually goes along with his crowning as tsar. There is one obstacle to becoming the king, however, and that is the old tsar, the princess's father. This obstacle is either avoided by having the old tsar and the young heir divide the kingdom in half, so the hero inherits the whole kingdom only after the natural death of the tsar, or else it is removed in a most decisive way: The old tsar is killed. Although such a case is relatively rare, we must still establish it as one that exists and proceeds naturally from the whole situation.[16]

Unity of Composition and Variety of Plots

Such is the internal structure and composition of the magical folktale. The schema laid out here is the unit of measurement by which folktales can be defined as wonder tales, not by eye and not approximately but with adequate scholarly accuracy. Wonder tales are distinct from others not in the feature of fantasticality or magic (other kinds of tales can also have these traits) but in their particular traits of composition, which other kinds of tales do not possess.

Thus the composition of wonder tales is always one and the same. Their uniformity, their regularity, resides in this. Not all the functions are present in all cases. More accurately, the fullness of functions is established only by way of comparison. The choice of function and of its form defines the plot; that is, the given compositional schema includes an enormous quantity of various plots, built on a single foundation. So, tales of stepmothers and stepdaughters are built on exile (the original misfortune), sending away, testing, reward and punishment, and return. Other tales, such as tales of battling dragons, are built on abduction, summoning a hero, sending off, battle with the dragon, and return. The third kind, exemplified by the tale of Sivko-Burko, is founded on the difficult task, testing and reward, solving a problem, marriage and becoming tsar, and so on. In this way, we see that uniformity of composition allows a broad space for creativity.

It is remarkable, however, that the genuine folkloric Russian tale, taking broad advantage of all the genre's creative possibilities, never violates the law of uniformity itself. This means that the wonder tale represents a kind of unity, that its plots are connected to one another. Therefore the methods of the Finnish school, which divides the complete material of folktales into plots (Aarne's index) and studies the plots in isolation, is defective in its foundation. Quite the contrary, all the plots are most intimately connected with one another and should be studied in that connection; study by individual plot is possible only on a foundation of study among plots. What has been laid out here may be called a syntax of the folktale. Just as a sentence falls into its component parts and a philologist must be able to distinguish the component parts of any sentence, so the folklorist must be able to distinguish the component parts of any folktale.

Examples of analyses: "The Magic Swan-Geese" (Afanas'ev 64); "Sivko-Burko" (Afanas'ev 105) (from Propp, *Morphology of the Folktale*, p. 106).

Sivko-Burko

Once there lived an old man, he had three sons. The third son, Ivan the Fool, did nothing; he only sat on the stove in the corner and snuffled (cinders, stove, ancestors). . . . The father began to die (not separation) and said, "Children! When I die, you each in turn come to my grave to sleep for three nights" (not Z-R, D-G, brought ahead), and died. . . . They buried the old man. Night comes; the big brother has to spend the night on the grave, but he's lazy, or else he's afraid, so he says to the little brother, "Ivan the Fool! Go to our father's grave, spend the night for me. You aren't doing anything." . . . The father asks who is sitting there. "Here, my son, is a good horse for you. And you, horse, serve him as you have served me." The old man said this, and he lay back down in his grave. . . . Suddenly a summons from the tsar: if anyone can pull the princess's portrait from the house through so-and-so many beams, that one will marry her.

At that time word came from the tsar that his daughter Elena, the beautiful princess, had ordered that a temple with twelve columns, with twelve crowns, be built for her; she will sit in that temple on a high throne and will wait for her bridegroom, a worthy young man, who on a flying horse, at one leap, can kiss her on the lips.

In the morning the tsar issues a summons: "Whoever can kiss my daughter princess Dear-Face on the lips while jumping up to the third floor on his horse, I will marry her to that man." (Note the transfiguration.)

Ivan mounted the horse, waved his hand, kicked with one foot, jumped up all three stories high, and kissed the tsar's daughter on the lips; she struck him on the forehead with a golden seal-ring. (Note that the external appearance of Ivan is unknown; he is only necessary for his service.) …

The next day the tsar ordered a feast for the whole world, and the princess began to look for her fated bridegroom. The fool came into the tsar's palace and crept in behind the stove. (Unrecognized arrival.) She went around all of them, brought them food, glanced behind the stove, and saw the fool: his head tied round with a rag, snot dripping down his face. (She recognizes the brand. Recognition. Sometimes there is a star on his forehead.)

Finally, there is the marriage, but there is no coronation.

Other Artistic Means of the Wonder Tale

We have examined the folktale from only one of its angles—from the angle of composition, as this turns out to be the decisive one for the wonder tale. But this does not exhaust its study. The folktale can also be studied from the point of view of language and style. People usually see the distinctiveness of folktale style in the way the wonder tale is larded with repeating formulas, among which introductory and concluding formulas attract particular attention. Several works have been devoted to these formulas.[17] However, even the most painstaking comparison and study of these formulas will not advance our understanding of the folktale if we do not assume the historical point of view. These formulas are not devices but indicators of a certain attitude toward reality. The introductory formula, as indicated, removes the tale from the sphere of real time and real space. This defines its fantasticality—its character and style. The study of concluding formulas should also be carried out in a framework of broad comparative-historical analysis. Some peoples, for example, have tales that end completely unexpectedly with the words, "I ran away." The narrator himself ("I"), who remains as a rule in the shadows in the wonder tale, always figures in these formulas. Along with this, these formulas contain a rejection of what is narrated in humorous and various forms. We can explain this only by the fact that the contents of the story once represented something sacred and forbidden. When this taboo ceased to be in effect, formulas were created whose original goal was to protect the reader from the possible consequences of this violation. When the Russian folktale says, "and I was there," this can be understood as a humorous attitude, whose primeval meaning was

"I was not there," because, of course, no one believes that "I was there." The formula "[the mead] ran down my moustache but did not get into my mouth" expresses in joking, reinterpreted form precisely the narrator's lack of participation at the final moment of the story and thus in the whole story.

In just the same way the other formulas of the folktale canon are not formulas at all in the proper sense. So, the formula of summoning a horse—"Stand before me as a leaf before the grass"—if given historical study, may turn out to be an incantation. As we shall see later, we have the formula of Baba Yaga meeting the hero, and her dialogue with him reflects extremely ancient ideas, connected with the fear of death and the guardians of the threshold, of entry into the kingdom of death, and so on.

The question of style is linked to the question of folktale images and heroes: Baba Yaga, the horse, the dragon, the grateful animals, and so on. They were all formed in historical layers, each with its own peculiarities (Baba Yaga has a bony leg, the horse breathes fire, the dragon has many heads, etc.), calling up corresponding verbal formulas. The study of formulas cannot proceed in isolation from study of the folktale characters who are characterized by these formulas.

Speaking of folktale style, we must touch on the question of trebling. In a folktale everything is triple. Parents have three sons, the king has three daughters, the princess sets three tasks, battle with the dragon happens three times, the three dragons have three, six, and twelve heads, and so on. Trebling occasionally occurs in other genres too (the *bylina*), but it is rarely encountered there; when it is, it is for the most part in archaic plots (e.g., in the *bylina* of Sviatogor). Trebling is at the origin of the most ancient of all genres, namely, the folktale. It is itself a sign of great antiquity. How can we explain this?

I must admit that I have no clear and convincing key to the question. We must seek an explanation in the history of the numbering system, of counting and sums. Our system is decimal. Up to 10, every figure has its own name. After 10, numbers are formed by adding to 10 ($12 = 2 + 10$) and by multiplying by 10 ($20 = 2 \times 10$). This system seems so simple and natural to us that we imagine it as objectively inherent in the nature of the numbers themselves. However, this system is the result of abstraction, of lengthy work by the human mind. It comes from counting on the fingers; two hands give this system its foundation. Study of the languages of primitive peoples shows that some languages do not possess numbers as abstractions. Thus one boat is signified by one word, two boats by another, and three boats by a third.

The concept of the number as an abstraction arose slowly. It passed from 1 to 2 and from 2 to 3. Human thought paused at this stage for a long time. As Lévy-Bruhl showed (in *Primitive Mentality*),[18] many languages of primitive peoples do not have numbers higher than 3. Three meant "many," as many as it was possible to count. Three became a holy number; it plays a particular role in religions of the whole world, among others in Christianity, where there is not a unitary God but a triune divinity, a trinity, consisting of the father, son, and holy spirit. Briefly, the period of counting by tens followed an extended period of counting by threes. Evidently, the plots of wonder tales were formulated in this very period. All this to some extent explains the constant presence of treblings in the folktale. It explains why they repeat up to three, but it does not explain why it is necessary to repeat at all, why three figures are needed rather than just one. Why does a dragon have three heads, and not one? Why are there three brothers, three tasks, three journeys—why not limit these to happening only once?

I can give only a preliminary answer to this. All the actions in ancient folklore are presented as quite intense, not the sort of thing an ordinary person does. But there are no means for expressing this intensity. The only means is to repeat the action several times.

That is how children or unrestrained people tell stories to this day. Repetition expresses the intensity of the action and also the strength of the speaker's emotional tension. I will limit myself to my own observations.

While an apartment was being cleaned, the couch was moved away from the wall and turned out to have a lot of dust under it. A little girl, about 5 or 6 years old, describing it, spoke this way: "And there it was all dust, dust, dust," and at each repetition she waved her hands up and down. She also composed a little tale like this: "Once there was a rooster and a hen. They lived, lived, lived, lived. . . . Once the little hen went off into the swamp and got lost. The little rooster went to look for her. He looked, looked, looked. . . . But the hen was in another swamp." The repetition of actions in folklore has the same significance as hyperbole. Hyperbole is an exaggeration of measure; repetition of action is a primitive way to express the strength and intensity of these actions and the power of the teller's emotions.

Looking closely into folktale trebling, we can uncover a certain contradiction. Contemporary thinking does not demand repeating thrice. Therefore in tales with three brothers, only one genuinely acts. The trebling takes the shape of the schema 2 + 1, and the three links of the tripling are not equal in their rights. One turns out to be decisive—the last one. So, of three brothers only one is the hero of the narration. The other two brothers serve as a contrasting background for him. Of the princess's three tasks the third is the hardest; of the three battles with a dragon the hardest and decisive one is the third. In all these cases we have the scheme $2 + 1$ (the number of dragon's heads is 3, 6, or 9, which equals 3×1, 3×2, and 3×3; or perhaps 3, 6, or 12, which equals 3×1, 3×2, and $3 \times 2 \times 2$). Occasionally we encounter the schema $3 + 1$. There is no schema $1 + 1 + 1$. In other words, repetition has the character of an increase. This increase is a later addition, when the trinity turns into unity. There is, in essence, only one active link—the last one.

Trebling is one of the questions of folktale style. We cannot resolve all the questions of the style of folktale narration here. We can isolate only some of them, those that are most characteristic.

The question of style is a question of the relationship to reality and to what is narrated. On this level we may permit the question of humor in the wonder tale, for example. The wonder tale possesses a most subtle, entirely characteristic humor, colored by light, warm-spirited irony. The character of this humor should also be investigated in connection with the general theory of the comic. Humor is founded on a certain distorted or transfigured transmission of reality. To an even greater extent, this is the foundation of the character of folktale fantasticality. We attempted earlier to define certain features of this fantasticality: ascribing actions to actors that are not typical for them (animals speak, a ball of yarn shows the way, etc.). This fantasticality too is not a mere poetic device; it is the result of a very complex and protracted process of acquaintance with reality.

This attitude to reality is defined by a worldview. The complex question of the ideology stored up in the folktale is linked first and foremost with the question of the character of the tale's hero himself and which ideals he follows. Upon closer examination, he turns out not to follow the ideals of contemporary life; he expresses the ideals of the distant past, and the artistic and entertaining character of the contemporary wonder tale is a recent phenomenon.[19] In this way, we can see that none of the most important questions in the study of the wonder tale can be solved outside the question of its origin and most ancient foundations.

If we have established the unity of composition of the wonder tale, its single type and persistence, then we should ask, How can this kind of persistence be explained? It is entirely obvious that all the accessories of the wonder tale, all these magical objects—flying horses, fire-breathing dragons, beautiful princesses, and so on—were not thought up by a contemporary peasant but inherited by him. This confronts us with the task of historical study of the folktale. The key to the folktale is not in the present but in the past. The folktale reflects not only contemporary aesthetic tastes and peasant creativity but also the inheritance of earlier eras, and we will have to establish precisely what these are. All further tasks in the descriptive study of the folktale can be resolved in a satisfyingly scholarly way only through the historical approach.

A BRIEF SURVEY OF PLOTS

Earlier, I contrasted the interplot study of the folktale to study of the folktale by plot. Although plots are linked in the tightest possible way, because elements of some plots enter into other plots, and although it is sometimes hard (and at times impossible) to draw a line between plots, plot types still do undoubtedly exist, and we should pause to mention the most important plots of the Russian wonder tale. I have already noted the fundamental series of plots: plots that develop through battle with an opponent, then plots founded on the solution of a difficult task, and, finally, plots that are of neither the first nor the second kind.

I will not touch on the question of classification but will simply select a few vivid artistic plots from each indicated group and linger on them in detail.

Let me begin with the model of the tale of the abduction of the princess and the hero's battle with a dragon (A-T 300 A; Afanas'ev 136). This tale is disseminated throughout the world; numerous Russian versions have been recorded (according to data from 1957, more than forty).[20] The tale has been the object of major research in Kurt Ranke's *Two Brothers*[21] and Edwin Hartland's *Legend of Perseus*. The motif of fighting dragons enters the composition of various plots and it exists in folk books and spiritual verses, but we cannot linger on it now. Let us take only one text as an example, namely, the folktale "Buria-*bogatyr'*, Ivan the Cow's Son" (Afanas'ev 136).

A king and queen have no children. From the formal point of view, the motif of childlessness is an epic enlargement of the original situation. From the ideological and artistic point of view, it expresses the people's aspiration to have children. Why? The folktale formula says, "In youth for amusement, in old age to be fed, and in death—to remember your soul." If we think deeply about this definition, we will understand its whole inner beauty. But here is what is curious. This motif develops according to all the laws of folktale composition. The spouses have been living together for ten years, but they must find a way for the queen to become pregnant. And so, in pure folktale style, they issue a summons: Who can find the cure for childlessness?

The council of princes and boyars cannot think of anything, so a peasant's son takes up the problem, even though he "hasn't even dreamed" of how to remedy this misfortune. He sets out from home to seek the necessary means. We already know that, according to the canon of the folktale, the hero should now be subjected to a test, and in fact he meets an old woman. "Tell me, peasant's son, why are you so pensive?" He answers her angrily, "Be quiet, you old bat, don't pester me," but he regrets it at once. "Why did I scold her? Perhaps she really knows something?" Briefly, the old woman tells him how to catch a golden-tailed pike. "When the king catches it and cooks it and the queen takes a taste, then she will become pregnant with a great child." Cures for childlessness were once widespread, and they go back to the primitive times when the laws of biology were not fully understood. People thought in analogies. All peoples considered fish a particularly strong means of stimulating fertility, because fish produce roe that consists of thousands of individual eggs, from which fish hatch.

All kinds of fruits—apples, nuts, seeds—are in second place, also for entirely understandable reasons. Green peas were particularly highly regarded, because of their ability to cause swelling. A woman who ate peas would soon begin "to get fat" (*Pokatigoroshek*). Fruits and seeds should be given with the proper words; one must only be careful of double nuts, which might cause twins to be born.[22] In our tale they catch the fish, but something unexpected happens. After the pike is cleaned, the washing water is poured out the window and a cow drinks it. They fry the fish, and a servant girl brings the plate to the queen, but on the way she eats the fins. On the same day and at the same hour the queen, the servant girl, and the cow each give birth to one boy— three brothers who all look very much alike: "voice for voice and hair for hair" (*golos v golos i volos v volos*). "Marvelous boys were born." One is called Prince Ivan; the second, Ivan the Servant Girl's Son; and the third, Buria-*bogatyr'*, Ivan the Cow's Son. They grow quickly—not by the day but by the hour, the way "yeasted dough rises." I will leave out the details, but I do want to pause and discuss one of them.

Earlier I said that tripling never falls into a schema of 1 + 1 + 1 but always into a schema of 2 + 1. This explains the quarrel of the three brothers over their superiority. One should be the senior one or the leader, that is, the basic hero. In these cases the brothers each throw a heavy metal beam into the air or—as in "Buria-*bogatyr'*, Ivan the Cow's Son"—a ball, to see who can throw it highest. The senior one turns out to be not the king's son and not the son of the servant girl, but the cow's son. Once again we are dealing with archaic notions. The hero of wonder tales turns out to be an animal's son in other cases too. Thus in "Ivan the Bear-Cub" he is the son of a girl who was abducted by a bear.

So ends this introductory episode. Curiously, it represents a kind of tale within a tale and is constructed according to all the laws of folktale composition: a lack, a summons, setting out, a test, gaining the sought object, return. But this is only the introductory episode; the tale is still to come.

The brothers leave home without any motivation, without any errand. It is obvious that here some element has been omitted. But this gap is not an oversight, not forgetfulness, but an intentional lacuna. The brothers travel "to such places—to the dragon regions, where three dragons ride out of the sea, a six-headed, a nine-headed, and a twelve-headed one." The dragons here have not abducted anyone, and they seem to have done no harm. But they are evil, and the brothers have come to battle this evil. How they came to know about the dragons does not trouble the tale-teller. There is no originating idea here, no preface, only the departure. The logical plot has suffered, but the artistry of the tale is not defined by logic, rather the opposite: Strict logic spoils it.

As I have already said, I am leaving out the details. The tale is very long, befitting a taste for detailed elaboration.

The brothers come to the dragon regions. The landscape is not described, only a snowball-berry bridge. The snowball-berry bridge is a constant detail in this type of tale. I will not attempt to explain it; I will only say that a river is usually imagined as a kind of boundary between worlds. Baba Yaga is at the beginning of the path, and a dragon is at the end. The dragon always lives in water. The bridge is a passage to the dragon regions, and this bridge is guarded by dragons. A hut stands here, recalling the hut of Baba Yaga, but it does not fulfill the same functions. The brothers settle down to spend the night in the hut. For three nights dragons appear, and the hero vanquishes them all while his brothers are sleeping. The third battle is the most terrible. Here is the description: "As the third night approached, Buria-*bogatyr'* prepared to go stand guard. He put a candle on the table, stuck a little knife into the wall, hung a towel on it, gave his brothers a deck of cards, and said, "Play cards, lads, but don't forget about me: when the candle starts to burn down and you see blood gathering in the dish, then run to the bridge as fast as you can to help me." The brothers do not hold out, of course; they fall asleep while Buria-*bogatyr'* battles the dragon alone.

This picture is full of mystery and significance. The towel that drips with blood is one of the fabulous objects into which the hero has placed a part of his essence (a connector). When the hero is in peril, this object begins to drip blood. Now let us imagine the scene: the square window of the hut, a table by the window, and a candle on the table. On each side of the table sit two *bogatyri*, resting their heads on their arms on the table and sleeping deeply. A knife is driven into the wall, a towel hangs on the knife, and blood drips from it into a bowl. It is the hero's blood. Outside the window is a blazing flame. The hero is doing battle there with the dragon. A terrible battle is going on between good and evil, but here the men who are called to take part in it are plunged into a deathlike sleep. The arrival of the dragon and the battle with it are described this way: "Suddenly the duck quacked [*kriaknula*], the banks rang [*zviaknuli*], the sea began to shake [*vzboltalos'*], the sea began to heave [*vskolykhnulos'*]—the marvelous monster [*chudo-iudo*], dangling lip, was climbing out: a twelve-headed dragon." Let us pay attention to the wording. There are three pairs of rhymes.

There is no description of the dragon, but we can imagine it from other folktales. In this case it is mounted on a horse, which does not suit its form and is not encountered in other tales. The hero is also on a horse, moreover a magic one, white and shining. The dragon has a brief dialogue with his horse. It rides out onto the bridge, the horse stumbles under it: "Why do you trip, raven's meat? Or have you sensed an enemy?" The horse is prescient; it understands what people do not understand. "It is our enemy—Buria-*bogatyr'*, the Cow's Son." "Be quiet, the raven hasn't even brought his bones here in a bladder!" To this the hero replies, "You lie, *chudo-iudo*, dangling lip! I've been strolling here for three years now."

This dialogue is full of significance. The dragon somehow knows that he has an enemy. The hero too knows when he rides into the dragon regions that he has an opponent there. It is as though a mortal battle of two forces is predestined. It is as though the fate of a separate hero turns out to be drawn into the fate of the world, where truth and evil, purity and filth, the bright hero and the monster meet, and where victory is always with the hero (St. George the Victorious).

The unclean one does not give in at once. The dragon is killed, but the dragon has a family of his own: his young serpent-wife and her mother, a horrible witch, who will take vengeance for him. Having killed the dragon, the three brothers return home. According to the folktale canon, now we should see pursuit or persecution. One form of persecution consists of an illusion that comes over the brothers. It gets terribly hot, and the brothers ride out into a beautiful meadow with a well in it. And a silver drinking horn is floating in the well. The hero's brothers are about to slake their thirst, but the hero strikes the well with his sword and blood spurts out of it. It is the younger of the two dragonesses, who has taken the form of a well. If the brothers had drunk its water, they would have exploded into bits the size of poppy seeds. The second dragoness turns into a beautiful orchard with juicy fruits, and the third into a hut. If the brothers try to taste the fruits or go into the hut to spend the night, they will be blown into pieces the size of poppy seeds. Here too the hero turns out to be farsighted and prescient. He slashes at the orchard, slashes at the hut, and they spurt with blood—they are the witches, who had taken on those forms. Thus he saves his brothers and himself and drives evil out of the world.

This motif undoubtedly has a deep hidden meaning. It is not the apparent, not the symbolic image of evil, but real evil, which has taken on real forms, and the hero really destroys it.

This is the end of the story, internally. Externally, it continues. The fairytale ending demands that the heroes get married, and so in this tale the heroes find themselves wives (the third move). I will not linger on this continuation. The presence of such an ending can be explained quite simply. The canonical form of folktales about fighting dragons has a hero who, after killing the dragon, rescues a woman, whom he marries. But in this case the battle with the dragon is not for the sake of a woman—it is as though she were removed from the narration but reintroduced in the form of the short story of the marriage of the heroes. They make war against a king who has three daughters, and they win them for themselves in battle. From the artistic point of view this sort of ending looks a bit pallid.

This folktale about Buria-*bogatyr'* is a model for folktales with a battle as the culminating point.

Another series of tales is founded on resolution of some kind of difficult task. There are a great many such tales; we will take only one example: the tale "Elena the Wise" (A-T 329; Afanas'ev 130a).[23] This tale is quite popular in Russia; there are twenty-four recorded versions.[24] It has been the topic of a dissertation in the Federal Republic of Germany (Göttingen). The research was carried out according to the methods of the Finnish school. The author (I. Hartman) knew only twenty-two variants, which clearly does not reflect reality.

This folktale begins not with an ordinary introductory situation but differently. The hero is a soldier. He is standing guard at night by a stone tower. Suddenly he hears a voice from the tower:

"Hey, soldier!"

The soldier asks, "Who's calling me?"

"It's me, the unclean spirit," answers a voice behind an iron grating. "I've been sitting here for thirty years, without anything to eat or drink."

"What do you want?"

"Let me out; when you're in need, I'll be useful to you. Just say my name and that moment I'll appear to help you."

Then and there the soldier tore off the seal, broke the lock, and opened the doors—the unclean one flew out of the tower, soared upwards, and vanished faster than lightning.[25]

What is this element? The formula "When you are in need, I'll be useful to you" recalls the words of grateful animals. This is a test, which here takes the form of a folktale favor. The hero does a good turn for the unclean one and thus acquires him as a magical helper. Here a middle element has been shifted to the beginning. The figure of a soldier, of course, is a more recent one. In just the same way, the figure of the unclean one in the role of a helper is a rethinking of earlier forms. We have something else in variants of these motifs. An eagle is sitting locked up, or a forest spirit or a dragon, that is, a mythological figure, and it is not a soldier who releases it but a prince. But, be that as it may, the hero has acquired for himself a magical helper. Fearing that he has made a mistake that the tsar might punish, the soldier runs away, following his nose. The unclean one offers to take him into service: "In my household you'll have a free life; drink, eat, and relax as much as your soul desires; just look after my daughters—there's nothing else I require."[26]

The soldier agrees. The unclean one grabs him under the arms, lifts him high up in the air, and carries him over thrice-nine lands to the thrice-tenth kingdom, to white-stoned halls. The unclean one has three daughters, all beauties. He orders them to obey the soldier and to give him as much to eat and drink as he wishes, and he himself flies off to do bad things; you know—he's the unclean spirit.[27]

We expect a romance to unfold between the soldier and the devil's daughters, but no, the development is completely different. Everything is going well. The soldier has a wonderful life, but then there is a problem: Every night the girls disappear somewhere. The soldier spies on them through their keyhole and sees the following:

> The beautiful girls took out a magic carpet. They spread it out on the floor, struck the carpet and turned into doves, leapt up and flew out the window. (Disappearance; search.) What a marvel, thought the soldier, let's see, I'll try it too. He jumped into the bedroom, struck the carpet, turned into a robin, and flew out the window after them. The doves settled down in a green meadow, and the robin alit under a currant bush, hid in the leaves, and watched from there. The place was filled with so many doves he couldn't count them; the whole meadow was covered. A golden throne was standing in the middle. A bit later heaven and earth lit up with a great light—a golden chariot was flying through the air, drawn by six fiery dragons. In the chariot sat queen Elena the Wise—so indescribably beautiful that you couldn't even think it up, or guess at it, or tell it in a tale! She got down from her chariot and sat on the golden throne; she began to call the doves over to her one at a time and teach them various wise things.[28]

This whole section is not specific to the given plot.

The image of Elena the Wise is one of the grandest and most splendid images in Russian folktales. This image, undoubtedly, is ancient. It reflects exceedingly archaic concepts of the power of women.

I cannot here go into the essence of the question of matriarchy, that is, of that period in the development of human society when power was in the hands of women, or when woman was in any case considered a wiser and more powerful being than man. The archaic quality of this image is confirmed by the fact that her chariot is drawn by dragons. The dragon is the same kind of dualistic creature as Baba Yaga, but its nature is more markedly hostile to man. At the same time the dragon is a guardian of wisdom, of prescient knowledge. Elena too is not simply a wise woman. She possesses sorcerous knowledge and spells. The soldier loses his spiritual calm.

The robin came to the green meadow, hid under the currant bush, and looked at Elena the Wise, admiring her incomparable beauty and thinking, "If I could have a wife like that, there would be nothing in the world left to desire! Let me fly after her and find out where she lives."[29]

The soldier, in the form of a robin, flies after Elena to her palace and lets himself be caught. Elena puts the robin in a cage and hangs the cage in her bedroom.

The day went by, the sun set. Elena the Wise flew to the green meadow, returned, began to take off her garments, undressed, and lay down in her bed. The robin looked at her white body, at her indescribable beauty, and shook like a leaf. No sooner had the princess fallen asleep that the little robin turned into a fly, flew out of the golden cage, struck against the floor, and turned into a goodly youth. The goodly youth walked over to the princess's bed, looked and looked at her beauty, couldn't resist and smack, kissed her on her sugared lips.

So they begin to become closer, but there are still many obstacles. It seems to Elena that she has had a dream, but the third time she takes her book of magic and sees the truth there: "Ah you ignorant one! . . . Get out of the cage. You'll pay me for your deception with your life!"[30] She calls a headsman with a scaffold. A terrible giant with an axe and scaffold appears and is all ready to cut off the soldier's head. Then the soldier begs with tears, "Let me sing one final song." "Sing then, and be quick about it!"

The soldier started up a song that was so sad, so plaintive, that Elena the Wise herself burst into tears. She became sorry for the good youth, and she told the soldier, "I'll give you ten hours, and if you manage in that time to hide so craftily that I can't find you, then I'll marry you; but if you aren't able to do it, I'll order them to cut off your head."[31]

Here we finally recognize a motif that is widespread in folklore: when a hero who has been condemned to death asks permission to blow his horn or play his fiddle or sing, and so on. The motif's interpretation is clearly not folkloric—it is a bit sentimental. The place where this version of the tale was recorded is not indicated, but one senses an urban setting.

The soldier is helped by the unclean one, whom he had set free. The unclean one turns into an eagle and bears him away to his own place under the sky. But Elena has the book of magic. "Elena the Wise took the magic book, looked, and she saw everything as if it were on the palm of her hand."[32] Then the unclean one turns the soldier into a pin and sticks it into the magic book, behind the pages where she is looking. In variants it is not a magic book but a mirror. He hides behind the mirror, and she cannot see him in her magic mirror—this comes out better. The tale ends this way:

Elena the Wise opened her book of magic, looked and looked, but the book did not show her anything. The princess became angry and threw the book into the stove. The pin fell out of the book, struck the floor, and turned into the goodly youth. Elena the Wise took him by the hand. "I'm crafty," she said, "but you're even craftier!" They did not bother to think it over for long; they got married and began to live together happily.[33]

The words are telling: "I'm crafty, but you're even craftier!" Here we have a competition in magic between the hero and Elena. Elena is strong in the beginning, we would say—strong as a woman who is credited with sorcerous charms. The hero has magical equipment of a different kind. He possesses a helper who does everything for him. Taming a powerful woman before marriage is one of the most widespread motifs of world folklore. The power of woman must be broken, and it is sometimes destroyed in the harshest way; for example, she is tormented with whips. In those cases the woman is depicted as treacherous and dangerous. After entering the marriage, her sorcerous powers disappear; she throws her book into the stove and becomes peaceful. Things happen this way in the *bylina* too: Dobrynia and Il'ia and Dunai come upon a *polesnitsa*, that is, a female *bogatyr'*, riding in the field. They do battle with her, vanquish her, and one marries her, after which the woman loses her power.

A marriage of equals.

The historical foundations of this motif demand special research. We can say only that this is one of the moments in the transition from matriarchy to patriarchy. Woman is deprived of her power.

I have given one model of the tale, based on the assignment of difficult tasks that lead to a marriage. Many tales include this motif. I will name a few and, without going into details, describe them briefly, simply to remind you of them.

Princess Never-Laugh (A-T 559; Afanas'ev 297)

The tsar's daughter never laughs. The tsar promises her hand to the man who can make her laugh. The princes and boyars cannot do it. It is a peasant's son or a merchant who succeeds, helped by grateful animals. The tale is complex and interesting in many respects. I have devoted a specialized study to it, and I would recommend it to anyone who is curious: "Ritual Laughter in Folklore."[34]

In this tale the difficult task is placed in the foreground and used as the opening. Here the difficult task is the equivalent of the form of opening where the hero, for example, is sent in search of something.

Sivko-Burko (A-T 530; Afanas'ev 179)

The tsar promises his daughter to the man who can leap on horseback up to her window in the high tower and kiss her. A fool manages to do this, after sitting for three nights on his dead father's grave and receiving a magical horse from his father in exchange. The princess strikes him on the forehead with a ring. A star begins to burn on his forehead, and the princess recognizes him by that star when he tries to hide himself.

I have already pointed out that the test of the hero here comes from the cult of the dead, in particular, the cult of ancestors.

The Flying Ship (A-T 513 B; Afanas'ev 137–138)

A paper comes from the tsar: "I will give the princess in marriage to the man who can build a flying ship." A fool sets off, meets an old man on the road, and shares his meager rations with him. The old man tells him where and how to fall asleep; when he wakes up, he sees a flying ship and flies off in it. Along the way he sees various tricksters on the earth: Runner, whose leg is detached, because he runs so fast; Sharp-Eyes and Sharp-Ears, who see and hear everything; Archer, who shoots without ever missing; Eater-Up and Drinker-Up, who can eat a whole herd and drink a whole lake; Frost-Freeze, and others. He takes them along on the ship. The princess does not want to marry a peasant: "I'll give him all kinds of difficult tasks." She summons him to a competition in running and shooting, forces him to eat and drink a lot, puts him in a red-hot bathhouse, and so on. The tricksters do all of that for him, and he marries the princess.

Here the motif of difficult tasks even doubles. The tale begins with one, and, in addition, the princess assigns more tasks on her own behalf before entering the marriage. This tale is related to another, the tale of the Seven Simons, or, in folktale style, Simeons.

The Seven Simeons (A-T 653; Afanas'ev 145–147)

A father has seven sons. He sends them to study. One learns to steal, the second to be a blacksmith, the third to shoot well, the fourth to make ships, the fifth to heal wounds, and so on. Although no difficult tasks are formally assigned in this tale, they are still there in essence. The tsar sends the Simeons to get a princess for him.

Each son fulfills some part of this task. The princess, for example, flies away after turning into a swan. The archer shoots her in the wing, and she falls into the water. They catch her, the physician heals her, and so on. She does not want to marry the tsar, because he is old, and she chooses the thief who managed to steal her as her husband.

The Tale of Tsar Berendei (According to the Title Vasilii Zhukovsky Gave It) (A-T 313; Afanas'ev 219–226)

A young man is promised to the water spirit. The tsar bends over to drink, and the water spirit grabs him by the beard and says, "Give me the thing in your house that you don't know," and that turns out to be a newborn son. The water spirit gives the prince a task: "Hello there, my friend! Why have you taken so long to come see me? I got tired waiting for you. Now get to work. Here is your first task: You have one night to build a big crystal bridge, so that it's done in the morning! If you don't build it, off with your head!" The water spirit's daughter, Vasilisa the Wise, helps him. Next, he has to plant a green orchard. "Choose your bride from among my twelve daughters." The prince fulfills everything and runs away with Vasilisa. The water spirit cannot catch up with them.

Pushkin's recording (Pushkin, 1949, III, 458). Used by Zhukovsky.[35]

The motif of difficult tasks is always linked with courtship. However, there may also be no courtship in the direct sense of the word. Thus in this case the hero is not courting, but as he fulfills the tasks, he in essence wins himself a wife.

This link is clearer in the tale "The Little Humpbacked Horse," on which I will not dwell because it is well known in Pëtr Ershov's version (A-T 531; Afanas'ev 169–170). The hero gets hold of a magic pony, which helps him achieve all the tasks the tsar requests: He gets the Firebird for him and the princess and then carries out her orders for the wedding. One of those is bathing in boiling water. He comes out of the water a beautiful man; the tsar tries to do the same thing and perishes. The hero wins the hand of the princess.

Amor and Psyche

I will move along to tales that include neither B-P nor Z-R.[36] In these tales the test takes on a special role. There are two large groups of these tales: tales of the Amor/Cupid and Psyche type and tales involving stepdaughters.

The first group of tales is about a girl who by the will of fate winds up in a monster's power in a luxurious garden or a magic palace. Here we recall Pushkin's "Ruslan and Liudmila," with Liudmila in the power of Chernomor. Unlike Pushkin's long poem, in the folktales the monster turns out to be an enchanted handsome youth, who is freed from his enchantment thanks to the girl. These are tales of the same type as "Cupid and Psyche." They are especially famous in the history of world culture and have undergone literary reworking. One of the most ancient belongs to the Roman author Apuleius, who included the tale in his novel *The Golden Ass, or Metamorphoses.* The name for this tale type comes from his title. Apuleius has a characteristically light, playful tone. Pushkin wrote of him:

Back when in the Lyceum gardens
I was serenely flowering,
I read Apuleius with gusto,
But did not read my Cicero

There are treatments by Molière, Corneille, Lamartine, and Wieland. One reworking of this plot belongs to Jean de Lafontaine in "Les amours de Psyché et de Cupidon," from which Ippolit Bogdanovich borrowed for his "Sweet Soul" (Dushen'ka). Goethe decorated his room with drawings from Apuleius's tale. There are many sculptures (e.g., by Canon and Torvaldsen); one of these is in the Summer Garden in St. Petersburg. The tale of Cupid and Psyche was invested with deep, symbolic meaning. Tales of this cycle are distinguished by particular beauty, and one can understand their popularity, although the tale owes its symbolic interpretations first and foremost to the names: "Amor" means love, and "Psyche" the soul.

These tales form a whole cycle. Among the Russian examples are "The Little Scarlet Flower" and "The Tale of Finist the Bright Falcon." But first I will linger briefly on Apuleius's tale.

Apuleius lived in the second century A.D. (he was born around A.D. 124). Some scholars date the tale to this era. At the same time, Apuleius's tale represents the first, most ancient written record of the folktale, but the tale itself is undoubtedly much more ancient. Apuleius's text is a literary reworking, made by a thinker and philosopher. It allows us to establish which elements of this tale were already present in the second century. As a whole, however, the Russian tale gives a more archaic form of the plot.

Apuleius's characters are the Greek gods of Olympus: Venus, the goddess of earthly love and beauty, and her son Amor (or Cupid); Ceres, the goddess of agriculture and fertility; Jupiter and his spouse, Juno; and others. But this is not evidence of antiquity at all; rather, exactly the opposite. These names are a literary introduction of his own time by a philosopher, an initiate in all the antique cults. As it happens, they have nothing to do with folklore.

Apuleius's plot canvas comes down to the following. A king has three daughters. The youngest of them is distinguished by such beauty that she is given divine honors. This attracts the envious wrath of the goddess Venus. Because she has been given divine honors, no mortal dares to marry her. Then her father asks the oracle and begs the great divinity with prayers and sacrifices for a spouse for his bypassed daughter. The oracle tells him to take his daughter away, decked out in funeral finery, to a high cliff. His son-in-law will be a wild, savage, fierce winged creature whom all the gods fear.[37]

Here we see the curious detail that a girl destined to be married should be dressed in funeral garb. In general, marriage and funeral rituals possess a relationship that is fairly clearly expressed in folklore.

The wind sweeps Psyche off the cliff. In this whole motif, through comparative study of various materials, we can establish that Psyche enters the realm of the dead. But that is from the genetic point of view. In the tale, she winds up in a marvelous garden. The palace and garden are described in great detail. She sees all kinds of dishes and wines on the table and fortifies herself. She hears the voice of an unseen creature, who suggests that she take advantage of all this. She is the mistress of this castle. At night she becomes the wife of this invisible creature and they get to be friends. She converses with him by night.

A great deal of time passes in this way. On the earth her sisters mourn her as if she were dead, and Psyche hears of this (they are on the cliff and she hears their lamentation). She asks her spouse to let her sisters come visit her. He tries to persuade her not to do this but gives in to her. The same wind that brought Psyche now brings her sisters. They see all the marvels and envy her. They begin to speak badly of her spouse, convince her that he is a monster, and advise her to kill him—to light the lamp at night and stab him with a dagger. At the same time, her husband has forbidden her to see him. In the morning he becomes invisible, and she does not know what he looks like. At night Psyche takes a lamp in one hand, a dagger in the other; she lifts the lamp and sees before her not a monster but a most handsome youth. It is Amor, the son of Venus. This is the moment most often depicted in art. The dagger freezes in her hand. A drop of oil falls from the lamp onto the god's shoulder. He wakes up and disappears forever.

Here the first part of the tale ends and the second part begins: the search for the vanished spouse. Before we move on to this part, we must pause over a few details that will help us understand the Russian folktale better and that are also important in their own right. The first thing to note is that in Apuleius's telling Psyche's spouse is not a monster, not a beast. In the folkloric tradition, including the Russian folktale, he *is* a beast. Apuleius presents him as a beast in the text of the prophecy. But prophecies of gods tend to be ambiguous. The prophecy says that he has wings, that he is venomous and evil, that the gods themselves are afraid of him. Flying on his wings through the atmosphere, he brings everything to a state of exhaustion. Yet this is no beast but the winged god of love. Yes, all the gods fear him; yes, he is crafty and treacherous, but he is not a monster.

The artificiality of this motif is immediately obvious. Apuleius was a great mocker of the official religion, and here he is laughing at the practice of fortune-telling, prophecy, and oracles, which were widespread in Greece and Rome. To escape reproach, the priests gave ambiguous answers, which could be interpreted both this way and that.

The second detail concerns Psyche's own feelings. We already know that folktales seem to involve no personal love. Nevertheless, a wife will set off in search of her husband only if she loves him. In Apuleius she is actually pierced by love for her husband when she sees him for the first time and he disappears. According to antique notions, love is inculcated by Amor, or Cupid, the god of love who fires arrows at his victims. He is therefore depicted with a quiver and a bow. Psyche too must be wounded with this arrow. In Apuleius this occurs at the moment when she sees her spouse, sees his quiver and arrows. Apuleius explains this as follows:

At the foot of the bed lay a bow and a quiver of arrows—the beneficent weapon of the great god. The insatiable and curious Psyche could not look away from her husband's weapon, she examined it and touched it, pulled one arrow out of the quiver, tested its point with her fingertip, but, as her trembling made her movements stronger, pierced herself deeply, so that a droplet of scarlet blood stood out on the surface of her skin. Thus, without knowing it herself, Psyche began to burn with love for the god of love.[38]

Here again the artificial addition of Apuleius is perfectly obvious. Thus, comparing this with the Russian tale allows us to separate the Roman literary work into its folkloric and literary layers.

Speak about the works of Ivan Tolstoi.[39]

The second part of this tale is less interesting, and we can limit ourselves to a quick retelling. Apuleius's version is rhetorical and ornate.

Psyche wants to kill herself in despair, and she leaps from the cliff into the nearby river. But a miracle occurs: "The timid stream, no doubt in honor of the god who is capable of making even water burst into flames and out of fear for itself, immediately bore her on its wave unharmed to the shore, covered with flowering greenery."[40] She sets off to wander and searches for Amor. She passes through countries and nations but cannot find him.

At the same time, Venus learns of her son's escapades—a seagull tells her. This is also a general motif in folklore. The prescient bird, horse, or some other animal tells the heroes what has happened. Venus discovers that the same Psyche who received divine honors for her beauty has become the lover of her son Amor.

Amor disappeared at the moment when he woke and saw Psyche holding a dagger above him. Now it turns out, quite unexpectedly, that he is lying ill in his mother's chamber (he had come to visit her). By the way, Apuleius violates one of the laws of folklore poetics: that the story always follow the hero. Here, as he tells about Amor's fate, the narrator must abandon Psyche for a time. Venus, infuriated, reproaches her son and sets out to look for Psyche in order to punish her.

It is clear to the reader that there can be no punishment. But neither can Venus tame her fury. New characters are introduced to unravel this knot. As she wanders, Venus meets Ceres, goddess of agriculture and fertility, and

Juno, wife of Jupiter, and they persuade her: After all, Venus is the goddess of love herself. How can she object to her son's marriage?

At the same time Psyche continues her quest and finally makes her way to Venus's home. Venus is furious, but she does not destroy Psyche. Instead she assigns to her a series of impossible tasks. This is the familiar motif of the difficult task before the conclusion of a marriage. For example, she spills a heap of various seeds—rye, wheat, millet, poppy, and so on—and says, "It seems to me that such a hideous slave could not please a lover with anything other than diligent service; I want to test your ability. Sort this pile of mixed seed and, once you have arranged everything properly, seed to seed separately, present your work before evening comes for my approval."[41] We must say that the motivation is fairly weak, but the aesthetics of early Roman literature demand logical motivations in places where folklore does not demand them. Psyche is helped by ants. Venus assigns her three more tasks: to bring the golden fleece from a miraculous flock of sheep; to bring a cup of water from a terrible river, the river of death (Cotsit); and to bring a healing ointment from Hades, from the goddess Proserpina. Psyche carries out all these tasks; it is all described in great detail. With this she moves the gods to take her side. Jupiter calls together all the gods and admonishes his daughter Venus. The tale ends with a depiction of the married pair on Olympus.

Why do we need to become acquainted with Apuleius in the course of Russian folklore? Obviously, we could choose not to do so. But the tale shows what great significance folktale plots may have in world culture. It helps us to understand Apuleius and the error of West European classical philologists and so on.[42] Besides, I would like to introduce you to a few questions in the comparative study of the folktale. Such a comparison not only is important for classical philology and the history of literature but also instructive for folklorists and, in particular, for Russianists who work on folklore.

The tale "The Little Scarlet Flower" will serve as the nearest Russian equivalent (note: it is not a variant!). I will move on to it now. According to my incomplete data, we can cite ten Russian variants of this tale.[43] The most famous is the recording made by Sergei Aksakov. Aksakov published it in the form of a supplement to *The Childhood Days of Bagrov, Grandson* and called it "The Little Scarlet Flower (A Tale of the Housekeeper Pelageia)." He had, by his own admission, heard this tale in the village "at least a dozen times." He also writes about it in a letter to his son Ivan: "I am writing down a folktale I knew by heart in my childhood and told for everyone's amusement with all the amusing rhymes of the tale-teller Pelageia. . . . I have set out to restore this tale."[44] We know that Aksakov possessed a phenomenal memory for all kinds of minute details, and we can entirely believe that this tale is recorded word for word, or at the least nearly word for word. The tale-teller's style is preserved; we see an indubitable individual manner not only in the performance but also in the form of the narration. The tale begins this way:

> In a certain kingdom, in a certain state, there once lived a rich merchant, a man of standing. He had great riches of all kinds, expensive goods from beyond the seas, pearls, precious stones, gold and silver treasure; and that merchant had three daughters, all three great beauties, but the youngest was the best of all; and he loved his daughters more than all his wealth, pearls, precious stones, gold and silver treasure—because he was a widower, and he had no one else to love. He loved the older daughters, but he loved the youngest daughter more, because she was the prettiest of all and most affectionate to him.[45]

We recognize the standard initial situation, but it is complicated by the tale-teller's manner. Undoubtedly this marvelous housekeeper was a good-natured creature who knew how to love. Love is also ascribed to family members, and the father's love in particular is motivated by the fact that he is a widower. The father travels away to trade, and each daughter asks him to bring her something. The oldest asks for a crown of gems that glows in the dark. The crown is a fairly clear symbol of marriage. The middle one asks for something else: "You bring me a toilette of eastern crystal, carved from one whole piece, without any flaw, so that when I look into it I can see all the beauty under the sky and, when I look at myself in it, I will not grow old and my maidenly beauty will increase."[46] This is clearly a deformation, drawn from the way of life of upper-class landowners. For a housekeeper a toilette is the extreme of luxury. The style of narration clearly comes from the *lubok* folktale.

The youngest daughter requests a completely different present: "My dear lord and father! Do not bring me gold and silver brocade, nor black sable from Siberia, nor a pearl necklace, nor a necklace that glows in the dark, nor a crystal toilette, but bring me the little scarlet flower that is the most beautiful in the whole white world."[47] This is also a symbol, but what kind is not yet clear.

It is not hard for the merchant to get hold of the first two presents. He departs. He sends these presents to his daughters on ships, but he himself sets off to search for the little scarlet flower. The difficulty is that this flower should be the best one in the world, so that there had never been a finer one in "the whole white world." The elder sisters are concerned about their own beauty. The youngest is concerned with some other kind of beauty. This is a symbol of something wonderful.

Bandits fall upon the merchant and rob him, and he winds up alone in the forest, walking farther and farther through this dark forest. The dark forest begins to thin before him. He sees some kind of light ahead, and there before him is a marvelous castle.

> There stands a house—no, not a house, a mansion—no, not a mansion, but a king's or tsar's palace, all lit up in silver and gold and in glowing stones. It all burns and shines, but you can't see any flame, like the beautiful sun, so it's hard on the eyes to look at it. All the windows in the palace are wide open, and harmonious music is playing inside, the likes of which he has never heard. He enters the broad courtyard, through the wide gates, wide open; there is a road of white marble, and along the walls fountains of water spurt high, big and little ones. He enters the palace by a stairway covered with crimson cloth, with gilded banisters; he enters the main room . . . the décor is all imperial, the likes of which has never been seen or heard of: gold, silver, glowing gems, ivory from elephants and mammoths.[48]

The description of the palace is quite detailed. The father is hungry—a table of food appears before him. He eats and then lies down to sleep. In the morning he goes out into a marvelous garden with all kinds of flowers and fruits, and suddenly he sees "on a little hill of green a scarlet-colored flower was flowering, of unseen and unheard-of beauty; you could not tell it in a tale or describe it with a pen. . . . The flower's scent was all through the garden, as if a stream were flowing."[49]

This flower is also a symbol. But a symbol of what? We recall Garshin's red flower; there it is the incarnation of the evil that has poured into the world. Here it is something else. This flower is so splendid, so wondrous, that it embodies all the beauty of the world and the highest possible happiness on earth.

Now let us think a bit about what is going on. It is obvious that the father has found his way to the enchanted palace and garden where Psyche stayed. Even details such as that sudden appearance of a table covered with food and the bed for sleep at night coincide. But how does his daughter know about the little scarlet flower, which grows in this garden alone? Apparently, she was destined to be in this garden. This is her fate. The tale-teller says nothing about this directly. But we sense it, as people of logic and rational thought. Apuleius sensed it as well. Apuleius put all this into the form that was available to a person in antiquity. Such is the will of the gods, and their will is expressed in the prophecy, the oracle. And although this form is not folkloric at all, the motivation of the prophecy is contained in the very essence of the folktale's situation.

Comparison with "Amor and Psyche" leads us to other thoughts as well. There are two worlds: first, the world of people, the world of home, which is drawn as the initial situation; and there is another world, represented in the given tale by the enchanted palace and garden. In Apuleius they are divided by a space of air, which can be crossed only by the god of the winds, Zephyr. In the Russian tale they are separated by an impassable forest. But their function is identical. Both forest and the space of air divide the two worlds, making the faraway world unattainable. It is reachable only for those who are fated to be there. The impassable forest opens before the father of the girl for whom he is, in essence, laying a trail.

But I have digressed from the thread of narration. It goes on as follows.

The merchant's arms and legs began to tremble, and he spoke in a joyful voice: "Here is the little scarlet flower, the fairest one in the whole world, which my youngest and favorite daughter asked for." And, having said these words, he walked over and picked the little scarlet flower. At that very moment, out of a cloudless sky, lightning flashed and thunder struck so that the earth reeled under his feet—and before the merchant's eyes, as if out of the ground, arose a beast—not a beast, a person—not a person, but truly some kind of monster, terrible and shaggy, and it howled in a wild voice, "What have you done? How dare you pick, in my own garden, my cherished, my favorite flower?"[50]

The merchant explains why he needs the little scarlet flower, and then the monster demands that the merchant send him one of his daughters.

This differs from "Amor and Psyche," for in Apuleius the castle's master is not a monster but Amor, a handsome youth. Here the folkloric tradition is observed: The master is a monster. But the housekeeper Pelageia digresses from the folktale canon in another place. The monster demands not a wife but a companion; that is, here the presence of marriage relations is rejected, although they are stressed in Apuleius. It is obvious that the housekeeper Pelageia, telling this tale to children, and being of a tender and delicate nature herself, apparently, changed this moment. The tale suffers from this, for the genuine folkloric tale is never afraid to call things by their own names, but the change does honor to the tact of the tale-teller.

The agreement between the monster and the father of the girl represents a kind of contract. Such contracts occur in the system of various plots ("give up the thing in your house that you don't know"). The contract in the case at hand is transferred to the magic garden. This is a unique case, unusual, and, quite likely, not entirely successful. The father is compelled to agree.

The girl reaches this garden in a different way from her father. The monster gives the father a ring to take along, and as soon as his youngest daughter puts it on, she finds herself in the magic garden. Once again all the wonders are described in great detail. The monster has a talk with her. First fiery words appear on the wall: "Is my lady satisfied with her gardens and chambers, meals and servants?"[51] But later she asks him to speak with her in his own voice. He does so, and he has a terrible voice, but she is not afraid. So peaceful life goes on for a certain time.

The complication begins in more or less the same way as in Apuleius. "The merchant's young daughter, the wonderful beauty, began to wish to see with her own eyes the forest beast, the sea monster, and she began to beg and plead with him about this."[52] In Apuleius this desire is suggested to Psyche by her evil sisters, but here the wish appears by itself, a natural consequence of the friendly relations between her and "the forest beast, the sea monster." He does not want to show himself to her, but he gives in to her request. He looks like this: "And the forest beast, the sea monster was frightful: crooked arms, beastly claws on his hands, horse's legs, before and behind great camel lumps, all shaggy from top to bottom, from his mouth hung boar's tusks, nose in a hook like a golden eagle's, and owl's eyes."[53]

The girl faints. We expect a catastrophe, that the beast will disappear as Amor disappears. But that is not the case in this tale. When she comes to, the girl hears the beast weeping, and the Russian Psyche behaves entirely unlike the Roman Psyche, who is wounded by the arrow of Cupid. "And she felt sorry and conscience-stricken, and she overcame her great fear and her timid girlish heart, and she spoke in a firm voice, 'No, do not fear anything, my good and affectionate master, I am no longer afraid of your terrible appearance, I will not leave you, I will not forget your kindnesses; show yourself to me now in your usual form; I was only afraid at first.'"[54]

So the folktale unexpectedly reveals the soul of a girl, a good-hearted girl who feels pity. This may strike us as contrary to nature. But in Aksakov's variant this generosity later develops into another feeling. This happens as follows: She dreams that her father is unwell and begs for permission to go home. The beast gives her a ring that will take her home and back in a moment, and sets her a term: three days and three nights, and no longer. If she does not return by that deadline, the beast will die of longing. At home the envious sisters reset the clock, she arrives one hour late and sees the beast dead; she laments over him, drops tears onto him, grieves. And a miracle happens: Lightning flashes, thunder rumbles. She loses consciousness, and when she comes to herself, she sees herself on a throne, with a prince embracing her. It is none other than the beast. He was bewitched, and only the love of a girl could return his human form. The tale ends with their wedding feast.

This tale has not attained the same worldwide fame as Apuleius's. But, if we compare the two, we cannot help preferring the humble Russian folkloric tale. A few things in the tale of the housekeeper Pelageia are distorted compared with the folk original. But it traces the image of a Russian Psyche who does not need Cupid's arrow in order to win true love, regardless of all obstacles.

Apuleius's tale differs from Russian tales in that the spouse disappears, and Psyche sets out to search for him.

The tale of the spouse who disappears is, in fact, a different tale. In Apuleius they contaminate one another. In the Russian folklore tradition the quest for a vanished spouse makes up the plot of a separate tale that is possible in various forms. The most splendid of these is the tale of Finist the Bright Falcon. Aarne, like Andreev and Thompson after him, considered it a separate tale, distinguishing it from Amor and Psyche (A-T 432).

I will move on to examine the tale of Finist the Bright Falcon. Finist is the phoenix, an immortal bird. In its old age the phoenix burns up and rises from the ashes even more youthful and beautiful. This is not the case in the tale. How the name came to the Russians is not clear. It is fixed in the tale. The tale is quite popular (there are ten variants)[55] and is spread over the whole world. In Europe it has been known since the fourteenth century.[56]

I will examine this tale according to the first variant in Afanas'ev (Afanas'ev 234; there are only two variants in Afanas'ev's classification); in particular cases I will draw attention to other sources.

The opening has an old man with three daughters. The older two are fine dressers, "while the youngest was always working around the house." This detail is interesting in that later the younger daughter receives gifts without any test. She is completely different from her sisters from the beginning. Their father travels away to the city; the older sisters ask him to bring them fancy clothes, but the younger wants "a feather of Finist the Bright Falcon." Here the same question arises as in the tale of the little scarlet flower. How does she know about Finist? This is a matter of generally irrational folktale poetics. We shall see how the variants attempt to rationalize this moment.

What this feather is, and why the girl asks for it, is not yet clear, but it will become clear soon.

How can one get hold of the feather?

In the Afanas'ev variant it is acquired simply. The father meets an old man, who is carrying a little box, and in that little box is the feather of Finist. The father buys the box for a thousand rubles and brings it home. We feel clearly that the motif of acquiring is simplified and deformed.

The secret qualities of this feather reveal themselves immediately. The girl takes the little box into her bedroom. "The little feather of Finist the Bright Falcon flew out right away, struck the floor, and a handsome prince appeared before the maiden." In this way, this feather is a part of the whole. The notion that someone who possesses part of a person has power over the whole person is ancient. Some forms of charms (*zagovory*) and sorcerous practices are based on it. It is enough to have a little hair or part of a person's clothing in order to have power over the whole person. Here the bridegroom once again has an animal form. But unlike in "The Little Scarlet Flower," where this form is horrible, here the form is attractive. In all lyrics the bright falcon is a metaphor for a fine young man. A bridegroom, or a spouse in general, with the form of an animal is a widespread folktale motif (compare "The Frog Princess"). It can be explained through totemic concepts.

Unlike "The Little Scarlet Flower" and "Amor and Psyche," life together takes place not in a marvelous palace or garden but in the home of the bride. This is also characteristic not just of this plot. In the tale of the Frog Princess the frog wife lives for a time in the home of the prince.

Afanas'ev gives an interesting variant. Here the girl asks her father to bring her not a feather but the little scarlet flower. The father brings it, but later it turns out that this flower is the equivalent of the feather. When it is placed in water on the windowsill, Finist comes flying. We might suppose that the flower is also a part of the monster bridegroom, that is, in essence, of the prince. This could be the topic of a specialized study. In the tale such connections are presented as mysterious, and this mystery holds one of the charms of the tale. At the same time, we may encounter attempts in folklore to rationalize some elements of the tale. Thus the teller sometimes asks him- or herself the same question that a contemporary reader would ask: How does the girl know about Finist? In the second variant in Afanas'ev (Afanas'ev 235), the old man asks his daughter, "Do you really know him?" "I know him, I know him, father! Last Sunday he was at mass. He kept on looking at me, and I spoke with him. He loves me, father!" This is a clear and complete violation of folktale poetics.

The action pauses for a time. The girl is happy with Finist. But the older sisters come on the scene. They spy on her and eavesdrop, and they see Finist flying through her window. To destroy her happiness, they do this: "In the evening, when it was completely dark outside, they set up a ladder, gathered sharp knives and needles and stuck them into the window of the beautiful maiden." The falcon struggles, he cannot get in, he wounds his wings and flies away with these words: "Farewell, beautiful maiden! if you think to look for me, then seek me beyond thrice-nine lands, in the thrice-tenth kingdom. You'll sooner wear out three pairs of iron boots, break three forged staves, gnaw through three stone wafers, than you'll find me, the goodly youth."

This detail is interesting in its historical relationship. It reflects some features of the ancient funeral rite. It was supposed that the deceased would make his way on foot into the other world. Therefore in the grave he was given a staff to lean on and sound footwear, which with the advent of the Iron Age becomes iron boots; finally he would be given bread to take along. Stone bread, by analogy with the iron staff and the iron footwear, is a substitute for the ordinary bread that once was found here. The girl sets out on her wandering.

All this is the opening. Misfortune and setting out on a quest are its fundamental elements.

We wait for the heroine to undergo a test now and to receive magical things. But our expectations are realized only in part. Along the way she sees a hut with an old woman in it. The old woman asks her about everything and rewards her without any sort of test at all. This happens three times. The test has clearly dropped out of the story here. It has become unnecessary because the listener already knows who this girl is. Wearing out the footgear and so on can be considered the equivalent of a test. The first old woman gives her "a silver wheel, a golden spindle; when you start spinning a golden thread stretches out." The second gives her a silver plate and a golden egg, and the third "a golden embroidery frame and needle: you just hold the frame, and the needle stitches by itself." In variants other objects are named, but their character is the same everywhere. These are not magical objects; they are wonders, but these wonders will help the heroine obtain what she seeks.

The third old woman also tells the heroine where Finist can be found. In the given variant he is quite close by: He has married the daughter of a wafer baker, and the old woman advises the girl to find work as the wafer baker's servant. In other variants something more fabulous happens: Finist is beyond thrice-nine lands (this makes more sense given the worn footgear and all). "There was the dark-blue sea—like a glowing coal the golden roofs burned on the white-stoned chambers. 'This must be the kingdom of Finist the Bright Falcon,' thought the girl" (Afanas'ev 235).

Then comes the dénouement. The girl finds Finist's wife and tempts her with the first of the marvels: She sits down to spin with her golden spindle. Finist's wife wants to buy this marvel, but the girl will not sell it; she demands something completely different: "Let me spend the night with your husband." The wife agrees, because she intends to put Finist to sleep with soporific herbs. So everything comes to pass. The girl is allowed in to see Finist, who sleeps without waking. The girl cries over him, and this is one of the most touching and splendid moments of this tale. I will cite it verbatim from Afanas'ev's first variant: "'Wake up, wake up, Finist bright falcon! I, the fair maiden, have come to you, I broke three forged staffs. I wore out three pairs of iron boots. I gnawed through three stone loaves, and I kept on searching for you, my dear!' But Finist slept, he heard nothing, and so the night passed."

This tale says nothing in words about love. It gives the image of a girl who is true to her love and capable for its sake of the highest sacrifices. She is separated from him through ill will; her fate is tragic and provokes the deepest sympathy. The image of the girl in this tale is one of the most beautiful in the entire Russian folktale epos.

Things happen in the same way three times. On the third night a burning tear falls onto Finist's cheek, and he suddenly wakes up. After this things move quickly. "They talked until they agreed and ran away from the wafer baker." The wafer baker tries to catch them on their horses, but their tracks have grown cold.

At home there is a wedding, but before this the tale gives one episode that is superfluous from the point of view of composition or plot development but internally necessary. When Finist whistles, clothes, decorations, and a golden carriage appear. He himself turns into a prince, and this way they drive to the church. No one recognizes them. This happens three times. After the third time they are recognized, and now they get married.

Why is this last episode necessary—the moment of transformation? It expresses a deep and lovely fairytale philosophy. Things, as well as people, look completely different to us from what they really are. There is a lack of correspondence between external appearance and internal contents. The creature who is most unattractive, humble, last in line, scorned by everyone is the one who turns out to possess internal beauty. This plot is common to all folktales. Such are Ivan the Fool, Ivan Behind-the-Stove; such is Cinderella; such is the stepdaughter persecuted by everyone. Such is the heroine of this tale. This heroine usually does not have a name. But there comes a moment when her internal beauty seems to burst out and take on its real form, now at last visible to everyone. So the heroine of this tale, after withstanding all the tests and showing the beauty and strength of her soul, turns into a queen.

This lack of correspondence between external appearance and essence, according to the folktale, also penetrates the world of things. This world is not what it appears to be. Things may contain an unusual power, hidden from everyone. We have already said that in the folktale any object can be magical. So too the little scarlet flower is not at all a mere flower. It embodies the beauty of the world and the beauty of a human being. The difficulty of getting hold of the flower is that it must be the most beautiful, the most splendid one in the whole world, that there is none more beautiful in the world. The daughter requests precisely this kind of flower; her father seeks this kind of flower; she presses this kind of flower to her heart and kisses it, once she receives it. But this flower is not merely a flower. It is mysteriously linked with the beast, and, in essence, the prince who is fated to be hers. It is a kind of residence for his soul. We have already said that this reflects animistic conceptions of the soul, that the soul may be hidden in a plant or an animal. Rudiments of this concept have been preserved in other motifs as well; not only may the hero's antagonist possess such a soul, so may the hero. The same thing affects the image of Finist, which conceals a prince. He may be incarnate not just in a bird but even in a feather. Once she possesses the scarlet flower or the feather of Finist, the girl already possesses the one represented by this flower or this feather. This is how it appears in the text: "But that feather was magical; it was a tsar's son."[57]

These remnants of totemism could not be preserved if they did not correspond to the teller's worldview or sense of the world, according to which the everyday world we see is an envelope for something splendid, which may be revealed at least in the folktale.

This, historically and philosophically, may resolve one of the puzzles set for us by the tale of Finist the Bright Falcon.

But there is still a series of other riddles. I have said that the concept of the two levels of the world corresponds to the teller's worldview, if only in imagination. But this tale has details that do not correspond to the people's contemporary consciousness and contemporary morals. How, for example, does it explain that its hero, Finist, not only abandons a girl who is blameless in anything but also marries another, whom he abandons in turn to return to the first one? From the point of view of contemporary morality such behavior provokes no sympathy at all. At the same time, in the tale itself there is never even a shadow of judgment, not in a single variant. By the way, one variant shows some attempt to rehabilitate the hero at least in part.[58] After three nights and after recognizing the girl, Finist gathers his council (here he is a tsar) and says, "Listen, good guests! Which wife is more true to me: the one who betrays me for pleasures, or the one who walked, sought me out, wore out three pairs of boots, broke three ploughs, gnawed away three iron wafers?" The wife is tied to the tail of a horse. "And with the other one he had a wedding on the spot." However, this case is the only one, and even here his marrying after living with the girl is not judged. The bad wife is guilty, not he, who married someone else.

We should seek an explanation in the real history of family relations and forms of conducting a marriage. It is discussed in more detail in my book *Historical Roots of the Wonder Tale*, and I refer anyone who is interested to that.[59] Here the matter is precisely in the details; a brief, schematic outline of the essence of the matter would not seem convincing. But for general orientation I will nonetheless say that in the clan system both young men and young women were supposed to have two marriages. Married life began not in the family, at home, but in a distant sacred place, where the girl became, as it were, the wife of a god. Such is the preform of the fairytale palace where a girl lived with a monster, a creature of divine order and a human creature at one and the same time. It is as though she receives a marriage consecration. Once she returns home, she may enter into an ongoing marriage and begin a family. But with the development of the paired family, such an order collided with its interests,[60] which allowed no form of mutual life other than the married one. So a plot arises in which the beast-husband or god-husband is not replaced by a man but becomes one and thus turns into the heroine's ongoing husband. So arises the tale of Amor and Psyche, of which one variety is the tale of Finist. But, again, this explanation cannot be satisfactory in such a brief outline.

The tale of Finist includes elements that even today do not yield to any historical, historical-ethnographic, or historical-social explanation. This is the motif of the three purchased nights, when the wife appears to the sleeping youth and regains him for herself. Perhaps this motif will be explained, but for now there is no explanation, and folklore scholars have not spent much time pondering it.

Making the acquaintance of plots. The importance of studying plots, and what to do in order to know folktales. Beauty. Comparative study in light of regularities (Apuleius—the Little Scarlet Flower—Finist). Minor observations by the way.

I would like, quite briefly, to dwell on one more tale that includes the motif of difficult tasks. This is the tale of the Firebird, one of the most perfect and interesting tales with regard to form (A-T 550; Afanas'ev 168). It is very popular in the East and in Western Europe but less so in Russia. Andreev knew four Russian variants, and by 1957 twelve were already known.[61] The best version of this tale is in Afanas'ev. Vasilii Zhukovskii and Nikolai Iazykov's literary treatments are well known. Both of them, however, used the German text of the Grimm brothers; apparently they did not know the Russian texts. Afanas'ev's text goes back to a *lubok* edition from the eighteenth century; he borrowed it from the anonymous collection *Grandpa's Strolls*.[62] The *lubok* editions are distinguished by a particular rhetorical and artificial bookish style, although far inferior in artistry to the immediately narrated folkloric tales, but we may encounter true pearls among these woods, and one of these is the tale of the Firebird.

A tsar has three sons. He has a splendid garden, "And the tsar had one favorite apple tree, and golden apples grew on the tree." But the Firebird visits this tree at night: "Its feathers are gold, and its eyes like eastern crystal" (Afanas'ev 168).[63] The tsar promises the throne to whichever of his sons can catch this bird alive. The elder ones, as always, fall asleep and see nothing, but the youngest manages to seize the bird by the tail. It tears loose, leaving a golden feather in his hand. "This feather was so marvelous and bright that if you took it into a dark room, then it would shine as if a great multitude of candles were lit in that room."[64] The two oldest sons set out one after the other to seek the Firebird, and after them the youngest son also gets permission to go. We expect him to be subjected to a test and to receive a magical object or a magic helper. But our expectations are not entirely realized. He comes upon a pillar in the road with this notice: "Whoever rides straight forward from this pillar will be cold and hungry; whoever rides to the right will be safe and sound, but his horse will die; and whoever rides to the left will himself be killed, but his horse will remain safe and sound."[65]

A specialized study of the motif of the pillar beside the road would be very interesting. It appears both in the folktale and in the *bylina*, but its treatment varies a great deal both between the genres and within them. In the given tale it replaces the test; it corresponds to it functionally. Where will the hero ride? The hero reasons quite rationally, not at all in fairytale style. "Prince Ivan read this sign and rode to the right, keeping in mind: Although his horse would be killed, he would remain alive and with time he could find another horse."[66] This tale-teller, an eighteenth-century rationalist, ascribes his own views to the hero. A true hero always takes the road to death, meets mortal danger, and overcomes it. In the given case the hero is thinking of his own life. In fulfillment of the prophecy a huge gray wolf runs up, tears the horse in half, and disappears. It would seem that the test was not passed. But the tale-teller thinks otherwise. Now the magical object or magical helper is supposed to come into the hands of the hero. This is told as follows: "Suddenly the gray wolf caught up with him and said to him, 'I feel sorry for you, Prince Ivan, since you are so exhausted. I am also sorry that I ate up your good horse. Well! Climb on me, on the gray wolf, and tell me, where I should take you and why.'"[67] It is clear to us that the moment of the test and the receipt of the magical helper have been deformed here. What do variants show? The variants confirm our guess. In Onchukov the wolf is clearly linked with the motif of grateful animals: "The wolf said, 'I'm going to eat you.' But he (the prince) said, 'Don't eat me, I'll be useful to you.' Well, then he got onto the wolf and rode to the kingdom" (Onchukov 88).[68] In this kind of form the motif makes no sense (how could Prince Ivan be useful to the wolf?), but this does not stop the teller; he has simply mixed up the motif of grateful animals.

In some variants the action develops in the same way as in Afanas'ev. But there are also others. So, in the cited variant the pillar says, "Whoever rides to the right will find happiness, whoever rides to the left will find two happinesses, but whoever rides straight ahead will find unhappiness" (Onchukov 88). The clever brothers ride along the happy paths, and the youngest takes the road of unhappiness, but he is the one who finds happiness. This treatment corresponds more exactly to the folktale canon. After this, the tale develops without hindrance in Afanas'ev's variant. The wolf takes Prince Ivan to the garden where the Firebird lives in a golden cage. The wolf orders Ivan to take the bird but not the cage; however, Ivan, of course, violates that prohibition. There is a string tied to the cage; crashing and thunder resound, and the guards catch him and bring him to their king. The king is ready to forgive Ivan if he brings him a golden-maned horse. The wolf takes him to the stables where the golden-maned horse lives, and everything happens again as if by rote. The wolf forbids him to take the golden bridle hanging on the wall. Prince Ivan once again disobeys; once again a string makes noise, and the whole dialogue repeats with the tsar who owns the horse: He is prepared to forgive him if he brings him the princess Elena the Beautiful. But the action cannot develop in the same way for a third time. It must be crowned with success. This time the wolf steals the princess. She and the prince climb onto the wolf and ride away.

Expressed in the language of the tale, here is what happens next: "Prince Ivan, sitting on the gray wolf next to the beautiful princess Elena, came to love her with all his heart, and she to love Prince Ivan."[69] Now it is already impossible to exchange Elena for the horse; Elena must be brought home. The wolf finds a way out. He makes himself look like Elena, Prince Ivan hands him over and receives the golden-maned horse, and then the wolf turns back into a wolf, and they travel farther. The Firebird is also obtained through deception: The wolf turns into the horse, and Prince Ivan receives the Firebird. They are returning home, the wolf disappears, and everything should be fine, but, as they are approaching his home city, Prince Ivan and Elena sit down to rest. This is a typical folktale motif, sewn with white threads. The hero falls asleep just so that he can be tricked. At that very moment, the older brothers are returning with empty hands. They take away Elena, the horse, and the Firebird from Ivan, and they chop him up into little pieces. From somewhere the wolf appears, finds a raven, and forces it to get hold of the water of life and the water of death; the wolf brings Prince Ivan back to life, and the truth is made clear. The brothers are put in prison, Ivan marries Elena, and the tale ends not entirely stereotypically with the words: "Meanwhile Prince Ivan married the beautiful princess Elena and began to live with her in love and friendship, so that neither of them could live even a single moment without the other."[70]

In its simplicity, transparency, and elegance of composition this Russian variant of the tale of the Firebird is the best of all the variants in the world. From the comparative point of view it has certain defects, but only the specialized researcher will notice them. In Western European variants the wolf is a cursed prince, which makes the plot too heavy and complicated. Russian variants are characterized by an unusual simplicity.

Truth and Falsehood (A-T 613; Afanas'ev 115–122)

"Truth and Falsehood" is one of the most popular Russian tales. In it no task is expressed in words, but it contains a task in essence. The tale is popular not only in Russia but all over the world. It was already known in the Middle Ages, but it is apparently much more ancient than that. Its plot has been found in an ancient Egyptian papyrus. The tale is interesting because it directly and immediately expresses a certain philosophy. That is fairly rare in the folktale, where philosophy usually flows from the plot and the nature of the characters but is never uttered directly. I will dwell briefly on this tale in the form of Afanas'ev's first variant. The tale occupies, as it were, an intermediate position between the wonder tale and the novellistic tale.

There are two peasant men. In Afanas'ev's variant 118, the two peasants are named Ivan and Naum. In variant 115, they are described as "two of our brother peasant men, who were awful-awful poor." One of them is described as living any old way; he carries out all kinds of falseness, and he is fond of deceptions and of tricking people. In variant 116 instead of peasants we have two merchants: one who lived by falseness, the other by truth.

The two men argue over which of them is right. Such a beginning is not typical for the wonder tale. In Afanas'ev's variant 116, Falsehood says one day, "Listen, Truth, you know it's better to live in the world by falsehood!" "No!" "You want to argue?" "Let's argue."[71] In Afanas'ev's variant 115, one of the men says that it is better to live by falsehood; but the other one says that you cannot live your whole life by falsehood; it is better to live however you can, but with truth.[72] They decide to go out on the road and ask people they meet how to live better—by truth or by falsehood. Here they sometimes conclude a deal.

In Onchukov's variant (no. 158),[73] the deal takes the form of a bet. If the people they meet say three times that it is better to live by falsehood, then Falsehood will gouge out Truth's eyes. Sometimes, however, the two men do not make any deal.

After this deal follow the encounters. The two peasants have various kinds of meetings on the road, and curiously there are no variants at all. Each tale-teller forms this motif in his or her own way, based on personal experience. In Afanas'ev's variant 115, a merchant says, "I used to live by truth, but badly; now I live by falsehood. Falsehood is better." A peasant man says, "You can't earn even a crust of bread with truth!" At the third meeting they are told just the same thing.[74]

Instead of the meetings, sometimes the peasants seek out advisers. In Afanas'ev's variant 115, the merchant says, "They deceive us, and so we too deceive, you hear."[75] A landlord's peasant

says, "You can't live your whole life by truth; there's more profit in living by falsehood." A priest
says, "There, they've found something clever to ask about. Everyone knows that it's falsehood.
What kind of truth is there nowadays? For truth, you hear, you'll wind up in Siberia; they'll call
you a scandal-monger."

In Afanas'ev's variant 116, the two peasants meet two people (here, there is no third meeting). A clerk tells them, "In our times it's better to live by falsehood." A judge says the same thing.

The situation is a bit different in Afanas'ev's variant 158. Here the two peasants meet a dog
who was driven away from home, a horse who was driven away from home, and a peasant man,
who says: "There's not even a rumor of truth on earth now, and if any is still wandering around
here, then it's wearing bast shoes."

The peasant, the merchant, the clerk—they all say it is better to live by
falsehood. After that Falsehood usually blinds Truth, according to their
agreement. But sometimes there is no agreement. This is how things go in
Afanas'ev: Truth and Falsehood are in the woods; they are cold. Truth has
nothing to eat, whereas prudent Falsehood has had the foresight to bring
along some bread. Truth asks him for a piece of bread, and Falsehood gives
him first one piece, then another; for the first piece he burns out one eye,
and for the second the other. We encounter this form fairly often. It does not
sound very convincing to the contemporary listener. Why would Truth let
his eye be taken, agree to give his eyes for bread? But the tale-teller thinks
otherwise. He needs to show the whole depth of Falsehood's criminality: He
is unable to share his bread without a reward. He burns out a man's eyes in
exchange for bread. However, some tellers understandably tell the tale differently. The blinding is part of the bargain from the beginning: Whoever turns
out to be wrong will be blinded. In a tale from Viatsk (Zelenin 69)[76] the characters are two merchants. One does fair business; the other is unfair. The latter blinds his competitor out of envy.

Be that as it may, Falsehood is triumphant. There is no truth on the earth.
Falsehood is right and Truth is blind, abandoned, wandering alone in the forest, running into trees, in the depths of humiliation and misery. But Falsehood's triumph is superficial and temporary. The tale-teller could not allow
Falsehood to triumph. Night comes, and Truth sits down on a stump or lies
down under a tree, an oak or a pine, or climbs into a tree to spend the night
there safe from beasts. Some devils fly to roost in this oak tree. They boast of
their black deeds ("who has arranged which intrigues"). One brags that he
got two cousins to marry, another that he stopped the water that was running

a mill, the third that he made Falsehood blind Truth, and finally, one of them brags that he has taken up residence in a woman—a princess or a merchant's daughter—and torments her at night (a vampire). This list of misdeeds is fairly various; there is no need for us to exhaust it. But here the devils, or "little sinful ones" (*okaiashki*), the evil, unclean ones, expose one another. It turns out that people can correct all these deeds: One can restore vision by rubbing one's eyes with the dew from under the oak tree, or "all you need is to rub with that grass over there—the eyes will be healed again" (Afanas'ev 117), or you must wash them from a thundering spring (Afanas'ev 115), and so on. The princess can also be cured, and the means are quite various. For example, you have to hold an icon of God's Mother of Smolensk to her breast (Afanas'ev 115), or "catch a frog, fry it up, give it to her to eat; she'll be well" (Khudiakov 47);[77] or you must find a special flower, "a fire-flower" (Afanas'ev 116), whereupon the tale-teller adds: "It's the kind of flower that when it flowers the sea gets rough, and the night is brighter than day: devils fear it." The devils also talk about how the water can be released or how to defend against all the other kinds of dirty tricks they do.

Truth hears all this. What comes next is obvious. He restores his vision, and he corrects the evil the devils have done: releases the water, heals the princess, and in most cases wins her hand in marriage (task and solution in a hidden form), but sometimes he refuses the princess and receives a lot of money. In all cases Truth is triumphant; the hero begins to live well.

But that is still not enough. Falsehood must be punished. Truth returns home healed and wealthy (sometimes he has become the king), meets Falsehood, and tells him everything. Falsehood goes to the same oak tree where the devils gather, but they discover him and punish him for eavesdropping. "They tore him up into little pieces" (Afanas'ev 116). "And so it turns out that it's better to live by truth than by falsehood" (Afanas'ev 116).

Tales of the Persecuted Stepdaughter

I have examined some tales with difficult tasks in various forms. I did not give a morphological analysis—that was not the point of the description. It is not easy in all cases, but it is always possible.

I move on now to another group of tales that have neither battle with an opponent nor difficult tasks linked with courtship and marriage. The basic element of these tales is the test, in particular, the test of a girl or of children.

These tales are brief. The test, as we know, takes place, as a rule, right away after the opening. We could say that these tales go no further than the test, reward, and return.

Here, for example, belong tales about the stepdaughter who is taken away into the forest. Baba Yaga, Jack Frost, the Forest Spirit, the Bear, or other creatures test and reward her, but the blood daughters of the old woman are punished. I spoke of these tales when I was looking at the function of test and reward in general, and I will not repeat myself now. These tales trace the image of a meek and long-suffering but hardy and spiritually strong girl and the opposite image: the old woman's arrogant, lazy, shameless blood daughters, who think only of their own well-being.

Cinderella Cinderella (Zolushka) (A-T 510 A) represents a different type from this group. Here too we have a stepmother, her blood daughters, and her stepdaughter, but unlike the other tales, this stepdaughter is not led away into the forest; all the action takes place in one setting. The test occurs in the house itself. The stepmother assigns the stepdaughter all kinds of impossible tasks (e.g., to pick grain out of the cinders), which she fulfills thanks to the help of doves. These doves appear in a way that is externally accidental; their help is not motivated by anything but the character of the heroine, her meekness, goodness, her inner beauty. It is precisely this image, this inner womanly beauty that makes the tale so attractive and therefore so widespread and popular.

In many variants Cinderella has a helper from the other world: her own dead mother. The girl goes to cry on her mother's grave, and there she finds the dresses and jewels she wears to the king's ball. This reflects the general folktale law of a certain initial lack of correspondence between external form and internal meaning. The word *Cinderella* is linked with the concept of cinders. By the way, in the Russian folkloric tale she is called Zamarashka (Filthy-Face), not Zolushka (Cinderella, from *zola*, "cinders"). Zolushka is a translation from the German Aschenbrödel or Asche (cinder) or the French Cendrillon (from the French *cendre*) or the English Cinderella (from *cinder*). In Czech her name is Popeluska, in Serbo-Croatian Pepeljuga, in Bulgarian Pepeleshka, and in Polish Popiełucha.[78] In Russian folktales the male equivalent of this name is Ivan Popelov—the name of a hero who, until he carries out his feats, lounges on the stove and is smeared with ashes and soot. But Zamarashka does not lounge on the stove. She is exiled to the kitchen and does all the dirty work there. Therefore she is dirty—Zamarashka. But at the end of the tale this external lack of correspondence always winds up with transformation of the externally unprepossessing hero or heroine into a handsome prince or a beautiful princess. This happens here as well.

I will not dwell on the plot since I consider it well known. This tale is spread over the whole world, and recordings of it are extremely numerous. It has been the topic of several studies. In 1951 a specialized work researching the whole cycle of these tales came out in English in Sweden, under the title *The Cinderella Cycle*.[79] In 1893 M. R. Cox's work appeared, examining a whole complex of related plots rather than only one.[80] However, many of the motifs are even more widespread than Cox knew. The king arranges a ball. This motif is characteristic not just for tales of the given type. It is present, for example, in the tales of Sivko-Burko, Emelia the Fool, and others. A ball or party is always arranged so that the false hero can be distinguished from the true one. In this case the genuine hero takes advantage of a magical helper's cooperation. In the tale of Emelia it is a pike; in Sivko-Burko it is a horse that the hero's dead father gave him; in the tale of Cinderella it is her own deceased mother. On her grave she finds one after the other three marvelous dresses, which shine like stars, like the moon, and like the sun. The motif of the lost slipper is the sign by which the true hero is recognized. Thus Ivan the Fool in "Sivko-Burko" is recognized by the star on his forehead; in the tale of Zamarashka this role is played by the slipper. The prince will marry only the girl whom the lost slipper fits, and this turns out to be Cinderella. In this way, the cycle of tales about Cinderella belongs to the order of wonder tales as a whole, and it cannot be studied and understood outside it.

The Little Brown Cow (Burenushka), Crooked-Arms, and the Handless Maiden (Kosoruchka) The tales of "Little One-Eye, Little Two-Eyes, Little Three-Eyes," or "Burenushka" (A-T 511; Afanas'ev 100, 101) are close to the tale "Cinderella." A stepmother has two daughters—one-eyed and three-eyed. The stepdaughter has two eyes. She is sent out to tend the livestock. But she has a magical helper, the cow Burenushka. How she came to have this cow, the tale does not tell us. Some hints in separate variants let us establish that this cow was left to her, as in the tale of Cinderella, by her own dead mother. The sisters spy on her, the old woman orders the cow slaughtered. But the girl buries some part of the cow's body (the intestine), and a wondrous tree with wondrous fruits grows from it. A prince is traveling past and sees the tree. He wants to marry the girl who can pick a fruit from the tree. The tree lifts its branches when the evil stepsisters approach it, and lowers them when the girl herself comes. The prince marries the stepdaughter.

I have promised to examine tales that include no difficult tasks. Strictly speaking, the condition that the prince will marry only the girl who can pick him a fruit from the wondrous tree morphologically represents the difficult task before the wedding. The same thing can be said of the slipper in Cinderella. The prince will marry only the girl whose foot fits the slipper.

However, in the given survey it is thematically more fruitful to put all the tales about innocent people who are persecuted into one group, although such a combination may be debatable from the formal point of view.

The group of tales about the innocent persecuted also relates to the famous tale of Snow White, in the Russian repertoire better known under the title "The Magic Mirror" (A-T 709; Afanas'ev 210, 211). I will pass over this tale because Pushkin's poetic treatment is well known ("The Tale of the Dead Princess and the Seven *Bogatyri*"). Petr Ilyich Tchaikovsky's ballet was not based on the Russian tale, however, but on the French text from Charles Perrault's collection.

The innocent persecuted one may turn out to be not only a stepdaughter but also a sister or a wife. She is subjected to slander and driven from her home; she suffers all kinds of miseries, but all the blows of fate and unjust persecutions always end with the persecuted one's full triumph.

One of these tales is "Crooked Hands" or "The Handless Maiden" (A-T 706; Afanas'ev 279–282). Its plot comes down to the following: A brother and sister are living together in peace. But the brother marries, and the two women become enemies. This is a typical situation in peasant families, but not just peasant families. The beginning is entirely realistic. But we should consider this realistic family situation a later introduction. Such cases of enmity between members of the family are more characteristic of the ballad. There slander leads to a tragic plot development. Things go differently in the folktale. Apparently, the fundamental ancient folktale canon demands without fail that a young girl or woman be driven from her home, and the reason for this happening is added later. The husband leaves because of his business and hands over the household not to his wife but to his sister. From that moment the hatred takes on active forms. In this way, the opening has a psychological basis. The husband departs three times, and three times, in ascending order, the wife slanders her sister-in-law. In Afanas'ev she first ruins the furniture, then cuts off a horse's head, and then cuts the head off her own newborn child. When her husband returns she blames his sister. On the pretext of making a trip to church, the brother takes his sister into the woods and leaves her there. This whole scene is described in great detail. The tale-teller knows how to depict the growing fear and horror of the girl, who begins gradually to understand that her brother is taking her not to church but to some terrible deed. The brother pushes his sister off the wagon, but she grabs hold of the side, and at that moment he chops off her hands and drives away.

The girl remains in the forest alone. In some variants she lives there for several years, grows wild; her clothes gradually wear out and fall off her, but her hair grows long, and she wraps herself in it. In this part the tale crosses with another tale, called "The Pig Coat" (A-T 510 B), and is very close to "Cinderella." The girl lives in a hollow tree or in a tree's branches. The prince's dogs catch her scent during a hunt. The prince takes her with him and marries her, even though she has no hands. A different development is more typical for the given tale: Crooked-Hands comes out of the forest and becomes a beggar. A merchant's son falls in love with her and marries her. But the tale cannot stop at this point. Crooked-Hands also must be healed and justified, and the sister-in-law must be punished. Crooked-Hands suffers new misfortunes. The situation repeats itself. The husband's parents (or other relations) hate her because she has no hands, because their son has married a handless beggar. The husband leaves home, and at the same time she gives birth to a wonderful baby: "On his sides many stars, on his forehead a bright moon, against his heart the beautiful sun" (Afanas'ev 279). This miracle shows the listener that the mother is no simple, ordinary person; she belongs to some other world. The evil relatives slander her once again. They send word to the child's father that she has given birth to a child who is "half dog, half warlock; she got him when she was in the woods with the beasts" (Afanas'ev 279). They also replace the letter he sends in answer. The in-laws bind the infant to his mother's breast and drive them from the house. They wander through the world. And a miracle occurs. I cite the text word-for-word from Afanas'ev:

> She set off walking, she cried bitter tears, walked for a long time or for
> a short time—it was all bare fields, no forest or village anywhere. She
> walked up to a hollow, and how thirsty she started to feel. She took a
> look to the right—there stood a well. She wanted to quench her thirst,
> but she was afraid to lean over, so as not to drop the child. Then it
> seemed to her that the water came closer (i.e., the water in the well rose
> up). She leaned over, the child slipped out and fell into the well. And

she walked around the well and cried: how could she get the child out of the water? An old man came up to her and said, "Why are you crying, God's servant?" "How can I not cry? I leaned over the well to take a drink of water, and my baby fell into the water." "Go, bend over, get him." "No, father, I have no hands, only up to the elbows." "But go over, bend down and take the child!" She went over to the well, started to stretch out her arms, the Lord took pity on her—and her arms became whole. (Afanas'ev 279)

She lifts the infant out and they go onward. Unrecognized, she comes to her brother's house, where they had driven her away, and she asks to spend the night. Her brother does not recognize her and lets the beggar woman in to spend the night. He asks her to tell some kind of tale, and she tells the whole story of what happened to her as if it were a tale; the folktale is repeated almost word for word. From the point of view of folktale morphology, this is one of the forms of exposure. They unwrap the child, "and the whole room was lit up." The brother ties his wife to a mare's tail, and she is dragged through the field until she dies. He gives his sister a troika; she arrives home in triumph. In Afanas'ev's version her return is not described.[81]

As I said before, every folkloric tale text, as a rule, possesses some kind of defects that are usually immediately clear to the contemporary reader or researcher but that the tale-teller does not notice. This is how things stand with Afanas'ev. The schema of this tale, which becomes clear only when we make a comparison of variants, possesses a high degree of artistic perfection. The tale may not be as popular in literate circles as "Cinderella" or "Sleeping Beauty," but among the folk it is more popular: "Cinderella" (A-T 510) is known in nine Russian variants; "Sleeping Beauty" (A-T 709) is known in eighteen Russian variants; "The Handless Maiden" (A-T 706) is known in thirty-four Russian variants.[82] "Crooked-Arms" did not undergo literary reworking in nineteenth-century Russian literature. But it has a place in many early Western European reworkings,[83] with as many as nineteen literary treatments from the thirteenth to the sixteenth centuries. In Western European folklore this tale is also extraordinarily popular.[84]

Other Groups of Tales

I cannot, of course, characterize every Russian wonder tale. I will linger on only a few of the categories and their groups, illustrating these categories with individual images. A survey of plots, a brief acquaintance with the plot contents, willy-nilly, becomes clipped and incomplete and fails to reflect the whole plot richness of the Russian folkloric tale. But a full survey would take up a great deal of time. Moreover, it is unnecessary.

My task is not to count the tales but to introduce an understanding of them. I will indicate a few of the most popular or most significant plots of the Russian wonder tale, and at the same time I will give their names in the order of the plot index. Here are the tales I consider it most necessary to name:

301. The Three Kingdoms
302. Kashchei's Death in an Egg
307. The Girl Who Rose from the Grave (Gogol uses the plot in "Vii")
315. The Feigned Illness (beast's milk)
325. Crafty Knowledge
327. Children at Baba Yaga's Hut
400. The husband looks for his wife, who has disappeared or been stolen (or a wife searches for her husband)
461. Mark the Rich
465. The Beautiful Wife
519. The Blind Man and the Legless Man
545B. Puss in Boots
555. Kitten-Gold Forehead (a gold fish, a magical tree)
560. The Magic Ring
567. The Marvelous Bird
707. The Tale of Tsar Saltan (marvelous children)

THE MOST ANCIENT FOUNDATIONS OF THE WONDER TALE

I will move on to another question: the most ancient basis and origins of the wonder tale. This question is complicated. My book *Historical Roots of the Wonder Tale* is devoted to it. I will not retell the book but will lay out only a few conclusions and some supplementary thoughts and observations.

This question of origins is complex for various reasons but especially because in genetic study of the folktale one must not forget that the plot may be older than the genre. The plot may have roots in myth. Primitive people did not have fairytales. They had only myths. Individual motifs, episodes, or events may reflect ancient concepts that existed before the creation of the folktale. The folktale did not yet exist, but those concepts, those images, those fantastic or real events that it tells about, could have had a place in formations that preceded the folktale or even in reality. This way, the question splits in two: (1) How did the plot arise, and (2) how did the folktale arise?

Let us look initially at the first of these. It also splits in two: (1) the question of sources and (2) the question of the work's genesis. Let us examine some of the folktale's most ancient elements, which go back to primitive concepts. And we will take a concrete example: fighting dragons.

I have already spoken of dragons. According to the concepts of many peoples in the early stages of agriculture, the dragon is master of the element of water—both earthly and heavenly. In the folktale he lives in water, and when he comes to the surface, the water rises three yards along with him. In ethnography such creatures are called masters of the elements. The dragon is master of the element of water. In the *bylina* of Dobrynia the Dragon-Fighter, it is clear that the dragon controls the rain.

> At that moment, at that time
> There is no wind, a cloud was carried past,
> There is no cloud, but the rain rains,
> There is no rain, sparks are pouring.
> The great dragon is flying—*Gorynishche*
> Besides the dragon with twelve trunks.
> The dragon wants to burn him and his horse.[85]

The dragon's link with rain is completely clear. As controller of the watery element, people assumed that the dragon, the serpent, had power over the rain. The harvest was dependent on water. Therefore, to propitiate the master of the element of water, they brought him gifts and sacrifices. They brought girls to the shores of rivers or lakes and left them there or drowned them. They were given to the dragon to be devoured or for marriage. This custom was witnessed and widespread where agriculture depended on rivers—for example, in the valleys of the Nile, the Ganges, the Euphrates, and the Tigris. Clearly, as long as this custom was actually in force there could be no tales about it.

Religious and mythological concepts of the harvest's dependence on the masters of the elements would gradually, with development of techniques of agriculture, become more tenuous, waver, and disappear. The custom that was once considered necessary and useful became repellent. People began to create stories about how a girl was given to a dragon to eat (or, later, how a dragon stole a girl), but a brave rescuer appeared, who had acquired special powers and abilities, who possessed either talismans or animals. He searched out the dragon, threw himself into battle with it, vanquished it, and freed the girl who had been brought as a sacrifice. Had such a hero appeared when the custom of bringing a sacrifice for the dragon still existed, he would have been torn apart and destroyed as the greatest disgrace, a threat to the fundamental conditions of existence, to the harvest. The plot of dragon fighting is born from an action against custom or ritual, which was once considered sacred and necessary but which became horrifying and unnecessary. The plot of fighting dragons arises where such rituals and customs existed, at a stage of agriculture when primeval concepts begin to disappear. At first it appears in myths, in whose reality people believed. Their heroes are gods and demigods, whose cult was respected. The plot can be traced in antiquity.

I will mention the myth of Perseus and Andromeda. The king of Argos, Acrisius, is told that his daughter's child will rob him of his life and throne. The king has a daughter, Danaë. To hide her from men, the king locks his daughter into a high tower. We easily recognize the motif of the girl who is locked in and surrounded by prohibitions. But this prohibition does not succeed. So too, in the tale "The Wooden Eagle," the prince flies to a girl on an eagle. They catch him and want to kill him, but he flies away from the place of execution along with the princess. In the Greek myth things go differently. In the myth a god—Zeus himself—makes his way to Danaë through the window in the form of a shower of gold. (This moment is depicted in Rembrandt's famous painting. Titian's picture is also widely known.) A son is born (the king's grandson), Perseus. To save himself nonetheless from the prophecy, the king locks the mother and son (his own daughter and grandchild) in a chest and orders this chest thrown into the sea, just as in the tale of Tsar Saltan, where mother and son are put into a barrel. Danaë addresses the sea, pronounces an incantation: "Let the sea fall silent, let the terrible danger pass." Here let us remember Pushkin.

But the child hurries the wave:
"You, my wave, oh wave of mine,
You are booming and you're free;
Wherever you wish, you splash,
Sharpening stones in the sea.
You wet the shore of the land,

Do not be our souls' ruin:
Splash us out onto dry land!"[86]

The wind carries the chest to the shore of an island in both myth and folktale. The myth is known in numerous variants, as is the folktale. According to one, Perseus is raised on the island by the brother of the island's king, Polydectes. Polydectes falls in love with Danaë. Perseus grows bigger, and, to get rid of him, Polydectes assigns him perilous and impossible tasks. Scholars of the folktale will immediately recognize the plot. In the folktale the evil king sends the hero away from home, to get his wife; in the myth he is sent away so the king can take his mother. In the folktale the hero is a prince; in the myth he is the son of the god Zeus. He is sent to cut off the head of the monster Medusa and bring it to the king. I will not go into details of the narration. Perseus has various adventures, which I omit. However, we expect the hero to obtain magical gifts: a magical object or magical helpers. And this is in fact what happens. Perseus is the son of the god Zeus; therefore other gods, Hermes and Athena, help him. Hermes gives him a sickle, Athena a mirror, and the nymphs give him winged sandals, which enable him to fly, a bag, and the helmet of the god of the underworld, Hades, which makes a man invisible—an invisibility hat.

The Medusa is a fright. Instead of hair she has snakes; tusks protrude from her mouth; she has iron hands and golden wings. Her gaze is so terrible that anyone she looks at turns to stone. With the help of the invisibility hat, the mirror (he does not look directly at her but sees her in the mirror), and the other gifts, Perseus cuts off the Medusa's head. Once again I am omitting the details. After fulfilling this task, Perseus does not return home, as we would expect, but flies farther. We hear about his main feat—rescuing a girl from a dragon. Here we must add that the magic horse Pegasus leapt out of Medusa's body after her head was cut off. We also know the magical horse from the folktale, only there he is obtained in a different way. Perseus flies farther and comes to Ethiopia. We will note, by the way, that in the myth, unlike the folktale, all the characters and places where the action takes place are named. This means, as I already said, that the events of the myth were considered real. Perseus sees a beautiful girl bound to the cliff with chains. She is so beautiful that at first he takes her for a marble sculpture (the Greeks painted their sculptures). She is completely motionless, but when he comes closer he sees tears flowing from her eyes; she is not a sculpture but a living person. He asks who she is; she says she is Andromeda and tells him her story. Andromeda's mother boasted that she was better and more beautiful than the Nereids. The Nereids were the daughters of Nereus, the old man of the sea, sea maidens distinguished by their unusual beauty. The Nereids became enraged, and the sea god Poseidon took their side. He sent a flood and a sea monster in the form of a fish that devoured everything. An oracle told the king of Ethiopia that the country could be saved from the monster and the flood if the king gave up his daughter for the monster to devour. While Andromeda is telling all this, a wave rises and the sea monster appears. With the help of his magical gifts, Perseus vanquishes the monster (this is described in detail), frees the girl, and then marries her. The delighted king not only gives him his daughter but hands over his kingdom. In all this we recognize the plot of a folktale. Perseus also kills his rival, Andromeda's former fiancé, and then returns with his wife to his mother Danaë. Later he comes unrecognized to his grandfather, who once drove out him and his mother. The prophecy comes to pass: Perseus accidentally kills his grandfather and becomes his heir. He gives up the kingship in the land of his father-in-law. Thus this remarkable story ends.

Almost against our will we are drawn to compare this myth with the folktale on the one hand and with ritual on the other. It leads us to conclude that in the oldest form there are no gods yet; that is, it is the ritual. In the myth it is the god Poseidon who provokes the flood and the monster's appearance. In the archaic form it is the monster, of course, who provokes the flood. The maiden is taken out for the monster to eat by the oracle's command. This oracle is clearly a later introduction. At first Perseus inherits his wife's kingdom, but later it is the kingdom of his grandfather. Here before us we see the shift of one form of inheritance—from king to son-in-law through the hand of his daughter (a more archaic form, which once existed in reality)—to another, later form of inheritance—from father to son, from son to grandson through the male line.

Thus the descent and origin of one of the most widespread folktale plots— the plot of fighting a dragon and rescuing a girl—opens to us in its general outlines. We see the plot in three stages. The first stage is the ritual, which was carried out in fact. The second stage is the myth. The ritual has already moved into the past and is perceived as something repulsive and dishonorable. A hero appears, the son of a god, and destroys the monster to whom the girl was to be handed over. The people believed in the myth; its contents have a sacral character, representing a people's sacred tradition. The third stage is the folktale. Some traits of the plot change, but the core remains. The story is perceived as an invention. The hero's image is delightful in its manliness and handsomeness—not as a god but as a person, a prince, idealized and splendid.

But sometimes belief in the event does not disappear. Then a different kind of evolution occurs. A plot from one religious system makes its way into another. Pagan sacrality is replaced by Christian belief. The feat of vanquishing the dragon is now carried out not by a pagan deity but by a Christian saint: Saint George the Victorious (the patron saint of Muscovy), Dmitrii of Thessaloniki, or the Archangel Michael. This is narrated not in a folktale but in hagiography. In accord with the new character of the plot, the woman disappears. Actually, in some cases she still remains. George is a Christian, whereas the liberated girl is a pagan. George does not marry her but converts her, her father, and the whole country to Christianity. This plot is found in spiritual verses. St. George's battle with the dragon is often depicted on icons, picturesque and colorful. St. George's impetuous movements as he thrusts his spear into the dragon are given with particular artistry, as well as the rush of the horse, who is shown in action, rearing up on its hind legs.

I have traced the appearance of one plot.[87] The question is, Do all the plots of the wonder tale have such a detailed history?

Asking the question this way seems entirely logical. But, from my point of view, it is nonetheless illegitimate. I have attempted to show that the wonder tale is constructed according to a single system, according to one compositional schema, regardless of its plot. Before asking about the descent of individual plots, we must speak of the descent of the entire system as a whole.

My book *Historical Roots of the Wonder Tale* is devoted to this question. I am not going to lay out that book's contents here, but I will linger a moment on some of the most essential points. From the example of the motif of fighting dragons it is clear that what we perceive as pure fantasy reaches back to reality. It is true that this is not the everyday reality reflected, for example, in realistic novels; it is the reality of the distant past, mixed with a fantasy that, in turn, is also explained through some kind of unreal details. False conceptions are not born of themselves, independently of reality. They can always be explained by the reality that produced them, although it is not always easy to do so.

If we cast a glance at the compositional system of long, complicated folktales, where the action concludes with the hero's marriage and crowning as ruler and contains all the elements of the folktale, then we might confirm that the existence of two worlds of some kind serves as a presupposition for these tales. It is not a separate motif or plot but a compositional foundation. The tale begins with people's earthly life "in a certain kingdom, in a certain state," and some tale-tellers will add, "that is, in the one where we live." It is true that the addition is made as a joke, with an ironic tone, and this ironic tone is entirely well founded. The "certain kingdom" with which the tale begins is not like our land. And although realistic old men and old women live in it, peasants go out to work, sow, and mow, and soldiers pace on sentry duty, entirely fantastic kings and queens live in the kingdom alongside them, golden apples grow in their gardens, and the Firebird flies there. In this way, it is by no means the world the tale-teller lives in. But be that as it may, this world is opposed to another. The other world is located over thrice-nine lands. Thrice-nine is a typical folktale trebling. The other world is far away. It might also be called the thrice-tenth kingdom. It does not come in threes; it is unique. And there, if the original kingdom where the tale begins does not much resemble the land in which we live, then the thrice-tenth kingdom corresponds perfectly to the conceptions people once created of the world on the other side, the world where people go after death.

The concept of two worlds exists in absolutely every religion, beginning with the most ancient and ending with Christianity. It is one of the bases of religious thinking and concepts, and it disappears only with the development of science, scientific atheism. These concepts change over the course of history, with the development of forms of thinking that depend on a society's economic, cultural, and social level. But old concepts do not disappear right away as new ones appear. Most peoples at early stages of development have quite various and contradictory concepts, old and new ones. We see a picture like this even in the era of development of the slaveholding state of ancient Greece. The folktale also presents this kind of various and contradictory picture.

The most ancient form of religion known to us is totemism. We use the term *totemism* to describe a religion in which people deify an animal and consider it a more perfect being than they are themselves. This religion is characteristic of the stage of a hunting economy and the earliest forms of clan structure. In accord with these concepts, people count their own descent from the animal. Every clan has its own animal, from which it traces its origin and which it considers sacred. Such an animal is called the totem, and the corresponding religion is totemism.[88] The totem animal, as a rule, is not used for food. The totem is considered the protector of the clan. After death people come to a world where the animals rule. This is also preserved in the folktale.

The tale, of course, may change the "nomenclature" of the animals. It is rich enough: There is a kingdom of lions, of bears, of dragons, of eagles, of falcons, of ravens, of mice, of chickens—all these examples are taken from Afanas'ev. These are the most ancient forms of the other, or in folktale terms, the thrice-tenth kingdom.

We also have the totemistic form of hunters. Gardening precedes agriculture. There are figs and banana palms. Eden, and then palaces, and finally cities. But there is no agriculture. We are in the land of plenty. Everyone and everything comes from there: the culture hero, the first seeds, knowledge of rituals and ceremonies, fire (stolen), and so on. How is this land to be governed? By the people themselves. This is transformed into rule by an invisible woman, the queen or perhaps the tsar-maiden. She is a powerful female. Later, she is replaced by the king.

Where is this other kingdom? Most often in the folktale it is far away, somewhere over the horizon, over the sea, over thrice-nine lands. But it may also be located under the earth. For example, "For a long time, for a short time—Ivan came upon a way into the ground. By this way he went down into a deep abyss and came to the underground kingdom, where a six-headed dragon lived and ruled" (Afanas'ev 237). It may also be located in the mountains: "They climbed onto him, and the bear-king took them to mountains so steep and high that they reached up to the sky itself; it was completely deserted, no one lived there" (Afanas'ev 201).[89] It may also be located under the water, as in the tale of the sea king and Vasilisa the Beautiful.

All these concepts are entirely historical. Thus, for example, in antiquity the far distant kingdom (in Greece, Elysium) is an island of the blessed. In the folktale (e.g., in the tale of Tsar Saltan) the other kingdom is also located over the sea on an island. People live there without labor in eternal bliss. There is no snow, no storm, no rain; for the Greeks, snow and cold are a misfortune. Sometimes this paradise is called the Elysian land or the Elysian fields. Along with this paradise the Greeks have another: the underground kingdom of the dead. There Hades rules with his wife Persephone, whom he stole away and brought to his realm. He is the ruler of the bowels of the earth and of earthly riches, and Persephone is a goddess of fertility. This kingdom is sometimes set apart by a river, across which the dead are ferried by the gloomy and silent Charon. The motif of being brought across is found in the folktale too, for example, in the tale of Mark the Rich (type 461). Mark sends his nephew to the other world to get rid of him, and he is taken across by such a ferryman.

There is some lack of agreement between these two concepts. The Greeks attempted to explain it in various ways. Later on, Christianity divided the other world in two. One part is located in the skies. That is paradise, where the righteous go. There God rules and the winged angels live. The other is hell, the underworld; sinners go there to eternal torment, and there the devil rules. The Catholic Church added Purgatory too, but this is a late concept; it does not exist in the folktale. All these medieval concepts are depicted in detail by Dante in his *Divine Comedy*.

Antiquity knows the mountains as one form of the other world; this is Olympus. There the gods sit and feast; there Zeus rules. This concept too is significantly later.

How do people get to the other world? Let us see what kind of picture the folktale gives and what concepts this corresponds to in the historical past. One way to get there is when the hero turns into an animal. For example, "Buria-*bogatyr'* struck the earth, turned into an eagle, and flew to the palace" (Afanas'ev 76). Most often it is precisely a bird. This concept is clearly of to-temistic origin. According to these concepts, after death a person turns into an animal. At first it can be any kind; later on the animal is most often a bird, because a bird is capable of flying over the sea. Later, as concepts of the soul develop, the soul is represented in the form of a bird—not the whole person, just the soul flies away to the other world. Then develops the concept of winged angels, who carry the soul to heaven. With the domestication of horses, the horse becomes this kind of bearer to the other world. As it replaces the bird, the horse acquires wings. So we see the image of the winged horse, known in both religion and the folktale. The Slavs buried the dead along with their horses so that the horse could take the deceased to the other world. In the tale of Sivko-Burko the hero's dead father gives him such a horse.

In the folktale any fast-moving animal, able to move by land, sea, or air, may take the hero to the thrice-tenth kingdom. He flies on an eagle, sails on a whale, runs in the form of a deer. Later the ship appears. It may be a flying ship, and there are also notions of a ship of souls. Later the folktale ship turns into an ordinary vessel, and the hero becomes a merchant who travels to trade in distant places.

I would like to dwell on two more forms of transit in the folktale, for which we may find an equivalent in the religious and historical past. The hero steps into the skin of some kind of animal, most often a bull, sometimes a horse. He is seized by an eagle and taken to a mountain peak. In funeral rites we encounter the practice of sewing the dead into a skin. This represents a development of the concept of turning into an animal. I will not cite examples here.

Finally, I would like to mention the motif we met in the tale of Finist but also found in other tales: The heroine must wear out three pairs of iron shoes, break three iron staffs, and gnaw on iron bread.

The tale grows out of social life and its institutions. One of them is the ritual of initiation. It forms part of a system. It is reflected in the motif of the children at Baba Yaga's hut. Here I have moved from the tale to the ritual (the dragon). Now I will move in the opposite direction. We may assert that children who spend time in the forest reflect a ritual of initiation in the clan system. What did the ritual consist of?[90] Such are the general conceptions. Now the details, the factual side of the matter.[91] Perhaps it is kidnapping[92] or the witch is a bird who steals Tereshichka or the Brave Youth. What has happened? Perhaps madness.[93] Perhaps a finger is severed (or the whole hand).[94] Perhaps the children avoid being shoved into Baba Yaga's stove,[95] or the witch is burned. There might be a magical gift.[96] Then the hero returns unrecognized[97] or simply returns home.

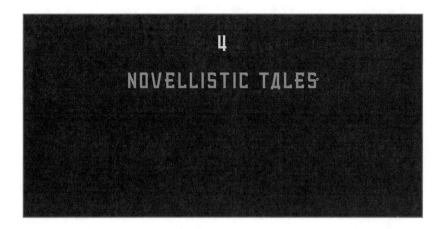

4

NOVELLISTIC TALES

GENERAL DESCRIPTION OF NOVELLISTIC TALES

I will move on now to another major type of folktales: everyday, realistic, or novellistic tales. They are completely different in character from the wonder tale. Why do they have three names, and which of the three is best? Terminology has great significance in any branch of scholarship. It should be as precise as possible. But here we encounter a great difficulty. All three names are possible, but no one of them possesses the precision of a scientific term, and each of them may be applied only conditionally and with limitations.

Folktales could be called realistic because the characters in them are not fantastic creatures from another world but real people. But despite that, as we will see, these tales are far from what we would call realism. They can be called novellistic because they are entertaining, interesting short narratives. But they are still not novellas but real folktales. Finally, they could be called everyday tales, because they give the everyday life of peasants before the Great

Reforms a fairly broad depiction, although their goal was never to describe everyday life.

These tales differ so sharply from wonder tales that we could ask whether the two forms of folktales might be two different genres of folk narrative art.

If we saw a certain quality of dual levels in the wonder tale, the presence of two worlds, here there is only one. It is our own world, the one we live in. True, describing everyday life was never the goal of these tales. For example, they give no description at all of the setting where the action takes place. The setting is not described; it is only thought of or imagined or given as a kind of background against which the action develops, and it is dashed off with sketchy strokes. But although such tales offer no direct descriptions, everyday life makes up not only their background but also the material, the arsenal that the everyday tale makes use of for artistic goals. For this reason, the everyday tale has the most intimate connection with reality. It is impossible to evaluate the condition of the prerevolutionary Russian village according to the material of wonder tales, but everyday tales do offer this possibility. The characters always belong to a definite social category. The hero of everyday tales is already not a prince, not the youngest of three sons. He is a young lad, a villager, a soldier, a worker, a peasant. His antagonist is a nobleman, a landowner, a priest, a judge, a rich peasant, a magnate. Therefore these tales often have a character marked by class. They give a vivid reflection of the class antagonism of the old village.

These tales may serve as a means to study the peasant worldview and the peasant philosophy of life. Just like wonder tales, they are thoroughly optimistic. The hero always triumphs over his opponents. But the character of the struggle here is different, as is the morality of these tales. In the wonder tale good always triumphs. Evil appears in the form of fantastic creatures: dragons, Kashchei, Baba Yaga, and so on. In the everyday tale earthly people are the bearers of evil. Evil is represented not by Kashchei, a dragon, or a witch but by the antagonists a peasant sees in his own life. These are most often the peasant's social enemies. All kinds of methods are good in the struggle with them. The hero's opponent is socially powerful but worthless in his essence. The hero is worthless socially; he stands on the bottom rungs of the social ladder. He is deprived, poor, oppressed. There is no idealization in his depiction. It is as though his appearance holds nothing beautiful, nothing markedly heroic. He is the most ordinary person. But at the same time he is the embodiment of bravery, decisiveness, invention, and inextinguishable power of the spirit and the will to struggle, sometimes of unusual craftiness. Therefore he always wins.

One basic trait of these tales is the absence of the supernatural. As a rule, the laws of nature are not violated. In wonder tales the hero acquires some magical object and achieves his goal with its help. In so-called realistic tales there is never any magical object, and this may serve as one feature to distinguish realistic tales from magical tales. For example, there are no magical horses, no magical objects, or spirits who appear out of a ring; there are also no enchanted kingdoms, no people who marry animals, and in general none of what makes up the contents of fairy tales. Nevertheless, the supernatural is present in these tales, just drawn into the orbit of ordinary, everyday life and always with a comic coloration. Thus, for example, the devil is a character in some of the tales, but this devil is not at all like the magical personages of the fairy tale. It is always a devil who is fooled, deceived, bested by a person, as in "The Tale of the Priest and His Workman Balda." Aarne's index sets aside a whole group of tales about the stupid devil. The devil in the folk consciousness possesses a different degree and a different quality of reality from, say, Baba Yaga or a dragon. Thus in the tale "An Old Woman's Worse Than a Devil" (A-T 1165 [1353]; Gospodarev 59),[1] profoundly researched by Jiri Polívka,[2] the devil is bested by an evil peasant woman, and the devil is depicted just as realistically as she is.

To gain the most basic concept of the character of these tales, of their style, and of how they combine what is real with the fantastic, we will linger on the plot of this tale. The tale describes a man and his wife who have lived in peace and harmony for twenty years. The devil finds this repellent; he cannot get them to quarrel no matter what he does. He talks it over with an old peasant woman. In Gospodarev's version it goes like this: "For three years I've been walking around in your neighborhood there. Where there's a murder, they praise me; where there's a fight, there I am; but here, with that peasant, I can't get him even to argue with his wife. I've already sat under their table, but I can't take them that way either." The old woman agrees to make the spouses quarrel.

"And what will you give me, if I get them to start fighting in three days?" "What do you want, old woman?" the devil cheered up. "Buy me some red boots." "I'll buy them, old woman, just do your best!"

The old woman really does get the couple to quarrel. She tells the wife that the husband is cheating on her, that he goes to see such-and-such a woman at night. She advises the wife to take a razor and cut off the three hairs that grow out of a wart on her husband's neck. She has to say a charm over those three hairs, and then her husband will love no one but her. The old woman tells the husband that the wife is "stepping out" and wants to get rid of him. At night she will take a razor to cut his throat. The idea succeeds. The husband pretends to be asleep and catches his wife lifting the razor to his throat. The spouses have a fistfight. "And the imp starts to run around and rejoice that they're fighting. Now he enjoys the glory." The devil brings the old woman the red boots he promised, but he holds them out to her on the end of a pole, because he is afraid to touch a woman like that. In Gospodarev's rendition the tale ends with the saying, "You know, where the devil can't make it, the old woman manages."[3]

This tale is quite typical of the whole genre of everyday tales. It depicts the devil not as a being from the other world but as entirely earthly and real. He and the old woman are the two main characters. The dialogues are in living, everyday peasant speech, expressive and emotionally colored. In its unexpected ending the tale is not far from the anecdote.

This tale is fairly rare on Russian soil. It is known in only two variants that differ greatly from each other. But in the West the tale has been known since the end of the twelfth century; that is, it is one of the oldest. It is often encountered in edifying manuscript literature and in sermons as a monastic weapon against women, who, according to the church's teaching, are the vessels of every kind of evil. However, in the Russian interpretation there is no such idea. The tale is directed not against women in general but against those who love family arguments, intrigues, and scandals, and they are the ones it mocks. We can cite other examples of how the everyday novellistic tales treat the supernatural in an entirely realistic way.

Transformations are possible in these tales, however. Still, if in a wonder tale Baba Yaga turns a hero or his brother into a stone, it is perceived as the most tragic misfortune. The very setting (the forest, Baba Yaga) is fantastic and frightening. In the novellistic tale an evil wife, when her husband finds her with her lover, turns him into a hound dog with a blow of her stick. This is told in the following manner: "When it got dark I heard my wife and her friend making merry in the house. I ran into the house and just wanted to teach my wife a bit of a lesson when she grabbed a stick, hit me on the back, and said, 'Till now you were a peasant man, but now be a black hound!' That moment I turned into a dog. She took the oven tongs and started to give it to me on both sides; she hit me, hit me and drove me out" (A-T 449; Afanas'ev

254–255). In the wonder tale a first-person narration is impossible. Here this device seems to bring events into the realm of reality. The contrast of the everyday setting with the fantastic contents establishes the comic quality of the situation. In Aleksandr Afanas'ev's collection the tale is called "The Wonder," and it is characterized by contamination with other adventures, just as marvelous and unusual, that happen to the most ordinary people. But, regardless of the everyday setting, the events are not at all presented as real; they represent an artistic invention.

The character of realism in these tales is defined by the fact that the way they are narrated; their style is realistic, but the events depicted are far from always realistically possible. The realism of such tales is quite relative. The novellistic, or realistic, tales are first and foremost folktales in the way that they can pile up the most monstrous improbabilities. As we already know, it is precisely the unusual that serves as the tale's topic. The everyday tale does not violate the laws of nature (with small exceptions), and if it does violate them, then this is depicted as something entirely possible. Nevertheless, the events narrated in the everyday tale are completely impossible in life because of their unusualness. They are so unusual that no one believes in them. This is what gives the tales their appeal.

The aesthetics of realism come down, in brief, to the desire to depict typical characters in typical situations. The typical is a generalization of the usual. Just the opposite is true in the everyday tale. It is not attracted by the usual at all. It is true that the setting, the background of the everyday tale, is completely real. The figures who feature in the tale also have a realistic character. But the actions of these figures move outside the framework of what really happens in life. Everyday tales are atypical, unheard-of stories, stories of things that are completely impossible.

We need only mentally translate the capers of crafty thieves or the harshest jests of a joker or the tricks played on the corpse of the hero's mother (sometimes after he himself has killed her) to the plane of the real to see at once how incongruous these and similar plots are with real actuality. Finally, in all kinds of cock-and-bull stories (*nebylitsy*) this reality is turned inside out.

Novellistic tales contain a great many everyday elements, cunningly depicted observations, lifelike details. With a certain literary reworking, we could easily turn them into novellas. They share with novellas the fact that they are short entertaining stories from life. Yet they are not novellas all the same. To see the difference between the tale and the novella, it is enough to compare one and the same plot in a folktale treatment and in a literary reworking. Let us take, for example, one of Boccaccio's novellas and compare it with its original folklore source (see the article "Folklore and Reality," the plot of dirty tricks played on a corpse in folklore and literature).[4] Boccaccio or Basile, Chaucer, or other authors move the action to definite places with definite names; that is, they transfer it to the plane of real events, whereas the folktale never does and cannot do that. The everyday tale is a particular poetic function. Its goal is not the depiction of reality but artistic entertainment.

But, although these tales always speak of completely unlikely events that could never take place in reality, they are narrated in such a way, with such intonation and with such artistic means of expression, saturated with such realistic everyday details, that it is as though it all took place in reality. This incongruity produces a comic effect. And really, all the everyday tales are strikingly humorous. They respond to the healthy desire to laugh, to chuckle. Therefore everyday tales may be used as the sharp and keen-eyed tools of satire, particularly social satire. The everyday tale tends toward the anecdote. This tendency is so strong and there are so many anecdotes in folk narrative art that it can erase the boundary between anecdotes and everyday tales. Aarne dedicated a large place in his index to anecdotes, but some of these represent typical folktales, and vice versa. Here we will not attempt to draw the line between everyday tales and anecdotes. I presume that folkloric anecdotes can be classed entirely with everyday tales, but first we must get acquainted with the plots of everyday tales.

A few words about the composition of folktales. In Chapter 3, while examining the composition of wonder tales, we noted certain regularities. The composition of folkloric wonder tales is monotonous and complex; the typical traditional wonder tale is always long. The composition of everyday tales is much more various. It is defined not so much by internal regularities as by the variety of events narrated. As a rule, everyday tales are distinguished by simplicity and brevity. The intrigues are extremely uncomplicated. The complex development of action typical of the wonder tale—complication through peripeties and so on—is alien to the everyday tale. Some everyday tales consist of several episodes mechanically strung together. The sequence of such episodes may be arbitrarily changed. Thus the hero, convinced of his wife's stupidity, sets out to search the world for stupider people. A series of meetings with even more stupid people defines the course of subsequent events.

Incidentally, there are nonetheless certain compositional regularities. So, for example, we will see that the predominating majority of plots consist in someone making a fool of someone else, but I will discuss that later.

Correspondingly, the everyday tale has none of the trebling so typical of the wonder tale. The everyday tale is alien to the formulaicity (so to speak) of the wonder tale; it has no introductory or concluding formulas, no clichés, and no general formulas—those would not match its style. All of what I have said—closeness to life, entertainingness, wit, and humor—also explains the extraordinary popularity of these tales. Judging by Afanas'ev's collection, the wonder tale would be the most widespread and beloved form of the folktale. But this is not so. Everyday tales could not always be published. Only after the 1905 revolution, when strict tsarist censorship temporarily eased, could these tales begin to make it into print in large quantity. We find especially many in Nikolai Onchukov's collection.[5]

The extraordinary popularity of the everyday tale is confirmed by statistical data. According to Nikolai Andreev's count, they compose 60 percent of the plot matter of Russian tales; 30 percent is made up of wonder tales, and 10 percent are tales about animals, cumulative tales, and so on. These data, of course, are not precise, and by now they are outdated, but the general picture is nonetheless accurate.[6] The repertoire of every people includes both international plots (i.e., plots known to many peoples) and national plots (which are the property of only one people).

Although there are many international plots among the wonder tales, the everyday tales of each people include many plots that are national. The everyday tale is not only the most popular but also the most nationally specific type of folktale.

ORIGIN AND HISTORICAL DEVELOPMENT
OF THE EVERYDAY TALE

The question of the wonder tale's origin could be answered by comparing its images, motifs, plots, and composition with the forms of social organization, rituals, concepts, and forms of thinking in primitive society.

The everyday tale has nothing in common with the primitive way of life, although in individual cases one might find ancient relics in it. These tales were created not in a primitive communal societal structure but later. We do not find it at all among the peoples characterized by totemistic concepts; it is also not found among peoples with shamanistic religion, such as the Paleo-Asiatic. But it is widespread in Africa, among peoples who know primitive agriculture. It is clear that it existed in ancient Egypt from the story of the crafty thief who looted the treasury of the pharaoh Rampsinit, preserved for us by Herodotus. It is true that in Herodotus's version the tale of Rampsinit is extremely close to the wonder tale (the hero marries a princess) and does not bear a strictly everyday character. I will have more to say about this tale later. But we can judge the presence of the purely everyday tale in Egypt by other sources too. Among the tales collected by G. Maspero,[7] some are typically novellistic, such as "The Complaints of the Salt-Boiler," who, after he is beaten and robbed while traveling, complains so picturesquely that the ruler keeps inciting him so he can hear more and more new complaints. The accumulation of complaints makes up the main plot of the tale. All this compels us to deduce that the everyday tale appears when agriculture emerges from its primitive stage and the clan structure is replaced by a slaveholding state.

This is confirmed by materials from antiquity. In antiquity realistic tales were quite broadly distributed, with a whole series of direct and indirect witnesses. There is a series of specialized studies of this in both Russian and Western European scholarship. Bolte and Polívka, in their commentary to the Grimm brothers' tales, give a rich list of folktale motifs, among them motifs of farcical character, that were preserved in antique literature.[8]

Another heir of the novellistic folkloric tale is comedy. Aristophanes's creative work is shot through with folklore. As Bédier rightly indicates, we know only an insignificant part of the antique comic literature. If we knew it all, we could more bravely assert that antique comedy is "the fabliau, brought into action." It is also likely that in the antique era the merry erotic tale, a type that still lives on in Russian villages, was already flourishing. We know that anecdotes were widely disseminated in antiquity from the collection of anecdotes of Hierocles, an Alexandrian scholar of the fifth century. The anecdotes he relates have no corresponding numbers in Russian folklore, but they do have them in Western European folklore (e.g., the anecdote about the stupid man who wants to see how he looks when he is asleep, so he closes his eyes in front of the mirror, is witnessed in England in the seventeenth century). But on the other hand, Hierocles, like other writers, includes stories about stupid people corresponding to our country bumpkins (*poshekhontsy*). Residents of the city of Abdera (Abderites) were considered stupid in the ancient era. In brilliant and cultured Athens, it was the relatively provincial Thebans who had the reputation of being none too bright. We will touch on the question of the tale in the clan system and in antiquity only in the most general outlines, because it is the Russian folktale we are studying. From this point of view it is more important for us to look at the folktale traditions of the Middle Ages.

In the Middle Ages it would never have occurred to anyone to write down folktales. The culture of Rus' and then of Muscovy had a primarily clerical character, and the folktale was not reflected in literature until the seventeenth century. Nonetheless there is no doubt at all that merry tales with realistic style were in circulation alongside church literature, along with the hagiographies, apocrypha, and moralizing tales, and in part as a counterweight to this literature. We can judge this from a few indirect data and also by analogy with Western Europe, where there is more testimony to the circulation of the folktale. We know of similar folktales beginning in the tenth century (the stories of Ol'ga's revenge[9] and so on).

The clerical character of early medieval culture both in Eastern Europe and in Russia interfered with the written, literary, properly artistic use of folktale plots. Things changed in Europe with the arrival of the Renaissance and in Russia in the seventeenth century. True, there are still no direct records, but we can nonetheless judge what kinds of folk traditions existed in the Middle Ages by the rich novellistic literature of the fourteenth to seventeenth centuries, a literature that was to a great extent folkloric in its foundation. In the late Middle Ages in Western Europe and Russia, the everyday tale circulated not only among peasants but also in urban spheres, among the middle and upper classes. It was disseminated by wandering performers: *jongleurs* in France, *Spielmänner* in Germany, minstrels in England, *skomorokhi* in Russia. They transmitted entertaining stories that entered the literature of European countries. Verse treatments of such stories received the name *fableau* (or *fabliaux*) in France, *Schwank* in Germany, *facecie* in Italy, a term that passed on to Muscovy. These terms for the most part include the jesting genre (the Jolly Monastery has sixty-one literary treatments, of which the most ancient is from the eighth century). This genre is represented in Italy by Poggio's famous *Liber facetiarum*, a book that was published and imitated more than once. A whole series of collections appeared in Germany beginning in the fifteenth century. The most significant collections of *Schwanke* are Pauli's.[10] The largest of these collections is Hans Wilhelm Kirchhof's (in seven volumes).[11]

TALES OF TRANSITIONAL CHARACTER

I move on now to examine the Russian everyday, novellistic, or realistic tales recorded in our collections, beginning with Afanas'ev and his occasional predecessors.[12]

One great difficulty arises here. Any survey, whether strictly scholarly or popular-scientific, demands preliminary classification, sorting, or division of material into some kind of groups. However, the everyday tale has been studied so little that it is still impossible to give an irreproachably correct sorting. Therefore we will limit ourselves to dividing the material into plot-thematic groups. Such a division is convenient because it visibly represents the kinds of plots one finds as the everyday tale circulates in a folk milieu. We will linger on the major ones, the most popular and widespread. The makeup of the novellistic everyday tale is extraordinarily colorful and various, and it can be divided and classified in a variety of ways. Studying it by plot is only one way to resolve this question. But we may not leave aside or ignore the question of composition either.

As we study folktales by their composition, we discover that some novellistic tales are extremely close to the wonder tales. They make up a kind of transitional or intermediate group. The boundary between wonder tales and novellistic tales is purely conventional here; it should be regarded not as a formal boundary but as a historical one, the result of a protracted process of transformation of one kind into another. The morphological relationship between some novellistic tales and wonder tales also allows us to assert the descent of the novellistic tales from the wonder tales. Briefly, among the everyday tales some are structured according to the same compositional schema as the wonder tale, with the sole distinction that they contain nothing supernatural or magical. Here are a few examples of such transitional tales.

Let us take the tale "The Marks of the Princess" (A-T 850; Afanas'ev 238). In Afanas'ev's variant the tsar lets it be known that he will give his daughter in marriage to the one "who finds out the marks on my daughter." We recognize in its form the typical difficult task, characteristic of the magical tale, although the task in itself involves nothing supernatural or magical. Van'ka, a peasant's son, has gotten hold of a magical pipe or the self-playing *gusly*. We recognize the magical object. He received this magical object from an old man after doing him a favor. He herds swine, and the swine dance to the music of this pipe. Even before the tsar makes his announcement, the princess sees Van'ka and asks him to sell her one of the swine. "Pigherd, pigherd, sell me a piggy!" "My pigs are not for sale; they are secret." "And what is the secret?" "Well, princess, if you want to have a pig, then show me your white body up to the knees." The princess thought for a while, took a look in every direction and saw that no one was around; she lifted her dress up to her knees, and on her right leg she had a small birthmark. This way, the task is solved even before it is assigned. Aarne, like Andreev and Thompson after him, assigns this tale to the division called novellistic. In fact, the tale does bear a novellistic character. But we would call such tales novellistic or everyday, whereas there is nothing everyday in this tale. Its composition is typical of wonder tales: A difficult task is solved with the help of a magical object, leading to marriage with a princess. We must recognize that Aarne's definition is clearly mistaken. This tale could be assigned to the novellistic or to the wonder tales equally well, but it is closer precisely to the wonder tales.

Other case may be more dubious and difficult. Such, for example, is the tale "Unanswered Riddles" (A-T 851; Afanas'ev 239). A princess undertakes to answer all the riddles people pose to her. If she guesses someone's riddles, he loses his head, but whoever asks her an insoluble riddle will get to marry her. This once again is a difficult task. Ivan the Fool, the youngest of three sons, solves it. He sets out without having prepared anything. Along the way he sees that a horse has gotten into a field of oats and is trampling the field. He chases it out with a knout and says to himself, "There's a riddle." He poses that riddle in this way: "As I was coming here to see you, I saw on the road a good (i.e., the field of oats), in the goods a good (the horse): I took a good (i.e., the knout), and with the good I drove the good out of the good: the good ran away from the good out of the good." He asks another similar riddle, and the princess is obliged to marry him. For us the link with the system of the magical tale is entirely obvious, although it stands even further from the magical tale than "The Marks of the Princess." Once again we see a difficult task, its resolution, and a peasant's son marrying a princess. True, there is no magical object here and there is nothing magical in it at all; the hero solves the task with his own mind, his own cleverness. Nonetheless, this tale too may not be grouped entirely among the novellistic tales. Three brothers and the marriage of a fool to a princess are typical compositional elements of the wonder tale, and it would hardly be correct to assign this tale to the class of novellistic tales without qualification.

The same might be said of the tale "The Husband at His Wife's Wedding" (A-T 974). A husband leaves his wife for a long time (he is traveling). While he is away, he finds out (sometimes in a marvelous way, from the birds or from a horse) that his wife plans to marry someone else, and he hurries home. In some variants a forest spirit or a devil brings him at lightning speed. Other variants, however, include no wonders at all. He happens to arrive home on the very day of his wife's new wedding. He comes unrecognized, in the form of a beggar, pilgrim, or a singer. His wife recognizes him by various signs and chases the new groom away. This plot is found all over the world. It lies at the root of the *Odyssey*: Odysseus returns home as Penelope is besieged by suitors. The same plot occurs in the *bylina* about Dobrynia and the failed wedding of Alyosha. The same plot is the basis of the tale "Ashik-Kerib," which was adapted by Mikhail Lermontov. Academician Ivan Ivanovich Tolstoi wrote a splendid scholarly study of this plot.[13] Comparison of material on an international level leaves no doubt about the fact that this tale that is not at all an everyday one (cf. also "The Underground Princess" [A-T 870, Sd. 66], "Eustathius Placida" [A-T 931], "Ballak Boris'evich" [A-T 946; Afanas'ev 180], "The Robber Bridegroom" [A-T 955; Afanas'ev 200], and others).

A SHORT SURVEY OF PLOTS

Tales of Wise Maidens

The study of tales that preserve the compositional schema of wonder tales but in which the properly magical elements gradually grow weaker and finally completely disappear leads us to consider that the wonder tale has evolved, that some tales can take on the form of everyday tales or novellistic ones, and thus that some everyday tales arose as the wonder tales evolved toward realism.

Among the motifs of the wonder tales, the one most likely to receive realistic reworking turns out to be the motif of difficult tasks. Solution of a difficult task is a condition of marriage in the wonder tale. In the novellistic tale this link is sometimes broken. The difficult task is interesting in itself, in its difficulty, and its resolution leads to the most various kinds of rewards.

Some novellistic tales center on the motif of the difficult task, already completely detached from its original link with courtship and used in some other framework, although its link with the original basis is nonetheless clear to the researcher. The difference in principle of wonder tales and novellistic tales is that in wonder tales the hero acts not alone but with the mediation of his magical helpers or magical objects. These helpers are distinguished by unusual abilities, sometimes prescient wisdom or omniscience, such as the prescient horse. As the magical helper falls away, his qualities pass to the hero. Thus the type of the wise hero is created in folklore. This wisdom no longer has anything magical or wondrous about it. It is human wisdom. In the wonder tale the hero's wife often possesses such wisdom. In the novellistic tale it is a young woman or even a little girl, with the child's age clearly used as an element of contrast, underlining the wisdom. Correspondingly, in the "man's" tale the hero is a wise boy.

One difficult task that appears more frequently than others in novellistic tales is solving a riddle. There is nothing supernatural or magical in such a task; it is entirely human. Thus a whole series of novellistic tales is constructed on the motif of riddles and wise solvers. Such everyday tales, which have not yet lost the compositional elements of the wonder tale, include "The Seven-Year-Old" (A-T 875; Afanas'ev 328). The tsar sets four riddles to his boyars or other people: What is stronger and faster than anything else? What is richer or more satisfying than anything else in the world? What is softer than anything else? and What is dearer than anything else? The boyars answer that the fastest is a light chestnut mare, the richest is a spotted boar, the softest is a featherbed, and the dearest is grandson Ivanushka. The tsar drives them out. They look for someone to help them solve these riddles. In their search they come to a yard where a 7-year-old girl lives. She is a wise maiden who gives the correct answers. It turns out that the wind is fastest and strongest and that the earth is richest and most satisfying. From here on I cite the text: "The softest of all is the hand: no matter where a man lies down, he still puts his hand under his head; and there is nothing in the world dearer than sleep!" The tsar sees at once that the boyars have not solved these riddles themselves, and he orders them to bring this clever girl to him. He tests her with other riddles, and in the end he marries her. The connection with the wonder tale is fairly obvious. Its compositional heart is the solution of difficult riddles, which have a hidden life and philosophical meaning. The boyars' answers are wrong because they all come from the sphere of personal experience and personal well-being, limited by the circle of one's own ego and its material interests: my mare, my boar, my featherbed, my grandson Ivanushka. The girl's answers come from the sphere of the working life of the peasant.

In variants where boyars or merchants take part, the tale has the character of a social satire. The riddles are given precisely in order to shame the boyars or the rich men. They are solved by a peasant girl. Her being 7 years of age presents no obstacle; seven is a purely conventional figure in folklore.

Closer to everyday tales, although clearly sprung from the wonder tales, is the tale "The Wise Bride" (A-T 921; Afanas'ev 327). In this tale a peasant man hears about a wise girl and goes to court her for his son or nephew. They ride into the yard and ask where to tie the horse. She answers, "Toward winter or toward summer, as you wish." They do not understand. "Toward winter" means by the sleigh; "toward summer" means by the wagon. They come into the hut, sit down on the bench, and the old man asks the girl where her father is. She answers, "He's gone to change a hundred rubles for fifteen kopecks." Again they do not understand, but this means that "he's gone to trap hares: if he traps a hare, he'll only earn fifteen kopecks, but if someone steals his horse, he'll lose a hundred rubles." When they ask where her mother is, the girl answers that she has gone "to cry on loan." This means that she has gone to cry for a dead person, but someday they will cry over her. The old man is so struck by her intelligence that he betroths her to his son. There are no longer any difficult tasks here. The marriage of a tsar or the marriage of a princess have turned into a real-life peasant wedding: The father or uncle arranges to marry the girl to a son, and riddles were once part of the marriage ritual in the Russian village. Both tales—"The Seven-Year-Old" and "The Wise Bride"—are often assimilated, with the tasks and riddles moving from one to the other.

Tales About Testing Wives

In the previous section a girl was subjected to a test, and moreover this test was followed by marriage.

Difficult tasks or riddles are a condition of marriage or crowning and come before them. However, difficult tasks can also be set after the wedding, and in that case they serve to test one of the spouses. Such cases are possible even in the pure wonder tale. So, in a tale of the Frog Princess type the tsar requires his sons' wives to perform various tasks, all of which lead to the ascendancy of the frog-wife, who until then was scorned by everyone (A-T 402; Afanas'ev 267–269). We rarely encounter such cases in the wonder tale, but in the novellistic tale the moment of testing a spouse is a fairly frequent phenomenon. Usually it is the wife who is tested and displays unusual wisdom and meekness, cleverness and inventiveness.

Tales in which a test occurs after the wedding make up a special subgroup of tales about wise answers to riddles. Among them, for example, belongs the tale "The Wise Wife" (A-T 875; Onchukov 49). It is rarely encountered in the Russian repertoire. Sometimes it occurs as a continuation of the preceding tale; sometimes it figures as a freestanding tale. To test his wife, a husband goes away and orders his wife to bear a son begotten by himself and to have his mare bear a foal from the pacing horse he is riding away on. As he leaves, he locks the chests and takes the keys with him, ordering his wife to fill these chests with gold and so on. She disguises herself as a man, follows him unrecognized, and fulfills all the tasks he has set.

Read Onchukov 49 and others and briefly tell how this is achieved.

This tale is close to another, in which the wife also dresses as a man and rescues her husband from disaster. Properly speaking, there is no task here, or more exactly it is not formulated as such. But in fact the wife is confronted with the task of saving her husband from misfortune, and she carries it out brilliantly. This is the tale "The Hussar Queen" (A-T 888; Afanas'ev 338). A tsar rides away to Jerusalem. He is captured and subjected to torture (they plough on him and so on). The tsar writes to his wife in secret, asking her to rescue him. Here the difficult task takes on the form of a plea for help. The queen puts on a hussar's uniform, enchants everyone with her playing, and asks for one of the captives as a reward. She chooses her husband, who does not recognize her. On the way home they separate, and she arrives home first. When he comes home, he condemns his wife. "Ministers, gentlemen! Judge my unfaithful wife by justice, by truthful justice. Where was she traveling all over the world? Why wouldn't she ransom me?" and so on. The truth becomes clear, and a feast follows, corresponding entirely to the wedding feasts of the wonder tale. This tale's plot is also known in the *bylina* form ("Stavr Godinovich"). In the tale the king does not test his wife, he does not intend to, although what happens does in fact represent a test for her.

But there are other plots too in which a tsar intentionally tests his wife, subjecting her to all kinds of made-up misfortunes. This is the famous plot of "Griselda" ("The Patient Wife"), more widespread in Western European folklore but also known in Russia (A-T 887; Afanas'ev 335). The tsar is enchanted with the beauty of a peasant girl and marries her. When their children are born, the tsar pretends to order them killed and, finally, even acts as though he is preparing to marry another woman and orders his wife to work at the wedding as a servant, all under the pretext that she is a peasant's daughter and not his equal and the children cannot be his heirs. But the wife meekly bears all the tests. The supposed bride turns out to be her daughter, and for her long suffering the wife is reinstated in the rights of a king's wife.

This plot has not taken root in Russian soil. Only one Russian variant and one Ukrainian variant are known. The test, set by the husband, is perceived as mockery of a perfectly innocent wife. The plot was more popular in the Middle Ages; many literary treatments of it are known (among others, the novella of Boccaccio), and at that time, against the background of literature about evil wives, it had great significance as an attempt to extol the dignity and beneficence of women. But the plot is no longer in harmony with contemporary consciousness, and it has been little disseminated among the people.

Tales About Clever and Lucky Guessers

From what I have laid out, it is clear that riddles are a kind of organizing principle, the foundation of an entertaining plot. Tales about wise guessers are one form of such tales. The guesser in them is a wise man who reveals not only an unusual mind but also a heightened morality. Another group includes tales in which the guesser is not wise in the higher sense of that word but has a practical cleverness, craft; he is cunning and sometimes solves the riddle or task entirely by accident. If the reward in the first group of tales is often a marriage, here the guesser primarily gains material benefits from solving the riddle.

This group includes the tale of Gorshen', which Aleksandr Veselovskii studied. The tsar is no longer a fairytale king but entirely real—the Russian tsar Ivan Vasilievich, Ivan the Terrible. This plot is attached to Ivan the Terrible not at all by chance; it brings the action close to reality and reflects the popularity Ivan enjoyed in folk memory. The tale vividly reflects an antiboyar tendency. This is precisely why it is linked with the name of Ivan the Terrible; the people remembered his struggle against the boyars. The tale is also known without Ivan's name.

In one variant in Afanas'ev (no. 325),[14] reprinting a tale recorded by Nikolai Iazykov and published in the journal *The Muscovite* from 1843, the tale is told this way. Gorshen' (i.e., a potter) is riding along the road, dozing, with a wagon full of pots. The tsar overtakes him and asks him about his craft, how he manages to make a living, about his family. This dialogue has a purely realistic character. Gorshen' is pleased with his life. The tsar says that "all the same, there's no life on earth without evil." Gorshen' replies that there are three kinds of evil: a bad neighbor, a bad wife, and a bad mind. "But tell me, which evil is worse than the others?" "You can get away from a bad neighbor ('a scraper'), from a bad wife too ... but you can't walk away from a bad mind; it's always with you." The tsar likes this answer: "You're a brain-catcher." The tsar says to him figuratively (in a riddle) that "the geese will fly in from Rus'" and offers to let the potter pluck them. The meaning of these words becomes clear later. The tsar orders the boyars "to have dishes at all their feasts made not of silver, not of lead, not of brass, not of wood, but only of clay." Now the boyars are forced to buy pots from Gorshen', and he sets the price: "Fill each vessel full of money." Thus he unriddles the tsar's figurative speech: The geese are the boyars, and he "plucks" them, in the tsar's words. When one of the boyars tries to haggle, he offers another form of payment instead of money: The boyar should be hitched to the wagon in place of the horse and pull him home. The boyar agrees, Gorshen' rides on the boyar's wife and sings songs. The tsar looks out his window, asks, "And what are you riding on?" and the answer is "On a bad mind, sire." The tsar deprives the boyar of his rank and makes Gorshen' into a boyar. The boyar has to take off his clothes and put them on Gorshen' (A-T 321*E; Afanas'ev 325).

This tale already offers not only types but human characters—the clever and merry Gorshen', the foolish and unintelligent boyar—and it is precisely human character that defines the actions of the personages. The sting of satire is directed here against the boyar, whereas the tsar is presented as a tsar of the people, who sides with the poor man against the boyars.[15]

Among tales about lucky guessers we also find the famous tale "The Merry Monastery," or in Western European terminology "The King and the Abbot" (A-T 922; Afanas'ev 326). It has a compositional character different from the tales examined here, but its basic theme places it right in the group of tales about clever and crafty guessers. I will choose as our starting point one of the best Russian variants, recorded from the Siberian tale-teller E. I. Sorokovikov, also known as Magai (*The Tales of Magai*),[16] but as I tell the tale I will also consider other variants.

A peasant got the idea of going to pray, and he set out for a monastery. The gates were locked fast, but he could hear the monks singing something, although it wasn't very godly. The peasant thought to himself, "Well, well, the monks are having a party." He puts a sheet of paper on the gate with the inscription "The Merry Monastery" and leaves. The tsar too comes to pray, and he sees this sign. The tsar summons the Father Superior. The prior says, "It was just someone making fun or someone feeling spiteful at the prior who went and wrote that and stuck it here." The ruler does not believe him and says that there is nevertheless a bit of truth in it. "So here's what, father superior, you have to feel a bit sad and do some praying. I'll give you a small grief—three problems that you and your brethren must solve." These problems can vary quite a bit, but the following predominates: "How many stars are in the sky? How much am I, the tsar, worth? What am I, the tsar, thinking?" The tsar gives them a deadline of three days and departs. The father superior goes to the tavern in sorrow and orders a lot of vodka. The tavern keeper asks, "Why do you need so much vodka?" The prior tells him everything; the tavern drunk says he will answer the three questions. The drunk demands a stack of paper, pencils, a liter of vodka, and locks himself in one of the cells. When the tsar comes, the drunk switches clothes with the prior and answers all the questions. The answers generally come down to the following: Asked how many stars are in the sky, the drunk hands over the pile of paper, all written with figures. To the tsar's reply, "You've made a mistake in something here," he answers, "So you check it." To the second question he answers that the tsar is worth twenty-nine rubles. The tsar gets angry, jumps to his feet, and shouts at him, "Where did you get that price—twenty-nine rubles, when any ordinary workman gets thirty rubles for a month's work?" And the "prior" says, "Tsar! You listen first, sire, and then you may get angry at me. I set your price this way: Judas betrayed Christ, the king of heaven, for thirty rubles, but you are an earthly tsar, and that means you should be a ruble cheaper." To the third question he answers that the tsar is thinking that the prior is before him; the tsar says that he truly does think so, to which the drunk answers, "But I am a drunk from the tavern." The prior is always punished, and the guesser is rewarded. In Sorokovikov's variant the prior runs away, and the tsar makes the tavern drunk father superior.

This remarkable tale was fundamentally studied by Estonian scholar V. N. Anderson.[17] He established 492 variants of the tale, including 65 independent literary treatments of the plot.[18] Anderson could not have known that there would be at least two more treatments in Soviet literature: Samuil Marshak's "The King and the Shepherd" (a transmission of the English variant) and M. B. Isaakovskii's "The Tsar, the Priest, and the Bear." Anderson's monograph is striking for its abundance of material and the erudition of its author. It is carried out according to all the laws of the Finnish school. Anderson groups the recordings into redactions and establishes that the riddles can be posed by a tsar, a king, a president, a pope, a bishop, etc., and in one case a professor. The riddle is posed to the abbot of a monastery (most frequently), to monks, to a bishop, to a cardinal, to priests, to courtiers, and so on. The answers come from a miller, a shepherd, a sexton, a peasant, a soldier, etc. (about forty different cases in all). The number and variety of riddles posed are extraordinarily great; there are questions not only about the number of stars, about how much the tsar is worth, and what he is thinking but also about how far it is to the sky, how deep the sea is, how many drops are in the sea, how far it is from happiness to unhappiness, and so on—altogether, seventeen questions that repeat and about sixty-five that occur only once. The variants of the tale encountered most often are considered the basic ones or the most ancient ("the archetype"), whereas the others are derivative. Anderson establishes which peoples have which forms and combinations ("ecotypes"), and then he makes conclusions about the homeland of the plot and its wanderings. He takes into account how many times the plot was recorded in each nation.

At the same time, these conclusions, founded on statistical calculations, are not persuasive for the Soviet researcher. In my opinion, no plot can be isolated from others. The plot's ideological contents are completely ignored. It testifies to striking anticlerical feelings, an inimical attitude toward the clergy. It is interesting that this plot takes exactly the same direction among Catholics, Orthodox, and Lutherans as well as among Muslims and Jews.

The tale "The Seer" (A-T 1641; Afanas'ev 379–381) also belongs among the tales of clever or lucky guessers. Its hero, "a poor and improvident peasant man," makes a living by stealing horses, cloth, and so on and hiding them, after which he pretends to be a seer and shows people where to find what was stolen. His fame reaches the tsar, whose pearl ring has gone missing. He summons this seer. The tsar orders him locked in so he can perform his magic. The seer finds himself in a difficult position and thinks that now his trickery is bound to be discovered. But this is not what happens. Quite by chance he manages to catch the thieves. There are many variants, and his good fortune is described in a variety of ways. In one of them a lackey, who stole the ring, is eavesdropping, peeking to see how the seer will do his magic. The seer says to himself, "You're caught, my friend." But the thief thinks that he is talking to him, and he tells the seer everything. They come to an agreement. The thief tells where the ring is hidden but begs the seer not to give him away. The tsar rewards the peasant richly. Sometimes there is not a single thief but three of them. Sometimes the tsar tests the trickster further: He invites him to his table, has a covered bowl brought to the table, and asks what is in it. The supposed seer answers with some kind of proverb ("You're in it, like a cock in cabbage soup"), and very luckily. The bowl turns out to hold cabbage soup with chicken. The tsar rewards the seer richly and lets him go.

The hero of this tale is a poor man who is brought to despair but has unusual good luck. An introductory episode about hiding horses is characteristic of the Russian versions. Here the hero is a rascal, but he is a trickster out of poverty. This is just the kind of hero fate favors. Therefore his good luck with external chance is not internally accidental. Fate elevates not the wise or the meek, as in tales from the previous group (about testing wives), but those who are to some extent strong and clever, who do not submit to their deprivation.

Tales of Clever Thieves

Tales of crafty thieves are easily separated into a special group of everyday, or novellistic, tales. We should, however, qualify this right away by saying that the heroes of these tales can by no means be compared with real thieves or criminals from any era or epoch of Russian life. These tales arose not as stories of real thieves but as quite the opposite. Some of them possess an undoubtedly morphological relationship with wonder tales. It can be shown that the basis of these tales is also the motif of the difficult task; the thief attempts a robbery not by his own will but because it is assigned by someone else, and he handles it artistically. This will be clear once we become acquainted with plots from this cycle.

It is curious to note that theft, robbery, and kidnapping play an enormous role in even the most archaic wonder tales. Just as difficult tasks turn out to be a cell in the body of the folktale organism that is capable of independent life and new formations, the motif of kidnapping too turns out to be just such a cell. Kidnapping plays an ambivalent role in the wonder tale. On the one hand, the kidnapper turns out to be the hero's enemy—a dragon who has kidnapped girls, brothers who steal his magical objects, and so on. On the other hand, the hero may be a kidnapper himself. Abduction leads to counterabduction. Even when there is no initial kidnapping, just departure on a quest, the hero gets what he seeks by way of abduction. In the tale of the Firebird he steals the Firebird, the golden-maned horse, and Elena the Beautiful. In the tale of the apples of youth he steals the apples and the water of life. Children steal Baba Yaga's magical kerchief, her comb, her vial, and so on. The heroes of similar tales may with full right be called clever thieves. Such "thieves" are distinguished from the kind found in the novellistic tale by the facts that the object of the quest in wonder tales is won in the other world (the thrice-tenth kingdom), the theft is achieved by magical means (with magical objects or helpers, shape changing, incantations that put guards to sleep, and the like), the object of the theft is typically of a magical character (the apples of youth), and this object cannot be won anywhere but in the other world. These motifs have great antiquity, reaching back to concepts that the first things, the first seeds, and also arts and crafts, as well as cults, are brought from the other world by heroes, human benefactors. Among the abductors belongs Prometheus, who stole fire from heaven and brought it to people. Antiquity gives the example of deification of a thief (making a thief into a divinity) in the person of the god Hermes, who while still in his diapers stole fifty head of divine cattle that Apollo was herding. Hermes is an embodiment of craftiness, a god-thief, but it is characteristic that precisely he is the one who mediates between two worlds; he is the god of inventions, letters, numbers, crafty speech, and trade. The novellistic tale does not oppose two worlds. The stolen object and the means of theft have no magical character, and heroization follows the same line as in tales about lucky guessers; the person robbed always turned out to be socially inimical to the hero. In distinction from the lucky guessers, the clever thief gains no material benefit from his actions. He is an artist at his business, and his actions satisfy an elementary sense of fairness, shaming, and making fools of the powerful in this world.

Historically the concept of theft as an illegal and reprehensible act could arise only with the appearance of private property. Appropriation, taking what nature gives that belongs to no one, is the most elementary act of a primitive economy. But when private property appears, the act of appropriation, from the point of view of the property owner, is an amoral act, whereas from the point of view of a person who lacks something it is a simple act of restoration of downtrodden fairness. This explains why in a folktale the one who is robbed always belongs to the upper social classes.

The most ancient recording we know of a tale about clever thieves is the ancient Egyptian tale of the treasury of the pharaoh Rampsinit, which we have already mentioned. This tale is cited by Herodotus, who spent time in Egypt, in his history. The tale of Rampsinit's treasury (A-T 950; Afanas'ev 390) is so called because the person robbed here is the Egyptian king, or pharaoh, Rampsinit.

The Egyptian version is valuable to us not only because it is the most ancient recording but also because it is close to a wonder tale, representing a kind of transitional step from wonder tales to novellistic tales. The summons of the king, who promises to give his daughter in marriage to the person who can achieve such-and-such a feat, and the subsequent marriage of the hero to the king's daughter relate this tale to the wonder tales, leading us to suppose that it descended from wonder tales, evolved from them.

A huge literature has been devoted to this tale. One work belongs to the Italian scholar Stanislav Prato, who wrote a specialized book about it (*The Legend of the Treasury of Rampsinit in Various Italian and Foreign Redactions*).[19]

Veselovskii wrote an interesting review of the book.[20] Veselovskii recognizes that Prato collected a great deal of material and that this is his book's achievement. For his part, Veselovskii added to Prato's list several Russian variants that the Italian scholar did not know. But, as a whole, Prato's book did not satisfy Veselovskii. The material is not systematically presented, and no attempt is made to define the plot's origin and history. Since this review was written, many new materials have come out. The plot was known in antiquity, in the Middle Ages. It has been recorded in the East (India, China), in North Africa, and among all the European peoples in a significant number of variants. We know of more than ten Russian recordings in the basic collections. There is also a series of new studies.[21] Nonetheless, at present we do not yet have an exhaustive monograph. Veselovskii indicated a way to solve this problem too. Variants should be compared according to their degree of ancientness. He established that Herodotus's version is the most ancient only in the date of its recording, not in its contents. Many folkloric texts are more archaic. Here is an example: In folk versions the tsar orders that the corpse of a thief with his head cut off be put outside in order to catch the ones who will come to lament over him. In the folkloric tales the lamentation always occurs; the mother or wife of the slain one comes to weep for him, but thanks to the hero's tricks, she is never caught. Herodotus omits this motif. If we apply the approach that Veselovskii suggests and bring not only the given motif but also all the others into the comparison and then compare this tale's structure with the structure of the wonder tale, or if we bring into our study, besides this, the whole cycle of tales about clever thieves in general and examine all the real historical details, then the question of the descent, evolution, and dissemination of this plot can in all probability be resolved.

There is little everyday material in the tale of the treasury of Rampsinit. It could just as soon be called a novellistic tale as an everyday one. The king of these tales, or the pharaoh in the Egyptian version, has little in common with real kings. The presence of the figure of the king is one sign of the archaism, the ancientness of the plot.

We will now examine other tales from this cycle, where one of the characters is a king. Ivan the Terrible, who is popular not only in historical songs but also in folktales, figures in one of the Russian tales. We have already met the figure of Ivan in the tale of Gorshen'. There is an essential difference between the songs and the tales about Ivan. The songs are based on historical events: the taking of Kazan', Ivan's marriage to Mar'ia Temriukovna, Ivan's struggle with betrayal and the boyars, and so on. Events in the tales are completely fantastic, but they are nonetheless historical, though already in a different sense. Veselovskii speaks well about this: "The people's unconscious creativity is distinguished by its faithful tact, which moves it to attach to its hero only those long-familiar tales and anecdotes which truly corresponded to folk understanding of the historical figure. In this sense, and in this sense alone, the tales may contribute to the historical description."[22] We noted the historicity of the character of Ivan the Terrible while analyzing the tale of Gorshen'. Another tale about Ivan is preserved for us by the Englishman Samuel Collins, the physician of Tsar Aleksei Mikhailovich. Upon his return from Russia in 1667, Collins put out the book *The Present State of Russia in a Letter to a Friend at London*. The book was translated by Petr Kireevskii. Collins conveys the plot of the tale, considering it a real event. I cite according to Veselovskii: "Sometimes the tsar would join a band of robbers in disguise, and once he advised them to rob the keeper of the tsar's treasury. 'I'll show you the way,' he said. But one of the thieves lifted his fist and struck him in the face with his whole hand. 'Scoundrel! How dare you suggest that we rob our lord, who is so merciful to us? Better that we rob some boyar, who himself is ruining the tsar's treasury.'"[23]

From its language it is immediately clear that this is not a folktale text. Collins recounts what he heard in his own words. The tale has a continuation that is unrelated to the cycle of tales about clever thieves. The tsar exchanges hats with a thief and orders him to wait for him on the palace square. The thief comes, and here he sees that he is speaking with the tsar himself. The tsar rewards him with a horn of vodka and mead and makes him his servant, taking advantage of the thief's help to discover gangs of thieves.

What we have before us is really a folktale; this is clear from the fact that variants of it were recorded in the nineteenth century (A-T 951; cf. Bolte and Polívka, no. 2).[24]

Tales in which an apparent robber turns out to be the tsar are interesting in their historical connections. They are rare in Russian folklore. Much more often, the one who is robbed turns out to be a nobleman, a landowner. Such tales have a more strongly expressed everyday character. They have a high rate of international migration and are motley in their variants. Andreev's *Index* indicates fourteen various subtypes under just one type of this ring of tales (A-T 1525, "The Clever Thief").[25] The most characteristic case is the one in Afanas'ev, "The Thief" (A-T 1525 A; Afanas'ev 383). The tale's beginning is realistic not just in the folktale sense of that word. An old man and woman complain to a landowner about their son, who will not feed them. The nobleman summons the son, but the son makes excuses for himself: He has no way to feed his parents. "Do you really command me to go out robbing!" "I don't care what you come up with, let it be robbery, but feed your father and mother. I don't want to hear any more complaints about you." The hero steals the gentleman's boots on the spot and takes them to his parents. This is the introductory episode. In the given recording it serves to justify the hero morally. Similar introductory episodes to this tale are various. From the compositional point of view they are needed to motivate subsequent events. The nobleman summons the clever thief and suggests that he carry out a series of tricky robberies: "Steal my black bull from under the plough." "Now steal my favorite yearling." "Now steal the Kerzhensk teacher" (i.e., an Old Believer priest). And so on. In other variants the suggestions include stealing a sheet from under the landowner and his wife and stealing the service from his table. The hero carries all this out with extraordinary cunning and aptitude.

In these tales the clever thief gains no material benefits from his tricks. Rather the opposite: He undergoes the risk of harsh punishment, and in case he fails to succeed, he is threatened by the lash or even by execution. Theft serves the goal of making fun of the nobleman. The nobleman is mocked; the listeners laugh at him. Making fun, as we will see, is one means that every people has for expressing scorn and hatred for the nobleman.

In some tales the thief really is a thief who commits real crimes. But in these cases he fools and robs a rich man or a priest and therefore delights the listeners. Such tales come close to anecdotes. In one (A-T 1525; Afanas'ev 386), two thieves creep up to a general by night and rifle his house. One of them puts on the robe and slippers of the nobleman and walks through the courtyard in that guise. The watchmen take him for the nobleman himself. He starts a conversation with them: "What, lads, is it cold now?" "It's cold, your Excellency." "But no sound of thieves?" "No, we haven't heard anything." "Well, if you haven't heard anything, then off you go to sleep." The guards go away to sleep, and this thief and his helpers empty the barns and carry out all the best things.

In other tales it is not a nobleman but a stupid peasant woman who is robbed, as thieves easily fool her (A-T 1525 P; Afanas'ev 504, 505, 517). The peasant woman, for example, is bleaching linen canvas. Two soldiers agree to steal it. One talks nonsense with her while the other steals the cloth. The tale is sympathetic to the soldiers, because in prereform Russia soldiers served for twenty-five years and could own nothing. In another tale (Afanas'ev 502) the soldiers rob a peasant woman in a different way. She is driving her wagon to the market to sell butter. One asks her, "Hey, auntie, hitch me up, please." The woman gets down from her wagon and helps the soldier put his belt on. He asks her first to make it tighter, then looser, and then again tighter while the other soldier steals the butter from the wagon. "Well, thank you, auntie, you've belted me well enough for the whole of carnival," says the soldier. "To your good health, serviceman!" The woman gets to the city, she takes a look—and it's as though the butter had never been there!

Tales of this type already have no connection with wonder tales, nothing in common with those tales' morphology. Their heroes are thieves not by necessity but, we might say, by vocation or inspiration. Their art transcends everything a person could imagine in this field. This vocation is apparent from youth. A father takes his three sons into the forest. The oldest sees a birch tree and says, "Father! If this birch were burned to charcoal, I'd start up a smithy and go off to strike with my hammer and knock out some money." The second sees an oak and says, "Father! If that oak were cut down, I would start working as a carpenter. I would earn money with my axe." The youngest one is quiet, and only when they come out of the woods and see butchers leading a cow, says, "Father! How can I steal that cow?" The father drives his son away (Afanas'ev 383–390).

Thus the urge to steal is an innate tendency. Often the tales describe how such a thief goes to apprentice with a master of his trade, but he always immediately surpasses him in mastery. The teacher, for example, climbs a tree to show how to steal the eggs out from under a magpie without her noticing. The pupil climbs after him and, while the older one is stealing the eggs, the pupil cuts the soles off his boots and even takes his pants off so skillfully that the other man does not notice anything. The teacher admits that he has been bested. The competition with the teacher makes up a kind of introductory episode. In tales of this type the thief usually steals horses or oxen, even a whole herd of bulls or other animals.

Sometimes such dirty tricks are played on a bet. In one tale of this kind (Afanas'ev 390), peasants are driving a herd. A thief takes off one of his boots and throws it into the road. The herders see the boot and say, "Eh, too bad there's only one!" "If I had a pair of boots like that, I'd put them on and be a gentleman." They do not take the boot but drive the livestock farther. The thief runs ahead and throws down his other boot. The drovers go back to pick up the first one, and meanwhile the thief steals the bulls.

I will not cite all the variants of these tales. They vary quite a bit. The thief's ways of evading capture and fooling his persecutors are likewise various. In this, such tales echo and respond to tales about jokers, which I will speak about later.

A competition among thieves may become the subject not only of an introductory episode but also of a whole narrative of anecdotal character.

Tales of Robbers

We have seen that tales about clever thieves do not originate in real life, in the sense that they do not depict criminals carrying out actual thefts. They are folktales, not detective novels, not stories from real life, although they do reflect many everyday details. The same can be said of those tales whose main characters are robbers. These robbers also do not spring from the phenomenon of robbery, which represented one of the social miseries in old Rus' and later. This form of robbery is reflected in songs, not folktales; folktale robbers have nothing in common with it. They live in the forest in large houses; they live in brotherhoods. They are presented as abductors of women, whom they treat with great cruelty.

The Aarne-Andreev-Thompson index puts tales about robbers and thieves in one group (types 950–973). This is unfounded. The crafty thief is a hero who has an aura, and he takes vengeance for social inequity, whereas robbers are terrible people who commit monstrous crimes and meet a well-earned punishment. Stories about them are appealing precisely in their atmosphere of mystery and horror. A brave and clever girl saves herself from robbers by overcoming her fear, and she not only saves herself but also exposes the robbers. These tales were especially popular among women.

One of them was reworked in a poem by Pushkin, "The Bridegroom." For some reason it does not figure among Pushkin's *skazki*, although it is clearly related to them.[26]

Briefly, in the robber-bridegroom tale, a girl gets lost in the forest. She finds a big house in the forest and hides in it. She watches the robbers drag in a girl and kill her. They cut off her hand. A ring rolls into the corner where the girl is hiding. The robber leader comes to court the girl, and she shows him the ring. Pushkin wrote his ballad based on the Grimm brothers' tale.

In Russian folklore this tale has the following form (A-T 955; Afanas'ev 344). In Afanas'ev's Belarusan variant twelve suitors pay court to the tsar's daughter. In other variants the heroine is not a tsar's daughter but a merchant's or a peasant's. The suitors ask the girl to come visit them. They live in a palace in the forest. The girl dresses up richly and goes. There is no one in the yard; in the chambers she sees barrels full of blood, severed arms, legs, heads, and torsos. She hides under a bench. From here she sees the robbers appear. They bring a girl in with them, lay her on the floor, and cut her apart. They try to take the ring off her finger but cannot do it and cut off the finger. It flies under the bench where the girl is hiding. Because of the darkness the robbers do not want to crawl under the bench. In the morning the girl runs back home. After a few days the robbers come to visit and dine at her house. She tells everything that happened in the form of a dream, but at the end pulls out the severed finger with the ring. The robbers are caught and executed.

This folktale cannot at all be explained by the Russian everyday life of any era whatsoever. Nonetheless, it reflects historical reality, only it is that of an earlier era—that of the clan system.

Retell from *The Historical Roots*.[27]

This tale does not represent pure fantasy. It reflects prehistoric reality, ritual cannibalism, and cutting apart as a form of temporary death. The plot represents a reflection of ritual actuality. There is no longer any resurrection of the persons chopped apart, and therefore cutting apart human bodies is presented as a crime. In *legendy* of the type of "The Unsuccessful Doctor," cutting apart leads to the renewed youth of old people or to healing the sick, and therefore it is ascribed not to robbers but to Christ and the saints and is presented as a miracle.

The everyday elements of these tales are quite pallid. They are more developed in tales of the type "The Girl and the Robber" (A-T 956 B; Afanas'ev 342), which can be seen as a freestanding tale close to the previous one (here the motif of cutting apart is used as punishment for the robbers, and the whole plot has a more realistic everyday coloration). In this tale the girl Alyonushka invites a party of friends over for a spinning bee while her parents are out. One girl drops her distaff, and it falls through a crack into the cellar. Alyonushka goes down into the cellar and sees a robber sitting behind a tub. When the bee is over and everyone leaves, she waits for the robber to come out, and the moment he puts his head out the door, she cuts it off, cuts his body into pieces, and puts them into a bag.

Here it is not the girl who is cut apart but the robber. At night his comrades gather under the window and order him to throw them his loot. The girl throws them the bag with the corpse. The robbers discover the deception and, in order to take vengeance on the girl, come courting her. They take her away, intending to kill her, but the girl tricks them and escapes. A chase scene follows, resembling the chases in wonder tales but with more realistic coloration. The tale ends with the exposure and execution of the robbers.

The famous tale "Ali Baba and the Forty Thieves" (A-T 676; Afanas'ev 345) from *The Thousand and One Nights* belongs among the tales about robbers. There are two *lubok* editions of Russian versions of this tale (published in 1763 and 1771). I will remind you of the contents of this tale, according to *The Thousand and One Nights*.

The contents of this tale in Russian folklore correspond on the whole to the Arab folktale. When the Russian tale-teller, not understanding the original "Open Sesame," says instead, "*Sazan, otvoris'*" (open, carp) or "*Sam otvoris'*" (open by yourself), the borrowing is entirely obvious. However, it would be premature to assert that all the versions of this tale (among them some from Russia), which is extraordinarily widespread not only all over Europe but also in Asia and Africa, descend from *The Thousand and One Nights*. The tale could also have been in circulation independently of *The Thousand and One Nights*, and the folk tradition may turn out to be more ancient than its most famous but not necessarily original form in *The Thousand and One Nights*. Its relationship to the tale of Rampsinit is fairly clear: robbery of a treasure trove by two heroes, neighbors, or brothers; the slaying of one of them during a second robbery; saving the body; searching for the guilty person; marking the guilty one, who, in order to escape discovery, makes other marks—all these motifs in various forms are common to both folktales. The difference in form corresponds to the different interpretation of heroism. In tales of the Rampsinit type the thief is a crafty rascal; in the tale of Ali Baba the hero is an unwilling burglar, an honest person, and the keepers of the treasury turn out to be robbers. Killing one of the burglars is given the character of just recompense for greed. To solve the question of the tale's genesis, we may pose the question of the tale's connection with the widely disseminated belief in treasure troves that are preserved in mountains and caves. Sometimes poor and honest people who possess "breach-herb" (*razryv-trava*) or other means manage to penetrate these mountains and get hold of the treasure.

Tales About the Master and the Hired Laborer

One group of tales is not set apart in any scholarly indexes but is nonetheless quite distinct. These are tales in which the antagonists are a householder and his hired man. Although fantasy also plays a large role in these tales, they are nonetheless extremely realistic, and through all the fantasticality of the action it is easy to guess at the real life that it conceals.

These tales can be divided into two subgroups. In one the master is a landowner, and the hero is his serf; in the other the master hires the worker for money, entering into certain contractual relations with him. This entirely corresponds to historical reality. Serfs could be held only by nobles. Everyone else had to hire workers for money. In folktales this always means either merchants or priests, and this too corresponds entirely to reality.

There are fairly many types, not always distinguished by high artistic qualities (A-T 1538, "The Peasant Gets Revenge on the Nobleman"; Afanas'ev 497). The nobleman buys a canary for 50 rubles. The peasant thinks, a big goose must be worth more. He asks the nobleman for 100 rubles for the goose. The noble beats him and takes the goose. The peasant pretends to be a carpenter and gets himself hired to build a bathhouse. He lures the noble into the forest, ostensibly to choose trees. He saws down a pine tree, pegs out (or ties up) the nobleman, and beats him up. Afterward he pretends to be a doctor. He beats the nobleman up again. He lets the nobleman know who he is. The nobleman buys him off for a great deal of money.

In popular scholarly literature "social protest" is much advertised. The artistic value of these tales is lower than the value of the wonder tales: (1) They are unbelievably artificial; and (2) they are individual protests. This is a typical peasant limitation: The peasant wants only to get revenge on his own landlord. There is not even a rebellion here, only vengeance. Such tales confirm Vladimir Lenin's insight that the peasantry alone cannot complete a revolution. At the same time, they testify to class hatred. Examples of tales of this type are "The Noble and the Peasant,"[28] and "The Falcon (Nightingale) Under the Hat" (A-T 1528; Afanas'ev 391). In this last tale, a peasant man comes to a noble's yard. He sees a swine with piglets. On his knees, he bows to the earth. The lady sends to ask him why. "Tell the lady that your mottled swine is my wife's sister, and my son is getting married tomorrow, so I'm inviting her to the wedding." The lady gives him a carriage and horses and lets the swine and her piglets go to the wedding. "Let people have a good laugh at him." She also gives him her fur coat. The nobleman comes back. He understands everything. He mounts his horse to chase the peasant. The peasant hides the carriage in the forest. He puts his hat on the ground in front of him. "Have you seen a peasant in a carriage?" "He went by a long time ago. You can't catch him; you don't know the roads." "You ride, brother, catch me that peasant." "No, sir, I can't do that at all. I have a falcon under my hat." "Let it go." He gives him 300 rubles as a pledge. The peasant gallops home on the pacer. At home he tells his wife, "I got a carriage with a horse, a fur coat, a pig with her piglets, and a riding horse." There are other tales of the same type in which the nobleman is made a fool of or the noblewoman is fooled.

Tales in which the master hires a day laborer have a somewhat different character. The hirer is socially powerful. The worker, the day laborer, is socially deprived. But the weaker one wins. The master, who thinks he is hiring a workman for nothing, does not understand that he has met a power that will sweep him from the face of the earth. The hero's power is not in his social position but in his craft and cleverness. Usually he also possesses monstrous physical strength. For the listener he is already strong because he is in the right. The employer perishes at the hands of his servant.

The tale "The Day Laborer" (A-T 1045, 1063, 1071, and 1072; Afanas'ev 150–152) can serve as the most striking example. This tale is extraordinarily popular in Russia. It is the source of Pushkin's "Tale of the Priest and His Workman Baldá." The satire in this tale, in both Pushkin's version and the folk one, is extraordinarily vivid. It is well known that Pushkin's tale was not published during his lifetime. Vasilii Zhukovskii changed the priest to a merchant, and it was printed in that form until 1882. In numerous Russian anticlerical folktales the conditions under which the workman is kept are described in detail: They wake him along with the roosters; they don't feed him; they dump all the work on him, and so on. The situation traced in the folktale corresponds entirely to reality. As Iurii Sokolov shows, the village clergy did not possess the right to own serfs individually.[29] Relations between the priest and workman were the relations of a hirer and a hired man. This explains why work for the priest is based on a contract or deal, with the greedy clergyman hoping to get off cheaply but paying harshly for his greed. In Pushkin the pay is three blows. The Afanas'ev version is somewhat different: "I'll live here for a year—one smack for you and a little pinch for the wife." The hirer is pleased: "What a blessing! How cheap that is, how cheap!" But he soon comes to regret this. He sees how his workman handles the bull; it takes four men to lead this bull, but they still cannot manage him. The workman kills the bull with a smack, and he skins him with a pinch. Only now does the master understand what danger threatens him. To get rid of his workman, the hirer gives him various dangerous and unfulfillable errands. In the variants there is a great variety of motifs; I will mention only a few. For example, the masters send the workman into the forest to find a cow that is supposedly lost. "Let the fierce beasts eat him up." The workman brings a bear out of the forest instead of a cow and locks him in the barn along with the cows. Overnight the bear tears up all the cows. The master sends the workman to the mill to collect a debt from the devils. The devils are ready to pay, but first they demand that he have a contest with them. All the kinds of competition in Pushkin are completely folkloric; that is, they exist in folklore. In the folkloric tales a little devil suggests that they compete in racing, and the workman enters a hare in his place; in the fight he sends the devil to fight a bear; in competitions of strength ("if you can carry this horse all the way around the lake"), the workman sits on the horse; in whistling competitions the workman hits the devil on the head instead of whistling, and so on. The devils want to pay; the workman holds his hat out for them, but the hat is full of holes, and he is holding it over a pit. The workman brings his master a whole wagonload of money but then finishes him off according to their agreement.

Comparing Pushkin's tale with the folk versions shows that Pushkin followed the original exactly. He equipped his manuscript with drawings depicting the old demon, Baldá with the hare on his knees, the little devil, and the face of a bearded priest in a skullcap, with an arm reaching for him, ready to give him the smack. Boris Tomashevskii's assumption that Pushkin borrowed the plot from the Grimm brothers' collection *The Young Giant* is completely unfounded.

This tale is a complete whole, both in folklore and in Pushkin. At the same time, the plot is not in Aarne's index. There the tale is broken up into motifs (a competition in running, in whistling, etc.), and each such motif receives a separate number. There are a great many such motifs, and the index gives them in the section "Tales of the Stupid Devil" (types 1000–1199). Although there is in fact a stupid devil in these tales, the tale is still not about him but about the workman and his master, though the index keeps silent about that. Breaking the tale up into types diminishes the social point of the narration.

The workman may bring his master to death and ruin in another way too: by fulfilling all his commands literally. Thus, for example, as the master leaves, he orders the workman to keep a good watch on the barn door. The workman takes the door off its hinges, brings it to the tavern and guards it there. Meanwhile the tavern drunks clean out the barn. The master orders him to slaughter a ram. To the question, "Which one?" he answers, "Whichever one looks at you." But all the rams in the flock look at him, so he slaughters the whole flock. Carrying out orders literally, he kills the master's children.[30] Sometimes the master and mistress try to run away from home to escape their workman. The traditional folktale motif of flight changes here: It is not the hero who flees, pursued by his enemy, but, on the contrary, the enemy flees. But the hero catches him, destroys his wife (he pushes her into the water or over a cliff as she sleeps), and he cuts a belt out of his master's back. The workman's dirty tricks, as he carries out all his master's orders literally, recall the tricks of Eulenspiegel. However, the Russian hero is not satisfied with petty mockery, like Eulenspiegel, who when he is driven away by his master finds another master and does the same thing. The Russian workman ruins and destroys his master. The element of social conflict is precisely what makes up the content of the Russian tales.

Tales About Priests

In tales of masters and hired workers the workman's hirer is already often a priest. However, the master there is not necessarily a clergyman. In some tales the plot itself is linked with the spiritual rank as such (mockery of the liturgy and so on). These tales confirm the words of Vissarion Belinsky about the clergy, from his deathbed letter to Gogol about Gogol's *Selected Passages from a Correspondence with Friends*. Belinsky wrote, "Could it really be that you do not know that our clergy is held in universal scorn by Russian society and all the Russian people? About whom does the Russian people tell scabrous tales? About the priest, the priest's wife, the priest's daughter, and the priest's workman. . . . Is not the priest for all Russians in Rus' a representative of gluttony, miserliness, servility, shamelessness? And can it be that you do not know all that? Strange!"[31]

Belinsky did not print folktales of that sort in his lifetime. Afanas'ev printed tales like it in Geneva, under the title *Obscene Folktales*, mentioned earlier. Belinskii knew them in oral performance. His assertion regarding the scorn of the Russian people for the clergy is, of course, correct. But he is wrong about one thing: Scorn for priests is not a Russian national feature but an international one. The strength of this scorn depends on a people's stage of historical and cultural development. The influence of the clergy is especially strong in backward countries. In countries with developed capitalism it is artificially supported by the government with the goal of suppressing protest against the existing system.

It is obvious that the people's negative attitude toward the clergy is an international trait from the fact that some satirical plots about priests have international currency. Such, for example, is the tale of the crafty beauty whom the priest notices at confession. The deacon and the sacristan also come to court her. She invites them all to come at different times, on the same evening, and then hides them one after the other in a trunk full of soot. Her husband takes them out in the trunk and shows or describes them as devils. He lets them out of the trunk in front of a crowd (A-T 1739).

This plot is quite popular. It is found in Old Russian narrative literature (the tale of Karp Sutulov) and in Gogol (where only the sacristan is left from the clerical triad), and it apparently figured in folk comedy. In *Notes from the House of the Dead*, Dostoevsky has the convicts give a play based on the given plot. In Western Europe the rise and development of such plots was aided by the forced celibacy of the Catholic clergy; its violation provoked sharp attention and heightened interest and led to all kinds of stories and anecdotes, which began to be widely disseminated in the Renaissance in connection with the era's anticlerical mood (Boccaccio). In Russia the clergy often entered into forced marriages, because when a priest died, the place was reserved for his son-in-law. The young priest was assigned a place and also a wife by the spiritual leadership. Such marriages were not always happy. A widowed priest did not have the right to remarry. All these conditions, in part, explain the widespread plots about licentious priests. Under such conditions priests' wives likewise did not always observe marital fidelity, and some tales narrate precisely the adventures of the priest's wife. The folktale often mocked other flaws, including greed, stinginess, and bribe taking. In the article "On Village Poverty," Vladimir Lenin wrote, "Our priests preach unacquisitiveness and restraint to the peasants, but they themselves have taken an enormous quantity of land by hook or by crook."[32] One direct satire of bribe taking is the tale of the funeral of the hound or the goat, which Afanas'ev placed in his *Obscene Folktales*. A hound happens to discover a kettle of gold in the ground. A peasant wants to bury the hound according to the Christian rite. For a bribe the priest buries him, and for an even bigger bribe the archbishop puts aside the complaint of the sacristan, with whom the priest did not share his bribe.

A fair number of plots in the Russian repertoire deal with priests (cf. A-T 1725–1830). They outline the unappealing qualities of the old prerevolutionary clergy, who led a pathetic existence, living on bribes—qualities that reveal greed, lack of culture, indecency, and lack of principle.

In these cases the satire bears a peasant character. It is directed against the clergy, not against religion as such. But other tales mock the divine liturgy. Such tales, of course, could be told only by those who did not believe in God. They undermined not only the authority of the priests but also the pious attitude toward the church, the liturgy, and along with them religion itself. These tales make fun of the liturgy and priests as servants of a cult. The rural clergy stood at an extremely low level of culture. Priests in far-flung places were sometimes chosen from among the peasants, who were illiterate. From here we have such tales as "Priest Pakhom." All the spice in these tales is in the performance. They are often chanted to the tunes of church singing.

So, a priest and a deacon are coming to an agreement about a bribe or a theft. They look out the window. Is anyone coming? Are they bringing something? An old woman is coming; she's bringing some butter. "Give it, oh Lord!" Or, a peasant man is coming, he is bringing an oak cudgel for the priest's back. "For Thee, oh Lord!" (Onchukov 262). At one and the same time the clergy's greed and mockery of the church service are illustrated.

Another tale is "The Illiterate Village." Here, everyone is illiterate—the whole village, the priest, the deacon, the sacristan. The archbishop comes. The priest sings in a drawn-out manner, "Oh, oh, oh, from behind the island of Cell Island / Ran an aspen boat, / Its bow, its stern painted," and so on. The deacon likewise sings: "From behind the island of…" and the sacristan in the choir joins in "Along the grass yes along the ant-hill, / Over the azure flowers."[33] The archbishop comes out; he shrugs. "Keep on serving as you have been giving the service," and then he drives away.

In the tale of the priest Pakhom, there is a parish without a priest. The lay people are choosing. "Well, Pakhom, you be the priest." Everyone is invited to service on Sunday. Many people are curious: How will he manage the service? "As the priest is, so then is the parish." Pakhom is censing. A coal falls out and lands in his boot. The priest begins to stamp his feet. The coal works its way in deeper. "Flop! to the ground, legs up, he starts kicking his legs." One man is coming out of the church as another is going in. "Is the service already done?" "No, not done yet! The stamping's done, now they're on the kicking."

Tales About Fools

Tales with heroes who are unusual fools of some kind, who perform the most absurd actions, form a special group both thematically and compositionally. These tales occur in two kinds. In one kind, whole ethnic groups or the residents of some city or locale are distinguished by stupidity; in the other type it is individual people who are fools. It is impossible to draw an exact boundary here, because in the final analysis the unusual actions are nonetheless performed by individual people. Still, plots or motifs will tend somewhat toward one or the other group.

In wonder tales the fool is usually the youngest brother, but this only serves as a contrasting background for his subsequent heroization: The fool carries out magical feats. In the everyday or novellistic tales the folktale fool represents something completely different: His deeds provoke laughter, and the stories amuse listeners. They contain a certain element of satire, but as a whole they cannot be called a satire on human stupidity. The actions of the fool are too unlikely for this, and the laughter is not scathing but good-natured. The fool in such tales, regardless of the laughter, wins the listener's sympathy. It often happens that the hero achieves great success. But if in the wonder tales this success is achieved by the internal qualities of the seeming fool, here it is achieved quite accidentally and unexpectedly. The unexpected ending brings these tales close to the anecdote.

Such, for example, is the tale "The Fool and the Birch Tree" (A-T 1643; Afanas'ev 402). A fool inherits a bull. He takes it to market to sell it. In the forest he passes an old dried-out birch tree. "The wind blew and the birch started to squeak." "Why is the birch squeaking?" wonders the fool. "Is it bidding on my bull?" He demands 20 rubles, "but the birch does not say anything, it only squeaks; and it seems to the fool that it is asking to buy the bull on credit." The fool agrees to let it go for 20 rubles on credit; he ties it to the birch and comes back the next day for the money. But the bull has been eaten by wolves, and the birch tree is standing there as before. In irritation the fool knocks the birch tree over, and under its roots he discovers a treasure trove—a pot of gold.

In other tales the hero achieves no success at all. Thus in the tale "The Fool Makes Purchases" (A-T 1681; Afanas'ev 400; compare Loorits 1689),[34] the brothers send the fool to the city to buy household things for the holiday. Ivanushka bought some of everything: He bought a table, and spoons, and cups, and salt; he filled a whole wagon with all kinds of things. Further, the tale is told this way: He rode home, and the nag was, you know, not very peppy; she pulled without pulling much. "So what," Ivanushka thought to himself, "the horse has four legs, and the table also has four; so the table can go the rest of the way by itself!" He took out the table and stood it in the road. He rode, rode, near or far, and the ravens kept on circling above him and cawing. "That means my sisters feel like eating and dining, that's why they're yelling so," thought the little fool. He laid out plates with the food on the ground and began to invite them: "Sisters, my little doves, eat to your good health!" But he himself went on and on. Ivanushka was riding along a forest path; along the road were all kinds of burned stumps. "Eh," thought the fool, "the kids have no hats; they'll catch cold, the dears!" He took the pots and earthenware and put one of them on each stump." He continues acting in the same spirit. The brothers give him a thumping.

This tale is quite interesting in many ways. The fool sees the world in a distorted way and makes wrongly reasoned decisions. But his internal motivations are the very best. He pities everyone, he is ready to give away his last possession, and this provokes indubitable sympathy.

Another kind of stupidity is depicted in the tale "The Utter Fool" (A-T 1696; Afanas'ev 403–404). The fool here does and says everything wrong, too late. The tale is brief, and it can be cited here as a whole.

> Once there lived an old man and an old woman. They had one son, and a fool at that. His mother told him, "You should go, sonny, out among the people and rub against them to get some sense into you." "Wait, mama, I'll go right now." He went through the village and saw two men threshing peas; he ran right over to them. First he rubbed against one, then against the other. "Quit your fooling," the men told him. "Off you go, back where you came from." But he kept on rubbing. The men got angry and started to treat him to the flails. They gave him such a whipping that he could hardly crawl home. "Why are you crying, child?" the old woman asked him. The fool told her his sorrow. "Ah, sonny, you are such a fool! You should have said to them, 'God help you, good people! May you carry it and never tire of carrying, may you drive and never tire of driving.' They would have given you some peas; we would have cooked them and eaten them." The next day the fool was walking through the village; a funeral procession was coming toward him. He saw it and started to shout, "God help you! May you carry and never tire of carrying, may you drive and never tire of driving!" Once again they beat him up; he came home and began to complain. "There, mama, you told me what to do, but they beat me up." "Ah, child! You should have said, 'Rest in peace!' And taken off your hat, and started to cry many tears and make deep bows; they would have let you eat and drink your fill." The fool set off through the village; he heard noise and merriment in one house: They were celebrating a wedding. He took off his hat, and himself started to cry and cry. "What kind of ignoramus has come," said the drunken guests. "We are all drinking and celebrating, and he seems to be crying for a dead man!" They jumped up and gave his sides a good pounding! (A-T 1696 A; Afanas'ev 403)

This tale is also not void of philosophical meaning. Lenin cites it for its description of details that act without being in concert. The fool of this tale is polite and well-meaning and wants to please everyone. But he is always oblig-ing too late, he applies the past to the present, and, regardless of his polite-ness, he provokes anger and gets nothing but a beating. The folk love people who are good but a bit stupid, and they have no pity for the clever ones who think only of themselves.

The theme of stupidity is widely disseminated in the folktale, and there is no need to pause in detail here on all the plots.

Absolutely anyone, regardless of age, sex, and social position, may turn out to be a fool. In the examples cited the fool is presented actively as a character. But in some tales the fool turns out to be duped by more crafty people, who take advantage of his stupidity. Old women, for example, are distinguished by stupidity, even when they are good and soft-hearted. Such an old woman lets in a soldier who calls himself "Non-End, from the other world" to spend the night. She tells him to go back to the other world with cloth, money, and all kinds of things for her dead son (A-T 1540; Afanas'ev 391). An old woman sells bulls on credit but keeps one of them to ensure payment for the oth-ers. The purchasers vanish forever. This exhausts the patience of her husband, who sets out to find people who are even more stupid, and he usually finds them. Setting out like this is an extremely simple compositional device, al-lowing tale-tellers to string all kinds of episodes together one after another. Tales about stupid noblemen and the cumulative tale of the stupid peasant girl and so on fall into such a chain. Tales that present a nobleman as stupid, in which a peasant makes a fool of him, acquire a sharp satirical character. In their compositional schema these tales echo and respond to tales about jok-ers, although their meaning is completely different.

I will not retell all the plots in which fools appear. The cited examples give a sufficiently clear impression of them.

Another group of tales is about fools and idiots. The actors in them are not one person but a group. These are either non-Russians (Tatars, Gypsies, Germans) or residents of some particular place.

Tales about stupid peoples are an international phenomenon. Old schol-arship considered tales of this kind to be a manifestation of nationalist an-tagonism and used them for reactionary purposes. However, ethnographic collectors know quite well that a mocking attitude is found not only with respect to representatives of other nationalities but also with regard to the residents of neighboring settlements, whose quirks provoke a good-natured smile, one that does not at all exclude friendly, neighborly relations. Such plots arise from the natural desire to make fun of one's neighbor. These plots are largely international; the direction of the nation at which fun is poked is subject to fluctuation and is different for different peoples. This makes clear that the essence and basis of the plot is not national antagonism but the comicality of situations. This is particularly true of Russian materials. *Poshekhontsy* (i.e., residents of the Poshekhonsk region of the Iaroslavl' *guberniia*) have the reputation in Russia of being none too bright; their name even came to mean country bumpkins. However, such an assignment is not folkloric and does not belong to the people itself. We would search in vain for the word *poshekhontsy* in any of the folktale collections known to us; it is not known among the people. We must presume that such an assignment arose in Russia not in the folk sphere but as a result of the literary reworking of folk plots. The first edition of Vasilii Berezaiskii's book *Anecdotes, or the Merry Adventures of the Poshekhontsy* appeared in 1798; it was republished many times and enjoyed great popularity.[35] In Western Europe anecdotes of that kind were gathered and reworked much earlier than in Russia; they make up the foundation of several folk books, such as the one about the *Schieldbürghers* (i.e., residents of the city of Schielde, first edition 1597) and the one about the seven Schwabians.

Speaking of these folk books and others like them, Friedrich Engels rates them highly: "This wit, this naturalness of conception and performance, the good-natured humor that always accompanies the always biting mockery, so that it does not become too cruel, the striking comicality of the situations— all this, in truth, could outdo a good part of our literature."[36]

Of the anecdotes applied in the West to their own *poshekhontsy* and in Russia simply to fools without specifying their nationality, the most widespread are the following: fools who drag a cow up onto a roof where grass is growing; fools who try to drive a horse into its collar and are unable to harness it; fools who, in building a house, forget the windows and try to bring in sacks of light; fools who sow salt; fools who try to milk chickens, and so on. In these cases the hero of the tale helps them, tells them what to do, and they thank him and reward him. But often such fools perish or suffer from their own stupidity. A fool cuts the branch he is sitting on, regardless of a peasant's warning, and falls into the water. Fools are getting ready to shoot, and one of them looks into his muzzle. Taking a millstone down a mountain, one of them puts his head into the opening to see where the stone is rolling to. Such tales are told in realistic style, but their realism bears a conventional character, just like the realism of other kinds of novellistic tale. They are far from being copies from reality. The stupidity of the heroes makes it possible to realize one of the basic principles of folktale poetics. What is impossible for an ordinary person becomes possible for a fool, and the folktale strives precisely for what is unusual, what is impossible under everyday conditions. These everyday conditions are drawn realistically, but the event itself is usually absolutely impossible in real life.

Separating out tales about fools and looking closely at their heroes, we conclude that the stupidity here is something greater, something more significant than a simple artistic device for creating unusual situations and comical events. These tales belong to a broader circle of comic folktales, whose comicality sometimes produces a strange impression on a contemporary person. Thus among the anecdotes about fools there is one in which the hero thinks he has died. He is convinced that he has died, and this permits comical responses. A good blow from a whip brings him to himself. We have a mix-up of consciousness in episodes telling how one member of a married couple brings the other to the workplace, usually the harvest, in his sleep. They cut his hair, smear him with tar, and stick feathers on him and so on, so that when he wakes up the hero does not even recognize himself. He is no longer himself; he asks the others who he is. If we also include in this comparison tales about jokers and the terrible tricks they play on their neighbors without any purpose, simply for the sake of some grandiose mockery, then we are willy-nilly compelled to suppose that this orgy of stupidity and jest is somehow connected with the so-called medieval feast of fools (*festa stultorum, fêtes des foux*).

Tales of Bad Wives

Finally, we can single out a special group of tales about obstinate, lazy, evil, and unfaithful wives. Such tales are satiric in coloration. They note some negative sides of the everyday family life of the patriarchal village. Application of hyperbole lends them a vividly comical character. We have already mentioned the tale "An Old Woman's Worse Than a Devil." Among the tales of evil wives, for example, we find a plot such as "The Evil Wife in a Pit" (A-T 1164; Afanas'ev 433–437). To get rid of his evil and quarrelsome wife, a peasant throws her to the devils in a pit. After a while he goes back to the pit and sees the devils climbing out of it one by one, because they cannot tolerate the company of this woman. There are many tales about lazy, stubborn, or quarrelsome wives. A husband searches for the corpse of his drowned wife, going upstream against the current because he is convinced that even after dying, she will do everything against the grain (A-T 1365 A; Afanas'ev 439). Such a woman would rather be buried or drowned than agree with her husband. For example, she reproaches her husband for shaving badly (he is not "shaven" but "mown"). The husband throws her into the water from a bridge, but she lifts her hand above the water to show that it is *mown* (A-T 1365 B; Afanas'ev 440). A woman was distinguished for her quarrelsome nature even before marriage. Her suitor or young husband sets out to correct her and does this decisively: He harnesses her into a sleigh in place of the horse and makes her pull him to visit his father-in-law (A-T 901; Afanas'ev 519) (cf. Shakespeare's *Taming of the Shrew*).

Among the tales of unfaithful wives there are two notable groups. In some the unfaithful wife is exposed, and the husband triumphs and punishes his wife; in others, on the contrary, the clever wife fools her husband, and he is left deceived. The plot of the "Matron of Ephesus" is international and ancient; it was examined by Fedor Buslaev. An inconsolable widow is mourning her husband in the crypt but betrays him with a criminal, who has come to take refuge in the crypt, and gives him her husband's corpse (A-T 1510). She is ready to marry the man who brings her news of her husband's death (A-T 1350; see also Afanas'ev 272). Even King Solomon has an unfaithful wife, whom he punishes (A-T 920).

In Western Europe such plots about unfaithful wives were already well known in the Middle Ages, as we know from preserved Latin monastic sermons. From the point of view of church asceticism, woman is the source of all evil, the vessel of the devil, and this was proved with stories about wives' infidelity. The folk morality expressed in them, however, is of a completely different kind. The stories condemn debauchery; it is presented in a comic way in the form of entertaining stories, but in folklore there is no kind of asceticism. On the other hand, the plot of the wife who succeeds in fooling a silly or despotic husband, a jealous old man, reflects later views of women from the era of the Renaissance. Such plots were used by Boccaccio. The tale of the Guest Terentii, known in Russia both in the form of a folktale and in the form of a *bylina* sung by *skomorokhi*, is also international. A wife sends her husband out to get medicine. Advised by the *skomorokhi*, he returns home in their basket, catches his wife feasting with her lover, and cures her with a whip (A-T 1360 C, "Terentii the Guest"; Afanas'ev 445). This plot was being performed in puppet theaters in Holland as early as the eleventh century. To these plots we might also add the tale "The Expensive Skin." While selling a hide, a poor man happens to be in the house of a rich man whose wife is with her lover. They are not discovered. The poor man saves the lover and winds up richer (A-T 1535; Afanas'ev 447). The plot "Nikola in the Hollow Tree" also enjoyed great popularity. A wife asks a tree how to get rid of her husband. The husband answers her from the hollow tree in place of St. Nikola, and then he kills her lover (A-T 1380; Afanas'ev 446).

Tales About Jokers

Tales about jokers make a somewhat strange impression on a contemporary person who has grown up reading realistic literature. The hero of the tale, a joker, brings people to crime and death with his deceptions; he provokes fires and ruin—and all with a belly laugh of schadenfreude. Such plots may provoke not only perplexity but also indignation. However, the impression changes as soon as we recall that we have before us a folktale, whose action cannot be immediately and directly correlated with reality. Such tales spring from the desire for mischief. At its roots this desire indicates a certain strength that has nowhere to go, that cannot find proper application. Mischief maker and anarchist Vasilii Buslaevich is hymned in the *bylina*; he plays "no-good jokes—he grabs someone's arm and the arm comes off, he grabs someone's head and the head comes off." However, theoreticians who consider that the image of Vasilii Buslaevich only lauds individualistic anarchism, strength that is sufficient in itself, are nonetheless mistaken. Vasilii Buslaevich's strength finds release in a struggle with Novgorod's old, patriarchal, and clerical system, the struggle with religious prejudices (he blasphemes in Jerusalem), the struggle with Novgorod's social leadership—and all that in the form of a vicious rebellion, whose depiction has the character of powerful grotesquerie. No determined social struggle is so vividly expressed in the folktale.

Folktales about jokers take to an extreme a general narrative device that runs through all kinds of folktale narration: the device of making cruel fun of one's opponent. We observe it in animal tales, where the crafty fox fools all the beasts and saves herself. This narrative principle is one basis for the tales of clever thieves. The people are not calling for rebellion in them; they are not calling for the ax. But in a way the tale prepares the psychological groundwork for rebellion, prepares a rebel consciousness. This is done with the means that folklore has had at its disposal for a long time. Laughter is a means of destroying one's opponent. In tales about jokers, such destruction by laughter may go along with actual destruction of the opponent, although it is somewhat softened by the power of laughter and pleasure in laughter.

Curiously, the psychological state that leads to tales about jokers is expressed musically in Sergei Prokofiev's symphonic poem *The Fool Who Out-Fooled Seven Fools*. Professional literature also knows the image of the joker and rogue; these are the so-called picaresque novels. But they express social struggle more sharply than the folktale. Their hero is a joker who fools his noble master. This genre flowered especially in Spain beginning in the sixteenth century, when the famous novel *Lazarillo de Tormes* appeared (1554). The plot basis of the novels is folkloric to a significant extent, but their grotesquerie bears shallower, softened, and, as it were, more civilized forms, whereas Russian folklore knows no softening and gives full freedom to the most merciless laughter.

Tales about jokers, like some other forms of folktales (about animals, about fools) are multistructured. Individual dirty tricks represent freestanding tales, but they may also figure as episodes in other tales. Several such tales are collected in the first edition of Afanas'ev under one number (223, 397–399). One such tale is "Left His Jokes at Home" (A-T 542 P). A joker lives in a village. The priest says, "We should go see the joker, he might make a jest." The joker says, "As you will, father; only I left my jest with the seven jesters, so dress me up nice and warm and give me a horse so I can go get it." The priest gives him a horse, a fur coat, and a hat. "The joker drives to the priest's wife and tells her, "Mother! The priest has bought 300 pounds of fish; he sent me on his horse to get the money from you, he wants 300 rubles." The priest's wife gives him the money, and the joker takes it home. The priest, seeing no jest, goes home to his wife, and there he finds out what kind of joke the joker has played on him, and in response to his own request at that. After this, the joker continues to make other jokes, which we will not retell here, as the priest asks for them. For example, he dresses up as a woman and starts to work as a serving maid at the priest's house, leading to a series of misunderstandings (A-T 1538*). After the priest he fooled gives him 300 rubles, the joker now makes jokes not about the priest but about other people who are jokers just like him.

Another such tale is "The Joker and the Seven Jokers" (Afanas'ev 397). A joker receives 300 rubles from a priest he has fooled. He makes a coffin and carries the money in it. Here come the seven jokers; they ask where he got the money. "Where'd I get it? See, I sold a dead man and now I have a coffin full of money." The jokers kill their wives, put them into coffins and drive off to sell them. They drive along shouting, "Dead for sale, dead for sale! Who needs some dead people?" The Cossacks beat them and drive them out of town. The fooled jokers now want to get revenge on the joker. He fools them again. He sells them a goat or a horse who supposedly defecates money. At home they discover the deception and go back to him. Now he shows them a "living" whip, which supposedly brings people back to life. First, he tells his wife what to do, hides a bladder of blood under her shirt, and stabs the bladder with a dagger; then, afterward he "brings her back to life." The jokers buy the whip for 300 rubles. In variants where the jokers have already killed their wives, they now try to bring rich dead people back to life, but they get a beating, whereas in the variants where their wives are still alive, they kill their wives but cannot bring them back to life. They try to drown the joker, but this also comes to nothing. They put him in a sack and take him to the water, but he asks them to wait and to bring his family so he can say goodbye. They put the sack down by the water. A shepherd walks by with his flock. The joker says that they have put him in the sack in order to make him the chief, the mayor, but he doesn't want to do it. The shepherd asks him to put him in the sack instead; he is ready to become the chief. The joker throws the sack with the shepherd into the water and starts driving his flock home. When the jokers ask where he got hold of the flock, he says that he found it under the water. They jump into the water in order to get some livestock too, and they drown.

The joker's dirty tricks vary. For example, he sells a kettle that supposedly cooks by itself or a hat that lets the wearer eat and drink in the tavern without paying. The joker tells the priest's wife that her husband has bought a new house and wants her to burn the old one, and the priest's wife actually burns down their house.

Seventeenth-Century Russian Tales of Literary Origin

I noted in the introduction that folktale tradition supplied the origin of artistic literature. In Western Europe this process began during the Renaissance, whereas in Russia it began in the seventeenth century. It was precisely in the seventeenth century that the clerical culture of the Russian Middle Ages began to grow obsolete. Russia began to form connections with Western Europe. The Petrine reforms and the shaping of a powerful empire concluded a process that had begun in the first quarter of the seventeenth century. A new secular literature was needed, and it was created on the basis of the people's narrative art.

This process took place differently in Russia than in Western Europe. Only one plot has passed directly from folklore into written literature, but it was widely read. This is the tale of Karp Sutulov, which originates in the plot of the tale of the clever beauty who fools the priest, deacon, and sacristan.

Other literary tales of the seventeenth century that are linked with folklore spring not from folkloric plots but from the vivid dynamic narration of folklore, the images and language of the folktale, and its humor and jollity. Three of these are "Shemiaka's Judgment," "The Tale of Ruff, Son of Ruff," and "The Tale of the Hen and the Fox," works whose authors remain anonymous. The folktale style is caught and transmitted so well and vividly that these works have entered folk circulation. They have become part of folklore, turned into folktales. We see here a kind of spiral process: Works that grew up on a folkloric base once again return to folklore.

These tales form part of the course on Old Russian literature, and they are well illuminated in Gudzii's textbook.[37]

I will begin with the tale "Shemiaka's Judgment." Gudzii considers this a plot that arose in the East, linked with a cycle of narrations about the wise judgments of Solomon. I think that the plot has nothing at all in common with the judgments of Solomon. It comes down to the following. There are two brothers, a poor one and a rich one. The poor one asks the rich one to lend him a horse so that he can bring home some firewood. The rich one lends him a horse but does not give him a horse collar. The poor one drives to his gate but forgets to remove the board under the gate. The horse gets stuck, keeps pulling forward, and tears off its tail. The rich brother does not want a horse without a tail and goes to complain to the judge, Shemiaka, who lives in the city. He brings his brother along, taking him to court. They spend the night at a priest's house. The priest gives food and drink to the rich brother, whereas the poor one lies on the top sleeping bench and watches. He leans out to see better, falls from the bench right onto the cradle, and kills the child. The priest comes along to complain to Shemiaka. They cross a bridge over a cliff. The poor brother is in despair; he expects to be condemned. He jumps off the bridge, meaning to kill himself, but falls into a sleigh that an old man and his son are driving. The son is taking his sick father to the bathhouse. The poor brother falls right on the old man and kills him, but he himself is not hurt. The old man's son joins the others going to court. Now there are three plaintiffs.

The poor man gets the idea of bribing the judge. He has nothing, so he takes a stone from the road and wraps it in a handkerchief. Every time the judge asks a question he picks up the stone and shows it to the judge. The judge thinks it is gold and judges in the poor man's favor as follows: He tells the rich brother to give the poor one his horse until its tail grows back; tells the priest to give him his wife until he gets a new child with her; and he suggests that the son of the old man jump off the bridge and crush the poor man just as his father was crushed. Afterward the judge demands the bribe he was promised. The poor man shows him that he had a stone wrapped up in the handkerchief and that he was ready to kill the judge with it. The judge expresses his happiness at avoiding that fate. The poor man demands that the sentences be carried out, and the plaintiffs buy him off for a lot of money.

The tale has been studied by historians of Old Russian literature. It has the most intimate links with Russian everyday life and reproduces details of Old Russian court proceedings quite exactly, representing a satire of court proceedings and the corruptibility of the judges. But the folktale has not been studied at all. At present there are twenty oral Russian variants,[38] which testifies to its wide dissemination (A-T 1534; Afanas'ev 319–320). Stith Thompson, in his edition of Aarne's Index, names Estonian, Latvian, Lithuanian, Czech, Serbian and Croatian, Hungarian, and other variants of the folktale besides. In the Romano-German world the tale does not exist, but it does exist in Turkey. Historians of Old Russian literature are wrong to study this plot outside folklore. It is possible that the tale is not the work of a single author but rather folkloric, and precisely Russian at that, and that the authorial treatment of the plot took place in the seventeenth century.

Another seventeenth-century tale that is also known in folklore is "The Tale of Ruff, Son of Ruff." Afanas'ev called it a folktale and included it in his count of animal tales (Afanas'ev 77–80). Andreev also placed it among these tales, setting aside a new, special Russian type for it, 254*. There is a splendid book by a corresponding member of the Academy of Sciences of the USSR that also investigates this tale: Varvara Adrianova-Peretts's *Studies in the History of Russian Satirical Literature of the Seventeenth Century.*[39] Adrianova-Peretts knew twenty-one written texts and five folkloric recordings. At present the number of folkloric recordings has reached twenty-three. There are four independent redactions (versions). I will touch on the redaction represented in folklore.

"The Tale of Ruff, Son of Ruff" is also a satire on court proceedings. But if "Shemiaka's Judgment" laughs at bribery and injustice, the tale here mocks the very process of court proceedings with their bureaucracy, red tape, and crotchetiness. The tale is written in the language used for judicial acts, and this same language passed into the folktale. Here we see a satirical depiction of the suits over land that were especially common in the mid-seventeenth century. A bream, an inhabitant of the lake of Rostov, is presented as the plaintiff. The bream is a nobleman, and the Lake of Rostov is his ancestral estate. The defendant is a ruff, who has set up a large family in the Lake of Rostov and gives no one any peace. The large, ponderous bream is opposed here to the small and nimble ruff. The judges are a beluga and a sturgeon, and the witnesses for the bream are a whitefish and a *lodoga* (Vladimir Dal' identifies the *lodoga* as a northern fish). The judges' decision is to hand the ruff over head first to the plaintiff, to punish him with a merchants' execution—beating with a knout and after that hanging for thievery and slander in the sun at the hottest time of year. The ruff is not dismayed, and he answers, "My lords, judges, you have judged me not according to justice but according to a bribe. You have justified the bream with his comrades, but you have condemned me." The ending goes this way: "The ruff spat in the eyes of the judges and leapt into the undergrowth: and that's the last they saw of him."

The spice of this tale is not in the plot but in the parody of the whole process of a court trial. Here we also have a perch as the bailiff, a chub and an ide as witnesses, a carp as the scribe, a crucian as the summoner (i.e., investigator), a loach as the clerk, and so forth. They are all artful dodgers and rogues, but inept rogues, whereas the ruff is a clever rogue who escapes from their court. The language, both in the written tale and in the folktale, parodies the language of court acts; the exposition is enriched with rhymes and rhymed sayings.

To understand this folktale better, we must keep in mind that the judges were not officials but rich boyars and landowners. Suits over land and landholding rights were numerous, and judges judged in favor not of the smallholders but of rich agriculturists, the class to which they themselves belonged. Both bribery and injustice flourished in such courts. The folktale could not have become so popular if it did not reflect judicial practice that had spread from Moscow to the whole country. This explains the presence of different versions and the multitude of variations, whose analysis I cannot dwell on. Both copyists and tale-tellers contributed their share of creativity in the exposition of this folkloric written tale.

The third folkloric written tale I would like to linger on is the tale of the hen and the fox. Adrianova-Peretts's book studies this tale in detail.

There are twenty-nine manuscript texts and three redactions: in prose, in verse, and of mixed style. Adrianova-Peretts also knew of eight Russian folklore texts and one Ukrainian text. At the present time we know thirteen Russian folklore texts (Andreev 61 A; Afanas'ev 15–17). This folktale is a satire of ostentatious, sham piety and the clergy. The plot scheme in folklore comes down to this: A fox tries to steal a peasant's hen, but the rooster raises the alarm, and the fox runs away.

To give you some conception of the language of this folktale, I will cite Nikiforov's recording (Adrianova-Peretts 200). The fox goes into the forest, lies down under the bushes, and stays there for three days. Lifting her eyes, she sees the rooster sitting in a tree. She pretends to be repentant and suggests that the rooster come down to the ground and confess his sins, of which the main one is polygamy and lack of respect for the church (he does not go to confession). When the rooster says that the fox recently wanted to steal a chicken, she says that it was another fox, not her. The fox grabs him in her claws, carries him away, and mocks him. The rooster promises the fox that he can fix her up with the wafer baker. They will eat their fill and live richly. The fox lets the rooster go; he flies up into a tree, and, in turn, makes fun of the fox.

I have cited the brief version of the folktale. There is a more extensive redaction of the written tale and a version of the folktale where both the rooster and the fox cite holy scripture and interpret it in their own ways. This tale is a satire.

Moralistic Tales

I would like to point out the kind of folk prose that has the most intimate relationship to folktales. I have in mind stories of terrible sinners who are punished. If members of the people always know that folktales are inventions that cannot be believed but that provide tremendous enjoyment, then stories about sinners express some truth that is very close to the people and entirely real, so strong that the question of belief or disbelief in what is being narrated cannot even be asked. The people believe in the truth of these stories and tell them with a feeling of dread and reverence, without pondering whether such events could actually happen or not, although the events narrated are just as unverisimilar, fantastic, and improbable as the ones described in folktales. Standing close to folktales, their ideological tendency is close to the *legenda*, and they form a kind of intermediate link with it.

Russian peasants have always been distinguished by high moral demands on themselves and others, and they reproved the sins that were found in the peasant milieu with all the strength of their being. Despite the poverty and difficulty of their existence, internally they lived by ideals of a higher order of worldview as well as by the ideals of everyday life. These ideals touch on the family, for example. The family is a kind of primary cell of the peasants' societal and productive life, and peasants have a clear concept of the purity and moral norms of family life and familial relationships. An inharmonious, unfriendly family is not only a misfortune but also a heavy sin. This disharmony tends to be hidden from those outside, but it appears to the wise, old, and pure like a vision. "A little old man was walking through the world and asked one peasant to let him in to spend the night"—this is the beginning of the folktale-legend "Night Visions" (A-T 840; Afanas'ev *Legendy* 17 a, v).[40] They let him in. The family sleeps while the old man sees various things in the darkness: A snake is lying between the master's son and his wife and breathing on them; a cat is sitting on another son's wife, "its mouth is gaping at the husband." These visions signify that the spouses feel enmity for one another. The cat means that "the wife wants to get rid of the husband." Between the youngest son and his wife lies an infant; he and his wife are in a state of grace. There are interesting variants and details. In one of the variants the passerby sees that in the space where the oldest son sleeps "a cudgel is beating from the floor all the way to the ceiling." Yet "it is not a cudgel beating, but his mind and reason." "That is because he wants to be the big man" (i.e., the senior member of the family). The rooms of such a family are full of vermin: snakes, frogs, lizards. The passerby goes out to spend the night in the barn. But here he hears moaning in the hay because the hay was stolen. The peasant mowed someone else's parcel of land. The livestock will die off after eating this kind of hay. The old man lies down under the sheaves of grain, but here too he hears a voice, which says that the lazy master did not collect the ears neatly from his field—he left a great deal of seed. So the symbolic images reveal the unappealing life of an unharmonious peasant family: enmity between father and son, enmity between spouses, theft, laziness at work—all that is invisible to the eye is concealed by the apparently peaceful life of such a family.

The sinners in this family are not punished. As he leaves, the pilgrim speaks to the master about his visions and tells him what he should do, how to live. The story has a certain allegorical quality, which is characteristic not of folktales but of *legendy*.[41]

But there are also more horrible tales about crimes between members of a single family—not only between spouses but between parents and children. One of these stories begins this way: "In one village a girl fell in love with a young man and got pregnant by him. When her time came, she secretly gave birth to a live child, took it into the woods, and buried it there in the ground." In its linguistic style this recording gives the impression of a retelling by someone educated. Nonetheless the authenticity of the plot is undoubted. The narration develops as follows: The girl gets pregnant three times, and three times she buries her living children. After the third time, as she is returning home, she suddenly feels three snakes jump on her. "Two of them crawled briskly onto her breast, started to suck at her nipples and began to suck the milk greedily, choking, too hurried to swallow it all—milk mixed with blood dripped out of their mouths." The third one wraps itself around her neck. They take turns. Once they have sucked their fill, they all wrap around her neck. They cannot be removed, and the girl goes along covering them with her kerchief. The story ends with her repenting her sin and going to wander from monastery to monastery.

Children may also turn out to be guilty. Onchukov recorded the folktale "The Greedy Sons" (A-T 779*C; Onchukov 280). Three sons are dividing their inheritance, but none of them wants their old mother: "No one needs mama." The brothers live and eat together, "and not one of them sits their mother down at the table; mother lies on the stove." A little old beggar man comes to the hut. In the folktales too this is typically the bearer of truth and the reproacher who is invested with some kind of higher powers. He hears the old woman exclaim, "Lord, if only you would let me die." The old man suggests to the brothers that they sell their mother—they don't need her. The sons are glad to. They lead her out, two taking her arms, one pushing her from behind. When they try to let go of her arms, they cannot do it: "The old woman has grown into them."

Another typical flaw of the peasant is stinginess. This is perhaps less typical of Russian peasants than of German and French peasants (we might recall some of Maupassant's peasant stories). Stinginess is provoked by poverty. However, regardless of their poverty, real peasants despise extortion, greed, and miserliness, and the heroes of their folktales are unmercenary poor men and the acquisitive are mocked and disparaged. In the folktale "The Poor Man" (A-T 750*, subtype 1; Afanas'ev 347) the hero is the peasant Nesterka, who has six children (*"Nesterka, u kotorogo detei shesterka"*). He has nothing to live on. He loads his children into a wagon and sets off to pick scraps. Along the road he meets a poor man, a legless beggar, and they take him along. They ask permission to spend the night in a rich hut. The housewife orders the children to lie down under the bench and puts the legless man on the highest sleeping bench. The man of the house comes home: "What sort of people have you let in?" "They're beggars. They asked to spend the night." "Indeed they did! They could have spent the night outdoors!" The beggars are not invited to dinner; they have to feed themselves on dry crusts. In the yard stands the master's wagons with goods; the horses are hitched and chewing oats. At night the legless man talks Nesterka into leaving. He loads his children into their own wagon and goes. And a miracle occurs. The horses hitched to the wagons full of goods leave by themselves and follow Nesterka's wagon. A second miracle happens. The legless man sends Nesterka back, saying he forgot his gloves. "Nesterka got to the house—and it wasn't there, it had sunk into the earth! Only the gloves were left on the stove pipe." The legless man explains that these wagons are full of goods acquired unjustly. "Take these twelve wagons with everything in them for yourself," says the legless man, and he disappears before their eyes.

Thus the peasants expressed a dream of the redistribution of wealth. The rich and miserly man is destroyed, and property passes to the poor man. True, the peasants dimly understand that such redistribution does not yet signify fairness. In some stories a poor man who has grown wealthy becomes a *kulak* (a rich, exploitative peasant) himself and begins to persecute the poor (A-T 751*C; see Afanas'ev 122, 262).

In the pure peasant style the miser is punished not in this life but after death, as in the story "The Miser's Death" (A-T 760*A; Afanas'ev 370). This is the only story of its kind. It exists in a single recording in Afanas'ev. The story is brief, so I will cite it in full.

> There was once a miserly skinflint, an old man; he had two sons and a great deal of money. He heard death coming, locked himself alone into his hut and sat down on his chest, started to swallow gold coins and eat paper bills, and so he ended his life. The sons came, laid out the dead man under the holy icons and called the sacristan to read the Psalms. Suddenly right at midnight the Evil One arrived in the form of a man, picked up the dead old man on his shoulder, and said, "Sacristan, hold out your skirts. The old man started to get scared. The devil said, "The money is yours, but the sack is mine!" He took him away, and disappeared.

In some ways this story gives the impression of a retelling by the one who recorded it ("in the form of a man," "he had two sons and a great deal of money"). However, the plot is undoubtedly genuine. The story was written down in Saratov *guberniia*. The image of a miser who locks himself in his hut and swallows coins and bills conveys the last, horrifying stage of a terrible sin and is related with enormous artistic power.

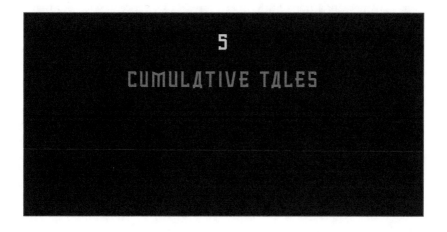

GENERAL DESCRIPTION OF CUMULATIVE FOLKTALES

As we have seen, Afanas'ev's separation of wonder tales into a special subgroup is justified by analysis of these tales. Afanas'ev often proceeded by way of intuition, whereas the modern division is based on study of the internal structural traits of the folktale and can be carried out with adequate scholarly precision.

We should be able to separate out other kinds of folktales according to their particular traits as well, but we cannot do this yet, because the structural particularities of other kinds of tales have not been studied sufficiently.

However, one not very common kind of folktale has compositional and stylistic particularities so specific that it can be separated into a separate variety without any doubts. This is the so-called cumulative tale.[1]

The existence of cumulative tales as a special type was noted long ago, but no one made corresponding conclusions for either classification or study of the folktale. In revising and translating Aarne's index of folktale types into English, American scholar Stith Thompson set aside 200 numbers for them (Cumulative, 2000–2199). Translating the same index into Russian, Professor Nikolai Andreev introduced one general number for all cumulative tales, calling it "Cumulative Tales of Various Kinds." In this way, both researchers addressed the need to distinguish this material in some way, but they used opposite tactics: One foresaw 200 tale types; the other only 1. At the same time, however, it is still not clear which folktales should be called cumulative, and a large number of typical cumulative folktales are scattered among the other subtypes. An especially large number of cumulative tales are found among animal tales. Aarne's system does not let us separate them exactly, and attempts to make corrections in the index have had a compromised character. It is not corrections that are needed here but an essentially new system of classification, founded on the study of folktale poetics.

Our data suggest about twenty different types of cumulative tales in the Russian folktale repertoire. However, before we move on to analyze the Russian material, we must establish what in fact cumulative folktales are. Vagueness about this question leads not only to mix-ups in classification but also to erroneous conclusions about the nature of the material. Thus Boris Sokolov devotes a special chapter in his course on folklore to the composition and style of animal tales. This chapter is entirely based on cumulative tales, however, and literally not a single example represents any other kind of animal tale.[2] A. M. Smirnov's article "Verbal Creativity in the Folk Tale" likewise examines only cumulative folktales without appearing to notice this and without ever mentioning it to the reader.[3] Neither of these authors uses the term.

The basic compositional device of cumulative folktales is some kind of constantly increasing repetition of one and the same action, until the created chain breaks or unravels in the opposite, diminishing direction. The simplest example of an increase that leads to breaking the chain may be the widely known story "The Turnip" (A-T 2044 + AA 1960*D1); the tale "The Rooster Choked" (A-T 2021 = AA*241 1; A-T 2032; A-T 2021 A) is one example of opposite development of the chain. Besides the chain principle, other forms of gradual growth or piling up may lead to an unexpected comic catastrophe. Hence too the term for these tales, from the Latin *cumulare* (to pile up, accumulate, increase). In English they are called cumulative or accumulative stories, in German *Kettenmärchen*, *Häufungsmärchen*, or *Zählmärchen* and in French *randounées*.

In fact, it is the piling up that constitutes the entire interest and content of these tales. They have none of the interesting "events" of a plot type. On the contrary, the event itself is trifling, and its triviality sometimes contrasts comically with the monstrous growth of consequences proceeding from it and with the final catastrophe (an egg breaks and the whole village burns down).

These tales tend to be ambiguous in style and in their manner of performance. We would call some formulaic in the English style (formula tales), whereas others are epic. The first kind, the formulaic, are the most characteristic and typical cumulative tales.

COMPOSITION OF CUMULATIVE TALES

The composition of cumulative tales is exceedingly simple. The exposition is most often some insignificant event or ordinary life situation: An old man plants a turnip, an old woman bakes a loaf of bread, a girl goes to the stream to rinse out a whisk broom, an egg breaks, a peasant man takes aim at a hare, and so on. This exposition cannot even be called an opening because there is no way to tell what will start the development of the action. It develops unexpectedly, and that unexpectedness is one of the main artistic effects of the folktale. There are a great many ways to connect the chain with the exposition. In the tale of the turnip, narrative creation is stimulated when the old man cannot pull it out. In "The Fly's Bedchamber" (Andreev 283*; Afanas'ev 82, 84), a fly builds a chamber or settles into an abandoned glove, a dead animal's head, and so on. Then other creatures appear one at a time (generally in order of increasing size) and ask to come into her home: first a louse, a flea, a mosquito; then a frog, a mouse, a lizard; then further a hare, a fox, even a wolf and others. The last to appear is a bear, who puts an end to the whole business by sitting on the little house.

In the first case (the tale of the turnip), the chain's creation is motivated and internally necessary; in the second case (the little house) there is no internal necessity at all for the arrival of more and more animals. We can distinguish two kinds of cumulative tales according to this trait. The second kind predominates; the artistry of such tales does not demand any logic.

The principles of the chain's growth are also exceedingly various. In "The Rooster Choked," we have a series of dispatches. The rooster sends a hen to the river for water, the river sends her to the linden to get a leaf, the leaf sends her to the girl for a thread, the girl sends her to the cow for milk, and so on. We have a similar situation in tales of the type "The Nanny Goat with Nuts Is Missing" (A-T 2015 1; Afanas'ev 60, 61 [535]). A nanny goat is sent to get nuts. A wolf is sent after the goat, after the wolf a bear, and so on in ascending order up to a blizzard, which chases everyone else back. The tale "The Little Lad Made of Clay" (A-T 2028 = AA 333*B; Onchukov 102) is based on a series of devouring. A little boy, made of clay, eats a ball of thread with a spindle, then an old woman with a sheaf, an old man with an axe, Kat'ka with a bucket, peasant women with rakes, until a goat appears and butts the boy, who falls into dust. Everyone the boy has devoured comes back out. In this tale the little boy eats up everyone he encounters.

In "The Bread Bun" (cf. The Gingerbread Man) (A-T 2025 = AA*296), creatures that the hero meets threaten to eat him, and the tale ends when the bun is actually devoured. We have a sequential series of consumption (without meetings) in "The Wolf's Singing" (A-T 163 = AA*162; Afanas'ev 49, 50, 58) and "Beasts in a Pit" (A-T 20 A; Afanas'ev 29–30). On closer analysis, "Beasts in a Pit" reveals a triple application of the principle of accumulation (a gathering of beasts, falling into the pit, devouring one another).

Other tales rely on a series of exchanges that either proceed in decreasing order—from something better to something worse ("The Trade," A-T 1415)—or move from worse to better ("A Duck for a Hen," A-T 170). The increasing exchange may occur in reality, or someone may only dream of it. A peasant man who has not yet killed a hare dreams of how he will sell the hare; he will buy a piglet for the hare, and so on. Meanwhile the hare runs away (A-T 1430). The milkmaid with the pitcher of milk on her head has similar daydreams (Onchukov 271).

A whole series of cumulative tales is built on the sequential appearance of uninvited guests. A hare, a fox, a wolf, and a bear ask a peasant man or a fox to let them get on and ride, until the sledge breaks. The wolf asks to put one paw, another paw, a third paw, a fourth paw, and his tail on the sledge, and the sledge breaks (A-T 158). Similarly, a persistent peasant woman asks to get in a man's wagon (Afanas'ev 251 v). More and more new animals ask to come into the fly's house, until finally a bear sits on it (A-T 283*B = AA*282). In the opposite case, a stubborn goat takes over a bunny's home and cannot be chased out by a dog, a boar, a wolf, an ox, a bull, or a bear. A mosquito, a bee, a rooster, or a hedgehog manage to chase her out (A-T 212; Afanas'ev [14], 62, 63). "The Beasts' Winter Lair" contains four cumulative episodes: gathering, building a hut, spending the winter, and driving off the uninvited guest, usually a wolf (A-T 130, 130 A, 130 B = AA 139; Afanas'ev 63–65).

A special kind of tale is constructed on the creation of a chain of human or animal bodies. In "The Turnip," everyone falls over, pulling out the turnip (A-T 2044; Afanas'ev 89). Wolves stand on top of each other to eat a man who is up in a tree. The man says, "The lowest one will get me!" and they all fall down (A-T 121; Afanas'ev 56, 555 [V]). Country bumpkins want to get water from a well and grab onto one another. The one at the top lets go to spit on his hands, and everyone else falls into the well (A-T 1250).

Finally, we can distinguish a special group of tales in which more and more people are killed over trifles. An egg breaks and the old man cries; a peasant woman, the wafer baker, the deacon, the sacristan, and the priest all join in, not only raising a lament but also expressing their despair in some absurd way: They tear up books, ring the bells, and so on. Things end up with the church or the whole village burning down (A-T *241 III). A doleful peasant girl goes to the river to rinse out a whisk broom. "If I have a son, he'll drown." A peasant woman, her mother, her father, her grandmother, and so on join in her crying, and her fiancé leaves her (A-T 1450).

We can also count as cumulative tales those in which the whole action is based on various endless comical dialogues (A-T 241, 2015 II, 2041, and others).

STYLE OF CUMULATIVE FOLKTALES

Besides their distinct compositional system, cumulative folktales are also different from other tales in their style, their verbal decoration, and the form of their performance. We should keep in mind, however, that there are two forms of these tales in their performance and style, as we indicated earlier. Some are told with epic calm and slowness, just like any other folktale. They may be called cumulative only because of their fundamental composition. Examples are "The Exchange," which is usually considered a novellistic tale, and "A Duck for a Rolling-Pin," which is placed among the animal tales. The tale of the little boy made of clay, the day-dreaming milkmaid, and so on also belong among the epic tales.

Alongside these is another, more vivid and typical kind of cumulative tale. In it the accumulation or growth of events corresponds to an accumulation of words. These tales can be called formulaic. The boundary between the two kinds is unstable. One and the same plot may be performed by different tellers in either manner. But tale types indubitably tend toward one or the other manner of performance. Formulaic tales often repeat all the preceding links in the chain with the connection of each new link. Thus in "The Fly's Bedchamber" each new arrival asks, "Chamber, little chamber, who lives in the chamber?" The one who answers lists all the others, that is, first one, then two, then three animals, and so on. The whole charm of these tales is in the repetition. Their whole purpose is the colorful artistic performance. In "The Fly's Bedchamber" each beast is described with some well-chosen word, often in rhyme: *vosh'-popolzukha* (louse-crawler), *blokha-popriadukha* (flea-tress-climber), *myshka-noryshka* (mousy-little hole), *mushechka-tiutiutiushechka* (little fly-tiutiutiukins), *iashcherka-sherosherochka* (lizardy-roughkins), *lia-gushka-kvakushka* (croaky-froggie), and so on. Performance of these tales demands great mastery. They can approach tongue twisters, and sometimes they are sung. The whole attraction is the appeal of the word as such. Piling up words is only interesting if the words themselves are interesting. Therefore such tales tend to include rhyme, verse, consonance, and assonance, and they do not hesitate to make brave new word formations. Thus the hare is called "leaper-away on the mountain," a fox "jumper everywhere," a mouse "sneaker-around-the-corner," and so on.

These traits of cumulative tales make them favorites with children, who are so fond of new, witty, and vivid words, tongue twisters, and the like. For this reason cumulative tales can quite justifiably be called primarily a children's genre.

ORIGIN OF CUMULATIVE TALES

Because cumulative tales have not been correctly described and are often not even recognized as a special subgroup, the problematic of the cumulative tale cannot yet be completely resolved. We sense that the principle of accumulation is a relic from long ago. A contemporary educated person, it is true, will read or listen to a series of tales like these with pleasure, delighted mainly at their verbal tissue, but the tales do not correspond to our own forms of consciousness and artistic creation. They are a product of earlier forms of consciousness. We have phenomena arranged into a series where contemporary thinking and artistic creation would no longer count up the whole series but would jump over all the links to the final and decisive one. A detailed study of folktales needs to show precisely which series are here and which logical processes correspond to them.

Primitive thinking does not know space as a product of abstractions; it knows no generalizations at all, only empirical distance. Both in life and in fantasy, it does not conquer space by leaping from the first link to the last but goes through concrete, truly given sequential links, the way blind people walk by making their way from one object to another. Stringing together is not only an artistic device but also a form of thinking that has consequences not just in folklore but in linguistic phenomena as well. In language it would correspond to agglutination, that is, stringing together verbal particles without inflection. At the same time the folktales already show a certain tendency to overcome this stage, making artistic use of it in humorous forms and purposes.

Accumulation as a phenomenon is typical not just of cumulative tales. It enters into the structure of other tales, for example, the tale of the fisherman and the fish, where the increasing wishes of his old wife represent pure accumulation (A-T 555), or tales about Never-Laugh, where the princess laughs at people who stick to each other one at a time (A-T 559). It is more important for us to note that accumulation also occurs in the system of certain rituals, reflecting the very same manner of thinking through intermediate links. As Ivan Tolstoi indicates, Athenian ritual buffoonery was structured on the principle of accumulation.[4] A bull is killed, and the guilt for its death is passed sequentially, on the principle of accumulation, from one participant to another until it comes to the ax, which is subjected to punishment. Tolstoi also points out the correspondence of our little clay lad to the myth of Erysichthon, who was punished by the gods with an insatiable hunger: "Erysichthon eats one dish after another and cannot be sated. He gradually devours all the food supplies and all the animal inventory in the courtyard and in the field. First he eats up the animals in the byre, then the ones grazing in flocks, then the mules unhitched from their wagons, then the special cow that is being fattened for sacrifice to the goddess Hestia, then the racing horse, then his father's warhorse, and, finally, to crown it all—the house cat."[5]

These examples sketch out the problem but do not resolve it, just as it is not resolved by the purely cumulative folktale-song that appears in the Hebrew Haggadah and is performed at Passover.[6] Here a cat eats a goat, a dog bites the cat, a stick beats the dog, fire burns the stick, water puts out the fire, and so on up to God, after which there is an opposite series of another order. We may suppose that the goat eaten by the cat was once a scapegoat and that we have here the same kind of reassignment of guilt, according to the principle of accumulation, found in Athenian ritual buffoonery.

Along with everything I have outlined here, future research should establish all the kinds of accumulation present in folklore. These kinds should be contrasted with the same kinds of principles in language and in thinking. Ritual reflections of the same principle should be found, and if there turns out to be sufficient material to arrange them all in a historical sequence, then the problem may be solved.

6

ANIMAL TALES

GENERIC DIVERSITY OF ANIMAL TALES

We have separated out wonder and cumulative tales according to the category of their structure. With regard to animal tales, no such division is yet possible. We will separate them on the basis of another trait, namely, the fact that their main characters are animals. Logically this is incorrect because it introduces a different principle into the basis of division. But we are forced to take this step, given that the properly generic traits of animal tales have not yet been studied. We shall see that tales about animals, with few exceptions, nonetheless make up a natural group, although on closer examination they reveal great generic diversity. Some of the tales that are usually classed as animal tales belong among the cumulative tales, such as the tales of the ice and bast hut (A-T 43; Afanas'ev (1), 10, 11, 13, 14), the wolves who climb a tree to catch a tailor (A-T 121; Afanas'ev 56, 555 [V]), the simpleton wolf (A-T 122 A; Afanas'ev 4 [V], 6 [V], 7, 8), trading a goose for a rolling pin (A-T 170;

Afanas'ev 1, 8), the rooster's death (A-T 241*I), the fly's chamber (A-T 283*B = AA *282; Afanas'ev 82–84), and some others.

"The Wolf and the Seven Baby Goats" can be counted as a wonder tale in its structure. Here we have the absent older generation, a prohibition and its violation, misfortune and rescue, and punishment of the wolf (A-T 123; Afanas'ev 53, 54). A few animal tales might count as fables, which characteristically include not only animals but also objects and people, which all act on an equal footing. One such tale is "The Old Hospitality Is Forgotten" (A-T 155; Afanas'ev 27).[1] The animal tales also include some that might be considered folktales only with considerable reservations. So, the "The Tale of Ruff, Son of Ruff" is a literary tale, written by a single author, from the second half of the seventeenth century. It is not a folktale but a political pamphlet in folktale form. Insofar as this tale spread among the people in an altered form and in different variants, it is subject to study by folklorists as well, but it is not an animal tale in the proper sense of the words; it should be studied alongside other monuments of literary work that later began to circulate in the form of folktales. The folktale "The Fox Confessor" also has literary provenance, as we have established.

CONDITIONAL CHARACTER OF ANIMAL TALES

The particular conditional quality of division of animal tales into a special form or category becomes even clearer if we examine the separate plots and motifs of these tales. It turns out that their characters are not always animals. Tales about animals are subject to the same law of transferability of actions from one set of characters to another, and consequently one or another animal or even person cannot serve as the fundamental trait for definition of a genre. Animals and people are interchangeable.

"The Tomcat, the Rooster, and the Fox" (A-T 61*B = AA *61 II; Afanas'ev 37–39, 106–107) has the same beginning as the magical tale "Baba Yaga and the Young Lad" (A-T 327 C; Afanas'ev 106–108, 109 [V]). Baba Yaga drags the boy off, and then he is rescued. In the animal tale the fox carries off the rooster, who is lured by its song; the tomcat sets out to save him. In the tale I mentioned, "The Old Hospitality Is Forgotten," a fox forces a wolf to climb back into a sack exactly as a fisherman forces the genie he released to go back into the jar in *The Thousand and One Nights*. Similarly, another folktale that is usually counted as an animal tale but is actually about a deceitful division of the harvest, where a bear receives the tops and the peasant the roots, is told not only with the bear as the fool but also about a devil. In the latter case there are no animals in the tale at all. A tale that usually figures a fox, "A Goose for a Rolling Pin," in which a fox uses trickery to exchange a rolling pin for a goose, a goose for a turkey, and so on right up to a bull (A-T 170; Afanas'ev 1, 8), was recorded not long ago as a folktale about a crafty old woman (the Aleksandr Nikiforov manuscript collection).

GENERAL CHARACTER OF ANIMAL TALES: ANIMALS AND PEOPLE

For all its difficulties and conditional nature, the division of animal tales nonetheless has a certain justification because, after excluding the cases listed, there remains a series of tales that cannot be counted among any other kinds and that, as we will see, possess specific traits.

We understand the heading of animal tales to mean tales in which animals are the basic objects or subjects of the narration. Afanas'ev already began with this understanding,[2] and it is repeated, in essence, in the 1936–40 edition of Afanas'ev's tales.[3] This trait distinguishes animal tales from others in which animals play only an auxiliary role and are not the heroes of the narration.

However, this trait is not absolutely dependable either. It encompasses, undoubtedly, all the animal tales with only animal characters, such as "The Fox Midwife" (A-T 15; Afanas'ev 4 (V), 9–13), "The Fox and the Crane" (A-T 60; Afanas'ev 33), "The Fox and the Thrush" (A-T 56 B; Afanas'ev [32]), "The Fox Confessor" (A-T 61 A = AA *61 I; Afanas'ev 1, 15, 17), and "The Simpleton Wolf" (A-T 122 A = 47 B = AA 122).

Besides tales with only animal characters, some have both people and animals. Counting these tales among the animal tales may raise objections. In some cases Afanas'ev's definition applies easily and without interference. Thus in the most popular animal tale, the one about a fox who steals fish from a peasant's wagon, the fox herself is without a doubt the heroine, whereas the peasant is only the object of her actions. The same is true in the tale "The Wolf by the Ice Hole" (A-T 2; Afanas'ev 1–3, 4 [V]); it is the adventures of the wolf that are depicted, not those of the peasant women who come to the ice hole and beat him. In the tale "The Dog and the Wolf" (A-T 101; Afanas'ev 59) a dog is driven out because of old age; she makes friends with a wolf, and the wolf tells her how to regain her master's good graces. The wolf carries a child out of the house, and the dog, as they have agreed, brings the child to the parents, who welcome the dog back. Here there are some adventures with the people whose child is taken, but the narration is conducted form the point of view of the dog and the wolf, not the dog's owners (cf. "The Peasant, the Bear, and the Fox," A-T 157, Sd. 58, and others).

But along with these are tales in which people and animals are on an equal footing, and ascribing these tales to the animal tales is sometimes dubious and sometimes clearly erroneous.

As we study the animal epos, we must be wary of one widespread misconception: that animal tales really represent stories from the lives of animals. As a rule, animal tales have little in common with the real lives and ways of animals. Animals are usually no more than conditional bearers of the action. It is true that to some extent the animals act according to their own nature: The horse neighs, the rooster sings, the fox lives in a burrow (though this is far from always true), the bear is slow and sleepy, and so on. All this gives the tales a quality of realism, makes them truthful and artistically convincing. The depiction of animals is sometimes so persuasive that from childhood we get into the habit of defining animals' characters according to folktales. This is where we find the concept that the fox is an exceptionally crafty animal. Any zoologist knows that this opinion has no foundation. Every animal is crafty in its own way. Alfred Brehm rejects the superior craftiness of the fox and asserts that the wolf is craftier.[4] Craftiness is a folkloristic question, not a zoological one, and we will return to it again later.

The power of artistic realism is so great that we do not notice that, regardless of their subtly depicted traits, animals in the folktale often act not at all the way animals do and that their actions do not agree with their nature. Animal tales should be recognized as essentially fantastic tales. Thus the fox or some other animal builds a hut of ice, and the hare builds itself a hut of bast (A-T 43); the tomcat marries the fox; the wolf has a long conversation with his prey before he leaps on it, and so on. Beasts form friendships and keep company in ways that are impossible in nature. A bull, a ram, a pig, a goose, and a rooster set out together to roam; a dog is friends with a woodpecker (A-T 248 = AA 248 A), the fox with a crane (A-T 60), and so on. In other words, along with features and behavior that truly are typical of animals, we also observe in folktales a complete incongruity with reality, and this last trait is predominant in tales about animals.

This leads us to suppose that animal tales arose not from direct observation of the life and character of animals but in some other way. Although it is not correct to say that animal tales depict the lives of animals, the opposite point of view, that these tales represent people in the guise of animals, that the tales have an allegorical meaning (i.e., that they are in essence fables), is not correct either. The fable and the folktale are entirely different genres in their essence. Individual tales about animals might be used in the composition of fables, and we have plenty of examples of this in the fables of Ivan Krylov ("The Raven and the Fox," A-T 57; "The Lion and the Mouse," A-T 75; "The Frog and the Bull," A-T 277 A; "The Wolf and the Crane," A-T 76), but the folktale is not a fable, although it is easy to add a moral to it. In one case in Afanas'ev (A-T 1030, 154; Afanas'ev 23) we find, "So it often happens: even the head can be lost by the tail." However, the moralizing element of animal tales is no greater than the moralizing element in any other kind of folktale. We know that Perrault added morals to all the tales he published.

If animal tales are not didactic, then to the same extent they are not satirical either. True, there are purely satirical folktales ("The Tale of Ruff, Son of Ruff," "The Fox-Confessor"), but if we investigate them, these tales turn out to have literary origins. They can be used with satirical goals, just as tales of other kinds can be used, but they are neither moralizing nor satirical in their essence.

Human life, with its passions, thirst, greed, treachery, stupidity, and craftiness but at the same time with friendship, fidelity, gratitude—that is, the broad spectrum of human feelings and characters—finds a broad reflection in the animal epos, as does the realistic depiction of human and, in part, everyday peasant life.

SCOPE AND CONTENTS OF RUSSIAN ANIMAL TALES

About 140 types or plots of animal tales are known in world folklore (or, more accurately, European folklore), according to data from the Aarne-Thompson index. The Russian folktale animal epos is not very rich; according to Nikolai Andreev's data, there are sixty-seven types of animal tales.[5] They make up about 10 percent of the whole Russian folktale repertoire, but at the same time this material is characterized by great originality. Of the sixty-seven Russian types only thirty-six (53.7 percent) are international, whereas thirty-one (46.3 percent) are specifically Russian, not known in international dissemination. These figures overturn L. Z. Kolmachevskii's theory, which claims that the Russian folktale epos, with few exceptions, was borrowed from the West.

It is true that these figures are somewhat conditional, and correctives may be introduced as the material grows broader, but nonetheless the general picture is clear.[6]

The Russian animal tale is distinguished not only by the repertoire's originality but also by its particular nature. The commonality of many plots with Western ones does not at all mean that they were necessarily borrowed. Vladimir Bobrov underlines the Russian folktale's originality, counting the Russian folktale's basic particularities in comparison with the West.[7] The Western animal tale is anthropomorphized to a greater extent. It is personified; it reflects medieval everyday life with its castles, tournaments, and so on. Our beasts live in burrows and do not reflect human everyday life as much as the beasts in Western tales. Therefore they give the impression of greater freshness and immediacy. We may only object that Bobrov treats the properly folk Russian tale on an equal basis with novels about the fox, which we will speak of later. These novels are not folktales but medieval reworkings of folktales. Nonetheless, Bobrov's observation is correct, as is the general idea of the originality of the Russian animal epos. We will note, based on other observations, that Western animal tales ascribe only inimical and deceptive actions to their heroes. The beasts are all in a competition of mutual hostility. In Russia, hostility is noticeable in some cases among hunting and domestic animals. "In the West, as Grimm already noted, animals bear only corrupt traits, while their good qualities are fleeting."[8] Our animals, though, are typified by good qualities, such as compassion and selfless friendship. Thus in the typical Russian folktale "The Tomcat, the Rooster, and the Fox," the tomcat, the rooster's friend, saves the rooster from danger several times.

However, regardless of their originality and freshness and also of their high poetic qualities, Russian animal tales are little disseminated. Their small proportional weight shows up even more vividly if we subject not only the number of plots but also the number of recordings of each plot to quantitative analysis. The absolute majority of plots is represented by one to three recordings, and very few (three plots in all) have been recorded more than ten times; in comparison, the wonder tales in general are each represented by much more numerous records. This speaks of the relatively small dissemination of the animal tales.[9] Such a phenomenon requires interpretation. Andreev links "the wealth of animal tales in the West (compared with the Russian material) to the development of the medieval animal epos."[10] He repeats this explanation in his commentary to the Afanas'ev collection. Pointing to medieval European poems about the fox, Andreev writes, "These poems in turn exerted, evidently, a significant influence on the folktale tradition and supported the existence of animal folktales in Western Europe."[11] We cannot accept such a view as correct. The novels and long poems about the fox were themselves created on a wholly folk foundation. They were created in an urban milieu, partly in Latin; they circulated in a small quantity of manuscripts and printed editions, and they would hardly have reached the illiterate or barely literate peasant milieu of the feudal Middle Ages. The given explanation is also undermined by the simple fact that among Ukrainians, for example, who had no medieval novels of the fox, the national animal epos not only equals the volume of the international repertoire but also significantly exceeds it (314 types).[12]

Consequently, variations of repertoire cannot be explained just by the presence of a medieval literary tradition. However, if we reject Andreev's explanation, we cannot counter it with any other that is more persuasive. Apparently, the solution must be sought in the sphere of the social function, the role the folktale plays in the life of each people. The animal tale is now primarily the property of children. At the same time, the Russian folktale still lives a full life among adults, primarily men. A great tale-teller such as M. M. Korguev not only represents an exception in the degree of his unusual talent but is also characteristic as a type of Russian tale-teller. Of seventy-eight folktales from Korguev, only two tales about animals were recorded, and they are not among his best. They are not in his style. On the contrary, as we see from Aleksandr Nikiforov's *Children's Folk Tale of the Dramatic Genre*,[13] the children's repertoire consists almost exclusively of animal tales. The childish character of some of these tales was noted already by V. Bobrov.[14] In countries where the folktale has already been crowded into the nursery—and this has taken place in the West to a greater extent than in Russia—the proportional weight of tales about animals will be greater than in places where the folktale still represents a broad phenomenon of the whole people. The richness of the Ukrainian repertoire is connected with Ukraine's general folkloric wealth.

SOURCES OF THE CONTEMPORARY ANIMAL EPOS

The makeup of each people's animal epos is always complex in its historical roots, its international connections, and the variety of forms of its development, and the materials that one can adduce for a comparative-historical study of the animal epos are correspondingly various. On the one hand, the animal epos is represented by remnants of primitive totemic myth. One of the urgent tasks of our branch of scholarship is comparison of the contemporary folktale with myths. In connection with the wonder tale, as we have seen, Soviet scholarship has already begun this work, and it has produced certain results, casting a certain light on the origin of the wonder tale. So far as the animal tale is concerned, this kind of work has not even begun. It is difficult because the animal in primitive consciousness is not at all the real animal as we perceive it. It is endowed with supernatural powers. We should expect the myths of primitive peoples to form one source of the animal epos, but they are not the sole source. The folktale epos is made up of not only one's own materials but also other people's. Along with primordial, ancient plots there are also new arrivals, borrowed in more recent times, already in folktale form. The borrowed plots in their turn can also be exceedingly ancient but were received only later by a given people. For example, the role played in Western European folklore by the lion, which never roamed in Europe, raises the question of the migration of plots that belong in one nation. The lion is not part of the Russian animal epos (although it is in the Ukrainian). Nonetheless, part of our plots are undoubtedly borrowed from the West. Kolmachevskii devoted his work to this question.[15] The material needed to resolve the question was still far from sufficient, and Kolmachevskii, who was entranced by the theory of migrations, used imperfect methods. The question has not been revisited since the days of Kolmachevskii and his reviewers, and it demands a new, critical solution.

In studying the animal epos, we also cannot ignore the great heritage left to us by antiquity. We saw earlier that with regard to the wonder tale this question has already been addressed in both Western European and Soviet scholarship, but with regard to the animal tale the question has not been broadly posed. Meanwhile, antiquity left us a rich inheritance of fables (Aesop, Babrius, Phaedrus) in which animals play a large role. In Aesop, for example, we find plots that are also represented by Russian tales, such as "The Fox and the Crane" (A-T 60; Afanas'ev 33), "The Dog and the Wolf" (A-T 101; Afanas'ev 59), "The Stupid Wolf" (A-T 122 A = 47 B = AA 122; Afanas'ev 55, 56, 555 [V]), "The Old Hospitality Is Forgotten" (A-T 155; Afanas'ev 27), and "The Fox and the Crab" (A-T 275; Afanas'ev 35). If we include international material, the number of correspondences turns out to be significantly greater. The presence of these plots in Aesop was noted long ago. Benfey considered the homeland of these tales to be not the East but the antique world, from where they supposedly penetrated into India and then from there into Europe: "As far as sources are concerned, it turns out that the majority of animal fables in general originates in the West, that they are more or less reconstituted so-called Aesop's fables."[16] From our point of view, the question cannot be resolved on the plane where it is posed. We cannot correlate the creation of only two peoples or two cultures. The question can be solved only if we do not limit ourselves to two cultures but instead introduce folklore material on an international scale, arranging it, first, according to its stage of historical development and, second, without predetermining the question of a plot's literary or folkloric origin (both cases are possible) and only then deciding the question of sources in each individual case through critical analysis. In Russian scholarship Kolmachevskii took Benfey's position. For him Aesop is the original point of development. Thus, speaking of the tale "The Dog and the Wolf," he considers, "It is hardly necessary to linger on the fact that all variants that develop this episode spring from Aesop's fable 'The Dog and the Wolf.'"[17] This view of Aesop is held to this very day. So, a propos of the tale "The Fox and the Crab" (also known as "The Race"), Bolte and Polívka write, "The original form is in Aesop's fable."[18]

At present, however, I am inclined to a different opinion. It is not the folk tradition that borrows from Aesop or descends from him but Aesop who drew from that tradition in antiquity. But Aesop's fables are important not just for judging the antique form of the plot. Aesop's and Phaedrus's fables were favorite reading matter in the Middle Ages and were published, translated, and reworked many times. Aesop was translated and read in Russia as well.[19] Aesop's influence could show up not directly (as Kolmachevskii and others thought) but through medieval literary translations and their reworkings.

In the Middle Ages the animal world figures not just in fable literature. Concepts about animals are reflected in the so-called physiologies and later (on French soil) in bestiaries—forerunners of our zoologies, which give sometimes completely fantastic information and stories about animals, especially biblical ones, and also fabulous ones, such as the unicorn, the phoenix ("Finist the Bright Falcon" of our folktales), and the siren (the Russian "Sirin"). The first physiologies date from the second century A.D., the Alexandrian epoch, and their number is fairly high in the Byzantine, Slavic (including Russian), and Romano-Germanic Middle Ages. Their connection to the folktale epos has not been studied. It may be asserted or denied, but the question should be raised.

Finally, the question of the folktale's interrelations with the medieval novel about the fox belongs among questions about the sources of animal tales. As we have seen, a series of studies assign it great significance in the creation of the animal epos (Kolmachevskii) and its preservation (Andreev).

These novels have been much better studied than the folkloric tale proper, and a significant number of works have been devoted to them. The old discipline traced them from Aesop for the most part while seeing the folk tradition as dependent on the literary one, but later opinions changed. Adolf Graf said, "*Reineke Fuchs* and the medieval *épopées* about animals have a dual foundation: the antique fable and European folk tradition, whose root is local, on the one hand, and on the other hand reaches back to the East."[20] This point of view is clearly eclectic, but all the same the given work puts particular stress on the significance of the folkloric tale. Examples of this epos were spread for the most part through France, the Netherlands, and Lower Germany and to a lesser extent in Italy and England. The first monument of this literature was the Latin poem *Echasis captivi* (The Rescued Captives), which appeared in 940. The poet was a Lotharingian monk who had fled his monastery and then returned to it. He describes his adventures as the adventures of animals. A calf runs away from its stall and winds up in the clutches of a wolf, who takes it to his lair.

A series of brief works testifies to the tradition in formation. The Latin poem *Yzengrimus*, whose author may be considered the monk Magister Nivardas, has great significance. It was created in Ghent around 1148. It gives the animals their names for the first time: Isengrim the wolf, the fox Reinard. It is an elegant combination of plots about the fox and the wolf, whose performance is distinguished by artistry and humor. It is important for us to establish that plots of this cycle were orally reproduced by wandering entertainers (*jongleurs* in France, *Spielmänner* in Germany), like our *skomorokhi*.

The French *Roman de Renard*, by an unknown compiler, dated around 1230, is connected with this oral tradition. It is a less artistic combination of separate plots or episodes, here called *branches*. The center of the action is moved from the wolf to the fox (Reinard, renard = *Reinardus* [fox]).

The Dutch poem *Von den Vos Reinaerde* (About the Fox Reinard), compiled around 1250, was the European nursery for the epos of the fox. We will omit the less significant revisions and translations. The Low German translation, which came out in Lübeck, where the diminutive Low German form *Reineke* (*Reynke de vos*) appears for the first time, has great significance. It gives the whole epos a sharply anticlerical, satirical character, scourging the monastic order under the mask of the wolf and the lion as feudal powers. A High German translation appeared in 1544, and a wonderful Latin iambic one was published in 1567. The Latin translation was adapted in German prose by Gottsched (1752), and the Gottsched text was decanted into German hexameters by Goethe in his *Reineke Fuchs* (Reineke the Fox, 1794). The compositional backbone of these works is the complaint of the beasts to the king, the lion, about the dirty tricks of Reineke, the trial and triumph of Reineke, and the shaming of the wolf.

Unlike the early Latin texts, here the animals live in a state—a trait that is completely unlike Russian folktales about animals.

Novels about the fox circulated over the course of several centuries. Such longevity is explained by the fact that they are distinguished as a whole by high artistic quality, aptness of observations, and lively satire and humor, which met the demands of the era. "The grandeur and clarity of conception," says Nikolai Dashkevich, "were gradually perfected because people worked on them for centuries, as on almost every major artistic idea, such as, for example, legends of the Grail or of going to the land of the dead, crowned by Wolfram von Eschenbach's *Parzifal* and Dante's *Commedia*."[21]

As I have already indicated, the epicenter for dissemination of novels about the fox was the Netherlands, France, and Germany. Echoes of it can be found in England and Italy. There are no traces of this epos in Russian medieval literature. Nonetheless, it is important for study of our folklore tradition too, and it has often been mentioned in the study of Russian tales. Among the plots of the Russian repertoire that are represented in the Western European medieval animal epos, as we can see from Kolmachevskii's comparisons, are such popular plots as the theft of fish from a wagon, catching fish by lowering a tail into the water, unfair division of a harvest, the frightened bear and wolves, the old hospitality forgotten, the simpleton wolf, and the fox and the woodpecker. However, as we have established, correspondence is far from always meaning borrowing.

Composition of Animal Tales

The composition and style of animal tales have still not received specialized study in either Russian or Western scholarship. We have some observations in Aleksandr Nikiforov's *Children's Tale of the Dramatic Genre*, although the work is dedicated to a broader theme.[22] Boris Sokolov's observations refer exclusively to the cumulative tale.[23] At the same time, the question of composition is important for understanding these folktales.

Earlier, as we were examining wonder tales, we could establish the regularity of their composition and define it as one that follows certain laws. No such unity can be established in animal tales. Their composition is various; in any case we observe no unity at this time.

Tales about animals are built on elementary actions, which form the basis of the narration and present a more or less expected or unexpected ending, prepared in a certain manner. These most simple actions represent phenomena of a psychological order, increasing their realism and proximity to the people's life, regardless of the complete fantasy of the treatment. So, for example, many tales are built on perfidious advice and an ending that listeners expect, although it is unexpected for the character who follows the advice. Hence we get the humorous character of animal tales and the need for a crafty and perfidious character, like the fox, and a silly hoodwinked character, who in Russian tales usually turns out to be the wolf. The fox advises the wolf to catch fish by putting his tale in a hole in the ice. She tells the pig to eat her own intestines or to break her head open and eat her own brains. A chain of ill-intentioned advice like this might be combined in a single tale with variations in the individual links ("The Stupid Wolf"). A goat tells a wolf to open his maw and stand at the bottom of a hill, so the goat can jump into it. The goat knocks the wolf over and runs away. A fox forces a wolf to kiss the bait after he sticks his head in a trap (A-T 122 = 47 B = AA 122). In Western European folktales there is a plot or episode in which a fox tells a bear to stick his paw into a split log; then she removes the wedge that held the split wood open.

Another such narrative unit is the motif of sudden fright. The tale "The Bast Hut and the Ice Hut" (A-T 43; Afanas'ev 1, 10, 11, 13, 14) is built on this. A fox takes over the hut of a hare. A dog, a bear, and a bull cannot chase her out; a rooster chases her out by singing a threatening song that frightens her, or a horsefly suddenly bites the fox in a sensitive place. The tale "The Beasts' Winter Lair" (A-T 130, 130A, 130B = A-T 130; Afanas'ev 63–65) has the same thing. In some cases an owner is driven out through fear (in "The Musicians of Bremen" the animals stand on top of each other and start singing, so that the robbers flee in fright); in others fear drives away an enemy who wants to take over a house (cf. also "Verlioka," Afanas'ev 301). Ways of causing fright are extremely various. In the tale "The Frightened Bear and Wolves" (A-T 125; Afanas'ev 18, 44 [45], 46 [47], 554 [V]) the animals, already warned by the fox, are so afraid of a cat's dirty tricks that they cannot see a bear fall out of a tree and a wolf run out of the bushes. In a similar tale, a cat and a ram show the wolves a severed wolf's head they have found on the road. The wolves scatter in fear.

Frightening represents a particular case of deception. A whole series of other plots relies on various kinds of deception, such as "The Fox Midwife" (A-T 15; Afanas'ev 4 [V], 9–13), "The Race" (A-T 30; Afanas'ev 1), "The Fox and the Thrush" (A-T 56 A, B [V]; Afanas'ev 32), "The Fox Confessor" (A-T 62A = AA *61; Afanas'ev 1, 15, 17), and "The Dog and the Wolf" (A-T 101; Afanas'ev 59). In some cases characters disregard good advice, and the tales end with their deaths. A wolf comes to visit a dog. The dog warns him not to make noise. But the stupid wolf, after eating and drinking his fill, starts to howl; he is found and killed (A-T 100; Afanas'ev 59).

In this way a variety of plot situations come down to one psychological premise or foundation. We also encounter the opposite: Identical plot situations or motifs are founded on differing psychological premises. Thus tales in which animals drop something for various reasons can be brought together. A crane is teaching a fox to fly, but he drops her, and she is smashed (A-T 255 A; Sd. 53, 54). A crow finds a crab and flies away with him. The crab flatters the crow, who starts to caw and drops him into the sea (A-T 227* = AA *242; Afanas'ev 73 [V]). Here, of course, we recollect the fox who tricks the crow into dropping its cheese, as in Krylov (A-T 57, not witnessed in the Russian repertoire).

A study of composition reveals that there are two kinds of animal tales. Some tales represent something completed, integral, with a definite initial situation, development, and dénouement; as a rule, they do not enter into combination with other plots but represent complete works in themselves; these are folktale types in the general sense of that word. Such, for example, are "The Old Hospitality Is Forgotten," "The Fox and the Crane," and "The Crane and the Heron." It is easy to see, however, that these tales form a clear minority. Most animal tales do not possess plot independence but only a certain special combinability, a tendency toward one another; although they could be told independently, they are in fact never told separately. One might ask why one part of the animal epos represents a whole, which among the folk is never brought to complete unification but is only unified in parts. The term *animal epos* is therefore completely possible and accurate. There are plots that are never narrated separately. Thus the tale of the fox who steals fish is united with the tale of the wolf who catches fish with his tail, although externally they are separate from each other. This combinability is an internal trait of the animal epos that does not belong to other genres. Hence we have the possibility of novels or epics that, as we have seen, were created so broadly in medieval Western Europe. The persuasiveness and artistic quality of the use of possibilities embedded in the tales themselves will depend on the artistry of the compiler. Wonder tales allow no such combination. The combinations of wonder tales that we possess follow the tendency to external contamination of various plots, or else the combination is made on the principle of a frame tale, as in *The Thousand and One Nights* or *The Magical Dead Man*. Tales about animals, on the contrary, are internally combinable into a single whole. This is also apparent in that some types that are separated in the index not only never empirically occur separately but also, in essence, cannot exist as independent folktales. Thus the types "The Beaten One Carries the Unbeaten One" (A-T 4), "The Fox Smears Her Head with Sour Cream" (A-T 3), "Beasts (in a Pit) Devour One Another" (A-T 20 A), "Devouring One's Own Innards" (A-T 21), "The Dog Imitates the Bear" (A-T 119*), "The Wolves Climb a Tree" (A-T 121), "The Fox and the Tail" (A-T 154* 1), and some others do not represent folktales or types or plots. They are only fragments, parts, motifs that become comprehensible or possible only in a whole system of some kind. Hence we can see that the Aarne-Thompson *Index* is put together incorrectly: From an index of types it unnoticeably breaks into an index of motifs. This error, however, is indicative because it reflects the character of the material itself.

We can observe another phenomenon as well: Plots or motifs do not have exact boundaries; that is, they are not clearly and exactly separated from one another. On the contrary, they shade into one another, so that, if we compare two folktales, it is sometimes difficult and sometimes impossible to say whether we have two distinct plots or two variants of one plot. The phenomenon of combinability of plots and their tendency to pass into one another represents a great problem, which the old mythological scholarship already sensed but which later works did not even ask, so rooted did study by plots in isolation become when it was elevated to a principle by the Finnish School. The mythologists solved this problem easily. Afanas'ev writes in his commentaries to tales 1–7: "Tales about the fox, the wolf, and other beasts (*Tiermärchen*) comprise fragments of the ancient animal epos."[24] Buslaev explained proverbs in just the same way: as scattered parts of a lost epic tradition. It is clear to me that such an explanation is incorrect. The question can be resolved only by the methods of stadial historical study of the folktale. It is intimately linked to the question of the origin of animal tales.

Origin of Animal Tales

After the mythological scholars, the question of the origin of the animal epos, as I have said, was not raised. The phenomenon of international parallels and the study of borrowings and migration eclipsed all other problems in the study of folktales. Nonetheless, there were individual statements on the question of the ancestry of the animal folktale. Nikolai Dashkevich was inclined to ascribe a totemistic descent to these tales, and he gave a brief outline of existing views on the nature of totemism. But we find no decisive opinion in Dashkevich, far less any proof of this position. Volodymyr Hnatiuk, in the preface to his collection of Ukrainian animal tales, also asserted that totemism was one of the historical components of the animal epos.[25]

In the current state of scholarship, the totemistic ancestry of the animal epos can be neither fully overturned nor completely proven. The only thing we are sure of is the totemistic ancestry of animal motifs in the wonder tale. The category of the magical helper, for the most part in animal form, is clearly of totemistic ancestry. The motif of grateful animals has the same origin. The motif of a wondrous birth from an animal also descends in part from totemistic beliefs and concepts. The motif of an animal's marriage to a person (a woman conceives a child with a bear) goes back to these too. But all these motifs concern the wonder tale.

Most researchers consider it possible to separate animals from the whole composition of the folktale without paying attention to generic distinctions. Wundt does so, for example. In the chapter "Mythological Animal Tales,"[26] he asserts the totemistic ancestry of animal tales but proves it with motifs from the wonder tale. Totemism is a certain kind of relation between people and animals, and Wundt examines the forms of this relation (the bases of contracts, marriage, the animal ancestor, turning into animals, sacred animals, winning mercy by bringing a sacrifice, and so on). He includes the study of fantastic animals—the dragon, among others—here too. However, from our point of view this has little to do with the animal tale, which involves no marriage to, transformation into, or birth from animals. The animal tale remains unexplained. Nonetheless, although the animal tale's generic traits have not yet been completely studied, the animal tale represents a completely different phenomenon from the wonder tale; consequently, the possibility that it has a different origin should be considered. It reflects different cognitive categories from the wonder tale; therefore it may spring from different social-historical roots.

Observing the kinds of animals who appear as characters in the animal epos, we note a predominance of wild and, especially in the Russian epos, forest animals. These are the fox, the wolf, the bear, the hare, and birds (crane, heron, thrush, woodpecker, crow, etc.). Domestic animals appear far more rarely: dog, cat, goat, ram, pig, bull, horse, and domestic fowl, most often the rooster. Domestic animals appear in combination with forest ones, not as independent or leading characters. For examples, we have the combinations of the cat, rooster, and fox (A-T 61 B; Afanas'ev 37–39); the sheep, fox, and wolf (A-T 122 C, A; Afanas'ev 28); and the dog and woodpecker (A-T 248; Afanas'ev 66, 67). The main characters, as a rule, are forest animals; in most cases domestic animals play a supporting role. There are no folktales at all that concern solely domestic animals in the Russian repertoire, and the international repertoire includes no more than five or six of them (A-T 200, 203, 204, 206, and 210). We may conclude that the animal epos is an epos about the wild forest and other animals, not domestic animals. It is important for us to note this because it leads us to suppose that animal tales arose at a stage of development of human culture when forest animals were the objects of primitive kinds of economy (i.e., of hunting) and also the objects of cognitive and artistic activity; either there were no domesticated animals, or they did not yet play an essential role. Consequently, creation of the animal epos should be assigned to the preclass stage of societal development.

Several other peculiarities of the animal epos agree with this. Even cursory morphological examination of these tales has shown us that their fundamental compositional backbone is trickery of the most varied kinds and forms. Trickery presupposes the dominance of the crafty over the stupid or simple. From our point of view, trickery is morally reprehensible. In animal tales, on the contrary, it arouses delight, as a form of expression of dominance of the weak over the strong. This forces us to suppose that the animal tale was created when trickery not only was not blameworthy but also represented one form of the struggle for existence. At the center of the animal epos stands a crafty animal who surpasses and vanquishes the rest. If we look over the epic creations of preclass peoples from this point of view, we find the same picture there. Among the North American Indians the mink is such an animal; among the Chukchi, the crow, and so on. At the same time these animals are not totems.[27] But the myths in which they are active do not have an entertaining role. The tricks of crafty animals bear the character of a joke, but they mean something completely different. Such folktales were performed before the hunt. Although they were narrated, the craftiness was supposed to pass magically to the participants in the narration. We cannot say now why some peoples give preference to one group of animals and some peoples prefer other ones. The central animal is neither especially powerful nor especially crafty. A crow may aid success at the hunt just the way an otter or a mink does, or a rabbit. This confirms that the animal epos does not arise from observation of the real powers and abilities of animals. The animal is the hero because of the powers ascribed to it, which are not at all real but magical. Thus the transferability of actions from one animal to another is a purely formal and artistic phenomenon with roots in the peculiarities of primitive thinking.

All this leads us to confirm the great ancientness of the animal tale as a whole, although both ancient and new plots exist. We cannot establish an immediate genetic link with totemism, but if the actors are not people but animals, endowed with power and abilities that are inaccessible to people, then this could testify to a link with totemism, which does not distinguish human beings from animals.

The point of view laid out here is still subject to elaboration based on a large body of comparative material, which would include the myths of primitive peoples in various stages of their societal development. This work demands the efforts not of one person alone but of a whole school—of our whole Soviet folkloristics. When we assert the ancient ancestry of animal tales, we confirm the ancient ancestry of the genre itself. But this does not mean that subsequent eras did not contribute new formations. Individual plots may also be of more recent origin. Comparing the repertoire of primitive peoples with those of more developed peoples will show which line animal folktales followed in their development.

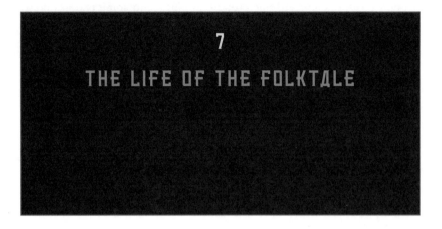

7
THE LIFE OF THE FOLKTALE

Posing the Problem

Just as a song is sung, a folktale is told. A folktale is intended not for reading with the eyes but for aural reception. And just as studying the text of a song alone is one-sided and insufficient (and for full knowledge one must study the melody), thus too the folktale must be studied by investigating the forms and manner of its performance. A text that may seem pale and not very expressive in reading gains full resonance only in a suitable performance.

Performance is inseparable from the performers. Performers are not abstract figures who create arbitrarily. They belong to a certain social milieu and a certain era, and these condition their creative work. This is a phenomenon of a social order, subject to certain regularities. But all the same the boundaries set by the milieu and the era are not fixed eternally, once and for all. They change along with historical developments and are themselves broad enough to allow room for individual creativity within certain boundaries.

The question of performers and performance is closely tied to the question of the content and size of the repertoire. In studying performance, we encounter the same phenomenon we saw in the tales themselves: a meeting of two opposite tendencies. On the one hand, we have a certain fixity, traditionality, and boundedness that make it possible, for example, to compile catalogs and indexes of plots and motifs. On the other hand, within the bounds of regularity we have an endless variety of variants, often connected with the individual particularities of the performers. This is a typically folkloric phenomenon. Both sides, both problems, are subject to study: the problem of uniformity and the problem of diversity.

Russian scholarship raised the question of the life of the folktale and living bearers of the epic tradition as early as the 1860s. It is true that Aleksandr Afanas'ev, who compiled his collection almost exclusively from written sources, naturally could not yet know almost anything about the function of the folktale. True to the views of his school and seeking primarily reflections of the primitive era in the folktale, he was not curious about that side of the matter. But, in his review of Afanas'ev's collection, Nikolai Dobroliubov was already writing, "Each person who has written down and collected works of folk poetry would do a very useful thing if he did not limit himself to simply writing down the text of a tale or song, but conveyed the whole setting, both the purely external one and the more internal, moral one, where he happened to hear this song or tale."[1] We know that the first volume of Pëtr Rybnikov's *Songs* provided a "Collector's Note" in which he introduced the Russian reader to such remarkable performers of *byliny* as Trofim Riabinin.[2] Aleksandr Gil'ferding began for the first time to arrange *byliny* according to their performers in his *Byliny of Lake Onega* (see Anna Astakhova's works for details).[3] Dmitrii Sadovnikov transferred this tradition in part to the folktale.[4] He almost always noted the performer's name underneath the text. This seemingly trivial circumstance signals a shift to new principles. Sadovnikov managed to find a remarkable tale-teller—Abram Novopol'tsev, from whom he wrote down about seventy texts in various genres. Sadovnikov died before he could prepare his collection for print.

The principle of arranging folktales according to their performers was fully applied for the first time by Nikolai Onchukov in his *Northern Tales* (1908).[5] Onchukov was already preparing for this in an edition of Pechora *byliny*, in which his arrangement of material follows Gil'ferding.[6] Onchukov prefaced his collection of folktales with the chapter "Tales and Tale-Tellers in the North," which described the economic and geographic particularities of the region and the north's folktale creativity. He introduced each teller's tales with a biography and description.

This approach entered firmly into Russian collecting practice (in the collections of Dmitrii Zelenin, Boris and Iurii Sokolov, Mark Azadovskii, Irina Karnaukhova, and others; see Chapter 2). We now record not only the folktale but also the place and time of performance and information about the performers. In this way, collecting practice has created a firm basis not only for textual but also for comprehensive study of the folktale. The activity of the folktale commission of the Russian Geographical Society, headed by academician Sergei Fedorovich Ol'denburg, imparted this direction to Russian folktale collecting. In his article "The Collection of Russian Folk Tales in Recent Times," Ol'denburg asserted that materials published without exact indications of the place and time of recording, without information about the tale-tellers, "can have only quite conditional scholarly significance."[7] He also gave a brief history of Russian collecting and underlined the superiority of Russian methods over Western European ones. He later repeated his words in a 1929 address at the Sorbonne.[8]

After the October Revolution, a new type of collection appeared in the Soviet Union: the collection devoted wholly to the work of a certain performer, whose repertoire the collectors attempted to record completely. These include collections of the tales of Matvei Korguev (two volumes),[9] Anna Baryshnikova (known as Kuprianikha),[10] Egor Sorokovikov (Magai),[11] and Filipp Gospodarev.[12] Azadovskii's collections are of the same kind, devoted, on the whole, to two tale-tellers: Vinokurova and Aksamentov (for more detail on these editions, see Chapter 2).[13]

This method of collection also lays the groundwork for scholarly study of the folktale that addresses all its aspects. For a long time, however, theoretical elaboration of the question lagged behind actual collecting. We see separate works that only elaborate individual questions. E. V. Gofman's "On the Question of the Individual Style of the Tale-Teller"[14] is devoted to two (of five recorded) tales of the Belozërsk tale-teller Bogdanov. It shows how the presence of traditional devices goes along with realism, motivation, details of the situation, and psychologism. These traits are all ascribed individually to Bogdanov.

Sofiia Mints's "Traits of the Individual and Traditional Creative Work in the Tale of King Solomon"[15] has a somewhat broader character. On the basis of twelve variants of one plot, Mints attempts to define types of tale-tellers according to their "artistic manner." She enumerates four such types (everyday-life realists, professional jokers, epic tellers, and schematicists). Irina Karnaukhova's "Tale-Tellers and Folktales in the *Zaonezh'e*"[16] divides tale-tellers into types according to their relationship to the text (improvisers, masters of a set text, and destroyers). She gives a general picture of the tale's functional life in the north and a short description of four tale-tellers.

Boris Sokolov's course in *Russian Folklore*, in a volume devoted to the folktale, undertakes a more detailed solution of the question of types of tale-tellers. Proceeding primarily from his own observations, Sokolov divides tale-tellers into epic tellers, moralists, realists of everyday life, jokers, and satirists. This schema is imperfect and unevenly elaborated, and to some extent it is impossible to agree with Sokolov's opinions. For example, he makes repertoire the basis of his division. The epic tellers tell wonder tales, the moralists tell *legendy*, realists relate novellistic tales, jokers the anecdote, and satirists also anecdotes plus the novella, but in a satirical light. However, the relationship of living people to the types indicated is not always entirely clear. Thus A. M. Ganin—an epic teller—told only one fantastic folktale. More than half his tales are folktale-*byliny*, and he has a completely different type of repertoire from Semënov, introduced here by Sokolov, who tells only wonder tales. This error is possible because the principles for defining each type are awkward and because the manner of performance is not taken into account along with repertoire.

As though sensing the insufficiency of his assertions, Boris Sokolov also supplements these "types" with "groups," divided according to no definite system. Such groups include tale-tellers who tell tales of the obscene (*zavetnye*) type, dramatists who act out the roles in their folktales, bookmen who speak in literary language, and, finally, women, who are distinguished, according to Sokolov, by particular sentimentality. It is no longer possible at present to make assertions like these.

Now that the individuality of tale-tellers has been thoroughly studied on the basis of a series of models, the question of the influence of individuality on tradition can be answered on a broad scale. Even though study of the folktale by performer began in the 1860s, no one suspected how great the significance of the performer would prove to be. This is clear in a number of splendid descriptions of individual performers (cf. the introductory articles to the editions cited).[17]

At the same time, preoccupation with the tale-tellers, and with the best tellers at that, may risk not only one-sidedness but also erroneous understanding of the essence and specificity of folk creativity.

Publication and study of folktales narrated by the best masters represents a kind of selection, and selection is dangerous in any branch of scholarship because it may lead to incorrect concepts and conclusions. Studying the tales of the finest performers, we learn nothing about the mass life of the folktale. Meanwhile, the tale lives its full life not just in the person of expert narrators. Its life is all around; everyone knows it. A selective principle of collection and study will not reveal the character of this mass existence, and it is therefore insufficient by itself.

Soviet scholarship also knows another tendency, that of all-around (*splos-hnoe*) collecting. Recording and study should encompass not only individual, selected people but whole settlements and, more broadly, whole regions, ideally a whole country. Aleksandr Nikiforov stood for this point of view. He supplied its theoretical foundations,[18] and he applied the principle in practice in his collecting work.[19] This kind of recording and study reveals the picture of a folktale's broad life. The stationary method of all-around recording allows us to judge the degree of dissemination of the folktale in general, the life of the folktale, the forms and relative dissemination of individual plots through regions, the distribution of material according to sex and age, natural forms of the folktale's life, and so on. For example, it exposed the unusual intensity of the folktale's life among children, allowing Nikiforov to distinguish the particular genre of the children's folktale, defined through both the aspect of contents and the aspect of performance.[20] All-around recording makes it possible to establish the predictable connection of repertoire and its forms with geographic particularities and the economy of a region.[21]

With this manner of collection, it is not necessary to publish everything that is recorded. Tales can be kept in archives, accessible for special research and queries. For scholarship it is not just the best material but all of it as a whole that is important for comprehensive and various study.

In this way, we can avoid the one-sidedness that occurs if we limit ourselves to only the finest examples. But studying material according to performers risks exaggerating the role of individuals and forgetting the specifically folkloric side of the matter. Just as the history of literature is not the sum of biographies and works, even less so is folklore the sum of texts that well-known performers are acquainted with. The performers and their texts reflect certain processes that are still insufficiently studied but regularly occur in folklore. What is sometimes depicted here as the creative work of individuals (psychologization, introduction of motivations, rapprochement of the fantastic to real, everyday life, use of landscapes, etc.) in fact reflects general processes in folklore. Studying the work of individuals merely creates a foundation for study of these processes; it should lead to the identification of these processes and their forms and varieties. Such work has not yet been accomplished. Thus, as Nadezhda Grinkova wrote as early as 1934, "If we look closely at articles about tale-tellers and the biographical notes provided with the texts of this or that tale-teller in a collection, we get the impression that it is all still just outlines, rough drafts, showing only a general tendency in the collector's work. We still do not have an exhaustive elaboration."[22]

Sometimes our scholars consider the old doctrine of folklore's lack of individuality as opposed to the new understanding of the deep role of creativity that is precisely individual. Opposing one to the other is definitely incorrect. We should instead oppose the old understanding of nationality (especially as represented in the teachings of the Grimms) to the new understanding of nationality. We must not set aside the problem of folk creativity, replacing it with the study of work by individuals. Maxim Gorky understood the power of folk creativity as such when he called it, perhaps not entirely successfully, collective. Gorky said, "The power of collective creativity is proven most vividly of all by the fact that over the course of centuries individual creativity has created nothing equal to the *Iliad* or the *Kalevala*, and that individual genius has not provided a single generalization without the people's creativity at its root, nor a single world type that did not already exist in folk tales and legends."[23] Here it would be appropriate to recall Lenin's words after he read Nikolai Onchukov's collection: "This is genuine folk creativity, so necessary and important for the study of folk psychology in our days."[24] It is telling that Gorky does not separate himself from Buslaev's point of view; he proceeds from it, relies on it. Buslaev's "romantic" point of view turns out to be not so romantic after all but quite advanced and correct in many respects.

In this way, the question of the folktale's existence is not simply an ethnographic or a literary one; it is a complicated question, a major theoretical problem.

FORMS OF FUNCTION OF THE FOLKTALE

The folktale was not created all at once as a complete genre. As we have seen, its roots are in a people's ritual and cultic life; it develops out of myth. Correspondingly, the forms of its performance, as we have observed today, also developed from the myth's forms of function. But it is not our task to study the life of primitive myth. Because of the philological traditions of Western European scholarship, in most cases we have only the texts of myths, and the means of their use have not been illuminated. For now it is sufficient for us to note that myths have magic and incantatory significance; they were used for practical purposes.

Traces of such utilization of the texts that preceded folktales have been preserved to the present day among many peoples. Western European scholarship has noted this.[25] Vera Kharuzina, in her work "Time and the Setting of Telling of Narrative Works of Folk Verbal Arts,"[26] was the first to mention this question in Russia, but it was broadly illuminated in Dmitrii Zelenin's remarkable "Religious and Magical Function of Folkloric Tales."[27] Zelenin noted the seasonality that is found in some peoples' telling of folktales. Sometimes tales can be told in summer but are forbidden in winter. We know of prohibitions on telling tales at night. Zelenin showed that these were prohibitions based in hunting that had been preserved, and he gave new significance to prohibitions such as "Don't tell tales in the summer; the sheep will fall down."[28] This shows that at one point the folktale had the significance of a protective amulet, an incantation, and was part of a ritual.

However, at present, such prohibitions are possible on Russian territory only as relics; they are not what defines the character of the folktale's life. Speaking of the folktale's ritual ancestry, we know almost nothing about its ritual performance and the historical development of these forms of performance. At the same time, Zelenin's study leads one to think that it is not just the function of the folktale that is connected with the early use of plot and the act of narration for practical magic. The performer was not just anyone but someone who belonged to a particular professional caste.[29] However, as we have already noted, at present the folktale has freed itself from its ritual connections, and tale-telling has become an act of pure artistic creation, free from the limitations and prohibitions of earlier stages of development.

We have sparse information about the life of the folktale in old Rus'. We know of church prohibitions on tale-telling. They testify to the fact that folktales existed and were told widely enough to demand the intervention of church powers. The church suspected sin in this telling, a sin that consisted of more than the entertaining character of the folktale. The church sensed its inimical worldview; the sermons of Kirill of Turov mention tale-telling along with belief in wizards, prognostication by birdsong, and so on.

We have little information about the life of the folktale at that time. The rich kept tale-tellers as a cure for insomnia (twelfth century). There is no doubt that folktales, "shameful" folktales among them, were told by *skomorokhi*. Ivan the Terrible kept three blind tale-tellers; each one would tell him a tale as he went to bed. Tsar Vasilii Shuiskii kept a tale-teller named Ivan. We know of Tsar Aleksei Mikhailovich's tale-tellers: Klim Orefin, Pëtr Sapogov, and Ivan Putiatin. These are the earliest known names of Russian tale-tellers. From the housekeeping ledgers we see that they were rewarded with footwear, caftans, and cloth.[30] Later, tale-tellers were also known in the landowners' milieu (see, for example, Azadovskii on Arina Rodionovna, Pushkin's nanny).[31] But all these data still tell us nothing about how folktales functioned in the folk milieu.

I must admit that, despite the vast collecting work and attention that has been paid to the performer in Russia, the question has still not been exhaustively studied. This insufficiency results from the methods of collection. Usually the collector, after arriving on the spot, looks for a tale-teller. If the search is successful, the collector goes to him; or else the tale-teller comes to the new arrival and the collector works with him, that is, makes a recording from his words. Having finished with one tale-teller, the collector turns to another. It is clear that this method can teach us nothing about the natural forms of life of the folktale. The personality of the collector, a "gentleman" or scholar from the city, also undoubtedly influences the tale's contents. The Sokolov brothers observed that if they paid the performer for his time, the tales turned out long; if they paid by the tale, they were short. According to Nadezhda Grinkova, family members tend to get upset if a worker is taken away from his work and the recording takes too long. Under such conditions the performer will hurry and make a hash of things, just to get rid of the insistent, uninvited guest. Great tact and the ability to approach a person are needed to get fully valid material. Ideally, one must find out the situations when people tell tales on their own initiative, in a natural setting, when the teller does not know he is being recorded. Despite these and other difficulties, which collectors know well, enough material has been collected to draw some conclusions.

As Aleksandr Nikiforov observed, some professions encourage the performance of folktales.

Among the whole range of professions of the adult population in the northern village, we see the folktale utilized to make work easier by creating a group around the workers. Many craftsmen do this: tailors, cobblers, carpenters, cobblers, stove menders. The majority of these, moreover, are the most mobile part of the peasantry: tailors, for example, do not work in their own homes but at the homes of their clients. The biographies of tale-tellers in N. Onchukov's and D. Zelenin's collections of folktales, and of the Sokolnikov brothers in my collection, definitely show that the professions listed often include good tale-tellers. One of the many tale-tellers from the Zaonezh'e region, the stove mender Riabov, said as much: "I love to tell tales at work. It's easier and more cheerful to work—people gather round, they listen, and the work goes faster."[32]

In this way, the folktale goes along with labor. This is one of the forms of its existence. Given the slow tempo of life and the handicraft character of work in the old village, folktales must have had a drawn-out, lingering character; this must have been illustrated in both the text and the style of performance. This form of existence leads to refinement of details, to a measured flow of narration, with pauses and stops.

Some kinds of work tend to experience forced, extended interruptions and unwelcome idleness, and this idleness is filled with folktales. The work of lumbermen in the conditions of the north was like this. Short winter days and long dark nights, nights spent far from home in forest huts—under these conditions a folktale was highly valued. According to Aleksandr Nikiforov's testimony, a good tale-teller was freed from part of the work; people shared their earnings with him in exchange for evening and nighttime storytelling. Similar conditions of enforced idleness occur when the lumber is floated down the long northern rivers and the workers while away the time with folktales. Fishing far from home also sometimes has breaks in work filled with story-telling. The same is true of hunting. Zelenin observed that folktales were told at a mill while waiting for the grinding. In short, northern trades create fertile soil not only for the folktale's existence but also for its cultivation. In these cases the milieu is exclusively male. It may tend to prefer the novellistic, amusing, witty, joking tale, but that does not exclude interest in the wonder tale as well. Audience and performer are in the most intimate contact. The performer thrills the audience with his mastery and, in turn, depends on its approving cooperation and influence. The thirst of his listeners inspires him, and he displays the highest degree of his mastery.

This may in part explain why the Russian folktale lives primarily in male company. Primarily, but not exclusively. There are also female professions that encourage the performance of folktales. The work of milkmaids, if livestock is driven far from home and does not return home at night, is one such profession. Milkmaids, like lumbermen, spend the night in forest huts, and besides conversation they also pass the time with tales. Spinners at spinning bees not only sing songs but also tell tales.

One special realm of the female folktale is composed of tales that nannies and grannies tell children. Acquaintance with and love of tales are inculcated from childhood. The village is splendidly aware not only of the entertainment value of folktales but also of their pedagogical significance. Nikiforov confirms the presence of a special genre of children's folktale, and he defines it not only by repertoire (here we find primarily cumulative tales, animal tales, and tales with children as heroes) but also by the manner of performance. Such tales are acted out; they are rich in embedded songs and distinguished by rhythmic quality and a particular style. Children easily pick up such tales and pass them on splendidly. Karnaukhova's and Nikiforov's collections include a number of tales recorded from children.

Finally, given the long distances in our country and the occasional difficulties of communication, the folktale would accompany certain types of migration. We know not only the coachman's song but also the coachman's folktale. Nikiforov observed that the labor of the drovers on cattlemen's and shepherds' migrations was eagerly and frequently accompanied by tale-telling.[33]

However, some kinds of labor not only do not encourage the folktale but, on the contrary, hinder and delay its development. These are agricultural labor, which demands the greatest concentration of strength, and women's domestic work in housekeeping. This may in part explain the greater folkloric riches of the Russian north, with its trades, compared to the agricultural central regions, where the folktale is possible only in short periods of rest, on holidays, and when people are not at work. In those cases they gather in houses, sometimes according to sex and age, and here the folktale flourishes alongside the usual peasant conversations.

But the folktale does not circulate only in a peasant milieu. We must distinguish the soldier's tale as a special kind of folktale. It is true that we have no information about forms of the folktale's existence in prereform and postrevolutionary barracks. But there is no doubt that it existed there widely and in specific forms, with a definite repertoire and special stylistic traits. One of Azadovskii's best tale-tellers was Fedor I. Aksamentov, a retired soldier. The soldier's element, so strongly reflected in folk theater, for example, was also reflected in the folktale. Even in Afanas'ev's "faceless" collection we can recognize some soldiers' tales.

Speaking more briefly, each social group, each profession, is reflected in the character, style, and sometimes repertoire of the folktale. Thus we may speak of the pilgrim's folktale in Siberia (Azadovskii 216).[34] A region's geographic setting is also quite clearly reflected. Tales of the Urals (Zelenin's collections) are distinct from tales of the north.

TYPES OF TALE-TELLERS

The personality of the performer is one factor that conditions the diversity of folktale texts. As I have already pointed out, this personality is defined by social factors, profession, and so on. It is also defined by a person's life experience. A sailor who has been around will tell different things and in a different way than an elderly nanny. But even so the folktale is also defined by people's psychological particularities, their character, their preferences, the degree and originality of their talent.

Some Soviet scholars have tried to establish certain types of tale-tellers. Collectors often relate their performers to one or another type. Such a desire is fully regular and justified. However, it will have genuine scholarly significance only when the concept of a type is defined with complete exactness. A tale-teller's type might be established according to the most various traits, and all these traits might be considered equally important and decisive.

Thus a tale-teller's type might be defined by the character of his repertoire. In this case the types of performer are defined by genres of the folktale itself. This arrangement is possible only to the degree to which a genre has been studied. We may speak of epic tale tellers, who prefer wonder tales; novellists, who prefer everyday and anecdotal folktales; moralists, who tend toward the didactic *legenda,* and so on. However, as a matter of fact we see that most tale-tellers who have been recorded with sufficient completeness know tales of several kinds. We can say only that this or that genre predominates or is preferred. Such great masters as Filipp Gospodarev know absolutely all kinds of tales. His publisher, Nikolai V. Novikov, calls him a universal type. This definition, in essence, erases the very concept of type.

Collectors have also advanced another, most essential trait, and that is the manner or means of performance. We have a series of splendid descriptions of such manners (Nadezhda Grinkova, *The Tales of Kuprianikha*; Irina Kar-naukhova, *Tale-Tellers and Folktales of the Zaonezh'e*). Undoubtedly, this aspect of the life of folktales is also subject to detailed examination and study. It is also obvious that the manner of performance and the character of the repertoire have a certain connection. The wonder tale is narrated differently from the sharply satirical, jesting or joking tale. However, this is not a general rule. A joking-tale teller can tell a wonder tale too, but he will fill it with elements of realism and comicality, changing it until it is hard to recognize. Thus we have advanced another aspect of the creativity of performers, namely, their style. Tale-tellers are often defined as realists. This phrasing of the question demands preliminary study of various kinds of style present in the Russian repertoire.

Finally, tellers may be categorized by the degree of independence of their work. Some tale-tellers are brave innovators, improvisers who tell a story in a new way every time, whereas others blindly follow tradition and reproduce a text they have learned once and for all without intentional changes. Such performers are not always among the worst; they are preservers of tradition. But some among them cannot remember and reproduce an oral text well. In their mouths the folktale is subject to corruption, abbreviation, and disintegration.

In this way, the arrangement (typologization, classification) of performers still encounters significant difficulties. More often than not collectors generate a typology for their own performers, without much interest in the materials from other collections. Existing attempts at arrangement do not agree with one another. Here difficulties in principle are multiplied by insufficiency of material.

Judging the character of a performer requires recording a significant quantity of his material, and the performer himself must be exhaustively studied from the scholarly point of view. In most cases we have only sparse records of texts from individuals accompanied by a laconic biography or description that is not scholarly. The Sokolov brothers recorded 163 texts from 47 performers. This works out to an average of three or four texts per performer. That is not enough material to make judgments about the true face of the tale-teller.

Judging by what we have laid out here, for the time being it would be more correct not to speak about the types of tale-tellers; such an examination first requires detailed examination of the performers with whom we are well acquainted. We will linger on the most indicative models of performance.

SOME GREAT MASTERS

Zelenin recorded twenty-seven folktales from the Perm′ tale-teller Aleksandr D. Lomtev. The introductory note to Zelenin's collection gives a thorough description of Lomtev. There is plenty of material for us to reach some conclusions about him. The make-up of his repertoire is characteristic. Among twenty-seven folktales, twenty are wonder tales, two are legendy, one is a folktale-*bylina*, two are tales with anecdotal content, and two tales cannot be assigned to the usual types of folktales (one is a soldier's; the other a convict's tale). This make-up already characterizes Lomtev as a lover of the old wonder tale. Zelenin says of him:

> Lomtev takes folktales very seriously. He would never call brief stories and everyday anecdotes *skazki* [tales] but, deprecatingly, *pobasen′ki* [tall tales]. He also dislikes tales with "a lot of indecency" [*briazg*], and he told me "Mikula the Joker" only after having a bit to drink, and then with apologies: this, he said, is a tale "only to make men laugh [literally, "neigh"]." . . . Lomtev considers real *skazki* to be only those that tell in detail about the wondrous feats of *bogatyri*. Lomtev is proud of his knowledge of precisely this kind of tale. If a tale has no real *bogatyri*, then there should at least be tsars, kings, generals, and highly placed figures in general; otherwise the tale is "for peasants."[35]

These last words vividly describe Lomtev's aesthetics, and to a certain extent the aesthetics of the wonder tale in general. If the folktale assigns such a large role to tsars, princes, and princesses, this is not a sign of the folktale's aristocratic ancestry, as is sometimes mistakenly assumed, and even less a sign of kowtowing feelings, as the representatives of reactionary folkloristics thought. The tsars match the golden palaces, wondrous gardens, fountains, and all the other scenery of the wonder tale. This is an international phenomenon; fairytale kings have nothing in common with European monarchs.

Zelenin tells us almost nothing about Lomtev's manner of performance. His tales have an epic calm; he observes all the norms of traditional folktale poetics. Lomtev consciously refrains from altering his tales. On the contrary, it is a question of pride for him to keep the tale the way he heard it. "Lomtev considers changing the foundation, the framework of a folktale to be a kind of crime and always holds quite accurately to the same course of events that he first heard in a given folktale."[36] However, changes occur nonetheless, not by the will of individual people but as a result of historical development. An element of realism breaks powerfully into Lomtev's wonder tales. Lomtev possesses the gift of observation and invention, and he reworks details, introducing elements of the everyday life that surrounds him. Thus he has Il'ia Muromets work for a while as a merchant's shop assistant.

If in Lomtev we see the everyday element intruding into the wonder tale, then with Abram Novopol'tsev, a major Russian tale-teller recorded by Sadovnikov in the Samara region, it is an uncharacteristically joking manner that creeps into the wonder tale. However, this manner is so perfect in him, it shines so with merriment and wit, subtlety and refinement of style, that Novopol'tsev is among the best Russian tale-tellers. We know nothing about him besides his tales. His repertoire is quite large; seventy-two folktales of the most various genres were recorded from him. A large part of these are wonder tales, and on that basis Boris Sokolov calls him an epic tale-teller. After analyzing his style and artistic devices, Mark Azadovskii (in *Russian Tale-Tellers*) ranks Novopol'tsev among the entertaining tale-tellers. One of his constant devices is rhyming. "His basic manner is rhyming, which appears to be one of the most typical devices of this joking style. The tendency to rhyme spreads through almost all parts of his tales; he has rhymed openings, endings, typical folktale formulas, and even descriptive passages and sections of dialogue."[37] This corresponds to his treatment of both characters and plots. The wonder tale loses its elevated style. Novopol'tsev displays the whole brilliance of his talent in the novellistic folktale. He also tells some animal tales outstandingly.

The observation that major tale-tellers tend to prefer the wonder tale is confirmed by another significant and talented performer: Filipp P. Gospodarev. Gospodarev's creative work displays a phenomenon that is interesting and completely regular in our time: The old wonder tale collides with contemporary ideology. If Aleksandr D. Lomtev and Matvei M. Korguev, N. O. Vinokurova, and others invest the wonder tale with elements of everyday life, and Novopol'tsev with jokes, then Gospodarev invests it with elements of ideology. His mastery and talent are clear in the artistically persuasive and realistic results as he combines the old folktale with new ideology. He was prepared for such treatment by his life story as well as by his convictions. Arrested in 1903 for participating in peasant disturbances on the eve of the 1905 revolution, in 1906 he was exiled for life from his native Belarus to the former Olonetsk *guberniia*, to the village of Shuia. After that he received a residence permit to live in Petrozavodsk and worked for ten years at the Onega factory, first as an assistant and digger and later as a stamp operator and welder. A fire at the factory led to a reduction in the workforce. Gospodarev became a blacksmith and then a carter; after a crippling accident, he was disabled and ended his life as a watchman and worker in a *sovkhoz*.

Thus Gospodarev is not a peasant; in his maturity he is a worker, and this defines the internal contents of his folktale creativity. Gospodarev's consciousness of reality is different from that of the peasants who came before him. Conditionally magic, folkloric reality turns into complete reality in his tales. We no longer have a succession of elements from everyday life but instead a different kind of quality. The tsars of wonder tales, whom Lomtev treasures precisely because they are magical, are impossible in Gospodarev. His tsars are real tsars, and he describes and treats them correspondingly. The anticlerical tendency we also find in the prerevolutionary folktale becomes antireligious in him. Gospodarev does not condemn the evil landowner or nobleman, who is left looking like a fool; he condemns the feudal landowning system. For him, love for the old folktale is love for his cultural heritage. He treasures the folktale. He knows about forty wonder tale plots, contaminating and combining them in various ways.[38] He preserves both plot framework and the treatment of details. Nonetheless, his wonder tales resemble novellas in a number of their stylistic devices. If Gospodarev had received an education and become a writer, he could have been a significant novelist. Baba Yaga's hut, dragon fights, the hero's marriage—he depicts everything as though it really took place. This is encouraged by his lively and natural language, the abundance of dialogues, and the extraordinary level of detail. Here, for example, is how he treats the motif of the heroes in the monster's house, as the monster's mother hides them from the monster and asks them questions:

> "Come with me," said the old woman, "I know you've been traveling, you'll want to eat."
> "Yes, granny, we do."
> "Well, eat quickly, or my son will be home soon, and he'll kill you."
> She feeds them and sees her son coming. She goes and hits them on the head, one and then the other, turns them into sticks and puts them behind the cupboard.[39]

Here absolutely everything—hurrying them with the food, hitting them on the head (compare sprinkling with water and pronouncing incantatory formulas in other cases), hiding them behind the cupboard, and expressions such as "come with me"—all this reveals a new worldview and a new style.

Hence it is understandable that despite Gospodarev's preference for the wonder tale, the novellistic folktale nonetheless predominates in the quantity of his plots. Of ninety-four published texts, the absolute majority are novellistic tales. Hence it is also understandable that Gospodarev, although on the whole he values tradition, nonetheless does not actively preserve it; in repeat performances he tells the tale in different ways and sometimes creates new folktales ("The Red Eaglets"). In this regard he is the opposite of Lomtev, who consciously treasured tradition and rejected authorship of some of the tales Zelenin wanted to ascribe to him.

We see that most major tale-tellers are men. This does not yet mean that appearance corresponds to reality. It could be a result of the fact that most collectors are men, which could make women feel shy and refuse to perform their tales for them. The question of whether men or women predominate in Russia in the quality of performances can be resolved only by an all-round stationary investigation.

According to Irina Karnaukhova's observations, almost every woman tells folktales, whereas not all men do. However, if a man does know folktales, he knows more of them than women do, and men's repertoire is richer, because they leave home in the wandering trades, enriching their repertoire, whereas women rarely leave the boundaries of their home areas.[40] However, among women one also encounters major masters, although they tend to be more difficult to find. The most important Russian female tale-teller, Anna Baryshnikova, nicknamed Kuprianikha, was discovered in the summer of 1925 in the Voronezh region by a woman who had a knack for approaching her and getting her to talk: Nadezhda Grinkova. The fifty-six folktales recorded from her in 1925 have remained unpublished. Following in Grinkova's footsteps, A. I. Novikov and I. A. Ossovetskii recorded her a second time (*Kuprianikha's Tales*).[41] Kuprianikha was a 50-year-old grandmother with grown children and grandchildren; she no longer worked but looked after her grandchildren and kept house. Grinkova, describing her creativity, notes rhyming as one of her basic devices. Kuprianikha learned folktales from her father, who was apparently a joker of the same type as Abram Novopol'tsev. But at the same time her tales are feminine. The makeup of her repertoire is quite varied. Anecdotes and novellistic tales predominate; after them come wonder tales, and there are a few *legendy, pobyval'shchiny*, and stories with purely everyday contents. Her repertoire is clearly her father's, a man's. But she brings to that repertoire a lyricism that is hers alone: a sense of measure and beauty, a rhythmic smoothness of speech, a melodic and dramatized manner of performance, often interrupted with singing performance. In her life she also values beauty, loves flowers, and speaks of the loveliness of plants, and she brings this natural gift to the folktale. Her audience is primarily children. In her performance, risqué anecdotes lose their sharp character and become amusing stories.

The number of significant masters in Russia is extraordinarily large. The whole country knows such masters as Matvei M. Korguev, the White Sea taleteller, from whom seventy-six texts were recorded, mostly combinations consisting of several plots. He is a monumentalist, an enormous talent, worthy of a special monographic study. Among the greatest masters are Egor I. Sorokovikov (Magai) and Natalia O. Vinokurova, who were recorded by Azadovskii, and many others. We can only regret that prerevolutionary scholarship was often satisfied with a partial recording and did not try to mine its sources fully. But what has been done until now, after the October Revolution, allows us to assert that the power and range of folk creativity are superior to all the assumptions of our old and early scholarship and that after the revolution the folktale flowered with a new, unusually rich, and splendid bloom.[42]

NOTES

Several writers contributed to the notes in Propp's text. First, of course, is Propp himself. His notes appear with no special markings. The notes added by Kirill Chistov and Valentina Eremina, editors of the 1984 Russian edition of Propp's book, appear in brackets and are identified with the initials CE. I have also added a few notes to Propp's text, and these appear in brackets with the initials SF.

Notes to Foreword
1. See Uther, *Types of International Folktales*. These three volumes constitute a revision of Antti Aarne and Stith Thompson's work.

Notes to Preface
1. Propp, *Morfologiia skazki*. The English translation is *Morphology of the Folktale*, Svatava Pirkova-Jakobson, ed.; Laurence Scott, trans. (Bloomington: Indiana University Research Center in Anthropology, Folklore, and Linguistics, 1958). The second

edition was published by the University of Texas Press (Austin) in 1968, was revised and edited by Louis A. Wagner, and includes a new introduction by Alan Dundes.

2. Olshansky, "Birth of Structuralism."

3. This example is drawn from an actual astronomy textbook I perused in a Moscow bookshop in 1982, more than a decade after Propp's death.

4. Using folklore to study the distant past might be compared not only to historical linguistics but also to the turn of some Soviet writers to the historical novel.

5. Ivanov, "Podniavshii perchatku" (Taking up the Gauntlet), 10–11, 12–13, 14–15, 16–17. The final section of the article (available at http://www.spbumag.nw.ru/2005/14/18.shtml, accessed November 5, 2011) includes links to the earlier sections.

6. As memorably symbolized by Vera Mukhina's famous 1937 statue, *Worker and Peasant Woman*.

7. Propp, *Theory and History of Folklore*, li–lii (Liberman was the editor of this volume).

8. For elements of political incorrectness in Russian jokelore, see Draitser, *Taking Penguins to the Movies*.

9. The term *fakelore* originated with American scholar Richard Dorson. See F. J. Miller, *Folklore for Stalin*.

10. Laura J. Olson's *Performing Russia* shows this complexity in the sphere of folk music. Some old women in the village assert that songs from Stalinist musicals are folk songs because that is what they remember and love to sing, evoking their own shared past.

11. See Bogatyrëv and Jakobson's 1929 article "Folklore as a Special Form of Creativity." For information on the surprising state of preservation of folkways, though not of folktales, in some Russian villages, see Paxson's *Solovyovo*.

12. Propp, *Neizvestnyj Propp*, p. 290 (entry for August 12, 1962).

13. Propp, *Theory and History of Folklore*, p. xliv. As Liberman mentions (Propp, *Theory and History of Folklore*, p. lxxxi), *The Russian Folktale* had been promised for two years but had not yet appeared as his collection went to press.

14. Propp, *Neizvestnyi Propp*, p. 333 (entry dated 30.VI.1970).

15. The *skaz* is now almost universally considered a variety of Soviet fakelore, created by genuine tale-tellers or epic singers in response to the new postrevolutionary situation and the encouragement of folklorists who were surely motivated by the desire to make their own livelihoods more secure.

16. Moreover, Propp does not neglect to mention Nikolai Marr and Aleksandr Veselovskii, who had been attacked in earlier decades.

17. Ivanov, "Podniavshii perchatku." In 1932 Propp began a lightly fictionalized autobiography he called "The Tree of Life," but he destroyed the sections concerning

the years after 1918 ("Drevo zhizni," published by N. A. Prozorova in Propp, *Neizvestnyi Propp*, pp. 25–159). Much of what we know of Propp's life thereafter comes from a diary he kept in his last years and from the memoirs of his students and younger colleagues, which were necessarily limited sources.

18. Propp, "Drevo zhizni," p. 26. All translations from Russian are mine, unless otherwise noted.

19. Propp, "Dnevnik starosti, 1962–196 . . . ," in Propp, *Neizvestnyi Propp*, pp. 289–333.

20. Boris Eikhenbaum (1886–1959) was a major Soviet literary scholar and historian and a member of the formal school. Dmitrii Zelenin (1878–1954) was a Russian and Soviet linguist and ethnographer. Viktor Zhirmunskii (1891–1971) was a Soviet literary historian and linguist and another representative of the formal school.

21. For information on Russian formalism—a title the school itself rejected—see Erlich, *Russian Formalism* or Steiner, *Russian Formalism*.

22. See, for example, the entry for January 27, 1965, in Propp, *Neizvestnyj Propp*, p. 298.

23. Afanas'ev, *Narodnye russkie skazki v 3-kh tt.*

24. Propp, *Russkaia skazka.*

NOTES TO INTRODUCTION

1. [As Propp was writing, three volumes of *Enzyklopädie des Märchens* had appeared: Bd. I–III.—CE]

2. [The Institute of German Folk Studies was later renamed the Department of Ethnography and History of Culture of the Central Institute of History of the Academy of Sciences of the German Democratic Republic (Wissenschaftsbereich "Volkskunde und Kulturgeschichte" des Zentralinstituts für Geschichte der Akademie der Wissenschaften der DDR). The title of the annual was changed to *Jahrbuch für Volkskunde und Kulturgeschichte.*—CE]

3. [*Fabula: Zeitschrift für Erzählforschung (Journal of Folktale Studies)* (West Berlin and New York, 1957–80).—CE]

4. [*Russkii fol'klor*, vols. 1–21 (Leningrad, 1956–81).—CE]

5. [Mel'ts, *Russkii fol'klor.*—CE]

6. [The Sorbs, a Slavic people of eastern Germany, are also known as the Wends.—SF]

7. Bolte and Polívka, *Anmerkungen*, v. 2, no. 61.

8. [Dmitrieva, *Povest' o Petre i Fevronii.*—CE]

9. [See Aarne, *Verzeichnis der Märchentypen mit Hilfe von Tachgennossen ausgearbeitet*; Andreev, *Ukazatel' skazochnykh sjuzhetov po sisteme Aarne*; and Varag et al.,

Sravnitel'nyi ukazatel' sjuzhetov.—CE.] [The Aarne-Thompson tale-type numbers are given with the abbreviation A-T, followed by the type number and sometimes by additional letters or numbers that clarify the subtype of the example. Propp frequently follows this combination with the number of examples of the tale type present in the Afanas'ev collection, source of the wonder tales on which his own *Morphology of the Folktale* was based.—SF]

10. [See Adrianova-Peretts, *Russkaia demokraticheskaia satira*; and Skripil' and Eremin, *Russkaia povest' XVII veka.*—CE]

11. Sipovskij, *Ocherki iz istorii russkogo romana*, v. 1, issues 1 and 2. [For further studies, see Kuz'min, "Literatura petrovskogo vremeni"; Berkov, "O tak nazyvaemyx 'petrovskix povestiax'"; and Moiseev, *Russkie povesti.*—CE]

12. For example, Blagoi, *Istorija russkoj literatury* (1945).

13. Lupanova, *Russkaia narodnaia skazka*.

14. The source for Iarullin's ballet *Shurale* is G. Tukai's tale by the same name, written on the basis of Tatar folktales.

15. [Propp wrote about this in more detail in an unpublished article on Vrubel'.—CE]

16. Honti, *Volksmärchen und Heldensagen*, p. 3.

17. For example, Vladimirov, *Vvedenie v istoriiu russkoi slovesnosti*; Pypin, *Istoriia russkoi literatury*, v. 3; Speranskii, *Russkaia ustnaia slovesnost'*; and Zamotin, *Russkaia narodnaia slovesnost'*.

18. Pypin, "Aleksandr N. Afanas'ev, *Russkie narodnye skazki,*" p. 57.

19. Bolte and Polívka, *Anmerkungen*, v. 4, pp. 1–3.

20. Savchenko, *Russkaia narodnaia skazka*, p. 37.

21. Dal', *Tolkovyi slovar' velikago russkago iazyka*.

22. Bolotov, *Zhizn' i prikljuchenija Andreja Bolotova*.

23. Turgenev, *Polnoe sobranie sochinenij*, v. 4, p. 141.

24. For the complete text, see Pypin, *Istoriia russkoi literatury*, v. 3, 23 ff.

25. A special journal, titled *Fabula*, was published in Germany in the nineteenth century. It printed all kinds of unlikely and implausible stories.

26. Bolte and Polívka, *Anmerkungen*, v. 4, pp. 1–3.

27. Bolte and Polívka, *Anmerkungen*, v. 3.

28. Nikiforov, "Skazka," p. 7.

29. Anikin, *Russkaia narodnaia skazka*, p. 46 and elsewhere.

30. Belinsky, "Stat'i o narodnoi poèzii," v. 5, p. 354.

31. For more detail, see Propp, "Fol'klor i deistvitel'nost'."

32. Anikin, *Russkaia narodnaia skazka*, p. 10.

33. Anikin, *Russkaia narodnaia skazka*, p. 218.

34. Anikin, *Russkaia narodnaia skazka*, pp. 40–41.

35. Bethe, *Mythus, Sage, Märchen*; and Bethe, *Hessische Blätter für Volkskunde.*

36. Wundt, "Märchen, Sage und Legende."

37. Brinton, *Myths of the New World.*

38. Cushing, *Zuni Folktales.*

39. Rand, *Legends of the Micmacs.*

40. Boas, *Indianische Sagen.*

41. [For broad information about the mythology of peoples of the world, see *Mify narodov mira.*—CE]

42. [Propp has in mind the 41st rune of the Kalevala. See *Kalevala*, pp. 284–87.—CE]

43. Schwab, *Die schönsten Sagen*, v. 1, p. 113.

44. Trencheni-Val'dapfel', *Mifologiia*, pp. 107–8 (Virgil, *Georgics*, bk. IV, verses 494–98).

45. Tronskii, "Antichnyi mir," p. 534.

46. [These are figures in Russian folk belief, considered relics of pre-Christian belief. For more detail in English on these figures and others, see Ivanits, *Russian Folk Belief.*—SF]

47. Sadovnikov, *Skazki i predaniia Samarskogo kraia.*

48. [From the introduction to Aleksandr Pushkin's mock-heroic epic poem, *Ruslan and Liudmila.*—SF]

49. Iu. M. Sokolov, *Russkii fol'klor* (1941), pp. 292–373.

50. The Aarne-Andreev index will be discussed in more detail later in this chapter.

51. Simonsuuri, *Typen und Motivverzeichnis der finnischen mythischen Sagen.*

52. Interest in these problems has grown in recent years. See, for example, Tokarev, *Religioznye.* [See also Pomerantseva, *Mifologicheskie personazhi.*—CE].

53. Afanas'ev, *Narodnye russkie legendy*, v. 1.

54. Andrejew, *Die Legende von dem zwei Erzsünder.* [For more recent literature, see Grin, "O dvukh legendakh," pp. 25–26; and Grin, "Spor o velikom greshnike."—CE]

55. Sadovnikov, *Skazki*, p. 229.

56. Shein, *Materialy*, v. 2, pp. 371–73.

57. [Propp has in mind part II ("Pir vo ves' mir" [A feast in the whole world]), ch. 2 ("Stranniki i bogomol'niki" [Pilgrims and men who pray to God]), of Nikolai Nekrasov's long poem *Komu na Rusi zhit' khorosho* (Who Lives Well in Rus'?). See Nekrasov, *Polnoe sobranie sochinenii i pisem*, v. 3, pp. 363–66. For more recent literature, see Grin, "O dvukh legendakh," pp. 19–27.—CE]

58. B. M. Sokolov and Iu. M. Sokolov, *Skazki*, p. 297 (no. 163).

59. Engels, "Nemetskie narodnye knigi."

60. Pypin, *Ocherk literaturnoi istorii.*

61. Mirer and Borovik, *Rasskazy rabochikh o Lenine.*

62. Akimova, *Skazy o Chapaeve.*

63. Nikiforov, "Skazka," p. 13.

64. [Propp has in mind the most archaic folktales of the peoples of Africa, whose heroes may be simultaneously zoomorphic and anthropomorphic (totem, beast, person). See Kotliar, *Mif i skazka Afriki*, pp. 14–71.—CE]

65. Andreev, *Ukazatel' skazochnykh siuzhetov po sisteme Aarne.* [See also Varag et al., *Sravnitel'nyi ukazatel' siuzhetov.*—CE].

66. Thompson, *The Types of the Folktale* (1927).

67. For the most complete list of national indexes, see Varag et al., *Sravnitel'nyi ukazatel' siuzhetov*, pp. 411–15 ("Spisok ukazatelei i materialov k ukazateliam siuzhetov skazok i drugikh povestvovatel'nykh zhanrov"). See also "O sistematizatsii siuzhetov vostochnykh slavian i sravnitel'nom ikh izuchenii," pp. 3–28 [in Varag et al., *Sravnitel'nyi ukazatel' siuzhetov*—SF].

68. Thompson, *Types of the Folktale* (1927).

69. Iu. M. Sokolov, *Russkii Fol'klor* (2nd ed., 1941).

NOTES TO CHAPTER 1

1. The exact text of this part of Kirill's sermon is reproduced in the Introduction.

2. For pointers to the literature, see Bazanov and Azbelev, *Russkaia literatura i fol'klor*, pp. 69–86 (the chapter "Narodnaia poeziia na rubezhe novoi epokhi" [XVII v.]).

3. For recent research, see Derzhavina, *Velikoe zertsalo.*

4. Gudzii, *Istoriia drevnei russkoi literatury* (1941), pp. 357–62, esp. 361.

5. Gudzii, *Istoriia drevnei russkoi literatury* (1941), p. 362.

6. Gudzii, *Istoriia drevnei russkoi literatury* (1941), p. 362.

7. For a summary, see Gudzii, *Istoriia drevnei russkoi literatury* (1941), pp. 364–65.

8. Gudzii, *Istoriia drevnei russkoi literatury* (1941), p. 366.

9. See Zhdanov, *Russkii bylevoi epos*, v. 1, pp. 152–92.

10. Savchenko, *Russkaia narodnaia, skazka.*

11. [Propp is referring to Sipovskii, *Ocherki iz istorii russkogo romana.*—SF]

12. [Propp is referring to Savchenko, *Russkaia narodnaia skazka.*—SF]

13. *Facejce polskie, żartowne a trefne powieśći biesiadne* was translated in 1680 in several manuscripts with differing titles: "Frashki, sirech' izdevki: fatsetsii ili zharty pol'ski, izdevki smekhotvorny moskovskii" [*Frashki*, so to speak mockeries: Face-

tiae or Polish jests, laugh-inducing Muscovite mockeries—CE], "Fatsetsi, ili zharty pol'skij, povesti, besedki, uteshki moskovskij" [Facetiae, or Polish jests, tales, *besedki*, Muscovite rhymes—CE]. On Russian translations of the facetiae, see Derzhavina, *Fatsetsii*.

14. Chulkov, *Peresmeshnik, ili Slovenskie skazki*. [After this, Propp planned to provide a survey of the editions of literary folktales of the second half of the eighteenth century, making use of the information provided in Dmitrii Blagoj's textbook, *Istoriia russkoi literatury XVIII veka* (pp. 266–69), and S. V. Savchenko's monograph, *Russkaia narodnaia skazka* (pp. 61–113). For a later critical survey and texts, see Novikov and Pomerantseva, *Russkie skazki v rannikh zapisiakh.*—CE]

15. [Chulkov, *Peresmeshnik*; Levshin, *Russkie skazki*; Blagoi, *Istorija russkoj literatury*; Savchenko, *Russkaia narodnaia skazka*, pp. 76–77; Kurganov, *Pis'movnik.*—SF]

16. [Propp is referring to Blagoi, *Istorija russkoj literatury*; and Savchenko, *Russkaia narodnaia skazka.*—SF]

17. [Propp is referring to Savchenko, *Russkaia narodnaia skazka.*—SF]

18. [Savchenko, *Russkaia narodnaia skazka.*—SF]

19. In recent years, surveys of eighteenth-century collections have been published: Pomerantseva, *Sud'by russkoi skazki*, pp. 32–61 (the chapter "Russkaia skazka v XVIII veke") [and Novikov and Pomerantseva, *Russkie skazki v rannikh zapisiakh.*—CE].

20. Novikov, *Russkie skazki v zapisiakh*, pp. 117–36, 351–61. [For indications of more recent literature, see Priima, *Russkaia literatura i fol'klor*, pp. 143–209.—CE]

21. This is "The Legend of the Arab Astrologer," by American writer Washington Irving, which, as Anna Akhmatova established, was the source of Pushkin's "Skazka o zolotom petushke" [Tale of the Golden Cockerel—CE]. For more details, see Azadovskii, "Istochniki 'Skazok Pushkina,'" pp. 85–89.

22. Novikov, *Russkie skazki v zapisiakh*, pp. 132–33, 359–60. [After this, Propp cites information about the sources of Pushkin's tales, using information given by Novikov [see the table in the text—SF].—CE]

23. From the introduction to *Ruslan and Liudmila*. [Propp cites Pushkin without attribution because Russian listeners or readers would simply recognize the quotation.—SF]

24. Pushkin, *Polnoe sobranie sochineniia*, v. 13, p. 121.

25. Lupanova, *Russkie narodnye skazki*.

26. Bronnitsyn, *Russkie narodnye skazki*.

27. Vanenko, *Skazki russkie*.

28. Belinsky, *Polnoe sobranie sochinenii*, v. 2, pp. 506–11.

29. Belinsky, *Polnoe sobranie sochinenii*, v. 2, p. 70.

30. Belinsky, *Polnoe sobranie sochinenii*, v. 2, p. 415.

31. Dal', *Russkie skazki*; and Dal', *Povesti*.

32. Afanas'ev, *Narodnye russkie skazki* (1936), v. 1, p. 499.

33. Sakharov, *Russkie narodnye skazki.*

34. Belinsky, *Polnoe sobranie sochinenii*, v. 5, pp. 420 ff.

35. Avdeeva, *Zapiski i zamechaniia o Sibiri.*

36. Avdeeva, *Zapiski o starom i novom russkom byte.*

37. Avdeeva, "Ocherki maslenitsy v Evropeiskoi Russii i Sibiri, v gorodakh i derevniakh."

38. Avdeeva, *Russkii pesennik, ili Sobranie luchshikh i liubopytneishikh pesen, romansov i vodevil'nykh kupletov.*

39. Avdeeva, *Russkie skazki dlia detei, rasskazannye nianiushkoiu Avdot'ei Stepanovnoi Cherep'evoi.*

40. Maksymovych, *Tri skazki i odna pobasenka.*

41. Maksymovych, *Malorossiiskie pesni.*

42. Gogol, *Sobranie sochinenii*, v. 6, p. 67.

43. Afanas'ev, *Narodnye russkie skazki* (1855–64).

44. [Vladimir Propp was the editor of the 1957 edition of Afanas'ev's tales.—SF]

45. [Propp does not mention the tales that were included in this edition (and excluded from the three-volume publication) because of their sexual context; these were not included in Soviet editions of Afanas'ev.—SF]

46. Afanas'ev, *Narodnye russkie legendy.*

47. Count A. P. Tolstoi cites a letter from Filaret. See Filaret, *Sobranie mnenii i otzyvov*, supplemental volume, pp. 527–31. See also Gruzinskii, *Bibliografiia Afanas'eva*, v. 1, pp. xxii–xxiii; and Chernyshev, "Tsenzurnye iz"iatiia iz 'Skazok,'" p. 315.

48. [Censorship laws forbade a second edition of Afanas'ev's *Narodnye russkie legendy*, which was being prepared for publication the same year, 1860.—CE]

49. Khudiakov, *Velikorusskie skazki.*

50. Khudiakov, *Velikorusskie zagadki.*

51. For an interpretation of Belinskii and Khudiakov's relations, see Azadovskii, *Istoriia russkoi fol'kloristiki*, v. 2, pp. 117–22.

52. Khudiakov, *Verkhoianskii sbornik.*

53. Pryzhov, *Ocherki.*

54. Sadovnikov, *Zagadki russkogo naroda.*

55. Novopol'tsev, *Skazki.*

56. Onchukov, *Severnye skazki.*

57. Rybnikov, *Pesni.*

58. [In his article "Lenin on Poetry" (*Na literaturnom postu*, 1931, no. 4), Vladimir Bonch-Bruevich recalls Lenin's comment on Onchukov's collection: "I took a quick look at these books, but I see that, evidently, people lack the time or the desire to generalize from all of this, to look at all of this from the sociopolitical point of view; you know this material could be the basis of a splendid study of the hopes and expectations of the people. Look in N. E. Onchukov's folktales, which I leafed through—there are really marvelous moments here. This is what our historians of literature should be paying attention to. This is the most authentic people's creativity, so necessary and important for the study of the people's psychology in our day" (p. 4). On Lenin's comment, see also Bonch-Bruevich, "V. I. Lenin ob ustnom narodnom tvorchestve," p. 118; Chistov, "Zametki"; Pomerantseva, "Russkaia skazka "; and Pomerantseva, *Sud'by russkoi skazki*, pp. 131–50.—CE]

59. Zelenin, *Velikorusskie skazki Permskoi gubernii*; and Zelenin, *Velikorusskie skazki Viatskoi gubernii*.

60. B. M. Sokolov and Sokolov, *Skazki i pesni Belozerskogo kraia*.

61. B. M. Sokolov and Sokolov, *Skazki i pesni Belozerskogo kraia*, p. viii.

62. The letter was published with detailed commentary by Aleksandr I. Nikiforov. See Commentary in *Uchenye zapiski pedagogicheskogo instituta im. A. I. Gertsena*.

63. [See Propp's introductory article, "A. I. Nikiforov."—CE]

64. [Akimova, *Seminarii*, pp. 101–37. For the most complete listing of collections of Russian folktales, see Varag et al., *Sravnitel'nyi ukazatel' siuzhetov*, pp. 29–51.—CE]

65. [This is Baryshnikova, *Skazki Kupriianikhi.*—SF]

66. [Korguev, *Skazki M. M. Korgueva*; and Gospodarev, *Skazki F. P. Gosporadeva.*—SF]

67. Gofman and Mints, *Skazki Kovaleva*. Detailed references to the other editions will be given in the text.

68. [For a list of the most important studies of the Russian folktale in recent years, see the chapter "Vazhneishie issledovaniia o skazkakh vostochnykh slavian" in Varag et al., *Sravnitel'nyi ukazatel' siuzhetov*, pp. 402–10.—CE]

Notes to Chapter 2

1. Pypin, *Istoriia russkoi ètnografii*; Speranskii, *Russkaia ustnaia slovesnost'*; Iu. M. Sokolov, *Russkii fol'klor*; and especially Savchenko, *Russkaia narodnaia skazka*.

2. Azadovskii, *Istoriia russkoi fol'kloristiki*.

3. [*Bibliothèques* was the name of various serial editions (e.g., the blue library, the light-blue library, the universal library of novels), which included literary fairytales, retellings of adventure novels, and the like.—CE]

4. [Levshin, *Russkie skazki.*—CE]

5. [Sakharov, *Skazaniia ruskogo naroda.* See also Ukhov, "K ustorii termina 'bylina.'"—CE]

6. Pushkin, *Polnoe sobranie sochineniia*, v. 13, p. 121.

7. Merzliakov, *Kratkaia ritorika*, p. 79.

8. *Dedushkiny progulki; Lekarstvo ot zadumchivosti i bessonitsy.*

9. Tsertelev, "Vzgliad na starinnye russkie skazki."

10. Ostolopov, *Slovar' drevnei i novoi poezii*, pt. III, p. 146.

11. Shishkov, *Razgovory o slovesnosti mezhdu dvumia litsami Az i Buki.*

12. Makarov, "Dogadki ob istorii russkikh skazok"; Makarov, "Listki."

13. Sreznevskii, "Vzgliad na pamiatniki ukrainskoi narodnoi slovesnosti."

14. [The triune ideology of "Orthodoxy, Autocracy, and Nationality," also known as Official Nationality, was the tsarist state-promoted reactionary position after the Napoleonic Wars.—SF]

15. Shepping, "Ivan-tsarevich, narodnyi russkii bogatyr'."

16. Shepping, "Ivan-tsarevich," p. 37.

17. K. S. Aksakov, "O razlichii mezhdu skazkami," v. 1, p. 399.

18. K. S. Aksakov, "O razlichii mezhdu skazkami," v. 1, p. 399.

19. Shepping, "Otvet K. Aksakovu."

20. Bessonov, *Pesni, sobrannye P. V. Kireevskim*, vyp. 3, pp. xi ff; vyp. 4, pp. xix ff.

21. Kotliarevskii, *Starina.*

22. Buslaev, *Istoricheskie ocherki*, v. 1, p. 310.

23. Buslaev, "Lektsii po istorii russkoi literatury," pp. 247–48.

24. Shepping, "Kosmogonicheskoe znachenie russkikh skazok i bylin."

25. O. F. Miller, "Razbor 'Sbornika russkikh skazok.'"

26. Veselovskii, "Tri glavy iz istoricheskoi poetiki," in his *Istoricheskaia poetika*, p. 317.

27. Veselovskii, *Istoricheskaia poetika*, pp. 73–199.

28. Veselovskii, *Poetika siuzhetov.*

29. Veselovskii, *Poetika siuzhetov*, p. 500.

30. Veselovskii, "Iz lektsii po istorii èposa," in his *Istoricheskaia poetika*, p. 455.

31. Veselovskii, *Istoricheskaia poetika*, p. 459; see also p. 454.

32. Veselovskii, *Sobranie sochinenii*, v. 16 (1938).

33. Bédier, *Les fabliaux.*

34. Basset, "Les formules dans les contes."

35. Usener, "Rhein," p. 59; Lehmann, "Dreiheit und dreifache Steigerung"; and G. Polívka, "Les nombres."

36. Petsch, *Formelhafte Schlüsse.*

37. Kahlo, *Die Verse.*

38. Eleonskaia, "Nekotorye zamechaniia o roli zagadki"; and Kolesnitskaia, "Zagadki v skazke."

39. Bolte, *Name und Merkname.*

40. Shklovskii, *O teorii prozy.*

41. Olrik, *Epische Gesetzte.*

42. Shklovskii, *O teorii prozy*, p. 27.

43. Propp, "Transformatsii volshebnykh skazok." [The same work is in Propp's *Fol'klor i deistvitel'nost': Izbrannye stat'i.*—CE]

44. Volkov, *Skazka.*

45. Nikiforov, "K voprosu o morfologicheskom izuchenii narodnoi skazki."

46. Propp, *Morfologiia skazki.*

47. Nikiforov, "Vazhneishie stilevye linii"; and Nikiforov, "Motiv."

48. Nikiforov, "Struktura chukotskoi skazki kak iavleniia primitivnogo myshleniia."

49. Nikiforov, "Rosiis'ka dokuchna kazka."

50. Nikiforov, *Obzor rabot skazochnoi kommissii.*

51. Nikiforov, "Skazka."

52. Nikiforov, "Zhanry russkoi skazki."

53. Sreznevskii, "Vzgliad," p. 144.

54. Snegirev, *Lubochnye kartinki russkogo naroda*, pp. 78–114.

55. Bessonov, *Pesni, sobrannye Kireevskim.*

56. O. Miller, "Razbor 'Sbornika russkikh skazok,'" pp. 72–107.

57. O. Miller, "Razbor 'Sbornika russkikh skazok,'" p. 107.

58. O. Miller, "Razbor 'Sbornika russkikh skazok,'" p. 106.

59. O. Miller, *Opyt istoricheskogo obozreniia russkoi slovesnosti.*

60. Drahomanov, *Malorusskie narodnye predaniia i rasskazy.*

61. Romanov, *Belorusskii sbornik*, v. 3 (Vitebsk, 1887); v. 4 (Vitebsk, 1891).

62. Sumtsov, "Otchet o piatom prisuzhdenii premii Makariia."

63. Vladimirov, *Vvedenie v istoriiu russkoi slovesnosti.*

64. Vladimirov, *Vvedenie v istoriiu russkoi slovesnosti*, p. 155.

65. Sumtsov, "Skazka," pp. 162–64.

66. See Galakhov, *Istoriia russkoi slovesnosti.*

67. Khalanskii, "Skazki," p. 144.

68. Smirnov, "Sistematicheskii ukazatel' tem i variantov russkikh narodnykh skazok."

69. Hahn, *Griechische und albanische Märchen.*

70. Gomme, *Handbook of Folklore.*

71. Christensen, *Motif et thème.*

72. Thompson, *Motive-index of Folk Literature*.

73. Aarne, *Verzeichnis der Märchentypen mit Hilfe von Tachgennossen ausgearbeitet*.

74. Nikiforov, "Zhanry russkoi skazki."

75. Nikiforov, "Zhanry russkoi skazki," pp. 233–59.

76. Creuzer, *Symbolik und Mythologie der alten Völker, besonders der Griechen*.

77. Görres, *Mythengeschichte der asiatischen Welt*.

78. Makarov, "Dogadki ob istorii russkikh skazok"; and Makarov, "Listki."

79. Makarov, "Listki," p. 23.

80. Makarov, "Listki," p. 23.

81. Makarov, "Listki," p. 23.

82. Grimm, *Deutsche Grammatik*.

83. Grimm, *Deutsche Mythologie*.

84. Buslaev, "Èpicheskaia poèziia," p. 55.

85. Buslaev, "Èpicheskaia poèziia," p. 55.

86. Buslaev, "Èpicheskaia poèziia," p. 1.

87. For more details on these views, see Azadovskii, *Istoriia russkoi fol'kloristiki*, v. 2, pp. 53–70.

88. Buslaev, "Slavianskie skazki"; and Buslaev, "Perekhozhie povesti i rasskazy."

89. Kulish, *Zapiski o Iuzhnoi Rusi*.

90. Wenzig, *Westslavische Märchen*.

91. Schott and Schott, *Walachische Märchen*.

92. Schleicher, *Litawische Märchen*.

93. Buslaev, "Slavianskie skazki," p. 308.

94. Buslaev, "Slavianskie skazki," p. 308.

95. Buslaev, "Slavianskie skazki," pp. 309–10.

96. Buslaev, "Slavianskie skazki," p. 310.

97. Buslaev, "Slavianskie skazki," p. 310.

98. This and subsequent references are to Afanas'ev's book *Narodnye russkie skazki v 3-kh tt*, and the number indicates the specific tale.

99. Buslaev, "Slavianskie skazki," p. 310.

100. Buslaev, "Slavianskie skazki," p. 311.

101. Buslaev, "Slavianskie skazki," p. 311.

102. Buslaev, "Slavianskie skazki," p. 315.

103. Buslaev, "Slavianskie skazki," p. 320.

104. Buslaev, "Slavianskie skazki," p. 318.

105. Buslaev, "Slavianskie skazki," p. 317.

106. Kuhn, *Die Herabkunft des Feuers und des Göttertranks*.

107. Schwartz, *Die poetische Naturanschauung der Griechen, Römer und Deutschen in ihren Beziehung zur Mythologie der Urzeit.*

108. Afanas'ev, *Poèticheskie vozzreniia slavian na prirodu.* For a list of articles, see Iu. M. Sokolov, "Zhizn' i deiatel'nost' A. N. Afanas'eva," v. 1, pp. ix–lvii.

109. Afanas'ev, *Poèticheskie vozzreniia slavian na prirodu*, v. 1, p. 5.

110. Afanas'ev, *Poèticheskie vozzreniia slavian na prirodu*, v. 1, pp. 7–8.

111. Afanas'ev, *Poèticheskie vozzreniia slavian na prirodu*, v. 1, p. 55.

112. Afanas'ev, *Poèticheskie vozzreniia slavian na prirodu*, v. 2, p. 311.

113. Afanas'ev, *Poèticheskie vozzreniia slavian na prirodu*, v. 1, p. 171.

114. Afanas'ev, *Poèticheskie vozzreniia slavian na prirodu*, v. 1, p. 529.

115. Pypin, "Afanas'ev," p. cxvi.

116. Veselovskii, "Zametki i somneniia," p. 10.

117. Kotliarevskii, "Desiatyi (1888) i trinadtsatyi otchety."

118. Kotliarevskii, "Razbor sochinenii A. Afanas'eva," p. 334.

119. Kotliarevskii, "Razbor sochinenii A. Afanas'eva," p. 330.

120. Potebnia, "O mificheskom znachenii," p. 234.

121. Potebnia, "O Dole i srodnykh s neiu sushchestvakh."

122. Pypin, *Ocherk literaturnoi istorii starinnykh povestei i skazok russkikh.*

123. Graesse, *Die großen Sagenkreise des Mittelalters.*

124. Pypin, *Ocherk literaturnoi istorii*, p. 6.

125. Pypin, *Ocherk literaturnoi istorii*, p. 9.

126. Pypin, *Ocherk literaturnoi istorii*, p. 13.

127. Benfey, *Pantschatantra*, v. 1, p. xxii.

128. Kolmachevskii, *Zhivotnyi èpos.*

129. Liebrecht, *Jarhbuch für romanische und englische Literatur zur Volkskunde.*

130. Köhler, *Aufsätze über Märchen und Volkslieder*; and Köhler, *Kleine Schriften.*

131. Paris, *Les contes orientaux dans la literature française du moyen age.*

132. Cosquin, *Contes populaires de Lorraine.*

133. Veselovskii, "Lorrenskie skazki," pp. 212–13.

134. Cosquin, *Etudes folkloriques*; and Cosquin, *Les contes indiens et l'Occident.*

135. Stasov, "Proiskhozhdenie russkikh bylin." Also in Stasov, *Sobranie sochinenii*, v. 3.

136. Azadovskii, *Istoriia russkoi fol'kloristiki*, v. 2, pp. 160–69; and Astakhova, *Byliny*, pp. 32–34.

137. Stasov, "Proiskhozhdenie russkikh bylin."

138. For a list of reviews, see Savchenko, *Russkaia narodnaia skazka*, p. 417.

139. Veselovskii, "Zametki i somneniia," p. 39.

140. Veselovskii, *Slavianskie skazaniia o Solomone i Kitovrase i zapadnye legendy o Morol'fe i Merline: Iz istorii literaturnogo obshcheniia Zapada i Vostoka* (see also Veselovskii, *Sobranie sochinenii,* v. 7, no. 1 [Prague, 1921]).

141. Veselovskii, "Slavianskie skazaniia," p. 177.

142. Veselovskii, *Slavianskie skazaniia,* p. 1.

143. Savchenko, *Russkaia narodnaia skazka,* pp. 435–45.

144. Veselovskii, *Sobranie sochinenii,* v. 16, p. 214.

145. Veselovskii, *Sobranie sochinenii,* v. 16, p. 221.

146. Buslaev, *Narodnaia poèziia,* pp. iii–iv.

147. Buslaev, "Retsenziia," pp. 56–57.

148. Buslaev, "Perekhozhie povesti i rasskazy."

149. Buslaev, "Perekhozhie povesti i rasskazy," p. 405.

150. See, for example, Iu. M. Sokolov, *Russkii fol'klor* (1941), p. 56.

151. Drahomanov, *Rozvidky pro ukrainsku narodnu slovesnist' i pis'menstvo.*

152. Drahomanov, "Kordeliia-Zamarashka"; Drahomanov, "Luchshii son"; Drahomanov, "Sholudivyi Buniaka"; Drahomanov, "Turetskie anekdoty."

153. Drahomanov, "Slavianskie povesti o pozhertvovanii svoego rebenka."

154. Drahomanov, "Slavianskie povesti o rozhdenii."

155. Drahomanov, "Slavianskie pererabotki istorii Edipa"; Drahomanov, *Rozvidky,* v. 4.

156. Drahomanov, *Rozvidky,* v. 4, p. 7.

157. Kolmachevskii, *Zhivotnyi èpos,* p. 54.

158. Kolmachevskii, *Zhivotnyi èpos,* p. 84.

159. Kolmachevskii, *Zhivotnyi èpos,* p. 173.

160. Veselovskii, "Kolmachevskii," p. 204.

161. V. F. Miller, *Ekskursy v oblast' russkogo narodnogo èposa.*

162. V. F. Miller, *Osetinskie ètiudy.*

163. V. F. Miller, "Spisok trudov"; see also Speranskii, "Spisok uchenykh trudov V. F. Millera."

164. V. F. Miller, "Vostochnye i zapadnye paralleli odnoi russkoi skazki."

165. V. F. Miller, "Kavkazskie skazaniia o velikanakh, prikovannykh k goram"; and V. F. Miller, "Kavkazskie skazaniia o tsiklopakh."

166. V. F. Miller, "K skazkam ob Ivane Groznom."

167. V. F. Miller, "K pesniam, skazkam i predaniiam o Pëtre Velikom."

168. V. F. Miller, "Vsemirnaia skazka v kul'turno-istoricheskom osveshchenii."

169. Cf. Shklovskii, O teorii prozy, pp. 28 ff.

170. Bédier, *Les fabliaux.*

171. Potapin, *Ocherki severo-zapadnoi Mongolii.*

172. Potapin, *Vostochnye motivy v srednevekovom evropeiskom èpose.*

173. Ol'denburg, "Buddiiskie legendy i buddizm."

174. Ol'denburg, "Fablo vostochnogo proiskhozhdeniia."

175. Ol'denburg, "Stranstvovanie skazki," p. 158.

176. Ol'denburg, "Stranstvovanie skazki," p. 160.

177. [Oldenbourg, "Le conte dit populaire: problèmes et methodes."—CE]

178. Zhdanov, "K literaturnoi istorii russkoi bylevoi poezii" (also in Zhdanov's *Sobranie sochinenii*, v. 1, pp. 485–743).

179. Zhdanov, *Russkii bylevoi èpos.*

180. Zhdanov, *Povest' o Vavilone i skazanie o kniaziakh Vladimirskikh.*

181. The best recording is in Sadovnikov, *Skazki*, no. 3.

182. Sozonovich, *Pesni o devushke-voine i byliny o Stavre Godinoviche.*

183. Sozonovich, *"Lenora."* (Also in Sozonovich's book *K voprosu o zapadnom vliianii.*)

184. Sozonovich, "Poèticheskii motiv o vnezapnom vozvrashchenii muzha ko vremeni svad'by svoei zheny, sobiravsheisia vyiti zamuzh za drugogo."

185. Sumtsov, "Otgoloski khristianskikh predanii v mongol'skikh skazkakh."

186. Sumtsov, "Muzh na svad'be svoei zheny."

187. Sumtsov, "Muzh na svad'be svoei zheny," p. 19.

188. Sumtsov, "Muzh na svad'be svoei zheny," p. 21.

189. [Aarne, *Leitfaden der vergleichenden Märchenforschung.*—CE]

190. [Krohn, *Die folklorische Arbeitsmethode.*—CE]

191. Aarne, *Verzeichnis der Märchentypen.*

192. Thompson, *The Types of the Folktale* (1964). [Thompson's index generalizes the data from a number of national indexes.—CE]

193. Andreev, *Ukazatel' skazochnykh siuzhetov po sisteme Aarne.* [See also Varag et al., *Sravnitel'nyi ukazatel' siuzhetov.*—CE] Also, cf. the list of national indexes in Andreev on pp. 411–15.

194. Wesselsky, *Märchen des Mittelalters.*

195. Zelenin, "Mezhdunarodnaia konferentsiia fol'kloristov-skazkovedov."

196. Anderson, *Imperator i abbat.*

197. Andrejew, *Die Legende von den zwei Erzsündern*; and Andrejew, *Die Legende vom Räuber Madej.*

198. Nikiforov, "Finskaia shkola pered krizisom"; see also Konkka, "'Finskaia shkola' o skazke" (in the series "Trudy Karel'skogo filiala AN SSSR"), pp. 3–29. [Propp has in mind Anderson's monographs *Kaiser und Abt* and *Swank vom alten Hildebrand.*—CE]

199. See von der Leyen, "Indogermanische Märchen."

200. Mackensen, *Handwörterbuch des deutschen Märchens*. Because of the start of World War II, this dictionary was not completed.

201. Waitz, *Anthropologie der Naturvölker*.

202. Bastian, *Der Mensch in der Geschichte: Zur Begründung einer psychologischen Weltanschauung*.

203. Bastian, *Die heilige Sage der Polinisier*.

204. [On the subsequent development of ethnography in the countries of Western Europe and in America, see Tokarev, *Istoriia zarubezhnoi ètnografii*; Averkieva, *Istoriia teoreticheskoi mysli*; *Ètnografiia za rubezhom*; and others.—CE]

205. *Folklore World* (London, 1878–82); *Folklore Journal* (London, 1883–89); *Folklore* (London, 1890–1913).

206. Hartland, *Legend of Perseus*.

207. *Melusine* (Paris, 1878–1912).

208. Lévy-Bruhl, *Les functions mentales dans les sociétés inférieures*; Lévy-Bruhl, *La mentalité primitive*; and Lévy-Bruhl, *Sverkh″estestvennoe v pervobytnom myshlenii*.

209. Saintyves, *Les contes de Perrault et les récits parallèles*.

210. Veselovskii, "Poètika siuzhetov," p. 493.

211. Veselovskii, "Poètika siuzhetov," p. 514.

212. Voevodskii, *Kannibalizm v grecheskikh mifakh*.

213. Komarov, *Èkskursy*.

214. Kirpichnikov, *Poèmy lombardskogo tsikla*.

215. Sumtsov, *Kul'turnye perezhivaniia*.

216. Eleonskaia, "Nekotorye zamechaniia o perezhitkakh pervobytnoi kul'tury v skazkakh."

217. Engels, "Proiskhozhdeniia sem′i, chastnoi sobstvennosti i gosudarstva."

218. Veselovskii, "Iz lektsii po istorii èposa," in his *Istoricheskaia poetika*, p. 450.

219. Andreev, "Izdanie skazok"; and Andreev, "Novoe izdaniia skazok." [See also Varag et al., *Sravnitel'nyi ukazatel' siuzhetov*, pp. 402–10.—CE]

220. Lur′e, "Dom v lesu."

221. Propp, "K voprosu o proiskhozhdenii volshebnoi skazki."

222. Propp, "Muzhskoi dom."

223. [Propp, "Ritual'nyi smekh v fol'klore."—CE]

224. [Propp, "Motiv chudesnogo rozhdeniia."—CE]

225. [Propp, "Èdip v svete fol'klora."—CE]

226. Propp, *Istoricheskie korni volshebkoi skazki*.

227. Morgan, *Ancient Society*.

228. [For a contemporary summary of the theory of primitive society, see the book *Pervobytnoe obshchestvo*. See also Pershits, "Periodizatsiia pervobytnoi istorii";

and Bromlei, "Voprosy sotsial'noi istorii pervobytnogo obshchestva v sovremennoi sovetskoi ètnografii," in his *Sovremennye problemy ètnografii.*—CE]

229. A summary of European scholarship in this regard is in Bolte and Polívka, *Anmerkungen*, v. 4, pp. 95–127.

230. Klinger, *Skazochnye motivy v "Istorii" Gerodota.*

231. Klinger, *Zhivotnye v antichnom i sovremennom sueverii*; and Klinger, "Dve antichnye skazki ob orle i ikh pozdneishie otrazheniia."

232. F. F. Zelinskii, "Antichnaia Lenora."

233. F. F. Zelinskii, "Zakon khronologicheskoi nesovmestimosti"; F. F. Zelinskii, "Starye i novye puti"; and F. F. Zelinskii, "Die Behandlung gleichzeitigen Ereignissen."

234. Pokrovskii, "Opyt novogo tolkovaniia komedii Plavta."

235. Tolstoi, "Zakoldovannye zveri Kirki v poeme Apolloniia Rodosskogo."

236. Tolstoi, "Neudachnoe vrachevanie: Antichnaia parallel' k russkoi skazke."

237. Tolstoi, "Vozvrashchenie muzha v 'Odissee' i v russkoi skazke."

238. Tolstoi, "Obriad i legenda afinskikh bufonii."

239. Tolstoi, "Tragediia Evridipa 'Elena' i nachalo grecheskogo romana."

240. Tolstoi, "Sviazannyi i osvobozhdennyi silen."

241. Tolstoi, "Gekal Kallimakha i russkaia skazka o babe-iage."

242. Tolstoi, "Iazyk skazki v grecheskoi literature."

243. Tronskii, "Mif o Dafnise."

244. Tronskii, "Antichnyi mir i sovremennaia skazka."

245. Tronskii, "Antichnyi mir," p. 530.

246. Tronskii, "Antichnyi mir," p. 534.

247. Marr, *Izbrannye raboty.*

248. Marr, *Tristan i Isol'da*, p. 202.

249. Marr, *Tristan i Isol'da*, pp. 12 and 92.

250. Marr, *Tristan i Isol'da*, p. 15.

251. Marr, *Tristan i Isol'da*, p. 1.

252. Marr, *Tristan i Isol'da*, pp. 201–4.

253. Freidenberg, "Slepets nad obryvom"; Freidenberg, "Mif ob Iosife Prekrasnom"; and Freidenberg, "Fol'klor u Aristofana."

254. Freidenberg, *Poètika siuzheta i zhanra: Period antichnoi literatury.* [See also the posthumous collection of selected works from Freidenberg's archive, *Mif i literatura drevnosti.*—CE]

255. Erlikh, "Skazka o lovkom vore."

256. Sovetov, "Odin iz obrazov 'ognia' i 'vody' v serbskikh i slavianskikh skazkakh."

257. Bolte and Polívka, *Anmerkungen*, v. 4, pp. 95–102.

258. Vikent'ev, *Drevneegipetskaia povest' o dvukh brat'iakh.*

259. Frantsov, "Zmeinyi ostrov"; and Frantsov, "Drevneegipetskie skazki."

260. Frank-Kamenetskii, "Gruzinskaia parallel'."

261. Frank-Kamenetskii, "Gruzinskaia parallel'," p. 54.

262. Western European materials are indexed by Bolte and Polívka, *Anmerkungen*, v. 4, pp. 127–76.

263. Wesselsky, *Märchen des Mittelalters*; and Wesselsky, *Mönchslatein*.

264. Nikiforov, "Russkaia literatura." See also Propp, *Russkoe narodnoe poèticheskoe tvorchestvo*, v. 1 [and Bazanov and Azbelev, *Russkaia literatura i fol'klor.*—CE].

265. Andreev, "Problema istorii fol'klora."

266. Andreev, "Fol'klor i ego istoriia."

267. [For additional literature, see Propp, *Russkoe narodnoe poèticheskoe tvorchestvo*, vols. 1 and 2; and Putilov, *Metodologiia*. On the folktale, see Meletinskii, *Geroi volshebnoi skazki*; Novikov, *Obrazy vostochnoslavianskoi volshebnoi skazki*; and Pomerantseva, *Sud'by russkoi skazki.*—CE]

Notes to Chapter 3

1. Thompson, *Motive-Index of Folk Literature*.

2. References of this type are to tales in Afanas'ev, *Narodnye russkie skazki v 3-kh tt.*

3. See Propp, *Morfologiia skazki*, pp. 28–29.

4. See Propp, *Istoricheskie korni volshebnoi skazki*, ch. 2, pt. 2 ("Calamity and Counteraction"), pt. 8 ("Misfortune"), and pt. 9 ("Equipping the Hero for His Travels"), pp. 25–34.

5. The functions of divining and handing out (Propp, *Morfologiia skazki*, p. 30).

6. The functions of a dirty trick and abetting (Propp, *Morfologiia skazki*, pp. 31–33).

7. Onchukov, *Svernye skazki*, p. 8.

8. See Propp, *Istoricheskie korni volshebnoi skazki*, pp. 46–47 ("The Hut and Baba Yaga").

9. Afanas'ev, *Narodnye russkie skazki v 3-kh tt*, pp. 279–80.

10. Afanas'ev, *Narodnye russkie skazki v 3-kh tt*, p. 280.

11. Afanas'ev, *Narodnye russkie skazki v 3-kh tt*, p. 280.

12. [Propp is referring to the functions that he first defined in his *Morfologiia skazki.*—SF]

13. [Propp, *Morfologiia skazki.*—SF]

14. Cf. Propp, *Istoricheskie korni volshebnoi skazki*, ch. 5, pt. 1, para. 3–12.

15. [For a contemporary systematization of plots, see Meletinskii, "Strukturno-tipologicheskoe izuchenie skazki," pp. 161–62.—CE]

16. Frazer, *Golden Bough*, vols. 1–4. [See also Frazer, *Zolotaia vetv'.*—CE]

17. [For a listing of the literature, see Rosianu, *Traditsionnye formuly skazki.*—CE]

18. Lévy-Bruhl, *La mentalité primitive.*

19. [For pointers to recent literature, see Meletinskii, *Geroi volshebnoi skazki;* and Novikov, *Obrazy vostochnoslavianskoi volshebnoi skazki.*—CE]

20. [In *Sravnitel'nyi ukazatel' siuzhetov,* Varag et al. give information on thirty published Russian recordings. There are more than a hundred recorded versions of type A-T 300 in total.—CE]

21. Ranke, *Die zwei Brüder.*

22. Cf. Propp, "Motiv chudesnogo rozhdeniia" [original publication in *Uchenye zapiski Leningradskogo universiteta* in 1941—SF]. [See also Propp's book *Fol'klor i deistvitel'nost',* pp. 205–40.—CE]

23. Afanas'ev, *Narodnye russkie skazki v 3-kh tt,* v. 2, p. 236.

24. [In *Sravnitel'nyi ukazatel' siuzhetov,* Varag et al. cite thirty-two Russian recordings.—CE]

25. Afanas'ev, *Narodnye russkie skazki v 3-kh tt,* v. 2, p. 247.

26. Afanas'ev, *Narodnye russkie skazki v 3-kh tt,* v. 2, p. 247.

27. Afanas'ev, *Narodnye russkie skazki v 3-kh tt,* v. 2, p. 248.

28. Afanas'ev, *Narodnye russkie skazki v 3-kh tt,* v. 2, p. 248.

29. Afanas'ev, *Narodnye russkie skazki v 3-kh tt,* v. 2, p. 249.

30. Afanas'ev, *Narodnye russkie skazki v 3-kh tt,* v. 2, p. 250.

31. Afanas'ev, *Narodnye russkie skazki v 3-kh tt,* v. 2, p. 250.

32. Afanas'ev, *Narodnye russkie skazki v 3-kh tt,* v. 2, p. 250.

33. Afanas'ev, *Narodnye russkie skazki v 3-kh tt,* v. 2, p. 250.

34. Propp, "Ritual'nyi smekh v fol'klore" [original publication in *Uchenye zapiski Leningradskogo universiteta* in 1939—SF].

35. [Here, Propp refers to Pushkin, *Polnoe sobranie sochineniia,* v. 3, p. 458; and Zhukovsky, "Skazka o tsare Berendee," pp. 729–40.—SF] [Zhukovskii's tale is written in hexameters.—CE].

36. [According to the significance assigned in Propp's *Morphology of the Folktale,* this signifies the absence of a block of paired functions: "Battle/Victory and Task/Solution of the Task."—CE]

37. Apulei, *Zolotoi osel,* p. 96.

38. Apulei, *Zolotoi osel,* pp. 111–12.

39. See Propp, "Trudy I. I. Tolstogo po fol'kloru"; and Tolstoi, 1966, pp. 3–17. [Propp has in mind a series of comparative articles by Ivan I. Tolstoi, "Drevnegrecheskii fol'klor i literatura."—CE] [These articles are included in Tolstoi, *Stat'i o folklore.*—SF]

40. Apulei, *Zolotoi osel,* p. 113.

41. Apulei, *Zolotoi osel*, p. 123.

42. [For pointers to further literature, see Megas, *Das Märchen* (A-T 425, 428, 432); and *Enzyklopädie des Märchens*, Bd. 1, u. 2, pp. 464–72.—CE]

43. [*Sravnitel'nyi ukazatel' siuzhetov*, by Varag et al., contains information about eighteen Russian records (A-T type 425 C).—CE]

44. Aksakov, *Sobranie sochinenii*, v. 1, p. 630.

45. Aksakov, *Sobranie sochinenii*, v. 1, p. 583.

46. Aksakov, *Sobranie sochinenii*, v. 1, p. 584.

47. Aksakov, *Sobranie sochinenii*, v. 1, p. 585.

48. Aksakov, *Sobranie sochinenii*, v. 1, pp. 586–87.

49. Aksakov, *Sobranie sochinenii*, v. 1, p. 588.

50. Aksakov, *Sobranie sochinenii*, v. 1, p. 588.

51. Aksakov, *Sobranie sochinenii*, v. 1, p. 595.

52. Aksakov, *Sobranie sochinenii*, v. 1, p. 597.

53. Aksakov, *Sobranie sochinenii*, v. 1, p. 599.

54. Aksakov, *Sobranie sochinenii*, v. 1, p. 599.

55. [In *Sravnitel'nyi ukazatel' siuzhetov*, Varag et al. provide information on eighteen Russian recordings (A-T 432).—CE]

56. [Propp has in mind the reflection of the plot (A-T 432) in written sources (see Bolte and Polívka, *Anmerkungen*, v. 2, p. 261).—CE]

57. Khudiakov, *Velikorusskie skazki*, v. 1, p. 5.

58. Khudiakov, *Velikorusskie skazki*, tale 39.

59. Propp, *Istoricheskie korni volshebkoi skazki*, ch. 9 ("Nevesta").

60. [That is, it contradicted them.—CE]

61. [In *Sravnitel'nyi ukazatel' siuzhetov*, Varag et al. give information on twenty-seven published Russian recordings.—CE]

62. *Dedushkiny progulki*.

63. Afanas'ev, *Narodnye russkie skazki v 3-kh tt*, v. 2, p. 415.

64. Afanas'ev, *Narodnye russkie skazki v 3-kh tt*, v. 2, p. 416.

65. Afanas'ev, *Narodnye russkie skazki v 3-kh tt*, v. 2, pp. 416–17.

66. Afanas'ev, *Narodnye russkie skazki v 3-kh tt*, v. 2, p. 417.

67. Afanas'ev, *Narodnye russkie skazki v 3-kh tt*, v. 2, p. 417.

68. Onchukov, *Severnye skazki*, no. 88.

69. Afanas'ev, *Narodnye russkie skazki v 3-kh tt*, v. 2, 419.

70. Afanas'ev, *Narodnye russkie skazki v 3-kh tt*, v. 2, p. 423.

71. Afanas'ev, *Narodnye russkie skazki v 3-kh tt*, v. 1, p. 195.

72. Afanas'ev, *Narodnye russkie skazki v 3-kh tt*, v. 1, p. 191.

73. Onchukov, *Severnye skazki*.

74. Afanas'ev, *Narodnye russkie skazki v 3-kh tt*, v. 1, p. 195.

75. Afanas'ev, *Narodnye russkie skazki v 3-kh tt*, v. 1, p. 191.

76. Zelenin, *Velikorusskie skazki Viatskoi gubernii.*

77. Khudiakov, *Velikorusskie skazki*, no. 7.

78. Bolte and Polívka, *Anmerkungen*, v. 1, p. 183.

79. Rooth, *Cinderella Cycle.*

80. Cox, *Cinderella.* For a guide to recent literature, see Weehee, "Cinderella (A-T 510 A)."

81. Read "*Popović: Pripovetka o devojci bez ruku*, Belgrade, 1905, A. I. Iatsimirskii" (a detailed review) in *Izvestiia otdela russkogo iazyka i slovestnosti Akademii nauk*, v. 16, bk. 3, 1911, pp. 328 ff.

82. [According to *Sravnitel'nyi ukazatel' siuzhetov*, by Varag et al., correspondingly, eighteen, twenty-eight, and forty-six variants.—CE]

83. For example, Bolte and Polívka, *Anmerkungen*, v. 1, no. 31.

84. For more details, see Thompson, *Types of the Folktale* (1964), pp. 240–41.

85. Rybnikov, *Pesni v 4-x tt*, no. 25.

86. Pushkin, *Polnoe sobranie sochineniia*, v. 4, p. 316.

87. For information on more recent literature on fighting dragons, see Roerich, "Drache, Drachenkampf, Drachentöter"; and Varag, "Drachenkampf auf der Brücke (A-T 300 A)."

88. Frazer, *Totemism.*

89. Afanas'ev, Narodnye russkie skazki v 3-kh tt, v. 2, p. 91.

90. Propp, *Istoricheskie korni volshebkoi skazki*, pp. 43–44.

91. Propp, *Istoricheskie korni volshebkoi skazki*, pp. 68–71.

92. Propp, *Istoricheskie korni volshebkoi skazki*, p. 71.

93. Propp, *Istoricheskie korni volshebkoi skazki*, p. 75.

94. Propp, *Istoricheskie korni volshebkoi skazki*, p. 76–77.

95. Propp, *Istoricheskie korni volshebkoi skazki*, pp. 83–84.

96. Propp, *Istoricheskie korni volshebkoi skazki*, p. 91.

97. Propp, *Istoricheskie korni volshebkoi skazki*, p. 120.

NOTES TO CHAPTER 4

1. Gospodarev, *Skazki*, no. 59.

2. Polivka, "Baba khuzhe cherta."

3. Gospodarev, *Skazki*, pp. 515–17.

4. Propp, "Fol'klor i deistvitel'nost'" [original publication in *Russkaia literatura* in 1963—SF]. [Also in Propp, *Fol'klor i deistvitel'nost': Izbrannye stat'i*, pp. 83–115.—CE]

5. Onchukov, *Severnye skazki.*—SF]

6. [According to updated data in Varag et al., *Sravnitel'nyi ukazatel' siuzhetov*, the Russian plot repertoire, out of a combined figure of 1,233 plots, has 119 animal tales, 225 wonder tales, 106 *legendy*, 137 novellistic works, 84 tales about the stupid devil, and 562 anecdotes.—CE]

7. Maspero, *Les contes populaires.*

8. Bolte and Polívka, *Anmerkungen*, v. 4, p. 116.

9. [In the *Primary Chronicle.*—SF]

10. Pauli, *Schimpff und Ernst*, originally published in 1519 and reprinted in 1876.

11. Kirchhof, *Wendungmyth*, originally published in 1565–1603 [and later reprinted in 1869—SF].

12. [For a critical edition of tales before Afanas'ev, see Novikov and Pomerantseva, *Russkie skazki v rannikh zapisiakh*; and Novikov, *Russkie skazki v zapisiakh.*—CE]

13. Tolstoi, "Vozvrashchenie muzha."

14. Afanas'ev, *Narodnye russkie skazki v 3-kh tt*, v. 3, no. 325.

15. Cf. Veselovskii, "Skazki ob Ivane Groznom."

16. Sorokovikov, *Skazki Magaia*, no. 13.

17. Anderson, *Kaiser und Abt*. In 1916 the first part of this study was published in Russian in a more complete form: Anderson, *Imperator i abbat.*

18. Anderson, *Kaiser und Abt*, p. 426.

19. Prato, *La leggenda del tesoro di Rampsinite nelle varie redazione italiane e straniere.*

20. Veselovskii, "Retsenziia."

21. Cf. Andreev's commentary to Veselovskii's review of Prato's book in Veselovskii, *Sobranie sochinenii*, v. 16, pp. 316–18.

22. Veselovskii, "Retsenziia."

23. Veselovskii, "Retsenziia."

24. Bolte and Polívka, *Anmerkungen*, v. 3, p. 393.

25. [In Varag et al., *Sravnitel'nyi ukazatel' siuzhetov*, it is tale type 1525, with twenty-seven subtypes.—CE]

26. Lotman and Kukulevich, "Istochniki ballady Pushkina 'Zhenikh,'" p. 90. [For more information, cf. Novikova and Aleksandrova. *Fol'klor i literatura*, pp. 70–71.—CE]

27. Cf. Propp, *Istoricheskie korni volshebnoi skazki*, ch. 3, para. 18 ("Otrublennyi palets"), pp. 76–77.

28. Iu. M. Sokolov, *Barin i muzhik.*

29. [Propp is speaking here of the tale "The Priest and the Peasant."—CE]

30. Cf. the commentary to Afanas'ev 150 in Afanas'ev, *Narodnye russkie skazki v 3-kh tt*, v. 1, pp. 496–97.

31. Belinsky, *Polnoe sobranie sochinenii*, v. 10, p. 215.

32. Lenin, "K derevenskoi bednote," v. 7, p. 146.

33. [The singing is a parody of misheard liturgical phrases that sounds like traditional folk songs.—CE]

34. Loorits, *Livische Märchen- und Sagenvarianten*.

35. Berezaiskii, *Anekdoty, ili Veselye pokhozhdeniia poshekhontsev*.

36. Engels, "Nemetskie narodnye knigi," p. 348.

37. Gudzii, *Istoriia drevnei russkoi literatury*. [See also Adrianova-Peretts, *Russkaia demokraticheskaia satira*.—CE]

38. [Besides this, *Sravnitel'nyi ukazatel' siuzhetov*, by Varag et al., contains information on ten Ukrainian and five Belarusan recordings.—CE]

39. Adrianova-Peretts, *Ocherki po istorii russkoi satiricheskoi literatury XVII veka*. Commentary to Adrianova-Peretts's collection *Russkaia demokraticheskaia satira XVII veka* includes information on thirty-four recordings.

40. [Thompson, in *The Types of the Folktale* (1964) lists it as a folktale type; it is published in Afanas'ev's *Narodnye russkie legendy*.—SF]

41. Cf. Smirnov, *Sbornik velikorusskikh skazok*. [There are no texts in the collection with the plot type A-T 840 ("Night Visions"). Propp probably has in mind text 98 with plot A-T 840*C (also with the title "Night Visions").—CE]

NOTES TO CHAPTER 5

1. [For a listing of the types of cumulative tales, see Propp, *Fol'klor i deistvitel'nost': Izbrannye stat'i*, pp. 248–57.—CE]

2. B. M. Sokolov, *Russkii fol'klor*, pp. 60–61.

3. Smirnov-Kutachevskii, "Tvorchestvo slova v narodnoi skazke."

4. Tolstoi, "Obriad i legenda" [originally published in *Sovetskii fol'klor* in 1936—SF]. See also Tolstoi, "Obriad i legenda" [1966 reprint in Tolstoi's *Stat'i o fol'klore*—SF], 80–96.

5. Tolstoi, "Obriad i legenda" (1966), p. 93.

6. Bolte and Polívka, *Anmerkungen*, v. 2, p. 104.

NOTES TO CHAPTER 6

1. [In the title, *kleb-sol'* (literally "bread-salt") can be translated as hospitality.—SF]

2. Afanas'ev, *Narodnye russkie skazki* (1936), v. 1, commentary/note to nos. 1–7.

3. Afanas'ev, *Narodnye russkie skazki*, p. 513.

4. [Propp does not cite Brehm, but this information could have come from Brehm et al., *Brehms Tierleben*.—SF]

5. Andreev, "K obzoru russkikh skazochnykh siuzhetov."

6. [According to new and more precise data, animal tales make up 119 plots (9.6 percent) of the Russian plot repertoire (cf. Varag et al., *Sravnitel'nyi ukazatel' siuzhetov*, p. 15).—CE]

7. Bobrov, *Russkie narodnye skazki*, pp. 29 ff.

8. Bobrov, *Russkie narodnye skazki*, p. 33.

9. Andreev, "K obzoru russkikh skazochnykh siuzhetov."

10. Andreev, "K obzoru russkikh skazochnykh siuzhetov," p. 64.

11. Afanas'ev, *Narodnye russkie skazki v 3-kh tt*, v. 1, p. 514.

12. Andreev, "K kharakteristike ukrainskogo skazochnogo materiala." [According to Varag et al., *Sravnitel'nyi ukazatel' siuzhetov* (p. 15), there are 336 types.—CE]

13. Nikiforov, *Narodnaia detskaia skazka*, pp. 49–63.

14. Bobrov, *Russkie narodnye skazki*, p. 35.

15. Kolmachevskii, *Zhivotnyi epos*.

16. Benfey, *Pantschatantra*, v. 1, p. xxi.

17. Kolmachevskii, *Zhivotnyi epos*, p. 145.

18. Bolte and Polívka, *Anmerkungen*, v. 4, p. 341.

19. See Adrianova-Peretts, "Basni Ezopa v russkoi iumoristicheskoi literature."

20. Graf, *Die Grundlagen des Reineke Fuchs*.

21. Dashkevich, *Vopros*, p. 3.

22. Nikiforov, *Narodnaia detskaia skazka*.

23. B. M. Sokolov, "Kompozitsiia i stil' skazok," pp. 60–61.

24. Afanas'ev, *Narodnye russkie skazki* (1855–64).

25. Hnatiuk, *Ukraïnsky narodny baiky*, pp. 37–38.

26. Wundt, *Völkerspsychologie*, v. 2, pp. 155–224.

27. [For pointers to further literature, see Meletinskii, *Paleoaziatskii mifologicheskii èpos*.—CE]

NOTES TO CHAPTER 7

1. Dobroliubov, "Narodnye russkie skazki," p. 591.

2. Rybnikov, *Pesni*, v. 1, pp. x–cii.

3. Gil'ferding, *Onezhskie byliny*. Cf. Astakhova's collection, *Byliny*.

4. Sadovnikov, *Skazki*.

5. Onchukov, *Severnye skazki*.

6. Onchukov, *Pechorskie byliny*.

7. Ol'denburg, "Sobiranie russkikh narodnykh skazok."

8. Oldenbourg, "Le conte dit populaire."

9. Korguev, *Skazki*.

10. Baryshnikova, *Skazki Kuprianikhi*.

11. Sorokovikov, *Skazki Magaia*.

12. Gospodarev, *Skazki*.

13. Azadovskii, *Verkhnelenskie skazki*; and Azadovskii, *Skazki iz raznykh mest Sibiri*.

14. Gofman, "K voprosu ob individual'nom stile skazochnika."

15. Mints, "Cherty individual'nogo i traditsionnogo tvorchestva v skazke o tsare Solomone."

16. Karnaukhova, "Skazochniki i skazki v Zaonezh'e."

17. Azadovskii, *Russkaia skazka* (the introduction, in somewhat revised form, is in Azadovskii's book *Literatura i fol'klor*, pp. 196–273.); Azadovskii, *Eine sibirische Märchenerzählerin*; Azadovskii, *Pohádky z Hrnolenskeho kraje*; and Azadovskii, *Stat'i o literature i fol'klore*.

18. Nikiforov, "K voprosu o zadachakh i metodakh."

19. Nikiforov, Sv'otochasna pinez'ka kazka"; and Nikiforov, "K voprosu o kartografirovanii skazki." [Propp published Nikiforov's collection as *Severnorusskie skazki v zapisiakh A. I. Nikiforova* in 1961.—CE]

20. Nikiforov, *Narodnaia detskaia skazka*, pp. 49–63.

21. Nikiforov, "Finskaia shkola pered krizisom."

22. Grinkova, "Vopros o skazochnike," p. 175.

23. Gor'kii, "Razrushenie lichnosti," v. 24, p. 27.

24. Bonch-Bruevich, "Lenin o poèzii," p. 695.

25. Sartori, "Erzählen als Zauber."

26. Kharuzina, "Vremia i obstanovka rasskazyvaniia povestvovatel'nykh proizvedenii narodnoi slovesnosti."

27. Zelenin, "Religiozno-magicheskaia funktsiia fol'klornykh skazok."

28. Zelenin, "Religiozno-magicheskaia funktsiia," p. 217.

29. See Brodskii, "Sledy professional'nykh skazochnikov."

30. Savchenko, *Russkaia narodnaia skazka*, pp. 42 ff. [See also Savchenko's bibliography.—CE]

31. Azadovskii, "Skazki Ariny Rodionovny."

32. Nikiforov, "Zhanry russkoi skazki," p. 239.

33. Nikiforov, "Zhanry russkoi skazki."

34. Azadovskii, *Literatura i fol'klor*.

35. Zelenin, *Velikorusskie skazki Permskoi gubernii*, v. 11, p. xxxiii.

36. Zelenin, *Velikorusskie skazki Permskoi gubernii*, v. 11, p. xxxiv.

37. Azadovskii, *Literatura i fol'klor*, p. 222.

38. In all, 103 texts were recorded from Filipp Gospodarev (94 of them have been published). There is information suggesting that he knew seven more tales (Gospodarev, *Skazki*).

39. Gospodarev, *Skazki*, p. 65 (the tale "The Soldier's Sons").

40. Karnaukhova, *Skazki*, pp. xxiv–xxv.

41. Baryshnikova, *Skazki Kuprianikhi*.

42. On the existence of Russian folktales in recent decades, see Pomerantseva, *Sud'by russkoi skazki*, pp. 151–201. [Also see Vedernikova, *Russkaia narodnaia skazka*, pp. 116–33.—CE]

SELECTED REFERENCES: PROPP, RUSSIAN FOLKLORE AND
ETHNOGRAPHY, AND TRANSLATIONS OF RUSSIAN FOLK TALES

Afanas'ev, Alexander. *Russian Fairy Tales*, Norman Guterman, trans., with commentary by Roman Jakobson. New York: Pantheon Books, 1973.

Balina, Marina, Helena Goscilo, and Mark Lipovetsky, eds. *Politicizing Magic: An Anthology of Russian and Soviet Fairy Tales*. Evanston, IL: Northwestern University Press, 2005.

Bogatyrev, Pet[e]r, and Roman Jakobson. "Folklore as a Special Form of Creativity." In Peter Steiner, ed., *The Prague School: Selected Writings, 1929–1946*, pp. 32–46. Austin: University of Texas Press, 1982.

Draitser, Emil A. *Taking Penguins to the Movies: Ethnic Humor in Russia*. Detroit, MI: Wayne State University Press, 1998.

Erlich, Victor. *Russian Formalism: History, Doctrine*, 2nd ed. The Hague: Mouton, 1965.

Haney, Jack V., ed. and trans. *An Anthology of Russian Folktales*. Armonk, NY: M. E. Sharpe, 2009.

Ivanits, Linda. *Russian Folk Belief*. Armonk, NY: M. E. Sharpe, 1989.

Miller, Frank J. *Folklore for Stalin: Russian Folklore and Pseudofolklore of the Stalin Era*. Armonk, NY: M. E. Sharpe, 1990.

Olshansky, Dmitry. "The Birth of Structuralism from the Analysis of Fairy-Tales." *Toronto Slavic Quarterly* 25 (summer 2008). http://www.utoronto.ca/tsq/25/ Olshansky25.shtml (accessed April 15, 2010).

Olson, Laura J. *Performing Russia: Folk Revival and Russian Identity*. London: Routledge, 2004.

Paxson, Margaret. *Solovyovo: The Story of Memory in a Russian Village*. Washington, DC: Woodrow Wilson Center Press, and Bloomington, IN: Indiana University Press, 2005.

Propp, Vladimir. *Morphology of the Folktale*. 2nd ed. Rev. and ed. Louis A. Wagner. Austin: University of Texas Press, 1968.

———. *On the Comic and Laughter*, Jean-Patrick Debbeche and Paul J. Perron, trans. Toronto: University of Toronto Press, 2009.

———. *Theory and History of Folklore*, Anatoly Liberman, ed.; Ariadna Y. Martin and Richard P. Martin, trans. Minneapolis: University of Minnesota Press, 1984.

Steiner, Peter. *Russian Formalism: A Metapoetics*. Ithaca, NY: Cornell University Press, 1984.

BIOGRAPHICAL INFORMATION IN RUSSIAN

Ivanov, M. V. "Podniavshii perchatku." *Journal of St. Petersburg University*, 2005, no. 8, pp. 10–17. http://journal.spbu.ru/2005/16/12.shtml (accessed August 10, 2009).

Martynova, A. N., ed. *Neizvestnyj Propp: Nauchnoe izdanie*. St. Petersburg: Izdatel'stvo Aleteia, 2002.

WORKS CITED

Aarne, Antti. *Leitfaden der vergleichenden Märchenforschung*. Folklore Fellows' Communications no. 13. Helsinki, 1913.

———. *Verzeichnis der Märchentypen*. Folklore Fellows' Communications no. 3. Helsinki, 1911.

———. *Verzeichnis der Märchentypen mit Hilfe von Tachgennossen ausgearbeitet von Antti Aarne*. Helsinki, 1910.

Adrianova-Peretts, Varvara P. "Basni Ezopa v russkoi iumoristicheskoi literature XVIII veka." *Izvestiia ORIaS*, 1929, v. 2, no. 2, pp. 377–400.

————. *Ocherki po istorii russkoi satiricheskoi literatury XVII veka.* Leningrad, 1937.

————, ed., comp. *Russkaia demokraticheskaia satira XVII veka,* 2nd ed. Moscow, 1977.

————. *Russkoe narodnoe poeticheskoe tvorchestvo.* Moscow, 1953. (Subsequent volumes were published under different titles.)

Afanas'ev, Aleksandr N. *Narodnye russkie legendy.* Moscow, 1860.

————. *Narodnye russkie skazki.* Moscow, 1936.

————. *Narodnye russkie skazki,* 8 vols. Moscow, 1855–64.

————. *Narodnye russkie skazki v 3-kh tt,* Vladimir Propp, ed. Moscow: Gosudarstvennoe izdatel'stvo "Khudozhestvennoi literatury," 1957.

————. *Poèticheskie vozzreniia slavian na prirodu,* 3 vols. Moscow, 1865–69.

Akimova, Tat'iana M. *Seminarii po narodnomu poèticheskomu tvorchestvu Saratova.* Saratov, 1959.

————, comp. *Skazy o Chapaeve.* Saratov, 1951.

Aksakov, Konstantin S. "O razlichii mezhdu skazkami i pesniami russkimi." In his *Polnoe sobranie sochinenii,* v. 1, pp. 399–408. Moscow, 1861.

Aksakov, Sergei T. *Sobranie sochinenii v 4-kh tomakh.* Moscow, 1955.

Anderson, Valter N. *Imperator i abbat: Istoriia odnogo narodnogo anekdota,* v. 1. Kazan', 1916.

Anderson, Walter. *Kaiser und Abt: Die Geschichte eines Schwanks.* Folklore Fellows' Communications no. 42. Helsinki, 1923.

————. *Schwank vom alten Hildebrand.* Dorpat, 1931.

Andreev, Nikolai P. "Fol'klor i ego istoriia." In his *Russkii fol'klor: Khrestomatiia dlia vysshikh pedagogicheskikh uchebnykh zavedenii.* Leningrad, 1936 (2nd ed., Leningrad, 1938), pp. 20–21.

————. "Izdanie skazok za poslednee piatiletie." *Sovetskii fol'klor,* 1936, no. 2–3, p. 409.

————. "K kharakteristike ukrainskogo skazochnogo materiala." In Petr Emel'ianovich Skachkov and Sergei Fedorovich Ol'denburg, *Sergeiu Fedorovichu Ol'denburgu: k piatidesiatiletiiu nauchno-obshchestvennoi deiatel'nosti, 1882–1932,* pp. 61–73. Leningrad: Izdatel'stvo Akademii nauk SSSR, 1934.

————. "K obzoru russkikh skazochnykh siuzhetov." *Khudozhestvennyi fol'klor,* 1927, v. 2–3, pp. 59–70.

————. "Novye izdaniia skazok na russkom iazyke." *Sovetskii fol'klor,* 1941, no. 7, pp. 221–22.

————. "Problema istorii fol'klora." *Sovetskaia ètnografiia,* 1934, no. 3, pp. 28–45.

————. *Ukazatel' skazochnykh sjuzhetov po sisteme Aarne.* Leningrad, 1929.

Andrejew, Nikolai P. *Die Legende vom Räuber Madej.* Folklore Fellows' Communications no. 69. Helsinki, 1927.

――――. *Die Legende von dem zwei Erzsünder.* Folklore Fellows' Communications no. 54. Helsinki, 1924.

Anikin, Vladimir P. *Russkaia narodnaia skazka.* Moscow, 1959 (2nd ed., Moscow, 1977).

Apulei [Lucius Apuleius]. *Zolotoi osel: Metamorfoza.* Moscow, 1956.

Astakhova, Anna M. *Byliny: Itogi i problemy izucheniia.* Leningrad, 1966.

Avdeeva, Ekaterina A. "Ocherki maslenitsy v Evropeiskoi Rossii i Sibiri, v gorodakh i derevniakh." *Otechestvennye zapiski,* 1849, v. 12.

――――. *Russkie skazki dlia detei, rasskazannye nianiushkoiu Avdot'ei Stepanovnoi Cherep'evoi.* St. Petersburg, 1844.

――――. *Russkii pesennik, ili Sobranie luchshikh i liubopytneishikh pesen, romansov i vodevil'nykh kupletov.* St. Petersburg, 1847.

――――. *Zapiski i zamechaniia o Sibiri.* Moscow, 1837.

――――. *Zapiski o starom i novom russkom byte.* Moscow, 1842.

Averkieva, Iuliia P. *Istoriia teoreticheskoi mysli v amerikanskoi ètnografii.* Moscow, 1979.

Azadovskii, Mark K. *Eine sibirische Märchenerzählerin.* Folklore Fellows' Communications no. 68. Helsinki, 1926.

――――. "Istochniki 'Skazok Pushkina.'" In his *Literatura i fol'klor: Ocherki i ètiudy,* pp. 85–89. Leningrad, 1938.

――――. *Istoriia russkoi fol'kloristiki,* 2 vols. Moscow, 1958–63.

――――. *Literatura i fol'klor: Ocherki i etiudy.* Leningrad, 1938.

――――. *Pohádky z Hrnolenskeho kráje,* pt. 2, *Vestnik Narodno pisny československy.* 1928, pp. xxi–xxii.

――――. *Russkaia skazka: Izbrannye mastera,* 2 vols. Moscow, 1932.

――――. "Skazki Ariny Rodionovny." In his *Literatura i fol'klor: Ocherki i etiudy,* pp. 273–93. Leningrad, 1938.

――――. *Skazki iz raznykh mest Sibiri.* Irkutsk, 1928.

――――. *Stat'i o literature i fol'klore.* Moscow-Leningrad, 1960.

――――. *Verkhnelenskie skazki.* Irkutsk, 1925 (2nd ed., Irkutsk: 1938).

Baryshnikova, Anna K. *Skazki Kuprianikhi,* Anna M. [*sic*] Novikova and Iosif A. Ossovetskii, eds. Voronezh, 1937.

Basset, René. "Les formules dans les contes." *Revue des traditions populaires,* 1902, v. 17, pp. 233–43.

Bastian, Adolf. *Die heilige Sage der Polinisier.* Leipzig, 1881.

――――. *Der Mensch in der Geschichte: Zur Begründung einer psychologischen Weltanschauung,* 3 vols. Leipzig, 1860.

Bazanov, Vasilii G. "Nakanune 'khozhdeniia v narod.'" In Ivan A. Khudiakov, *Velikorusskie skazki v zapisiakh I. A. Khudakova*. Moscow-Leningrad, 1964, pp. 7–49.

Bazanov, Vasilii G., and S. N. Azbelev. *Russkaia literatura i fol'klor, XI–XVIII vv.* Leningrad, 1970.

Bédier, Joseph. *Les fabliaux: Etudes de littérature populaire et d'histoire littéraire du moyen age*. Paris, 1893.

Belinsky, Vissarion G. *Polnoe sobranie sochinenii*, 13 vols. Moscow, 1953–59.

———. "Stat'i o narodnoi poèzii." In his *Polnoe sobranie sochinenii*, v. 5. Moscow, 1956.

Benfey, Theodor. *Pantschatantra*, 2 vols. Leipzig, 1859.

Berezaiskii, Vasilii. *Anekdoty, ili Veselye pokhozhdeniia poshekhontsev*. St. Petersburg, 1798 (2nd ed., St. Petersburg, 1821).

Berkov, Pëtr N. "O tak nazyvaemyx 'petrovskix povestjax.'" *Trudy Otdela Drevnerusskoi Literatury*, 1949, v. 7, pp. 419–28.

Bessonov, Petr A., ed. *Pesni, sobrannye Kireevskim*, v. 4. Moscow, 1862.

Bethe, Erich. *Hessische Blätter für Volkskunde*, bd. 4. Leipzig, 1905.

———. *Mythus, Sage, Märchen*. Leipzig, s.a.

Blagoj, Dmitrii D. *Istorija russkoj literatury XVIII veka*. Moscow, 1945 (4th ed., 1960).

Boas, Franz. *Indianische Sagen von der Nord-Pazifischen Küste Amerikas*. Berlin, 1895.

Bobrov, Vladimir. *Russkie narodnye skazki o zhivotnykh*. Warsaw, 1909.

Bolotov, Andrei T. *Zhizn' i prikljuchenija Andreja Bolotova, opisannye samim im dlja svoikh potomkov*, 3 vols. Moscow-Leningrad, 1931.

Bolte, Johannes. *Name und Merkname des Märchens*. Folklore Fellows' Communications no. 36. Helsinki, 1902.

Bolte, Johannes, and Georg [sic] Polívka. *Anmerkungen zu den Kinder- und Hausmärchen der Brüder Grimm*, 4 vols. Leipzig, 1913–32.

Bonch-Bruevich, Vladimir D. "Lenin o poèzii." In his *V. I. Lenin o literature i iskusstve*. Moscow, 1976.

———. "V. I. Lenin ob ustnom narodnom tvorchestve." *Sovetskaia ètnografiia*, 1954, no. 4.

Brehm, Alfred Edmund, Eduard Oskar Schmidt, and Ernst Ludwig Taschenberg. *Brehms Tierleben: Allgemeine Kunde des Tierreichs*, 10 vols. Leipzig: Bibliographisches Institut, 1876–1879.

Brinton, Daniel G. *Myths of the New World*. New York, 1868.

Brodskii, Nikolai L. "Sledy professional'nykh skazochnikov v russkikh skazkakh." *Ètnograficheskoe obozrenie*, 1904, no. 2, pp. 1–18.

Bromlei, Iulian V. *Ètnografiia za rubezhom: Istoriograficheskie ocherki*. Moscow: Nauka, 1979.

————. *Sovremennye problemy ètnografii (Ocherki teorii i istorii)*. Moscow, 1981.

Bronnitsyn, Bogdan. *Russkie narodnye skazki*. St. Petersburg, 1838.

Buslaev, Fedor I. "Èpicheskaia poèziia." In his *Russkaia narodnaia poèziia*. St. Petersburg, 1861.

————. *Istoricheskie ocherki russkoi narodnoi slovesnosti i iskusstva*, v. 1. St. Petersburg, 1861.

————. "Lektsii po istorii russkoi literatury, chitaemye ego imperatorskomu velichestvu nasledniku tsezarevichu Nikolaiu Aleksandrovichu 1859–1860 gg." *Starina i novizna: Istoricheskii sbornik*, 1904, v. 8

————. *Narodnaia poèziia: Istoricheskie ocherki*. St. Petersburg, 1887.

————. "Perekhozhie povesti i rasskazy." In his *Moi dosugi*, v. 2, pp. 259–406. Moscow, 1886.

————. "Retsenziia na 'Slavianskie skazaniia o Solomone i Kitovrase . . . ,' soch. Akad. A. Veselovskogo." In his *Otchet o shestnadtsatom prisuzhdenii nagrad grafa Uvarova*, pp. 56–57. St. Petersburg, 1874.

————. "Slavianskie skazki." In his *Istoricheskie ocherki russkoi narodnoi slovesnosti i iskusstva*. St. Petersburg, 1861, pp. 308–54.

Chernyshev, Vasilii I. "Tsenzurnye iz''iatiia iz 'Skazok' A. N. Afanas'eva." *Sovetskii fol'klor*, 1935, no. 1–2, pp. 307–15.

Chistov, Kirill V. "V. Ya. Propp: Legend and Fact." *International Folklore Review* 1986, v. 4, pp. 8–17.

————. "Zametki o sbornike N. E. Onchukova *Severnye skazki*." *Trudy Karel'skogo filiala Akademii Nauk SSSR*, 1957, v. 8, pp. 5–29.

Christensen, Arthur. *Motif et thème: Plan d'un dictionnaire de contes populaires, de légendes et de fables*. Folklore Fellows' Communications no. 59. Helsinki, 1925.

Chulkov, Mikhail D. *Peresmeshnik, ili Slovenskie skazki*, 4 vols. Moscow, 1766–84.

Clouston, William A. *Popular Tales and Fictions: Their Migrations and Transformations*, 2 vols. London, 1834.

Collins, Samuel. *The Present State of Russia, in a Letter to a Friend at London*. London, 1667.

Cosquin, Emmanuel. *Les contes indiens et l'Occident*. Paris, 1920.

————. *Contes populaires de Lorraine, comparés avec les contes des autres provinces de France et des pays étrangers et précédés d'un essai sur l'origine et la propagation des contes populaires européens*, 2 vols. Paris, 1887. Published in Russian as E. Kosken, *Issledovanie o proiskhozhdenii i rasprostranenii skazok*, D. Dmitriev, trans. (Kiev, 1907).

————. *Etudes folkloriques*. Paris, 1920.

Cox, Marian R. *Cinderella: 345 Variants of Cinderella, Catskin, and Cap o'Rushee Abstracted and Tabulated, with a Discussion of Medieval Analogies and Notes*. London, 1893.

Creuzer, Georg Friedrich. *Symbolik und Mythologie der alten Völker, besonders der Griechen*. Leipzig, 1843.

Cushing, Frank H. *Zuni Folktales*. New York, 1901.

Dal', Vladimir I. *Povesti, skazki i raskazy Kazaka Luganskogo*. St. Petersburg, 1846.

———. *Russkie skazki, iz predaniia narodnogo izustnogo na gramotu grazhdanskuiu perelozhennye, k bytu zhiteinomu prinorovlennye i pogovorkami khodiachimi razukrashennye Kazakom Vladimirom Luganskim: Piatok pervyi*. St. Petersburg, 1832.

———. *Tolkovyi slovar' velikago russkago iazyka*. Moscow, 1861–67.

Dashkevich, Nikolai P. *Vopros o proiskhozhdenii i razvitii èposa o zhivotnykh po issledovaniiam poslednego tridtsatiletiia*. Kiev, 1904.

Dedushkiny progulki, soderzhashchie v sebe 10 russkikh skazok. St. Petersburg, 1786.

Derzhavina, Ol'ga A. *Fatsetsii (Perevodnaia novella v russkoi literature XVII veka)*. Moscow, 1962.

———. *"Velikoe zertsalo" i ego sud'ba na russkoi pochve*. Moscow, 1965.

Dmitrieva, Rufina P., ed., comp. *Povest' o Petre i Fevronii*. Leningrad, 1979.

Dobroliubov, Nikolai A. "Narodnye russkie skazki." In his *Sobranie sochinenii v 3-x tt.*, v. 1. Moscow, 1950.

Drahomanov, Myhailo P. "Kordeliia-Zamarashka." *Vestnik Evropy*, 1884, no. 2, pp. 53–71.

———. "Luchshii son." *Kievskaia starina*, 1885.

———. *Malorusskie narodnye predaniia i rasskazy*. Kiev, 1876.

———. *Rozvidky pro ukrainsku narodnu slovesnist' i pis'menstvo*, vols. 1–3 and 7. Kiev, 1899–1907.

———. "Sholudivyi Buniaka v ukrainskikh narodnykh skazaniiakh." *Kievskaia starina*, 1887, no. 8, pp. 676–713; no. 10, pp. 233–76.

———. "Slavianskie pererabotki istorii Èdipa." *Kievskaia starina*, 1889, nos. 5–6.

———. "Slavianskie povesti o pozhertvovanii svoego rebenka." *Sbornik za narodny umotvorennia*, 1889, v. 1.

———. "Slavianskie povesti o rozhdenii Konstantina Velikago." *Sbornik za narodny umotvoreniia*, 1889, v. 2–3.

———. "Turetskie anekdoty v ukrainskoi narodnoi slovesnosti." *Kievskaia starina*, 1886, no. 2–3, pp. 209–36.

Dunlop, John. *History of Fiction*, 3 vols. Edinburgh, 1814.

Eleonskaia, Elena N. "Nekotorye zamechaniia o perezhitkakh pervobytnoi kul'tury v skazkakh." *Ètnograficheskoe obozrenie*, 1906, no. 1–2, pp. 63–72.

———. "Nekotorye zamechaniia o roli zagadki v skazke." *Ètnograficheskoe obozrenie*, 1907, no. 4, pp. 78–90.

Engels, Friedrich. "Nemetskie narodnye knigi." In Karl Marks and Fridrikh Engels, *Iz rannikh proizvedenii*, pp. 344–52. Moscow, 1956.

———. "Proiskhozhdeniia sem'i, chastnoi sobstvennosti i gosudarstva." In Karl Marx and Fridrikh Engels, *Sochineniia*, 2nd ed., v. 21. Moscow: Gosudarstvennoe izdatel'stvo politicheskoi literatury, 1955.

Enzyklopädie des Märchens, bd. 1, u. 2. Berlin, 1975–81.

Èrlikh, R. L. "Skazka o lovkom vore." *Iazyk i literatura*, 1932, v. 8, pp. 199–200.

Ètnografiia za rubezhom: Istoriograficheskie ocherki. Moscow, 1979. Filaret [Vasilii M. Drozdov]. *Sobranie mnenii i otzyvov*. St. Petersburg, 1887.

Frank-Kamenetskii, Israel' G. "Gruzinskaia parallel' k drevneegipetskoi povesti o dvukh brat'iakh." *Iafetinskii sbornik*, 1926, issue 4, pp. 39–71.

Frantsov, Iurii P. "Drevneegipetskie skazki o verkhovnykh zhretsakh." *Sovetskii fol'klor*, 1936, no. 2–3, pp. 159 ff.

———. "Zmeinyi ostrov v drevneegipetskoi skazke." *Izvestiia Akademii Nauk, otdela gumanitarnykh nauk*, 1929, no. 10, pp. 817–38.

Frazer, Dzh. [James]. *Zolotaia vetv'*. Moscow, 1981.

Frazer, James G. *The Belief in Immortality and the Worship of the Dead*, 3 vols. London, 1913–24.

———. *The Fear of the Dead in Primitive Religion*. London, 1933.

———. *Folklore in the Old Testament: Studies in Comparative Religion*, 3 vols. London, 1919. Published in Russian as D. Frezer, trans., *Fol'klor v Vetkhom Zavete* (Moscow-Leningrad, 1931).

———. *The Golden Bough*, vols. 1 and 2, London, 1890; vols. 1–3, London, 1900; vols. 1–13, London, 1911–15. Published in Russian as D. Frazer, trans., *Zolotaia vetv'*, vols. 1–4 (Moscow, 1928); V. K. Nikol'skii, ed., *Zolotaia vetv'*, v. 1 (Moscow-Leningrad, 1931); and S. A. Tokarev, ed., *Zolotaia vetv': Issledovanie magii i religii* (Moscow, 1981).

———. *Totemism and Exogamy*, 4 vols. London, 1912.

Freidenberg, Ol'ga M. "Fol'klor u Aristofana." In Petr Emel'ianovich Skachkov and Sergei Fedorovich Ol'denburg, *Sergeiu Fedorovichu Ol'denburgu: k piatidesiatiletiiu nauchno-obshchestvennoi deiatel'nosti, 1882–1932*, pp. 549–60. Leningrad: Izdatel'stvo Akademii nauk SSSR, 1934.

———. *Mif i literatura drevnosti*. Moscow, 1978.

———. "Mif ob Iosife Prekrasnom." *Iazyk i literatura*, 1932, v. 8, pp. 137–58.

———. *Poètika siuzheta i zhanra: Period antichnoi literatury*. Leningrad, 1936.

———. "Slepets nad obryvom." *Iazyk i literatura*, 1932, v. 8, pp. 229–44.

Galakhov, Aleksei D. *Istoriia russkoi slovesnosti, drevnei i novoi*, v. 1, sec. 1. St. Petersburg, 1880.

Gil'ferding, Aleksandr F. *Onezhskie byliny*, 3 vols. St. Petersburg, 1894–1900.

Gofman, E. V. "K voprosu ob individual'nom stile skazochnika." *Khudozhestvennyi fol'klor*, 1929, no. 4–5, pp. 113–20.

Gofman, E. V., and Sofiia I. Mints. *Skazki Kovaleva*. Moscow, 1941.

Gogol, Nikolai V. *Sobranie sochinenii v 6-ti tt*. Moscow, 1953.

Gomme, George L. *The Handbook of Folklore*. London, 1890.

Gor'kii, Maksim. "Razrushenie lichnosti." In his *Sobranie sochinenii v 30-ti tt*, v. 24, pp. 26–27. Moscow, 1953.

Görres, Joseph von. *Mythengeschichte der asiatischen Welt*, 2 vols. Heidelberg, 1810.

Gospodarev, Filipp P. *Skazki F. P. Gospodareva*, Nikolai V. Novikov, ed. Petrozavodsk, 1941.

Graesse, Johann Georg Theodor. *Die großen Sagenkreise des Mittelalters*. Dresden, 1842.

Graf, Adolf. *Die Grundlagen des Reineke Fuchs: Eine vergleichende Studie*. Folklore Fellows' Communications no. 38. Helsinki, 1920.

Grimm, Jacob. *Deutsche Grammatik*, 4 vols. Leipzig, 1819.

———. *Deutsche Mythologie*. Göttingen, 1835.

Grimm, Jakob, and Wilhelm Grimm. *Kinder und Hausmärchen*, 3 vols. Berlin, 1812, 1815, 1822.

Grin, M. M. "O dvukh legendakh iz 'Komu na Rusi zhit' khorosho.'" *N. A. Nekrasov i russkaia literatura vtoroi poloviny XIX–nachala XX veka: Mezhvuzovskij sbornik nauchnykh trudov*, 1979, v. 56, pp. 25–26.

———. "Spor o velikom greshnike (Nekrasovskaja legenda 'O dvukh velikikh greshnikakh' i ee istoki)." *Russkij fol'klor*, 1962, no. 7, pp. 84–98.

Grinkova, Nadezhda P. "Vopros o skazochnike v russkoi fol'kloristike." In Petr Emel'ianovich Skachkov and Sergei Fedorovich Ol'denburg, *Sergeiu Fedorovichu Ol'denburgu: k piatidesiatiletiiu nauchno-obshchestvennoi deiatel'nosti, 1882–1932*. Leningrad: Izdatel'stvo Akademii nauk SSSR, 1934.

Gruzinskii, Aleksei E. *Bibliografiia Afanas'eva: Narodnye russkie skazki*, 3rd ed. Moscow, 1897.

Gudzii, Nikolai K. *Istoriia drevnei russkoi literatury*. Moscow, 1953.

———. *Istoriia drevnei russkoi literatury: Uchebnik dlia vuzov*. Moscow, 1941.

Gukovskii, Grigorii A., ed. *Istoriia russkij literatury*, 10 vols. Moscow-Leningrad, 1941.

Hahn, Johann Georg von. *Griechische und albanische Märchen*. Leipzig, 1864.

Hartland, Edwin S. *The Legend of Perseus*, 3 vols. London, 1894–96.

Hnatiuk, Volodymyr M. *Ukraïnsky narodny baiky*. Etnohrafichnyi Zbirnik, L'viv, 1916.

Honti, János [H.]. *Volksmärchen und Heldensagen*. Folklore Fellows' Communications no. 95. Helsinki, 1931.

Ivanov, M. V. "Podniavshii perchatku." *Journal of St. Petersburg University*, 2005, no. 8, pp. 10–17. http://journal.spbu.ru/2005/16/12.shtml (accessed August 10, 2009).

Kahlo, Gerhard. *Die Verse in Sagen und Märchen*. Berlin, 1919.

Kalevala: Karelo-finskii narodnyi èpos, L. P. Belskogo, trans.; with introduction and notes by E. G. Katarova. Petrozavodsk, 1940.

Karnaukhova, Irina V., ed. *Skazki i predaniia Severnogo kraia*. Moscow, 1934.

———. "'Skazochniki i skazki v Zaonezh'e': Krest'ianskoe iskusstvo SSSR." In her *Iskusstvo Severa: Zaonezh'e*, v. 1, pp. 104–20. Leningrad, 1927.

Keightley, Thomas. *Tales and Popular Fictions: Their Resemblance and Transmission from Country to Country*. London, 1834.

Khalanskii, Mikhail E. "Skazki." *Istoriia russkoi literatury*, 1908, v. 1, no. 2, p. 144.

Kharuzina, Vera N. "Vremia i obstanovka rasskazyvaniia povestvovatel'nykh proizvedenii narodnoi slovesnosti." *Uchenicheskie Zapiski Instituta istorii TANION*, 1929, v. 3, pp. 43–57.

Khudiakov, Ivan A. *Velikorusskie skazki*, 2 vols. Moscow, 1860–62.

———. *Velikorusskie zagadki*. Moscow, 1861.

———. *Verkhoianskii sbornik*. Irkutsk, 1890.

Kirchhof, Hans Wilhelm. *Wendungmyth*, 5 vols., H. Oesterley, ed. Tübingen, 1869.

Kireevskii, Petr V. *Pesni, sobrannye P. V. Kireevskim*, P. A. Bessonova, ed. v. 3, Moscow, 1861; v. 4, Moscow, 1862.

Kirpichnikov, Aleksandr I. *Poèmy lombardskogo tsikla*. Moscow, 1973.

Klinger, Vitol'd P. "Dve antichnye skazki ob orle i ikh pozdneishie otrazheniia." *Kievskie universitetskie izvestiia*, 1913.

———. *Skazochnye motivy v "Istorii" Gerodota*. Kiev, 1903.

———. *Zhivotnye v antichnom i sovremennom sueverii*. Kiev, 1911.

Köhler Rainhold. *Aufsätze über Märchen und Volkslieder*. Berlin, 1894.

———. *Kleine Schriften*, 3 vols. Weimar, 1898–1900.

Kolesnitskaia, I. M. "Zagadki v skazke." *Uchenye zapiski Leningradskogo universiteta*, 1941, v. 12, pp. 98–142.

Kolmachevskii, Leonard Z. *Zhivotnyi èpos na Zapade i u slavian*. Kazan', 1882.

Komarov, M. N. *Èkskursy v skazochnyi mir*. Moscow, 1886.

Konkka, U. S. "'Finskaia shkola' o skazke." *Voprosy literatury i narodnogo tvorchestva*, 1959, v. 20, pp. 3–29.

Korguev, Matvei M. *Skazki M. M. Korgueva*, 2 vols., Aleksandr N. Nechaev, ed. Petrozavodsk, 1939.

Kotliar, Elena S. *Mif i skazka Afriki*. Moscow, 1975.

Kotliarevskii, Aleksandr A. "Desiatyi (1888) i trinadtsatyi otchety o prisuzhdenii nagrad gr. Uvarova." In his *Sochineniia*, v. 2, pp. 256–358. St. Petersburg, 1889.

———. "Razbor sochinenii A. Afanas'eva." In his *Sochineniia*, v. 2, pp. 345–46. St. Petersburg, 1889.

———. *Starina i narodnost'*. St. Petersburg, 1861.

Krohn, Kaarle. *Die folklorische Arbeitsmethode*. Oslo, 1926.

Kuhn, Adalbert. *Die Herabkunft des Feuers und des Göttertranks*. Berlin, 1895.

Kulish, Panteleimon. *Zapiski o Iuzhnoi Rusi*. Kiev, 1857.

Kurganov, Nikolai G. *Pis'movnik*, 2 vols. St. Petersburg, 1790.

Kuz'min, V. D. "Literatura petrovskogo vremeni." In Grigorii Gukovskii, ed., *Istoriia russkoj literatury*, v. 3, pp. 118–34. Moscow-Leningrad, 1941.

Lang, Andrew. *Custom and Myth*. London, 1884.

———. *Magic and Religion*. London, 1901.

———. *The Making of Religion*. London, 1899.

———. *Modern Mythology*. London, 1897.

———. "Mythology." In *Encyclopedia Britannica*, v. 17. Translated into Russian as *Mifologiia*, N. N. Kharuzin and V. N. Kharuzina, trans., eds. (Moscow: V. Lind, 1901).

———. *Myth, Ritual, and Religion*, 2 vols. London, 1887.

———. *The Secret of the Totem*. London, 1905.

———. *Social Origins*. London, 1903.

Lehmann, A. "Dreiheit und dreifache Steigerung im deutschen Volksmärchen." Leipzig: Buchdruckerei R. Noske, 1914.

Lekarstvo ot zadumchivosti i bessonitsy, ili nastol'nye russkie skazki. St. Petersburg, 1786.

Lenin, Vladimir I. "K derevenskoi bednote." In his *Polnoe sobranie sochinenii*, v. 7, pp. 128–203. Moscow: Gosudarstvennoe izdatel'stvo politicheskoi literatury, 1958–65.

Levshin, Vasilii. *Russkie skazki, soderzhashchie Drevneishie Povestvovaniia o slavnykh bogatyriakh, skazki narodnye i prochie, ostavshiesia cherez pereskazyvanie v pamiati. Prikliucheniia*, pt. 1. Moscow, 1780.

Lévy-Bruhl, Lucien. *Les fonctions mentales dans les sociétés inférieures*. Paris, 1910.

———. *La mentalité primitive*. Paris, 1922. Translated into Russian as L. Levi-Briul', *Pervobytnoe myshlenie* (Moscow, 1930).

———. *Sverkh''estestvennoe v pervobytnom myshlenii*. Moscow: Gosudarstevnnoe antireligioznoe izdatel'stvo, 1937.

Liebrecht, Felix. *Jarhbuch für romanische und englische Literatur zur Volkskunde*. Berlin, 1879.

Loorits, Oskar. *Livische Märchen- und Sagenvarianten*. Folklore Fellows' Communications no. 66. Helsinki, 1926.

Lotman, L., and A. Kukulevich. "Istochniki ballady Pushkina 'Zhenikh.'" *Studencheskie zapiski filologicheskogo fakul'teta LGU*, 1937, pp. 90–111.

Lupanova, Irina P. *Russkaia narodnaia skazka v tvorchestve pisatelei pervoi poloviny XIX veka.* Petrozavodsk, 1959.

Lur'e, Solomon Ia. "Dom v lesu." *Iazyk i literatura*, 1932, v. 8, p. 177.

Mackensen, L., ed. *Handwörterbuch des deutschen Märchens.* Berlin, 1931.

Makarov, Mikhail N. "Dogadki ob istorii russkikh skazok." *Moskovskii telegraf*, 1830, pt. 36, pp. 157–64.

———. "Listki iz probnykh listkov dlia sostavleniia istorii russkikjh skazok." *Teleskop*, 1833, pt. 17, nos. 17, 19; pt. 18, nos. 21, 23, 24.

Maksymovich, Mykhailo A. *Malorossiiskie pesni.* Moscow, 1827.

———. *Tri skazki i odna pobasenka.* Kiev, 1845.

Marmontel, Jean-François. *Contes moraux*, 2 vols. Paris, 1761.

Marr, Nikolai Ia. *Izbrannye raboty*, v. 1. Leningrad, 1934.

———, ed. *Tristan i Isol'da: Ot geroini liubvi feodal'noi Evropy do bogini matriarkhal'noi Afrevrazii—Sbornik statei.* Trudy Institute iazyka i myshleniia Akademii Nauk SSSR, no. 2. Leningrad, 1932.

Maspero, Gaston. *Les contes populaire de l'Egypte ancienne.* Paris, 1882.

Megas, Georgios. *Das Märchen von Amur und Psyche in der griechischen Volksüberlieferung (AaTh 425, 428, 432).* Athens, 1971.

Meletinskii, Eleazar M. *Geroi volshebnoi skazki: Proiskhozhdenie obraza.* Moscow, 1958.

———. *Paleoaziatskii mifologicheskii èpos: Tsikl Vorona.* Moscow, 1979.

———. "Strukturno-tipologicheskoe izuchenie skazki." In Vladimir Propp, ed., *Morfologiia skazki*, pp. 161–62. Moscow, 1969.

Mel'ts, Mikaela Ia. *Russkii fol'klor: Bibliograficheskij ukazatel'*, 4 vols. Leningrad, 1961–81.

Merzliakov, Aleksei F. *Kratkaia ritorika, ili Pravila, otnosiashchiesia ko vsem rodam sochinenii prozaicheskikh.* Moscow, 1828.

Mify narodov mira: Èntsiklopediia, 2 vols. Moscow, 1980, 1981.

Miller, Orest F. *Opyt istoricheskogo obozreniia russkoi slovesnosti.* St. Petersburg, 1865.

———. "Razbor 'Sbornika russkikh skazok' A. N. Afanas'eva." *Tridtsat' chetvertoe i poslednee prisuzhdenie uchrezhdennykh P. D. Demidovym nagrad*, 1866, pp. 72–107.

Miller, Vsevolod F. *Ekskursy v oblast' russkogo narodnogo èposa*, 3 vols. Moscow, 1892.

———. "Kavkazskie skazaniia o tsiklopakh." *Ètnograficheskoe obozrenie*, 1890, issue 4, no. 1.

———. "Kavkazskie skazaniia o velikanakh, prikovannykh k goram." *Zhurnal Ministerstvo narodnogo Prosviashcheniia*, 1883, no. 1.

———. "K pesniam, skazkam i predaniiam o Petre Velikom." *Russkii filologicheskii vestnik*, 1909, v. 61.

———. "K skazkam ob Ivane Groznom." *Izvestiia Otdeleniia Russkogo Iazyka i Slovesnosti*, 1909, v. 14, no. 2, pp. 85–104.

———. *Osetinskie ètiudy*, 3 vols. Moscow, 1881–87.

———. "Spisok trudov." In N. A. Ianchuk, ed., *Iubileinyi sbornik v chest' Vsevoloda Fedorovicha Millera*, pp. xiii–xvii. Moscow, 1900.

———. "Vostochnye i zapadnye rodichi odnoi russkoi skazki." *Izvestiia Obshchestva liubitelei estestvoznaniia, antropologii i etnografii*, 1877, v. 28, pp. 174–90.

———. "Vsemirnaia skazka v kul'turno-istoricheskom osveshchenii." *Russkaia mysl'*, 1893, November, pp. 207–29.

Mints, Sofiia I. "Cherty individual'nogo i traditsionnogo tvorchestva v skazke o tsare Solomone." *Khudozhestvennyi fol'klor*, 1929, v. 4–5, pp. 107–13.

Mirer, Semën, and V. Borovik, recorders. *Rasskazy rabochikh o Lenine*. Moscow, 1934.

Moiseev, G. N. *Russkie povesti pervoj treti XVIII veka*. Moscow-Leningrad, 1965.

Morgan, Lewis H. *Ancient Society, or Researches in the Lines of Human Progress from Savagery Through Barbarism to Civilisation*. London, 1877. Translated into Russian as *Drevnee obshchestvo*, M. O. Kosven, ed. (Leningrad, 1935).

Müller, Max. "The Migration of Fables." In his *Selected Essays on Language, Mythology, and Religion*, v. 1, pp. 500–47. London, 1881.

Nekrasov, Nikolai A. *Polnoe sobranie sochinenii i pisem*. Moscow, 1949.

Nikiforov, Aleksandr I. Commentary in *Uchenye zapiski pedagogicheskogo instituta im. A. I. Gertsena*, 1940, v. 3, issue 2, pp. 253–54.

———. "Finskaia shkola pered krizisom." *Sovetskaia ètnografiia*, 1934, no. 4, pp. 141–44.

———. "K voprosu o kartografirovanii skazki." *Skazochnaia kommissiia v 1926 g.*, 1927, pp. 60–66.

———. "K voprosu o morfologicheskom izuchenii narodnoi skazki." *Sbornik otdela russkogo iazyka i slovesnosti*, 1928, v. 1, no. 8, pp. 173–77.

———. "K voprosu o zadachakh i metodakh sobiraniia proizvedenii narodnoi slovesnosti." *Izvestiia GRGO*, 1928, v. 10, issue 1.

———. "Motiv, funktsiia, stil' i klassovyi refleks v skazke." In *Sbornik statei k 40-letiiu uchenoi deiatel'nosti akad. A. S. Orlova*, pp. 287–93. Leningrad, 1934.

———. *Narodnaia detskaia skazka dramaticheskogo zhanra*. Leningrad, 1928.

———. *Obzor rabot skazochnoi kommissii za 1927 god*. Leningrad, 1928.

———. "Rosiis'ka dokuchna kazka." *Etnohrafiches'ky visnyk*, 1932, v. 10.

———. "Russkaia literatura XI–nachala XIII veka." In *Istoriia russkoi literatury*, v. 1, ch. 2. Moscow-Leningrad, 1941.

———. *Severnorusskie skazki v zapisiakh A. I. Nikiforova*, Vladimir Ia. Propp, ed. Moscow-Leningrad, 1961.

————. "Skazka, ee bytovanie i nositeli." In Ol'ga I. Kapica, *Russkaia narodnaia skazka*, pp. 7–55. Moscow-Leningrad, 1930.

————. "Struktura chukotskoi skazki kak iavleniia primitivnogo myshleniia." *Sovetskii fol'klor*, 1936, no. 2–3, pp. 233–73.

————. "Sv'otochasna pinez'ka kazka." *Etnnohrafichnii visnyk*, 1929, v. 8, pp. 52–96.

————. "Vazhneishie stilevye linii v tekste sev. russkoi skazki." *Slavia*, 1934, v. 13, pt. 1, pp. 52 ff.

————. "Zhanry russkoi skazki." *Uchenye zapiski fakul'teta iazyka i literatury ped. instituta im. Pokrovskogo*, 1938, issue 1, v. 2, pp. 233–59.

Novikov, Nikolai V. *Obrazy vostochnoslavianskoi volshebnoi skazki*. Leningrad, 1974.

————. *Russkie skazki v zapisiakh i publikatsiiakh pervoi poloviny XIX veka*. Leningrad, 1961.

Novikov, Nikolai V., and Erna V. Pomerantseva, comps. *Russkie skazki v rannikh zapisiakh i publikatsiiakh (XVI–XVIII vv.)*. Moscow, 1971.

Novikova, Anna M., and Evdokiia A. Aleksandrova. *Fol'klor i literatura: Seminarii*. Moscow, 1978.

Novopol'tsev, Abram K. *Skazki*. Kuibyshev, 1952.

Oldenbourg, S. "Le conte dit populaire: problèmes et methodes." *Revue des études slaves*, 1929, v. 9, fasc. 3–4, pp. 221–36.

Ol'denburg, Sergei F. "Buddiiskie legendy i buddizm." *Zapiski Vostochnogo otdela russkogo arkheologicheskogo obshchestva*, 1896, v. 9, pp. 157–65.

————. "Fablo vostochnogo proiskhozhdeniia." *Zhurnal Ministerstva narodnogo prosveshcheniia*, 1903, no. 4, pp. 217–38; 1906, no. 10; 1907, no. 5.

————. "Sobiranie russkikh narodnykh skazok v poslednee vremia." *Zhurnal Ministerstva narodnogo prosveshcheniia*, 1916, v. 14, no. 8, pp. 296–322.

————. "Stranstvovanie skazki." *Vostok*, 1924, no. 4.

Olrik, Axel. *Epische Gesetzte der Volksdichtung*. Helsinki, 1910 (?).

Onchukov, Nikolai E. *Pechorskie byliny*. St. Petersburg, 1904.

————. *Severnye skazki*. Zapiski RGO, v. 33. St. Petersburg, 1908.

Ostolopov, Nikolai. *Slovar' drevnei i novoi poezii*. St. Petersburg, 1821.

Paris, Gaston. *Les contes orientaux dans la literature française du moyen age*. Paris, 1875.

Pauli, Johannes. *Schimpff und Ernst: Nästbuchlein*. Strassburg, 1519 (later ed. 1876).

Pershits, Abram I. "Periodizatsiia pervobytnoi istorii: Sostoianie problemy." *Voprosy istorii*, 1980, no. 3.

Pervobytnoe obshchestvo: Osnovnye problemy razvitiia. Moscow, 1975.

Petsch, Robert. *Formelhafte Schlüsse im Volksmärchen*. Stuttgart, 1900.

Poggio, Bracciolini. *Liber facetiarum*. s.l., 1470.

Pokrovskii, M. M. "Opyt novogo tolkovaniia komedii Plavta v sviazi s voprosom o fol'klore i novoatticheskoi komedii." *Izvestiia Akademii nauk SSSR*, no. 4, 1932.

Polivka, Georg. "Les nombres 9 et 3 × 9 dans contes des Slaves de l'Est." *Revue des études slaves*, 1927, v. 7, pp. 217–23.

Polivka, Izhi. "Baba khuzhe cherta." *Russkii filologicheskii vestnik*, 1910, no. 2.

Pomerantseva, Erna V. *Mifologicheskie personazhi v russkom fol'klore*. Moscow, 1975.

———. "Russkaia skazka v nachale XX v." In her *Sud'by russkoi skazki*, pp. 131–50. Moscow, 1965.

———. *Sud'by russkoi skazki*. Moscow, 1965.

Potapin, R. P. *Ocherki severo-zapadnoi Mongolii*, 4 vols. St. Petersburg, 1883.

———. *Vostochnye motivy v srednevekovom evropeiskom èpose*. Moscow, 1899.

Potebnia, Aleksandr A. "O Dole i srodnykh s neiu sushchestvakh." *Chteniia Obshchestva istorii i Drevnosti rossiiskikh*, 1867, v. 1, pp. 153–96.

———. *O mificheskom znachenii nekotorykh obriadov i poverii*. In *Chteniia Obshchestva istorii i drevnosti rossiiskikh*. Moscow: Izdatel'stvo moskovskogo universiteta, 1865.

Prato, Stanislav. *La leggenda del tesoro di Rampsinite nelle varie redazione italiane e straniere*. Como, 1882.

Priima, Fedor A. *Russkaia literatura i fol'klor (pervaia polovina XIX veka)*. Leningrad, 1976.

Propp, Vladimir Ia. "A. I. Nikiforov i ego *Severnorusskie skazki*." In A. I. Nikiforov, *Severnorusskie skazki v zapisiakh*, pp. 5–24. Moscow-Leningrad, 1961.

———. "Èdip v svete fol'klora." In his *Fol'klor i deistvitel'nost': Izbrannye stat'i*, pp. 258–59. Moscow, 1976.

———. "Fol'klor i deistvitel'nost'." *Russkaia literatura*, 1963, no. 3.

———. *Fol'klor i deistvitel'nost': Izbrannye stat'i*. Moscow, 1976.

———. *Istoricheskie korni volshebkoi skazki*. Leningrad, 1946.

———. "K voprosu o proiskhozhdenii volshebnoi skazki (Volshebnoe derevo na mogile)." *Sovetskaia etnografiia*, 1934, no. 1–2, pp. 128–51.

———. "Legenda." In his *Russkoe narodnoe poèticheskoe tvorchestvo*, v. 2, bk. 1, *Ocherki po istorii russkogo narodnogo poèticheskogo tvorchestva serediny XVII–pervoi poloviny XIX veka*, pp. 378–86. Moscow-Leningrad, 1954.

———. *Morfologiia skazki*. Leningrad, 1928 (2nd ed., Moscow, 1969).

———. "Motiv chudesknogo rozhdeniia." In his *Fol'klor i deistvitel'nost': Izbrannye stat'i*, pp. 205–40. Moscow, 1976. Originally published in *Uchenye zapiski Leningradskogo universiteta*, 1941, no. 81, vyp. 12, pp. 67–97.

———. "Muzhskoi dom v russkoi skazke." *Uchenye zapiski Leningradskogo universiteta*, 1939, no. 20, pp. 174–98.

———. "Ritual'nyi smekh v fol'klore (po povodu skazki o Nesmeiane)." In his *Fol'klor i deistvitel'nost': Izbrannye stat'i*, pp. 174–204. Moscow, 1976. Originally published in *Uchenye zapiski Leningradskogo universiteta*, 1939, no. 46, pp. 151–75.

———. *Russkaia skazka*, Kirill Vasil'evich Chistov and Valeriia Igorevna Eremina, eds. Leningrad: Izdatel'stvo LGU, 1984.

———. "Transformatsii volshebnykh skazok." In his *Poètika*, v. 4, pp. 70–90. Leningrad, 1928.

———. "Trudy I. I. Tolstogo po fol'kloru." In Ivan I. Tolstoi, *Stat'i o fol'klore*, pp. 3–17. Moscow-Leningrad, 1966.

Pryzhov, Ivan G. *Ocherki, stat'i, pis'ma*. Leningrad, 1934.

Pushkin, Aleksandr S. *Polnoe sobranie sochineniia*. Moscow-Leningrad, 1949.

Putilov, Boris N. *Metodologiia sravnitel'no-istoricheskogo izucheniia fol'klora*. Leningrad, 1976.

Pypin, Aleksandr N. "Afanas'ev i ego trudy po izucheniiu russkoi stariny." In A. N. Afanas'ev, *Narodnye russkie legendy*, p. cxvi. Kazan', 1914.

———. "Aleksandr N. Afanas'ev: *Russkie narodnye skazki*." *Otechestvennye zapiski*, 1856, v. 105, pp. 47–48.

———. *Istoriia russkoi ètnografii*, 2 vols. St. Petersburg, 1891.

———. *Istoriia russkoi literatury*, 4 vols. St. Petersburg, 1899.

———. *Ocherk literaturnoi istorii starinnykh povestei i skazok russkikh*. St. Petersburg, 1857.

———. *Ocherk literaturnoi istorii starinnykh povestei i skazok russkikh*, pt. 4. St. Petersburg: Uchenye zapiski 2 otdela, Akademii Nauk, 1858.

Rand, Silas T. *Legends of the Micmacs*. New York, 1894.

Ranke, Kurt. *Die zwei Brüder*. Folklore Fellows' Communications no. 114. Helsinki, 1934.

Roerich, L. "Drache, Drachenkampf, Drachentöter." In *Enzyklopädie des Märchens*, v. 3, lf 2/3, pp. 787–820. Berlin, 1975.

Romanov, Eudakim G. *Belorusskii sbornik*. v. 3 Vitebsk, 1887; v. 4, Vitebsk, 1891.

Rooth, Anna B. *The Cinderella Cycle*. Lund, 1951.

Rosianu, Nicolae. *Traditsionnye formuly skazki*. Moscow, 1974.

Rybnikov, Pavel N. *Pesni v 4-x tt*. St. Petersburg, 1861–67.

Sacy, Silvestre de. *Calila et Dimna ou fables de Bidpay en arabe*. Paris, 1816.

Sadovnikov, Dmitrii N. *Skazki i predaniia Samarskogo kraia*. Zapiski GRGO, Ethnography Section, v. 12. St. Petersburg, 1884.

———. *Zagadki russkogo naroda*. St. Petersburg, 1875 (2nd ed. St. Petersburg, 1901).

Saintyves, Pierre. *Les contes de Perrault et les récits parallèles*. Paris, 1923.

Sakharov, Ivan P. *Russkie narodnye skazki*. St. Petersburg, 1841.

———. *Skazaniia ruskogo naroda*, v. 1. Moscow, 1836.

Sartori, Paul. "Erzählen als Zauber." *Zeitschrift für Volkskunde*, n.s., 1930, v. 2, pp. 40–45.

Savchenko, S. V. *Russkaia narodnaia skazka: Istoriia sobiraniia i izucheniia*. Kiev, 1914.

Schleicher, A. *Litawische Märchen: Sprichwörter, Räthsel und Lieder*. Leipzig, 1857.

Schott, Arthur, and Albert Schott. *Walachische Märchen*. s.l., 1845.

Schwab, Gustav. *Die schönsten Sagen des Klassischen Altertums*, v. 1, *Teil Gütersloh*. Leipzig, 1882.

Schwartz, Wilhelm. *Die poetische Naturanschauung der Griechen, Römer und Deutschen in ihren Beziehung zur Mythologie der Urzeit*, 2 vols. Volume 1, *Sonne, Mond und Sterne*, Berlin, 1864; v. 2, *Wolken und Wind, Blitz und Donner*, Berlin, 1879.

Shein, Pavel V. *Materialy dlia izucheniia byta i iazyka russkogo naseleniia Severo-Zapadnogo kraia*. Belorusskii sbornik, v. 2. St. Petersburg, 1891.

Shepping, Dmitrii O. "Ivan-tsarevich, narodnyi russkii bogatyr'." *Moskvitianin*, 1852, no. 21, pt. 3.

———. "Kosmogonicheskoe znachenie russkikh skazok i bylin." In his *Russkaia narodnost' v ee poveriiakh, obriadakh i skazkakh*, pp. 71–116. Moscow, 1862.

———. ["Otvet K. Aksakovu"]. *Moskvitianin*, 1853, no. 1, pt. 8, pp. 50–54.

Shishkov, Aleksandr S. *Razgovory o slovesnosti mezhdu dvumia litsami Az i Buki*. St. Petersburg, 1811.

Shklovskii, Viktor B. *O teorii prozy*. Moscow, 1929.

Simonsuuri, Lauri. *Typen und Motivverzeichnis der finnischen mythischen Sagen*. Folklore Fellows' Communications no. 182. Helsinki, 1961.

Sipovskii, Vasilii V. *Ocherki iz istorii russkogo romana (XVIII vek)*, v. 1, sections 1 and 2. St. Petersburg, 1909.

Skripil', Mikhail O., and I. P. Eremin. *Russkaia povest' XVII veka*. Moscow, 1954.

Smirnov, Aleksandr M. *Sbornik velikorusskikh skazok arkhiva Russkogo Geograficheskogo Obschestva*, 2 vols. Petrograd, 1917.

———. "Sistematicheskii ukazatel' tem i variantov russkikh narodnykh skazok." *Izvestiia otdela russkogo iazyka i slovesnosti*, v. 14, no. 4, 1911–12; v. 17, no. 3, St. Petersburg, 1912; no. 4, Prague, 1915.

Smirnov-Kutachevskii, A. M. "Tvorchestvo slova v narodnoi skazke." *Khudozhestvennyi fol'klor*, 1927, issue 2–3.

Snegirev, Ivan M. *Lubochnye kartinki russkogo naroda v moskovskom mire*. Moscow, 1861.

Sokolov, Boris M. "Kompozitsiia i stil' skazok o zhivotnykh." *Russkii fol'klor*, 1929, v. 1, pp. 60–61.

————. *Russkii fol'klor*, v. 2. Moscow, 1930.

Sokolov, Boris M., and Iurii M. Sokolov. *Skazki i pesni Belozerskogo kraia*. Moscow, 1915.

Sokolov, Iurii M., ed. and comp. *Barin i muzhik*. Moscow-Leningrad, 1932.

————. *Russkii fol'klor*. Moscow, 1938 (2nd ed., Moscow, 1941).

————. "Zhizn' i deiatel'nost' A. N. Afanas'eva." In A. N. Afanas'ev, *Narodnye russkie skazki*, v. 1, pp. ix–lvii. Moscow, 1936.

Sorokovikov, Egor I. *Skazki Magaia*, Mark K. Azadovskii, ed. Leningrad, 1940.

Sovetov, S. S. "Odin iz obrazov 'ognia' i 'vody' v serbskikh i slavianskikh skazkakh." In I. I. Meshchaninov, ed., *Pamiati akad. N. Ia. Marra*. Leningrad, 1938.

Sozonovich, Ivan P. *K voprosu o zapadnom vliianii na slavianskuiu i russkuiu poeziiu*. Warsaw, 1898.

————. *"Lenora" Biurgera i rodstvennye ei siuzhety v narodnoi poèzii evropeiskoi i russkoi*. Warsaw, 1893.

————. *Pesni o devushke-voine i byliny o Stavre Godinoviche*. Warsaw, 1886.

————. "Poèticheskii motiv o vnezapnom vozvrashchenii muzha ko vremeni svad'by svoei zheny, sobiravsheisia vyiti zamuzh za drugogo." *Varshavskie universitetskie izvestiia*, 1897, vols. 2–6; 1898, vols. 1–2.

Speranskii, Mikhail N. *Russkaia ustnaia slovesnost'*. Moscow, 1917.

————. "Spisok uchenykh trudov V. F. Millera." *Otchet imperial'nogo Moskovskogo universitetaza 1913 god*, 1914, pt. 1.

Sreznevskii, Izmail I. "Vzgliad na pamiatniki ukrainskoi narodnoi slovesnosti." *Uchenye zapiski Moskovskogo universiteta*, 1834, pt. 6, p. 134.

Stasov, Vladimir V. "Proiskhozhdenie russkikh bylin." *Vestnik Evropy*, 1868, no. 1–4.

————. *Sobranie sochinenii*. St. Petersburg, 1894.

Sumtsov, Nikolai F. *Kul'turnye perezhivaniia*. Kiev, 1890.

————. "Muzh na svad'be svoei zheny." *Ètnograficheskoe obozrenie*, 1893, v. 19, no. 4.

————. "Otchet o piatom prisuzhdenii premii Makariia, mitropolita Moskovskogo." *Zapiski Akadamii nauk*, 1895, v. 25, no. 41.

————. "Otgoloski khristianskikh predanii v mongol'skikh skazkakh." *Ètnograficheskoe obozrenie*, 1893, v. 6, pp. 1–20.

————. "Skazka." In *Èntsiklopedicheskii slovar' Brokgauza i Èfrona*, v. 59, pp. 162–64. St. Petersburg, 1900.

Thompson, Stith. *Motive-Index of Folk Literature*, 4 vols. Helsinki, 1932–34 (2nd ed., Bloomington, 1955–58).

————. *The Types of the Folktale*. Folklore Fellows' Communications no. 74. Helsinki, 1927.

———. *The Types of the Folktale: A Classification and Bibliography*—A. Aarne's *"Verzeichnis der Märchentypen"* (FFC no. 3), 2nd ed. Folklore Fellows' Communications no. 184. Helsinki, 1964.

Tokarev, Sergei A. *Istoriia zarubezhnoi ètnografii*. Moscow, 1978.

———. *Religioznye verovaniia vostochnoslavianskikh narodov XIX–nachala XX veka*. Moscow-Leningrad, 1957.

Tolstoi, Ivan I. "Drevnegrecheskii fol'klor i literatura (russkii fol'klor)." In his *Stat'i o fol'klore*. Moscow-Leningrad, 1966.

———. "'Gekal' Kallimakha i russkaia skazka o babe-iage." In his *Stat'i o fol'klore*, pp. 142–56. Moscow-Leningrad, 1966.

———. "Iazyk skazki v grecheskoi literature." In his *Stat'i o fol'klore*, pp. 29–41. Moscow-Leningrad, 1966.

———. "Neudachnoe vrachevanie: Antichnaia parallel'k russkoi skazke." In his *Stat'i o fol'klore*, pp. 42–58. Moscow-Leningrad, 1966.

———. "Obriad i legenda afinskikh bufonii." In his *Stat'i o fol'klore*, pp. 80–96. Moscow-Leningrad, 1966. Originally published in *Sovetskii fol'klor*, 1936, no. 4–5, pp. 251–65.

———. *Stat'i o folklore*. Moscow-Leningrad, 1966.

———. "Sviazannyi i osvobozhdennyi silen." In his *Stat'i o fol'klore*, pp. 97–114. Moscow-Leningrad, 1966.

———. "Tragediia Evridipa 'Elena' i nachalo grecheskogo romana." In his *Stat'i o fol'klore*, pp. 115–27. Moscow-Leningrad, 1966.

———. "Vozvrashchenie muzha v 'Odissee' i v russkoi skazke." In his *Stat'i o fol'klore*, pp. 59–72. Moscow-Leningrad, 1966.

———. "Zakoldovannye zveri Kirki v poeme Apolloniia Rodosskogo." In his *Stat'i o fol'klore*, pp. 24–28. Moscow-Leningrad, 1966.

Trencheni-Val'dapfel', I. *Mifologiia*. Moscow, 1959.

Tronskii, Iosif M. "Antichnyi mir i sovremennaia skazka." In Petr Emel'ianovich Skachkov and Sergei Fedorovich Ol'denburg, *Sergeiu Fedorovichu Ol'denburgu: k piatidesiatiletiiu nauchno-obshchestvennoi deiatel'nosti, 1882–1932*, pp. 523–34. Leningrad: Izdatel'stvo Akademii nauk SSSR, 1934.

———. "Mif o Dafnise." *Iazyk i literature*, 1932, v. 8.

Tsertelev, Nikolai A. "Vzgliad na starinnye russkie skazki i pesni." *Syn otechestva*, 1820, no. 59.

Turgenev, Ivan S. *Polnoe sobranie sochinenij v 28-mi tt*. Moscow-Leningrad, 1963.

Tylor, Edward B. *Anthropology: An Introduction to the Study of Man and Civilisation*. London, 1881. Translated into Russian as E. Teilor, *Antropologiia: Vvedenie k izucheniiu cheloveka i tsivilizatsii* (St. Petersburg, 1882).

———. *Primitive Culture: Researches into the Development of Mythology, Philosophy, Religion, Art, and Custom.* London, 1871. Translated into Russian as E. Teilor, *Pervobytnaia kul'tura* (Moscow, 1939).

———. *Researches into the Early History of Mankind.* London, 1866. Translated into Russian as E. Teilor, *Doistoricheskii byt chelovechestva i nachalo tsivilizatsii* (Moscow, 1868).

Ukhov, P. D. "K istorii termina 'bylina.'" *Vestnik Moskovskogo universiteta*, 1953, no. 4, pp. 129–35.

Usener, Hermann. "Rhein." *Museum f. Phil.*, Neue Folge, 1909.

Uther, Hans-Jörg. *The Types of International Folktales: A Classification and Bibliography*, 3 vols. Folklore Fellows' Communications no. 284. Helsinki: Suomalainen Tiedeakatemia, 2004.

Vanenko, Ivan. *Skazki russkie, raskazannye Ivanom Vanenko.* Moscow, 1838.

Varag, Lev G. "Drachenkampf auf der Brücke (AaTh 300 A)." In *Enzyklopädie des Märchens*, v. 3, lf 2/3, pp. 825–34. Berlin, 1975.

Varag, Lev G., I. N. Berozovskij, K. N. Kabashnikov, and N. V. Novikov, comps. *Sravnitel'nyj ukazatel' sjuzhetov: Vostochnoslavjanskaija skazka*, Kirill V. Chistov, gen. ed. Leningrad, 1979.

Vedernikova, Natalia M. *Russkaia narodnaia skazka.* Moscow, 1975.

Veselovskii, Aleksandr N. *Istoricheskaia poetika.* Leningrad, 1940.

———. "Kolmachevskii L. *Das Tierepos in Occident und bei den Slaven.*" In his *Sobranie sochinenii*, v. 16, p. 204. Moscow-Leningrad, 1938.

———. "Lorrenskie skazki." In his *Sobranie sochinenii*, v. 16, pp. 212–30. Moscow-Leningrad, 1938.

———. *Poetika siuzhetov*, volume 2 of his *Sobranie sochinenii*. St. Petersburg, 1913.

———. "Retsenziia na kn. Stanislava Prato." In his *Sobranie sochinenii*, v. 16, pp. 185–90. Moscow-Leningrad, 1938.

———. "Slavianskie skazaniia." In his *Sobranie sochinenii*, v. 8, pt. 1. Moscow-Leningrad, 1938.

———. *Slavianskie skazaniia o Solomone i Kitovrase i zapadnye legendy o Morol'fe i Merline: Iz istorii literaturnogo obshcheniia Zapada i Vostoka.* St. Petersburg, 1872.

———. "Skazki ob Ivane Groznom." In his *Sobranie sochinenii*, v. 16. Moscow-Leningrad, 1938.

———. *Sobranie sochinenii.* Moscow-Leningrad, 1938.

———. "Zametki i somneniia o sravnitel'nom izuchenii srednevekovogo èposa." In his *Sobranie sochinenii*, v. 16. Moscow-Leningrad, 1938, pp. 1–82.

Vikent'ev, Vladimir M. *Drevneegipetskaia povest' o dvukh brat'iakh.* Moscow, 1917.

Vladimirov, Petr V. *Vvedenie v istoriiu russkoi slovesnosti: Iz lektsii i issledovanii*. Kiev, 1896.

Voevodskii, Leopol'd F. *Kannibalizm v grecheskikh mifakh*. St. Petersburg, 1874.

Volkov, Roman M. *Skazka: Razyskaniia po siuzhetoslozheniiu narodnoi skazki*, v. 1. Kiev, 1924.

von der Leyen, Friedrich. "Indogermanische Märchen." *Zeitschrift für Volkskunde*, 1929, no. 1.

Waitz, Theodor. *Anthropologie der Naturvölker*. Volumes 1–4, Leipzig, 1859–65; vols. 5 and 6, Leipzig, 1867–72.

Weehee, R. "Cinderella (AaTh 510 A)." In *Enzyklopädie des Märchens*, v. 3, lf. 1, pp. 39–57. Berlin, 1975.

Wenzig, Josef. *Westslavische Märchen*. Leipzig, 1857.

Wesselsky, Anton. *Märchen des Mittelalters*. Berlin, 1925.

———. *Mönchslatein*. Berlin, 1909.

Wundt, Wilhelm. "Märchen, Sage und Legende als Entwicklungsformen des Mythus." *Archiv für Religionswissenschaft*, 1908, Bd. 11, pp. 200–22.

———. *Völkerpsychologie*, v. 2, *Mythus und Religion*, Abt. 1. Leipzig, 1903.

Zamotin, Ivan I. *Russkaia narodnaia slovesnost'*. Rostov na Donu, 1919.

Zelenin, Dmitrii K. "Mezhdunarodnaia konferentsiia fol'kloristov-skazkovedov v Shvetsii." *Sovetskaia ètnografiia*, 1934, no. 1–2, pp. 223–25.

———. "Religiozno-magicheskaia funktsiia fol'klornykh skazok." In Petr Emel'ianovich Skachkov and Sergei Fedorovich Ol'denburg, *Sergeiu Fedorovichu Ol'denburgu: k piatidesiatiletiiu nauchno-obshchestvennoi deiatel'nosti, 1882–1932*, pp. 215–40. Leningrad: Izdatel'stvo Akademii nauk SSSR, 1934.

———. *Velikorusskie skazki Permskoi gubernii*. Petrograd, 1914.

———. *Velikorusskie skazki Viatskoi gubernii*. Petrograd, 1915.

Zelinskii, F. F. (Tadeusz Zielinski). "Antichnaia Lenora." *Vestnik Evropy*, 1906, no. 3, pp. 167–93.

———. "Die Behandlung gleichzeitigen Ereignissen im antiken Epos." *Philologus*, 1900, suppl. 8, pp. 1, 2.

———. "Starye i novye puti v gomerovskom voprose." *Zhurnal Ministerstva narodnogo prosveshcheniia*, 1909, v. 5.

———. "Zakon khronologicheskoi nesovmestimosti i kompozitsiia 'Iliady.'" In *Sbornik v chest' F. E. Korsha*. Moscow, 1896.

Zelinskii, Th. *Märchenkomödie in Athen*. Leipzig, 1885.

Zhdanov, Ivan N. *K literaturnoi istorii russkoi bylevoi poezii*. Kiev, 1881.

———. *Povest' o Vavilone i skazanie o kniaziakh Vladimirskikh*. St. Petersburg, 1891.

————. *Russkii bylevoi èpos: Issledovaniia i materialy,* 4 vols. St. Petersburg, 1895.

————. *Sobranie sochinenii,* v. 1. St. Petersburg, 1904.

Zhukovskii, Vasilii A. "Skazka o tsare Berendee, o syne ego Ivane Tsareviche, o khitrostiakh Koshcheia Bessmertnogo i o premudrosti Mar'i Tsarevny, Koshcheevoi docheri." In his *Stikhotvoreniia,* pp. 729–40. Biblioteka Poèta, Bol'shaia seriia. Leningrad, 1956.

INDEX OF AUTHORS, CREATORS, AND TALE-TELLERS

INDEX OF SUBJECTS AND TALES